Praise for Sylvia Engdahl's **Children of the Star** *novels!*

This Star Shall Abide

(published in the UK as *Heritage of the Star*)

Winner of a Christopher Award

(given for "affirmation of the highest values of the human spirit").

"This is not the electronic-light-flashing-exterminate-him-thing from outer space type of science fiction. It is an allegory which poses one of the most heart-searching dilemmas of the human race, perhaps in the C.S. Lewis tradition. I mean *Perelandra* rather than *Narnia*. This is a thought-provoking book distantly related to *Lord of the Rings* and *The Glassbead Game,* and may appeal to a similar readership."—*The Junior Bookshelf,* London

"An excellent plot and remarkable character development make this tale of the future highly satisfying and thought-provoking."
—*Top of the News,* American Library Association

"An excellent work of fantasy. So many of our human needs and qualities are examined by this adventure that one cannot fail to be affected by reading it. It would certainly make a non-lover of fantasy think again about trying the genre. The characters of this work are well drawn and evoke pride from the reader who shares their dreams and struggle."—*Maine State Library*

"In another superior and thoughtful science fiction novel, the author has created a believable civilization on a far-off planet in a far-distant time."—*Chicago Daily News*

"Imaginative, carefully created science fiction."—*Dallas Times Herald*

"Individual characters and the society as a whole are credibly developed and suspense is well maintained in an above average science fiction tale for which a sequel is planned."—*Booklist*

"Superior future fiction concerning the fate of an idealistic misfit, Noren, who rebels against his highly repressive society. Although there is little overt action, the attention of mature SF readers will be held by the skillful writing and excellent plot and character development."—*School Library Journal*

"...[T]he story is noteworthy for its dramatization of the crucial meeting of man, science, and the universe."—*Horn Book*

"Tension-filled, beautiful and haunting."—*Commonweal*

"...Both logically and consistently suspenseful.... *This Star* **will** *Abide* a good deal longer than most here today, gone tomorrow sci-fi."—*Kirkus Reviews*

"The concept of the culture is imaginatively and convincingly detailed, the story line moves with brisk momentum, and the characters have solidity."—*Bulletin of the Center for Children's Books,* University of Chicago

"...[A] powerful novel for any science fiction buff, but especially written for the teenager. Technology, truth, knowledge and freedom are words given new meanings and could offer opportunities for today's reader."—*North American Moravian*

"I read this, fascinated, right to the end."—*Christian Science Monitor*

"This is more than an exceptionally fine book about outer space. It is a wonderful book, perhaps telling the subtle story of many faiths."—*Fresno Bee*

"...[T]he depth of insight Noren is required to reach pushes this story beyond most current writing for young people."—*Provident Book Finder*

Beyond the Tomorrow Mountains

"Andre Norton fans will definitely be interested in the books of Sylvia Louise Engdahl. The present book [on a preceding list of 20 recommended as the best original novels of 1973] is a sequel to *This Star Shall Abide* which I unfortunately missed when it appeared. I'll try to make up for it by not missing any more."—*Locus*

"Engdahl has carefully worked out the social structure and ecology of a scientific society that has been transferred to a planet without metals. What's more, she wrestles with deeply adult problems of an apparently meaningless universe and of a people's right to know facts that may destroy everything they hold dear." —*Psychology Today*

"More than most science fiction writers for young people, Engdahl's books are concerned with individual motivation and ethical conduct; the writing style is often heavy...but it offers depth and provocative ideas for the mature reader who wants more than just action."—*Bulletin of the Center for Children's Books*

"The well-developed characters will interest many young adolescents whose thoughts and questionings are similar to Noren's." —*School Library Journal*

"Introspective readers will identify with Noren and his doubts and sense of despair while the general science fiction buff will appreciate the further experiences of Noren within the credibly developed society on a planet unlike Earth."—*Booklist*

"Engdahl's science fiction I cannot praise highly enough. Anyone truly interested in books of philosophical and moral depth for young people should fix her name in his mind. The questions posed are not easy, the answers are rarely pat, but surely in a time of moral, social, economic and ecological crisis they are extremely relevant."—*Provident Book Finder*

"In a tribute to the intelligence of teenagers the author asks some thought provoking questions. The ideas of power, heresy, self-knowledge, and acceptance are thoroughly examined in a book that is a testimony to the human spirit."—*News-Gazette,* Martinez CA

"[A]sks some of those bigger questions that men like Buckminster Fuller, Paul Tillich, Barry Commoner, John Galbraith and Noam Chomsky are asking in more abstract terms. The answers Engdahl gives to such vast religious questions may not please all readers, but the book is well worth reading even if just to see how one modern writer conceives of life in this complex era."—*Vanguard,* Toronto

The Doors of the Universe

"Although it is the third book of a trilogy, *The Doors of the Universe* stands powerfully by itself as a quest for survival on a planet that is basically alien to the Six Worlds' life forms. This is much more than an adventure story. It is one man's realization of the need for change and his slow acceptance of the responsibility to lead that change… This is a contemplative book, but one never gets bored with the story and it haunts the reader long after it is finished."—*Journal of Reading*

"This Star Shall Abide and *Beyond the Tomorrow Mountains* serve as solid foundation for this powerful culminating volume that treats in far greater depth the philosophical/ethical/religious issues raised in the earlier books. Almost as much a character study (albeit of a very special individual) as science fiction, Engdahl's latest story is certain to appeal to the thoughtful good reader."—*Booklist*

"While this is a sequel, it more than stands on its own as an exquisite story of the lonely quest for knowledge and the burden of unsought leadership. Noren is the archetype of the impetuous, brilliant, promising kid, prone to rebellion and despair, and abhoring the pressure and reverence alternately accorded to him—in other words, the ultimate 'different drummer' and ideal adolescent protagonist. The technological, social, religious and philosophical landscape of the planet is carefully depicted, but not overly detailed."
—*Voice of Youth Advocates*

"Engdahl again proves herself a master storyteller in this third book of her sci-fi trilogy. As a converted sci-fi hater, I am again impressed with the depth of ideas that she explores. The constant twists and expansions of plot keep the reader's attention from lagging."—*Provident Book Finder,* Scottsdale PA

"...[T]he last few chapters become compelling, showing a power and mythic 'rightness'..."—*Locus,* May 1981

"Author Sylvia Louise Engdahl makes you care about her characters. They are not perfect, nor are they too cute to take seriously. Readers will find themselves caring for [Noren] and his problems. They will want him to succeed, to mature, to pull himself together and survive. Engdahl can make a reader forget her characters are on another planet, forget that they may not be human in precisely the way the people on this planet are, forget that the problems Noren is facing are simply fiction. Humanity, she says, transcends the definitions of outward form and physical location."
—*Ypsilanti Press*

"This book and its companions, *This Star Shall Abide* and *Beyond the Tomorrow Mountains,* will become classics of science fiction. They will not, unfortunately, be popular [with young people] because the intellectual level and reading difficulty will restrict their circulation to the more intelligent high school students. I admire the care and precision with which Engdahl has worked out the limits of the environment of this alien world, but especially the careful delimiting to its morality: what is in the best interests of the long-term survival of the race. Right up to the end of the book I had no clue as to the brilliant way in which all the problems raised would be resolved. And that makes a good book!"—*Children's Book Review,* Brigham Young University

"This is a very sophisticated and technical book... The subject is definitely popular, but the average child in eighth or ninth grade will not be able to comprehend the theme. This book will do better as an adult novel."—*Association of Children's Librarians*

Children of the Star

by

Sylvia Engdahl

Meisha Merlin Publishing, Inc
Atlanta, GA

CHILDREN OF THE STAR

An MM Publishing Book
Published by Meisha Merlin Publishing, Inc.
PO Box 7
Decatur, GA 30031

Editing & interior layout by Stephen Pagel
Copyediting & proofreading by Teddi Stransky
Cover art by Tom Kidd
Cover design by Neil Seltzer

ISBN: 1-892065-15-0 (hardcover)
1-892065-14-2 (softcover)

http://www.meishamerlin.com

First MM Publishing edition: January 2000

Printed in the United States of America
0 9 8 7 6 5 4 3 2 1

Table of Contents

Children of the Star

"...The land was barren, and brought forth neither food nor pure water, nor was there any metal; and no one lived upon it until the Founding. And on the day of the Founding humankind came out of the sky from the Mother Star, which is our source. But the land alone could not give us life. So the Scholars came to bless it, that it might be quickened: they built the City; and they called down from the sky Power and Machines; and they made the High Law lest we forget our origin, grow neglectful of our bounden duties, and thereby perish. Knowledge shall be kept safe within the City; it shall be held in trust until the Mother Star itself becomes visible to us. For though the Star is now beyond our seeing, it will not always be so...

"There shall come a time of great exultation, when the doors of the universe shall be thrown open and everyone shall rejoice. And at that time, when the Mother Star appears in the sky, the ancient knowledge shall be free to all people, and shall be spread forth over the whole earth. And Cities shall rise beyond the Tomorrow Mountains, and shall have Power, and Machines; and the Scholars will no longer be their guardians. For the Mother Star is our source and our destiny, the wellspring of our heritage; and the spirit of this Star shall abide forever in our hearts, and in those of our children, and our children's children, even unto countless generations. It is our guide and protector, without which we could not survive; it is our life's bulwark. And so long as we believe in it, no force can destroy us, though the heavens themselves be consumed! Through the time of waiting we will follow the Law; but its mysteries will be made plain when the Star appears, and the children of the Star will find their own wisdom and choose their own Law."

—from the Book of the Prophecy

This Star Shall Abide

Chapter One

Three orange crescents hovered above the fields and Little Moon was rising over the Tomorrow Mountains when Noren and Talyra left the schoolhouse. Laughter blended with the music of flutes drifted out across the stony area as they walked toward the sledge.

"By the Mother Star, it's hot!" exclaimed Noren as he swung himself to the wicker seat and held out a sturdy hand to the girl.

"Don't swear," she reproved gently, climbing in beside him. "You never used to swear."

Frowning, Noren reproached himself for his carelessness. He hadn't meant to offend her, but it was hard to remember sometimes that she, so spirited in other ways, still held the conventional beliefs on a subject about which he had long ago formed his own. He'd planned to discuss that subject on their way home, and he was already off to a bad start.

He jerked the reins; the work-beast snorted and headed reluctantly down the sandy road away from the village. "We're free!" Talyra said exultantly. "How do you feel?"

Noren considered it. Their schooling was finished for good; having reached mid-adolescence, they were free citizens: free to claim new farmland or to seek any work they chose; free even to move to some other village. And they were also free to marry. So why should he feel less satisfied than ever in his life before? "I don't know how I feel," he told her.

She stared at him, surprised and a little hurt. Suddenly Noren was ashamed. This was not a time to worry about freedom, or knowledge, or the Prophecy. He let the reins fall slack and drew Talyra toward him, kissing her. But there was a restlessness in his mind that refused to slip aside. Talyra felt it, too. "You're angry," she accused. "Is it because of the Technician?"

"I'm not angry."

"You fume whenever you catch a glimpse of one of them," she said sadly, sliding over on the seat. "I wish he'd never shown up at the dance. I can't imagine what he's doing in the village tonight, anyway."

"What does a Technician ever do?" Noren retorted with undisguised bitterness. "He comes either to inspect something or to inform us of some duty to the High Law that we may not have noticed."

"That's not true. More often the Technicians come with Machines, or to hold devotions, or cure someone who's ill—"

"No one was ill at the schoolhouse." Noren's voice was sharp, for inwardly he knew she was right; the High Law was enforced not by men of the Technician caste, but by the village council.

"You're funny, Noren," Talyra said. "Technicians aren't unkind, ever; why do you hate them?"

He paused; it was a hard thing to explain. "They give no reasons for what they do. They have knowledge we're not allowed to share."

"Reasons? They are Technicians!"

"Why are they Technicians? They're men and women like us, I think."

Talyra withdrew her hand from his, shocked. "Noren, they're not; it's blasphemy to think of them so! They have abilities we can't even imagine. They can control Machines for clearing land, and quickening it, or for building roadbeds, or—or *anything.* They talk to radiophonists from a long way off; they travel through the air from village to village...it's been said they can go to the other side of the world! And they've all sorts of marvelous things in the City. Why, they know nearly as much as the Scholars, who know everything."

"And tell us almost nothing."

"What would you expect them to tell us?" asked Talyra in surprise. The Scholars, as High Priests, were the acknowledged guardians of all mysteries. "We know all we'll ever need to," she continued. "You wouldn't want to go to school any more, would you?"

"No, I already know what the teacher knows," Noren agreed. "I've read all the books, and Talyra, I've worked out math problems the teacher couldn't even follow. But there is more knowledge than that. I want to know different things, like—like what Power is, and why crops can't be grown till a Machine's quickened the soil, and what good it does for Technicians to put clay into a purifying Machine before the potter's allowed to shape it."

"People aren't meant to know things like that! Not yet."

"Yet? You mean before the time given in the Prophecy?"

"Of course. The time when the Mother Star appears."

"Talyra," Noren said hesitantly, "do you believe that?"

"Believe in the *Prophecy?*" she gasped, her shock deepening. "Noren…don't you?"

"I'm not sure," he temporized. "Why should there be a time, generations in the future, when our descendants will suddenly know all the secrets? Why should knowledge be reserved for them? I want to know *now.*"

"There isn't any 'why' about it; that's just the way it is. *'At that time, when the Mother Star appears in the sky, the ancient knowledge shall be free to all people, and shall be spread forth over the whole earth. And Cities shall rise beyond the Tomorrow Mountains, and shall have Power, and Machines; and the Scholars will no longer be their guardians.'*"

"How do you know that's true?"

"It's in the Book of the Prophecy."

Noren didn't answer. What he'd been thinking during the past years would horrify Talyra, but if they were to marry, he must not conceal it any longer. He was firmly convinced of that, though such an idea was no less contrary to custom than many of his other unconventional ones. Girls promised themselves to men they respected, and if they were loved and returned that love, so much the better; they did not expect to be told of a prospective husband's feelings on other subjects. Yet because he did love Talyra, he'd decided that he owed her the truth. He had also decided that this was the night on which he would have to tell her.

At the edge of an open field he reined the work-beast to a halt and threw himself flat on the straw that filled the sledge, pulling Talyra down beside him. For a while neither of them said anything; they lay looking up at the stars, the faint but familiar constellations with puzzling names from the old myths: the Steed, the Soldier, the Sky-ship…

It was very still. A slow breeze rustled the grain and mingled dust with the warm, rich odor of growing things.

Soberly Talyra ventured, "Why couldn't you be happy tonight? Even before the Technician came you weren't having fun. Everyone at the dance was happy except you. I kept trying to get you to laugh—"

"I'm very happy." He fingered her dark curls.

"Don't you care enough for me to share what's bothering you?"

"It's not easy to put into words, that's all." He must proceed slowly, Noren knew; he would frighten her if he came out with the thing before explaining the reasoning behind it. Probably he would frighten her anyway. "You say everybody at the dance was happy," he went on. "Well, I guess they were. They're usually happy; they've got plenty to eat and comfortable homes and that's all they care about. They don't *think.*"

"Think about what?"

"About how things really are—the world, I mean. They don't mind not knowing everything the Technicians know. The Technicians bring the Machines we need and help us if we're in trouble, so they think it's all right for them to run things. They're content with being dependent."

"What's wrong with it? It's part of the High Law."

"Suppose we knew how to build our own Machines?"

"We couldn't," Talyra objected. "Machines aren't *built,* they just *are.* Noren, you're mixed up. Technicians don't run things in the village; our own councilmen do that."

"We elect councilmen to make village laws," admitted Noren, "but the Scholars are supreme, and the Technicians act in their name, not the council's. They're outside village law entirely."

"Has a Technician ever interfered with anything you wanted to do?"

"That's not the point."

"Then what is? Technicians don't interfere, they only give; but no matter what they did, it would be right. Keeping the High Law's a sacred duty, and the Scholars were appointed at the time of the Founding to see that it's kept. The Technicians are their representatives."

Noren hesitated a moment, then plunged. "Talyra, I don't believe any of that," he stated. "I don't believe that the earth was empty and that people simply sprang out of the sky on the day of the Founding. It's not—well, it's just not the way things happen. It's not natural. I think people must have been here for much, much longer than the Book of the Prophecy says, and to begin with they knew as little as the savages that live in the mountains—the ones we studied about, you remember; the teacher said they were once like us, but lost everything, even their intelligence, because they refused to obey the High Law?"

"Yes, but—"

"Let me finish. I think it was the other way around. You don't forget something you once knew, but you can always learn more. I think we were like the savages until someone, maybe one of the Scholars, found out how to get knowledge. Only he didn't tell anybody except his friends. He told the rest just enough to make them afraid of him, and made the High Law so that they'd obey."

Talyra sat up, edging away from him. "Noren, don't! That isn't true; that—that's heresy."

"Yes, it's contrary to the Book of the Prophecy. But don't you see, the Scholars wrote the Prophecy themselves because they wanted power; it didn't come from the Mother Star at all."

"Oh, Noren!" Talyra whispered. "You mustn't say such things." Raising her eyes devoutly, she began, *"'The Mother Star is our source and our destiny, the wellspring of our heritage; and the spirit of this Star shall abide forever in our hearts, and in those of our children, and our children's children, even unto countless generations. It is our guide and protector, without which we could not survive; it is our life's bulwark... We will follow the Law until the time when the Mother Star itself shall blaze as bright as little Moon—'"*

Noren seized her angrily, swinging her around to face him. "Stop quoting empty phrases and listen! How could a new star appear when the constellations have been the same since before anyone can remember? And even if it could, how could the man who wrote the Prophecy know beforehand? How did he know there was a Mother Star if he'd never seen it?"

"Of course it's invisible now; the Prophecy says so."

"We don't need a prophecy to tell us *that.* We do need one to tell us that it will someday be as bright as Little Moon, since common sense tells us that can never happen."

"But the Prophecy gives the exact date."

"When the date arrives, there will be a new Prophecy to explain the failure of the old one. Can't you see, Talyra? It's the Scholars' scheme to make us think that their supremacy's only temporary, so that we won't oppose it. As long as we accept the story, they can keep their knowledge all to themselves and no one will protest; but if we rebel against it, we can make them give knowledge to everyone! We could have Cities and Power and Machines now; there's no point in waiting several more generations only to find that there'll be no changes after all."

"I don't want you to talk that way! What if someone should hear?"

"Perhaps they'd believe me. If enough people did—"

"They wouldn't, any more than I do. They'd despise you for your irreverence, They'd report you—" Her dark eyes grew large with fear. "Noren, you'd be tried for heresy! You'd be convicted!"

He met her gaze gravely, glad that she had not forced him to say it himself. "I—I know that, Talyra."

It was something he had known for a long time. He was a heretic. Decent people would despise him if he was found out. And eventually he would no longer be able to keep silent; to do so as a boy was one thing, but now that he was a man, his search for truth would take him beyond the safe confines of his private thoughts. Then, inevitably, he'd be accused; he would stand trial before the village Council and would be found guilty, for when put to the question, he would not lie to save himself.

And once convicted, he would be turned over to the Scholars. Under the High Law, the religious law that overrode anything village law might say, all heretics were taken into the custody of the Scholars, taken away to the City where mysterious and terrible things were done to them. No one really knew what things. No one had ever entered the City where all the Scholars and Technicians lived; no one had ever seen a Scholar except from a distance, during one of the various ceremonies held before the City Gates. Noren longed to go there, but he was not anxious to go as a condemned prisoner. He'd awakened in the middle of the night sometimes, drenched with sweat, wondering what that would be like.

He reached out toward Talyra, more gently this time, suddenly noticing how she was shaking. "Talyra—oh, Talyra, I didn't want to scare you—"

"How could you not scare me by such ideas? I—I thought we were going to be married, Noren."

"We are," he assured her, hugging her close to him again. "Of course we are."

She wrenched away. "No, we're not! Do you suppose I want a husband who's a *heretic?* One I'd always be afraid for, and who—"

"Who could put you in danger," Noren finished slowly, chilled with remorse. "Talyra, I just didn't think—it was stupid of me—" He dropped his head in his hands, realizing that in his concern for being honest with her, he'd forgotten that if he was ever tried for heresy, she would be questioned, too. She would be called to testify. Wives always were, yet she would be called whether they were married or not, for everyone knew they were betrothed, and she could no longer say that she knew nothing. "I've compromised you," he whispered in anguish. "You could be punished for not reporting me."

Talyra gave him a pained look. "Darling, don't you trust me? Don't you know I'd never tell anyone? I love you, Noren!"

"Of course I trust you," he declared. "It's you I'm afraid for. It's not only that you'd be suspect because you hadn't told; it's that I've said enough to open your eyes. Before, you might never have thought of doubting, but now—well, now you're not innocent, and if you're questioned on my account you'll have to admit it."

"What do you mean, I'm not innocent?" she protested. "Do you think I believe any of those awful things, Noren? Are you suggesting that I'll become a heretic myself? I love you and I won't betray you, but you're wrong, so wrong; I only hope that something will restore your faith."

Noren jumped to his feet, angry and bewildered. He had not thought she'd consider him mistaken. It had never occurred to him that Talyra wouldn't accept the obvious once it was pointed out to her. She was brighter than most girls; he'd liked that, and only because of it had he dared to speak of his conviction that the orthodox faith was false. To be sure, not even the smartest village elders ever questioned anything connected with religion, but he'd attributed that to their being old or spineless.

"I don't want my faith restored," he said heatedly. "I want to know the truth. The truth is the most important thing there is, Talyra. Don't you care about finding it?"

"I already know what's true," she maintained vehemently. "I'm happy—I was happy—the way we are. If I cared about anything besides you I could have it, and if you're going to be like this—"

"What do you mean, you could have it?"

She faced him, sitting back on her heels. "I kept something from you. I know why the Technician came tonight. He spoke to me; he said I could be more than the wife of a farmer or a craftsman. He asked if I wanted to be more."

"Well, so there are rewards for blind faith in the righteousness of Technicians!"

"He said," she went on, "that if I liked, I could go to the training center and become a schoolteacher or a nurse-midwife."

Noren's thoughts raged. If he were to ask for even a little knowledge beyond that taught in the school, he'd be rebuffed, as he had been so many times, times when his harmless, eager questions had been turned aside by the Technicians who'd come to work their Machines in his father's fields. But Talyra, who seldom used her mind for wondering, had been offered the one sort of opportunity open to a villager who wanted to learn! To be sure, the training center vocations were semi-religious, and he was known to be anything but devout; yet it did not seem at all fair.

"I knew you'd be furious; that's why I didn't plan to mention it." She got up, brushing the straw from her skirt, and climbed back onto the seat. "When I told him I was pledged to marry, he said I was free to be whatever I chose."

"Even a Technician or a Scholar, maybe?" Noren said bitterly.

"That's blasphemous; I won't listen."

"No, I don't suppose you will. I can see how fraud has greater appeal than truth from your standpoint."

"You're questioning *my* piety, when you're calling the High Law a fraud? You had better take back what you've said if you expect to go on seeing me!"

"I'm sorry," he conceded. "That was unfair, and I apologize."

"Apologizing's not enough. I don't mean just the angry things."

Slowly Noren said, "I guess if I were to swear by the Mother Star never again to talk of the heretical ones, you'd be satisfied."

Her face softening, Talyra pleaded, "Oh, Noren—will you? We could forget this ever happened."

He knew then that she had not understood any of what he had revealed. In a low voice he replied, "I can't do that, Talyra. It wouldn't be honest, since I'd still be thinking them, and besides, an oath like that wouldn't mean anything from me. You see, I wouldn't consider it—sacred."

Talyra turned away. Her eyes were wet, and Noren saw with sadness that it was not merely because their marriage plans were in ruins, but because she really thought him irreverent. She did not put a reverence for truth in the same category as her own sort of faith.

"T–take me home," she faltered, not letting herself give way to tears.

He took his seat, giving the reins a yank, and the work-beast plodded on, the only sound the steady whish of the sledge's stone runners over sand. Neither of them said anything more. Noren concentrated on keeping to the road; two of the crescent moons had set, and the dim light of the third wasn't enough to illuminate the way ahead.

What now? he wondered. He had intended to go to the radiophonist's office the next morning and submit his claim for a farm, but without Talyra that would be pointless. He did not want to be a farmer; he'd worked more than half each year, between school sessions, on his father's land, and he had always hated it. Since he didn't want to be a trader or craftsworker either, he had thought farming as good a life as any; a man with a wife must work at something. He had planned it for her sake. Now he had no plans left.

None, that is, but an idea he scarcely dared frame, the exciting, irrepressible idea that although there was no way to get more knowledge himself, he might someday manage to convince people—as many as possible, but at least *some* people—that knowledge should be made free to everyone without delay. He was not sure how to put such an idea into action, much less how to avoid arrest while doing so. He was not sure that arrest could be avoided. Noren was sure of only one thing: if and when he was convicted of heresy, he was not going to recant.

Most heretics did, he knew. Most of them, after a week or two in the City, knelt before the Scholars in a ceremony outside the Gates and publicly repudiated every heretical belief they'd ever held. And that was no great surprise, Noren thought, cold despite the oppressive heat of the evening. It was all too understandable, when the penalty for not recanting was reputed to be death.

It was close to dawn when Noren unhitched the work-beast in his father's barn and went in to bed, undressing silently to avoid waking his brothers. He did not sleep. Talyra...it was hard to accept what had happened with Talyra. He had never been close to other people; he had always felt different, a misfit; but he'd had Talyra, whom he loved, and for the past year he had looked forward increasingly to the day when he would have her as his wife. Now, with the day almost upon him, his one hope for the future had been dashed. If only he'd been less honest!

But he could not have been. It was not in him to live as a hypocrite, Noren realized ruefully. The only thing in the world that meant more to him than Talyra was...Truth. He thought about it that way sometimes—Truth, with a capital letter—knowing that people would laugh at him if they knew. That was the difference between himself and the others: he *cared* about the truth, and they did not.

Looking back, he could not remember just when he'd started to reject the conventional beliefs; he was aware of much he had not known in the beginning, and could not trace the development of his doubts, which at first had been only a vague resentment at the fact that knowledge existed that was unavailable to him. Perhaps he'd begun to formulate them on the evening the Technician had come unannounced to his father's farm.

That had been before his childish admiration of Technicians had turned to inexplicable dislike; he'd been quite a young boy, and the sight of the aircar floating down over his own family's grainfield had thrilled him. The Technicians who quickened the soil at the start of each growing season seldom arrived in aircars, for they simply moved on from the adjacent farm, pushing their noisy Machines back and forth over the continuous strip of cleared land. So, with his brothers, Noren had run excitedly to meet the descending craft.

The man had asked lodging for the night, and had offered to pay well for it; Technicians never took anything without paying. Noren's father would have been within his rights to refuse the request. But of course it would never have occurred to him to do that, any more than it would have occurred to him to wonder why a Technician needed lodging when the aircar could have taken him back to the City in no time at all. Nobody ever questioned the ways of Technicians.

This Technician had been a young man with a pleasant smile and a friendly manner that had put the boys immediately at ease. He had allowed them to come close to the aircar, even to touch it. At least Noren had touched it; his brothers had hung hack in awe, as people generally did in the presence of a Machine. He would have liked to climb inside, but that, the Technician would not permit. Noren had to content himself with running his hand over the smooth, shining surface of the craft and, later, with fingering curiously the green sleeve of the Technician's uniform, so different from the coarse brown material of which ordinary clothing was made. And still more wondrous were the metal tools that the Technician carried, for metal was sacred and few villagers had opportunity to see it at close range. Only if wealthy or especially blessed might one possess a small metal article of one's own.

Those things, however, had not been what impressed him most about the Technician, for to his surprise Noren had found that this was a man he could talk to. Even in childhood he had found it difficult to talk to his friends about anything more significant than their day-by-day activities. Certainly he couldn't talk to his family. His father, though intelligent enough, cared for nothing but the price of grain and the problems of getting in the harvest; his brothers were stolid boys who spoke of happenings, but never of ideas. At times he'd felt that his mother had deeper interests than they; still, she was not one to go against women's custom by displaying such interests. She gave him love, yet could communicate with him no better than the others. The Technician was not like any of these people. The Technician spoke to Noren as if the use of one's mind was something very important. They had talked for a long time after supper, and Noren had felt a kind of excitement that he had never before imagined.

But in the morning, when the Technician had gone, the excitement had turned to frustration; and that day he had done a great deal of thinking.

He'd sprawled under a tall outcropping of rock in the corner of the field where he was supposed to be cutting grain, staring at his laboriously-sharpened stone scythe with the thought that a metal one—if such a thing existed—would be vastly more efficient. And gradually, with a mixture of elation and anger, he had become aware that Technicians were not the unique beings people presumed them to be. They were *men!* What they knew, other men could learn. Noren had been convinced, as surely as he'd ever been of anything, that he himself would be fully capable of learning it.

He'd also known that he would not be allowed to.

Someday, he'd decided fiercely, *someday I'll...* He had not let himself complete the thought, for inwardly he'd been afraid. Inside he'd already sensed what would happen someday, though he had not recognized his heresy for what it was until the following season.

He'd assumed that there was nobody in the world with whom he could talk as he had with the Technician, but he'd been mistaken. That year he had at last found a real friend: not just a companion, but a friend who had ideas, and spoke of those ideas. Kern had been much older than Noren and in his final year of school; but once during noon hour, when Noren had asked to borrow a book not available in his own schoolroom, they'd discovered that they had more to say to each other than to their contemporaries. Instinctively Noren had avoided mentioning his opinion about Technicians to anyone else, but Kern he'd told freely and gladly, only to find that Kern was already far beyond him.

He had looked up to Kern as he'd never been able to look up to his father and brothers. Not that Kern had been considered admirable by the villagers, for he'd been a wild boy, a boy who laughed a great deal, belying the true gravity of his thoughts; and he had defied as many conventions as he could get away with. Though he'd spent much of his time with various girls—too much, their families felt—it was to Noren that he had turned with the confidences to which no ordinary person would listen. He'd been recklessly brave and proud of his secret heresies. He had said terrible things, shocking things that Noren had never expected to hear from anyone. He'd said that Scholars were as human as Technicians. He'd said that they were not immortal, but were vulnerable to the same injuries as other people. He had even said that they were not all-wise and were therefore unworthy of the reverence accorded them. But Kern had been careful to whom he expressed such views, at least until one night when he'd forgotten himself to the extent of telling a blasphemous joke within the hearing of a respectable tavernkeeper.

Noren had been in the village that night; he'd seen the marshals arrest Kern, and he'd seen the crowd gather around the jailhouse with blazing torches held aloft. There was to be a heresy trial the next day, but everyone had known that there could be no doubt as to its outcome. Kern himself had known, for once apprehended, he'd abandoned caution and vaunted offenses that even Noren had not suspected. He had gone so far as to boast of having drunk impure water—water neither collected from rain nor sent from the City—a claim few had believed, since had it been true he would most assuredly have been transformed into a babbling idiot. Having dared to laugh at an inviolable provision of the High Law, however, he'd incurred still greater contempt than heretics usually did.

Sick with dread, Noren had stood in the shadows watching the enraged mob. Kern would not cringe at his trial, he'd realized; Kern would laugh, as always, and when the Technicians took him away to the City, he would go with his head high. The terror of such a fate had overwhelmed Noren, but he'd tried very hard to look upon it as an adventure, as Kern surely would. They had often talked about the City, and there had been more to Kern's speculations than idle bravado. One time, in a more serious tone than usual, he had said, "There are mysteries in the City, Noren, but we mustn't fear them. Our minds are as good as the Scholars'. We can't be forced to do or to believe anything against our will. Don't worry about me, because if I'm ever condemned I'm going to find out a lot that I can't learn here."

Kern never did find out. He'd never reached the City; he'd received no chance to explore the mysteries and test himself against the powers he had defied. There had not even been any trial, for the mob was inflamed, the councilmen were not present, and though the High Law decreed that all heretics must be turned over to the Technicians, there were no Technicians present either. Somehow the thatched roof of the jailhouse had caught fire—Noren had known how, as had everyone, but there'd been no particular man who could be accused—and when the Technicians had come, they'd found only the blackened stones.

At first Noren had blamed the Technicians because they hadn't arrived in time to claim the prerogative given them by the High Law; later he'd blamed them for that Law itself. Who was to say that death by fire had not been the most merciful alternative? That thought had haunted Noren. School, which he'd once liked, became dreary, for having abandoned all friends but Kern, he was too absorbed in his bitterness to accept the inanities of his classmates. Besides, his liking for Kern was well known, and he was wary of talking much lest he arouse the suspicion with which, had he been older, he would certainly have been viewed. There had been little left for the school to teach him in any case. He began to seek elsewhere for answers, but soon learned that they could be found only within his own mind. The villagers were ignorant of things that interested him, and the Technicians who came to the farm were unlike the young man who'd once taken lodging there. They would not respond to his questions even when he bridled his resentment, approaching them with deference for the sake of the knowledge he craved. Sometimes it had seemed as if they were deliberately trying to frustrate him.

And then, the next year, his mother had died. She'd fallen ill suddenly while gathering sheaves at the outermost edge of their land, and he had found her lying there, her face contorted with pain, arms cruelly scratched by the wild briars into which she had fallen. The Technicians sent for had declared that she'd been poisoned by some forbidden herb, but Noren had been sure that she, of all people, would never have tasted anything not grown from seed blessed by the Scholars. They'd tried to save her, at least they'd said they were trying, but afterwards he'd never been quite certain. All knowledge was theirs; if they'd truly wanted her to live, surely they could have cured her illness as they did ordinary maladies. Or perhaps it was merely that they had again come too late. If he, Noren, had possessed the syringes they'd brought—if he'd known how to use them—he might have saved her himself; it was not right that such things should be only in the hands of Technicians!

He had said so to their faces, too stricken by grief and rage to care what they did to him. Surprisingly, they had not done anything. They had simply stated that he must not aspire to knowledge beyond his station; and from that moment, his aspirations had increased.

Yet as they'd increased, so had his realization that those aspirations could never find fulfillment. Soon he would have to choose a way to make his living, and there was no work he wanted to do. He despised farming; he was too inept at working with his hands to became a successful craftsworker; he had neither the money nor the inclination to go into business as a trader. He had talent only for the use of his mind, and in the village that was more of a liability than an asset. The best he could hope for was that some trader or shopkeeper would hire him to keep accounts, since the few people who worked as schoolmasters, radiophonists and so forth obtained their posts only after appointment to the training center by Technicians. Noren had perceived that he would get no such appointment, for each year the school examiners had treated him more scornfully beneath their outward courtesy. They'd guessed his heretical thoughts, perhaps, though they could not take him into custody unless he was first convicted in a civil trial.

The world had grown steadily darker. Noren had turned still further inward after his mother's death, but because her loss was not his deepest pain, his grief had taken the form of an intensified search for some one good thing to make the future seem worth looking toward. And he had found it, for a time, in Talyra.

They'd known each other since childhood, for she lived on a neighboring farm, but he had not paid much attention to girls. Then all of a sudden he'd noticed her, and within a few weeks he had been in love. Never before had anyone cared for him, needed him, as Talyra did; nor had he ever received such joy from another person's presence. He'd no longer been lonely. He'd no longer considered the life of a farmer an intolerable one. His secret ideas had still been the core of his thoughts, but they'd been submerged, overshadowed by new and more powerful feelings. Underneath he had known that if forced to choose, he would not forsake those ideas, but he hadn't anticipated any choice. He'd told himself that Talyra would accept them, that he could share them with her as he had with Kern and, by the sharing, keep them from bursting forth to destroy him.

But it wasn't going to be that way. He'd been deluding himself, Noren perceived bitterly. He should have known that no girl, however deeply in love, would marry someone who admitted to being a heretic. Such a thing was unheard of. He had been selfish to ask it of her, for he had exposed her not only to possible peril, but to the scorn of the whole village even if her personal innocence was never placed in doubt. And she was indeed innocent. Why should she take his word against that of the venerated High Priests, the Scholars?

So it had come to a choice after all, and now the futile search would begin again; yet to Noren it would not be the same. He was a man now. He had nothing left to wait for. And he knew that from this night forward he would always be torn, for he still loved Talyra, and truth or no truth, he would never be happy without her.

Chapter Two

When sunlight glared through the window opening, Noren rose and went out to wash his face. The air was already hot, and the smoke of moss fires mingled with the ever-present barn smells. Behind the farmhouse, the jagged yellow ranges of the Tomorrow Mountains were flat against a hazy sky.

At the cistern, he jerked the spigot handle impatiently and water splashed onto the dusty earth. Noren paid scant attention. It was wrong to waste pure water; his father would be angry, for there would be a reprimand from the village council if the family took more of what came from the City than was usual to supplement the rain-catchment supply, besides the extra trips to the common cistern that would entail. But after this morning what went on at his father's farm would no longer concern him.

That was the decision Noren had reached during his sleepless hours: whatever happened, he could not stay at home. Though he wouldn't claim a new farm without Talyra, to continue working for his father was not to be endured. He would have to find some other way to earn his living.

He looked around him, surveying the place that for so many years he had found hateful. It was just like all other farms he'd ever seen, though perhaps larger than most, since his family had bought the adjoining one in his grandfather's time. The undulating grainfields, their ripened stalks orange in the sun, stretched away on three sides, and beyond, to the south, lay rolling wilderness of purple-green. Close by, however, was the grayish fodder patch that surrounded the area bordering the road. That area was ugly, for nothing grew in it but a few scrawny purple bushes. It was reserved for buildings. There was the stone farmhouse with its thick thatched roof; the cistern, also of stone, topped by a huge, saucer-shaped catchment basin; and the wattle-and-daub barn where the work-beasts and the sledge were kept, along with the rows of wicker cages that contained fowl.

Noren grimaced. He disliked all farm chores, but in particular he despised the job of taking fertilizer from the fowl cages to the fields: filling the great baskets that hung on either side of a work-beast and then, with the same pottery scoop, sprinkling it between the furrows left by the Technicians' soil-quickening Machines. Worst of all was the digging in, which required crawling on hands and knees, as did cultivating. He'd often thought there should be an easier way to hoe; once, in fact, he had envisioned a long, stiff handle for the stone triangle, and had tried to improvise one. Like similar experiments of his younger days, it had been a dismal failure. No plant existed with stalks strong enough not to bend under the pressure, even when several were bound together. His mother had remarked that since the purpose of all large plants was to provide wicker for the weaving of baskets, furniture, and the like, nature had done well to make them flexible. His father, more sharply, had declared that if hoes had been meant to have handles, people would have been taught to make handles at the time of the Founding, just as they had been taught to do everything else. His eldest brother had berated him for fooling around with plant stalks instead of getting on with his share of the work. His other brothers had simply laughed at him.

To Noren it did not seem reasonable that people could have discovered the best way to do everything all at once, whether at some mythical moment called "the Founding" or at any other time; yet he'd been taught in school that this was so, and he had found no evidence to the contrary. People did comparatively few things, after all, and no one had ever heard of their being done differently. Farmers planted, hoed, harvested and threshed; he'd learned from hard experience that the ancestral methods of performing these tasks could not be improved upon. Neither could the equally onerous ones of skinning dead work-beasts, preserving the hides and bones, rendering the tallow, and burying the remains in unquickened ground. Nor was there any imaginable way to make building less laborious: stones must be gathered and joined with mortar; the lightweight, porous softstone used for sledge runners and tables, among other things, must be slowly cut with sharper stone tools; wattles, thatch and wicker were as they were, and one could hardly handle them in a more efficient fashion. The village mill and brewery had existed unchanged since time out of mind, and so had the potter's shop. Even women's work remained the same from generation to generation. He had watched his mother, and later Talyra's, cut trousers, tunics and skirts from City-made cloth with stone knives, stitching the pieces together with needles of polished bone, and he had been sure that there *must* be a quicker way. But he could think of no such way—except one.

Metal! If knives, needles and other tools could be made of metal, that would obviously solve a great many problems. It was *wrong* that there should be no metal for anyone but Technicians!

He had wondered where the metal came from. It certainly did not come from the wilderness; the wilderness contained only dust, sand and stone, covered by mosses and other plants that didn't grow in quickened soil—some gray-green like the fodder patch, some purple-green, but none the bright, clear green of young grain shoots. He knew traders who'd gone far afield to collect the dry moss used for fuel, and they had not seen any metal either. The Book of the Prophecy said that all metal had come into the world during the Founding. Whispered legends suggested that some might be found in rock, but that couldn't be true; Noren had examined every kind of rock there was, and not a speck of it was in the least metallic. The Technicians, he'd concluded, must obtain their metal on the other side of the world.

A very few people did have metal articles, people whose ancestors had been specially favored at the time of the Founding, or who'd bought them from such blessed ones at great cost. Talyra herself owned a narrow silver wristband that had been bequeathed to her by her great-aunt, who, although in every way a pious and deserving person, had borne not a single child, leaving her husband no choice but to petition the council for divorce. Over the years many had said that a barren woman was unworthy to have custody of anything so holy as a metal wristband, but Talyra had felt more sympathy than scorn for the old lady, so in the end the treasure had come to her. She had shown it to him, and she'd promised to wear it at their wedding, along with the blue glass beads that symbolized devotion to the Mother Star and the red necklace, also City-made, that he'd bought for her with the savings of past Founding Day gifts—red, the color of love tokens…

Determinedly Noren wrenched himself back to the present. He must decide where to go. He knew of no open jobs or apprenticeships, but that was just as well, for there was too much restlessness in him to remain nearby; and besides, he could not bear to see Talyra if she was unwilling to marry him.

It was a temptation to leave at once, without seeing anyone, for there was bound to be an argument; yet Noren could not bring himself to do so. There was little love between himself and his father; still the old man had never treated him unkindly. He owed him a farewell. Resignedly, he finished washing, filled the pottery cook-jug, and went in to prepare breakfast.

Since their mother's death, the boys, having no sisters, had taken turns with the kitchen chores. This morning they were Noren's; his five brothers were already in the fields, and would be back soon, ravenously hungry and eager to joke with him about his impending marriage. They were expecting him to bring Talyra home, he knew, for the farm had been too long without a woman and he had not confided his plan to claim new land. It hadn't occurred to them that he would not ask his wife to be a drudge for the whole family, though their own willingness to do so might well account for the fact that the older ones had as yet found no wives for themselves. So they'd have been furious in any case, but he dreaded their derision now that she had turned him down. His being the first pledged to marry had given him a status among them that he, always the different one, had never before attained.

By the time they came in, he had the food ready: porridge, eggs, and large slabs of cold bread to be washed down with tea. Tea was expensive, since the herb from which it was brewed wasn't grown near the village and had to be bought from the traders, but Noren's father was not so poor as to give his sons unflavored water with their meals. Meals were monotonous enough as it was; it had sometimes occurred to Noren that it would be nice if there were some source of food besides grain and fowl.

From long habit the boys stood motionless behind their benches and raised their eyes upward while the words of the Prophecy were said: "*'Let us rejoice in the bounty of the land, for the land is good, and from the Mother Star came the heritage that has blessed it; the land has given us life… And it shall remain fruitful, and the people shall multiply across the face of the earth, and at no time shall the spirit of the Mother Star die in the hearts of its children.'*" Noren repeated them mechanically with the others. They meant nothing to him, yet in a way they recalled the presence of his mother, who had said them with warmth. He found himself thinking of the ceremony held for the sending of her body to the City, when he'd cried not because he was moved by the presiding Technician's intonation of the ritual phrases, but because she had believed them; it had seemed horrible for her to die believing something that wasn't grounded in truth.

The blessing complete, everybody sat down and turned noisily to eating. Noren had little appetite, but he knew he must take advantage of the meal, for it might be a long time before he could get another so plentiful. He had no money of his own. If he'd claimed land, he would have been paid in advance by the Technicians to cultivate it, in return for his promise to sell them most of the first year's harvest. Now, he realized, he would have to earn his keep day by day until he could find some sort of steady employment.

"Have you set the day for your wedding, son?" asked his father.

"No," replied Noren shortly, "I haven't." Everyone's eyes were on him, and he knew that there was nothing to be gained by delaying the inevitable. "There's not going to be a wedding," he continued resolutely.

"Oh, so you've lost your nerve?" remarked his eldest brother, and there were good-natured guffaws. No one had taken the declaration seriously. Every man, after all, had occasional fights with his girl; but a betrothal registered with the village council was seldom broken.

"Perhaps he hasn't lost his nerve," suggested another brother. "Perhaps Talyra lost hers; maybe she decided she could do better for herself than to marry a lazy dreamer who sits and thinks when he might be working."

Noren clenched his fists beneath the table and did not answer. He was well practiced in controlling his feelings; he had learned from Kern's recklessness that one must not reveal one's inner rage at things, at least not if one expected to accomplish anything of value. So many more vital issues angered him that he was used to hiding fury, and taunts from his brothers were nothing new.

There was an awkward silence. "I'm leaving today," Noren announced abruptly. "I'll be seeking work in another village, I think."

"Work? You?" sneered one of them. "Who will hire a boy who has neither stamina nor skill?"

There was no use in pointing out that if he hadn't applied stamina to farm work, it was not from any lack but because he had never chosen to. "I can keep accounts," said Noren in a level voice. "Or—or perhaps I'll hire on with some trader who's delivering a load to the markets outside the City." This last was pure improvisation, but as he spoke he wondered why he had not thought of it before.

His father stared at him. "You can't do that. You're needed here. The harvest is just starting."

"I'm of age, Father. I finished school yesterday and that makes me a free citizen." As free as anybody could be in a world where people were barred from all that was reserved for Technicians and Scholars, he added inwardly.

"Two of your brothers came of age, and stayed."

"They chose to work for wages on the farm, which was their right. It's mine to leave it."

"Let him go, Father," the eldest brother said. "He never pulled his weight in any case; he wouldn't be worth a man's wage."

"He's my son, and however addlebrained he may be at times, I'll not have him ruin his life. The only sign of responsibility he's ever shown is his betrothal to Talyra; I'll not see him break it."

"There's little either of us can do about that," Noren admitted bitterly. "It's already been broken, and not by me." He did not say that his own honesty had precipitated the break.

"She changed her mind?" demanded his brother. "I must say, I'm less surprised than when she accepted you in the first place. But I'm disappointed."

"I don't wonder," retorted Noren, "since I won't be bringing you the housemaid you expected. Let me tell you that if I'd gotten married, I'd have taken my wife to a place of our own. Nothing's changed as far as you're concerned."

"*You* cultivate your own land, you who've spent most of your life with your head in the clouds?" the eldest burst out. "You're unfit for any work, least of all that. Talyra's well out of it."

"No doubt we're all well out of it," added the next-eldest. "I've doubted all along that she was the sort we should bring into the family. No girl could think this brother of ours a good provider, so it's clear she chose him for love, and she can find plenty of that without doing a farmwife's work. Once she tired of him, she'd have left to seek it elsewhere."

Noren's rigid control gave way; before he knew it he was out of his seat and his fist was swinging into his brother's face. All the pent-up rage of the past years went into the blow, and the older boy had no time to be surprised. As he slumped to the floor, the others grabbed Noren's arms. They would not have interfered with a fight, but the blind fury in his eyes told them that he was scarcely aware that his opponent was already unconscious.

"I–I'm sorry, son," his father said helplessly. "That was ill-said; Talyra is a fine girl and would have borne you many fine children. I would have been proud to have her here." The other boys stood back, staring at Noren, realizing that they did not really know this brother who had always seemed such a weakling to them.

Noren hardly knew himself. He was numb, dazed; yet he was also free in a way he had not been before. His anger vented, he was sorry for all of them, sorry because they truly did not understand the thing they were lacking. They could not see that there was more to life than working, eating, and making love. "I'll go now," he said dully.

"I won't hold you, if that's what you want; but this will always be your home."

"You couldn't hold me. I don't need your consent, and as for a home, I don't have one. I never will." He turned and walked through the door, not looking back at them, not even stopping to think that he was taking none of his few belongings. He knew that what he had said was true; wherever he went he would be a stranger, for there was no home in the world for such as he.

He took the road toward the village center, not because he wanted to go there, but because it was the only road there was. To travel cross-country was dangerous, for the wilderness was full of forbidden things. Wild plants held peril; as he'd grown older, Noren had learned that the herb that had killed his mother had not been tasted, but had been a contact poison that attacked her through the scratches on her arms. Ordinarily Technicians with Machines destroyed any such herbs that could be reached from roads or fields, but that rare one had evidently been missed.

The farm was some distance from the village, more than an hour's walk, and the road was one of many spokes radiating out from that center. Whenever anybody started a new farm, the Technicians brought their Machines to extend some spoke road a little farther—his own land, if he'd claimed it, would have been several hours out, bordering the wilderness on two sides instead of one.

There were also continuous roads that connected the various villages; a large map of them had hung between the schoolroom windows. Farmland on one of these connecting roads was not open to claim. It was already cleared and very expensive, particularly if it lay on a main radial, which was a direct route to the City.

Noren had spoken of traveling to the City on impulse, but once the words were out, he'd known that was what he would try. Traders did go there—not inside, of course, but to the great markets outside the walls—and one of them might well hire a man to drive a string of work-beasts or an extra sledge. Work-beasts were exasperating creatures, so slow and stupid that it was odd the Scholars were credited with having created them; one would think people would expect guardians of all wisdom to have done a better job of it. But he could put up with a driver's work if the City was his destination.

The City was beautiful. There had been a painting of it in the schoolroom next to the map. It had high lustrous walls, a ring of scallops, within which stood towers that were much, much higher, so high that the Technicians who lived in them must fly from top to bottom; and those towers had windows: not mere openings like ordinary windows, but sheets of what almost appeared to be glass. The towers of the City were made not of stone or even of metal, but of some sparkling silvery substance that Noren judged to be akin to the surface of the aircar he had once touched. He had always wanted to see them for himself, and there was no reason why he should not make such a journey.

A thrill spread through him, rousing him from the dazed state in which he had left the farm. The City! The City had more than beauty; it was where knowledge was. The Prophecy even said so: *Knowledge shall be kept safe within the City; it shall be held in trust until the day when the Mother Star becomes visible to us.* And that, at least the first half of it, was very likely one of the few statements in the whole thing that was accurate. The Scholars were keeping their knowledge safe within the City, all right, and though looking at the place from the outside wasn't going to get him any of that knowledge, there was a certain excitement in the idea of being so close.

But to reach the City, he must be hired by a trader, for it was a journey of many days, and were he to set out alone, he would starve along the way if he failed to find work at the farms he passed.

He must therefore wait in the village until a trader came through who would take him on. Since it might be a long wait, he would have to have a means of paying for food, water and lodging while he was there. If he was lucky, the innkeeper, whose kitchen-maid was expecting a child soon, might have a place for him; he knew old Arnil for a kindly man, unlike the keeper of the brewery's tavern who'd denounced Kern.

Noren straightened and began to walk faster. As he did so, he was struck by the thought that he might never again pass over this road. Having walked it three days a week to school, except during the long season of harvest and replanting, he seldom noticed its landmarks; but if he was having his last view of them, he ought to. There were none he expected to miss, yet there was a pleasantness in the panorama of purple-clad knolls seen from the rise just before the softstone quarry. Then too, the pond where the workbeasts were watered, with its dense edging of rushes, held memories from his early childhood. Purple knolls; rush-lined ponds, springs, streams; spongy mossland; gray-green fodder plants and wicker plants and others with webbed stems; white rock, yellowish rock…on and on forever… Was the whole world like this? In school he'd learned that the world was round and that it was all wilderness except for the circle of villages and farms spreading outward from the City—but did one piece of wilderness look like another?

The Technicians knew, he thought with rancor. The Technicians looked down on it from the air. No doubt they had already traveled beyond the Tomorrow Mountains, where the Prophecy claimed that more Cities would someday arise. The Scholars almost certainly had, for although it was rumored that they never left the City, it was ridiculous to suppose that they, who could do as they pleased in all respects, would not take advantage of the opportunity.

At the Gates of the City, Noren reflected, he might see Scholars. Robed in brilliant blue, the color reserved for them, they would appear as High Priests: not merely to conduct devotions as their representatives the Technicians did, but to receive the homage of the people. And the people would give it with gladness! On holidays like Founding Day, the periodic Blessing of the Seed, and the Day of the Prophecy—which celebrated the Mother Star's appearance in advance—hundreds walked to the City just to participate; and in the presence of Scholars those people knelt. Noren knew he could not look upon a Scholar without hating him.

And perhaps he might see more than just Scholars. Perhaps, he recalled in dismay, he'd witness some other heretic's recantation...

Resolutely he set the thought aside. Ahead, over the next rise, he glimpsed the thatched roof of Talyra's house. A sudden, foolish hope came to him: might not Talyra have had second thoughts? Mightn't she too have spent a sleepless night, deciding in the end to marry him in spite of his heresy? Much as he feared the answer, he could not leave without finding out. When it came right down to it, Noren realized, he could not leave without seeing her once more.

He crossed the farmyard and stood by the familiar door. At his call, Talyra's mother drew back the matting. "Oh, Noren," she said, obviously flustered, "Talyra can't come out. She—she isn't feeling well today."

"She's not ill!" he exclaimed, panic-stricken.

"No—no, not really. Only she won't see anybody."

Noren dropped his eyes dejectedly. "Look," he persisted, "I'm on my way to the City. I don't know when I'll be back. I've *got* to see her."

The woman frowned. "Well," she said slowly, "I'll do what I can."

He sat at the scrubbed softstone table drinking the tea she gave him, hearing the low murmur of women's voices and, to his anguish, occasional muffled sobs. In the corner of the room was the wicker couch, its frame stuffed with moss and covered with softened hides, where he and Talyra had sat not many weeks ago to plan their marriage; now red fabric lay there, her unfinished wedding dress. Skirts of red, the color of love, were worn only by brides.

Finally Talyra's mother returned. "I'm sorry, Noren," she reported unhappily. "Though she's refused to tell me why, she says that—that you must not come back for her sake."

Mumbling something, he got up and strode to the door. "The spirit of the Mother Star go with you, Noren," Talyra's mother added with feeling.

The words, though customary, were an unfortunate choice. Once again Noren departed without a backward look, torn between distaste for the naive sincerity with which they'd been spoken and an irrational sense of hurt because his own father, in pronouncing him free to go, had not thought to say them.

* * *

The village center was a cluster of unadorned stone buildings, facing upon a sanded street graced by neither shrubs nor moss. It was a gray place, enlivened by color only on festival days when people wore brilliant clothes instead of their ordinary brown ones: green for holidays, yellow and orange for parties, red-trimmed white for weddings and births. On this particular day there was no festival, and the village, deserted by everyone who had harvesting to begin, looked empty as well as drab.

Noren reached it just ahead of the scheduled rain. The first four mornings of each week, except during the final week of harvest season, it rained for exactly one hour, stopping at noon. In school he'd been taught that the Scholars arranged this; but lately he had wondered, for if there were no rain, would not all wild plants have perished before there were any Scholars?

Rain did not bother him; it was a pleasant contrast to the parching air. He walked down the street as the first drops spattered the sand, entering the inn less for cover than to talk to Arnil, the innkeeper.

"A trader?" Arnil said when Noren explained his purpose. "That's too bad, Noren. There was one here only last night looking for an extra driver. He planned to ask again in Prosperity."

Noren cursed inwardly; the village was not on the main route and there might not be another for days. "Could I catch up, do you think?" he inquired.

"Perhaps," Arnil told him. "He got a late start this morning and his two sledges were hitched together. Besides, the road's past due for sanding."

"I'll try, I guess," Noren said. Work-beasts did not walk much faster than men, certainly not when hitched as a team—which they stubbornly resisted—and pulling laden sledges over a road that hadn't enough sand to make the runners slide smoothly. If he pushed himself, he could reach the next village, Prosperity, before the trader had time to find anyone there.

"If you miss him, come back," said Arnil. "You can work in the kitchen until my regular girl's child arrives; I can't afford to pay you, but I'll give you bed and board."

"Thanks," Noren said, "but I hope I won't have to."

He went on through the center, passing a row of craftsworker's shops: the potter's, the wickermonger's, the shoemaker's and the stonecutter's. Beyond was the shop that sold common City goods—fabric, thread, paper, matches; the powder one used to keep cistern water clear; utensils of glass and of the opaque material that resembled polished bone—as well as rarer products like colored glass necklaces and books. Books...Noren could never go by that shop without wishing that he had the money for just one book of his own. Maybe he'd been foolish not to have worked on the farm for wages at least until the harvest was finished; that should have given him plenty, though books, aside from the Book of the Prophecy, were even higher priced than the love-beads he'd bought Talyra. It was because so few people cared about them, the shopkeeper had told him. Books were heavy, and when there wasn't much demand, a trader wouldn't bring them all the way from the City unless he could be sure that they'd sell for enough to make the trouble worthwhile. Most families did little reading; they sent their children to school only because it was considered a religious duty. Why was it? Noren wondered suddenly. Why did the High Law *encourage* learning, and then withhold knowledge from people who did care? No book, at any price, would tell the things *he* wanted to know...

Chagrined, he turned away from the shop and headed quickly for the outbound road. He'd been daydreaming again; there was, he realized, some truth to his brothers' accusations. On the farm it might not matter, but if he wanted to catch up with that trader he must hurry!

He did not catch up. Some three hours later, thoroughly exhausted from a grueling trip during which he'd alternately walked and jogged without pausing, he arrived in Prosperity only to find that the trader had just left, having hired a driver without difficulty. Harvest season was already over in Prosperity; the main radial on which that village was located happened to be a seasonal boundary line. Long ago, Noren had heard, all villages had planted grain at the same time, but there were now so many that the Technicians could not take soil-quickening Machines everywhere at once, and the crop cycle was therefore staggered. Though he'd known that in theory, it was startling to find that in Prosperity it was Seed-Offering Day.

The village was jammed with people. Leaving the inn where he'd inquired for the trader, Noren walked toward the center, which in Prosperity took the form of a square. Nearly everyone in sight wore festive green. A woman with a basket approached him, smiling. "Will you have a Festival Bun, neighbor?" she asked. Noren accepted gratefully; he'd eaten nothing since breakfast, and Festival Buns, baked in fancy shapes and decorated with seeds, were always free.

In the square an aircar rested while a procession of farmers passed by, depositing clearly-labeled seed bags before the presiding Technicians. That seed would be taken to the City, where it would be blessed in an impressive ritual before the Gates and then returned. The Scholars would not keep any. The portion of the harvest charged for soil-quickening, along with whatever extra the Technicians had bought, was always claimed immediately after threshing, for in the City there were gristmills run by Power. Seed-Offering was different. The High Law declared that all seed must be offered for blessing, since unblessed seed would not sprout into healthy grain.

Noren scowled. The Scholars had power over even that, he thought—even food, the one thing villagers could produce better than City-dwellers! To be sure, it could not be produced without the Machines that quickened the land...but did it really matter whether the seed was blessed or not?

Amid the light green of the crowd's clothing and the darker green of the Technicians' uniforms, flashes of color caught his eye. A group clad in red-trimmed white was approaching the aircar, led by a girl and boy, and from the girl's solid red skirt and headscarf he knew they were bride and groom. They, too, sought to be blessed. That, the High Law did not demand; weddings were performed by village councilmen, not Technicians; yet people always wanted a Technician's blessing on a marriage. Talyra would have wanted it, too! It would never have worked out, Noren thought in misery. He could never have brought himself to follow such a tradition.

The couple, surrounded by family and friends, stepped back, obviously happy with whatever the Technicians had said. Then, slowly, the aircar lifted; and as it rose, the crowd began to sing. Noren did not join in, though he knew the words well enough:

For blessing, now, we offer joyfully
The seed of our abundant harvesttide
To those who guard the heritage of the Star,
That in our hearts its spirit may abide.

He turned disconsolately away from the square, wondering what to do. The people would celebrate all evening; soon the flutes would start playing, and everyone would dance. Noren did not feel like dancing. Besides, there'd be no work available here, and he had too much pride to beg a night's lodging for which he could not pay. There was nothing to do but return to Arnil's.

Back on the road, he walked blindly, not noticing his surroundings until he came to the stone arch that bridged a stream. The heat of the day was still at its peak; he was terribly thirsty, especially after the dry Festival Bun, and the water below the bridge looked cool and fresh. Not for the first time, he wondered why it should be wrong to drink such water.

And then, suddenly skeptical, he stopped. A new and daring thought came to him: *was* it wrong? Could Kern's fantastic boast have been true after all?

People did not drink from streams. Animals did; the work-beasts were often watered in them. But people, like the caged fowl whose eggs and flesh were eaten, were not allowed to touch impure water. From earliest childhood Noren had been told that any person whose lips it passed would be turned into an idiot like the savages of the mountains. The most sacred precepts of the High Law decreed that one must not drink. But why? It wasn't reasonable to think that drinking what animals drank could turn a man into an idiot! That the Scholars fostered such a belief to keep people dependent on supplementing rainfall with water from the City was far more likely, for as long as no one could live without that water, their power was assured.

He stared at the stream, excitement rising in his throat. Did he believe in his own ideas or didn't he? Logic told him that to taste it would be harmless. To be sure, the world abounded in poisons, but if poisons were in the water, there would be no need for a taboo against it; illness and death would be threat enough. Furthermore, escaped fowl never died of poisoning—they were slaughtered and the meat was destroyed, as the High Law commanded. Noren scanned the deserted road. The thought of becoming an idiot was more repugnant to him than any physical danger, yet what good was a mind he dared not trust? If he, a grown man, let himself be ruled by nursery tales, his convictions were not worth the sacrifice he had made for them.

Leaving the bridge, Noren flung himself flat on the mossy earth beside the stream and, defiantly, drank long and deep. The water tasted pure; it tasted better than cistern water ever had. Rising, he wiped his face with the back of his hand and looked up at the sky. He had not become an idiot. He was himself, and if anything, he felt stronger and wiser than before.

Perhaps he was not so helpless as he'd supposed against the formidable power of the Scholars. Perhaps, if he lived his beliefs instead of merely holding to them, he could really find a way to make people see.

Chapter Three

Though the sun had gone down when Noren returned to his own village, it was yet early and the inn's tavern was not crowded. He sat at an empty table to eat the meal Arnil gave him, thinking only of how tired he was. He'd had no sleep for two days, and so much had happened...the dance; the ordeal of telling Talyra his secret, followed by their quarrel and the disruption of all his hopes; his long-awaited departure from home; the grueling, futile trip in the midday heat; the various disappointments and frustrations of the past hours...and the triumphs. There had indeed been triumphs—he'd at last proven himself not only against his brother, but against the High Law itself! He had drunk the forbidden water and was unharmed! Surely, in due course, he would get to the City.

His head drooped wearily; and since his back was to the door, he did not see the Technicians until their dark green uniforms loomed in front of him. There were two of them: the middle-aged one who'd appeared at the dance, and another who seemed very little older than Noren. "My greetings, citizen," said the first. "May we sit down with you?"

"I am pleased by your concern, sir," replied Noren. He was not pleased, but that was how one responded to the greeting of a Technician.

Arnil hurried over to serve the Technicians food and ale, and at their sign, placed a mug of ale before Noren also. "To the Scholars," said the young man, raising his.

Noren drank; it would have been unthinkable not to, though aside from his dislike of the toast he was unused to ale, having had neither the money nor the friends to spend much time in taverns. He found that it lessened his weariness. He looked across at the Technicians, irritated by the contrast between their situation and his own. It was unfair! Why should they have the right to know more than he did simply by virtue of their birth?

Wiping his brow, the young Technician declared, "Had I known the evenings were as hot as noon, I'd have been reluctant to stay the night."

Surely, thought Noren, these men could not think him so stupid as to suppose they'd chosen to sit at a villager's table merely to discuss the weather. "Is it less hot in the City, sir?" he asked.

"Since the Outer City is roofed over, its air is filtered," answered the other, "and it is therefore cool. My young companion has not lodged in a village before."

Noren had not been aware that the privileges of Technicians extended not only to education and the use of metal tools and Machines, but to unique physical comforts; his resentment grew. "You must excuse my ignorance," he said with ill-concealed irony.

The younger man smiled disarmingly. "Tell me, Noren, have you ever wished to learn more than you were taught in school?"

"More about what, sir?" The man's knowledge of his name was proof that they'd sought him out with a purpose; no doubt they'd seen him enter the inn.

"About—well, about the Prophecy, for instance. Where it came from, how it is that we have a Prophecy."

"I've wondered, yes."

"And developed your own answers, perhaps?"

Noren hesitated. One was not supposed to develop one's own answers. These Technicians could well be trying to trap him into an admission of heresy, and here, in a public tavern, such an admission would be fatal. He was exhausted, both physically and emotionally, and it was hard to think clearly; yet he knew he must be very careful. "There's much in the Book of the Prophecy that needs to be explained," he said levelly. "To an ignorant person like myself, much of it seems to have more than one interpretation."

"Yet it's hardly your job to interpret it," the older Technician said. "What are you going to do now that you've got to choose your work? Does farming satisfy you?"

"No, sir, it doesn't." Noren replied frankly. "I haven't decided exactly what I'll do." Inwardly he was in turmoil. He'd felt for some time that most Technicians suspected him and were watching him, but why should they want to provoke him into revealing his thoughts? Logically, they should try to prevent any unorthodox opinions from being heard. Was it possible that he was a threat to them? Could this mean that there was some way in which he could expose the Scholars' deceit?

If so, then he must at all costs stay free to do it; still he must at the same time take a calculated risk. He must play along with them, let them think they were succeeding, in the hope of finding a clue to what they feared.

"It must be hard to come to the end of your schooling when there's still a great deal you'd like to know," remarked the younger Technician with apparent sympathy. "I would find it intolerable myself."

Noren almost choked on a swallow of ale. The implied acknowledgment of equality astonished him; he had not thought they'd make such a statement publicly, whatever their reasons. Then, looking around, he saw that only two of the other tables were occupied, and that the men there were paying no attention to any talk but their own. Arnil was in the kitchen. For the moment, at least, they could not be overheard.

"It's indeed hard," he confessed. "I would give much for further learning."

"Villagers do learn more at the training center outside the City, where men and women are prepared to become radiophonists, schoolteachers, nurse-midwives, and the like. It is a virtue to so dedicate oneself."

"Are you offering to send me there?" Noren demanded. That was the proposal that had been made to Talyra; he had not expected it for himself, but crumb though it was, he would not reject such a chance.

"No," the Technician said. "Those to whom offers are made are chosen by the Scholars; we are merely envoys."

"How do the Scholars choose?"

"By school records, I suppose. They have everyone's school records, you know."

He hadn't known, but it was not surprising. There must be more to the choice than that, however, for he had led his class in school. Perhaps the Technicians actually weren't informed. "Don't the Scholars tell you?" he inquired casually.

"They tell us very little," the young man said. "We are trained in our work; that is all. Someone who does well can receive extra training if he wishes, but he is not taught the reasons for things."

The words sounded a bit rueful, and Noren was nonplused; he had not stopped to think that the Technicians themselves might long for more knowledge. Machines were obviously complicated and would require much wisdom to build. "Is it not necessary to know reasons in order to make the Machines function?" he asked.

"No, not at all. If a Machine is damaged, a specialist must repair it, and few of us do work of that kind."

Startled, Noren perceived that the men who operated the Machines might know very little about how they were made, though he had never before had cause to suspect such a distinction. "Do you choose the kind of work you want to learn?" he persisted.

"Yes, if it's available; we're as free as you are in that respect."

That seemed an odd way to put it. Maybe, Noren reflected, he had been mistaken about these men's motive for sitting down with him; they were less patronizing than most, and it was possible that they were simply making conversation. Glancing over his shoulder, he saw that the room was still nearly deserted. He paused, wondering how best to make use of this opportunity, while the older of the two men refilled the mugs with ale.

"I myself would like to know reasons as well as skills," the younger man continued. "I can't see what harm there'd be in it."

Noren stared at him. Somehow it had not occurred to him that he might find allies among the Technicians. He'd lumped them together with the Scholars, assuming them to be equally calculating in their support of the High Law. But that was not really very reasonable. If they were men, they had opinions and feelings like other men, and they too must resent being deprived of the whole truth! For he saw that apart from the specific jobs they performed, they did not know nearly as much as he'd supposed. They were only tools. They probably took the Prophecy as seriously as did the villagers.

He must find out! Alone he was powerless; even if he should succeed in convincing a handful of other people, they could do nothing against the Scholars. But if *Technicians* could be won over...

"You were asking me about the Prophecy," he said. "I've been told, of course, that it came to us from the Mother Star; but that's confusing. The Mother Star is not yet even visible. So how did it determine the words written in a book?"

"That is a mystery," said the other Technician. "We are not intended to understand such things as that."

He had said "we," Noren noted. And the more he thought about it, the more evident it was that the Scholars would not have confided in the Technicians. There were too many of them; if they suspected any fraud, they would no longer take orders. Technicians, being outside village law, were subject to the direct authority of the Scholars, whose power depended on their obedience.

"I suppose the Scholars understand."

"The Scholars understand everything," agreed the man.

"No doubt. Yet are they really more capable of understanding than wise men like yourselves? You, sir—" Noren turned to the sympathetic younger Technician with the tone of deference that he'd long ago learned to feign. "You have so much more knowledge than I do; I can't believe that there's anything you could not grasp if it were explained to you. Have you never wished that these mysteries were not hidden?"

"I have, sometimes," the youth admitted. "At times I'm weary of spending my days in the villages checking radiophone equipment; in fact I've requested Inner City work, which would give me opportunity to see the Scholars and perhaps learn from them. But that, for us, is an honor demanding self-dedication, as is the training center for you, and so far my request has been denied."

Noren was by this time wholly absorbed by the new and promising discovery he'd made; he had forgotten to watch over his shoulder. "Perhaps the Scholars fear you might learn too much," he suggested.

"Too much?"

"Maybe there are things you could indeed understand, but would make you less content to follow their orders. Would you be here in this inn tonight if you did not believe in the superior wisdom of Scholars?"

After a slight pause, the man dropped his eyes. "I—I never thought of it that way," he said, almost with chagrin. "No, I don't suppose I would."

"Nor would I," declared Noren. "If wisdom and Power and Machines were shared equally among all, as the Prophecy tells us will someday happen, we would both be freer and happier. Why should there be any delay?"

Abruptly, the Technician stood up. His expression had changed; he seemed stricken by a guilt he had not felt at first. "I spoke in haste," he said with evident distress. "We must discuss these matters with caution; the Prophecy covers them, and the Scholars are our betters—"

Noren too got to his feet, swaying unsteadily. He was in no condition to be cautious; his head was spinning with excitement, with prolonged fatigue, and perhaps with too much ale. "But Scholars are not our betters!" he exclaimed, unaware of how his voice had risen. "They're no better than you are, nor than the rest of us, either! Don't you see, the Prophecy's only an excuse; they made it up so that we wouldn't object to having them keep things from us."

There was dead silence. The young Technician looked positively ill, and following his anguished gaze, Noren turned to meet the scandalized stares of nearly a dozen men: those at the other tables, old Arnil the innkeeper, and in the open doorway, a newly-arrived group that included his own two elder brothers.

Noren's head swam dizzily. The room whirled, and for a moment he was sure he would collapse. It did not seem as if this could really have happened. How could he have been so rash as to say words that would condemn him?

Grimly, he reminded himself that he had always known it must happen someday. "Someday," however, was vague, and his fear of it could be pushed aside...whereas this was *now.* The damage was irrevocable; he would be tried tomorrow, and the next day he would reach the City without the effort of driving a trader's sledge.

The Technicians moved quietly into the background, for it was not their business to arrest heretics; under the High Law they could neither accuse nor give evidence. They would take charge of him only after his conviction. For the present he stood alone, facing the villagers' enmity.

"I knew the boy was worthless," announced one of his brothers coldly, "but I hadn't thought him guilty of heresy. It's a good thing he no longer lives under our roof."

The public disavowal did not surprise Noren; few families would stand behind a self-proclaimed heretic, and certainly not his. The morning's fight with this brother had nothing to do with it. He knew, however, that they were all too pleased by his downfall.

The dread word *heresy,* once uttered, spread through the group like fire out of control. There hadn't been a heresy trial in the village for some time, and the last case had been an old woman, falsely accused of disobeying the High Law by making cook-pots of unpurified clay, who had actually been acquitted. There was no possibility of acquittal when the charge was brought by many witnesses. "I'll fetch the marshals," cried one of his brothers' friends excitedly.

Several men advanced toward Noren, and one of them spat contemptuously. "So the Scholars are not your betters," he growled. "You'll learn differently, boy, when they get you inside that City of theirs."

"Why wait for that," said someone in an ugly tone, "when he can begin his recanting here and now?"

His brothers and their companions moved closer, their intent obvious, and despite himself Noren stepped backward against the table, leaning against it for support. Arnil came to his side. "There'll be none of that here in my inn," he declared vehemently. "The boy's dazed by ale; he doesn't realize what he's said. I'm sure he's no true heretic."

Raising his eyes, Noren admitted, "I do know what I've said, Arnil. Everyone heard; you can't save me now, and you'll only cause trouble for yourself by trying."

"But Noren," protested Arnil, "you couldn't have meant it the way it sounded. Not about the Prophecy—"

Arnil, Noren knew, was a devout man who would never believe anything contrary to the Book of the Prophecy and would be deeply shocked by the idea that anyone else might; yet neither would he enjoy seeing a person hurt for it. "I'm sorry I got you involved," Noren said sincerely, "but I did mean it, and it wasn't the ale. It's something I've thought for a long time."

"What am I going to do when they call me to testify?" Arnil mumbled in anguish.

"You must tell the truth," said Noren resolutely. "I shall."

"You will indeed," agreed his eldest brother, "after we're through with you. You'll be begging for mercy before you ever see any Scholars."

Sick fear enveloped Noren; he was fair game now, and he knew that his brothers would take their revenge for the surprise punch. They were restrained not so much by Arnil's protests as by the presence of the Technicians, but they would have their chance later, for they were well acquainted with one of the jailers.

A crowd was already gathering outside the inn; Noren could see it when the door matting swung aside to admit the marshals.

The night of Kern's death loomed vividly in his memory. He realized that he would not be murdered as Kern had been—he had neither a bad reputation nor any real enemies, and besides, while Technicians were lodged in the village not even the angriest mob would dare—but all the same, his heart contracted when he glimpsed the flame of a torch.

The marshals bound his arms with ropes and led him out into the torrid dusk. The jailhouse was some distance up the street, and the people followed them toward it, shouting. Most of the people had not heard what he'd said at the inn, and the story had grown rapidly; the present version of what he'd called the Scholars, of which he caught snatches, was not merely blasphemous, but ribald. All of a sudden Noren knew why these men could never forgive him. He had expressed what they dared not say! In misquoting him, they were echoing their own real inclinations; but they could not admit that even to themselves. Those noisiest in their denunciation were the ones most afraid of their own underlying feelings. The villagers who had no such feelings—people like Talyra, like Arnil—were not in the street.

Noren tried to keep his head up, he tried to bear the contempt unflinchingly for the sake of the truth that meant more to him than anything else, but he was unable to maintain much dignity. His exhaustion; his rage both at the world and at himself for having been caught without achieving anything; his irrepressible fear—together, they proved more than he could handle. Perhaps the ale did have something to do with it, but in any event he stumbled and fell; and the marshals half-dragged him the rest of the way.

The jailhouse was fairly new, all but the stone walls having been rebuilt after the burning of its predecessor, but it was filthy, for it was seldom used and even less often cleaned. There was little lawbreaking in the village, and anyone convicted of a serious crime such as murder was hanged without delay; so apart from men awaiting trial, the jail had few occupants. Marshals and jailers worked as such only when needed. On this particular evening they'd been called to the inn from the rival tavern run by the brewer, to which they were anxious to return.

Noren was thrown into the inner room, his legs tied as well as his arms, and the heavier-than-average door matting was lashed securely in place. The cell had no furnishings; he sprawled on a floor of rough stone. There were no windows, and the air, of course, was stifling. For a while he was too overcome to think rationally, yet despite his fatigue he could not sleep; the thought of what awaited him in the City would not let him. The hours passed slowly, till he judged it must be past midnight.

Eventually, as he lay there, Kern's words came back to him: *Don't worry about me, because if I'm ever condemned I'm going to find out a lot that I can't learn here.* To Kern it would have been an adventure. He too must think of it that way, Noren knew. Yet Kern, for all his bravery, had not felt the same sense of failure he did. He had not felt the compelling need to accomplish things, to *change* things, that had been growing in Noren of late. He'd been defiant, but he had not considered truth a trust that must be passed on.

Hearing heavy, menacing footsteps, followed by the unlashing of the door, Noren struggled to sit up. His brothers stood over him, flanked by the jailer who was their friend and another who'd relieved the one originally left on duty. They had spent the evening in the brewery's tavern and all of them had had more than enough ale. Noren was well aware of what was going to happen. His arms and legs were still bound tightly, and they would not be unbound. He was defenseless, for the Technicians were by this time asleep in the inn and though the High Law required that he be turned over to them unharmed, they would not intervene in a village affair unless he was in danger of serious injury. Perhaps if he yelled loud enough someone would come, since on the whole the people of the village were decent folk; but his pride was too great for that.

"Are you going to retract what you said?" his eldest brother taunted.

"No," said Noren. There was nothing else he could say. He bit down hard on his lip and took the beating with scarcely a sound, until at last, mercifully, the world went dark around him and he knew no more before morning.

When he awoke it was approaching midday; he could tell because before he'd mustered the courage to move, the sound of rain began. The trial, by long established custom, would be held an hour past noon, so he had two hours in which to prepare himself.

Painfully, Noren pulled himself to a sitting position. He was badly bruised, but as far as he could determine there were no bones broken. It could have been much worse; his strength had been so nearly gone at the outset, he judged, that he'd lost consciousness sooner than his assailants had expected.

The brutally tight ropes with which he'd been bound had been loosened slightly, no doubt so that he would present a better appearance at the trial; the jailers must have grown fearful of the Technicians' censure. Noren flexed his fingers and found that they worked normally. While doing so he was abruptly overcome by nausea and, crawling to the clay pot in the corner, was violently, wretchedly ill. After that he lay down again, tormented by thirst and unsure as to whether his fortitude would be equal to the challenges ahead.

The outcome of the trial, of course, was a foregone conclusion. He had not asked for an advocate to defend him, as would have been necessary had he been falsely accused. The coming judgment was a mere formality, for he was, according to village law, manifestly guilty, and he had no intention of denying it. An advocate's defense would not help. There was only one defense: the truth. He had no illusions; he knew that no such defense could save him; but truth—Truth, in the special sense in which he had always thought of it—was in itself worth proclaiming. If he came out with it boldly, perhaps his words might influence someone, and that way his life would not be entirely wasted.

He had resigned himself to dying, though he knew no actual death sentence would be pronounced. The sentencing of heretics, unlike that of people convicted of other crimes, was not within the jurisdiction of the village council; it lay with the Scholars, and the Scholars were thought to be merciful. That was why the accused was sometimes murdered without benefit of trial, for never within memory had any heretic been sentenced to die. The passing of sentence, however, was part of the ceremony of public recantation—and Noren did not intend to recant.

Nobody had been told what happened to heretics who refused to recant—there were not many such, and in fact it was doubtful whether one could be mentioned by name—but it was commonly assumed that they must be killed. That, after all, was the only fate worse than the doom of those who did recant, for on one thing all rumors agreed: no heretic who had entered the City had ever been seen again, except during recantation itself, where the chilling phrase "we hereby commute your sentence to perpetual confinement" invariably ended the ceremony.

The question of how heretics were persuaded to recant was discussed only in whispers. The threat of death presumably had a good deal to do with it, yet that could not be the whole story; many before Noren had been determined never to give in, declaring themselves entirely ready to die for their convictions, only to deny all those convictions a few weeks later. Enough strong men had done so to indicate that it was not merely a matter of losing one's nerve.

Determinedly Noren pushed such speculations from his mind. He must forget them; he must pull himself together for the trial. Drawing himself upright once more, he leaned against the wall of the airless cell, hoping he would prove able to stand alone.

A jailer—not one of those who'd come during the night—brought him water and untied his bonds, making it plain that plenty of assistants were within call. After drinking, Noren cleaned himself up as best he could. Then he was taken under guard to the village hall. There were no hecklers in the street, for everybody who had a free afternoon was already packed inside. A trial was something few would want to miss. As he entered, Noren saw to his dismay that Talyra was seated in the front row. He'd feared they would force her to attend, and he knew that his most difficult task would be to protect her. Now more than ever, he cursed himself for having revealed his secret and thereby placed her in jeopardy. She was alone; her parents were not present, nor was his own father, who was no doubt unable to face the shame.

All eyes were on Noren as he took the place designated before his six judges, the village councilmen. At the sight of the bruises on his face and arms, Talyra bent her head in anguish, but his battered appearance was ignored by everyone else, including the Technicians, who sat in the back of the room. Both of them avoided his glance. His feelings were confused in regard to the Technicians; they might have been sent to trap him, still the young man's discontent had seemed genuine.

One by one the witnesses gave their reports of what had occurred at the inn. A number of them had short memories and related the street version of Noren's remarks rather than what he had actually said, causing most of the women in the room to turn pale with horror at the blasphemy; Talyra, staring at him, seemed about to faint. Noren found himself blushing for her sake, but as far as he was concerned it was a matter of small significance; he had not used words of that sort, but he could scarcely deny that he had thought them.

Arnil spoke last, and he gave a faithful account. That it was an ordeal for him was obvious; yet he had been required to swear by the Mother Star that his testimony would be true and complete, and he therefore had no alternative. Noren was glad when the old innkeeper was dismissed, and he himself was ordered to stand. The judges' table was positioned so that in facing them, he still met the hostile gaze of the spectators. It did not shake him. For the first time in his life he was free to say what he really thought.

"You have heard your accusers," the Chief of Council said to him sternly. "Do you dare to deny your guilt?"

"I deny that I've done anything to feel guilty for," Noren said steadily, "but I don't dispute the testimony. The charges are true."

A gasp arose from the spectators; they had not expected him to be so brazen. "Do you mean to say you see nothing wrong in blaspheming not only against our High Priests the Scholars, but against the Prophecy itself?" demanded one of the judges incredulously.

"There isn't anything wrong in it," Noren replied. "The Scholars, as I said, are no better than other men; in fact they're worse, for it's they who've done wrong in keeping knowledge from us. The Prophecy blinds us to the absurdity of the High Law through which they've established their power, and that's exactly why they wrote it."

At once the room was in uproar; several people jumped from their seats, shouting angrily for immediate condemnation. "Silence!" ordered the Chief of Council, banging the table with his fist. "I agree that the provocation was very great, but under the law—the High Law as well as our own—this boy must receive a fair trial."

"What need is there to investigate any further?" protested another councilman. "We have evidence of his guilt from his own lips as well as from those of ten witnesses, two of whom are his brothers."

"One of those witnesses, the innkeeper, felt that the boy was not himself and was unaware of the import of his words," reminded someone.

"That is belied by the statement he has just made," the Chief of Council pointed out. "However, it is proper that we determine whether or not his heresy is of long standing." Turning to Noren he inquired, "How long have you held the false view you just expressed here?"

"It is not false," Noren declared calmly. "I have held it since childhood, but I never told anyone."

"Never? You have been a heretic for years and yet kept your pernicious ideas entirely to yourself? I would think rather that you might have corrupted others in secret."

Noren had known this issue would be raised, and he had decided how he must deal with it. The risk in telling the whole truth was less than that in attempting to evade it, for Talyra would be required to testify anyway, and she would not lie under oath; he must forestall any suspicion that she might have supported him. "As a child, I discussed my beliefs with another heretic who is now dead," he answered. "After his death, I was afraid. I spoke to no one until two nights ago. At that time I confessed them to my betrothed, whereupon she broke our betrothal and has refused to see me since."

Pain crossed Talyra's face, a look not merely of sorrow, but of deep hurt. Bewildered, Noren wondered why the truth should evoke such a look, for surely she knew that the fact she'd broken off with him was her best protection. And then he saw. She was blaming herself for his arrest! She thought he had not trusted her and had spoken in the tavern because he considered himself already doomed.

It was providential. Though he longed to say something reassuring, he knew he must do the opposite. His greatest fear had been that although her refusal to go through with the marriage would be corroborated by both his family and hers, she would be suspect because she'd failed to report him; now, by one small but cruel lie, he could ensure her safety.

"She told me she wouldn't reveal her reason for calling off the wedding," he went on, "but I could see that her piety was stronger than whatever love she had once felt for me. After that there was little point in caution, for though she was kept home by illness yesterday, she would surely have denounced me as soon as she was able to."

Talyra turned away from him, her suffering obvious to all. "The girl's piety is indeed well known," one of the councilmen said. "It is plain that in betrothing herself to this scoundrel, she was the innocent victim of his deceit. I see no need to subject her to questioning, since he has already admitted his crime. I see no need to question anyone else at all. The case is clear-cut."

The Chief of Council nodded. "That's quite true. However, the boy himself must be examined further. Not only did he say blasphemous and heretical things, but he said them to Technicians! It is fortunate for him, and for all of us, that the High Law toward which he shows such disrespect does not in itself forbid the voicing of wicked ideas, and that its enforcement is left to us in any case; otherwise he would have been instantly struck down by those Technicians' wrath. We would not have them think us tolerant of whatever other heresies he may be harboring."

There was a murmur of agreement. "We of this village," the man continued, "are respectable, reverent people, ever mindful of the High Law's demands. We must concede that although we may forbid heresy in our own laws, it is not ours to chastise; yet should we fail to root out this boy's errors and censure him severely for them, our name would be forever tarnished."

Noren waited with newly revived confidence. He had anticipated this and in fact had hoped for it; only under cross-examination would he be permitted to argue for his beliefs. He was fighting not for his freedom, which could not be won in any case, but to be heard; if this was to be his only chance, he was going to make the most of it.

All six of the councilmen glared at him reproachfully. "The Book of the Prophecy," one of them began, "tells us that at the time of the Founding, the Scholars in their wisdom made the High Law, and that although its mysteries will not be made plain to us until the Mother Star appears, we are nevertheless bound to follow it. It is possible that you are ignorant of the reason for this?"

"I am not ignorant of the reason that's given," said Noren. "It's claimed that without the High Law, people could not survive. But why should we assume that to be the real reason?"

"Because the book says so," declared the man, as if to a very stupid child.

Noren laughed. "That doesn't prove anything. When the Scholars wrote the book, they naturally put in a reason that sounded good."

"Have you no respect for anything sacred?" cried another judge indignantly.

"I respect truth," Noren said soberly. "I respect it too much to believe anything merely because some book or some person tells me I should. I want to really *know!* Maybe you'd rather accept stories that make you feel comfortable about the way things are, but I care more for truth than for comfort."

For a moment the councilman seemed incapable of reply. "I shall pass over the enormity of your arrogance," he told Noren after an ominous pause, "and simply point out to you that it is self-evident that we could not survive without the High Law. We live only by the grace of the Scholars. If they did not send us water, we would die of thirst. If they did not send Machines to quicken the land, no grain would sprout; and if they did not cause rain, the sprouts would die. For that matter, if the Scholars blessed no seed there would be no grain in the first place, nor would there be fowl if they had not favored our ancestors with the gift of fertile eggs. We would all starve."

"I too will pass over much," said Noren slowly, realizing that he could not possibly present the details of his thoughts about all these topics. "I will concede that we are dependent on the Scholars' knowledge and on the use of Machines. But knowledge and Machines should be shared by all of us. It is not right for them to be controlled by Scholars."

"Of course it is right! It is how things have been since the time of the Founding."

"I do not believe in the Founding," said Noren.

Once again the Chief of Council had to pound on the table to restore order, and this time it took quite a while to obtain it. No one in the village had ever heard of a heretic going so far as to deny the Prophecy's account of the Founding.

"Just how do you think people got here," inquired a councilman sarcastically, "if they did not come from the sky? Did they rise out of the ground, perhaps, like plants?"

With many interruptions, Noren attempted to explain his theory about the savages, noticing hopelessly that nobody was taking him seriously. "The savages are idiots," protested someone in an exasperated tone.

"Maybe our original ancestors were idiots, and as they learned more, became more intelligent."

That was the wrong thing to say. It was also a mistake to suggest that the ancestors of the Scholars and Technicians might have been idiots. Noren perceived that whatever secret support he might have gained had been wiped out; the spectators were now firmly united against him.

"You can achieve nothing by mocking us," the Chief of Council admonished. "You are exhausting our patience! Everyone knows that the savages are idiots because they disobeyed the High Law and drank impure water."

Noren hesitated only a moment; he had nothing to lose, and perhaps he could convince someone that in this respect at least, the High Law was foolish. "I doubt that," he asserted. "I myself drank from a stream only yesterday, and as you see I'm still quite sane."

There was an exclamation of horrified disbelief, and the judges scowled, as if they considered that last point to be somewhat questionable. "You are not an idiot *yet,*" one of them conceded, "but we know nothing of how long the process takes. Any morning you could wake up to find yourself transformed."

"It's indeed fortunate that the boy was apprehended before his marriage," stated another coldly. "Some say that if a man should drink impure water and remain unchanged, his wife would give birth to idiot children."

Noren looked out at the people in surprise; that story was not prevalent, and he had never heard it before. He caught Talyra's eye, seeing that she was more shocked and wounded than ever. *Oh, Talyra,* he thought wretchedly, *surely you don't believe such nonsense!* But he knew that she did, and that she would never marry him after this even if he were to recant and be miraculously released. He also, for the first time, understood the real reason for Kern's murder; Kern had been all too popular with girls.

The councilmen huddled together; Noren realized that they were about to pronounce the verdict and that he would have little more chance to speak. Desperately he said, "Forget about the Founding! Forget all I've said if you wish, but is it not a fact that the Prophecy itself admits that it's not good for the Scholars to keep things from us? Does it not say that someday they will no longer do so, that knowledge and Machines will come to everyone and that *'the children of the Star will find their own wisdom and choose their own Law'?* Why would the Scholars have made such a promise if not because they knew that's how the world should be? I don't deny that they're wise! They knew, and they also knew that the promise would keep us content to hope instead of seizing what's rightfully ours."

"The promise was not made by the Scholars," reproved the Chief of Council. "It came from the Mother Star itself. The

Prophecy will be fulfilled when the Star appears to us and not a day sooner; to believe that things should be otherwise is the worst sort of heresy."

It was not the worst sort, and Noren, seeing that his case was lost, took the ultimate step of defiance. "I do not believe that there is a Mother Star," he stated honestly.

He expected pandemonium, but instead, the room remained hushed; everybody was speechless. Finally the Chief of Council mustered the composure to proceed. "We'll waste no more time here," he said, "for it's plain that you are past redemption. I grow cold at the thought of the punishments that will be yours when you enter the City! Are you not aware that the Technicians present in this room have a Machine wherewith they have recorded every word you have said? When you face the Scholars, Noren, you will be forced to listen to those words spoken by your own voice; and it will then be too late to plead for the forgiveness you will crave."

Noren hadn't known of the Recording Machine, but though startling, the idea of hearing his testimony repeated did not strike him as the dire ordeal it was evidently intended to be. "Do you think I don't plan to be truthful before the Scholars?" he demanded. "If my words are recorded, then I'll be saved the trouble of saying the same things over."

"You are insolent now. Your life may be spared once your insolence has been crushed, but I'll wager you'll be made sorry to be alive." The Chief of Council rose. "We have reached a unanimous verdict. We pronounce you guilty as charged, and hereby remand you to the custody of the Scholars as is required of us under the High Law, though I have never seen anyone less deserving of their mercy."

The marshals stepped again to Noren's side. As he was led down the aisle, Talyra's eyes met his, and she was in tears; he saw that despite her revulsion at his beliefs, she still loved him and would grieve for him. No one else showed any sympathy. Even Arnil lowered his head when Noren passed. From behind, one of the judges added, "May the spirit of the Mother Star protect you, Noren, for it's sure that you'll find no succor among men."

Chapter Four

Noren was lodged in the jail that night; the Technicians, apparently, were not yet ready to take him away. After some hours he remembered that he had had no food since the previous evening. Perhaps that contributed to his faintness, though he felt no hunger.

Fear was rising in him again now that the trial was over. He'd suppressed it while there'd been something he had to do, but once alone, he could no longer keep it down. Too many of his nightmares in the past years had been centered on the unknown horrors that were about to confront him. *We can't be forced to do or to believe anything against our will,* Kern had said, but Noren could not help worrying.

The Scholars, he realized, would not view him as his judges had. They, after all, knew even more of the truth than he did; they would not consider it stupid or sinful not to believe in things like the Founding and the Mother Star. On the contrary, they would recognize the sharpness of his mind. They would recognize it as a threat to their supremacy. One way or another, they would have to silence him; it was no wonder that they required all heretics to be placed in their hands. Nor was it any wonder that no villagers seemed to care about truth, he saw with bitterness. Anyone who'd shown signs of caring had been trapped, as he had, and summarily disposed of.

His attempt to convince people at the trial had been an utter failure, Noren knew. Nobody had been impressed by his arguments; they had simply been incensed. Thinking of it, impotent rage burgeoned within him: rage at the defeat, the blindness of others, the whole injustice of the way the world was arranged. He strained against the tight ropes with which he was again bound until his wrists were raw and his body clammy with sweat. Was there no power that could stand against a system that was so *wrong?*

There was, he perceived suddenly. He would undoubtedly be hurt in the City; in the end he would be killed; but as long as he kept on caring, nothing could touch the freedom of his inner thoughts. With that one solace he fell at last into fitful sleep.

It was pitch dark in the cell when Noren awoke to the sound of voices and knew that the door matting was being unlashed. He sat up, thinking in despair that he had not the strength to endure another beating.

But the figure that appeared in the doorway was not one of his brothers, nor yet a drunken jailer. It was the young Technician.

He carried a lantern—not an ordinary one, but the mysterious kind that had neither tallow nor flame, being instead lit by Power—and as he approached, his face was illuminated; Noren saw that it was drawn. "Speak softly," the Technician cautioned, without formal greeting. "I've sent the jailer outside, but he's not far off, and I don't wish to be overheard."

"Are you going to take me to the City in the middle of the night?" Noren demanded, startled.

"No. You'll be taken about two hours after sunrise, but I want to talk to you alone beforehand." The man's anguish was evident. "I—I'm sorry, Noren," he continued through white lips. "I don't expect you to forgive me, but all the same I had to come."

"What happened wasn't your fault," Noren said. "We both spoke rashly. You too could be in trouble if the Scholars found out all you said to me."

"You don't understand," persisted the Technician. "It was a deliberate setup; I was instructed in what to say. At first I was only following orders, and then I—I found I meant what I was telling you, and I tried to stop the thing, but it was too late."

On the verge of fury, Noren paused. Despite the betrayal, this man might have had a change of heart, and if so, he might someday be able to actively oppose the Scholars; a Technician was in a far better position to do so than a villager. "Just what do you believe?" he asked slowly.

"I believe as you do," the Technician confessed. "I didn't know I did until I heard you testify today, but—well, that woke me up. It's wrong for the Scholars to conceal their knowledge! And it's wrong for you to be punished for saying what you think."

"Will you answer some questions?" Noren challenged. Above all, he needed information, and this was probably his one chance to get it.

"Yes, if I can." The Technician, to Noren's astonishment, drew the matting across the cell's door and without hesitation, removed the ropes by which his prisoner was kept helpless. Then he sat down on the dirty stone floor and placed the light between himself and Noren.

"Exactly what were your instructions?" Noren began.

"To watch you, wait till you were in some public place or else alone with your older brothers, and then trick you into an open declaration of heresy by pretending to sympathize."

Noren frowned; whoever had planned that had been very clever and very well informed. They had known his brothers would denounce him, and what was more, had been aware that he viewed Technicians as people rather than as the nameless, faceless beings most villagers considered them. The more obvious approach would have been to arouse his ire by an overbearing attitude, yet it had been foreseen that he'd be on guard against that. "Was the other man to do the same?" he inquired.

"I don't think so, but we were briefed separately. I assume he was told not to report me later for anything I might say." Meeting Noren's eyes, the Technician added painfully, "You'd best know everything. He admitted to me that it was hoped that offering your girl an appointment to the training center would upset your marriage plans, and perhaps make you vulnerable."

Noren clenched his hands, knowing that he could not afford to give in to anger, and demanded, "Were you told why they wanted me convicted?"

"Yes, at least they had an excuse that seemed plausible at the time. They claimed it was for your own good! They knew you were a heretic, and they said it would be better for you to get caught while we were on hand to see that you weren't harmed by the villagers."

"It would have been still better for me not to have gotten caught at all," said Noren dryly.

"They don't look at it that way. They think a heretic is happier after they've converted him, that he benefits from 'acknowledging the truth,' as they call it."

"Recanting?" asked Noren with a shiver.

"Yes. I believed it, Noren! I've always believed it, but now—after what you said at the trial—I can't."

"Who gave you your instructions?"

"The Scholar Stefred." There was awe in the Technician's voice, as if the name was of particular and terrible significance. "He's the Chief Inquisitor, and he's in charge of all heresy proceedings. I'd never seen him except from a distance, at ceremonies, until he sent for me. He seemed to know a lot about me, Noren—and he knew *all* about you."

That fit, Noren thought; things had been too carefully planned for it to have been otherwise. "What will happen to me in—in the City?" he faltered.

"I honestly don't know. We don't have any more information about that than the villagers. Ordinary Technicians aren't allowed in the Inner City, the Scholars' part; when Stefred sent for me, I went to a conference room in the exit dome where the Gates are, and that's Outer City. All I can tell you is that he'll make you recant."

"How? By torture?" Noren asked directly.

The young Technician averted his face. "I'm afraid it may be something like that," he admitted miserably. "When you talk to him, he doesn't seem like a cruel man, yet it's said that no heretic can hold out against him. I used to think he really convinced people, but I can see that wouldn't work with someone like you; and threats wouldn't, either."

"No," declared Noren grimly. "Look, if you know anything more specific—any rumors, even—go ahead and say so. Don't try to spare me, because I'd rather be prepared."

"I wish I could help. But there's—well, a strange sort of mystery about heresy. I don't know how to describe it except to say that we all feel there's some tremendous secret that's hidden from everyone but Scholars. Perhaps it's merely what you believe, that they made up the whole Prophecy to stay in power. I think there's more to it, though; I think it's connected with what becomes of heretics, both before they recant and afterwards. They're imprisoned in the Inner City, you see, and Outer City people don't have any contact with them."

Noren shuddered. The information he was getting was anything but reassuring. He was quiet for a few moments, then asked hesitantly, "Are you transporting me to the City yourself?"

"No," the Technician replied. "I can guess what you're thinking, and I'd like to let you escape; but it's impossible. They'll send an aircar for you. All we do is escort you to it, keeping you safe from the mob that'll gather to watch." There was an unhappy silence. Then suddenly he raised his head, saying in a low, excited voice, "If you were to escape, it would have to be tonight. Is there anybody who'd help you if I could get you out of here? Your family, maybe? I—I've just had an idea, but it depends on outside aid."

Noren thought. His brothers would not want to help him; his father would not dare. But Talyra...

Talyra loved him. She would not marry him, but neither would she abandon him to torture and death. To aid a convicted heretic would be a sin in her eyes; she would be torn; still, remembering her as he'd last seen her in the courtroom, he was quite sure that she wouldn't refuse him any help that was in her power to provide.

Yet he could not say so. His testimony at the trial had cleared her of involvement, and he dared not undo that. This Technician seemed sincere, but he had tricked him once; there was no real assurance that he would not do so again. The whole episode, including both the confession of remorse and the frightening suggestion of some unspeakable mystery in regard to his fate, might be a trick to get the names of other potential heretics; the Scholars' design was obviously complex.

"No," he said. "No, there isn't anyone."

The Technician's distress, whatever its cause, was unquestionably real. "I don't believe that," he said slowly, "but I can't blame you for not trusting me. Noren, you don't need to! I won't have to know from whom you get help. What I'm proposing is that you change clothes with me, here and now, then tie me up and simply walk out."

Noren stared at him, completely and utterly astonished. That a Technician should make such an offer was incredible even in the light of his own unprecedented view of their humanity. "But—but what would happen to you?" he stammered.

"Nothing. The aircar will take me back to the City, where I'll be recognized. The other Technician will recognize me first, of course; but the villagers won't, and to save face he'll put me aboard quickly, without letting them notice that I'm not you."

"Won't the Scholars punish you?" Noren protested.

"I'll say your ropes were loose and you overpowered me. That can't hurt you even if they recapture you, since under the High Law they can't accuse a villager of any crime for which he hasn't been convicted in a civil trial."

It made sense, Noren saw. They would certainly be more likely to believe that a heretic would overpower a Technician than that the Technician would voluntarily change places with him!

"In any case," the man went on, "they'll be looking for you before I get back; the aircar has radiophone equipment, and I'll have to let the pilot use it. That's why you'll need help. You've got to get other clothes and be well away from here when the alert's given. Can you arrange that?"

"Perhaps," Noren admitted. "What happens to me if I fail?"

"Nothing worse than what'll happen if we don't try it, at least not as far as the Scholars are concerned. The villagers—" The Technician frowned. "Officially I'm here to protect you from the villagers. If you're caught by them after I'm gone, you may be in trouble, especially if the story that you attacked me gets out."

Noren knew only too well what trouble he'd be in. If he should be caught masquerading as a Technician, he would incur even more wrath than Kern had. Yet it was that against certain doom, and even if he lived only a short while, he might manage to convince someone who would carry on after him. The fact that he'd convinced the Technician was encouraging, if he had indeed convinced him and this too was not an elaborate trap of some kind. It seemed odd that the man did not expect to be held in suspicion merely for having visited a prisoner's cell at this hour; still, what was there to lose by trusting him? "I'll try," he decided, "if you're sure you'll be all right."

"We'll make it look good," the Technician said with apparent confidence. He regarded Noren's bruises thoughtfully. "You're going to have to rough me up a bit. Otherwise I can't pass as far as the aircar, let alone fool the Scholar Stefred."

"You mean you'd just stand there and let me hit you?"

"It's necessary, Noren. Don't worry, I won't make any noise, and I ordered the jailer not to come back into the building till I called him."

They switched clothes first, Noren marveling at the strange feel of the green stuff of which the uniform was made. Fortunately its sleeves were long enough to conceal the bruises on his arms; only those of his face would have to be hidden, and he could not show his face anyway. The hat covered the ragged cut of his hair.

"Go ahead and let loose," the Technician told him, once he'd rubbed dirt on his own arms to simulate as much bruising as possible. He braced himself against the wall and added, "Think of how you felt toward me when I first admitted what I was doing at the inn."

After a brief hesitation, Noren complied. The Scholar Stefred, he judged, would demand real evidence of a struggle. The whole business was carried out in silence; the Technician didn't shrink from it, though he'd obviously had no prior experience with blows.

"Noren," he said when it was over, "I've got to be honest. You haven't much chance to elude Stefred, not if he really wants you. And I'm pretty sure he does. I could sense it in the way he spoke."

"I know. But before he gets me maybe I can win some people over to our side."

There was frank admiration in the Technician's gaze. "I'll try, too. We're up against something a lot stronger than we are, though—stronger than you realize. The Scholars have powers you can't even imagine. I agree that it's wrong for them to keep those powers for themselves, but I'm not sure I believe your idea about there never having been a Founding. You're just as smart as they are; could *you* have discovered such powers if you and everyone else had always lived as the savages do?"

"There's got to be more to it than intelligence," Noren conceded, frowning. "I don't quite see how it happened, yet it's more reasonable than people dropping out of the sky."

The Technician drew out several small objects that were hidden in the belt he still wore beneath Noren's tunic. "Hold this," he commanded, handing Noren an ordinary tallow candle stub and lighting it with a match. "The Power Cell in the lantern is weak; I must replace it before you leave." As Noren watched in fascination, he turned out the light, opened a panel in its bottom, and inserted a little red cube in place of an identical one that he stored carefully away in his belt. Then, once the lantern was burning with even greater brilliance than before, he took the candle back and produced a featureless flat disk.

"It's the recording of your trial," he told Noren. "Destroy it when you ditch the uniform."

Noren examined the thing closely, wondering how his words could possibly be preserved in such a form. "No," he said. "No, it will be better if you give it to the Scholars; if I'd overpowered you, I wouldn't have known enough to take it. I don't mind having them hear what I said."

"You're really not ashamed, are you…not even of having declared that there's no Mother Star." The young Technician's tone was troubled, though it carried no disapproval.

"I'm not," agreed Noren.

"I—I don't know what to say to you, then. I can't wish you its protection, yet—well, something's lacking. It's not enough just to learn what there *isn't,* we need to know what there *is.*"

"Let's just wish each other luck," Noren said, for though he understood the deficiency very well, his feelings about it went too deep for words. He gripped the Technician's hand, wondering if any villager had ever done such a thing before. When it was too late, the man having been securely tied and the jailer called, he realized that he did not even know his friend's name.

He held the light low when he left the cell, so that his face was in shadows, and he did not speak to the jailer, who nodded respectfully as he passed but did not question his actions. There was little chance of his being recognized; villagers did not look at the features of Technicians. To them Technicians were not men, but beings of a different order, and one was assumed to be like another. The idea of an ordinary person wearing a Technician's uniform would not enter anyone's mind.

The street was dark and silent. Noren walked rapidly through the village and headed out along the road toward Talyra's farm. He did not want to ask her help, for he knew she'd be shocked by the masquerade, but there was no one else from whom he could possibly get clothes. He'd be taking a risk: if he was caught by her family, he would be shown no mercy. He would have to reach her from a hiding place he'd used more than once in the past: the cluster of rocks on the knoll against which the farmhouse nestled. There had been an understanding between them that if a yellow pebble was tossed in between the woven mats that hung at her window, she would climb out and meet him there. She would no longer be expecting such a signal, however, and he hoped she wouldn't be too incredulous to respond.

All at once another thought hit Noren, and he stopped in the middle of the road, appalled. There was a worse risk than capture in contacting Talyra! With sickening chagrin he realized that he indeed had something to lose by trusting the Technician. Everything in the man's manner had indicated sincerity, yet if he'd misjudged...

He had been aware that the switching of places could be an elaborate plot, but no motive for it had occurred to him. Now he wondered. The two Technicians could be working together. The other man, who might not be going in the aircar, could be watching Talyra's house, expecting to get evidence against her; and he could have seen to it that there would be villagers there, too.

Noren could not take that chance. He was sure enough of the young Technician to gamble his own safety, but he was not willing to jeopardize Talyra's.

Yet what else was there to do? This was a spoke road; he could reach no other village except by way of the center he'd just left, and it was too late to return there, for dawn was already brightening the sky. He would have to lie low somehow until the next night. Though farms lined the road, to be seen from a distance by farmers would not endanger him; they would not approach unless faced by an emergency such as illness, since Technicians, whose ways were inscrutable, were left to their own devices. Real Technicians, however, would surely search the area. He'd have to hide in the wilderness, and he could not get to the wilderness without passing both Talyra's farm and his family's.

Despairingly, Noren trudged ahead. If there was anyone he did not want to encounter, it was one of his brothers; yet since Talyra's house might be under observation, he must go by it without a glance. What could he do if he ever did reach another village? he wondered. He could buy clothing without challenge, perhaps—though most people's clothes were made at home, a few shops did carry garments sewn by seamstresses—but he had no money and besides, Technicians would undoubtedly be expecting such a move. The shopkeepers would be either watched or warned.

Someone was coming toward him along the road. Noren felt a chill of apprehension, but he knew he must walk calmly forward. Though in the dim light he could not make out whether it was a farmer, there was no reason to suppose that it wouldn't be, and if he kept his lantern down and gave no greeting he would be ignored. To his surprise, as the figure came closer he saw that it was a woman. For a woman to be out alone before sunrise was very odd.

And the woman did not ignore him. "Sir!" she called out clearly. "Forgive me for presuming to approach you, but I could not wait at home. My parents don't wish me to accept midwife's training."

Noren froze, overwhelmed by astonishment. It was Talyra's voice.

As she approached, he was torn between his desire to run to her and the impulse to run away. When she recognized him, she would be stunned; he must reveal himself with care, lest she become too upset to cope with the situation. Setting the lantern on the ground, he raised one hand to his face, and disguising his voice as best he could, called back, "My greetings, citizen! May I be of service to you?"

She was by this time near enough to see him, but as was normal for villagers, she noticed only the uniform. "I am pleased by your concern, sir," she replied formally. "Are you not the Technician who is coming to take me to the training center? If I've erred in addressing you, I'm most sorry."

He reached for the large bundle she carried, turning from her to set it beside the lantern. "Talyra," he said quietly.

The girl let out a gasp, and Noren whirled; before she could speak, he had caught her in his arms and was holding her close to him.

As the first rays of sunlight touched the Tomorrow Mountains, gilding the uppermost ridges with gold, Noren and Talyra left the road for the shelter of a dense purplish thicket, for Noren realized that although a Technician alone would arouse no curiosity among the farmers, a Technician embracing a village woman would be a strange sight indeed. Though presumably, men and women Technicians embraced in the privacy of the City, villagers assumed they had no such feelings; no doubt the High Law forbade them to look upon ordinary people with love of that kind.

They sat on the ground, sinking into the spongy gray moss that grew beneath the webbed-stemmed shrubs, and kept low enough to be well concealed. At first Talyra sobbed hysterically, too overcome by Noren's miraculous appearance to care about anything else. After a short while, however, she pulled away, voicing the inevitable protest. "Noren," she exclaimed in wide-eyed horror, "to wear a Technician's clothes—it's blasphemy!"

"I'm already convicted of blasphemy, Talyra, and of heresy as well. Is this so much worse? I didn't steal the uniform; it was given to me."

Talyra dropped her head, her long dark hair hiding her face from him. "I—I'm all mixed up," she faltered miserably. "Everything you've been doing is wrong, but at the trial, I could think only of how I couldn't bear to have you punished. It was all my fault—" She began to cry again. "Why do you even speak to me, let alone kiss me? I thought you must hate me! And it's sinful—indecent—for me to be letting you touch me when you've committed such sacrilege; I hate myself both ways."

"Darling," he said gently, "you mustn't. It's not sinful! My arrest wasn't your fault, either; I never for a minute thought you'd report me. Don't you know why I had to say what I did? It was the only way to convince them that you're innocent."

"You—you lied? You wouldn't lie to save yourself, yet you did to protect *me?"*

"That wasn't the same kind of lying," he said gravely.

"I guess not," she agreed. "Noren, you were so brave to talk to the councilmen as you did I—well, I understand a little, I think."

"You see now how bad it is for the Scholars to keep things from us?" he asked eagerly. "You see how they've tricked people with the Prophecy?"

"No! I know you're mistaken, and I'll never see how you can believe the things you said. But I understand that you do believe them. I understand that being honest means more to you than anything else. Oh, Noren, I'm sure the Scholars won't punish you harshly! They couldn't!"

"I'm not going to give them a chance," he declared. "Talyra, you realize that I've escaped, don't you? That if I'm recaptured, I'll be killed?"

"Killed!" She stared, incredulous. "They've never sentenced anybody to die, not even for impenitence! It's a terrible thing to escape, but I just won't believe they'd kill you for it."

"Not for escaping," he explained patiently. "For refusing to recant."

"But all heretics recant," Talyra protested. "Whether they're penitent or not they at least retract whatever they've said."

"I'm not going to. Do you think that when I wouldn't deny the truth for your sake, I'd do so to save my life?"

"No," she said slowly. "No, I don't think you would. And the Scholars wouldn't want you to." Frowning, she went on, "I don't know how they get heretics to recant, but they surely don't ask them to lie. Your idea of the truth's twisted around, Noren, and somehow they'll make you see that. Perhaps…perhaps it's like the inoculations Technicians give; the needle hurts, yet without it we'd all get sick and die."

"Talyra," he demanded, "do you believe it's right for the Scholars to hurt people to make them see things their way?"

She averted her eyes. "I—I'm not sure," she confessed in a low voice. "It doesn't seem so, yet the Scholars are High Priests, and they know everything; how could they do anything wrong? You said yourself that truth's more important than comfort. Well, the Prophecy is *true—*"

Noren could see that she was genuinely unable to imagine that it might not be. "I'll put it another way," he said. "If you believe that what's done to heretics is for their good, then why didn't you denounce me? You would have called the Technicians if I'd been sick, even if it meant having me taken away to the hospital outside the City; why didn't you feel the same way about getting me cured of heresy?"

There was a brief silence. Then, baffled by a paradox she could not resolve, Talyra cried, "Because I don't *want* you hurt! I don't want you imprisoned! May the spirit of the Mother Star not forsake me; I want you to go free!"

"You'll help me, then?"

"I'll help you even if I'm condemned for it, Noren."

"You won't be, and you mustn't condemn yourself, either," Noren said with concern. "You must trust me, darling, as I'm trusting you. I know some things you don't, and there are Technicians who know them, too, like the one who gave me his uniform." He went on to tell her what had happened, hastily and with little detail, for he knew they hadn't much time. "You'll hear that I attacked him," he concluded, "but it's not true; we made up that story to save him from punishment."

The idea of a Technician taking a heretic's side against the Scholars was bewildering to Talyra, but she accepted Noren's word, giving her own that she would never repeat any of what he'd disclosed. "It's not going to be easy getting clothes for you," she said thoughtfully. "Have you any idea how we're to manage it?"

"Can't you get some of your brother's old ones?" he asked, puzzled. "By this time he and your father will be working in the fields."

"But I can't go back now. Mother would be there, and she'd not let me out of her sight again. I left a note, you see, when I came away this morning."

Noren frowned. He had forgotten for the moment what Talyra had said about leaving home against her parents' wishes. "You haven't told me why you changed your mind about the training center," he muttered, deciding that to reveal the reason she'd been appointed would be needlessly cruel.

"Do you have to ask?" she replied, blushing. "Being a nurse-midwife would be much better than living with my parents forever, or working in a shop or an inn. Mother doesn't understand. She thinks I'll get married someday."

"Won't you?" he inquired painfully.

"Noren! When I broke our betrothal, you surely didn't think I'd ever marry someone *else!"*

He held out his arms and she came eagerly, as if there had never been any rift at all. The ways of girls, Noren decided, were even more mysterious than those of Scholars.

"After the trial," Talyra continued softly, "when I knew they'd take you away and I'd never see you again, I spoke to the Technician who had offered me the appointment. I asked if I could still accept, and he said yes, he'd come for me today or send his partner. I was glad because I thought that while I was being trained, I'd at least be somewhere near the City where they were keeping you. But Mother was dreadfully worried. There are those stories, you know, about people who go to the training center and then just disappear—"

Noren held her tight. "I'm worried, too," he declared. It was quite true that there were occasional unexplained disappearances from the training center. To be sure, the Technicians always told families that they must not grieve, that the person who'd vanished was not dead, but had been honored by being given special and secret work of his own choosing. And it happened rarely; still, feeling as he did about the Scholars' secrets…

"Are you saying you don't want me to learn as much as they'll teach me?" she asked.

He could scarcely say that, Noren realized; he'd have gone gladly to the training center himself. Talyra would make a good midwife. She wouldn't mind following the orders of Technicians, for she'd feel no resentment at not knowing all that they did.

Nurse-midwives lived in every village to tend the ill and injured before the Technicians arrived, to carry out whatever treatment was prescribed, and to deliver babies; they were admired and respected by everyone.

"No, darling," he told her. "If you'll be happy as a nurse-midwife, that's what you must become."

She lay back against his shoulder. "I'll never be happy without you," she admitted. "But I would like the work, I think. I'm of age, and if I'd waited at home for the Technician, Mother couldn't have stopped me from going with him; but I thought it would be easier if I just slipped away."

"That puts your helping me in a different light," Noren said ruefully. "If you can't go home without being seen, we must forget it, for I won't have you do anything dangerous."

"Do you think I'm afraid?" Talyra demanded indignantly. "Noren, nothing matters to me but your safety! There must be some way I can get clothes for you in the village; no one even knows you've escaped yet."

There'd be no dissuading her, Noren saw. She had hesitated at first not from fear or unwillingness to defy convention, but from a real conflict of conscience; Talyra had never lacked spirit when it came to getting her own way. Having determined her course, she would hold to it.

"I could buy clothes and say they were for my brother," she suggested.

"I haven't any money."

"I have: the coins I've been given each Founding Day. And there's my great-aunt's silver wristband."

"I couldn't let you use those," Noren protested.

"They've always been yours," she said simply. "I was saving them for my dowry."

"But Talyra," he went on, "later, when they're searching for me, they would question the shopkeeper, and your brother, too. You'd be at the training center by then, and the Technicians there would make you tell them everything."

"I suppose they would," she agreed unhappily. "Whatever I do, they'll find out afterwards. Noren, there's just one way it will work; they've got to think you forced me. We've got to make up a story the way you did with the Technician."

"How could I force you even if I wanted to?"

She turned scarlet. "You're stronger than I am. You could make me swear by the Mother Star to do anything you say."

"But I wouldn't—not that way!"

"Of course you wouldn't, but people will believe just about anything of you now. After what you said about having drunk impure water, any girl would be scared to death of you. And besides, anybody who'd attack a *Technician—"*

That was all too true, Noren realized. It would be assumed that he had no integrity whatsoever. Yet Talyra's alleged refusal to break an oath by the Mother Star, even one forcibly extracted, would arouse no suspicion, for her piety had been acknowledged by the village council itself.

"Could you carry it off, Talyra?" he asked dubiously. "Accusing me, I mean?"

"I could to put them off your trail," she declared. "I won't wait for the Technicians to ask; I'll go to the councilmen as soon as your escape's made known, and send them to look for you in the wrong direction. It's the same sort of lie you told about not trusting me, isn't it? And since they're convinced you don't trust me, they'll be ready to believe that you'd try to get even."

"What if they require you to swear that it's true?" he objected.

Talyra laughed. "They won't. I'll cry and carry on so that nobody will even consider doubting."

"It might work," he conceded. "Yet oh, darling, if you were caught—"

"So what? I wouldn't be convicted of heresy, only of aiding an escaped prisoner."

"You'd be punished. You'd lose your appointment to the training center, too."

The girl scrambled to her feet. "We're wasting time, Noren! I've got to hurry if I'm to buy the clothes and bring them to you before that aircar arrives at the jail."

Noren got up also. "Talyra," he said sadly, "you can't bring them to me. It's already too late. You've got to hide them where I can pick them up tonight, and then look for the Technician, because he'll probably start out to your farm as soon as the aircar leaves. Even if he hasn't been planning to, he may suspect I'm hiding there when he finds out about the switch. We can't risk his catching up with you; and besides, I may not be able to wait here."

"Where would you go?" she asked, dismayed.

"Into the wilderness. I'll have to if they're hunting for me."

"The wilderness!" Talyra was horror-stricken. "That's so dangerous!"

"I'm in danger anyway."

She stared at him, beginning to take in the fact that he would always be a fugitive. "Where will you go after you get the clothes? What will become of you?"

"I don't know," he admitted frankly. "I won't pretend that I can ever come back, Talyra."

They were both aware of the likelihood of his recapture, and that it must not be mentioned; they must go on as if the escape could succeed. "Where shall I hide the clothes?" she asked, trying to keep her voice steady.

"At the schoolhouse." It would be deserted, he knew, since there was no school during harvest season; and it was on the opposite side of the village from the jail, where everyone would be gathering to see him taken away. "Put them in the hollow near the place we used to go for the afternoon break—remember?"

"I'll always remember," she whispered, caressing his bruised cheek. "Noren, it—it just wasn't meant to work out for us, was it? You couldn't ever have been happy with the life we'd have had. You're—well, you are what you are, and our loving each other wouldn't have made any difference."

"No," he said quietly. "But I love you more than I could ever love anyone else, Talyra."

"I—I'm proud. It's crazy, when I'm so sure you're wrong about things, yet I'm proud of you for being brave enough to be yourself."

He hugged her to him. "I don't feel brave when I think about not seeing you again."

"We've got to be. Let me go before I start crying." Talyra freed herself and resolutely picked up her bundle. "I know you don't want me to talk about the Mother Star," she told him, "but I'll say this anyway: may its spirit guard you. I've got to be myself, too, you see, and I couldn't let a person I love go off without a proper farewell. It's not so foolish as you think! Someday—well, maybe you'll find it's been with you all along."

Noren stood watching, his own eyes wet, until she vanished around a bend in the road, wondering in confusion how anything that meant so much to Talyra could be wholly false.

Chapter Five

Noren did not retreat into the wilderness that day; the thicket proved hiding place enough, though in order to watch the road he couldn't avoid exposing himself to view. Occasional farmers passed by and one or two of them looked at him curiously, but showed no signs of suspecting him to be anything but an ordinary Technician. There was no reason why a Technician should not sit quietly in the shade if he wished to, although it wasn't usual. The weather being suffocatingly hot, he was probably envied. Those farmers would be surprised, Noren thought ruefully, if they knew he was obliged to rest not by the heat, but by hunger.

It was his second day without food, and he was feeling the effects. He had not told Talyra, for there was nothing she could have done and it would only have worried her; but he knew that if he was to walk to the schoolhouse that night, he must reserve his strength. That was why, after much inner debate, he decided to risk waiting out the day where he was. If either villagers or Technicians had launched a full-scale search, he would have had no chance to elude them, but they apparently were convinced by Talyra's story to hunt elsewhere—either that, or they simply assumed that he would not stay in the area most likely to be combed.

That set him to thinking. He had made no plans as to what he would do once he got rid of the uniform, other than to leave the village far behind. It mattered little where he headed, for the problems of finding work and of avoiding recapture would be the same everywhere. In other localities he would not be recognized; however, since Technicians could talk not only with each other but with all villages by means of Radiophone Machines, they'd undoubtedly alert people to be on the lookout for a stranger of his description. It would be wisest to stick to farms, staying at each only long enough to earn a meal. Yet he could not travel the roads by day lest he be spotted from an aircar. He'd have to walk at night, or else go cross-country, which would be perilous at best. In his heart Noren knew that he could not move from farm to farm indefinitely. Sooner or later he would be caught.

He looked out through the clustered web of bushes toward the mountains. There? *Beyond the Tomorrow Mountains,* the Prophecy said...what did lie beyond? There was little point in wondering. In order to reach the mountains, he would have to go through an endless stretch of total wilderness, and while he'd learned that the water was drinkable, there would be no food. To be sure, the savages lived there, and they must eat something; but he had no way of guessing what it was. The High Law's prohibition against tasting any plant that grew in unquickened ground was not as absurd as the injunction against "impure" water, for most such plants were indeed poisonous. And a tale he'd once heard about savages eating creatures of the streams was too fantastic to be credited; Noren's stomach, empty though it was, turned over at the mere thought. The Tomorrow Mountains were tempting, but unattainable.

Moreover, his real aim was not to run but to talk with people, people who might question the Scholars' supremacy if not openly oppose it. There'd be few opportunities for that if he spent his life in hiding. And might he not last as long—perhaps longer—by using bolder tactics? The Scholars would expect him to hide. They had immeasurable power and would eventually be able to locate him, but their search would be systematic; they would begin where it was most logical for him to go. The last place they would look would be at the walls of the City itself!

Excitement rose in Noren. They'd tried to take him to the City and would therefore expect him to get as far away as possible. Yet the markets outside the walls were the one place where a stranger would be inconspicuous. The markets were unlike a village. There'd be different kinds of people there: not only traders, not only those anxious to attend the religious ceremonies, but men adventurous enough simply to want to see the fabled towers for themselves. Then too, there would perhaps be many Technicians, some of whom might listen to his ideas. His heart raced, and for the first time since his arrest he felt a surge of elation. Despite himself, he still felt drawn to the City. That was where knowledge was. If he hadn't many days of freedom left, he would take advantage of them! He would follow his original plan and go to the City not as a prisoner, but in his own time, of his own will.

An hour before noon the regular rain started, and to his amazement, Noren found that the smooth fabric of the

Technician's uniform in some strange way repelled the drops. He did not get wet at all. Often enough he'd been soaked to the skin and had not minded, for the scorching sun of afternoon dried clothes quickly; but it was galling to think that more comfortable ones existed. He would discard them with regret.

Fingering the lantern, he realized that he would discard that with regret, also. It was made mostly of the bonelike material and of glass, but inside the glass globe were metal parts. Metal was sacred; he, a heretic, was certainly the last person who'd be thought worthy to be in possession of any; yet he felt no more guilt than when he had drunk from the stream. He *knew* he'd committed no sin. All the High Priests in the world couldn't shake that conviction, no matter what Talyra thought.

Still...something was missing. There were pieces that didn't quite fit. The Technician's words came back to Noren: *It's not enough just to learn what there* isn't; *we need to know what there* is...

Holding out cupped hands, Noren let the rain fill them, thinking again how unreasonable it was to suppose that an event as natural and as predictable as sunrise could be controlled by the Scholars. Four days with rain, two without, week after week forever—one might as well believe they determined the hour of dawn! Rain, he mused, was obviously the source of pond and stream water, and could logically have been pronounced impure, as that was. Yet the Scholars could hardly have required people to transport enough City-purified water from village centers to keep the cisterns full, much less to carry cistern water into the grainfields. So they'd conveniently neglected to decree that rainwater was forbidden, and to explain the discrepancy had declared that they themselves made it rain. Why, he wondered, were people so gullible?

The clouds dispersed on schedule; the pungent smell of drying moss hung in the hot, thick air; the sparkling beads of moisture disappeared from the gray-green webbing that joined the stems of nearby shrubs. Slowly the afternoon dragged to its end. Noren watched the moons come up, noticing with illogical surprise that their crescents were not much fuller than on the night of the dance. That had been only three nights ago, yet it seemed a long way back.

When it was dark, he started for the village, pausing by the first bridge he crossed to assuage his thirst at a forbidden stream.

His body was stiff and sore from the beating and he was also weak from hunger, but he knew he must inure himself to that; it probably wouldn't be the last time he would have to go several days without food. The light of his Power-lit lantern, reflected in the dark water, dazzled him as he bent down to drink. He still found it incredible to be carrying such an object; it was the first Machine he'd been permitted to handle since the memorable day on which he had touched the aircar that had landed at his father's farm.

He dared not walk through the village before the taverns closed, so he waited on the outskirts until a lamp burned in only one building, the radiophonist's office. That was always open in case there should be need to summon the Technicians in some emergency, although ordinary messages to and from the City were transmitted only by day. Noren strode swiftly past, but to his dismay the radiophonist himself, having caught sight of the brilliant lantern, appeared in the doorway. "Sir!" the man exclaimed. "Sir, may I beg your assistance?"

Noren froze. He was not qualified to perform any task for which a Technician's help would be asked, and what was more, if he showed his face he might well be recognized, if only by his bruises. Yet neither could he ignore the request, for that too would arouse suspicion.

"My greetings," he said evenly. "How may I be of service to you?"

"I am pleased by your concern, sir," said the man, stepping into the street. "The Radiophone Machine has stopped working. I planned to send someone to Prosperity tomorrow to report it by way of their Machine, but if you would grant me a few moments, that would not be necessary."

In panic, Noren tried to think of some legitimate excuse, but he could not. To refuse would not be appropriate behavior for a Technician; if he did so the radiophonist, who had undoubtedly seen him at one time or another, might look past the uniform to his face. Yet how could he repair a Machine of which he knew nothing?

"I will examine it," he declared resolutely, and with a sense of helpless despair entered the dimly lighted room. There were two other men there, friends of the radiophonist on duty; any misstep could mean that an outcry would be raised. And the fact that no real Technicians could be called made it all the more certain that he, having had the unprecedented effrontery to pose as one, would be dealt with by the mob.

The Radiophone Machine rested on a small stone table in one corner. Noren had never seen it before, but he knew what it did: in some wondrous manner it transmitted the voices of faraway Technicians to whoever stood close to its grille, and vice versa. No one was permitted to touch it but the radiophonists; they alone among villagers were entrusted with the sacred task of Machine operation. A position of such prestige could be obtained only by those consecrated to it through appointment to the training center.

But though radiophonists were trained in the operation of the Radiophone Machine and in the rules governing the occasions upon which it could and could not be used, they were told nothing of its inner workings. Knowledge of that sort was, according to common belief, beyond the scope of the ordinary human mind and could be absorbed only by Scholars and Technicians. Noren did not agree, especially since he'd learned that not all Technicians had such knowledge; still he couldn't deny that he himself possessed none of it. He did not know anything about Machines except that they worked by Power, and that if Power was absent, they could no longer function.

He surveyed the Radiophone Machine thoughtfully. He must do something, he knew, and the maintenance of his disguise depended on doing it with apparent confidence. "Perhaps," he asserted boldly, "its Power Cell is dead."

"Yes, sir," replied the radiophonist. "I think, sir, that it's past due to be checked."

Encouraged, Noren recalled that the young Technician had remarked that his usual job was the checking of radiophone equipment. Very likely he would have checked this Machine had he not been taken away in the aircar. In his belt he had carried Power Cells, one of which he had inserted into the lantern, thereby causing the light to burn more brightly; could it be that the same one would make the Machine work again? It was a gamble, but if it failed he'd be no worse off than if he hesitated.

"I do not have any new Power Cells with me," he said, "but the one in my lantern may serve. I shall see." He switched off the light and carefully opened the panel in its bottom as he had seen the Technician do, withdrawing the small red cube that contained the mysterious Power. That part was easy. The problem would be to open the Radiophone Machine.

It was not reasonable, Noren decided, that a panel would be placed in its bottom; this did not look like a thing that should be turned upside down. The opening must be in the back. He grasped the Machine with trembling hands and started to turn it around, whereupon it gave forth loud crackling and hissing sounds. It took all his courage not to let go, but since the radiophonist and his friends did not draw back in terror, he concluded that these sounds must be normal.

The Machine's back did indeed have a panel, but it was evident that it could not be unlatched in the same manner as the one in the lantern. Noren cursed under his breath. If the radiophonist had watched the process of replacing Power Cells before, as he undoubtedly had, he must know perfectly well how to remove the back; yet he would not presume to advise a Technician and would be dumbfounded if his opinion were to be sought. On the other hand, he would be horrified by the sacrilege if the Machine was clumsily handled. Noticing in desperation that its sides curled over the panel whereas its top did not, Noren pressed upward and found that the entire back slid out easily. His relief faded quickly, however, when inside, amid a maze of appallingly complex devices, he saw not one Power Cell, but four.

He scowled, debating as to his next move. If there were four, then obviously four were needed; yet they appeared to be exactly alike. Would all four have died at the same time? Probably not, for if they had, that would mean their death was predictable, and "checking" would be unnecessary. He should therefore need to replace only one; but which? Was it possible to tell by looking? The Power Cell the Technician had removed from the lantern hadn't looked any different from its replacement, so perhaps it was usual to proceed by trial and error. Noren scrutinized the cube in his hand. One surface, he saw, was unlike the others in that it had a metal button in its center; he must take care to position it exactly as the Machine's old cubes were positioned.

One by one, Noren removed the Power Cells, putting his own in each successive place while the men watched reverently. Each time he held his breath; if it did not work anywhere, his ignorance would surely be exposed. But on the third try it did work. "There, sir!" exclaimed someone. "That's done it." Leaning over, Noren saw that a red light had appeared on the front of the Machine and was deeply grateful for the comment; he would not have known how to tell whether he'd succeeded.

"Thank you, sir," said the radiophonist. "It's fortunate that you passed by tonight."

"It is indeed," Noren replied, as he replaced the Machine's back panel.

"Will you not take the dead Power Cell away?" the man inquired anxiously, indicating the discarded red cube. "It cannot, of course, be left unprotected, and it would be irreverent for me to lay hands upon it."

"Certainly I shall," said Noren, suppressing a laugh, and thrust the thing casually into his pocket. "Goodnight, citizen."

He walked down the moonlit street, his now-useless lantern swinging from his hand, exhilarated by his triumph. There was nothing so awesome about Power! Surely anyone intelligent enough to be appointed a radiophonist ought to be able to replace Power Cells without the aid of a Technician...or was intelligence necessarily the basis upon which radiophonists were chosen?

Of course it wasn't, Noren perceived suddenly. A radiophonist's job, he saw, was not at all difficult. It demanded not skill, but willingness to follow instructions without overstepping certain prescribed bounds. Those who did the job were admired because they operated Machines, which most citizens viewed with awe and veneration; but far from being superior to others, the radiophonists were equally awed by the Power Cells. And that, no doubt, was the way the Scholars wanted them to be.

No wonder he hadn't been offered an appointment to the training center! No wonder the craftsworkers and traders he knew, most of whom were much shrewder than that radiophonist, had not been appointed either! The few people who disappeared from the place must be the ones who'd shown more initiative than the Scholars had anticipated. They must be the ones who had begun to learn too much.

He had no need to worry about Talyra's safety there, he realized with relief. Talyra was intelligent, but she would not ask for information beyond what she was given; furthermore, though a nurse-midwife's work was more demanding than a radiophonist's, it in no way infringed upon the Technicians' sole right to the Power and the Machines.

At the schoolhouse all was quiet. Noren made his way cautiously around the building, glad that the moons were up and yet fearful of being observed. The spot where he and Talyra had liked to sit was at the far edge of the schoolyard, half-hidden by a clump of shrubby growth. In the hollow there he found a neat pile of things: trousers, a tunic, and between the two garments, a carrying-jug of pure water plus a knotted kerchief. The latter was heavy; as he untied it, he saw the white gleam of coins—far more coins than could have been acquired in any way but by the sale of the treasured wristband. She had given him all she had. He paused a short while, staring at the flattened moss where they had spent happy moments together, and then firmly closed the door on a part of himself that could never be regained.

Smoke rose from the chimney of a sturdily built farmhouse and warm lamplight shone out through the dusk. The work-beast in the fodder patch raised its head as Noren approached, giving a warning bellow; he paid no attention. He could not go on without eating, and the only way to get a meal was to ask for it. Stumbling across the dusty yard, he called at the door in as firm a tone as he could muster.

The night before, after changing into the clothes Talyra had obtained for him and ditching the Technician's things in the depths of a pond, he had gone on until dawn, forcing himself despite his hunger to cover as much distance as he could. He'd passed straight through Prosperity, afraid that if he waited there to buy food, someone would remember him from his recent trip in pursuit of the trader. When morning came, he'd ventured to get breakfast at the first farm he had reached; but though he'd offered to pay, the farmer's wife had been surly and had given him only a stale chunk of bread. Noren had taken it to a depleted clay pit nearby, where he'd gulped it down ravenously and then, too exhausted to try another place, had slept through the day's heat, sheltered by sedges that grew out of coarse purple moss. Now it was evening again, and if he could not get supper, he would be unable to walk much farther. He had no choice but to make the attempt, dangerous though it might prove.

The matting of the door before him was pulled back and a motherly-looking woman exclaimed, "Lew! Lew, come here!" Noren found himself being propelled inside by a stout, brawny man who studied him briefly, then indicated a chair by the lamp. The room was thick with the dizzying odor of stewing fowl. Noren sat down. Nine or ten small children stared with interest, and he realized that his bruises as well as his presence would demand comment, though the only explanation he could think of was at best a flimsy one.

He forced the fear out of his voice. "I—I've been delayed," he told them. "I was to meet my cousin in Prosperity and help him take a load to the City markets, only I left the road to rest and—well, slipped into a quarry. He'll wait in the next village till tomorrow, and I'm sure I can catch up, but I'm awfully hungry. I can pay—"

"You don't need to," said the woman cordially. "I've fixed plenty; we'll just set another place."

"Thanks, I'd appreciate that."

"Cistern's out back, if you want to wash up," the woman said, surveying him. She fingered her apron. "Why, you're just a boy! The City's a long way off—"

"Not too far for a young fellow his age," her husband Lew interrupted. "I went to the City markets once, the year I finished school, right before we were married. It's really a sight. And the music—you never heard anything like that music they have at the Benison." He smiled, remembering. "Inspiring, it is."

No doubt, thought Noren, the Scholars could arrange inspiration with the same efficiency they employed in arranging everything else. He had heard often of the Benison, a ceremony held early each morning, before the Gates, to open the markets for the day's business; but it hadn't occurred to him that to avoid attracting notice he would have to attend. The idea dismayed him, for the crowd would be smaller than on holidays, and he did not believe that he could bring himself to kneel, as one must in the immediate presence of Scholars.

Lew grinned at him. "You're having a real adventure, I'll bet. Does it come up to your hopes, being on your own?"

"I guess so."

"We've got supper almost on," the woman put in. "Dorie, you take him out to the cistern."

One of the younger boys tagged along, and both children appraised Noren curiously as he splashed water over his bruised face and arms, then filled his stoppered carrying-jug. "I don't think I'd like an adventure," commented Dorie.

"I would," retorted her little brother promptly. "The City's where the Technicians live. Have you ever talked to a Technician, mister?"

"Yes."

"That's what I want to be when I grow up."

"Silly!" cried Dorie. "People don't grow up to be Technicians."

"But I want to run a Machine."

Noren looked at the small boy, who was as yet too young to know that wanting was not the same as getting, and his heart ached. This child, he sensed, was someone who would care. *You could grow up to run a Machine, or even to build one,* he thought, *and you wouldn't need the title of Technician, either.*

Would Lew and his wife listen to reason? Would they agree that their sons and daughters had a right to the knowledge that could give them Machines, and more? Maybe he should risk telling them; it might be his only chance. Suppose he never reached the City?

In the big kitchen, the woman was ladling hot stew into brown pottery bowls. Noren closed his eyes, leaning against the stone doorway; hunger was making him giddy. For an instant he was back in his own mother's kitchen, at home. Was he a fool to have given up everything that mattered to other people for the sake of a truth that would lead him ultimately to death?

The girl Dorie clutched at his hand. "What's the matter?"

"Nothing—nothing's the matter."

"Yes, there is." With the quick intuition of childhood she announced, "You're *afraid.*"

"No—"

"You shouldn't be," the child continued. "The Prophecy says the spirit of the Mother Star protects everybody, and as long as we believe in it nothing can hurt us."

"Does it?"

"Don't you *know?* Mother, he—"

"Yes, of course I do!" Noren said hastily. "*'It is our life's bulwark; and so long as we believe in it, no force can destroy us, though the heavens themselves be consumed.'*" So long as we believe in it. It was his misfortune, maybe, to believe in something a good deal less comforting.

They stood behind the wicker benches while the woman lit the table lamp and began the familiar words in a calm, unhurried voice: "*'Let us rejoice in the bounty of the land...from the Mother Star came the heritage that has blessed it...'*" With effort, Noren kept his voice steady and clear. These people would not understand his heresy. If he were to speak out, there would be more danger of harm to them than to him, he perceived; they would be lost without their faith. Perhaps the Scholars' greatest cruelty was in the way they deluded the good, kind people who were hoping in vain for the fulfillment of a false promise.

He tried to eat slowly, without revealing the urgency of his hunger, and to talk as a carefree traveler rather than an imperiled fugitive. "Your youngest son is a bright lad," he remarked to the mother, wondering if the spark he'd seen in the boy had been noticed by the parents.

"He is an adopted child," replied the woman proudly. "So is the littlest girl."

"My congratulations," said Noren, smiling at the youngsters. "They are fine children." It was a strange fact, he thought, that adopted children so often seemed brighter than most, as if the circumstances of their birth had been particularly fortunate to offset whatever tragedy had resulted in their becoming Wards of the City. There were many such babies—they were practically always adopted in infancy—and it was a mark of honor to have one, for it was well known that the women Technicians who were their official guardians placed them only with worthy families who would love them and give them good care. He wondered where they all came from, since although every village's foundlings became Wards of the City, there seemed to be more than could be accounted for in that way; it occurred suddenly to Noren that the Technicians' own orphans might be included. No one was permitted to know the parentage of those who had become Wards when too young to remember.

He scrutinized the little boy more closely. Could this child, who thought that ordinary people could become Technicians, possibly have been born as one? He had love in abundance; he seemed happy; yet had he somehow been deprived of his birthright? But that was nonsense, Noren realized with chagrin. It was no more unfair for him than for his foster brothers and sisters; knowledge was the birthright not only of Technicians, but of everyone.

"You must stay the night with us," said Lew, "We've an extra bed in our sons' room."

Noren shook his head. The thought of sleeping in a bed was tempting, but he could not accept; not only would it delay him, but to shelter him might somehow put this family in danger. "That's kind of you," he said regretfully, "but if I'm not in the next village by sunrise I might miss my cousin again. I'd best stay at the inn there."

The whole family walked out to the road with him after the meal. "Thanks for the supper," he told the woman. "You're surely a good cook."

She smiled and squeezed his hand. "May the spirit of the Mother Star be with you," she said.

"And with you," Noren answered, half-wishing he could mean more by the words than a courteous response to hospitality. He turned rapidly and started up the curving road, toward the top of the hill.

Noren stopped at many farms after that, for breakfast or for supper, but rarely more than once a day. Some families were cordial, as Lew's had been; others were less so and demanded payment. When possible he asked for work before offering money, for he knew he must save as many of Talyra's coins as he could to use at the markets, where there would be no farms and he would have to buy food from shopkeepers. That meant that he got little sleep, since he traveled by night, but working in someone's fields was safer than sleeping in them. It was increasingly hard to find hiding places, for the closer he got to the City, the fewer patches of uncleared land he found.

He passed through villages only in darkness. It amazed him that he encountered no Technicians searching for him, or even heard rumors from the farmers of such a search; and as the days went by the tension in him grew. If the Scholar Stefred wanted him caught, why wasn't a more intensive effort being made?

At last he could endure it no longer and decided to risk a deliberate inquiry. The people he ate with that day were friendly, but did not seem particularly devout; the subject, Noren felt, could safely be raised.

"I hear they're on the lookout for an escaped heretic," he said casually.

"Oh?" the farmer replied. "I was in to the center only yesterday, and nobody said a word about that."

"It was a trader who told me," Noren asserted. "Perhaps the man's not thought to be near here; traders pick up news from all over."

"I can't understand why anybody would get himself convicted of heresy," the wife declared.

"Some people just don't believe everything in the Prophecy, I guess," said Noren in a noncommittal tone.

"No doubt, but why do they admit it when they know what's bound to happen? It's all words anyway; is that worth suffering for?"

"Heretics must think so. Or else they think that the High Law's not what it should be, and that if they could get people to agree with them things could be changed."

"Rubbish," said the man. "The High Law is as it is, and the best way for a man to live comfortably is to follow it and keep his mouth shut."

"Once," Noren said slowly, "I heard a heretic say that he cared more for truth than for comfort."

"Goodness!" exclaimed the wife. "A nice boy like you shouldn't be talking to heretics. You could get yourself in trouble."

"He said it in public," answered Noren with a straight face. "It was at his trial."

"What happened to him?" she inquired.

"He was convicted and locked up to be turned over to the Scholars. Do you think he deserved it?"

"Frankly, I don't," the man admitted. "Live and let live, I say; I don't hold with punishing a man for what he thinks. But you'd not catch me talking that way in the village."

His eyes narrowed with sudden suspicion. "You wouldn't repeat it, would you?"

"No," Noren assured him, "I wouldn't."

It was apparent that his escape had not been publicized; perhaps Talyra had not even needed to use the story they'd concocted. If the inhabitants of villages along the road hadn't been alerted to watch for him, Noren concluded, it could only be that the Scholars were hoping he'd feel falsely secure and would grow careless. Their strategy was more subtle than he'd anticipated, which was all the more reason for him to move with caution.

Yet he could not resist sounding out more farmers as to their opinions. The first one's view seemed predominant; though there were some sincerely devout people, and others who took out a dislike of the Scholars' supremacy on anybody who dared oppose it, the majority of those he met couldn't have cared less whether the Prophecy was true or the High Law justified. Like his own father, they were interested only in practical affairs. Noren soon found that he could safely make comments bordering on heresy as long as he saw such people in the privacy of their homes, but he guessed that in a crowd they would be quick to clamor for his condemnation.

Would those he met at the City markets be any different? Noren wondered. If they weren't, he had no chance whatsoever to arouse opposition to the High Law; he must face that fact realistically. And what action could be taken even if he did succeed in convincing people? He had never gotten that far in his plans; he'd merely felt—and still felt, despite everything—that refusing to believe lies was in itself an act of importance.

During his none-too-frequent intervals of sleep he dreamed a lot. There were the old recurring nightmares of the City, now immediate and concrete: he would find himself bound hand and foot, facing the Scholar Stefred, who towered over him in a dark cavern filled with terrifying Machines; and he would wake trembling, telling himself that he could elude capture forever, yet knowing better. But there were also other dreams in which he was not afraid, but instead was on the verge of meeting secret, inexpressible things that he approached with joy—things concerning the ultimate, forbidden knowledge that was hidden behind the City's walls. Always, to his frustration, he woke just as he was about to learn the answers. On those occasions he could scarcely wait for dusk before starting off, and he drove himself to walk faster and faster through the night, knowing that it was foolish, yet seeing no real reason to resist his growing compulsion. The City and its mysteries had become a goal both feared and longed for; but the longing outweighed the fear.

It became harder and harder to locate spots where he could rest. Farms were small and crowded close together near the City, while villages were comparatively large; almost all the wild plants had been cut. Then too, there were no streams. Long, straight conduits stretched off into the distance from sandy beds that were thereafter dry, and the work-beasts were watered in unnaturally shallow ponds. At first that puzzled Noren, but before long he figured it out: the water was being channeled into the City itself, purified, and then sent out through the clay aqueducts that paralleled the main roads, from which pipes branched off to fill the huge village cisterns where people drew what they needed to supplement what was collected from rain. Fortunately he had the carrying-jug; he'd been replenishing it at farms in any case, since he might have aroused suspicion had he stopped for a meal without requesting water.

The day came when at first light Noren could see nothing around him but flat fields—newly-planted grainfields, the season zone being the same as Prosperity's—without a tinge of purple anywhere, nor yet of gray-green apart from fodder. There were a good many houses, but he'd had plenty to eat the previous evening and he never stopped for breakfast unless his shelter was already chosen, for he felt it was dangerous to walk far after sunrise. This time he had no choice; he must keep going.

The sky to his left was yellow. One of the moons, it was hard to tell which, traced a thin white curve above a silhouetted barn. Overhead a few fading stars displayed a faint, determined sparkle. Where was the Mother Star supposed to appear, anyway: in one of the constellations, or in some unnatural place like the zenith? Noren couldn't recall that the Prophecy told, and since whoever had written it had gone to so much trouble to manufacture details like the exact date, they might at least have mentioned where to look. Not that that wasn't a silly question to waste thought on when there were so many true enigmas, like what stars *were,* for instance—real stars! Having walked for countless hours under them, Noren had often stared upward in bafflement, wondering whether even the Scholars possessed knowledge of that sort.

The sun bulged over the horizon, blinding Noren momentarily, and in the same instant he heard an ominous sound. An aircar was floating toward him above the field! With the new-risen sun behind it, it was hard to see; but a long, dark shadow preceded it, and it was headed directly for him.

Noren did not have time to consider the situation; he reacted instinctively. Without stopping to think that if by any chance the men in the aircar weren't hunting for him, it would be unwise to attract their attention by an attempt to evade them, he threw himself headlong into the ditch beside the road. As he fell, a sharp rock stabbed into his knee, dazing him with pain, and he lay helpless while the aircar hovered and dropped lower.

Incredibly, it did not land. The Technicians saw him; Noren was sure of that, for as he turned onto his back their faces were clear, but to his astonishment the aircar rose abruptly and drifted off in the direction of the City. Bewildered, he tried to climb out of the ditch—only to find that the injured knee would not support his weight.

Chapter Six

For some time Noren remained in the ditch, at a loss to know what to do. He could go no farther alone. Once the worst of the pain subsided, he realized that he would be able to walk with the aid of a strong bandage; but the fabric of his tunic was too coarse to tear, and in any case, he could not climb. Moreover, the Technicians would undoubtedly be back for him. Though those particular ones apparently hadn't known that he was an escaped heretic, they would surely report what they had seen, for it was not normal for a villager to run from Technicians—and they would then be told that a fugitive was being sought.

As the sun rose higher, he propped himself against the stony bank and prepared to hail the first passer-by. As close to the City as he was, the road would be heavily traveled. He had no choice but to trust to luck in being found by someone who would help him without asking too many questions.

Luck was with him: a trader's sledge appeared before anybody else came by, and the trader was bound for the markets. He was a lean, brisk man who answered Noren's shout with cheerful alacrity. "I fell, and I can't walk till my knee's bandaged, I guess," Noren told him ruefully, "but I can drive. I'll spell you if you'll take me." Something in the man's manner warned him that it would be best not to mention his coins unless he had to.

"I'll do that," the trader declared. "I'd like to drive straight through, tonight, so's to get there by mid-morning." He boosted Noren to the seat and, yanking the reins, cursed casually at the work-beast.

After so many days and nights of effort, it was a relief to sit back and let himself be carried along. Also, he was less conspicuous, for on this road sledges and strings of work-beasts outnumbered people on foot. That would compensate, Noren hoped, for the peril of going through village centers in broad daylight. It was his first good look at the region's centers, which, like the local farms, had quite a few buildings of sun-dried brick instead of stone; clay must be more plentiful than at home, where all that could be found was purified by Machine for the making of pipe and pottery.

The sledge jarred, and a fowl squawked noisily; Noren twisted around. There were hens in back, in wicker crates. Did hens sense that they were on the way to the butcher? Of course hens weren't very bright, but then, there were times when brightness was a questionable advantage. He sucked in deep breaths, trying to dispel the fogginess from his mind; it was hard to keep his eyes open. He found himself wondering how long it had been since he had left his own village.

And then a new question worked its way into his thoughts: just how did the Scholars...kill a person? The rumors gave no hint. All the people he'd ever heard of—aside from the few who'd been hanged or who'd been victims of accidents, rare illnesses or murder—had died of old age. How Technicians died no one knew; and as for the Scholars themselves, it was generally supposed that they didn't, though that was probably untrue.

Throughout the long, hot day the work-beast plodded steadily forward, resting only during the pre-noon downpour. When the rain stopped, Noren took over the driving, but the dazed, lethargic feeling stayed with him. The trader was not a talkative man and for that Noren was glad, since between his drowsiness and the persistent ache in his knee it was all he could do to keep a firm grip on the reins. He ought to be more afraid, he thought. He ought to be watching with alarm for the inevitable approach of another aircar, but it all seemed too unreal to matter.

At sundown they halted again by a pond, where the work-beast was allowed to drink, and shared bread washed down with ale from a jug that had been stashed under the seat. The trader drank considerably more of this than Noren, and as a result drove only a short while after they started again; soon he was snoring in the back of the sledge, leaving Noren to keep the work-beast moving. The road was well lighted, for all three major moons were at full phase and even Little Moon seemed to shine with extraordinary brilliance. *The time when the Mother Star itself shall blaze as bright as Little Moon,* he thought wistfully; if there could indeed be such a time—a time when some immutable power would bring about the downfall of the Scholars and the fulfillment of all their empty promises—how different the world would be! *The ancient knowledge shall be free to all people...*why ancient? Noren wondered. Why had the Scholars who wrote the Prophecy used that particular word? It was almost as if there'd been a source of knowledge that had preceded them.

Long before he reached it, Noren could see the lights of the City. The whole valley seemed to glimmer. There were dozens of lights, white and yellow and green, swarming around a shining beacon that made him feel that if the Scholars wished, they could place the Mother Star in the sky themselves. He had known that the City was lit by Power, but he had not dreamed that there could be so much Power in the world at one time. He drew rein, overcome by emotions he could scarcely interpret. The moment he'd been anticipating was at hand: the end of his search was in sight, for better or for worse, and he looked upon it less with terror than with eagerness.

When dawn came, the trader roused himself and clambered back onto the seat to resume driving. Noren relinquished the job thankfully; the sights before him were too wondrous to claim anything less than his full attention. He was almost there! Ahead, the scalloped walls of the City stood tall behind a conglomeration of ordinary stone and brick buildings and the long, low wattle structures of the markets. As he watched, the rising sun illuminated the immense silvery barrier and the incredible spires behind it, shooting back dazzling streaks not merely from their widely spaced windows, but from the entire surface of each tower.

Noren stared, spellbound. There, in those soaring towers, was hidden all the knowledge he sought. Was it possible that other travelers could see them without feeling the unbearable desire they aroused in him? Surely even Talyra, who must have come days ago to the training center, could not have remained unstirred!

The trader thrust the reins back into Noren's hands momentarily and peeled off his outer tunic. "Going to swelter again," he remarked matter-of-factly. "Say, is this your first trip to the markets?"

"Yes."

"Quite a sight, huh?" The man waved a casual hand toward the spectacle that in Noren had evoked near-reverence. "You know someday villages'll be like that. Ordinary folks'll have all the stuff the Technicians've got, Machines of their own and everything."

Abruptly, Noren's head cleared. This man might be persuaded; at any rate, it could well be his last opportunity to try. "Do you believe in the Prophecy?" he asked directly.

His companion swore. "What d'you mean, do I believe it? I'm no fool heretic."

"I mean do you think it's right for us to wait all that time to have what the Technicians have? To be kept from knowing all there is to know? Knowledge isn't property; it should be free! We could have Machines right away, for instance, if—"

The man studied Noren intently. "We couldn't understand stuff like that," he said. "Someday folks'll be smarter than us, and then—"

"Technicians are men like other men, and so are Scholars! *They* understand, and we could, too, if we weren't afraid."

"Say, you better be careful. The way you talk, you could get yourself into a mess." He leaned over and spat into the street.

"Yes," admitted Noren levelly. "But if enough of us talked about it—well, maybe we could make something happen."

The trader turned, grabbing Noren's wrist with tense, calloused fingers. "You mean that? You don't like being bossed by Technicians that think they know everything; you don't fall for a bunch of phony stories about Mother Stars and sacred Laws, maybe?"

"You know they're not true, too!"

"Sure, I know. What's fair about them that live inside the walls having stuff the ones outside ain't got?"

"That's exactly what I mean! If there were only some way we could—"

Speculatively, the man asked, "Ever hear what happens to people that think your way once the Scholars get hold of 'em?"

Noren nodded slowly. The trader said nothing more, but took the reins and continued on in silence. Before long they drew to a halt in front of a wattle-and-daub shed. "This is where I unload," he announced. "Stick with me, and I'll introduce you to some pals of mine." He tied the work-beast and went around to the back of the sledge, lifting out one of the crates of cackling fowl and disappearing with it into the building.

Excitement exploded in Noren. At last, someone who shared his beliefs! And it had been implied that he would meet others who shared them! There was, of course, a possibility that the trader would betray him, perhaps even try to claim a reward for doing so; but since the Technicians must already have a good idea of his whereabouts, the risk seemed worth taking. Anyway, he had no choice but to wait, for he could go nowhere without something to bandage his knee.

When the unloading was finished, the man drove on to another section of the markets. Noren surveyed the long rows of open stalls with interest. Here the traders from many villages met to bring produce from the farms, for which the Technicians paid well. The traders would then purchase fine craftwork as well as the less common herbs, yeast, and the many commodities—glass, cloth, paper, writing styluses and the like—that came from the City alone, where they were made by Machines. Strangely enough, however, the place seemed nearly deserted. "There aren't a lot of people around," he observed, puzzled. "Is it always like this?"

"Most everyone's in the plaza," the trader said shortly. "A heretic's going to recant this morning, and they'll all be there to see the show. We will, too, soon's we can get you a bandage."

The sledge lurched ahead, its runners grating on sand already marred by countless tracks. Near the stable where they left it was a fabric stall, and Noren, in producing the money for a stout strip of cut cloth, could not avoid displaying his entire kerchief full of smooth white coins. The trader eyed them, but made no comment; he simply went ahead and wrapped Noren's leg tightly until it was stiffened by many layers of bandaging. When it was finished, Noren stood clumsily, his knee hurting fiercely as he shifted his weight, and hobbled along without objection. The last thing he wanted was to watch some other heretic being forced to go through the degrading ceremony to which he himself had sworn never to submit, but his companion seemed insistent, and the man was his only link to people who might prove kindred spirits.

They reached the plaza late, for the stabling of the work-beast had taken time and Noren was unable to walk fast; the ceremony was already in progress. Little of it could be heard, since they stood at the outer fringes of a vast, muttering crowd, so far back that to Noren's relief he was not made conspicuous by his failure to kneel. Though the majority of the spectators had done so, others like themselves had abandoned propriety for the sake of getting a good view.

The plaza faced a stretch of unobstructed City wall, in the center of which were the tall, majestic Gates. In front of them a white-paved platform surmounted a wide flight of steps. The backdrop of glittering towers, rising so high above the walls that Noren had to tip his head to glimpse their tops, was awesome, but he could devote little thought to it; his attention was focused on the occupants of the platform. They were Scholars. He knew they were because of the brilliant blue robes they wore, robes he'd seen in the paintings that adorned the village hall and schoolhouse: longer than women's skirts, but less full, with flowing sleeves that in the case of the center Priest were trimmed with bands of white. A number of Technicians were also present, and between them knelt the prisoner.

He faced the Scholars, his profile to the assembled people, with his hands bound behind him. His gray penitent's garments looked filthy; if his captors had any decency at all, he could at least have been given new ones! But there was no reason to suppose that they were that humane, Noren thought in sick despair. How could anyone who'd opposed them be so contemptible as to buy his life with obeisance?

This man had been convicted of heresy, which meant that he once had believed at least some things contrary to the Prophecy or the High Law. Yet he knelt there, unabashedly declaring that he acknowledged the Book of the Prophecy to be "true in its entirety" and retracting "all criticisms" that he might ever have made of anything! Either he was the lowest sort of coward or...or they had done something awful to him, something past any stretch of the imagination. Though no signs of injury were apparent, Scholars might well have more subtle means of inflicting pain.

Shuddering, Noren watched with growing contempt both for the High Priests and for their victim. He was not close enough to see faces, but the man's bearing was shameless. He spoke with seeming conviction rather than with reluctance. The Scholars were silent, impassive, accepting this submission as if it were no more than their just due. What had they done to change someone who'd once defied them into a consenting tool of their authority?

They will never change me, Noren promised himself grimly. *No matter what they do or what they threaten, I will not deny the truth; I will not become like that man; I will not recant!*

There was an atmosphere in the crowd that he did not like; it was akin to the temper of the people in the village who'd taunted him at the time of his own arrest. Only the presence of the Scholars, he guessed, prevented it from erupting into something uglier. The animosity was directed not toward them, but toward the heretic. And Noren could not help sharing it. He could not help feeling more scorn than pity: not, as with the majority, because of the prisoner's heresy, but because he had sold out.

"We missed the best part," the trader remarked cryptically during a pause in the ceremony. He had, Noren noticed, been talking to a friend who'd approached him some time back. "All that's left now is the sentencing, and that's always the same. Come on."

"Where?" questioned Noren.

"A bunch of us are getting together to eat," the man answered in his brusque, decisive way. "I'm taking you along; but by the Mother Star, you'll be sorry if you've lied to me."

The place to which the trader's friend took them was a ramshackle shed behind one of the market buildings. It was dark and dingy and smelled like a stable; in fact it probably had been a stable at one time. "Sometimes we sleep here when we haven't the price of a room at an inn," the trader said. "You can stay if you like, only don't repeat what you hear."

"I won't," promised Noren, with mounting excitement at this clear indication of the men's sentiments. It amazed him that heresy could be spoken aloud at any sort of gathering. But, he reflected, the Technicians weren't empowered to arrest anyone who hadn't been convicted in a civil trial, and though the people who lived permanently at the markets had a village government of sorts, they probably did not go out of their way to watch travelers.

The earlier arrivals had brought food and ale, which they proceeded to share informally. There were five or six of them, an ill-assorted lot, most of them men Noren would never have suspected of caring for the things that mattered; he had to remind himself that if they disbelieved the Prophecy and risked open criticism of the High Law, they must care. And it was evident that they did take such risks, for though the trader vouched for him, he himself was eyed with hostile suspicion.

A big, rough man clutched Noren's shoulders in a viselike grip. "What did you think of that weakling?" he demanded, in obvious reference to the heretic whose recantation they had all observed.

"He sold out," Noren declared.

"And you wouldn't?"

"No!"

The man released him. "You sound as if you mean it," he conceded. "They all do before they're caught, of course; but you've as much backbone as any. He did, too, once—used to be a friend of ours." He grinned unpleasantly. "Well, he got what he had coming, and don't think we didn't give him our share."

"Are you trying to scare me?" said Noren, covering his confusion with a laugh.

"Just making sure you know what you've gotten into," the big man said. "Lots of farm boys don't."

"I know, all right," Noren assured him. He wondered what these men would think if they knew he had already been tried and convicted; for some reason he couldn't explain, he felt that it would be unwise to tell them yet.

He sat silent, eating food he scarcely tasted and listening to the discussion of the others with elation that was tinged, somehow, by an uneasiness he did not understand. He didn't need to convince this group, for its members were saying just what he'd despaired of ever getting across to anyone! They hated the Scholars; they considered the Prophecy a fraud; and above all, they resented the exclusive rights of the Technicians. There was a great deal of talk, much of it lewd, on all these topics; and not until it had gone on for some time did Noren see what disturbed him about it.

There was nothing these men did believe in. They spoke of Power and Machines, but never of knowledge; and not once had anyone mentioned truth. Nor had they any plan for improving matters. To be sure, Noren had no plan himself; but he had always supposed that if this many heretics ever got together, their first move would be to form one. "Mightn't there be some way we could change things?" he ventured during a lull in the conversation.

One of the men gave a bitter laugh. "Change things, he says! Why, there's nothing we or anybody else can do against Scholars."

"All you traders ever do is talk," protested a younger man. "We should rebel openly, that's what we should do."

"And get arrested for it? What would that buy us?"

"I've told you before, the Scholars will have to deal with us in public. There'll be none of this nonsense about civil trials then! They'll show their hand, and people will begin to see them for what they really are."

"I haven't noticed *you* doing any rebelling."

"It won't work unless a lot of us take action at the same time."

"It won't work anyway."

"It might!" Noren argued. "If enough people would oppose the High Law—"

"Aw, people won't listen," said the trader. "Guys that quote the Prophecy at you every time you start to talk to 'em—they don't deserve no Machines anyhow. It's men like us should be getting that stuff."

"Knowledge and Machines should be for everyone!"

"Even the ones too dumb to care? What for? You and me, now— Well, no use talking about it. There aren't enough smart guys in the world. I heard once the Scholars have a way to blow the whole City up into clouds. Burn every last thing, all at once, see, so's the Technicians'd have nothing left better'n what the villagers got. If we could grab hold of *that*—"

"Destroy the City?" Noren was shocked. "That wouldn't be right; it wouldn't do any good at all. What we want is to have more Cities, Cities for everybody."

"We can't," said the young man with frightening intensity. "The Scholars and Technicians will be too powerful as long as anything of theirs remains. We can't have the kind of world we want without destroying this one; it's corrupt, evil."

"The High Law is," agreed Noren. "But that's no reason to smash the good along with the bad. If we did that, some knowledge might be lost."

"We want no part of the Scholars' knowledge!"

"Knowledge—truth—is the most important thing there is," Noren maintained. "The only trouble is that the Scholars are keeping it all to themselves when we should have it, too."

"You're right," put in another trader. "Why destroy what we could use? If we once got inside the City, we could take it over, maybe, and get rid of the Scholars. People would kneel to *us* for a change."

"I don't want anybody kneeling to me," said Noren, not bothering to point out that taking over the City was manifestly impossible. "No man should ever kneel to another. It'd be just as wrong for us to have that kind of power as for the Scholars to have it."

"I'd say it was our turn," someone asserted, and others muttered agreement.

In desperation Noren switched tactics. "The Technicians wouldn't obey us," he said.

"Them?" The young man laughed. "We'd kill them in any case. That's something we can start on right now."

Aghast, Noren exclaimed, "You're speaking of murder!"

"I didn't take you for the squeamish type."

"I'm no murderer," Noren declared. "And anyway, some of the Technicians are on our side."

The whole group turned on him with renewed hostility. "Where'd you get a stupid idea like that? All Technicians are our enemies."

"That's not true—" Noren broke off, helpless, for he might imperil the one who'd helped him if he told about his arrest and escape; it was becoming more and more apparent that these men were not the kind he was looking for. "I mean—well, they'd be on our side if we could talk to them, because the Scholars are hiding knowledge from them, too." In contrast to his hopes, he had seen few Technicians around the markets; there would be little opportunity for persuasion, yet they were still potential allies. Certainly they weren't to blame for a Prophecy by which they themselves were deceived or a High Law in which they had no voice.

"Look," the trader told him roughly, "you'd better get this straight. We don't trust no Technicians! If we get a chance, we'll kill as many as we can; they've been on top too long as it is."

"Killing people's wrong," insisted Noren.

"Since when are Technicians people?"

Noren stared, horrified. There was no real difference between these rebels and the villagers he'd known all his life! One kind thought Technicians were more than human; the other, less; neither had any true concern for the right of each man to be judged on his own merits.

Yet on second thought he saw that there was indeed a difference. His present companions were worse. They were even worse than the Scholars, who at least did not murder and destroy. There was a legend, he recalled, that told of how at the time of the Founding, before the Prophecy had been made known, an evil magician, whose name was unspeakable, had tried to rule the world by force—and of how he had been vanquished by the Scholar's establishment of the High Law, which forbade such rule. It was likely that they'd started that legend themselves to mask the Law's real intent; still, overthrowing them would hardly solve the world's problems if men like these were to seize power instead.

"We don't trust nobody that talks to Technicians, either," announced the big man in an ominous tone. "How do we know you're not a starcursed spy?"

"You'll have to take my word," said Noren heatedly. "I'm as much against the High Law as any of you, but I'll not go along with your ideas for what to do about it."

At that moment somebody glanced through the open door of the shed and cried, "Technicians! Outside, watching—"

"He must've brought them here; none ever came before."

Cold with dismay, Noren realized that they were right. He very probably had been followed, and instead of arresting him immediately, the Technicians were gathering evidence against his companions. He should have known that his presence would expose them to danger! Though they couldn't be seized directly, a trap could be arranged, as it had been for him; and little as he liked their talk, he had no desire to see them condemned for it. They had not, after all, actually done anything, nor were they ever likely to. They were powerless against the City, and if they tried to murder any Technicians, the villagers would deal with them in short order.

"By the Mother Star, he'll not leave here in one piece," growled the big man. They converged on Noren; then, abruptly, the light from the doorway was cut off by the Technicians' silhouetted figures. It was the last thing he saw.

When he came to, it was night, and he was lying on the dirt floor of the now-abandoned shed. He sat up, rubbing new bruises and realizing that only the entrance of the Technicians had saved him from worse. Why hadn't he been arrested? They must have known his identity; why else would they have followed him? It didn't make sense! Or perhaps...yes, perhaps they'd been unwilling to lay hands on him in the presence of the others. The men, being heretics unlikely to take their word, wouldn't have believed Technicians had authority to touch him, since it was unheard of for someone already in their custody to escape; it would have looked as if they themselves were disobeying the High Law.

Noren reached into the inner pocket of his tunic, knowing even before he did so that Talyra's coins were gone. He had no chance to make converts, for he was friendless, without money to live on, and there could be little doubt that his recapture was at best only a few hours away.

As the night waned, Noren wandered aimlessly; though his knee throbbed painfully under the bandage, he was able to limp, and some inner urge would not allow him to keep still. It was not merely an urge to evade capture. Rather, he was irresistibly drawn to a place where the great towers, the central one topped with its blazing beacon, were in full view.

Dawn found him back at the plaza. In front of him the City walls thrust up, solid and forbidding against the pale morning sky. He noticed that their surface was not straight, but curved, and wondered why they had been built that way. There were so many inexplicable things about the City, so many things that he longed desperately to understand...

At the lowest corner of the broad flight of steps leading to the Gates, he slumped wearily. What next? Arrest was imminent; he could neither buy food nor, because of his bad knee, could he work for it; and what hope was there of achieving anything if the only people who recognized the High Law's fallacies wanted either to destroy all that was good in the world or to set themselves up in the Scholars' place?

An aircar, sunlight catching its rotors, hovered briefly and dropped out of sight behind the high barrier. On either side of the steps, produce was being loaded into boxlike caverns in the walls; several Technicians were supervising. Noren eyed them nervously, then turned his back and sat on the bottom step, looking out toward the market stalls that lined the opposite side of the square. A crowd of people was again gathering. All at once music, loud and heart-stirring, burst from somewhere behind the Gates and reverberated through the plaza. It swelled in volume until Noren felt as if he might burst also; it was like nothing he had ever heard, and it made him want to sing or to shout or even to cry.

It faded; the crowd hushed. Above him the huge Gates parted and a blue-robed Scholar appeared, flanked by four Technicians. Immediately the people in the plaza fell to their knees.

Startled, Noren remembered too late the Benison that preceded the daily opening of the markets. The Scholar would read from the Book of the Prophecy. He had no desire to stay, but he would only attract attention to himself if he moved, for everyone was waiting, motionless, eyes raised toward the sky in sober respect. Yet he would *not* kneel! If he was reprimanded, he decided, he could state quite honestly that the injury to his knee made it impossible.

He turned toward the Gates and lifted his eyes with the rest. A trace of breeze fluttered the sleeves of the Scholar's robe as he opened the book. His voice, mysteriously amplified, floated past Noren, on out to the edge of the plaza with undiminished clarity.

"'Let us rejoice in the bounty of the land! For the land is good, and from the Mother Star came the heritage that has blessed it; the land has given us life—'"

The knowledge they were hiding could give people a better life, thought Noren bitterly.

"'Those who have brought forth life from the land are rich—'"

But not as rich as those who had access to the Power and the Machines.

"'For through the land's taming shall our strength grow, that we may be ready to receive the ancient knowledge—'"

No doubt, when the predicted date arrived, people would be told they weren't ready; the Mother Star would hide its face in shame! Noren scowled. He knew the words well and in fact had read the entire book many times, having been taught his letters from it as a child, but he had not spotted that loophole before. Whoever had inserted it had planned carefully.

"'...And the people shall multiply across the face of the earth, and at no time shall the spirit of the Mother Star die in the hearts of its children.'"

All the families, Noren reflected—all the good, sincere people who recited those words every time they sat down to eat—they'd been tricked by the Scholars into putting their trust in something false! Talyra trusted it implicitly, and she too was the victim of cold-blooded deception.

Glaring at the High Priest who stood above him, he was abruptly overpowered by the hot anger that had been building up in him for years. He could no longer contain it. What do *you* believe, Scholar? he raged. What is it that lets you stand up there and exhort people to attach their natural faith in goodness to what you know is a figment of somebody's imagination?

He looked back at the mass of rapt faces. Those people would never turn against the Scholars. There was no conceivable way he could make them listen, nothing he could do that would be even a small step toward changing the world into the sort of place the Prophecy described. And he was almost too weary to care. He almost wished the Technicians would arrest him and get it over with.

The spired towers glistened overhead, dazzling his vision. All mysteries were sealed away there...and he had a right to share those mysteries! Yet neither he nor anybody else would ever be granted that right. The idea of its depending on the appearance of a mythical Mother Star was too firmly entrenched. *The spirit of this Star shall abide forever*—there was a certain degree of truth in that declaration. By the success of their deceits, the Scholars had *made* it true.

People wouldn't oppose the High Law on being told that the Prophecy wasn't authentic because that would be acting not so much against bad rulers as against their own beliefs. The real trouble, Noren saw suddenly, was that most people had no reason to think the Scholars were bad. As High Priests, they did not interfere with ordinary villagers' lives. Yet if someone were to commit an act of overt defiance, wouldn't they have to interfere? Wouldn't they be forced to silence him immediately, without waiting for the formality of a civil trial?

Noren clenched wet fingers, an idea forming out of his desperation. They were going to kill him sometime. Why not in front of the whole Benison assemblage? Why not in a way that would provide the people who revered them with proof, real proof, of their underlying ruthlessness?

His heart raced. The Scholar was reading the last page of the Prophecy; within seconds after he closed the book, the music might surge up again. There wasn't time to deliberate, Noren rose from the step and moved forward.

"'*...through the time of waiting we will follow the Law—*'" As those words were reached he was part way up the flight, above the crowd; heedless of the pain in his knee, Noren found himself climbing without stumbling. He marshaled every bit of strength he could collect, throwing it all into his voice.

"No! We will not follow the High Law; it is evil! It's wrong for a few men to create a Law above village law and keep all the knowledge for themselves!" He glanced upward over his shoulder; the Technicians had left the Gates and were coming down toward him, unhurriedly and without any show of emotion. "There should be Machines for everyone, Power for everyone, and knowledge should be free!"

His words resounded hollowly from the walls behind him. Stunned silence pervaded the crowd; what would have been greeted with wrath on a less formal occasion evoked only shock when it came as an interruption of a ceremony like the Benison. "The Prophecy—is—a—fake!" Noren shouted. "It's a *fake!* There is no Mother Star!"

Something jolted him, thrusting him forward onto his injured knee, and its pain cut through him like the jab of a knife. The Technicians hadn't yet reached him; it was as if he had been assailed by some invisible force from within. Noren crumpled, his agony eclipsed by the growing numbness of his body. Just before the music overrode all other sound, he heard a gasp from the crowd and a woman's cry, "Blasphemer! See, the Star has struck him!" whereupon he realized that in the minds of the people he had been struck down not by the Scholar's order, but by supernatural intervention.

His eyes blurred; the incomprehensible thing they'd done seemed to have immobilized him. He tried to grip the edge of the step above, but his fingers would not move; they were frozen, somehow. None of his muscles would act. It occurred to him that this was very likely a natural part of dying.

The music exploded into the air, vibrating through his head. Hazily Noren was aware of the greenish shapes of the Technicians as they lifted him and carried him through the Gates, into the City itself.

Chapter Seven

Noren regained consciousness in a tiny room, without doors or windows but dimly lit by Power. It did not look like a jail cell: the walls were of a pale, clear green that was rather pleasant; the floor was covered with thick padding; and the couch on which he lay was smooth and soft. Moreover, everything was very clean. Even his garments were clean, for they were new ones, made of ordinary fabric but beige, not brown, and styled exactly like Technicians' clothing.

How had he arrived in this place? he wondered, getting to his feet. He had no recollection of anything else in the City. Strangely enough, his exhaustion was entirely gone and his arms and legs seemed to work normally; the pain in his knee had disappeared along with the bandage. Yet if he'd slept long, he should feel hungry, and he did not. What had happened? They'd lifted him from the steps…

He pressed his hand to his mouth, a surge of nausea rising in company with an overpowering sense of failure and of fear. His impulsive attempt to expose the Scholars' ruthlessness had not done any good; he was to be killed in secret after all. His death would be wasted: worse than wasted, for they'd managed to turn his words to their advantage by creating the impression that they'd had no hand in his falling, that the Mother Star itself had punished him.

He should have foreseen, Noren thought despairingly, that they would not kill him before making an effort toward getting his recantation.

Why hadn't he realized that? he asked himself in perplexity. Had he dreaded their unimaginable ways of coercion so much that he'd wished for immediate death…or had he actually *wanted* to be caught?

With honest self-appraisal, he saw that he had indeed wanted it. He had wanted to enter the City on any terms whatsoever! Furthermore, he'd known underneath that there was only one way left in which he could defy the Scholars: by confronting them and proving to them that not all heretics could be subjugated.

All right, he thought grimly, he was in their hands and totally helpless, but there would be certain compensations, compensations of which he'd been inwardly aware, and that gave him an edge of sorts. The circumstances of his recapture had been of his choosing, not theirs, and he was the stronger for it. It was impossible to guess how long it would be before they killed him, but he had little doubt that horrible things would be done during the interim. They would try to make him recant. He must not attempt to imagine how, for if he did, fear might sap his new-found strength; he must simply take the things as they came.

An opening appeared in the wall where a door, made of the same solid green material instead of matting, was swinging back. Two Technicians stood there; Noren straightened and, at their command, stepped into the corridor without protest.

He had hoped that he might see something of the City during his remaining days of life, but the room to which he was brought was as featureless as the hall leading to it. It was quite large, again lighted by Power, again with softly colored walls and floor. At one end was a dais upon which three Scholars sat at a curved table. Strangely, one of them was a woman; apparently the women among the Scholars shared in their decisions. All three wore the usual blue robes and their faces were indistinct; Noren had the impression that he might as well be facing a row of Machines. Certainly these judges showed no more feeling.

"Aren't you going to kneel?" asked one of the Technicians, who, oddly, had not done so themselves.

"I am not," replied Noren. He stood at the foot of the dais, his arms folded.

Nobody tried to force the issue; the Technicians left without restraining him in any way, and as yet none of the Scholars had spoken. He stood in silence for a long time before he realized that they were measuring his nerve.

Watching their faces, he saw that their apparent lack of feeling was deliberate, a mask. It was presumably meant to frighten him. But beneath the mask they were alert, intelligent people, people with whom a real argument might be held. At the trial he hadn't been able to argue with his judges; they'd simply labeled his statements as heresy and let it go at that. Though the Scholars might do the same, they would be capable of going further if they chose. They could not believe the Prophecy as the councilmen did. While they wouldn't admit that in public, mightn't they to a person who was going to die anyway? If he could convince them that he would never be coerced into recanting, he might at least have the satisfaction of hearing them concede that his theories were correct.

He had nothing to lose by trying, Noren decided. Taking the initiative, he began, "You must have been surprised when I gave you the chance to arrest me."

"Not at all," replied one of the Scholars. "We could have arrested you at any time since you left your village; we had you under constant surveillance. But it was more to our purpose to let you come to us."

Noren suppressed the dismay he felt. That must be a lie, for surely they couldn't have anticipated what he himself had not consciously intended! "You're wrong if you think I did it because I considered myself beaten," he declared.

"We don't. But you have learned that you cannot win support for your theories. You've also learned other things that you don't yet recognize. Frankly, Noren, we're glad you robbed that Technician of his uniform. Though we didn't plan it, your temporary escape will benefit us in the end."

"Mainly I've learned that I don't care what you do to me," asserted Noren, torn between relief that the Technician's story had been accepted and consternation over the untroubled confidence of this man. "I spoke at the Benison not only to tell others the truth, but to show them how far you'll go to hide it; I thought you might kill me then."

"It's not going to be that easy." The Scholar frowned. "Just what do you mean by 'the truth'?"

"What you call heresy. I understand it, so there's no point in pretending I'm as naive as most people. I know all about the Prophecy."

"You don't know nearly as much as you think you do," commented the Scholar dryly.

"Don't you think a villager can be smart enough to figure it out?"

"I don't think you have the background to figure it out."

"You mean because I was brought up to believe in the Mother Star, I should believe in it. But I don't. I'm admitting that I don't, that I know the whole Prophecy's a fake, a trick to make people content with having men like you keep all the knowledge for yourselves—"

The woman Scholar broke in sharply, "You're mistaken. The Prophecy's statements about the Mother Star are true. Everything you've been taught is true, except for a few exaggerated legends."

"Don't bother to say that, not with me."

"Why should you doubt it?"

"Because it's not logical or possible; magical things like new stars and people coming out of the sky don't happen, and they never will. If there were to be a new star, you couldn't know ahead of time, and anyway, even if you could, it would have nothing to do with your suddenly getting generous with the Power and the Machines!"

The Scholar's reply was delayed slightly, and when it came it carried an aura of flat finality rather than of anger. "What you're saying is false according to the Book of the Prophecy. You will suffer for holding such ideas. And you are wrong."

"The Book of the Prophecy is not sacred; you Scholars wrote it yourselves, the way *you* wanted it," insisted Noren, trying to match the woman's cool assurance. "You can do anything you like with me, regardless of my ideas, as you can with anyone. I have no choice about what happens."

"You had a choice between accepting what you were told and living out your life peacefully, or deciding to do your own thinking," the first Scholar said slowly. "Now you have a choice between admitting the error of your opinions without further ado, or admitting it later, after certain experiences that will persuade you to cooperate."

"I'll stick to my opinions," Noren declared. He hoped his voice sounded louder than it seemed to.

"The consequences of independent thought can be less inviting than you realize."

Noren didn't answer. After a short wait, the Scholars proceeded to play back the recording of his trial. He remained silent and impassive as he listened; to hear his own words repeated was strange, but not dreadful. He did not regret the statements he'd made. At the finish, when he was asked if there were any that he wished to modify, he declined without hesitation.

The third Scholar, the one in the center, hadn't said anything; he had simply watched, and yet had somehow given the impression that he was the most formidable of them all. Finally, in a soft but commanding voice, he spoke. "I must warn you, Noren," he said levelly, "that if you persist in your defiance, the consequences will be grave and irrevocable. You have no conception of the things that can happen to you here. This is your last chance to obtain our mercy."

"I don't want your mercy," said Noren angrily.

"Why not?"

"Because I'm not your inferior. To accept mercy would be the same as kneeling to you."

The woman Scholar turned. "The boy is bold enough, Stefred," she remarked. "Will you let such boldness pass?"

Noren's skin prickled. So this was the Scholar Stefred, the dreaded Chief Inquisitor who had given the young Technician his instructions. No heretic, it was said, could resist Stefred's methods.

"In time," Stefred said confidently, "this boy will kneel to me in public and retract everything he has ever said against the Prophecy and the High Law. Until then let him speak as he likes. I am interested in what he has to say." To Noren he continued, "We have a number of questions to ask you. Will you swear by the Mother Star to answer them truthfully?"

"I'll take no such oath, since we both know it to be a farce."

"You are frank, at least. Can I assume that you'll be equally frank in response to the other questions?"

Noren looked him in the eye. "I have nothing to hide," he said. "It's you who are hiding information; you, not I, have cause to fear the truth."

"Very well." Stefred leaned back, nodding to his associates to begin the questioning.

It went on for a long time. Noren answered candidly, having no desire to conceal anything aside from the details of his escape, which fortunately were not touched upon; and at first the game was not too disagreeable. The Scholars, instead of trying to extract heretical admissions, soon turned to opposite tactics: they tried to trap him into statements that could be construed as partial recantation. He refused to be trapped, and matching wits with them proved rather exhilarating.

After some hours, however, he was trembling with fatigue. The same questions had been repeated not once, but many times. Quite a few of them were foolish ones having nothing at all to do with the subject at hand; questions about his childhood, his family, his private thoughts about things entirely unrelated to the Prophecy or the High Law...

"No more of this," he declared at last, fearing that at any moment he might collapse. They had not told him he must stand throughout the inquisition, but there were no chairs in the room and to sit on the floor seemed akin to kneeling. "There is nothing more to say; I've told you the whole truth."

"We cannot be sure you have. Besides, there were a few questions to which you gave no responses at all."

"Some things," protested Noren indignantly, "are none of your business!"

"Everything is our business in an inquiry of this kind."

The details of his feelings toward girls, about which all too much interest had been expressed, could have no possible bearing upon heresy, Noren felt. Surprisingly, they had not mentioned Talyra specifically or asked anything that could conceivably be related to her having helped in his escape, though he'd dreaded it constantly, knowing that if they did, he would have to lie, since to remain silent might cast suspicion upon her. The questions he'd resented had been of a different sort. Most of them seemed stupid, for if Scholars knew anything at all about human nature, they could easily have guessed the answers; on second thought, however, it occurred to him that their aim might merely have been to catch him in an obvious falsehood.

"I will not answer anything else," he announced.

"You will," Stefred assured him, rising. Stefred himself had taken little part in the questioning, but he had listened with avid attention, hoping, no doubt, to detect some small inconsistency in Noren's responses. Now he touched a button on the table before him, summoning the Technicians. "We are specialists in the study of people's minds, Noren," he said, "and when someone does not tell us all we need to know, we have a way of compelling him to do so. You will find this frightening, but if you are sincere in your desire to be honest, you have nothing to dread from it."

The Technicians brought not a chair, but a low, padded bench on which they required Noren to lie. He complied without struggle; resistance was useless, he knew, and he was so tired that he scarcely minded. The needle that was stuck into his arm did frighten him, but not until a few minutes later did he become really terrified.

The thing that frightened him was the realization that he was speaking, speaking rapidly, yet without full conscious control.

Noren never knew exactly what he said under the influence of the drug. He knew only that it was Stefred who questioned him and that he was unable to hold anything back. He talked on and on for hours, yet the hours went quickly; he could not judge the time. He could not see anything but the blue-robed blur of the Scholar who bent over him, and who, surprisingly, spoke with a gentleness that had no cruel undertones. Hazily, he realized that the questioning was retracing all the same ground that had been covered before: his beliefs, his desires, his fears and above all, his reasons for what he had done. Why had he become a heretic? Why did he hate Scholars? Did he want to kill them, and if not, why not? Did he want to seize power for himself?

They had asked that last question constantly right from the beginning, disguised in different forms. It must be impossible, Noren had decided, for Scholars to conceive of anyone's not wanting power! They must think all heretics were trying to replace them. No wonder they cared so much about getting public recantations.

While drugged he could not reason that out, but he was aware that the point was being examined again from every possible angle. Then, eventually, he ceased to be aware of anything at all.

Later—perhaps a day later, perhaps more—he awoke in the small green room where he'd originally regained consciousness. Immediately terror engulfed him. What had he done? Had he spoken of Talyra or of the young Technician, or denied the things he had sworn to himself he'd never deny? Had they somehow *changed* him?

No, he realized. He was still himself. He was still sure that they could not force him to recant. If it were that simple—if they could do it merely by sticking a needle into somebody's arm—they would not bother with all the preliminaries.

The Technicians brought him food: good food, though he had little appetite for it. Then he was taken back to the large room to confront the same three Scholars. Again, he remained standing. He was no longer tired, he found, and his mind was absolutely clear. To his astonishment, his spirits were high. So far he had triumphed over these inquisitors; they weren't nearly so powerful as they pretended to be.

"We are satisfied that you have not lied to us," he was told. "It is impossible for anyone to lie while under the drug. A person can keep back information if he's determined to, but if you'd been concealing any we'd wanted from you, we would have known."

Relief lifted Noren's spirits still further. His worst fear had been that he might have been made either to betray those who had helped him escape or to say something he did not believe; but if he'd done so, they would surely boast of their success.

"We have learned a great deal about you," Stefred said. "We've learned, for instance, that you really want the knowledge we have here in the City. You long desperately for it."

"I've never denied that," Noren agreed. "Knowledge is the right of everyone; it should be available to all. Of course I want it."

"You want it not only because it's been kept from you, but for itself."

"Yes, I do."

Stefred eyed him thoughtfully. "Like everything else, knowledge has its price," he said. "Would you be willing to pay the price, Noren?"

On the verge of assent, Noren felt a vague sense of alarm. He'd already demonstrated that he was willing to pay with his life; what more could they ask? "That would depend on what it was," he said cautiously.

"In this case, it involves an ordeal that you would find quite difficult."

"No ordeal would be too difficult if it led to the truth you're hiding," declared Noren, with a sudden, irrational hope that they might actually decide to enlighten him.

"If you recant voluntarily," Stefred announced, "you will be given access to more knowledge than you can absorb in a lifetime."

Noren recoiled, stunned first by disappointment and then by his own stupidity in not having spotted the trap. That they could obtain recantations by bribery when threats had failed hadn't occurred to him, yet it was all too logical.

"Think before you answer," Stefred went on. "I know you're tempted. I know you well enough to be sure that it's a more painful temptation than the first offer you were made. Think: is your pride in your ability to hold out worth more to you than knowledge?"

Noren's head swam. Put that way, his determination to hold out seemed arrogant foolishness, a contradiction of everything he had said about what he was seeking. Yet there was a flaw; there had to be. That was not the way it should be put.

He raised his eyes. "Knowledge is worthless apart from truth. It's the truth I really value, but if I recanted, I'd be lying. Truth belongs to everybody; to recant would be to accept your right to keep it from the other villagers."

"That's your final word?"

"Yes."

Stefred did not seem disappointed; as a matter of fact he looked quite pleased. It was probable, Noren thought dejectedly, that they'd known all along that the bribe would be refused. If they'd analyzed his mind as well as they said they had, they must have known. They must also have known that the memory of this lost chance would keep on hurting right up to the end.

"Perhaps you're better off," said the other man. "Knowledge can be frightening, after all; sometimes people are better off without knowing everything. Sometimes they're aware of that underneath."

It was a skilled twist of the knife; Noren caught his angry reply just in time, realizing that to defend himself against the implicit accusation would be beneath his dignity. "Perhaps," he agreed, "especially since I have no reason to think you'd have kept your word in any case. Where do we go from here?"

"You know, I suppose, that we've hardly begun."

"I know," Noren replied grimly. They would not raise the subject of killing him yet, he felt, not while he was strong enough to laugh at them.

"Whatever you may think to the contrary," Stefred stated, "you are going to be compelled to recant. Your recantation will be wholly sincere and will be obtained by a means that you'll be powerless to resist. I shall not describe the procedure in advance; I'll merely say that it's beyond your present comprehension and that I judge you to be more vulnerable to it than average. You have until tomorrow morning to think that over."

The ultimatum was more unnerving than Noren had imagined it could be. He stood silent, utterly dismayed, while without another word the three Scholars left the room; then, blindly, he followed as the Technicians escorted him back to his own quarters.

There he collapsed on the couch, unsure of his ability to endure the hours of delay and thankful that no one was present to observe his lapse of self-control. *More* vulnerable than average? Stefred must have been lying, bluffing; surely he'd not displayed any vulnerability.

But the Scholar's eyes had not been veiled as for a bluff, and he had spoken with the force of total conviction.

When morning came, Noren was led through a maze of passageways and finally, after a puzzling wait in a small cubicle within which he felt an odd sense of motion, he found himself thrust through a tall door that, although also solid, had slid aside to admit him. There was light, brilliant daylight streaming through a window; Noren glanced out and drew a quick breath. The glistening towers were no longer above him, but stood directly opposite. He was high above the City walls! He looked down, seeing that they were merely the outer faces of a ring of domed structures. The huge silver circles dazzled him as he gazed across them to the busy markets and the grainfields beyond. This was what Technicians must see when they traveled through the air.

Reluctantly, Noren turned his attention to his surroundings. His guards had withdrawn, and at first he thought himself alone; but as he stepped further into the room, he saw that someone was seated behind a large desk made of some shiny white substance. Because the man was dressed in clothes similar to the ones Noren himself wore, it was a moment before he recognized the Scholar Stefred.

"Sit down, Noren," Stefred said, indicating a not-uncomfortable looking chair next to his own.

"I'd rather stand," replied Noren defiantly.

"As you wish. But we'll be spending a good deal of time together." Stefred's voice wasn't angry; it didn't even seem stern. Noren stood motionless, nonplused. The room was not the sort of place he had thought he'd be taken to; there was nothing particularly ominous about it. To be sure, he noticed a number of Machines that were incomprehensible to him, but he also noticed inviting shelves of books. One of the books lay open atop a pile of papers, as if hastily set aside. Did Scholars spend the time between ceremonies in rooms like this, unrobed, reading books as he himself might do if he had the chance? Though he'd denied their superiority, he had not pictured them as human in just that way.

Stefred leaned forward. "I believe you've been honest with us," he said. "I believe that when you say truth is more important to you than anything else, you mean it. We are now about to see whether you have what it takes to live up to what you claim."

Noren was silent. Would he? he thought, fighting for composure. He'd made up his mind that he would, no matter how much whatever they did to him might hurt; but suppose they really had a form of pressure against which he'd be powerless?

"You have courage," Stefred remarked, almost with warmth. "I shall challenge it; aren't you curious as to how?"

"I've got a pretty good idea," Noren said evenly.

"Really? You've heard all sorts of ghastly stories, haven't you, about the goings on here in the City—things that no one can describe, no one can even imagine?"

"They're part of the sham. If you believe me, you know you won't get anywhere by more talk, so you've no recourse but to put me to torture. There's no mystery about that."

"Does the prospect frighten you?"

"No," said Noren staunchly, hoping his knees wouldn't give way.

"That's the first lie you've told," the Scholar observed. He hesitated, giving Noren an appraising look. "I'll be frank with you, Noren. If I thought I had a chance of getting your recantation in that way, I could not proceed without trying it; there are some good reasons why we don't resort to the method I'm about to use with a person who can be made to cooperate through any other means. Fortunately, I already know you well enough to be sure that torture wouldn't work."

Astonished, Noren barely suppressed his breath of relief. This was undoubtedly another trap; still the admission restored not only his hopes, but his wavering self-esteem. Perhaps they had no mysterious means of defeating him after all, and he would *not* give in from mere fear of them!

Stefred regarded him soberly. "You're surprised. You weren't sure in your own mind, were you? You believed you could stand up under it, but you weren't absolutely sure." Keeping his voice level, he continued, "That's something one seldom knows about oneself, but we Scholars are usually able to tell. You see, we're interested not only in what people do, but in why they do it; and once we've determined why a heretic is holding out, we can judge what sort of persuasion he's susceptible to. In your case I am certain that physical discomfort, however severe, would have no effect. What I'm going to do is rather more complicated, and as I've said, it's undertaken only as a last resort."

They stared at each other, Noren resolving that he would not be the first to drop his eyes. There was something strange in Stefred's manner; though the words were cold, Noren sensed none of the calculated coldness he had felt during the inquisition. *Why, he admires me!* he realized suddenly. *This Scholar needs to break me, but underneath he admires me for standing up to him. He acknowledges me as a true opponent.* The thought was heartening; on the strength of it, he managed a forced smile.

Stefred returned it, his own smile looking surprisingly genuine. "You're wondering what can possibly be worse than the pain to which you'd steeled yourself. Tell me, what makes you think it's going to be?"

Caught off guard, Noren could only stammer, "Why—why—"

"You haven't an answer. You've got plenty of intelligence. but you haven't yet learned to make full use of it. You question a great many things that other people accept, but still, inside yourself, you're holding to premises for which you have no valid grounds. That's one of the ways in which you're vulnerable, Noren. I'm not going to treat you like a helpless victim; I shall fight on your own terms: the terms you chose when you stood before us and claimed intellectual equality as your birthright."

"I claimed the right to knowledge. There's no equality as long as it's hidden from me.

"True. You will be armed with what you need. But first, let's dispose of some of those false premises. Number one: we never said that you were our inferior, or for that matter, that any other villager was. Because many of *them* told you so, you assumed it was our idea. It wasn't."

Noren scowled, stricken by confusion. This was scarcely the kind of attack he'd been anticipating. "Number two," the Scholar went on, "we never threatened you with torture. We never threatened you at all. We merely told you that we could compel you to recant, and you assumed that we had no better weapon than fear. Like many of your other assumptions, that's wrong. Some of what I do to you will be terrifying, but you won't be swayed by that;

when in the end you recant, you'll do so of your own free will, because your innate honesty will leave you no choice."

"No," Noren insisted, "I'll never go back on what I believe."

"That's a very dogmatic statement, and it's unworthy of you. If you cling to it, you'll be going back on the key point in your defense: the assertion that you care more for truth than for comfort." Rising, Stefred fixed penetrating gray eyes on Noren. "The next few days aren't going to be comfortable; truth, when it conflicts with your personal opinions, is not easy to confront. Yet you maintained over and over again that you wanted to know the truth. All right. Your wish is hereby granted. My weapon is not like anything you ever expected, Noren. I'm simply going to give you what you asked for."

Noren shook his head. "You tried to bribe me before; I haven't changed my mind."

"This isn't a bribe. There are no strings attached, and you aren't being offered a choice. You've already passed the point of no return."

"There must be a catch," protested Noren skeptically. "As you yourself told me, there's a price for knowledge."

"Of course there is," Stefred agreed. "In the first place, once you've become privy to the secrets I'm about to reveal, you will be confined to the City for the rest of your life."

That, thought Noren, was unlikely to be long. "It would have happened anyway," he said. "No heretic has ever left the City."

"Not often, but there's a small chance when a person's repentance comes early. For an enlightened heretic, however, there is no release; our secrets must stay within these walls. And there are other consequences. You're in deeper waters than you realize; before I'm through with you, you're going to be shown things—unpleasant things—that even the Technicians don't know." The Scholar approached Noren, his tone carrying more force, yet at the same time more feeling. "Did you demand truth for its own sake, or merely to prove yourself right? Do you value it enough to take its consequences without protest?"

"I do," Noren declared, "if you can convince me that what you tell me is really true. I won't accept empty words." With chagrin, he saw that he had made a concession by admitting the possibility that Stefred might not lie; yet somehow he couldn't help feeling that this man was not like most Scholars. In any case, he could scarcely have answered otherwise.

Stefred sighed. "You'll receive more than words," he informed Noren, "and the consequences will be grimmer than you suppose. I warn you that a day will come when you'll be willing to give up everything you care most for in order to escape them."

Did they think he didn't know they were going to kill him? Noren wondered. Just because they'd never threatened to, did they think him naive? Aloud he said, "I made my choice long ago. I'll have no complaints as to where it leads."

"You're mistaken. I'm willing to bet that when the time is ripe you will stand here in this very room and give me all sorts of arguments as to why you should be let off."

Deliberately and with effort, Noren laughed. "I see what you're trying to do. If you could make me refuse your offer now, under these terms, it'd be the same as making me say that I don't really care about truth after all."

"You're very perceptive," the Scholar acknowledged. "However, as I explained, it's less an offer than a judgment. Hard as it may be for you to credit, you've convinced me that you do have the right to the facts about the Prophecy, which as you've guessed are not quite the same as the official interpretation. They are not the same as your interpretation, either; but then, your information has been very limited. It will be limited no longer, Noren. You've won what you wanted." With a strange note of sympathy he added, "I only hope you'll never be sorry that you did."

Chapter Eight

Noren sat in the chair Stefred offered him and waited with a mixture of excitement and resignation, aware that he'd been maneuvered into a position in which, for the time being, he had no choice but to play along. The Scholars' tactics were diabolically clever. He could not tell whether he would actually be given the truth or whether there'd be further attempts to deceive him, and if he was taken in by deception they would triumph; yet were he to resist truth when it was offered, they would achieve a final and ironic victory.

His spine tingled. To learn the real secrets—the underlying secrets that were kept not only from the villagers but from the Technicians—would be worth all he'd gone through. Perhaps Stefred was sincere; after all, what harm could it do the Scholars to enlighten him before he died? They might even see an advantage to it, for if the truth was as unpleasant as Stefred had intimated, they might think it a fitting punishment; but in that case the triumph would be his! Suddenly Noren recalled the remark that had been made during his inquisition: *Knowledge can be frightening…sometimes people are better off without knowing everything.* He was indeed being challenged, he decided. They were daring him to back up his conviction that it was always preferable to know.

He watched Stefred's movements curiously, seeing that the Scholar was handling a small Machine of some sort. Then, abruptly and without warning, the room was plunged into total darkness; the bright day of the City had somehow turned to moonless night. There was a penetrating humming sound. Noren clenched his icy fingers and tried to gulp down panic. He counted the seconds.

When he reached forty, a dazzling, fiery sphere burst into being in front of him. It dimmed slightly, so that he was able to look at it without blinking, yet at the same time it grew, tendrils of cold flame trailing out from its edges. It was about to envelop him, Noren felt. He wanted to hold his head up, but he could not bear the sight for more than a few moments; he closed his eyes and crumpled in the chair, biting his lip to keep himself from screaming.

The room turned black again, and Stefred's hand touched his shoulder. "We'll try again," the Scholar said, not unkindly. "We'll keep trying until you can watch it through, because you will soon be required not merely to watch, but to understand."

Noren drew himself erect and concentrated on understanding. The fire reappeared, larger and brighter than before; and this time, though his mouth was dry and his heart thumped as if it would burst, his eyes stayed open.

"Do you know what this is, Noren?" Stefred's voice went on.

"It—it looks like the sun, but there's no heat."

"Yes. But it's not our sun. And it's only a picture; this is a picture of a star, up close. Star, sun—they're the same thing."

"But the stars are much smaller," Noren protested.

"They look smaller because they are far away."

That was reasonable. But then how could the Scholars get pictures of them up close? How could they get such pictures in any case, pictures that moved, pictures that looked *real?* "Is this sun one of the stars we see in the constellations, then?" he asked.

"You have never seen this particular sun. It is the Mother Star."

Noren controlled his gasp of astonishment and did not reply.

"You've been told in school, haven't you, that the world is round and that it circles the sun?" the Scholar continued. "Well, there are many worlds, Noren; unnumbered worlds, circling other suns, the stars." The image was instantaneously extinguished and another took its place: a greenish globe, splotched with irregular areas of white and blue and brown. "Here you're looking at such a world. A whole earth; an earth with fields and streams and mountains—and Cities, hundreds of Cities, many of them larger and grander than you could possibly imagine."

As Noren watched, he saw the world come alive; the globe faded and it was as though he were flying over the land, and then he seemed to be walking through the streets of the Cities themselves. There were people dressed in exotic clothing like none he had ever seen; there were wide, deep streams with little houses floating on them; and once there was a vast expanse of blue water stretching all the way to the horizon. Even stranger, there were towering plants with dark green foliage and brown stems thicker than a man's arm! There were also other things that he could not begin to identify. He couldn't absorb the barest scrap of what he was seeing, and yet it filled him with an agonizing, irresistible longing to be part of it and comprehend it.

But it was gone. There was only the shining globe again, receding into the distance.

He knew then what Stefred's strategy must be. This glimpse of the forbidden, ultimate secrets was designed to tempt him past endurance; though not a bribe in itself, it was the prelude to a proposition that he would find very hard to stand out against. All the same, he could not regret having had the glimpse.

"Haven't you any questions, Noren?" Stefred asked.

He had so many questions that he would not have known where to begin, even if he had wished to reveal his craving for further knowledge; again, he resolved to remain silent. But Stefred, apparently, was not through tantalizing him. "I'll give you some of the answers anyway," he said.

When Noren didn't respond, the Scholar went right on. "A great many years ago," he began, "the world you saw had so many Cities and was so crowded that people were dying because they could not get enough food. There was no land left to grow more food. The Technicians of that world were able to travel to other worlds that circled the same sun, but on some of them they found only rock and ice, and some had no solid ground at all. The rest—five that were quite similar to the home world—were quickly filled up. They couldn't raise enough food there, either."

Despite himself Noren burst out, "How could they go from one world to another?"

"There is a way. They eventually came to use what was called a starship, a ship that enabled them to visit not only the worlds of their own sun, but those of far-off stars. Look." A shape grew out of darkness: a Machine, massive and cylindrical, a glistening thing that somehow resembled the towers of the City. "It is propelled by Power. Inside, there is space for hundreds of people to live and work; and in starships like this, Noren, our ancestors arrived at the time of the Founding."

No, thought Noren desperately. It couldn't be; the Founding was only a myth...

"They came upon this world only after years of searching. A new discovery had made it possible for them to reach other suns in less time than it had once taken them to circle their own, but there were few stars of the right type near theirs, and not all worlds are places where people can live. Some are barren; some are too hot or too cold, or have air that is poisonous; some are occupied by other forms of life. This was the first suitable one they found."

Again, Noren saw living scenes take form in front of him: first the interior of the starship, and then a smaller ship coming down out of the sky and the people getting out of it. In the background were the familiar yellow ridges of the Tomorrow Mountains.

After a long pause, the room grew light once more and the picture disappeared.

The Scholar smiled quizzically. "Well?"

Noren met his eyes. "Even if I were to accept these pictures—if I were to believe in the Founding, and concede that people came out of the sky instead of having once been savages as I guessed—I still couldn't believe in the Mother Star."

"But you have seen it. It is the sun of the world you were shown; it is, as the Prophecy says, our source."

"If that's so, how is it that we can't see it in the sky?"

"It is too far away."

"Will it come closer?"

"No. What will happen is as yet beyond your comprehension—"

Triumphantly Noren broke in, "If it's not coming closer, then how can you tell us it will someday appear? Nothing can change the fact that you've created the Prophecy as an excuse to keep what's here in the City away from people!"

Stefred returned to his desk, pausing thoughtfully. "Nothing can change that," he admitted. "Nevertheless, the entire Prophecy is true; you will accept it and revere it."

"I will not. These things—these pictures—should be for everyone; what right have you not to share them? If our ancestors all came together in a ship, what right have you to hide the knowledge that came with them?"

"You will concede us that right."

"To buy more enlightenment for myself? If you think so, you've underestimated me," Noren persisted.

"I doubt it," Stefred said. "If anything, I've overestimated you. As I told you, at present you have no option in regard to your enlightenment; it is going to proceed whether you like it or not, and it's quite possible that you won't. The next phase is considerably more painful."

"Oh," Noren said resignedly, "so you're threatening me after all."

The Scholar shook his head. "We don't want it to be painful for you, Noren. Parts of it will be; truth often is. But the pain won't be the sort you've anticipated, and I will not subject you to any that can be avoided."

"Which is another way of saying that if somebody won't go along with you, it's 'unavoidable' for you to punish him. Naturally you don't want to; you'd be much happier if we all agreed without making trouble—"

"Actually," Stefred interrupted with a strangely unreadable look, "we're delighted whenever a person proves willing to do his own thinking."

"Just so you can demonstrate your power over him?" Noren found, to his amazement, that he was disappointed; for some reason he had begun to think better of Stefred.

Quietly the Scholar replied, "You are not ready to understand why. I can't ask you to trust me because I'm aware that you have no basis for trust, but all the same, I hope you'll remember what I'm going to say to you." He leaned forward again, and his tone carried no trace of cruelty or deception. "You are about to undergo some very difficult and frightening experiences. During the course of them you'll learn a great deal that you've been longing to know, but you will suffer in the process. That can't be prevented. We Scholars have suffered in the same way. It is not punishment, but an inherent part of the truth you've chosen to seek out. You see, Noren, such truth involves not merely facts, but feelings. Some of the feelings aren't pleasant, but if you really mean the things you've been insisting—the things about its being better to know first hand than to believe because you're told you should—then you won't mind experiencing them."

Noren stared. The sympathy in Stefred's manner seemed too warm to be faked. "Are these experiences designed to make me believe the Prophecy?" he asked suspiciously.

"They are designed to show you the origin of the Prophecy. If you emerge from them believing, it will be because you've accepted the proofs; what a person believes is not subject to force."

"You're not talking as you did during my inquisition," Noren observed, bewildered.

"I am not," the Scholar agreed, "but in neither case have I lied." He smiled. "You have a quick mind. You've spotted an inconsistency between my ultimatum to you and the statement I just made; you think you have me trapped. Think deeper! If you understand your own system of values, you'll see that no inconsistency exists."

But it did, Noren thought. The bald assertion that his recantation would be sincere and that it would be obtained through means he'd be powerless to resist surely couldn't be reconciled with an admission that beliefs could not be forced; that is, it couldn't unless...

Unless real proof could be presented. If they could *prove* the Prophecy, he'd be unable to resist them. He was indeed vulnerable in that sense, for to ignore proof would be a violation not of their principles, but of his own.

He had never suspected that they might have proof. He'd given no thought to such a possibility; he'd feared only that they might torture him or, more recently, that they would practice some ingenious form of deception. And wasn't that still a danger? Wasn't it conceivable that they could make false proofs seem real? How, thought Noren in anguish, was he ever to judge?

"I've at last cracked your armor," Stefred was saying. "For the first time you doubt your convictions, and it hurts. You're beginning to realize that if by some remote chance we are right and you are wrong, it is going to hurt a great deal."

The man's analysis was all too accurate, Noren reflected ruefully. The idea of finding himself wrong was more upsetting than all the earlier warnings; Stefred had gained the upper hand.

"But consider this, Noren," the Scholar continued seriously. "You wouldn't be capable of feeling such hurts if you lacked the ability to evaluate what you're shown. You'd either label all the proofs offered you fakes, or, if we had some way of forcing them on you, you would accept them without question; in neither case would you feel distress. The fact that you do—that you're willing to open your mind to it—is evidence that your regard for the truth is reliable."

Noren looked up, seeing his antagonist with new respect. Why hadn't Stefred used his advantage? He was certainly shrewd enough to have done so, for he had uncanny knowledge of what went on in people's thoughts, yet he'd strengthened the defense he must destroy. He'd spoken as if truth was important to him, too!

Meeting the Scholar's gaze straightforwardly, Noren said, "I'm not afraid to be wrong about the Prophecy, sir. I won't deny it, if it's proven, but what difference will that make? I still won't recant, because recanting means more than accepting the Prophecy; it means accepting your right to keep things away from people. I won't acknowledge that no matter what you prove about the Mother Star."

Stefred showed no sign of disapproval; in fact he looked almost as if he'd received the answer he wanted. But his reply was impassive. "You'll be amazed at what you can be brought to do," he said dryly, touching a button at the corner of his desk.

The door of the room slid open, and the two Technicians reappeared. Noren's stomach contracted. All at once his fear rushed back, more debilitating than ever before. *He's playing with me,* he thought in despair. *He encourages me only to prolong the pleasure of breaking my spirit.* At Stefred's nod, Noren felt his arms gripped firmly; then he was being taken down a ramp and along a narrow, solid-walled corridor in which there was no apparent opening.

They ordered him to sit in a heavy, padded chair with a weird-looking leather headrest and an appalling assortment of unfathomable apparatus attached to it. Noren obeyed, seeing no use in resistance. He was tilted backward so that he was half-reclining. The cramped little room was windowless; light came, somehow, from the ceiling, dimly illuminating a panel of dials and switches on the opposite wall. One of the Technicians moved a lever at the top of the panel, causing a small red light to glow.

Resolutely, Noren told himself that they must not see his terror, and from somewhere he got courage to relax his muscles while they fastened various bands and wires to his head. He realized that this Machine would do something mysterious and overwhelming to him, and he was filled with foreboding; the interview with Stefred had left him deeply shaken. Yet part of him wanted desperately to believe Stefred. The Scholar had said the things he'd said as if he meant them, and some of them were things no one else—not even Talyra—had been willing to admit.

Thinking of Talyra, Noren felt a surge of sadness. He would never see her again. And what had he achieved? He had convinced only one person; he had not made the faintest dent in the

Scholars' aura of power; and he would die in the end, no matter how bravely he bore this ordeal. Why, he wondered, wasn't he sorry? Why was he still so determined never to give in?

A young woman entered, dismissing the Technicians, whom she evidently outranked although she wore no Scholar's robe. She carried a syringe; taking Noren's arm, she wiped it with a chilling, pungent solution. Her eyes avoided him, but there was pity in them as she plunged down on the needle.

The sting was intense, but brief; he felt a flash of heat spreading through his veins. It was not unduly unpleasant in itself. He lost awareness of touch and seemed to be falling through miles of emptiness, though he could see the unyielding walls and the woman standing before the control board, her hand on a switch below a winking yellow bulb. Then the room was black, and colored suns were expanding somewhere in his mind—not pictures, but images totally independent of sight. His eyes would no longer open, but he heard the switch close with a resounding metallic click.

He expected pain, but it did not come.

Instead, he was in the starship. He recognized it immediately and was perplexed over the sudden transference; then in the next moment he was conscious of the fact that he was not himself any longer. No…he was himself, but he was someone else too, simultaneously. The other person's thoughts and knowledge came naturally into his mind as if they were his own.

He was a Scholar. He stood at the round window of the ship—a viewport, it was called—and looked out at the earth, the other earth, the world of many cities. He could not see them from where he watched, but he knew what they were like; he knew countless things about them that had never been in the pictures. He knew the people, also, for they were his own people; he was a Scholar not of his world, but of theirs.

And in that world a Scholar had no rank, no secrets. All was as it should be: knowledge was free to everyone. The part of him that was Noren rejoiced. It *could* be that way, it was not a foolish idea! That was how it had been meant to be all along.

But his rejoicing did not last, for somewhere, buried deep inside him, lay knowledge so terrible that he dared not bring it forth consciously. It had nothing to do with High Priests or their secrets. It concerned something more basic than that, some horror too vast for contemplation. The Scholar could deal with such thoughts;

Noren realized that it was he, as himself, who lacked courage to let them surface. He must find the courage, he knew. He must not shrink from any knowledge that was available to him.

Deliberately, he suppressed his own identity, allowing the feelings of the Scholar to surge into his mind. He looked out at the green globe beneath him and thought of the people...millions upon millions of people, the people not only of this world but of its neighboring ones: their lives, their achievements, their hopes; their harrowing struggle to create a civilization in which everyone had equal rights to power and machines and wisdom; their audacious dream of interstellar expansion.

And he knew that the people were going to die. All of them.

It was not because they couldn't get enough food. That problem could have been solved. Though of the fifteen planets in the solar system, the six fertile ones were fully settled, already one world of a distant star was being explored; there would someday have been many more. But there was a far worse problem that he and his fellow-Scholars had discovered very recently, and it had no solution.

He, the Scholar, was counted among the wisest of his people, and everyone agreed that if he could not save them, no one else could. Nevertheless he had consulted all the other Scholars in all the cities of the Six Worlds, hoping that someone would prove wiser than himself. No one had. The tragedy that was about to strike was beyond the scope of human wisdom to prevent. It would take place soon, and instantaneously; there was no possible way to stop it. All that humankind had accomplished in the thousands of years since the first civilization had grown out of savagery was going to be wiped out—all, that is, but the knowledge preserved in the computers aboard the starship and its sister ships of the fleet. With sorrow he accepted the fact that there was *nothing* he could do, nothing but to stand at the viewport and passively observe what was going to happen.

Men approached him. "It's nearly time," said someone.

Noren nodded. "Take us out," he replied curtly, as if accustomed to command.

There was a peculiar sensation, not so much of motion as of dislocation. The green globe disappeared. After a little while the other men returned. "We are well beyond the solar system," one of them said. "Ten minutes to zero, sir." He added hesitantly, "Will you—watch?"

"I must." Noren was not quite sure why he must; he certainly did not want to. Even as the Scholar, he was afraid. Yet for some reason he felt a responsibility to do it. He could not save the Six Worlds, but he might perhaps save the people of the new and far-off research station, a handful of people who, with the fleet's passengers, would soon be the sole survivors of the entire human race. His plan for saving them was vague and very desperate. Somehow observation of the disaster would contribute to that plan.

"Maximum filters," he ordered. The glass in the viewport darkened. He could no longer see the stars. He could not even see the sun, which at this distance was no brighter than a large star in any case.

But it soon would be.

I'm dreaming, thought Noren in panic, *it's like other nightmares; before anything dreadful happens I'll wake up...* One did not feel nameless terror like this except in nightmares. One certainly did not become someone else, someone whose thoughts were beyond understanding.

His eyes were fixed on the center of the viewport; his companions had dissolved, as people do in dreams. The ship too was dissolving. Before him, a pinprick of light began to grow.

It grew as it had in the picture, but it was not harmless now, not cold; it expanded into a swollen mass of incandescence, a blinding, pulsating sphere of pure light and intolerable heat, and though his flesh was not burned, he felt the pain of burning. He had doubted when told that the picture showed the Mother Star. He could not doubt now, for he knew that this star was unlike others. Surely normal stars did not explode like this, engulfing their worlds, turning them not merely to ash, but to vapor! There was a word for such stars, drawn from the mind of the Scholar, and the word was *nova.*

Passage of time had no meaning. Even before the nova's light had become visible, the worlds circling that star had ceased to exist, and their people with them; yet the blazing brilliance of it would endure. It would someday reach far galaxies. The Scholar, perhaps, had watched in silence; but Noren was so overpowered by it that he could not hold back his screams.

When he awoke, Stefred was beside him. They were in the little room with the Machine, but the woman had gone and the apparatus no longer touched his body. He lay back in the reclining chair, sweating.

"Do you understand what happened to you?" Stefred asked quietly. His tone was concerned, compassionate; Noren turned to him with an instinctive, unreasoned conviction that the compassion was real.

"I—I was dreaming, I guess," Noren replied dazedly. "Those pictures you showed me must have brought it on. It was sort of a nightmare; did I cry out, or anything?" He averted his face, mortified at the thought that he might have done so.

"It wasn't an ordinary dream," Stefred told him. "You see, Noren, when there's need we can make people dream what we want them to."

Noren drew back, stunned less by surprise than by his own near-surrender. Once again they'd tried to weaken him through terror, and this time they'd come all too close to succeeding. Furthermore, if they'd done it once, they could do it over and over; no wonder they'd been so confident of their ability to break him without physical torture! "I do see," he said hopelessly. "You think I'll give in rather than go through worse nightmares."

Stefred's hand closed reassuringly on his. "You have it twisted. I think you'll consent to go through them, because dreams of this kind aren't mere nightmares; they are true. What happens in them once did happen; they will teach you much that would otherwise remain beyond your grasp."

Horrified, Noren whispered, "You mean it—it really was like that? The sun grew so big that it burned up its worlds...and all the people died?"

"Yes," Stefred admitted with sorrow. "I know how it feels to watch; I've dreamed the same dream myself. All Scholars have."

Noren frowned. It had never occurred to him that Scholars, despite their privileges, might undergo ordeals of their own. "Then you're not expecting to break me this way," he reflected. "Is it done to all heretics?"

"Just to those who will not be satisfied with anything less. Truth, Noren, can be quite terrible. Not everyone can face it. I'm exposing you to this only because you convinced me that you could."

For a long time Noren thought. He was not sure just how he knew that the dream was indeed true; it was partly that the feelings of the person he'd become had been real feelings, separate from his own terror—and partly that he could sense Stefred's sincerity. There was a subtle difference in the Scholar's manner that made plain that in earlier interviews, his emotions had been deliberately concealed.

Slowly Noren declared, "I—I believe you, sir. I believe that by keeping such secrets from the villagers and Technicians you're trying to be kind. But I don't think that's right. I don't think people need to be protected from the truth. Even when it does hurt, it's—well, it's how things *are.*"

"I agree with you," the Scholar said gravely. "In this case, however, the issue's not that simple. There's still a lot you don't know. Are you willing to dream again, Noren?"

"Do I have a choice? You said before that I didn't have."

"Your choice at that point had already been made. But you've had complete freedom to choose from the very beginning; the Technicians at the inn, for instance, couldn't have induced you to speak as you did if you hadn't wanted to. We don't control people. We don't even try. You would not be here if you hadn't chosen to seek knowledge that wasn't available elsewhere."

"I hadn't been fully informed about what I was choosing, though," Noren protested.

"No one ever is; information's a matter of degree. And as you become better informed, the decisions get harder."

Stefred paused and then asked again, "How about the dream?"

"It's…nightmarish?"

"Yes. Even more so than the first, but as you say, it's how things are."

"Then I guess I can't stop now. I don't want to stop."

"I thought not." The approval in Stefred's voice was unmistakable. He prepared a syringe, continuing calmly, "I'm going to give you something to make you sleep, and for many hours you'll sleep peacefully; you must have rest and nourishment, which you'll receive from injections, to regain your strength. After that you will find yourself back in the starship. What you hear and what you feel won't be faked; like the witnessing of the nova, it was recorded long ago from the memories of the First Scholar. He was a real person, and he actually experienced it. For him it wasn't a dream from which he could wake up."

"Why did he make himself watch the sun explode?"

"So that he could relive it in his mind later, while a Machine recorded his thoughts. He knew that we of the future could learn more from dreams than from words or pictures."

"But then why didn't I realize that while I was dreaming?"

"You cannot have access to his whole mind," explained Stefred. "The dream's content is limited both by what's in the recording and by your own reactions. Since you retain your personal identity, most of what you meet is strange to you; it can't all be comprehended at once."

"I didn't know what was going to happen at first," Noren reflected, "The First Scholar must have known all the time, but I had to—reach for it."

"Yes. The further you reach, the more you'll learn; but it takes courage." Stefred hesitated, then added, "The First Scholar had a great deal; you can draw on that as well as on his knowledge, and you'll need to. You will share his feelings fully, Noren, because it so happens that you are very much like him. He was older and wiser, but essentially he believed what you believe."

Then he must have been a heretic! Noren thought. No—no, in his world such beliefs hadn't been considered heretical. They'd been approved, and Stefred's respect for the man was clear. Incredulously he asked, "Are you—a Scholar—telling me that my heresy isn't wrong?"

"I can't tell you what's wrong and what's right. That's a decision every person must make for himself, though you may find it helpful to know how the First Scholar made his."

"I must be still dreaming," Noren murmured. "Everything's turned around."

"Not really. You are looking at sides you haven't seen before."

"But...some of what you've said supports *my* side, sir! Why should you side with someone who opposes you, someone who's got to be silenced?" Was it possible, thought Noren wonderingly, that there were secret opponents of the system among the Scholars themselves?

Smiling enigmatically, Stefred answered, "I've always been on your side. I couldn't let you know until I was sure of where you stood; but from now on I have nothing to lose by it, and everything to gain."

Chapter Nine

He was the First Scholar again. He was aboard the starship, but he no longer looked out through its viewports; instead, he sat at a large white table with a group of people, some men, some women. He knew them all, but their faces were dim and their names didn't matter. The only thing that mattered was the topic under discussion, which lay so heavily upon him that everything else was blurred.

"The colony will not survive," said someone.

"It must survive," declared Noren. "It is all that is left of humankind."

"Of course it must," another agreed. "Haven't we made every provision for its survival? Why else did we throw all our worlds' energies into the preparation of this fleet as soon as we learned that the sun would nova?"

"To put it bluntly," replied the first man, "we did so because there was nothing else to do. We had to keep busy at *something*. There were less than six weeks; we could not build new starships, we could merely recall and re-equip those we had. We've saved ourselves, only a few hundred of us. Our generation will live. The next will die."

"You speak as if our goal were self-preservation!" protested Noren angrily. "You forget that we were chosen by lot from among the best-qualified scientists of the Six Worlds, and that we were sent not for our sake, but for the colony's. The technicians at the existing research station don't have enough scientific knowledge to establish a permanent settlement; ours is needed."

"It may be needed, but it will prove useless. The research station is utterly dependent upon the arrival of a supply ship every five weeks. People can't live there without supplies; the environment of the planet is just too alien. Why, the soil itself is poisonous and has to be treated each season before it will produce edible crops, not to mention the fact that ground and surface water contains enough of the same poison to cause chromosome damage. If the water purification plant ever stops functioning, all future babies will be mutant idiots!"

"And purifying water on a larger scale won't be simple," added someone else, "even if we succeed in controlling the weather so that the need can be partially met by rain. We equipped the fleet as best we could, but the machines we have won't serve an expanding population—and since the planet has no useable metals, we can't manufacture more. The only hope is to synthesize metal, yet without proper research facilities we couldn't achieve that if we worked for several lifetimes."

"Yes," admitted Noren, frowning. "Yes, I know." He, the First Scholar, did know; and the knowledge had weighed on his mind ever since he'd been informed that he had been chosen to lead the final expedition. It had torn him inwardly, obsessed him so that he'd been barely able to sleep or to eat or even to talk with his wife. It was an insoluble dilemma: the planned colony could *not* survive, and yet it *must.*

Most of his companions had refused to recognize the hard truth, and that was understandable. More than thirty billion people—the entire population of the Six Worlds—had been doomed by the nova; it was too cruel a thing that the descendants of the few who'd escaped would also be doomed. The facts, however, were indisputable: only one planet with a breathable atmosphere had been found during the limited interstellar exploration accomplished in the short time since the invention of the stardrive, and that one did not have the natural resources needed to support human beings.

Through the permanent use of high technology, the planet could be made livable. But it was the world of a metal-poor star, and what little metal it had once, aside from that chemically unsuitable for fabrication of machines, had apparently been extracted in past ages by miners from some other solar system who had depleted it and gone on. Their origin was unknown; no contact had ever been made with another intelligent race; to continue the search for a better planet was impossible without a source of nuclear fuel and concentrated food. In any case, the fleet's ships would have to be dismantled to provide an adequate life-support system for the colony. They carried more equipment than people, since an opposite policy would have been self-defeating; still the equipment could not last forever, and without it, humanity would face extinction.

So far he had not tried to destroy anyone's illusions. The morale of the Six Worlds had been raised during those last terrible weeks by the thought of the expedition that was to save one remnant of humankind, and, within the starships' computers, the entire store of human knowledge. He'd known that if the real situation were to be grasped, the expedition's members might give up in despair. They must not give up! They must proceed as if survival were possible, so that somehow, a solution might be found.

But now the Six Worlds were gone; the fleet was en route to the new planet, and because the starships were not limited by the speed of light, they would get there very soon. A decision had to be made, a decision so appalling that Noren was unable to grasp its nature, however deeply he reached into his mind. The First Scholar did not want to think about the decision. To do so brought him pain, yet the people around the table must accept the fact that their mission was going to fail unless they made some drastic change in the plans formed by the Six Worlds' now-nonexistent government.

"It would be different," he said to them, "if the planet could support an independent colony. But it can't. No one ever expected people to live there without supply ships. Though foods can be raised if the soil is enriched and treated and the seed irradiated, without metal no industry can be established. Even the machines for inactivating native poisons must be imported. It's been assumed that tools and machines could easily be sent—the whole concept of expansion to worlds with insufficient resources was based on that assumption."

"With the food shortage at home so crucial, it seemed better to send the equipment than to wait for the discovery of worlds that could become self-sufficient," they agreed.

"But we've got to be self-sufficient now!" insisted one of the men. "Are you telling us we're stuck with a world we can't develop?"

Noren nodded gravely. "The old techniques, the ones that worked in our home solar system, won't do," he stated, not understanding half of what he, as the First Scholar, was saying. "We don't have enough equipment, and we don't have the means to build it. We have problems that never occurred on the Six Worlds: problems like the poison that permeates the soil, ground water and native vegetation; the need for irradiation of our grainseed to kill fungi; and above all, the lack of metallic elements suitable for industrial use. I believe those problems can be solved. But they can't be solved quickly! We must find a way to synthesize useable metals through nuclear fusion of other elements, and with inadequate facilities that will require generations of research. There is no shortcut.

"And," he added, "if we're to survive, the population must be built up during those generations. We're far too few to maintain the technology necessary for the support of such research, or to produce enough descendants with creative minds."

"How can the population be built up when we must ration our tools and machines merely to supply the population that already exists?"

"There's no easy answer," Noren admitted. "We can't save the human race unless the population grows, yet it can't grow without the equipment only technology can provide—"

"Why can't it?" a woman interrupted. "For thousands of years people lived on our mother world without any technology at all, and the population grew very rapidly."

"Our race evolved on the mother world. The environment wasn't alien. People could survive in the wilderness; they could eat the native plants, and they could kill and eat animals. The water didn't have to be purified. The trace elements essential to our form of life didn't have to be added to the ground, nor all wastes recycled to prevent loss of those elements. There weren't lethal diseases against which no one had natural immunity."

"And our forebears weren't used to the comforts of civilization as we are," another woman added.

"We're going to have to do without comforts," retorted somebody grimly.

"Yes. But it's not as simple as that." Noren sighed. From the First Scholar's mind came the realization that these people were all scientists, all highly educated and very intelligent. Their background was, in itself, blinding them to what a lack of such background would imply.

"Just suppose we did learn to live the way primitive peoples once lived," he said wearily. "Forget about luxuries like prefabricated shelters, powered transportation, communication networks, lighting, farm machinery, imported tools, clothing and medicines: all the things that colonists would normally have. Assume only that cropland was initially fertilized with the chemicals we've brought and treated each season to inactivate the native poison, that the grainseed was irradiated, that weather was controlled to provide enough rain for the crops, that a water purification plant of sufficient capacity to supplement rain catchment was built, and that provision was made for recycling of wastes. Of course, we must also assume nuclear power to maintain these essentials, and we must assume that vaccines for the local diseases could be developed before the drug supplies gave out. Under those conditions, do you think our descendants could last indefinitely?"

"Why not?" several men began confidently; but the faces of others grew thoughtful. "No," said one of the women in a low voice. "No, it wouldn't work. As long as we were alive, we could keep things going. Maybe we could teach our children enough so that they could. But our grandchildren, born into a non-industrialized world—"

"They wouldn't understand," another conceded, "The machines would be magic to them; they wouldn't be able to fix them if they broke dawn, much less find a way to synthesize the metal needed to supply an increasing population. They'd have to be nuclear scientists for that, and the people of primitive agricultural societies just can't be educated as nuclear scientists. They haven't the background, and what's more, they don't *care*. People care about things that seem relevant to the life they know."

"No community can be primitive and technological at the same time," someone else declared, "unless it's importing what its people can't make. Civilization and technology go hand in hand. We're going to be stranded on a planet where advanced technology is required if humanity's merely to stay alive—that is, if it's to stay human and not fall prey to the chromosome damage that would reduce its intelligence to the animal level. If our grandchildren lose that technology, they'll have no chance to start over from scratch; and they will lose it if they revert to primitive ways."

"Lose knowledge?" protested a young man skeptically. "The knowledge will be there in the computers; it will be preserved forever."

"The knowledge will not be retrievable from the computers," said Noren, "after the power plant breaks down."

For a moment nobody spoke; they sat horror-stricken, stunned by a fact so obvious that they did not see how it had been overlooked. They'd grown up believing that the memory of a computer was more eternal than the shape of the land; on the Six Worlds the information stored in the computers had remained accessible until the final holocaust. But they knew, of course, that electronically-stored data would be as meaningless without power as if it had never existed at all.

"We've been in a state of shock," Noren said. "Six weeks ago we learned that thirty billion people were about to die; it's hardly surprising if we failed to think rationally. But we must do so now—"

"All this talk is meaningless," a man broke in abruptly. "It doesn't matter how long the equipment lasts; it would make no difference if we had enough to supply endless generations. There won't be endless generations. The women among us are experienced scientists, too old to bear many children, and the people at the research station will begin to die when they hear about the nova."

"That's crazy," objected another. "Why should they?"

"What happened on the Six Worlds?"

"All right, there was panic. Some people went mad, some killed themselves. But that was different; they were going to die anyway, and they were afraid."

"The members of this expedition were chosen from the Interplanetary Association of Scientists," the man reminded him. "Medical and psychological screening tests were given to eligible couples, the same tests administered to those previously sent. Of the ones who passed, all had an equal chance in the lottery; yet some of them committed suicide even before the lots were drawn."

"I didn't know that!" several people exclaimed in dismay. Noren was silent; the First Scholar had known, but he had tried to forget.

"It was kept quiet," the man said. "But the fact is that most people who've grown up with the idea that they're part of an advanced culture with thirty billion citizens just can't live with the knowledge that it's gone."

"We're living with it," someone pointed out.

"That means nothing, since if we were among those who couldn't, we wouldn't be here."

"There might be another explanation for those suicides," someone else suggested. "They might have sacrificed themselves to give others a greater chance in the lottery."

"A few, maybe. Not very many." In a tone of unshakable certainty the man asserted, "Emotionally, the research station workers belong to the Six Worlds, not to the new world; they signed up for short tours of duty and never planned to settle there. They have no children, for they're waiting to start their families when they get home. They've been getting news from home on every supply ship. When they hear that all civilized planets have been destroyed—that humanity has been wiped out except at that one alien base—their spirit will be fatally crushed. They may not kill themselves, but they won't carry on the human race, either."

"They'll not have much choice once the supply of birth control drugs gives out. Besides, pioneers have always managed in the past."

"These people didn't choose to be pioneers. They weren't reared in the kind of society pioneers come from; the Six Worlds' was so complex that they never developed any independence. They had no desire to break away. Right now they're probably scared to death because the regular ship's late! Oh, they'll have babies in time—but a lot of those babies will be subhuman mutants because when the people learn the truth, their hope will die, and they'll stop bothering to avoid unpurified water."

"You're mistaken," Noren contended. "Surely it will work the other way. They'll know that they've got to be more careful than ever, that everything in the future depends on them."

"I wish I could agree. But they'll also know that there isn't likely to be much future, and not everyone has your courage, sir."

Noren did not feel very courageous; as the First Scholar he was tired and despondent, and he knew that a dreadful decision was soon to be made. "In any case," he said slowly, "we seem more or less agreed that the colony is in grave peril one way or another, and that if we can't come up with a solution, there's little hope for it."

"There is no solution. The colony will die, and humanity with it; and when the power goes off, humanity's knowledge will be lost."

"Is—is this all…futile, then?" a woman faltered. "Have we launched this expedition for nothing? I won't believe there's no way to save future generations!"

The time had come, Noren realized, to speak of his plan: the desperate, horrifying plan he did not wish to think of. "There may be one," he found himself saying, "if we dare to use it—"

Across the room from him a door burst open. A man stood there, a man who quavered, "Sir, we've illness aboard! Three people are stricken!"

Noren jumped to his feet. "Illness? That's impossible; we all had medical checkups and everything on this ship was disinfected."

"It hasn't been diagnosed yet." With still greater distress the man added, "One of those ill is your wife, sir."

Noren's heart lurched; the room swirled around him and then began to dissolve. He found himself transported to another, after the manner of dreams. For a brief instant he knew he was dreaming, but he was quickly engulfed once more by the emotions of the First Scholar.

He stood by a bed upon which a woman was lying. She had long, dark hair, like Talyra's, but he could not see her face. Only her voice came to him, the voice of the woman he loved.

"What use is there going on?" she demanded feebly. "Who are we, a mere scattering of people in a fleet of ships bound through emptiness to an alien world, to say that the human race is worth preserving? There is *nothing left,* darling! Don't you understand? Everything's gone; there's nothing to look back to any more."

"I understand," he told her, forcing the words through trembling lips. "I watched! I saw it, you did not—and I say that there is a reason to go on! If we don't, the colony has no chance at all."

"Why should it have? That world was never meant for humans. Our species wasn't meant to outlast the sun. We should have died when the others did."

He knelt beside her, holding her close to him. "Think of those who came before us," he insisted. "Think of all the labor, all the suffering of the generations past—"

"I am thinking of it! I'm thinking it will be better not to start that again; what end did it serve?"

"None, if we give up now. We have a responsibility."

"To whom? To the thirty billion dead?" She began to cry hysterically.

He felt tears on his own face. "Dearest," he murmured, "dearest, we can't know. We can't see what end we serve; we know only that there's no one but us to keep up the struggle."

"I—I *can't,*" she sobbed. "I can't, knowing what I do."

"You've known for weeks, as we all have. Nothing has changed."

"It has! Before, it was theory; we were told it would happen, but it wasn't real. Now all the worlds are consumed. The universe is empty—empty! No one can live knowing that! The people on that planet will die when they find out, as I am dying now."

"You're not dying," he said soothingly. "The doctors will cure you, and you'll feel differently when you're well. Trust me, dearest. I won't let you die."

"You don't understand," she whispered. "Darling, there's no cure. I...couldn't face it...I took some pills."

"Talyra!" he cried out. The sights and sounds of the dream were fading; he was aware only of the woman who had gone limp in his arms. Somewhere in the background he could hear voices, faint and far away: "An overdose...three people so far...if it's affecting *us* this way, we who knew beforehand and bore the knowledge, those who didn't know are bound to be crushed by it."

He looked down at his wife's colorless face, and it was Talyra's face; Talyra's eyes looked up at him, and she was not dying, but already dead. He wept, and the voices receded further into the distance. "The others may give up too, when they hear."

"No!" Noren exclaimed, his own voice as remote and unreal as the others. "They will not hear; I now see that we mustn't tell them. If we don't, they'll have no way of knowing, for the new world is so many light-years away that the nova will not be visible there for generations."

Noren awoke wrenched by sobs, deep, silent sobs over which he had no control. Talyra...he'd been holding her in his arms and she was dead, dead because civilization was gone and humankind was gone and it was futile to go on trying. The whole human race was going to die out.

At the sight of his surroundings, he came abruptly to himself. Talyra wasn't dead. It had been the wife of the First Scholar who had died. Moreover, the human race had somehow lasted after all. Why had it, when its doom had seemed so sure?

Stefred stood in a corner of the little room, his back turned. Noren sat up; his feet touched the floor and found it solid, though in the wrong place, somehow. "Why didn't things happen as the people of the fleet expected?" he asked.

"Do you think there was real danger?" Stefred replied, his voice giving no clue as to what he himself thought.

"There must have been," Noren said positively. "Even though the nova was kept secret—which I'm still not sure was right—there didn't seem to be any way around the other problems."

"The First Scholar found a way," said Stefred, coming to Noren's side. "If he hadn't, none of us would be here."

"It was something frightening, something he felt awful about," Noren recalled. "He—he had the idea, but I just couldn't get hold of it."

"His plan was not in this particular recording," Stefred told him. "It's hard when you reach for a thought that won't come; but Noren, many of the First Scholar's thoughts are too complex for anyone who knows little of the Six Worlds. They can't be made available until a person's ready to understand their significance."

"There are other dreams, aren't there?"

"Yes. But they keep getting rougher. You need not go on unless you choose to."

"I want to go on, sir." Noren took deep breaths, steadying himself, and then burst out, "Why did she have Talyra's face?"

"A dream is more than a recording," Stefred explained gently. "Each person experiences it differently, depending on what he or she brings to it. The recording contains no sounds, no pictures, but only thoughts; and when you as the First Scholar thought of the woman you loved, her face came not from his memory, but from yours."

"Will it work that way with other things?"

"It may." Stefred looked at him with sympathy. "Perhaps you've wondered, Noren, why it was necessary for me to give you drugs during your inquisition; perhaps you felt it an indignity. I had no choice. It wasn't that I suspected you of lying, but merely that I had to know more about what's buried deep in your mind than you could have told me while you were fully conscious. There is an element of risk in these dreams, for with some people they can stir memories better left untouched, and I don't want you to be harmed."

He spoke as if he cared, Noren noticed with wonder. Why should he care whether a heretic was harmed or not?

Another thought hit him, an appalling thought. "Sir, I—I've drunk impure water! I didn't believe before—"

"How often, Noren?" asked Stefred gravely.

"Five or six times, maybe."

"Don't worry about it. The damage is done only if you drink more than that."

Noren sighed with relief before he recalled that he was not going to live long enough to father children in any event. Somehow, despite his grim prospects, he had stopped thinking of what lay ahead. He even found Stefred's prediction that he wouldn't mind sharing the feelings of the First Scholar to be quite true. "What...became of him?" he faltered, as Stefred took his arm for another injection.

"You must experience it in order to understand. We'll proceed now; you're taking this well, and I see no reason to delay."

After that Noren lost track of time. He was never fed, but neither was he hungry; they controlled all bodily needs with injections as they controlled sleep. He was not plunged directly into the dreams without sedation as he had been the first time when, Stefred admitted, they had been making one last attempt to see if he could be panicked into capitulation. Since then they'd attached no apparatus to his head until he was unconscious. During his periods of awareness they questioned him searchingly as to his impressions; he was required to think the experiences through. Then he would sleep again, and dream again.

Someone was always with him when he awoke: usually Stefred, but occasionally the young woman who operated the Dream Machine. She was a Scholar, he was sure, for she knew what was in the dreams and discussed them. He no longer saw any Technicians; that seemed strange until it occurred to him that it was feared that he, who disapproved of secrets, might give some away.

At first he was puzzled because the woman Scholar wore no robe; but since Stefred rarely wore his either, he concluded that the robes, which he'd learned were mere outer garments that covered ordinary clothes, were put on primarily when it was necessary to impress someone. Except for the sexes dressing alike, Scholars looked just like anybody else. Noren had once thought them ageless, as did all villagers, but this woman seemed very little older than he was; and when he stopped to think about it, he realized that within the City there must be other young ones, even children. How did they feel about things? he wondered. Were they, too, frightened when they were first made to dream?

He was still frightened; he grew cold with apprehension every time he was given an injection, for being the First Scholar was not at all enjoyable; yet he wanted to keep dreaming. Stefred would grant him respite if he asked, Noren knew, but he couldn't do that.

It was not just a matter of pride. It was more a matter of an unquenchable desire to know all that had happened, however dreadful those happenings might have been.

He understood, of course, that dreams were proving certain aspects of the Prophecy; that had become evident when he'd absorbed the truth about the Mother Star. Gradually, Noren became aware that they were also proving something else. This awareness was painful, but the pain of giving up long-cherished theories was overshadowed by the First Scholar's suffering, which he found bearable only because of his knowledge that others—including the young woman—had borne it and had survived. If they could, so could he! After all, the First Scholar himself had borne it, and as Stefred had pointed out, for him it hadn't been a dream from which he could wake up.

But the First Scholar had not survived. Somehow, without being told, Noren knew that the final dream would end with the First Scholar's death.

He was back in the room with the white table, again surrounded by the members of his staff, and this time he knew he must present the plan. He must make them accept it, though he was well aware that they would not like it any better than he did himself.

"It's easy enough not to tell the research station people about the nova," someone was saying, "but it'll be a good deal harder to explain why no more supply ships are going to arrive."

"We won't explain," said Noren.

"But sir, we can't hide *that!* We mustn't even try to, because if we do, they'll wear out the equipment too fast. There's got to be rationing."

"There's got to be more than rationing. People must learn to do without any offworld equipment at all in their daily lives."

"That's impossible. We know they can't survive that way, at least not as human beings. If they drink unpurified water too often, the next generation will have subhuman intelligence."

"They can survive as long as somebody treats the soil, irradiates the seed, provides rain through weather control, purifies additional water, and vaccinates them against disease."

"Who's going to do that after we die?"

"Our successors."

The man at his left frowned. "We've been over all this. I thought it was agreed that our successors will lose their technology if they live in a primitive fashion."

"They will," Noren replied. "So the only answer is that they must not live in a primitive fashion. To develop the viewpoint they'll need to carry on our research, they must live in a city where technology is preserved: a walled city within which the power plant and the computers and all the essential equipment can be kept safe for posterity."

"That contradicts what you just proposed about learning to do without such equipment in everyday life," objected another man. "And besides, when the population expands, there won't be enough to go around."

"Within the city very little expansion will be possible."

"We need population growth," a woman protested. "You said so yourself only yesterday."

"For the world as a whole, yes. And outside the city we'll have it; a primitive agricultural society will expand there even more rapidly than the ancient ones, which knew nothing of medicine."

Everybody stared at him, suddenly grasping the implications of what he was saying. Their eyes were large with dismay; though their faces were indistinct, the eyes seemed huge. "You're suggesting a *caste system?"*

Noren paused; to the First Scholar, the thought of some people being allowed to live in a manner that others weren't permitted to share was serious heresy indeed. "Yes," he heard himself declare. "There is no other way."

There was a cold, shocked silence. "I think you're right, sir," one of the men finally conceded. "It could work; those in the city could act as custodians of the equipment and the knowledge, and at the same time they could do the research that would someday enable machines to be manufactured through synthesization of suitable metals. That would solve everything. It's a brilliant idea, but it has one insurmountable flaw: we can never get the majority to accept it."

"We certainly can't," others agreed. "People won't vote for a scheme that puts some in a city with all the equipment while the rest are left outside with none. They wouldn't even if they were aware of the emergency, let alone if we keep the nova secret."

"I know," Noren admitted painfully. "There is no possibility whatsoever of establishing such a system by vote."

"Then we'd better not even propose it. It would be tragic to let them vote down their only chance of survival."

"I'm glad you see that," he replied gravely. "I thought I'd have to argue more."

The faces were blank, for no one yet perceived his meaning. Noren was just beginning to perceive it himself, dipping deep into the First Scholar's memories in his efforts to understand. The government of the Six Worlds had been wholly democratic, he realized. For countless years no dictator had imposed his will on any of those worlds' people; the very concept of tyranny had all but died out; that he should suggest that they seize power was beyond his companions' comprehension.

Noren felt as if he were split in two. He was still the First Scholar, and he shared the First Scholar's misery; yet at the same time he was enough himself to see that the terrible, radical plan was simply that the Scholars should control the City and its contents without giving the villagers a voice in the matter. And to these Scholars, *that* was heresy! It was the worst heresy any of them had ever heard.

But it was a different sort of heresy from his own. The First Scholar did not believe that his plan was right; he did not believe that the world ought to be as he was trying to make it. He hated his own words even as he said them. Yet he knew that he must say them, for he was describing the one way in which humanity could be saved from extinction.

"There will be no violence," he continued. "We will simply build the city and bar the research station people from entering. They know as much as we do about how to utilize what natural resources there are; they can manage very well if we treat enough cropland, establish weather control and a supplementary water system, and provide them with seed and fertile eggs from our cargo. They are not armed, so they cannot resist us—"

The blank faces came alive with emotion: shock, horror, anger. "You're not serious! Impose this by *force?* We'd be setting ourselves up as dictators—"

"The people will remain free," Noren declared. "They will govern themselves; we'll assume no power over individuals, nor will we interfere in local affairs. We will control only the offworld equipment and the knowledge that would otherwise be lost."

Voices assailed him. "Control *knowledge?*" they cried, aghast. "You are taking us back to the Dark Ages! If there is anything that should never be controlled, it's the right of the people to know."

"Yes, a Dark Age," he admitted, "a Dark Age through which our knowledge will be preserved and passed from generation to generation in secret, while the people forget what they once knew. They must forget the Six Worlds; all memory of that vanished civilization must be wiped out so that a new and lasting culture can grow. Otherwise they cannot bear the loss, and there can be no second chance." He realized with despair that he was arguing against everything he had ever believed, everything he had cared about; yet he could not help himself. And Noren knew that this feeling was not his alone, but was also the First Scholar's, for to him, as to all his companions, the most sacred thing in life had been the free pursuit of truth.

"He is not himself," someone murmured. "The death of his wife has unbalanced his mind."

"His wife was right," the man opposite him said in an ominous tone. "If it's come to this, we should have died with the others."

Grief overwhelmed Noren: grief for his wife, for the Six Worlds, for the ordeals now confronting the survivors. "This plan has been in my mind ever since I assumed leadership of this expedition," he said quietly. "I shall bear full responsibility for it; I shall not put it to a vote even here among ourselves. Thirty billion people who are now dead charged me with the task of ensuring that something would outlast them. I must fulfill that mandate by the only means open to me."

"You are insane," asserted the man angrily. "We of the Six Worlds managed to abolish totalitarianism after centuries of oppression and strife; it was the greatest achievement of our civilization. It would be a poor memorial to those who died if the thing to outlast them was a renewal of that evil."

"There will be no totalitarianism. As I said, the people will have self-government."

"You advocate forced stratification of society! That's evil, too."

"It is an evil," Noren answered wretchedly, "but in our present situation it's a necessary one." He was appalled to hear such words from his own lips.

"Aren't you aware that nearly every dictatorship that ever came into power termed itself a necessary evil?"

"Yes, I am," said Noren, astonished by the things of which the First Scholar had been aware. "But by 'necessary' they meant something quite different from what I mean. They meant necessary to whatever they happened to value higher than human freedom."

"There is nothing of higher value!"

"True. And we're not going to abridge anyone's freedom, nor yet the freedom of the new world's society to develop in its own fashion. We'll merely be withholding things that cannot last long in any case if we fail to act." He hesitated; the plan was complex, and there were parts that could not yet be revealed even to his companions, parts that—as Noren—he found beyond reach. There were also justifications so foreign to his past experience that they slid by hazily in the dream…

"...we must choose between imposing a stratified culture and allowing the human race to die out," he found himself continuing. "Such a choice never arose before. It never could have arisen on the Six Worlds. But we face it now; have we really a choice at all?"

"Yes!" cried his antagonist with rising fury. "I'd prefer to die than to become a dictator."

"So would I," agreed Noren in anguish, "so would I. But I would not prefer to let our whole species perish, so I'll stake my life on the rightness of this course. I shall carry through the plan. If you want to stop me, you will have to kill me."

The man stood up. He had grown taller, it seemed; and though his features were still dim, he had become more real, more individual. "If I have to, I'll do it," he said. "I will kill us all, if need be! I'll blow this ship to space dust before I'll allow it to be used as an instrument of despotism."

Noren could no longer see any of the rest, for this opponent loomed too large in the dream; but he could hear their voices. "Perhaps we will all lose our sanity…perhaps suicides weren't the worst we had to fear…perhaps it's true that no one can endure to outlive the Six Worlds! Our two best leaders have become madmen."

In the man's eyes there was indeed madness; he looked at Noren with fanatical contempt, and then, abruptly, he turned and ran.

The white table disappeared, and Noren found that he too was running, running down a long bright tunnel toward a thing that the First Scholar knew to be the starship's main control board. He was dizzy with terror; his breath was torn from him in agonized gasps, for he was too old a man to run easily.

The antagonist whom he pursued stood before an array of switches, levers and flashing lights. "I mean what I say!" he shouted. "I will disable the safety circuits and put on enough power to blow this ship."

There was no time for argument, no time to wait for other men to come; Noren knew that before they could reach him, the starship would be vaporized. If he had been younger and stronger he could have fought the man and overpowered him, but as the First Scholar he was not. The First Scholar had no alternative. He saw that some of the lights had gone out and he saw hands thrust into an opening in the control board, entangled in bare-ended wires; he raised his arm to touch a single switch.

A flash of blue fire nearly blinded him. Noren shrank back, releasing the switch, and the man's form crumpled, fell; there was the stench of charred flesh. He stared down in horror. *I've killed a man!* he thought dazedly. *I said there would be no violence, yet already I've killed by my own hand…*

Others by this time had crowded around. He lifted his head, willing himself to assume the bearing of a leader. They would follow him, he knew; they would go along with the plan. But if this was how it had begun, where was it going to end?

Chapter Ten

Gradually, through many dreams, Noren experienced it all: the building of the City; the unloading of the starships; and the non-violent but rather ruthless way in which the research station people were transformed into villagers who, given the minimum essential technological aid, could fend for themselves in the wilderness of an alien world. But it wasn't easy. The First Scholar suffered intensely throughout, and as Stefred had predicted, Noren shared the agony fully.

Many of his sensations were pure nightmare. Because he was still partly himself, the impressions were often incoherent—he was experiencing mental reactions to events, rather than the events themselves, and though he could call on the First Scholar's knowledge, the facts that came into his mind were hard to interpret. Even the feelings were sometimes diffuse, chaotic ones that he could not put into words.

At first, during his periods of wakefulness, he found it hard to believe that keeping the secret of the nova had really been necessary. Surely few if any villagers would have gone so far as to kill themselves! Some of the men in the dreams shared this opinion. "Human beings have instincts that enable them to survive and adapt under almost any conditions," they insisted. "We owe these people the truth! Though some may not prove able to take it, the majority will."

"You're missing the point," others replied. "Of course they could survive physically, but their morale would be destroyed; suicide's just an extreme expression of the feeling almost everyone would share. And instinct wouldn't help in this case. To remain human here, we've got to *defy* instinct. People's instinct tells them that water that tastes pure is safe; it's mere training that stops them from drinking it. The shock of knowing about the nova would strip away their protective training, at least temporarily. And if they turned to instinct—the instinct that would let them drink the water and perhaps even adapt to a diet of native plants, as we expect to adapt the embryonic animals we've brought for beasts of burden—their children would suffer irrevocable brain damage. They'd survive, all right, but at the expense of generations yet unborn."

The First Scholar understood that. He knew that no evil was worse than extinction of the human race, and though dissidents reminded him that at certain points in the Six Worlds' history similar arguments had been invalidated, he knew such an analogy was false. There'd once been a time when his ancestors had claimed that abridging people's rights in order to prevent overpopulation of the mother world was essential to survival, but it had not been essential at all. On the contrary, voluntary reduction of the birth rate had worked very well, for if the mother world hadn't become overpopulated to some degree, interstellar travel would never have been developed—and in that case, nobody would have escaped the nova. This was different, for this was a matter not of how future humans would handle their problems, but of the terrible possibility that the next generation would be subhuman. Such a risk couldn't be taken. Moreover, he began to see other reasons why keeping the secret was important to the success of his plan.

He had known from the beginning that all offworld equipment would have to be preserved within the City if the colony was to last long enough for scientists to learn how to synthesize metallic elements suitable for the manufacture of machines. There were a number of reasons for this. In the first place, if that irreplaceable equipment fell into the hands of people unqualified to use and maintain it, it couldn't be kept operative; and while the research station workers were qualified, their descendants wouldn't be. Besides, recycling of worn metal parts, and indeed of all offworld materials, was going to be necessary over the years. If such materials were allowed outside the City, some would be lost. Some would be lost simply by being stored outside air-conditioned buildings, since the planet's atmosphere was corrosive to the metals of which certain machines were built. And of course, once the population began to expand, there would not be enough tools and machines to go around. Then people would start fighting over them. The colony was too small and weak to withstand much fighting.

But above all, the First Scholar knew that the existing equipment could not go on working forever even if it was carefully safeguarded, nor would it serve an expanding population forever. There would come a time when more *had* to be manufactured if survival was to continue. The supply of metallic trace elements for initial enrichment of cropland would also run out. Synthesization of metal had to be achieved by then, and that was utterly dependent not only on the education of future scientists, but on maintenance of research facilities and on preservation of the computers containing the Six Worlds' knowledge. Those things would be possible only within the City, and the City would need all the offworld equipment merely to function.

Depriving the people outside the City of that equipment, however, would be a terrible shock to them. The even greater shock of knowing about the nova might be too much—not simply because they had strong ties to the Six Worlds, but because if they knew, they'd be aware that there was nothing they could personally do to improve their situation. They couldn't face such frustration without being united by some immediate aim; he had realized that when he formed the plan, and had wondered what aim he could give them. By keeping the secret he solved that problem.

To Noren's dismay, he solved it by making them hate him.

Initially, the research station consisted of one large opaque dome in which people had been living and working, plus smaller ones containing power and water purification plants. Noren, as the First Scholar, looked down on them from the shuttlecraft in which he and some of the other Founders were descending, finding himself aware that such domes were standard equipment aboard all starships. They were easy to erect; an immense bubble was inflated, then sprayed with a substance that hardened to an impervious shell. The Outer City was to be composed of all the bubbles carried by the fleet.

As soon as the shuttlecraft landed, the captain, by radio, called a meeting in the existing dome; and when all the research station's people were inside, awaiting the newcomers' appearance, its doors were locked. They stayed locked—permanently sealed, in fact—during the days it took for the remaining passengers of the fleet to land and to build the huge circle of adjoining domes that formed the City's outer boundary.

Those imprisoned in the original dome were unharmed, but outraged and bewildered; they had no idea what was going on. They could not look out, and no one spoke to them. Then, once the City was fully enclosed, a new exit was cut in the outside of their dome, and they saw that they were at liberty to leave.

Unsuspecting, they did so, taking nothing but the clothes they wore and whatever articles they had in their pockets. It never occurred to them that they'd be unable to get back in. At the moment their fighting spirit was aroused, and all they wanted was their freedom. To find themselves in the wilderness, outside a vast ring of domes that had not been there previously, was so astonishing that at first they didn't understand the significance of what had happened. They encountered no people; they seemed to be free. And so they were. Nobody ever employed force against them again, but there was no way for them to enter the City.

The nucleus of the first village had already been prepared by the Founders: a large water cistern connected by pipe to the City, surrounded by enough cleared and treated land to support the existing population. There was also one stone building containing irradiated grain seed, the fertilized eggs of fowl with hens to incubate them, and enough concentrated rations to last until the first harvest. Inside that building were posted the rules of the game: the research station workers were to raise a larger crop than their previous experimental ones; they would receive no tools and no help except for essential medical supplies, which they could request by radiophone; purified water—for irrigating the fields as well as for drinking—would be supplied continuously, but no further food. No reason whatsoever was given for these instructions.

Though the people were stunned, they were not despairing. The only explanation they could think of was that they were the subjects of some fantastic psychological experiment, and they decided to play along, thinking that it would be an interesting challenge for which they'd eventually be well rewarded. They were all intelligent, highly-trained men and women who were ingenious enough to apply their technical knowledge to the fashioning of tools from stone. Some, in fact, began to have fun, for on their home worlds camping out had been considered a pleasure.

Meanwhile, the Founders within the City were working even harder and having considerably less fun. All of the equipment had to be brought down from orbit, meaning endless shuttlecraft trips; and after that some of the stripped starships, which were not designed to travel through the atmosphere, were dismantled and brought down piece by piece. These starships were reassembled inside the enclosure to become the City's towers. They were built of a special material that could not be reshaped by any means available on the planet, and all material was, of course, precious. The only solution was to make them into living quarters. It was a truly awesome task. The Scholars, unused to manual labor, worked to the point of exhaustion, and their knowledge of the tragedy and of the evils to come did not help.

All this time no villager had seen or heard any of the Founders; they were figures of great mystery. The people were not afraid of them. They assumed that the Six Worlds had decided to establish a major colony, and that while it was being built, the psychological effects of close contact with the alien environment were being evaluated. They were sure the experiment would not extend past harvest day. When the day arrived, they were weary of the game; still they felt satisfaction with what they'd accomplished, and they'd developed a strong sense of community. With pride they reported their success on the radiophone. And at that point, the First Scholar faced his most heartbreaking ordeal.

He knew that the people would not be willing to continue the "experiment" indefinitely. Furthermore, it was necessary for them to create permanent things: homes to replace the simple overhead shelters they'd constructed; gristmills to grind their grain; all the necessities of an ongoing life, including primitive clothing when their durable and easily-washed synthetic garments wore out. It was necessary for them to realize that no more contraceptive drugs would be available and that they would someday have to provide for children. Most important of all, it was time for irradiation of the seed and retreatment of the soil, which required go-betweens to ensure that the equipment would remain under the City's control. He longed to offer sympathy and encouragement, but there was none he could give. Instead, he must play the role of a dictator—he must assume the blame for their severance from home to conceal the fact that home had ceased to exist.

He spoke personally on the radiophone, the first voice that had been heard over it. He announced that he had established himself as absolute ruler of the planet, that his followers had successfully overpowered the crew of every supply ship that had arrived since, and that the Six Worlds, dismayed by the consistent and unexplained loss of ships, had written off this solar system and concentrated on exploring elsewhere. The people outside the City would be allowed to live only because they were needed to raise food. A token percentage of the harvest was to be delivered the next day to the gates; if it was not, the water supply would be cut off. By his manner as well as the words themselves, he deliberately made himself out to be insane.

At first the villagers laughed. Did the experiment's designer suppose that a season of living in the Stone Age would reduce citizens of the Six Worlds to a state where they'd swallow a ridiculous story like *that?* They didn't become frightened until two days later when the water supply was indeed cut off. Even then, they held out till the last moment; they knew how much unpurified water they could safely drink. But they were young couples who expected to have families someday when they got home, and—except for a few who eventually fled to the mountains, where their offspring became mutant savages—they did not take foolish chances. Since the planet's natural climate was dry and weather control hadn't yet been established, there might be no rain for weeks. Realizing that they could not wait, they capitulated and delivered the grain.

Noren was puzzled because although there were as yet no Technicians in the City, none of the Founders were allowed to risk disclosure of the secret by going out to treat the land. Someone would have to do it. He soon recalled, however, that the original villagers had been born as Technicians; they themselves knew how to operate the Machines. The process whereby they obtained those Machines and were forced to return them was shrouded in mystery, and he perceived that for some reason it was not in the recordings of the First Scholar's memories. When he asked Stefred about it during one of his conscious interludes, he was told only that the problem had been handled in a way beyond his present comprehension, a way that had made the villagers angry and afraid, but had brought harm to no one.

Lying there, waiting for the drug-induced sleep that would send him into the next dream, Noren wondered if he ought to take Stefred's word for such a thing. Instinctively, he felt that Stefred would not lie to him; still, the Scholars were admittedly trying to win him to their side… And then he realized that it did not matter whether he trusted Stefred. He trusted the First Scholar! Having shared the First Scholar's feelings, he knew with absolute certainty that the man could not have made plans that would hurt anybody.

But the villagers hadn't known it. To them, the First Scholar was a tyrant, a madman; as the dreams continued, their hatred of him flourished and the bonds of their community strengthened. Slowly, Noren began to see that by hating him, people were adjusting to their new way of life much better than they would have if they'd known his true motives. They still had hope of getting rid of the "dictator" and regaining the things of which they'd been deprived. To be sure, the lack of shuttlecraft traffic had become all too evident; there could be no doubt that the Six Worlds had abandoned the planet, and the towers that began to rise within the City seemed a clear indication that no starships remained in orbit. There was thus no conceivable means of communicating with home, since only starships could travel faster than light. They resigned themselves to their fate, knowing that even if they should succeed in overthrowing the "madman" and getting control of the City, they must make do with the world they had—still, hating him gave them the strength to keep struggling. In their hearts they cherished a hope of rescue. If they'd known the Six Worlds were gone, they would have had no hope at all.

As the First Scholar, Noren knew that once the struggle became easier, the hate would become dangerous. The First Scholar foresaw things he did not like to think about. Noren tried reaching for them and, without knowing why, was badly frightened; thereafter he resolved to take one step at a time.

Village life, he learned, was harder than in his own era. For instance, there were no work-beasts. The fleet had carried animal embryos, since the planet had no large native animals, but the poorly-understood process of altering their genetic makeup so that they could eat native plants wouldn't be completed for years, and there wasn't enough grain to feed more than were kept in the laboratory. To be sure, the original villagers lived close together and had no need to travel, but gathering stones for building wasn't easy when sledges had to be pulled by men. They thought at first they might make devices called "wheels," which they were used to, but soon found that since wheels made of softstone would not turn properly and wore away quickly from friction, these were less efficient than runners. That was a blow, for the wheel seemed somehow symbolic of civilization. Then too, there were no City goods at the beginning, aside from the cloth given in exchange for grain and wild fibers delivered to the gates. The Founders had brought machines to produce the City goods that would be needed, but it took time to find the right raw materials.

The villagers assumed that the Scholars were living in luxury, but that was far from the case. Actually they too were undergoing severe hardships. In the dreams Noren was almost always hungry. Before his escape from the village, he hadn't known what it meant to be hungry, and neither, it seemed, had the Founders. But the first harvests were not large, and the Scholars bought only the barest minimum to supplement the dwindling store of concentrated foods carried aboard the fleet, leaving most of the grain for the villagers. Within the City strict rationing was practiced, not only with food but with all supplies—especially anything made of metal—and the First Scholar felt called upon to set an example by following the rules more strictly than anyone else. He and his companions considered themselves stewards, custodians; they were preserving the City's equipment not for their own benefit but for that of future generations. They could not afford any waste.

Yet despite these handicaps they continued to work unceasingly, and their work wasn't simple. Top priority, after the enlargement of the power and water purification plants, was given to the guardianship of knowledge. The starships' computers were installed with extreme care at the heart of the City, in the first tower to be erected. Data stored in those computers encompassed all the past achievements of humankind, and was vital to the research work that in turn was vital to the ultimate survival of the colony. But the knowledge had wider significance. Like the equipment, it was held in trust; and to the Scholars, that trust was sacred.

Future villagers, however, would have to do without such knowledge—to children born and reared in a society shaped by the world's scant resources, it would seem irrelevant, meaningless. Since that could not be prevented, it was best that the break come soon, for only thus could the colony lose its dependence on the culture of the Six Worlds. For the time being, therefore, no books were provided. It was to be a Dark Age indeed; though the First Scholar knew that after a while books could be restored, his heart ached for the people of generations to come, whose education would remain limited. From time to time, when he felt especially depressed and discouraged, he tried to think of some way to give those people an abiding hope. In the recesses of his mind an idea glimmered, but always it eluded his grasp.

Dream followed dream. The plan was working. Technological capability was being preserved where mastery of the alien environment demanded it, but people were learning to do without technology in their daily lives. They were turning to the land; despite its lacks, it was a good land, a spacious land, and it was giving them something more basic than anything shut away in the City. They were creating a culture of their own. Though that culture would be unavoidably static, their children would thrive.

He had not deprived anyone of personal freedom, Noren perceived, nor had he robbed people of the right to develop their own kind of society. The limitations were imposed by the world itself, and not by him. He'd merely withheld the material things that could not have endured had he not guarded them.

Yet he had also withheld the truth, he reflected in anguish. To violate the right to truth was evil. Not everyone cared about knowledge as he did, yet for those few who did care, he must provide an avenue.

But there's still no avenue, thought Noren, waking. *We're still barred from knowledge!* And then he realized that that wasn't true. The avenue existed; wasn't he experiencing the dreams?

There came a moment—he was not sure whether he was awake at the time—when Stefred's eyes looked into his and Stefred's voice repeated softly, over and over, "You must not be afraid, Noren. What you face now will be frightening, but you must not give in to fear..." And the voice stayed with him until he was so much the First Scholar that he no longer had any knowledge of whose voice it had been.

He was standing at the entrance of a tower, the tall central one called the Hall of Scholars, which like the others opened into the courtyard of the Inner City. With the part of his mind that was still Noren, he realized that there had not been so many towers when last he dreamed; and looking into the First Scholar's memories, he found that years had passed. He was older and more weary. He was also more unhappy, though indeed he could not recall anything that had ever brought the First Scholar happiness.

Except perhaps one thing. He had been happy that the colony had been saved. And now, he knew, it was once again endangered, although the danger was one he'd anticipated and had arranged to deal with.

As always, he was surrounded by people, people whose faces weren't clear in the dreams and whose voices sounded alike. "We will not deceive you, sir," they said. "The situation is bad. You have been burned in effigy in the village squares, and this morning there's a mob assembling before the gates! The villagers will not accept our supremacy much longer; soon they'll be killing the Technicians who represent us."

Noren found he could reach no information about these Technicians' origin; there was a gap he couldn't fill. "But they can't live without the Technicians!" he heard someone object. "They know that!"

"Yes, but people don't always act reasonably, not when they're filled with hate," he replied. He had made the villagers hate him in order to unite them, to arouse their hopes and their will to strive; but the need for that was past. If they started killing Technicians, all that had been done would be for nothing. The Technicians would have to fight back, some people would defend them, and the villagers would fight among themselves. Whoever won, the colony would be fatally weakened, for it was still very small. The City was impregnable to attack. Within it, equipment and knowledge could be preserved; but what good were those things if the people themselves failed to survive?

The City's people couldn't survive without the farmers, and the farmers couldn't survive without the Technicians' aid. When hate prevented them from accepting aid, the hate must be discharged; he had realized that since the very beginning, and had made plans, plans kept secret even from his closest friends. "If I were no longer dictator," he said slowly, "their hatred would subside."

"They would merely transfer it to your successor."

"Suppose I had no successor, suppose Scholars stopped pretending to be tyrants and became—well, High Priests? Suppose we were viewed as figures of mystery and awe instead of as ordinary men who've seized power? By now enough's been forgotten for us to achieve that, for the emigrant generation is growing old; the native-born villagers hate me without knowing why. To them, stories of the Six Worlds seem mere legends." With sorrow, he thought of the grief this was causing the older people, who had tried hard to pass on their heritage to a generation that neither understood nor cared. Most of the native-born were truly content with village life, and for that their elders hated him most of all.

"High Priests?" echoed his companions. "Priests of what? Surely you would not establish a false religion!"

At their tone, he wondered if perhaps they thought him senile; he was, after all, a very old man who had outlived his time for leadership. Yet they had always supported him. He had not ruled as an autocrat; once the plan was underway, the other Founders had had equal voice in the decisions; still they had honored him and followed his advice.

"No," he assured them gravely. "Not a false religion, but a real one." He looked back on the years he had pondered it. This part of the design, too, had been in his mind for a long, long time, though he had told no one.

Most of the new world's people had no formal religion, for by and large neither the research station workers nor the scientists of the fleet had been strong adherents of the Six Worlds' traditional faiths. Now, however, their children and grandchildren were developing the kind of culture where a central religion would be needed and would be bound to flourish. It would be needed to sustain people's hope. It would be needed to make them follow rules of survival they could not fully comprehend, rules previously enforced by the elders: not using stream water or letting untreated clay come into contact with food or drink; delivering the grainseed to be irradiated; having respect for machines; all the things for which their daily lives offered no rational explanation. There were other reasons Noren couldn't grasp. But above all, it would be needed to keep the Scholars from becoming dictators in fact rather than as a mere pretense; he, the First Scholar, was sure of that.

"If we don't give people symbols for the truths we cannot express openly," he explained, "in time they'll fall prey to superstition. Their descendants may worship idols or practice barbaric rites of some sort. They won't look toward a changing future, since the inadequate resources of this planet permit them to make no progress—so they won't be prepared for the renaissance the completion of our research will bring. What's more, once the elder generation dies, we alone can ensure that the taboos essential to survival are observed. If we're not to employ any force, we can do it only by gaining the villagers' respect."

"That's all very well to say," his fellow-Scholars protested, "but not so simple to accomplish! We can't win people's allegiance by proclaiming ourselves High Priests; and even if we could, we wouldn't want such a role. It would be worse than the deceit we began with. What you suggest is impossible."

"There'll be no more deceit," he promised, feeling a strange elation mixed with his sadness. "Trust me in this; haven't I achieved things that were thought impossible before?"

They spoke warmly to him, nodding. "You have, sir. Without you we'd have failed long ago; who else could have founded a system like this without terror, without bloodshed?"

"It must remain without bloodshed," he declared grimly, "which it will not do if the villagers are in a mood to kill Technicians."

Noren knew inwardly that he had reached a decision, but he dared not probe deeply for it; it was one of the First Scholar's more frightening ideas. He let the words come to him without thought. "I will address the people," he stated.

"Very well, sir. We will prepare the radiophone."

"I will address them in person from the platform outside the gates."

"Have you lost your senses? Those people are violent, sir! We could not protect you even if we had weapons, and we have only a few tranquilizing guns."

"If you have any idea of abdicating, sir," one of the men added, "it won't work. The people will not be placated while you live."

He did not answer, since that was something he already knew and did not wish to discuss. Instead, he walked rapidly across the courtyard and into the exit dome's wide corridor, his companions following. "Please, sir—" they begged.

Turning to them, he said softly, "Did we do right, my friends? Was all this justified, as we believed, or were those who died aboard the starship wiser after all?"

"We did the only thing we could have done. The people are freer than they know, and someday there will be no more secrets. Someday there will be many cities, unlimited resources, education for everyone. This world will be like the mother world; someday we may even need spaceships again!" they responded.

They were the words he wanted to hear; he hoped they had not been said merely to humor an old man. Reaching the gates, he spoke solemnly to the others. "I have never asked you for unquestioning obedience," he said. "I do so now—" There was a break in his train of thought; Noren perceived that the First Scholar had given instructions that were inaccessible to him. "I must go out alone," he found himself concluding.

"Alone!" they cried, horror-stricken, but he ignored them. The next thing he knew the gates were open and he had stepped through; he was on a white-paved platform, and before him was the crowd. There was a roaring in his ears, and it was more than the outraged tumult of the people. It was the roar of his own fear.

The crowd was murderous. He raised his hand, hoping for silence in which to speak, but it had small effect. The villagers in that crowd did not want to hear anything from the hated, almost legendary "dictator;" upon recognizing his voice, they wanted only to kill him. For a few moments, stunned by his unprecedented appearance, they made no move; but their disbelief did not last long. They started up the steps, brandishing makeshift weapons—not only stones, but sharp stone knives—and though there was a newly-erected barrier at the top to keep people back, those weapons could be thrown over. Noren's terror was more intense than any he had ever experienced. *I'm dreaming,* he thought in cold panic, *and I'll wake up...before they can touch me I'll wake up...*

But he saw that he would not wake up. He was frozen in the dream. The blinding sunlight, the shouts of the faceless mob, the almost tangible hatred that assailed him—those would last until he died. His only recourse was to reach deep into the mind of the First Scholar, drawing out courage, for the First Scholar was stronger than he.

And the First Scholar had known what would happen.

He had known, Noren realized, from the time he'd first formulated his plan; and he had done this deliberately. The knife that struck him down was no surprise. It was not even unwelcome, for though he wanted to live, he knew that only his death could reconcile these people to the Scholars' supremacy. By this means alone could he prepare them for the new kind of leadership that must follow.

He fell, yet was still conscious; and the people went on hurling things while his blood spread onto the white pavement and he writhed under the pain of the blows. The pain was worse than he had expected. He had not really anticipated pain; he'd thought he would die quickly, the target of many knives. After he fell, however, most of the weapons that came over the barrier missed their mark, and within moments his friends pulled him back through the gates. Noren could not hear what they said. He felt himself dropping into a pit of silence and darkness, aware only of how much wounds could hurt before killing.

Then, desperately, he was fighting his way to the surface. He'd forgotten something; he had acted too soon! He should not have gone out while there was one thing left undone.

Time had passed. He lay on a couch, and people bent over him. "The knives were poisoned," they said gently. "It's a poison native to this planet; we can do no more than ease the pain." Someone held out a syringe.

Noren's own memories engulfed him, more powerful than the superimposed emotions of the dream. A native contact poison…it was thus his mother had died…she had felt such pain as this while he, a helpless boy, looked on. He wanted only escape—whether to wakefulness or death did not matter—but a voice within him kept repeating, *You must not give in to fear…* By tremendous effort he reached once more for the thoughts of the First Scholar.

"No," he protested. "No opiates; did we not agree to save what we have for injured villagers? Besides, there is a job I have not finished."

"Tell us," urged the others. "We will finish it for you, just as we'll carry out the instructions you've left for completing your plan. You must rest now."

"I'm dying!" he cried in anger. "Do you think I don't know I'm dying? What need have I of rest when I'm to get more than enough after tonight? Bring me the thought recording equipment; I have not yet recorded all I wish to."

"You would not have us record your death!" they exclaimed.

"I would have you record what I must think out before my death, since I haven't the strength to write it, or even to speak. It's there in my mind, but I've never been able to frame it as it should be—" He fell back against the pillows, exhausted, the pain overwhelming him. "I'm a scientist, not a poet," he whispered. "If I were a poet, I could find words."

"He's raving," said the voices. "We must give him sedation."

Noren struggled to rise. "No!" he cried again. "Do what I ask of you, but hurry—"

They obeyed, but he sensed their concern. "If he should die while he was recording, it would be dangerous; a dreamer could die, too."

Hearing that, Noren felt renewed terror, but he was detached from it, for the First Scholar was dominant in him now. The recording equipment was attached to his head, and his mind went momentarily blank; then all at once the detachment increased. Dimly, as Noren, he realized that he had never before dreamed anything that had been recorded while it happened; all the rest—even the episode just past, which must have been spliced into sequence—had come from the First Scholar's memories. This was different. This was real, immediate, and he knew that he *was* dying.

But he was no longer so afraid.

"It—is—evil, what we've done," he gasped. "To—to keep knowledge...from the people...is not right—"

"We know it's not right," his companions assured him. "We've always known; but if we had not done it, the human race would have perished."

"Yes, it was...necessary. But it will not be necessary forever. They hate us now—"

"They wouldn't hate you if they were aware of what you've given," a woman broke in sorrowfully. "They would honor you, as we do." She began to cry.

A burst of strength came into him; he must make them see, or they would not know how to use this last recording. "You don't understand," he said, mustering his waning resources. "They *should* hate us! They should keep on hating us, or at least the system we've imposed—but they won't. They will forget their birthright. When they forget the Six Worlds, as they must if they're to survive, they will forget that what we hold here in the City belongs to them. Then their hatred will fade."

"But you've sacrificed your life to achieve that!"

"Yes. Hate was destroying them." He paused; he was in no shape to explain the paradox coherently, yet he *must* make them see. "They must accept this system, still they shouldn't come to like it too much; and they may, since it will never be oppressive. That's the biggest danger in it! Benevolent controls are the most dangerous kind because the people forget what is theirs. We must not allow that to happen. Their hatred will fade, but their desire for what we hold in trust must never fade. We must tell them—"

"We can't," the others reminded. "Record more memories if you wish; tell all that you long to tell before you die; but you must know, sir, that nothing can be given to the people until our research succeeds."

"Not from my memories, no; we must keep the secret as long as our stewardship is required. But we must give the villagers a promise. They must be told that our control of the City is temporary."

"How could we tell them that without saying why? And even if we could, they would not believe us."

"They will believe," he declared. "If it's done right, they...will...believe..."

He could not do it right. He was too weak; there was too much pain; and besides, he was not a poet. "If I had a gift for poetry, I could do it as I've wanted to—"

"He speaks of poetry again," the voices said. "His mind is going. We had better remove the recording contacts before he dies."

"Please, please," Noren begged, "give me the time I have left to think out what I cannot say! Someday, someone will make a book of it; the people are not quite ready yet in any case. But when all who came from the Six Worlds are gone, their descendants will need a promise—"

They conceded to his wish; he was an old man whom they loved, and he was dying. Noren had not guessed how it would feel to die. It seemed as if one ought to be afraid, but the First Scholar was not afraid. He was only weak and tired, and of course, he was in pain. If he had let them stop the pain his mind would not be clear to think, and he must think; he must not give in until this task was done.

The people must have a promise! They must not be content with a Dark Age; they must hope for something more: machines, cities, free access to knowledge—they must want them, and they must not be allowed to forget that they wanted them. Furthermore, they must not forget the spirit that had once driven explorers out from their mother world—and eventually, from their mother star itself—toward something that must one day be sought again. That spirit must stay with them if the human race was to have another chance. They must believe in it without knowing that humankind needed another chance; they must do so until such time as their foothold was strong and their own culture well established.

He must give them the promise and the belief.

The mother star...the sun that gave humanity life...it would be visible someday, but by then, no one save the Scholars would understand what it meant. Yet they must understand! They must realize that it meant something very important! And perhaps—yes, almost surely—that would be time enough. If it was not, humankind was doomed, for the equipment could scarcely last longer; so wouldn't it be justifiable to gamble? *Symbols for the truths we cannot express openly,* he'd said to his friends, but though he had left them a plan formed in the dark nights of many years, the symbols themselves had eluded him. Now, in his last hour, the central one became clear...

The First Scholar had the idea and the purpose, and groped for words; but Noren already knew them. *"There shall come a time of great exultation, when the doors of the universe shall be thrown open and everyone shall rejoice. And at that time, when the Mother Star appears in the sky, the ancient knowledge shall be free to all people, and shall be spread forth over the whole earth. And Cities shall rise beyond the Tomorrow Mountains, and shall have Power, and Machines; and the Scholars will no longer be their guardians. For the Mother Star is our source and our destiny, the wellspring of our heritage; and the spirit of this Star shall abide forever in our hearts, and in those of our children, and our children's children, even unto countless generations. It is our guide and protector, without which we could not survive; it is our life's bulwark. And so long as we believe in it, no force can destroy us, though the heavens themselves be consumed! Through the time of waiting we will follow the Law; but its mysteries will be made plain when the Star appears, and the children of the Star will find their own wisdom and choose their own Law."*

For the first time he found comfort in those words. To the First Scholar, the thought behind them was a solace he had ached for during all the years of sorrow past. The tragedy had been surmounted. His work was finished; he could let go and sink into death, for the fierce, lethal explosion of the Mother Star had been made a symbol not of futility, but of hope.

The people crowded round, but he could not see them; he was too close to death. He was too weary, too crushed by the burden of leadership; too sick at the thought that people could survive only so long as he withheld from them that which was rightfully theirs. He'd done enough; why wouldn't they let him die in peace?

They would not. They called his name, urgently: "Noren! Noren!" Over and over they called until he opened his eyes and found that it was Stefred who was bending over him—Stefred and other men and women, all of whom seemed genuinely concerned for his life.

"I was...dying," Noren whispered. "I was *really* dying!"

"Yes," Stefred admitted. "The last dream is dangerous, and the more closely a person has shared the feelings of the First Scholar, the more dangerous it is. You would have died when he did if we hadn't been here to rouse you."

Why had they bothered? Noren wondered. They were going to kill him anyway. And yet of course they couldn't let him die while they were still hoping he'd recant.

"You would have died in spite of us," Stefred went on, "if you had not been brave enough to live. I knew that beforehand; I had to make the decision to let the last dream begin. I knew during our first interview that someday the decision would be mine. Do you envy me my job, Noren?"

That was when Noren looked into Stefred's face and knew, with chagrin, astonishment, and a kind of awe, that they were not going to kill him. There had never been any intention of killing him. Whether he recanted or not had nothing whatsoever to do with it.

The other Scholars had silently left the room. "Stefred," Noren said haltingly, "The rumors were false. I—I don't believe you've ever killed anyone. I don't believe you could."

"I'm glad to hear it," Stefred declared. "I knew, of course, what you've been assuming, but I hoped I could win your trust without bringing it up."

"You weren't trying to scare me into recanting?"

"At the beginning, yes. If you'd been susceptible, the truth would not have been shared with you."

"I—I guess I see," Noren said slowly. "You don't like the system any better than I do, but it's—necessary. You have to make people respect it. If somebody cares enough to give up his life, though, he earns the right to know why."

"It's something like that. As you know, the Founders didn't want to keep knowledge from people; they made provision for it to be given to anyone who values it highly enough."

"More knowledge than was in the dreams?"

"Yes."

"You've never lied to me," Noren mused. "When you said that if I recanted voluntarily I'd be given access to more than I could absorb in a lifetime, you meant it, didn't you?"

The Scholar was silent. It didn't add up, Noren realized. He'd been right to refuse the bribe; he was sure he had been, and even at the time it had been evident that Stefred was pleased by his refusal. "They just wouldn't have arranged it like that," he reflected aloud.

"How would they, then?"

"There are different sorts of knowledge," Noren said thoughtfully. "If I'd accepted the offer, I might have been told things Technicians know, but not the secret—not what's in the dreams. And now, well, now I can go on learning whatever else happens. Recantation isn't a condition."

"That's right. Still, you have problems ahead of you; there'll be difficult ones even if you do recant."

Noren shivered, knowing Stefred's warning that the consequences of truth would seem terrible must also have been sincere; but he was too overwhelmed to worry about it. He lay back, still weak and shaken by the death he had so nearly shared. "Why," he asked softly, "weren't people ever told that the First Scholar wrote the Prophecy? They look up to Scholars now; they would honor him even without understanding what he really did."

"They'd go beyond that," replied Stefred, "and it was his wish that the facts about him never be revealed. To be worshipped was the last thing he wanted; it's not what any of us want, though it happens. We try to remain as anonymous as we can."

That was true, thought Noren in surprise. They had never demanded obeisance; they had never claimed to be innately superior; they had never declared that to speak against them was blasphemy. All those ideas—the ones that weren't mentioned in the Prophecy—had been originated not by the Scholars, but by the villagers themselves. The First Scholar deserved every honor short of worship, but people wouldn't have stopped there. He had been a martyr; when their hatred faded, they'd have built statues of him and pronounced it heresy not to bow down.

Unjust though it seemed, it was better that he was remembered only in legend: the distorted legend about the evil magician who'd tried to rule by force and who had been vanquished by the proclamation of the High Law. He would be glad that forced rule was still thought evil.

"There's something I must explain," Stefred went on. "The First Scholar did not write the Prophecy, at least not the words. The idea was his, but the Book of the Prophecy itself was written later by a man who experienced that last dream many times."

"But the words were in the dream," protested Noren.

"No," Stefred said. "They are not in the recording, Noren; you supplied them yourself."

"If I did, if I put the idea and the words together, then—" Noren drew breath, suddenly taking in the implications of what he was about to say. "Then inside I must have known that they—fit."

"That the symbols are an accurate expression of the idea, yes. All words are symbols. These, being familiar to you, came naturally into your mind. They are figurative words, poetic words, and as such have more power than the scientific ones the First Scholar knew weren't suited to his purpose."

"I could say them and not be lying," Noren declared wonderingly. "The Prophecy is true!"

"You could; you passed that hurdle without even making an effort. The real question is whether you *should.*" Stefred looked down at Noren, his eyes filled with compassion and warmth, adding, "Remember that long ago you conceded that you would accept the Prophecy if I could prove it, and you were well aware that recanting means far more."

Chapter Eleven

Alone in his old quarters, the tiny green-walled room, Noren thought it through. He knew that he would receive no help from Stefred, much less any pressure; his decision was to be entirely free. It would be freer than it could ever have been while he hated the Scholars. Of all the strange things that had happened to him in the City, to have been granted this freedom was the strangest.

He had no idea what depended on whether or not he recanted, although reason told him that something must, some aspect of his personal future. "You're not permitted to know yet, Noren," Stefred had said. "As I told you, there'll be difficulties either way, but I can't explain them in advance."

"Why not?"

"You tell me why not," Stefred had replied, smiling.

"I'd say it'd be—well, the wrong basis for a decision."

"Anyone who's come this far has a better basis," Stefred had agreed. "You don't need any advice from me; your own mind is more than adequate to determine your course."

"If you believe that, Stefred," Noren had challenged, "then why do you make heresy a crime?"

"We don't. Heresy isn't forbidden by the High Law; the villagers ban it themselves." He'd hesitated. "The reason they do is complicated, and I can discuss only a little of it now. Later you'll learn more."

Stefred had gone on then, to tell what had happened after the First Scholar died. The Book of the Prophecy, and with it the High Law, had been given to the villagers the next year. That had been possible because in accordance with the First Scholar's instructions, all those who'd originally come from the Six Worlds had been admitted to the City as Technicians. It had been announced that only the "dictator's" insanity had kept them out in the first place—which was the last lie ever told by the Scholars. In the role of High Priests they had practiced no form of deceit.

The first-generation villagers had been warned that once inside the City they could never leave, but all the same they'd been happy, for they had missed the kind of life they'd been born to. The native-born, on the other hand, hadn't wanted to live in the City. They'd always been skeptical of their parents' claim to have been reared in such a place, and they'd known that with the elders gone, they would be the undisputed village leaders. So they'd been quite content with the distant promises of the Prophecy, which they had believed without question. There'd been nobody left who could refute anything it said—nobody who could distinguish symbols from science—and after all, it had been the first book they'd ever seen; they had learned to read and write by means of slates. Most had thought reading and writing a silly waste of time. Still, the Book of the Prophecy proved that the elders' insistence on school had not been entirely foolish, for if the Scholars themselves said the future would be unlike the past, was it not well to look ahead to that future? The Scholars who appeared as High Priests did not act like the "dictator" who'd been thought mad, and besides, the people knew that they were dependent on those Scholars' good will. They weren't anxious to jeopardize village welfare by letting anybody disobey the High Law, which set forth the same rules they'd been taught as children in any case. As time went on, however, they made rules of their own and became more and more intolerant.

"I don't quite see why," Noren had confessed.

"You'll have to study a good deal before you do. Essentially it was because village society reverted to a more primitive level not only as far as technology was concerned, but also in other ways. Attitudes that had been outgrown by the time the people of the Six Worlds built their starships came back, just as tallow lamps did."

"Couldn't you Scholars have prevented that?"

"No, no more than we could have prevented technological skills from being lost. Societies, like people, cannot be controlled without destroying their ability to grow and develop. All we can do is maintain an island of light amid the dark." With a sigh, Stefred had added, "Those of us on the island are not just basking in that light, you know. We're working against time to bring about the Prophecy's fulfillment."

Thinking about it, Noren knew that it was that—the research work—about which he really had to decide.

The Prophecy was true. He would gladly admit that publicly, though his reasons for doing so would be misconstrued by everyone but the Scholars themselves. He would affirm the Prophecy with pride; he knew that the First Scholar had created it in those painful last hours because only such a promise could ensure that the Dark Age would be temporary.

The High Law was also valid, and it too was necessary. It contained no provisions that were not essential either to the survival of humankind or to prevention of harm that might be caused by people's wrong interpretations. Stefred had given him a copy to review and, reading it in the light of his new knowledge, he'd seen that. The decree that convicted heretics must be turned over to the Scholars, he realized, had been placed there not to ensure their punishment, but to provide them with an avenue to the truth! The rules about Machines were all concerned with keeping people from damaging those Machines, or from going to the opposite extreme and worshipping them. There was nothing in the High Law that he was not willing to obey.

But recantation meant more than affirming the Prophecy and the High Law. It also involved affirmation of the system under which Scholars had privileges unavailable to others. It meant agreeing that they must remain supreme until the Prophecy's promises had been fulfilled—giving up all thought of changing the world immediately, letting people think he approved of things as they were...was that right?

It was not right! Yet the First Scholar had known better than anyone else that it was not; he'd established the system not because it was right, but because it was the lesser of two evils. And he had died at the hands of men whom he'd allowed to misunderstand him.

For the Prophecy was true only as long as the system was upheld. *The ancient knowledge shall be free to all people*—it couldn't happen unless the Six Worlds' knowledge was preserved. The Scholars were working to extend that knowledge so humans could survive on this world as they had on the old ones. They were striving desperately to create the kinds of metal needed to make the Machines that were essential to the support of life. They must finish the work; the world couldn't begin to change until they did.

To try to make it perfect overnight wouldn't make it perfect, it would only cause all that had been salvaged from the burning of the Six Worlds to be lost. Humankind would perish just as surely as if the First Scholar's plan had failed. Even revelation of the secret would be fatal, not for the same reasons as in his time, but because people were now as dependent on their belief in the Prophecy as they'd once been on the Six Worlds' culture. Through its fulfillment alone could the world be successfully transformed.

Between the dreams and what Stefred had told him, Noren knew something about why the research work was taking so long. It was harder than anything that had been achieved on the Six Worlds. There, they'd had plenty of metal; they had found it in the ground. Even people like the villagers had found it, and had used it to make tools and Machines of their own—slowly, generation by generation, they had improved them, before either Technicians or Scholars had ever existed, and by doing so they had learned more and more, until finally they *were* Technicians and Scholars. His theory about savages becoming smarter and discovering knowledge for themselves had been quite true on the mother world. That was the way human beings were meant to progress, and that was how all the knowledge in the computers had been accumulated.

But normal progress couldn't occur where there could be no technological innovation. On the mother world, tribes of people who never learned to get metal from the ground never improved their ways of doing things; once they'd gone as far as they could with stone, they stopped changing. And because this world's ground had no metal at all that was suitable for making tools, the villagers' situation was very similar. They could not develop better ways to use their limited resources, since their ancestors had already known the most efficient methods for everything from the fashioning of household implements to the building of bridges. Only within the City did the conditions for new discoveries exist.

And the discovery that must be made was extremely difficult even for the Scholars—they must learn how to create metallic elements through nuclear fusion. Noren hadn't really grasped what nuclear fusion was, but he could see that although it involved combining several substances to get a different one, it was not just a matter of stirring those substances together. The Six Worlds' scientists had known how to achieve nuclear fusion to get Power. Nuclear fusion to get metal had been beyond anyone's hopes. Here, however, it was the only hope there was.

No one knew when that hope would be realized. Conceivably it could be soon, and in that case new Cities would be built immediately; the Prophecy did not say that there would be no changes *before* the Star appeared! In the meantime, the Scholars must retain their stewardship if hope was to continue.

You would have died in spite of us, Stefred had told him, *if you had not been brave enough to live.* The words had been puzzling, but all at once Noren understood them. A person who'd seen the world through the First Scholar's eyes had to be brave, for no one who wasn't could face the hard truth about the world. But there was more to it. Only a brave person could face the awareness that his own honest attempt to fight injustice, if successful, would have accomplished the opposite of what he had been aiming for.

Noren faced it. He admitted to himself that overthrowing the Scholars would not have helped the villagers, but would instead have prevented Machines and knowledge from ever becoming available to them. To capitulate and recant would not be a defeat, he realized with surprise. His goals had not changed; his beliefs had not changed. What he'd wanted all along was for the world to be as the Prophecy said it would become. He would merely be conceding that it could not be that way before the time was ripe.

That evening he told the man who brought him food that he wanted to see Stefred. The Chief Inquisitor had been quite correct, he reflected ruefully, in predicting that in the end his innate honesty would leave him no choice.

It was dusk; the City towers were shafts of silver thrust skyward between the orange moons. Noren sat by the window in Stefred's study and watched the stars come out. "Will people ever travel between the stars again?" he asked wistfully. "Will there be more worlds to settle someday?"

"Someday," Stefred said, "if we don't fail on this one. It's the only permanent answer to our lack of resources here. The starships' design is stored in our computers, and in fact there are still stripped hulls in orbit; but there is much else we must accomplish first. It can't happen in our lifetime."

"Neither can the things I wanted people to fight for."

"No. There are some things fighting can't achieve."

"Is it always wrong to fight, then?"

"Not always. That can be necessary, too. If you study the history of the Six Worlds, you'll find that there are no clear-cut answers."

"There's a time to fight, I guess…and a time to surrender. I—I've come to surrender, sir." Noren sighed, glad that he had finally gotten the words out.

For quite a while Stefred was silent. Then, in a troubled voice, he asked, "Have you ever witnessed a public recantation, Noren?"

"Yes." Noren's heart chilled at the recollection.

"For some people it's worse than for others," the Scholar said, "and I can spare you nothing."

"I—I don't suppose you can."

"I must be sure you understand," Stefred persisted. "If you recant, I shall preside at the ceremony. You may think that because we know each other, trust each other, it will be less difficult for you; but it won't. It will be more so. You have never knelt to me, and I've never asked it; in fact I'd have thought less of you if you had. Can you do it before a crowd of villagers who'll think I've broken your spirit?"

"It's a form, a symbol, as the words of the Prophecy are symbols," Noren said. "It doesn't mean I'm your inferior. It means only that what you represent is worth honoring."

"Yes, you know that now. But the people in the crowd will not."

Noren swallowed. "It's necessary."

"Why, Noren?" demanded Stefred suddenly. "You know I won't force this on you. You must also know that you won't be punished for not doing it. Why take on such an ordeal? You came here seeking the truth, and you found it; what more do you hope to achieve?"

"I wanted truth not just for myself, but for everyone. I can't accept it without giving."

"Giving what? You won't be allowed to reveal anything of what you've learned; you'll stick to a prepared script."

"There won't be any lies in the script, will there?"

"No. The words you say will be literally true. But they'll be phrased in the language of the Prophecy, and the people have already heard those words."

"They've also heard me deny them. They've heard me ask *them* to deny them, and every heretic who does so strikes at the thing the First Scholar died for. I was wrong, Stefred! Would you have me conceal my error to save my pride?"

"No," answered Stefred. "I wouldn't have you do that. But though you were wrong, you were not without justification; and when a heretic recants no justification can be claimed."

"That doesn't matter. Truth is truth, and it's more important than what people think of me. Don't you see? I stuck to my heresy because I cared about truth; now I've got to recant for the same reason."

"I see very clearly," Stefred admitted, "but I had to satisfy myself that you do. This is no mere formality. It will be harder than you realize, Noren, and there will be lasting consequences."

"You warned me about consequences before," said Noren, smiling. "You thought I'd beg to be let off. You underestimated me after all."

"Don't be too sure. Your problems aren't over yet." The Scholar pulled a sheaf of papers from his desk and looked through them, handing one to Noren. "This is the statement you'll make. Read it."

Noren did so with growing dismay. He had not remembered the specific wording of the ceremony; the tone of it was something of a shock. Phrases like "I am most grievously sorry for all my heresies," and "I confess my guilt freely; I am deeply repentant, and acknowledge myself deserving of whatever punishment may fall to me," stuck in his throat. He went through it again, slowly and thoughtfully, before raising his eyes.

"Is it more than you bargained for?" Stefred inquired.

"Yes," said Noren candidly. "I thought I wouldn't be expected to say anything I didn't mean. Well, I was mistaken about the Prophecy and the High Law, and I'm willing to admit it; but I'm not *sorry* for having been a heretic. At the time I couldn't have been anything else."

"You agreed that there can be no self-justification."

"There'll be no self-abasement, either! To say my opinions were wrong is one thing, but to declare that I was morally wrong in holding them would be something else entirely."

"We will not ask you to lie," Stefred said slowly. "If there are things in the statement that are untrue, strike them." He held out his stylus.

Noren took it and did a thorough editing job; then, without comment, he handed the paper back. The Scholar perused it carefully. "You've removed all references to penitence," he observed.

"I'm not penitent, sir."

"You will wear penitent's garb, and your hair will be cropped short."

"I'll submit to whatever indignities are required of me, but I will not proclaim guilt I don't feel, Stefred."

Stefred eyed him. "What happens to an impenitent heretic, both during the ceremony and afterwards, is not quite the same as what is done with someone who repents," he said evenly.

"I can't help that."

"Aren't you being inconsistent? You tell me you must recant because heresy strikes at the cause for which the First Scholar was martyred; surely you're aware that a display of repentance would be far more convincing than the mere admission of error—"

"I've been perfectly consistent right from the beginning," Noren declared obstinately. "I said at my trial that keeping things from the villagers was wrong, and it *is*. I'm recanting only because I've learned that there's something worse. There will always be heretics, and there should be; I won't tell people that heresy's a sin. To affirm the Prophecy and the High Law is as far as I'll go."

"So be it, Noren," said Stefred. He rose, Noren following, and for a few minutes they stood side by side looking out at the darkening sky. "I know you're wondering what's going to become of you when this is over," the Scholar continued, "but I can tell you only that though the difficulties will be greater than you imagine, I think you'll prove equal to them. I must say no more until after the ceremony three days from now." As an afterthought he added, "You will not understand the whole ceremony at first; remember that I'm on your side, and that I'll have reasons for what I do."

"Three days?" faltered Noren. "I—I'd rather get it over with tomorrow."

"No doubt you would, but a little time for reflection will be good for you. You've shifted your whole outlook at a very rapid pace; this is a major step, and you mustn't rush into it."

Noren shuddered. Stefred was right, he knew; yet he was inwardly afraid that if he didn't rush into it, he would never have the courage to carry it through.

* * *

The next days were the longest Noren had ever spent. He was left entirely alone; the Technicians who brought his meals did not speak to him. At least he was now trusted to see Technicians, he realized. It was no longer feared that he'd tell them any secrets. What, he wondered, would happen if he ever encountered the one who'd befriended him? It would be hard to remain silent, but he knew that he would do so, although the man would be bound to draw the wrong conclusions.

Noren dared not speculate about the future in store for him, the mysterious fate about which he'd as yet been given no information. It would not be easy to face; Stefred had often warned him of that, and so far everything Stefred had said had proved to be true. He could not be forgiven and released. It had been clearly stated that the secret could not go outside the City walls. The Scholars themselves never went out, and if they didn't, they certainly wouldn't let *him* do it. To be sure, he'd been told that he would be allowed to go on learning; that was some consolation. It was also consoling to know that Stefred thought him equal to whatever was going to happen.

What was going to happen during the ceremony was inescapably grim, and he had apparently made it grimmer by refusing to declare himself penitent. He could understand that. Though the Scholars themselves tolerated heresy, they could not do so publicly, and it was Stefred's duty to persuade heretics to repent. An example must be made of those who would not. Yet Noren still wasn't sorry; only if he had yielded before learning the truth would he have felt guilty. The fact that the system was the lesser of two evils might excuse the Scholars for establishing it, but that couldn't excuse a person who didn't know the facts for accepting such a system!

On the third morning two Technicians came to him. "The Scholar Stefred sends you a message," one of them said formally. "First, you are offered a final opportunity to withdraw."

"No," said Noren steadily, inwardly angry. Did they want him to recant or didn't they?

"Very well," the Technician replied. "In that case, you are reminded that you must obey us implicitly, remembering that you have chosen to submit of your own accord."

Noren nodded, his indignation growing. There had been no need for such a reminder.

"Finally," concluded the Technician, "you are informed that there will be a departure from the script. After you read your statement, the Scholar will question you; he asks that you be told that he is relying on you to reply with absolute honesty."

Stefred ought to know by now, Noren thought, that he would scarcely do anything else! But why the change in plans? It had been emphasized that the ceremony would be formal and that no departures from the script would be permitted. Still, he'd sensed from Stefred's manner that he must expect further surprises; there was no guessing their nature.

The Technicians ordered him to change into the clothes they provided, the gray, unadorned penitent's garb that to the spectators would be a badge of shame. He did so grimly, then sat in stoic silence while they cropped his hair. But when they proceeded to bind his wrists behind him, using not ropes but strong inflexible bands, Noren protested vehemently.

"It's unnecessary," he raged. "You know I'm not planning to run away from you."

"We know, but all the same it must be done. It's a matter of form."

It was a matter of appearances, Noren realized miserably. The impression would be given that he was a criminal who had been browbeaten into submission; his voluntary choice of this course, his pride in honesty that overrode the sort of pride that could admit no error, would not be permitted to show. Abruptly he grasped the full import of Stefred's remark that he could be spared nothing. To the crowd, there would be no difference between his recantation and that of the man whom he himself had held in such contempt! And perhaps there was no difference. Perhaps that man, too, had experienced the dreams before capitulating; Stefred had never said that his case was unusual.

They walked through passageways Noren had not seen before, descended in the cubicle that he'd learned was called a lift, and crossed a small vestibule, finally emerging into the courtyard that surrounded the closely-placed towers. Looking back, he recognized the entrance of the Hall of Scholars from the last dream; he had been inside it all the time, he thought in wonder. He had been in the same tower in which the First Scholar had lived and died. In there were the computers, the awesome repository of the Six Worlds' knowledge, which he longed fervently to glimpse; would he ever be allowed to enter it again?

When they reached the dome through which one must pass to leave the City, Noren's guards did not accompany him into the broad, high-ceilinged corridor that stretched ahead; different Technicians took over, enclosing him within the formal rank of an escort of six. The eyes of the passers-by were all upon him. Noren straightened his shoulders and raised his head, trying not to notice. This was nothing, he knew, to what he must face outside the Gates, where he would be viewed with derision and scorn.

The Gates appeared before him all too quickly, and to his surprise he recognized their inner surface; the First Scholar had gone through those doors to his death. The memory was so vivid that he found himself shivering. A Technician pushed a button set into the corridor's wall and the huge panels began to slide back. At the same time another spoke, raising his voice to be heard above the rumble. "One more reminder: in public, the Scholar Stefred is to be addressed as 'Reverend Sir.'"

Noren pressed his lips tightly together, holding back the ire that rose in him. His own words echoed in his mind: *It is a form, a symbol, as the words of the Prophecy are symbols…*

He stepped forward into brilliant sunlight reflected from white pavement. Immediately a shout arose from the crowd, a hostile, contemptuous shout. And Noren froze, stricken by a terror he had never anticipated. It was like the dream! He was to stand in the very spot where the First Scholar had been struck down; he was being led directly and purposely to it. The sun, the noise, the enmity of the people: they were all the same—but this time there was no possibility of waking up.

The Technicians, after proceeding all the way to the platform's edge, moved back slightly, exposing Noren to full view. There was no barrier any more. Before him was the wide expanse of steps, the steps up which the First Scholar's assailants had come, where he himself had been immobilized at the time of his recapture. Men and women were swarming to the top. *Blasphemer,* they had called him then, and their mood had been one of shock; now they used more vulgar epithets. Their mood was not shocked, but ugly, as on the night in the village. The crowd was far larger, however, and the hecklers were bolder, knowing him to be helpless because of his manacled wrists and the vigilance of the Technicians. Noren struggled to master his panic, realizing that, ironically, the Technicians were there not to guard but to protect him. Whatever else happened, they would not allow him to be murdered.

As he looked around, he saw to his dismay that there were no Scholars anywhere. The people would not act like this in the presence of Scholars; why had Stefred sent him out alone before he himself was ready to appear? And why, when he was doing what they had wanted him to do all along, should he be deliberately terrorized by being forced to re-enact the dream? The likenesses were too precise to be accidental.

When the first clod of mud struck him, Noren was so stunned that he nearly lost command of himself; but he quickly regained his poise and stood erect, taking it impassively. That was the only way to take it, he saw. He must not flinch from anything to which he was subjected. The sun dazzled him and the heat of it shimmered from the glaring pavement, so that the steps, the crowd, and the markets beyond the plaza all blurred into a hazy mist. He focused his eyes on nothing and tried not to think. He'd been aware that he would be despised, reviled; but having watched only the latter part of the other recantation, he had not foreseen that he would be the target of such abuse as this. The significance of the prisoner's filthy garments had escaped him despite the traders' then-cryptic remarks. Yet looking back, he could see that exposure to the crowd prior to the Scholars' entrance must be a traditional part of the ordeal.

Why? The Scholars, he knew, did not believe that he or anyone else deserved punishment of this kind, and they could easily prevent it. Why didn't they, if they disapproved of the villagers' attitude as Stefred had claimed? Noren cringed inwardly as more and more mud was flung at him, but he let his bearing show no sign. He was meant to understand, he felt, and concentration on the effort to do so was the only defense open to him.

The Scholars could not prevent people from hating, he realized. They could only provide occasion for the hatred to be vented in relatively harmless ways. In the beginning, the First Scholar had taken it upon himself, and when it had become dangerous, he'd discharged it by allowing the villagers to throw not mud, but stones and knives.

Most villagers no longer hated Scholars. Now they hated heretics; they hated anyone who was not like themselves, either for daring to be different or simply for being so. What would happen if they were given no outlet for their hate, if those turned over to the Scholars suffered no public humiliation? Fewer heretics would reach the City! More of them would die as Kern had died! So it had to be this way, but the role of scapegoat was not forced on anyone. Stefred had not forced him; on the contrary, in the end he'd tried to dissuade him. Like the First Scholar, he stood in this spot only because he had given free consent.

As that thought came to him, Noren glimpsed a little of Stefred's design. The similarity to the dream was not intimidation; instead, it was meant to bolster his self-esteem. The villagers hated him, misunderstood him—but they'd hated and misunderstood the First Scholar, too, and he was facing them for the First Scholar's own reasons. The people who'd once been on his side now despised him most of all, for they thought recantation a coward's act, a sell-out; and though he knew better, it was hard not to feel that the surrender he'd fought so long would diminish him. The carefully arranged comparison was a reminder that it would not. Moreover, it was Stefred's subtle means of bestowing on him a status that the Scholars could not openly confer. To them, it must seem honorable to walk in those footsteps; the assumption that he too would find it so was a tacit endorsement of his inner equality.

With sudden insight Noren perceived that all he had ever believed, all he had ever done, had led inexorably to this moment. This, not the inquisition, was the true trial of his convictions. It was easy to uphold them when to do so meant merely to defy authority. To do so in secret, when not even his fellow-rebels would give him credit for it, was the only real proof that they meant more to him than anything else—and that he could trust himself to follow his own way.

He waited in silence, and the people went on pelting him with mud until his bare arms were splattered with it and the penitent's garb was no longer gray, but brown. He did not move; he did not bend his head; and somewhere inside he began to know that he was not really suffering any indignity. Dignity came from within; it could not be affected by a barrage of insults and filth.

And then, with cold shock, he glanced down at the steps and saw Talyra.

She had climbed more than halfway up them, heedless of the jeering mob, and she stood staring at him, her shawl pulled tight around her shoulders. In her face was more pain than he had ever seen in anyone's. His first thought was that he could endure no more of what to her would seem degradation, nor could he bear to have her think he'd betrayed the beliefs for which he had been willing to sacrifice their love. But at the sight of her grief he realized that he did not care about anything except the fact that she too was suffering. That she would witness the ceremony had not entered his mind; it hadn't occurred to him that she would ever know.

How could he have been so stupid? He'd known she was near the City, for she had told him she was going to the training center; and recantations were announced in advance. Talyra would have been heartbroken by his recapture, but relieved by the news that he was still alive. Yet her feelings must be mixed, for he'd convinced her that he would never recant of his own free will. Since she could not suspect the truth, there was only one thing she could possibly think: that he'd been tortured and had given in. There was no way he could tell her otherwise. She would think it for as long as she lived, and living with such a thought would be harder than resignation to his death.

Their eyes met. Talyra's face was wet with tears, and the anguish Noren felt surpassed anything he had previously undergone. She had come just to see him once more; she couldn't have stayed away; yet what was happening would hurt her far more than it was hurting him. He would break down, he thought in terror; he would lose all self-possession and run to her...

Just then, however, there was a loud surge of the City's overpowering music, and Scholars emerged from the Gates, taking their places on the low dais at the opposite side of the platform. At the last came Stefred, who, unlike the others, wore not solid blue but the presiding Scholar's ceremonial vestments with white-trimmed sleeves. He crossed to the central position and raised his hand. The people, instantly hushed, fell to their knees. The Technicians closed again around Noren, escorting him away from the mud-stained steps to the clean stone base of the dais.

He knew what was required of him. Keeping his back very straight he approached Stefred and, in a gesture more of courtesy than of obeisance, he knelt.

The ritual words, the formal words of invocation, were said; Noren scarcely heard them. Then Stefred looked down and his eyes were cold, a stranger's eyes. "You come before us as a self-confessed heretic," he announced. "Are you ready to admit the error of your beliefs?"

"Yes, Reverend Sir." Noren spoke out clearly; if he was going to do it, he was not going to be backward about it.

The script was placed in front of him by a Technician. It was, he noted with indignation, the unedited version; all of the self-abasing statements he'd crossed out were still there. Stefred's face remained absolutely impassive. Noren began to read, his voice sounding hollow and distant in his own ears. It made no difference whether those statements had been struck or not; he remembered the phrasing well and omitted them as he spoke, though the words swam dizzily before him.

"I confess my heresies to be false, misconceived and wholly pernicious; I hereby renounce them all... I no longer hold any beliefs contrary to the Book of the Prophecy, which I acknowledge to be true in its entirety and worthy of deepest reverence... I have blasphemed against the Mother Star, which is our source and destiny; I abjure all fallacies that I have uttered and freely affirm my conviction that this Star will appear in the heavens at the time appointed... I retract all criticisms I may ever have made of the High Law; I admit the error of my opinions and declare myself submissive"—he altered the phrase *most humbly submissive*—"to all of its requirements, affirming it to be necessary to the Prophecy's fulfillment..."

It went on and on; Noren's voice broke several times, and he began to wonder if he would ever get through it. But all the words were true words; not once did he let an expression of penitence slip out. He felt suddenly triumphant. If they'd thought they could trap him, they'd been mistaken!

There was a long silence after he finished; then finally Stefred spoke. "You have made no proclamation of repentance," be said levelly. "Do you feel no remorse for these many heresies?"

"None, Reverend Sir," replied Noren with equal coolness.

A murmur arose from the crowd; such shameless lack of contrition would surely call down dire retribution indeed. It was a pity, most felt, that the Scholars never imposed their mysterious forms of chastisement in public.

"Do you not agree that you deserve to be severely punished for having held such beliefs?" Stefred demanded.

"No, Reverend Sir, I don't."

"But you know that you must take the consequences in any case, do you not? If you were to show sorrow for the things you have confessed and plead our mercy, it might make some difference in your fate."

"I will not do that," Noren declared, forgetting the honorific in his anger. One of the Technicians clamped a firm hand on his head, pushing it slightly forward. Fury consumed him; just in time he recovered his wits and repeated with no audible irony, "I will not do that, *Reverend Sir.*" For the first time it occurred to him that Stefred, who had known perfectly well that he wouldn't do it, was checking his self-control in preparation for some more formidable challenge.

"Why are you so obdurate," the Scholar persisted, "when we offer you the chance to redeem yourself in the sight of the people?"

"Because, Reverend Sir, I have done only what I had to do. I was mistaken, but I thought my beliefs were true."

"You were not asked to think, but only to accept what you were told. Was it not wrong of you to set your own judgment above that of your betters?"

"It was not, Reverend Sir. What but his own judgment is to tell a man who his betters are?"

That was too much for the spectators; there were shouts of disapproval and several loud suggestions of advice as to suitable punishment. Stefred raised his hand, silencing them. "At your trial," he went on, "your accusers testified that you had claimed that even Scholars were no better men than yourself; and you did not deny it. In your recantation you have made no mention of this. Why?"

Noren frowned, perplexed. He had not been asked to mention it, and he could not imagine why it would be brought up without warning. Surely Stefred knew that he could not retract that particular opinion! If to answer truthfully would do any harm, that was too bad; there was no help for it. "Scholars know more than I do, Reverend Sir," he said without faltering, "and some of them may indeed be better; but they are not so by virtue of their rank. All men have equal right to earn the respect of others."

The crowd, scandalized, waited with hushed horror to see what the Scholar would do. Stefred addressed them, his voice heavy with sarcasm. "Behold the man who thinks himself as wise as a Scholar!" he exclaimed. "No doubt he fancies that he would manage more successfully than we do; it would be amusing to see how he'd proceed."

There was no sound; the people were confused, for this reaction was not at all what they'd expected. Relentlessly Stefred pressed on. "Perhaps we should be kneeling to him instead of the other way around," he said; and, mockingly, he laughed. They laughed with him: at first tentatively, unsure as to whether it was proper, and then in an uproarious release of tension that turned their outrage to mirth.

Noren's face burned crimson. The ridicule was even harder to bear than the hate. Why was Stefred doing this? It could not be mere cruelty; there was no cruelty in Stefred, and this derisive tone was totally unlike him. Always before he had treated Noren with respect. *I'm on your side,* he'd said; *I'll have reasons for what I do.* And, in the message given by the Technician, *I am relying on you to reply with absolute honesty...*

"Observe," Stefred continued, raising his hand once more, "that it *is* the other way around. This man's words are arrogant, yet despite his superior wisdom he kneels to me and acknowledges the truth of what he has been taught. I could humble his arrogance if I chose, but I do not so choose. He will receive discipline enough as it is."

All at once Noren understood what was taking place. Stefred was humiliating him, yes; impenitence could not be allowed to pass unnoticed. But in raising the question of the Scholars' alleged superhumanity, he was also doing other things, and he was doing them very cleverly. That idea was not part of either the Prophecy or the High Law—the Scholars themselves had never encouraged it, and to deny it was blasphemous only in the eyes of the villagers. To them such a denial merited not derision, but wrath. They would not have been surprised if Stefred had immediately pronounced an unprecedented death sentence. By forcing him to take the apparent risk, Stefred was demonstrating his own tolerance for the sort of "heresy" that should not be so labeled. Furthermore, he was vindicating him before the few who had ears to hear: those to whom such replies indicated not blasphemy, but human dignity and courage. Proof was being produced that the recantation had not been made from cowardice, and thus, perhaps, the seeds of faith would be planted in those who'd doubted its sincerity.

He met Stefred's eyes, and for the first time the Scholar responded; there was no overt smile, but Noren knew that whatever further ordeals might lie ahead, as far as Stefred was concerned he had done no wrong.

The ceremony resumed. This, the sentencing, was in the standard script, Noren realized; but it was a portion he had not seen. "We pronounce you an impenitent heretic," Stefred declared with austere formality, "and as such you are liable to the most extreme penalty we can decree. Yet since we bear you no malice, we hereby commute your sentence to perpetual confinement within the City, subject to such disciplines as we shall impose. Look your last on the hills and fields of this world, for you will never again walk among them."

Noren gazed out past the plaza and the markets to the countryside beyond. He had known beforehand, of course, but he had not really taken it in. The purple knolls; the scent of ripening grain; nights when Little Moon shone like a red glass bead overhead while he and Talyra lay side by side looking up at it…farmhouse kitchens, lamp-lit, with bread baking on the hearth…the fresh touch of free air…his whole being ached at the thought that he was forever barred from those things. Perhaps he would never see sunlight again! A few rooms in the towers, like Stefred's study, had windows; but there was no reason to suppose that he would receive such accommodations, or that he would be permitted access to the courtyard that was open to the sky. The domes of the Outer City were roofed over. Perhaps he would never see the stars…

A sharp cry broke in on his desolation. "No, oh no!" a girl's voice screamed. He turned; it was Talyra, who knelt at the topmost level of the steps, and she was sobbing violently, her face hidden by her hands. He could not comfort her. He could never touch her, never even see her from this day forward; and though he had known that, too, it suddenly became the greatest deprivation of all.

The music blared out again, drowning her sobs; Technicians surrounded him, and she was hidden from his sight. Stefred left the platform, followed by the other Scholars. But Noren remained kneeling, his own head bowed for the first time, and he did not even notice the jeers of the dispersing crowd. The sun shone hot on his shoulders, and overhead the sky was vast and blue. He made no move until his guards helped him to his feet and led him back into the City, closing the heavy Gates irrevocably behind.

Chapter Twelve

Once inside the City Gates, the Technicians who formed Noren's escort silently removed the bands from his wrists and, to his amazement, departed, leaving him alone in the wide inner corridor. Then he saw that Stefred was waiting for him. The Scholar came forward and gripped Noren's hand. "That took a great deal of courage," he said quietly.

Noren forced himself to smile. "I understood what you were doing, sir," he said. "And going through the paces of the dream—helped."

"I'm glad," Stefred declared, in a manner oddly more like a friend and equal than a Scholar. "The spectators despised you; I did not want you to despise yourself. Have you any regrets?"

"No. I was wrong about the Prophecy, but I was right to question it! I was right not to believe before I had proof. If I could start all over, I'd do just the same; you'll never get me to repent."

"I've never tried to, Noren."

"But the statement you wanted me to make—"

"Did I say I wanted you to make it?"

He hadn't, Noren realized suddenly. Stefred had not wanted him to make that statement any more than he'd wanted him to yield during the inquisition! He couldn't have, for never once had he implied that doubt was wrong; on the contrary, he'd endorsed it. He had achieved his end not by coercion, but by requiring Noren to live up to his own way of looking at things, and he had too much respect for honesty to want anyone to repent for the sake of appearances. The whole issue had been another calculated challenge. With surprise, Noren became aware that he'd been enjoying Stefred's challenges and that he was going to miss them.

"What happens to me now?" he asked resolutely, as they walked along the corridor and through the inner gates into the courtyard surrounding the towers.

"What do you think will happen?"

"I—I'm not sure. I can't leave the City, I know. And in the sentencing you mentioned discipline." Noren hesitated. He was guilty of no crime in their eyes, yet what could they do with him? The time had come when he could no longer put off facing the question. "Stefred," he burst out, "there's just no easy answer, is there?"

"No, there isn't." The Scholar's tone was very serious. "Much will be demanded of you."

Imprisonment, thought Noren in despair. There was no alternative. Weeks, years, in the small room in which he'd found a mere few days so trying, unless perhaps they made some arrangement whereby he could perform useful work. There must be other heretics somewhere; would he be allowed contact with them? Could discussion by non-Scholars of the secret truths be risked even within the City, when the Technicians weren't privy to those secrets? Solitary confinement was more likely, not as punishment but simply as a necessary precaution.

He would be well treated, he knew. He'd have every physical comfort, and would undoubtedly be permitted to read. All that recorded knowledge of the Six Worlds: he had been promised that more of it would be given to him, and the prospect was exciting. Yet to be shut up forever, alone…

He had been warned. All the ultimatums that he'd once considered threats had been true warnings. No Scholar had ever lied to him; when they'd told him he was incurring grave and irrevocable consequences, they had meant it. They would have to do what must be done to keep their secret.

Upon entering the Hall of Scholars they paused. Noren looked down at the mud-spattered penitent's garb in which he was clad, painfully aware of the glances of the people who passed to and fro in the vestibule. Stefred, watching his face, said compassionately, "Put this on. You'll be less conspicuous, and I want to talk to you for a while before we go upstairs." He handed Noren the robe he'd been holding, an ordinary blue Scholar's robe apparently carried to replace the ceremonial vestments that Stefred himself was wearing.

"*Your* robe? It's—not fitting, sir," Noren protested.

Stefred smiled. "I never expected to hear a statement like that from you!" he said. "Forget it, Noren. We're not stuffy about such things."

Noren put the robe on, reflecting bitterly on the irony of it. Talyra would think such an act the height of blasphemy, yet the Scholars themselves did not consider it so. How he'd misjudged them—still in guessing them to be people like himself, he'd not gone far enough. They had minds like his. He'd never met anyone who shared his views as closely as Stefred! If he'd been born a Scholar, he wouldn't have been such a misfit; why had fate made him a villager instead?

"Noren," Stefred was saying, "you've taken some big steps, but there are bigger ones ahead. You haven't yet been told everything."

Noren looked up, startled. More secrets? His spirits rose despite the cold tingle that spread through him.

"The dreams were edited," the Scholar announced bluntly, "edited not merely to remove thoughts too complex for you, but because before your recantation we could not give you the whole truth."

"Edited?" cried Noren furiously. "You—you didn't trust me after all; you got me to recant on false grounds?"

"No!" Stefred exclaimed, grasping Noren's arm. "Don't you see that we must have trusted you a great deal to send you out before the public as we did? What you were shown was true, and you could have betrayed it."

"How did you know I wouldn't?" Noren asked slowly.

"You had proved that you value the same things we do. If you'd been penitent, we could never have taken the chance; the heretics who show repentance publicly are those who agree to recant before learning any secrets. And only rarely can we rely on someone's quick wits enough to depart from the script as I did with you."

"I don't understand—"

"Think it through," the Scholar said.

Noren thought. "If I'd been penitent, it would have meant I valued something higher than truth. And it might have meant I cared more about what people thought of me than what happened to them; in that case I might have given away the facts to justify myself."

"Yes. But there's more to it. What if you'd refused to go all the way through with the ceremony? We made it a bit rougher than it needed to be, you know."

"I didn't know," Noren began with renewed anger, and then he stopped, perplexed. Many of the seeming ordeals—the re-enactment of the dream, the questioning, and even the use of the unedited script—had not made it rougher, but had served to give him the status of a free agent instead of a helpless victim. Still, the whole thing would have been less trying if Stefred had explained it in advance. Why hadn't he? "I couldn't have refused, because I want the Prophecy to come true," he reflected. "But a person who didn't care—"

"Would have missed the significance of what was happening and balked at allowing himself to be humiliated unjustly."

"If you already trusted me," Noren protested, "what point was there in putting me to such a test? My recantation was all you needed, and to be sure of getting it, you should have made it as easy for me as possible."

"You're holding to false premises again. Do you really think I've devoted all this time and effort merely to getting your recantation? Would I have engineered your arrest in the first place just for that?"

"What else could you have wanted from me?" questioned Noren in confusion.

"You of all people shouldn't have to ask that, you who've maintained from the start that your mind is as good as a Scholar's! Don't you realize how desperately such minds are needed if we're to transform this world by the time the Star becomes visible?"

"The research work...me?" Noren felt a rush of astonished joy. He had never dared hope that they would let him assist them; hadn't the Founders believed that villagers couldn't be trained as scientists? But that, he recalled, had been because they'd known most villagers wouldn't care about knowledge. All at once the system's logic became clear to him. No wonder the Scholars saw to it that the few who did care were arrested! Yet there were a few things that didn't fit.

"Sir," he continued, still baffled, "if you thought me worthy to do that work, why did you keep warning me that my future would be so hard to face? And why did you edit the dreams?"

Stefred paused, considering his words carefully. "I can't answer that until you've figured out what we concealed. I'll give you a clue: we showed you the true origin of the Prophecy, yet the key to its fulfillment was withheld from you. You haven't sensed that flaw because you've always thought of us as a group and not as individual people. But you're intelligent enough to frame the right questions; ask them now. You have nothing to lose by frankness."

Noren frowned. The fulfillment of the Prophecy obviously hinged not only on the completion of the work and the appearance of the Mother Star, but on the willingness of the Scholars to give up their power when the Star did appear. The mere fact that it was real and that the original Scholars hadn't wanted power did not disprove his longstanding doubts as to the present ones' motives. Why hadn't the First Scholar had such suspicions? What way had he had of knowing that the generations to come wouldn't decide that they liked being supreme; why hadn't he worried about it? He must have! His fears along those lines must have been in the edited portion, for men were men, and the First Scholar had known only too well that those who'd held power in the past had often misused it. Only because his personal loathing for tyranny had been so strong—and because Stefred had seemed so honest—had the omission not been apparent.

"I was right all along," Noren whispered in horror. "You deceived me; you knew I wouldn't recant unless I was distracted from your own aims by those of the First Scholar."

"You don't believe that, Noren."

Their eyes met. No, thought Noren, he didn't, not of Stefred. But what of the rest? How could any of them be sure of each other, much less of those who would follow them? Merely experiencing the dreams wouldn't have much effect on someone who didn't share the First Scholar's ideas to begin with.

Stefred went on looking at him, and the right questions began to rise in Noren's mind.

"What's to prevent a Scholar from having selfish aims?" he demanded. "Why couldn't some of you do just what I used to think you were all doing?"

"There's a safeguard," Stefred replied gravely. "We must prove ourselves, you see; we must stand up for our values in a series of situations where it costs something."

How, Noren wondered, did they ever encounter such situations? It couldn't happen unless it was deliberately arranged. "Are people simply born Scholars," he asked, "or must your children pass qualifying tests?"

"Neither one. We are not permitted to rear our own children; they are given to village families who want to adopt babies, and no one ever knows their true parentage."

"Wards of the City? *All* your children?"

"Yes; otherwise they would grow up believing they had the right to succeed us, and they don't."

"But sir, if they don't, then how does anyone become a Scholar?"

In a sober voice Stefred said, "There is only one way, Noren. Each of us must follow the path you have followed, and become first a heretic."

Incredulous, Noren could only stand frozen, incapable of speech, as the Scholar added with feeling, "That's not my robe you are wearing now; it is yours."

Later, after his first meal in the refectory of the Hall of Scholars, after he had been greeted as an equal by blue-robed dignitaries as well as by many younger men and women who were less formally dressed but apparently of equivalent rank, after he had received with stunned embarrassment the congratulations of countless people and was alone with Stefred in the elder man's study, Noren stood at the window and painfully, haltingly, said what he felt must be said. He had been too overwhelmed, too bewildered, to say it initially; he had, in fact, uttered scarcely a word, and Stefred had not pressed him. But once the shock started to lessen he knew there was only one course.

"Look," he began, "I'm honored…I'm—well, overcome… but—but this isn't right, Stefred. I can't accept it." He held out the robe, which he had not worn since bathing and dressing, but had carried over his arm.

Stefred regarded him thoughtfully. "The status, once earned, cannot be revoked. No one will force you to do anything against your will, but you won't be able to take part in the research work unless you at least accept training."

"I guess not. But I still can't become a Scholar."

"I thought you'd say that," Stefred said. "In fact I rather hoped you would; it seems the courageous thing to do at this stage, doesn't it?"

There was silence. Noren thought miserably of what he was rejecting: the chance to study not merely a small portion of the Six Worlds' science, but all of it; unlimited access to the computers and the films and perhaps to more dreams; exciting work that would be of real value to the world; exciting people to work with, all of whom looked at things his way, the searching way, and all of whom *cared*…

"At this stage," Stefred repeated. "Now we're going into it a little deeper. You haven't analyzed the issues as well as you think."

"I know you're my friend and you want to help me," Noren said determinedly, "but I can't let you."

"Have I ever led you anywhere except to truth?"

Noren sat down. It could do no harm to have one more talk with Stefred. He would be challenged to explore all the ramifications of his decision, but this time he was on firm ground, as he'd been in the matter of impenitence, and Stefred would respect his stand.

"You believe you're making a noble sacrifice for the sake of your principles," Stefred went on, "and I admire you for it. Once again, however, you happen to be dead wrong."

"But—"

"You will hear me out, Noren."

"Yes, sir. But you don't understand. I don't want to outrank anybody! I certainly don't want anybody kneeling to me. I see why Scholars have to control what's here in the City, but I still don't really approve of the system."

"Of course you don't. If you approved of it, you wouldn't be fit for the job." With a sigh Stefred declared, "Noren, there's just one kind of person who can safely be entrusted with power, and that's someone who's proven his contempt for tyranny by staking his life in opposition to it. From the very beginning this system has been made to work by one unbroken rule: the secrets are passed to those, and only those, who have done so. The First Scholar planned it this way; that was the decision we edited out of the dreams."

"From the beginning? What about the Founders' own children?"

"They had no contact with their parents; they were reared by teachers, in one of the domes, and became the first Technicians. The Founders chose successors as we do, from among people with what it takes to recognize and defy the system's evils."

Slowly absorbing this, Noren mused, "Some of the original research station workers must have qualified by defying the man they thought a dictator. And all Scholars since—even the women, like the one who operates the Dream Machine—have been brought here for heresy? They've been through the whole process and have remained impenitent?"

"Yes. They weren't called heretics in the early days before the Prophecy; those of the First Scholar's time entered the City as hostages for the land treatment equipment's return, which was the means he used to determine their worthiness. He took only volunteers, you see, and naturally those who offered themselves did so with the hope of learning something that would help to defeat him. There have always been rebels, and every one of them has faced an inquisition believing himself destined for death."

"Even you?" It was a startling idea, yet not so hard to imagine, Noren found. Stefred's defense would have been worth listening to!

"I myself was a year or so younger than you are," Stefred told him, "and I was guilty not merely of heresy, but of having taken part in a most irreverent demonstration of my feelings toward Scholars. In my particular village some rather grisly rumors had gotten started; I was fully convinced that I was to be burned alive." With a grim smile he added, "My partners in the escapade weren't caught; they were present at my recantation and all of them, even my closest friends, assumed I could have just one reason for making it."

"Oh, Stefred—"

The Scholar drew his chair closer to Noren's. "It's hard to give up one's visions of glorious martyrdom," he said quietly. "Even during recantation we're martyrs—we endure hatred and abuse, and picture ourselves dying not as we originally intended to, but as the First Scholar did. There's satisfaction in that, for we're still pitting ourselves against society. To become its respected agents is a far greater switch."

Noren bent his head. It was spinning; he felt unreal and without familiar footholds. "Do you suppose I wanted to accept the very role I had always despised?" Stefred continued. "I took it on only because I knew that if I didn't, I'd be betraying every conviction I'd upheld during my trial. And that's what you will be doing, Noren, if you refuse the trust that has fallen to you."

"Wait a minute. Isn't it the other way around?"

"What were you speaking for if not fulfillment of the Prophecy? You claimed we had no intention of fulfilling it, and we proved you wrong; still the promise cannot be kept unless the people who are qualified are willing to work toward that end. There's a lot to do, and though the time may seem long, it's barely enough for what must be accomplished. *'Cities shall rise beyond the Tomorrow Mountains,'* remember? Without suitable metal we can't build those cities! We can't even produce the machines to keep future generations alive! We've made progress, but we don't yet know how to synthesize it; new techniques—techniques different from anything the Six Worlds ever attempted—must be developed. The training for such work is very long and very difficult, and it's hardly surprising if you're not anxious to devote yourself to it—"

"You know I don't mind *that!*" Noren interrupted indignantly. "If being a Scholar meant only that, without—"

"Without the responsibility? Without the burden of representing a system you know is not as it should be?"

"I just don't think it's right for one group of people to be placed above another group," Noren maintained stubbornly.

"Neither do I, Noren. But you see, I don't consider myself better than the villagers; they merely think I do, just as they once thought me a coward who'd recanted to save my life. Which is more important, ensuring the survival of those people, or making sure they see me as I really am?"

There was no argument to that; the First Scholar himself, after all, had faced the same choice, and the living of it had been harder than the dying. Yet the First Scholar had been hated as an apparent villain. Even he had not been required to let people venerate him, kneel to him, under the impression that he agreed that was good!

In desperation Noren switched tactics. "But everybody should have a chance to be a Scholar," he protested.

"Everybody does have a chance. The way is open to anyone whose motives are sincere, but there is no great surplus of heretics pounding on the gates of the City demanding to be let in. How many people did you try to enlist in your cause, Noren, before you resorted to that last desperate gambit of yours?"

Noren dropped his eyes. "Most of them either weren't interested, or weren't willing to risk anything. And there were a few who wanted to destroy what they couldn't have, or else to seize power for themselves. If questioning things were encouraged, though, maybe more children would grow up caring."

"Encouraged by whom? The village leaders? You stood trial before a village council, so you must have a fairly realistic idea of the way they think. Yet they're elected by the people and we can't interfere with them. We don't tamper with democratic government in the villages; to do so would be exceeding our bounds. As High Priests we exert no influence beyond the sphere of the Prophecy and the High Law."

"Well, by Technicians, then. Some Technicians use their minds."

Stefred smiled. "A Technician encouraged you, didn't he, when you were still in school? A young man who spent the night at your father's farm?"

"I never told you that," Noren gasped. "I never told anyone!"

"The incident wasn't accidental," explained Stefred. "Neither were some of the less happy ones; there's more than one kind of encouragement, and at times we gave you cause to hate us. We've been watching you since you were a small child."

"You—you set me up for this…from the beginning? I didn't have free choice after all?"

"Oh, yes. You had free choice. We encourage every person who shows any spark of initiative, but most of them don't follow through. And the risks you took were real; if you'd fallen into the hands of certain fanatics, we might not have been able to save you. We failed with your friend Kern, for whom we had great hopes."

"You were watching Kern, too?"

"Of course," said Stefred unhappily, "but we were helpless; he was rash and spoke before we anticipated, before we'd arranged protection. Can you imagine how I felt when I heard you'd eluded yours?"

"That really was why you got those Technicians to trick me into getting myself arrested!" exclaimed Noren, realizing that despite the suspicions of the young man who'd switched places with him, Stefred had told them the literal truth.

"Yes. It was necessary for your safety that the time and place be of our choosing, but the decision to respond as you did was yours alone."

Noren frowned. "What if a Technician doesn't like the orders he's given?" he inquired, unable to forget the man's anguished remorse.

"It's a violation of the High Law to disobey. He is free to become a villager if he wishes, but otherwise he's subject to our authority and can be convicted by the Council of Technicians if he defies it."

But that was awful, Noren thought. And then he saw the implications of what Stefred was saying. Technicians too could be heretics, and could therefore go on to become Scholars! There must be more than one of them who opposed the system. Yet like the villagers they were reared to believe in the Prophecy and the High Law, and by the same token must believe that they could be killed for refusing to recant—which was as it should be if offering one's life was the only way to qualify.

"The men sent on such missions are very carefully chosen," Stefred went on. "Often the encouragement of heresy is intended to be mutual. You may have thought you weren't convincing anyone at your trial, but I suspect you convinced the Technician whose clothes you took; it was evident afterwards that he was tormented by the thought that he'd betrayed you. Someday soon, Noren, you'll be able to tell him that you weren't harmed by what he did, for the next time I give him such orders, he'll refuse them."

Stefred had painstakingly avoided the question of what that Technician had been doing in his cell in the middle of the night, Noren noticed. No doubt he'd guessed the truth from the beginning. Probably the man had never been given any instructions to pretend, but had simply not known how else to interpret the Chief Inquisitor's suggestion that he sympathize.

Torn, Noren struggled inwardly with the significance of what he had just heard. If Scholar status could be attained by anyone with the right sense of values, the scheme of succession was fair; and yet…

"I'm not trying to soften this," Stefred said, "because you want and need to face all its implications. But actually you are not going to be plunged abruptly into a position where people will worship you. I have not urged you to wear the robe, for the obligations it represents can't be imposed on anyone. The blue robe is a symbol of full commitment. It's your right to assume it whenever you choose, provided you're ready to make such a commitment formally. Most Scholars don't do that until they've passed through the first phases of training and seen what our work is really like. A few never do it at all."

"You mean I needn't become a High Priest?" asked Noren, relieved and yet confused.

"That's up to you to decide. You'll be ineligible for certain types of work unless you commit yourself; you will not even have a vote—and we Scholars vote not only to elect leaders, but on many issues that affect fulfillment of the Prophecy. Your fitness to participate is conditional on your being willing to share the accountability."

There was another distinction between novice Scholars and fully committed ones, Noren learned. A novice's true status was not revealed to the Technicians. He hadn't realized that there were Technicians who lived permanently in the Inner City. Stefred, however, explained that since they did not wear uniforms except for special duties, any more than committed Scholars wore their robes, and since everybody mingled freely outside the Hall of Scholars itself, people's rank could not be determined by looking at them. Nor could it be determined by the kinds of jobs they did, for not all heretics who earned Scholar status had desire or aptitude either for scientific research or any other field of study—some did less skilled work than some of the Technicians, who also had opportunity for education. The difference lay in knowledge of the secrets. Technicians admitted to the Inner City had to remain because they knew Scholar rank wasn't hereditary; yet because they didn't know anything about the process whereby it was conferred, they too were eligible to attain it.

"You realize, don't you," Stefred said, "that that's what would have happened to you if you'd recanted before learning the truth?"

"I'd have become an Inner City Technician?"

"Yes."

"What if I'd refused to recant after I learned? Or if I'd been penitent?"

"It very rarely happens, Noren. We don't enlighten anyone we're not sure of. Still, we're fallible, and your freedom of choice was real."

"You'd have had to isolate me."

"Unfortunately we would. The conditions wouldn't have been harsh—you'd have had our companionship whenever possible—and you'd have retained eligibility for a second chance, as does any person who's disqualified, for that matter."

"I might not have wanted one if I'd known what was ahead."

"No candidate knows. Incorruptibility can be proven only by taking all the steps without expectation of personal gain."

"That still doesn't make accepting a Scholar's role *right,*" Noren insisted.

"The question's not whether it's right for a special group of people to control the knowledge and equipment brought from the Six Worlds," Stefred said. "We're agreed that it isn't. Yet you conceded, when you decided to recant, that for the time being that's how it's got to be. You did so only because you'd been convinced that the Founders didn't want the job, and that those of us who are like them would prefer to be rid of it. Would you throw the whole burden on us—on me? Is it to be condoned only as long as you yourself can wash your hands of any involvement?"

Wretchedly Noren admitted, "If I refuse an active part. I'm condemning you all; I'm right back where I started. What's wrong with me, Stefred? Why do I feel this way, when only this morning I was willing to do anything that might be required of me?"

"If you don't know, you've less honesty than I've been giving you credit for."

Noren pondered it. "Some of the people hated me this morning," he said slowly, "because they thought I'd sold out. I could face that because I knew it wasn't true...but now I'm afraid it *is* true."

Stefred nodded, understanding. "You don't have to be," he said. "Why do you suppose we waited until after the ceremony to tell you, if not to spare you that fear? We were already sure of you; our final decision had been made; you were, in fact, a Scholar when you were exposed alone to the crowd, for we don't allow disqualified candidates to become targets of abuse. The final tests were not for our benefit but for yours, Noren! Would we have let you suffer them without good cause?"

"I thought maybe you wanted to see how much I could take before rewarding me with honor."

"This is not a reward. We kept you unaware because we knew you could accept nothing from us that was offered as payment."

"Sometimes I think you read my mind," Noren confessed ruefully.

"You forget that we've all traveled the same route. Every one of us, having refused to back down under pressure, has recanted for the sake of the future we're working toward—and that experience is just the beginning, for when we reenact the dream, we assume all the responsibility it implies. I took part in this morning's pageant, too, after all. I stood there and let the villagers kneel to me, pay me homage, while they despised and reviled you; and I well knew that the one was no more deserved than the other. Did you think I was enjoying myself?" Stefred's voice was sorrowful as he continued, "Noren, I watched you and looked back on my own recantation almost with nostalgia, thinking how simple life was for me then. Yes, we were judging you. No one who was secretly longing for my role could have borne yours as you did. But we never stop judging our own motives."

He rose and walked to the window, looking out across the shining towers of the City. "Before I revealed the secret of the Prophecy to you, I asked if you would accept the consequences without protest; and when you declared you would, I predicted that a day would come when you'd go back on those words. I warned you that in the end the consequences would seem so terrible that you'd be willing to give up all the things you cared most for in order to escape them—that you would stand here in this room and tell me so. You laughed. Even this morning you'd have laughed; you felt that by your voluntary participation in that ceremony you were proving me wrong. But you can't laugh now, Noren, for you have just fulfilled my prediction. If I'd made a bet with you, you would have to pay off."

"You meant—these consequences? All along?"

"Yes," Stefred said gently, "all along. They are the consequences not merely of your acts, Noren, but of everything you are."

"I—I can't escape, can I?" Noren said resignedly. It was more a discovery than a question, and Stefred did not reply; no reply was needed. Both of them already knew the answer.

For a while it was as though he were still in the dreams: he was himself no longer, but a Scholar; and he would be a Scholar forever. The idea was overwhelming, yet not entirely unwelcome. Looking around Stefred's familiar study, with its shelves of books and its many still-incomprehensible Machines, Noren felt a tremendous surge of excitement. All the mysteries were to be revealed to him! Whether or not he ever chose to wear the robe, he had both the right and the duty to understand them and someday to pass them on.

The training would be more challenging than anything he could imagine, Stefred warned. It would not be like the village school; there would indeed be discipline, rigorous discipline, for he would be given tasks that would tax his mind to the utmost. "There will be problems beyond any you've yet conceived," the Scholar concluded, "but though our life's far from easy, I think you'll find that it suits you."

Noren nodded. Knowledge was what he'd longed for, and he could not believe that the process of absorbing it would be anything but a joy.

"It is not a life of comfort. Like the Founders, we endure greater hardships than the people whose heritage we hold in trust, and we are confined here, remember. The decree that you can't leave the City still stands; that is one of the things we renounce. There are others."

"Marriage," murmured Noren, thinking again of Talyra.

"Not at all," Stefred assured him. "We are free to marry among ourselves, and fully committed Scholars, who have revealed their rank, can even marry Technicians."

"I—I won't ever want to marry anyone, Stefred."

"You don't mean that. You mean you don't want to marry anyone but the girl you're in love with." At Noren's astonished look he went on, "Yes, I know how you feel about Talyra, but even if I didn't, it would be easy enough to guess. The situation's not exactly unusual. Many of us, both men and women, have been very deeply hurt by it."

"I could bear that myself," Noren said unhappily, "but when I think of *her*— She was there this morning. She suffered more than I did; that was the worst part of the whole thing."

"I saw," Stefred said. "Her instructors forbade her to attend, but she disobeyed them." He hesitated, then added with abrupt candor, "Noren, there is one more fact you must know. There's no need for Talyra to go on suffering on your account. If she loves you enough to share your confinement, she can become a Technician."

Noren drew a breath of surprise. "Is that what happens to the people who vanish from the training center?" he asked, beginning to piece things together.

"Yes. That's one reason I appointed her to go there: so that if it worked out as I hoped, her disappearance from the village could be explained."

"But…we can't marry unless I accept the robe?"

"Would it be fair to make her your wife without telling her that a barrier of secrecy must always stand between you?"

No, reflected Noren, and certainly not without letting her know that they'd be unable to rear their own children. Besides, Talyra wouldn't want to be a Technician! The idea would shock her. She had been happy in the village, but in the City she'd be terrified and miserable. "Don't bring her here," he said resolutely.

"I couldn't even if you wished it," Stefred told him. "Those admitted must come of their own accord; they must request audience to plead clemency for someone who's imprisoned. A village-reared woman must show herself spirited enough to adapt to the Inner City, where women's roles are less restricted, as well as to see justification in the past actions of the man she loves. As a Technician, she'll always believe that we made him a Scholar not because of his heresy, but in spite of it; yet she must sense that he has proven himself worthy."

Then it was hopeless, Noren thought. He must put it out of his mind. Talyra was so very devout, so unwilling to question; she would never challenge the Chief Inquisitor! As he sat silent, remembering things she'd said, a new doubt came to him.

"Stefred," he began hesitantly, "there's something that bothers me. Lots of people believe in the Mother Star and it—well, comforts them. They've got the idea that it's a power that takes care of things. If they knew the truth, they might feel…lost. There'd be nothing up there any more. Mightn't that happen when the Time of the Prophecy comes?"

There was a long pause; Stefred, for the first time in Noren's memory, seemed at a loss for an answer. "That's a complicated question," he said finally, "and a very serious one. People have always looked toward something above and beyond them; they always will. They've called it by different names. Throughout the history of the Six Worlds there were many, and by the time of the Founding the right of all individuals to choose their own was almost universally accepted. The High Law still grants that right, but few villagers exercise it; most of them have forgotten all names but that of the Mother Star—which, used in such a way, would have seemed blasphemous to people of the First Scholar's day."

"I don't understand," Noren admitted.

"No, and you won't until you have studied much of the wisdom that is preserved here. What you can grasp now is that it's the idea that's important, not what it's called: the idea that there is something higher and more significant than we are. You, I think, would call it Truth. Later you may find another name more meaningful, as many of us do."

Comprehension stirred in Noren, making him glance again at the blue robe set aside. Stefred smiled. "Don't try to solve everything at once. You have quite a few surprises coming—even Talyra may surprise you—and in the meantime, there's plenty of work to get started on."

Noren raised his eyes to the window. Beyond the wall of glass, beyond the bright towers and beacons of the City, he could see the far-off rim of the Tomorrow Mountains. A whole new earth, and beyond the earth, a universe! One day, above those ridges, the Mother Star would appear in radiant splendor, and the annunciation of the old worlds' tragedy would become the confirmation of the new one's faith. *"And the spirit of this Star shall abide forever in our hearts..."* What did it matter if the truth was cloaked in a little symbolism? The idea behind it was the same! With sudden elation, he found himself looking forward to the tasks ahead.

Beyond the Tomorrow Mountains

Chapter One

The room was high in one of the City's towers. Its window viewed a vast panorama of grain fields dappling gray-purple wilderness, and of more wilderness beyond: a vista rimmed by the jagged yellow ridges of the Tomorrow Mountains. Noren was not looking at the view, however. His back to it, he sat nervously on the edge of a low couch, eyeing the closed-circuit video built into the opposite wall and thinking of the heavy responsibility that soon would fall to him. He was too young and unskilled to conduct an interview as crucial as the one to come; he had been told that frankly—still it was deemed best that he be entrusted with it. He'd accepted the job gladly, despite his inexperience. Only now, with the time at hand, had he begun to feel other misgivings.

The screen before him showed the ceremony taking place outside the City, on the wide stone platform before the Gates. It was a public recantation. The robes of the Scholars were brilliant blue against the white pavement, a sharp contrast to the green uniforms of the Technicians and the mud-stained gray garment of the prisoner whom they guarded. The crowd in the plaza was not visible, being behind the camera, but the audio picked up hostile murmurs. The sentencing was over and the people were beginning to jeer again, though they would throw no actual dirt in the Scholars' presence; it would not be seemly, for Scholars were High Priests and were revered.

The prisoner, Brek, knelt before the Scholars, his hands bound behind him. His hair had been cropped short, a sign of penitence and shame, but there was neither penitence nor shame in his bearing; he held his head high. Through the ordeals of the ceremony, his spirit had not faltered. The spectators might think that he'd been broken, but it was not true. On the contrary, Brek had just passed the final test of indomitability.

Noren's heart warmed with sympathy and admiration. It took courage to do what Brek was doing. He was a heretic: he had maintained that it was wrong for the Scholars to keep their knowledge secret and that the sacred Prophecy in which the villagers and

Technicians believed was a fraud, a foolish story invented to forestall rebellion against the priest caste's supremacy. He'd refused to recant despite his assumption that refusal was punishable by death. Yet now he was recanting after all, voluntarily denying most of his former convictions, though it meant exposing himself not only to the contempt of believers, but to the abuse and scorn of fellow-rebels who would think that he had sold out.

Noren understood how hard an act that was; he had recanted himself less than a year before.

Loud music burst forth, drowning the noise of the crowd, as the attending Scholars, in solemn procession, left the platform. Noren switched off the screen; Brek had been surrounded by a protective cordon of Technicians and was no longer in sight. A few minutes later the door of the room slid open and the Scholar Stefred, Chief Inquisitor, stood in the archway, still clad in his ceremonial robe. Unfastened, it flapped open to reveal plain beige clothing like Noren's own. "Brek's on his way up here," he said. "I'll leave you alone with him; you can help him more than I can at this point. Set his mind at ease, Noren."

Noren nodded. "I'll try. He must have caught the symbolism of what was happening to him out there; he took it well."

"Very well indeed, and it was a greater triumph for him than for you; he lacks your natural self-confidence. But as you know, the next step's difficult, and Brek has suffered more than you did. You had nothing in your past life to feel guilty about."

"Neither does he."

"No, but he thinks he does, and I couldn't let him know otherwise. In the early stages of his inquisition I had to play on it." Stefred sighed, troubled. "I was ruthless with Brek. I manipulated him more cruelly than I do most heretics; that's necessary in the case of a Technician. I wouldn't have done it if I hadn't been sure of him, and even surer of you. How you handle the next few days will determine whether it leaves lasting scars."

Alone once more, Noren paced back and forth with growing apprehension. He hoped fervently that Stefred's confidence would prove justified, for he owed Brek a great deal. The two had met only briefly, some time back, when as a villager Noren had never imagined friendship with a Technician. Technicians, who lived in the enclosed City and were permitted to handle Machines, were of a higher caste than villagers and were viewed by most of them with awe, though Noren himself had felt bitter envy. Yet Brek had defied both custom and religious law in an attempt to save him from the heretic's supposed fate: punishment, perhaps torture, at the hands of the Chief Inquisitor. In those days neither of them had shared the prevailing trust in the Scholars' goodness.

Once actually in Stefred's hands, one learned to trust, but the trust developed gradually. Terror had to come first. At the outset Stefred concealed his true sympathies, not only to test the prisoner's resolution but because he knew that no committed heretic who doubted his own ability to withstand terror would be able to make an objective decision about voluntary recantation. During the inquisition, before learning the secret facts about the Prophecy, a heretic must feel real fear: worse fear than of the rumored death sentence to which he was resigned. With Noren there'd been no need to generate that fear; as a villager to whom the forbidden City was awesomely mysterious and who had never before seen a Scholar at close range, he had been sufficiently terrified by his mere surroundings. For a Technician it was different. Noren knew what had been done to make Brek afraid, and he did not like to think about it; it was a grim piece of deception. Not that any lies had been told—but Brek's imagination must have tormented him in more ways than one during the solitary confinement he'd experienced.

Again the door opened, and this time it was Brek who appeared. His wrist manacles had been removed, but he still wore the gray penitent's garb; he'd had no opportunity to remove it or to wash the mud from his face and arms. Though at one time Noren would have raged at the idea of a person's being subjected to such degradation, he knew that what Brek had undergone had not been degrading. Stefred never degraded anyone. Heretics who agreed to recant under pressure were not exposed to the abuse of the crowd. Those permitted to face such abuse did not suffer from it; one mark of a person ready to share the Scholars' secrets was the ability to endure outward humiliation without loss of inner dignity.

Brek's difficulties weren't over, to be sure—nor, for that matter, were Noren's. The consequences of heresy were grave. They changed the course of one's whole life, and the interval since Noren's own recantation was still relatively short. During that interval he had acquired both privileges and burdens; to these he must now introduce Brek. *Set his mind at ease,* Stefred had said…yet, Noren reflected ruefully, he himself felt no peace of mind. There were certain things he dared not let himself contemplate, and it would be hard to keep them out of the coming discussion. In the past half-hour uncertainty had stricken him. Was it right to keep such things out, to conceal from Brek his recent fear that the Prophecy's fulfillment was less sure than one believed when, in recanting, one affirmed it?

The escort of Technicians withdrew. Brek stepped forward into the room, his drawn face lighting with startled recognition. "I didn't know whether they'd let me see you," he said, his voice low but steady. "I wanted to, Noren, though I don't suppose you can ever forgive me."

"No, I can't," said Noren, determined to keep worry from his smile. "There's nothing to forgive."

"But you were condemned because of me! You were living a normal life back in your village until I tricked you into a public admission of heresy."

"You did the job assigned to you, as you were bound to under the High Law. And then after the village council convicted me, you helped me to escape from jail; you gave me your Technician's uniform and stayed behind in my place! You claimed you weren't risking anything, but I know better now."

"I wasn't arrested for that," protested Brek. "Oh, I was accused of it later, but not until I'd balked at setting a trap for somebody else."

Noren sat down on the couch, offering a place to Brek, who after slight hesitation joined him. "You've gotten to know Stefred, and you've learned that he was sincere when he told you that it's better for a heretic to be trapped than to be caught accidentally when there are no Technicians around to protect him from his fellow villagers," Noren said. The High Law required anyone convicted of heresy to be turned over to the Scholars unharmed; but without Technicians to enforce this, there was real peril, for people who blasphemed against the Prophecy—or worse, against the Mother Star itself—were deeply despised by villagers and were occasionally murdered.

"I know Stefred tries to suppress heresy without hurting anybody," Brek agreed. "I know he doesn't torture or kill those who won't recant. But I didn't know it *then.*"

"So the second time, you defied him openly and were brought to trial for it?"

"Yes. Originally I was charged only with disobeying orders, but when the Council of Technicians asked me why I'd done it—well, I told them. From then on it was a full-scale heresy trial, though not much like the farce you went through with that self-righteous village council. Afterward, during the inquisition, the emphasis was on what I believe, not how I'd acted."

"Was it rough?" Noren inquired, knowing that it had been, and that talking about it would help to heal the wounds.

"No rougher than I deserved," Brek answered grimly. "It seemed ironic the way the punishment fit the crime: not heresy, which is no real crime at all, but the part I'd played in your conviction. You see, there was a time when they let me think they'd broken you."

"Stefred told me," said Noren. The stress of a heretic's inquisition was not intended as punishment, and Brek must be made to realize that. "I'd convinced you that I'd never recant, no matter what they did; you honestly believed that I could hold out despite the rumors that nobody ever has. So they showed you films of my recantation—edited films, the worst parts—without any comment at all, and then they locked you up to think it over."

In agony, Brek confessed, "I almost cracked up, Noren. I hadn't even known that you'd been recaptured! I'd been clinging to the hope that you'd escaped, that I hadn't really brought you any harm. But after those films, I could only think that heretics must be subjected to something more terrible than either of us had imagined. I knew you wouldn't have given in to save your life, or even to spare yourself pain, at least not beforehand—"

"Neither would you," Noren interrupted. "That's why it was done: to prove that you wouldn't."

"To Stefred?"

"No. He was already sure; if he hadn't been, he'd never have risked using that kind of pressure. His aim was to prove it to *you.*"

"But Noren," Brek admitted unhappily, "I wasn't sure at all! I was shaking so hard I could hardly stand when I was taken to see him again. I didn't know how I'd answer until I heard my own voice."

"That's the point. Stefred knew you weren't going to crack—but you didn't, not till the moment came. And you needed to know.

You wouldn't have felt right about recanting if you hadn't been shown that you could have held out if you'd chosen to."

Brek nodded slowly, "That's true. He never did try to force me to do anything against my will! I got the feeling that he respected me for defying him, even for disobeying his orders in the first place; I just wish I'd done it sooner." Bowing his head, he added miserably, "Nothing can change the fact that you'd be free now if I had."

Noren regarded him, concerned. This must be settled quickly, for his main task was to bring Brek face to face with a more difficult dilemma. "Brek," he asked seriously, "are you sorry you became a heretic? Do you regret speaking out against the Prophecy and the High Law when you were tried?"

"Of course not. They wanted me to say I was during the ceremony, but I drew the line there and was pronounced impenitent, though I was warned that that'll affect what becomes of me." He faced Noren with returning pride. "I don't care! I recanted because they proved that the High Law is necessary to keep people alive on this planet until the Prophecy can be fulfilled, but I'm not sorry for having challenged it."

"That isn't what I mean," Noren said. "I refused to fake penitence, too, and as a matter of fact that's what Stefred hoped we'd do. The official script we were offered was designed to give us the satisfaction of rejecting it. But are you sorry all this happened, that you've been told secrets that will keep you confined here in the Inner City for the rest of your life?"

"No," Brek declared. "It—it's worth whatever comes, I guess, to know the truth."

"Then don't you suppose it's worth it for me? Truth was what I cared most about, what I set out to find, and I couldn't have found it back in the village."

Brek stared at him. "I haven't looked at it that way. I thought only of your being imprisoned." He glanced around the room, with its comfortable though austere furnishings and its breathtaking view, for the first time aware of the strangeness of a prisoner being left unguarded in such a place. "What's it like, Noren? I've been told nothing."

Noren hesitated. He remembered only too well how it felt to be told nothing: to kneel on the hot shimmering pavement and hear the grim sentence: *Perpetual confinement, subject to such disciplines as we shall impose.* And to know that despite the Scholars' kindness, that sentence was no more a lie than any of the earlier and more frightening warnings. "It's hard to accept at first," he said frankly, "but not much like what you're expecting. You'll be surprised." This was not the time to mention that some of the surprises would be pleasant, since for someone in Brek's position the wished-for things were the hardest to accept of all.

"Stefred said I'd be equal to it," Brek reflected.

"He tells everyone that. He means it, too, because no one gets this far who isn't. People who don't qualify rarely get past the inquisition phase."

"Qualify? That's an odd way to put it."

"You didn't know you were being tested?"

"Well—well, yes, at some points. It was pretty clear that they wouldn't have let me in on any secrets if I'd been willing to recant under threat, or if I'd accepted the bribe they offered."

"It's more complicated than that. There are still secrets to learn, Brek. So far you've not heard the most important one. They think I'm the best person to enlighten you." Noren smiled, trying to seem reassuring, though he still found it incredible that he should tutor Brek: Brek, who was nearly two years older than he, who'd been born a Technician, trained in electronics instead of farming, and whom he had once addressed as "sir!"

"You enlightened me to start with," Brek told him. "I might never have known I was a heretic if it hadn't been for what you said at your trial."

"That's why you were sent to observe it," said Noren levelly.

"You mean Stefred *knew* how I'd react? But then why—" He broke off, appalled. "Noren, was I led into a trap, as you were? Was the whole thing planned?"

"Yes. From the beginning." Pausing again, Noren wondered what tactics to pursue. There were no hard-and-fast rules, but he must proceed carefully, he knew; he must cushion the shock. Brek must figure out as much as he could for himself.

Brek's eyes were anguished. "I'd come to trust them."

"Why?" Noren asked. "You've known all along that Scholars watch anyone suspected of having heretical ideas."

"They don't like the way things are any better than we do, though," Brek asserted. "They don't want to keep away from the villagers, and they don't want to hide their knowledge; they're doing it only because they have no choice. And as for being venerated as High Priests—well, they hate it."

"All of them? Or just Stefred?"

"Stefred's the only one I've ever really talked to, I suppose. But in the dreams—"

"In the dreams you shared the First Scholar's recorded memories and you knew what he believed, what the other Founders believed; you knew that they never sought power. Yet they lived long ago. What's to prove that all their successors are like them? What's to say some aren't out for personal gain, as you claimed at your trial?"

"Well, I—" Brek stopped, frowning. "*You* weren't at *my* trial."

"I've heard the transcript of it." Slowly, aware that having broached the key issue, he must say something more direct. Noren added, "I've also dreamed those dreams a second time, Brek, and they're—different. There are things in the recordings that only Scholars are permitted to know."

"Then how do you know them?"

Noren drew breath, his heart pounding. The most painful part of his job could be put off no longer. "I am a Scholar now, Brek," he admitted steadily. "I don't wear the robe, but I'm entitled to."

Stunned, Brek recoiled from him, then rose and walked away. "I've been naive," he declared dully. "Before revealing the truth they offered me further training in exchange for unqualified submission, and I turned them down...would they have gone *that* far if they'd wanted me enough?" With a bitter laugh he added, "You've a sharper mind than I have; you'll be useful to them. I don't wonder you could set your own price."

Fury spread in a hot wave through Noren, but he kept his face impassive. Brek couldn't be blamed. It occurred to him that Stefred would have foreseen this, that his own levelheadedness was no doubt being evaluated; the challenges of the training period were at times no less demanding than the qualifying ones. And if he failed to meet this one, it was Brek who would be hurt.

"My recantation was as sincere as yours." he said quietly, "and I knew no more of what was in store for me than you did. You see, the biggest secret—the one that was edited out of the dreams—concerns the scheme of succession. The status of Scholar is neither sold nor inherited; it is earned. No man or woman attains it whose trustworthiness is unproven. If you doubt that, remember that you could not have knelt to Stefred and the others, even ceremonially, if there'd been any question in your mind about their honesty."

Brek turned and for a long moment appraised Noren in silence, noticing the lines of weariness in his face, marks that made him seem older than his years. "There's no question about yours," he said finally. "I don't understand everything yet, but one thing's clear: somehow they recognized that, even in a former heretic, and bestowed rank and power where it was deserved." Approaching the couch where Noren still sat motionless, he continued, "I never knelt to Stefred in private, at least not after my arrest. While I hated him I ignored the conventions, and then later I sensed that he disliked them as much as I. Before the crowd I did it simply in honor of what he stood for. But I kneel to you, sir, as I now have new cause to beg your forgiveness." He dropped to his knees as was customary in addressing a Scholar, not subserviently but with dignity, his eyes meeting Noren's without flinching.

"No!" exclaimed Noren hastily, sliding to the floor himself and gripping Brek's outstretched hands. "Not to me, and never again to Stefred. And you don't call me 'sir,' either. Those customs don't apply; we're equals."

"Stefred's acknowledged me his equal in all the ways that matter. If Scholars must pass some special test of worthiness, it makes them all the more entitled to the courtesy due their rank. Do you think I'd want such status myself?"

"You have it whether you want it or not," said Noren gently, "since you too have earned it."

Brek drew back with incredulous dismay. "Scholar rank? But that's awful; it can't possibly work like that! I wouldn't have recanted if I'd known there'd be any such reward."

"Nor would the rest of us; that's one reason we weren't told."

"The rest of us…there are others?"

"All the others, even Stefred, when he was young! He wasn't born a Scholar; no one is. Scholars' children are given up for adoption. All candidates prove themselves in the same way."

Outraged, Brek persisted, "You mean the whole system's a sham—those chosen must demonstrate their outlook toward this setup, with all its evils, by humbly submitting to a ceremony of recantation?"

"No," Noren assured him. "Not by recantation, but by unrepented heresy."

It was past noon, and there was barely time left for Brek to bathe and dress before the refectory closed. That was just as well, Noren thought; there would be fewer people to confront than had greeted him during his own first meal as a Scholar. One was not permitted to retreat from one's new status; however great the strain, one was plunged immediately into the regular routine of Inner City life, and the adjustment was trying. It was supposed to be. Villagers and Outer City Technicians assumed that Scholars knew no hardship; the sooner a heretic learned that this was not the case, the sooner he could overcome his natural resistance to membership in a "privileged" caste. All the same, the traditional requirement that he appear in the Hall of Scholars' refectory shortly after recantation, maintaining his poise while receiving with bewildered embarrassment the congratulations of men and women hitherto viewed as a class apart, imposed arduous demands.

Brek bore up well, though his face was set and he spoke little as he and Noren made the rounds of the occupied tables. "The first few days are rough," Noren told him when they were settled with their food at a small table in a corner. "But once you get started on your training, you won't have time to worry about anything else. And you'll like it. Stefred says you're well-fitted to become a scientist; you always wanted to do such work, didn't you, even before you learned what the Scholars' main job is?"

"Not at the price of outranking people who have no chance to learn."

"We don't. Anyone on this planet is eligible to earn Scholar status; scientific aptitude has nothing to do with it. Some of us study other fields, or choose work that doesn't require study. The old lady who filled our trays, for instance—she was a basket-weaver in her village, and a grandmother; the council that convicted her of heresy thought she was a witch. Most women like that turn out to have no real heretical convictions, and they become Inner City Technicians without being required to recant, but not this one. She had her doubts about the justice of the High Law, and Stefred couldn't shake her. So he took her the whole way: the dreams, recantation in its most difficult form, everything. She works in the refectory kitchen now, but she ranks the same as a fully trained scientist and her vote has equal weight."

"Maybe so," Brek protested, "still, I'm never going to feel right about the system."

"Naturally you're not," agreed Noren. "Don't you see, Brek? A person who doesn't think anything's the matter with it isn't fit to hold power! The caste system necessary to human survival here is evil. The system whereby Scholars control all machines and all knowledge is evil, even though the villagers run their own affairs and enforce the High Law themselves through their elected councils. We who were heretics knew it was, and said so; we got ourselves tried and convicted and we refused to recant, believing we'd die for it. No one who's not that strongly opposed to such evils can qualify."

"But in the end we did recant."

"We're impenitent, though. We still have the same values, the same goals; we recanted only when we found that the other Scholars share them." Noren spoke firmly, doing his best not to rouse the conflicting feelings he'd suppressed during nearly a year of concentration on study. He had allowed the thrill of absorbing knowledge he'd always craved to engross him, but some of that knowledge had been disturbing. Some of it had raised questions that had not occurred to him at the time of his recantation, questions he did not want to think of, much less discuss with Brek.

He was still sure, of course, that the sealing of the City was necessary to human survival. Without its irreplaceable life-support machines, everyone on this colony planet would suffer chromosome damage; future generations would be subhuman. The First Scholar had not allowed that to happen. He'd set himself up as an apparent dictator, knowing that the villagers would hate him and eventually kill him for it. To preserve their hope, he'd kept silent about the nova that had destroyed the Six Worlds of their home system and deprived them of all that the City must safeguard for posterity. Even when he lay dying—when he recorded his idea for the religion through which an abiding hope was to be sustained—his wish had been that the truth about him should never be known to any but those judged fit for stewardship. He had not wanted to be idolized as prophet and martyr.

"What went on before the ceremony this morning was—arranged, wasn't it?" Brek asked. "I relived the dream where the First Scholar was killed; I stood in the same spot outside the Gates while people threw mud at me, just as they'd thrown stones and knives at *him.* At first I was so stunned I thought I'd lose control of myself, and then it dawned on me that Stefred meant me to feel—well, honored."

"Of course. He honored you by recognizing that you look at things the way Scholars do, that you'd understand the symbolism, as well as the fact that if people like the ones in the crowd were given no outlet for their hatreds there'd eventually be bloodshed. But he meant you to feel something more, Brek."

Noren glanced around the smooth windowless walls of the refectory—ancient walls that had been constructed on one of the Six Worlds, since the Hall of Scholars, like all the Inner City's towers, was in reality a converted starship. He raised his eyes to the prismatic glass sunburst, symbol of the Mother Star, which was fixed to the center of the ceiling. "We agreed to go through that ceremony," he continued slowly, "because we'd learned not only that the prophesied appearance of the Mother Star is based on fact, but that changes are honestly expected to occur when the Star does appear. The Prophecy is what keeps people hoping. It's the only means of telling them that the world won't always be as it is now. In time, when the light of the nova reaches this planet and the real Mother Star becomes visible, the Prophecy's promises must come true; yet they can't be fulfilled if we don't manage to synthesize usable metal by then, so that we can build enough machines for everybody."

Brek frowned. "Is there any question about it? The starships that escaped the nova got here generations ago and Scholars have been working ever since to create metallic elements through nuclear fusion. Haven't they been making progress?"

"Brek," Noren said sadly, "you can't say *they* any more; you've got to say *we.* We're working under terrible handicaps—even worse handicaps than you could guess from the dreams—and if those of us who've proven ourselves fit for the job don't do it, the Prophecy will become as false and empty as we thought it was when we laughed at what sounded like a silly legend."

The words seemed stiff. Was it really possible, mused Noren, that he was not giving Brek the whole truth? Was he hiding not merely fear, but fact? He was repeating what he himself had once been told; he'd been utterly convinced of its validity; yet deep inside, he sensed that dreadful doubts were stirring. Pushing them back, he went on, "When we re-enact the dream, we take on all the responsibility it implies. That's what we're meant to feel, not so much during the ceremony as afterward, when it seems that we've been duped into selling out."

Thoughtfully Brek said, "I'm willing to do any work I'm given, just as I was willing to do what had to be done to uphold people's respect for the Prophecy and the High Law. But becoming a Scholar is something else again. It means giving the impression that I'm in favor of the way things are."

"You've already done that; you made your decision when you consented to the ceremony. What's the difference now?" Noren averted his face as he spoke, for he knew perfectly well what the difference was; night after night he had lain awake for hours on end, unable to come to terms with it. He wondered if he was hoping that Brek would tell him that no real difference existed.

"The difference," declared Brek bluntly, "is that during my recantation I was hated, but most people don't hate Scholars nowadays. They worship them."

Their eyes met, and there was no need to say anything further; neither of them was wearing the blue robe of priesthood, and that was not merely because the occasion wasn't formal enough to warrant it. "It's rightfully yours," Noren had said when he'd given Brek the clean clothes set aside for him, "but you need not put it on unless you choose to. The robe's a symbol; among us it represents full commitment. Scholar status was conferred on us without our knowledge or consent, but we are free to decide how we'll use that status, and whether we'll reveal it to anyone besides our fellow Scholars. So far I'm committed only to scientific training."

He had agreed to train for the research work that must be done if synthesization of metal was to be achieved, for Stefred had convinced him that he'd betray his own principles if he refused to contribute actively toward the Prophecy's fulfillment. It had been a difficult step to take. Like Brek he'd longed desperately for the training and had been incensed at the idea of receiving such an incredibly high privilege as the result of having conceded that the world could not be transformed overnight; still, reason had told him that it was the only course. The work was an obligation, not a reward, and the fact that he would enjoy it did not make it any less vital. But to assume the role of High Priest—to share responsibility for the control of the City's contents, or to appear in public, when he was old enough not to be recognized as a former villager, and receive people's homage—of that he wasn't at all sure. Yet somebody had to do it. Stefred hated it, and for that matter, so had the First Scholar. And the First Scholar had been wise enough to arrange things so that nobody who wanted that kind of power would ever have it.

The First Scholar had been wise in many ways, but his greatest accomplishment had been the creation of a scheme through which power could be held only by those who, under pressure, had proven themselves incorruptible. Never in the history of the Six Worlds had there been such a scheme. Authoritarian systems, benevolent or otherwise, had always selected leaders from among their supporters instead of their opponents. The First Scholar had loathed the forced stratification of society he'd established. While he'd been aware that without it, the human race would be unable to preserve the essential life-support equipment during the generations when the growing population must live and farm by Stone Age methods, his plans had centered on the day when the system could be abolished. He had had the wisdom to know that it would never be abolished if people who approved of it wound up on top.

So through the years, the secret truths had been passed to those who approved *least:* those who had offered their lives in opposition to the supposed tyranny. To be sure, some heretics failed to qualify; they were motivated by desire to seize power for themselves or they weakened during the stress of the inquisition and its aftermath. But these people suffered no harm. Though they could not be released, they had the status of Technicians and did work of their own choosing.

And the Scholars themselves could not be released, neither from the physical confines of the Inner City nor from the unsought burden of representing a system that, while indispensable to survival in the alien environment, was abhorrent to them. It was they, not the villagers, who lived in bondage.

"It's not easy," Noren declared as he and Brek left the Hall of Scholars and walked through the Inner City's enclosed courtyard toward one of the other towers, where Brek was to lodge with him.

"Stefred warned me in the beginning that a day would come when the consequences of my choice would seem so terrible that I'd beg to be let off," Brek admitted. "I thought he was threatening to kill me, and I scoffed. Later I thought he'd been referring to the nightmarish parts of the dreams, or to the ceremony, or to imprisonment. But this—"

"This is worse than anything we envisioned," agreed Noren. "We dedicated ourselves to resisting the Scholars' authority, and now we've become what we most despised."

On leaving the lift at the level of Noren's compartment, they paused by the passageway window. The afternoon had gone swiftly; it was dusk, and the ring of large domed structures—the Outer City—that encircled the clustered towers looked dark and forbidding, an even more impenetrable barrier from within than it had once seemed from without. "Noren," Brek ventured, "in your village...there was a girl, Talyra, wasn't there? A girl you'd planned to marry?"

Noren lowered his eyes; it still hurt to think about that, and he did not want to speak of it. "Scholars aren't barred from marriage," he said. "We can even marry Technicians."

"But not villagers."

"No," Noren replied shortly. He did not add that when certain conditions were met, villagers already married or betrothed to heretics could become Technicians, and that he'd dismissed the matter because he'd felt that in the City Talyra would be fearful and unhappy.

For a few moments they were silent. Far away across the fields stood the sharp silhouette of the Tomorrow Mountains, now pale below three crescent moons. "*'And Cities shall rise beyond the Tomorrow Mountains, and shall have Power, and Machines, and the Scholars will no longer be their guardians,'*" Brek quoted softly. "How soon, I wonder? It's not all going to happen on the day the Star appears! If we're to be ready by then, the Prophecy must begin to come true long before."

Noren, upset by Brek's uninformed confidence, did not answer. Then, behind them, a voice said, "Maybe it will be sooner than you think, at least in a small way."

Turning to greet the Scholar Grenald, the oldest and most distinguished of his tutors, Noren demanded, "What do you mean? Could it start in our lifetime after all?" The Time of the Prophecy—fixed by the distance in light-years to the Six Worlds' exploded sun and chosen by the First Scholar not only for its symbolic value, but because survival without more metal could scarcely continue long past the time the light of the nova would arrive—was still several generations in the future.

Though Grenald smiled, the worry in his tone belied the hopefulness of his words. He looked at Noren intently, pleadingly, as if he somehow expected confirmation from a mere trainee. "It could," he said. "You're aware that it will start as soon as the research succeeds—"

"Of course," agreed Noren hastily. The old man had been engaged for years in a series of experiments that was soon to culminate, and its outcome would give an idea of how much more research was needed; some Scholars felt that the results might point the way to an impending breakthrough. "We could be close, Grenald," Noren declared. But as he spoke undeniable fear surged up in his mind, for he knew that if they were not close, they might not be on the right path.

And if that was the case, the Prophecy might never come true...yet he and Brek, like others before them, had publicly denied their heresy solely on the grounds that it would.

That night Noren dreamed he was the First Scholar again. It was not a controlled dream induced by the Dream Machine that fed recorded thoughts into his brain; but since experiencing those in which he'd shared the First Scholar's thoughts, their content had recurred often in his natural dreams, particularly when he was tired or troubled. The controlled dreams of the revelation hadn't been enjoyable; they had been nightmares. Though after the first Noren had submitted to them willingly, his hunger for the truth being stronger than his fear, the emotions they'd roused still frightened him.

So over and over, when he slept, he watched the nova explode into a blinding sphere of intolerable fire that filled the starship's viewport; and usually he awakened then, drenched with sweat and hoping that he had not cried out aloud. But this time he dreamed on, images from his personal past mingling with those from the controlled dreams. He was the First Scholar, weighed down with the grief of what had been and what he knew must come, yet he walked through a village the First Scholar had never seen: the village where he, Noren, had been born. He saw the place—the rough stone houses, the sanded roads marred by sledge tracks and the hoofs of plodding work-beasts, the desolate gray shrubby areas surrounding quickened fields—through a Scholar's eyes, and it seemed even more dreary than when he'd been growing up there. He had the First Scholar's memory of the Six Worlds, of a civilization that had built interstellar ships! He was a stranger in the world where he found himself...

Yet it had always been that way. He'd been a misfit since childhood, for most villagers were not unhappy; they did not crave the sort of knowledge he had craved, or care about truth as he had always cared. They were content with the life they had. The Technicians who brought Machines to clear the land and to quicken it never interfered with anyone's personal freedom, and who but the impious would envy their right to handle those Machines? Who but a presumptuous fool would be concerned over why even greater wonders were reserved for the City alone?

"You are a fool, a lazy dreamer," Noren's brothers said to him as, dreaming, he found himself back in the house of his family. They were right, he suspected; he had no aptitude for crafts or trading and he was ill-suited to be a farmer, though for Talyra's sake he was prepared to try. He must try something, for he had absorbed the meager offerings of the village school and was a grown man by his people's standards, although on the Six Worlds he would have been thought too young to work, much less to marry. Such wasn't the case in this land of more primitive custom. His impending marriage was the one thing to which he looked forward with pleasure…

But even Talyra could not understand the urge that drove him to question the Prophecy. And so he turned his face to the City, the impenetrable stronghold of all knowledge, compelled by some inner longing that outweighed his belief that to enter it would mean death. In the way of dreams, his view was abruptly transposed. He feared not the City, but a future that might imperil it. If there were no City everyone would die—and if none dared challenge its mysteries, there would be no Scholars to keep it functioning. The ground he trod was permeated with a substance damaging to life that had evolved elsewhere; because the mutations it caused reduced mental capacity to a subhuman level, no biological adaptation would ever be possible. Machines must continue to inactivate the substance so that imported grain could be raised. The City was needed to guard all machines: not only those used in the fields, but the more complex ones for rainmaking, for purifying additional water, for irradiating grain seed—and for generating the nuclear power upon which the other machines depended. And of course, the City must safeguard the computers. In those computers' memories was stored the accumulated knowledge of the Six Worlds, and if that were ever lost, there could be no second beginning. There would be no chance of achieving what must be achieved if the new world was to become a place where humans could thrive…

"And the land shall remain fruitful, and the people shall multiply across the face of the earth, and at no time shall the spirit of the Mother Star die in the hearts of its children." He, Noren, stood again at the table in his father's farmhouse and said the words automatically, as he'd done before every meal, disbelieving them, yet maintaining the pose because that was the way life was. Besides, had not his mother believed them? His dream-self recalled how she'd died believing, died slowly and in pain because the Technicians had not arrived in time to save her from the poisonous briars…

But it was a native poison for which there was no cure; as the First Scholar, he too was dying of it. The scene of the dream shifted once more, and he lay within the City, realizing that such poison had been on the knife that had struck him down. He'd faced the mob at the Gates knowing what would happen, and knowing also that he could nullify his people's hatred in no other way. He had not known, however, how much pain there would be, or how long it would take to die. *"There shall come a time of great exultation...and at that time, when the Mother Star appears in the sky, the ancient knowledge shall be free to all people, and shall be spread forth over the whole earth. And Cities shall rise beyond the Tomorrow Mountains, and shall have Power, and Machines, and the Scholars will no longer be their guardians. For the Mother Star is our source and our destiny, the wellspring of our heritage; and the spirit of this Star shall abide forever in our hearts, and in those of our children, and our children's children, even unto countless generations…"* They were comforting words! True words! His friends could stop the pain, but if he allowed that, he could not record the words that were so important. Yet how had he found them? He'd tried for years to frame such words, and had failed, for he was no poet; he was only a scientist.

"And so long as we believe in it, no force can destroy us, though the heavens themselves be consumed…" It was Talyra who was saying them now, although that could not be, for had not she whom he loved died aboard the starship, died because the Six Worlds were gone and humanity was gone and she lacked the courage to live in a universe that seemed so empty? When he, the First Scholar, had looked down upon his wife's lifeless form, the face had been

Talyra's face... Still Talyra stood before him, alive, believing, and her sorrow was not for herself but for him. "May the spirit of the Mother Star go with you, Noren..."

As the voice faded Noren awoke, dazed and shaken, lying still while he sorted the dream from the reality he had so recently begun to understand. "The First Scholar did not write the Prophecy," Stefred had told him. "The idea was his, but the words are not in the recording; you supplied them yourself." And also, much later, "The last dream was particularly dangerous for you, since as a child you watched your mother die by the same poison. I hesitated, Noren. All the rules of psychiatry said I should not let you proceed. Yet what was I to do? You had proven yourself fit to become a Scholar; was I to disqualify you on account of a tragic coincidence that had already caused you more than enough hurt?"

That Stefred himself could be hesitant and unsure was something Noren hadn't realized until then. Scholars, as guardians of all mysteries, were, in the villagers' eyes, omniscient, and though he'd once thought them tyrants, he had not suspected that they were ever doubtful about anything. After coming to trust Stefred, he had assumed that the human wisdom was limited only in regard to the basic problem of creating metal. Gradually, however, he'd begun to discover that this was not the case. In the first place, no single Scholar knew everything that had been known on the Six Worlds. The amount of knowledge was so vast that it was necessary to specialize, and Stefred, as a specialist in psychiatry, had little training in other fields. Furthermore, in every field there were areas not thoroughly understood by the experts. The existence of such gaps amazed Noren. Truth was far more complicated than he'd supposed it to be when he had demanded free access to it; the further he got into his training, the more evident that became. On mornings like this one the thought was frightening...

His surroundings seemed somehow unfamiliar; as he came fully awake, Noren saw that it was because the room's study desk was folded back into the wall. When it was out, there was scarcely space to turn around, so to accommodate Brek he'd put it away for the first time since entering training. That was probably why he'd dreamed as he had. In talking things over with Brek, he had allowed his worries to surface, as he had not done on previous days when study had absorbed his entire mind.

All his life he'd sought opportunity to study; and, Noren reflected, this aspect of being a Scholar had surpassed his greatest hopes. He had natural talent for it—especially for mathematics, on which he had so far concentrated as the first step toward specialization in nuclear physics—and though he'd been told he was progressing much faster than average, the days were not long enough for all he wanted to learn. Much of his time was occupied with more sophisticated training techniques than the reading of study discs; still he always kept a disc on hand to use in spare moments. Brek, on the upper bunk that had until now been unoccupied, was still asleep. Noren rose and restored the study desk to its normal position before even putting on his clothes. It made the cramped room more comfortable, for any link to the Six Worlds' huge store of knowledge was, to him, a marvel that compensated for all the difficulties and confusions of his strange new life.

But as he settled himself silently before the desk's screen, the mood of his dream failed to pass. Talyra's face loomed between him and the information he was perusing; Talyra's voice echoed in his ears. Irritably, he blamed Brek for having raised the subject. Brek had been persistent, unwilling to let it drop; they had talked on after bidding Grenald goodnight. "She was the one who got you clothes after you left the jail, wasn't she?" Brek had said. "After watching her at the trial, I guessed she would, though I saw why you couldn't trust me enough to say so."

"I'm the one who should be asking your forgiveness," Noren had muttered, recalling his unfounded suspicion that a trap might be laid for Talyra also. "Yes, she gave me clothes and money, too, in spite of believing that to aid an escaped heretic was sinful."

Talyra was very devout; they'd quarreled bitterly when he had first told her of his heresy. She had broken their betrothal then, declaring that she would marry no man who did not revere the Mother Star, and when at his trial he had denied the Star's very existence, she had been genuinely horrified. But she had grieved for him, knowing that he would not back down to save himself, and had gone counter to all she'd been taught in order to help him. "Talyra believed every word of the Prophecy," he'd remarked to Brek, "and she was *right!* I just wish I could tell her that."

Brek had looked at him, frowning. "Without telling her why? You were both right, but she would still think you'd been wrong to question! And anyway, she may well have heard that you recanted."

"She didn't hear," Noren had said grimly. "She saw. She was there, and she must have thought what you thought when you were shown the films." In anguish he remembered the pain that had filled her eyes when the public sentence was passed upon him. The harshest consequence of heresy was that one could not comfort one's loved ones.

To be sure, a reunion might be arranged at the price of permanent Inner City residence for Talyra, but Noren had told Stefred that he would prefer separation. Talyra had her own life to live. After his arrest she had accepted the Scholars' appointment to the training center where she was preparing for the semi-religious and highly respected vocation of a village nurse-midwife. Though that appointment had been made partly so that her disappearance from home could be explained if she chose to share his confinement—a fact of which she herself was unaware—he couldn't ask her to make the sacrifices entrance to the Inner City would entail. It was better that she should suppose him broken and condemned to prison.

Noren dropped his head in his arms, too disconsolate to turn back to the normally fascinating study screen. All thought of seeing Talyra again was foolish in any case, for the decision was not his; a villager not convicted of heresy could gain entrance to the City only by requesting audience to plead the cause of someone who was imprisoned. Stefred had seemed to think Talyra might do that, but Noren knew she would never question the rightness of the High Priests' decision.

There was a knock at the door; hurriedly Noren opened it and stepped into the corridor, greeting in a low voice the man who stood there. He did not want Brek disturbed, not when the ordeals of the previous day had been so great and when other demanding things lay ahead.

The man, a casual acquaintance, had merely stopped by with a message. "Stefred wants to see you," he told Noren. "Right away."

"Right away? That's funny; yesterday he said not till I'd gotten Brek initiated into our routines. We had the whole schedule planned."

"I wouldn't know about that, but he spoke to me at breakfast and asked me to send you over to his office. It sounded urgent; maybe it's something to do with tonight's meeting."

"What meeting?"

"You haven't heard? I suppose not, if you haven't been downstairs yet, but there's a notice posted. We're to assemble right after Orison—all Scholars, even the uncommitted—in one general session. And from the look of the executive council people, I'd say something important's come up."

Chapter Two

Noren was always glad of a chance to talk with Stefred, who, as head of recruiting and training, maintained close friendships with all the people he had guided through the steps leading to Scholar status. He had little free time; still Noren had dropped by to see him occasionally, and had often felt the better for it, although he was invariably offered not consolation, but challenge. And of course, they had had several discussions within the past few days about Brek.

On his way up in the Hall of Scholars' lift, Noren recalled what had taken place during the last of those discussions. Stefred had been quieter than usual, and there had been something in his manner reminiscent of their early interviews, before any of the secrets had been revealed. "You're hiding something," Noren had accused finally. "If I'm to help Brek, I've got to know all the facts."

"I've told you all that are pertinent," Stefred had replied slowly. "But there are—other issues, Noren, and I don't want you sidetracked right now. If things work out as I expect, you may soon be placed under rather more pressure than is usual for a trainee of your age. Once again I may have to gamble on your ability to withstand it."

"Won't I have a choice?" Noren had demanded.

"Of course. But knowing you as I do, I'm pretty sure you'll choose involvement—and you won't understand what you're getting into until it's too late." Soberly Stefred had added, "Think that over. In a few days, once Brek is settled, we'll talk again."

Noren had indeed thought it over, and had been more curious than worried. He wasn't bothered by the fact that Stefred evidently didn't plan to explain whatever it was he'd be getting into, for he had learned that many of the things a Scholar met could not be explained. They had to be experienced. All the experiences he'd undergone so far had proved worthwhile: unpleasant at times, but on the whole exciting or at least enlightening. Training did involve pressure, but it wasn't a sort of pressure he disliked. Just one comment of Stefred's had made him wonder.

"The issues I'm referring to have nothing to do with your training," Stefred had said. "They are real."

Now, entering the familiar study, which, like the conference room where he'd met Brek, was one of the few places in the City that had windows, Noren began to piece things together. He had been too absorbed in his own problems, in Brek's, to do so before; he'd dismissed Grenald's remark about the Prophecy's coming true as the kind of wistful speculation sometimes heard from older Scholars who had few years left in which to see the research progress. *Maybe it will begin sooner than you think,* Grenald had said... There could be a connection with the issues Stefred had mentioned, and with the unusual meeting to be held that night. Scholars did not meet formally except on matters of gravest importance, and even then the uncommitted—those who had not assumed the blue robe and the obligations of priesthood it symbolized, and who therefore had no vote—were rarely included. Sudden hope lifted Noren's spirits. Perhaps a breakthrough was imminent! Perhaps there was no need to worry that he might have sanctioned an empty promise.

One look at Stefred confirmed the hints that something crucial had arisen. He was obviously troubled, more troubled than Noren had ever seen him, and he did not seem at all eager to proceed. "I must do some things I'd like to put off," he declared without preamble. "First, there are questions I've got to ask you. If it were possible, I would wait until you're further along in your training; failing that, I'd at least delay until your responsibility to Brek is finished. That's no longer feasible. You must cope with them now. Bear with me, Noren, if this hurts; I won't probe deeper than I have to."

"I don't mind questions," said Noren, settling himself in the chair next to Stefred's. "We've always been honest with each other."

"Yes. You will be more honest with me than you've been with yourself lately; that's why I would prefer not to do this yet. In time, you would confront the difficult parts spontaneously, but you're not quite ready." Stefred sighed. "Your tutors confirm what I already knew from the computers' measurement of your aptitude. Grenald in particular tells me that, potentially, you have one of the most brilliant scientific minds of your generation, and that if I upset it, I'll be accountable for any effect on your future contribution to the research. He is probably right. Yet I promised you a choice, and even if I hadn't, it's guaranteed to you by fundamental policy—which Grenald knows as well as I. Given such a choice, do you want me to continue?"

Confused, Noren groped for an answer. Stefred, he knew, expected more of him than simple assent; he must attempt to analyze the problem. It would not be spelled out for him. At length he ventured, "You couldn't upset my mind except by telling me something I'm not aware of. And if you're asking whether I'd rather not be told, well, you know the truth's more important to me than anything else."

"More important than the scientific work on which fulfillment of the Prophecy depends?"

"Is there a conflict?"

"For the sake of argument, assume there is."

"Then the truth—the whole truth—is more important. A part couldn't be more important than the whole."

Stefred, with evident reluctance, fixed his gaze directly on Noren and in one skillful thrust stripped away the armor built up through many weeks past. "Is that consistent with the fact that you've devoted practically every waking moment to technical studies since the day after your recantation?" he inquired softly.

Noren gasped, overcome by the extent of his own self-deceit. How had Stefred known? He had never hinted to Stefred that doubt about the work's ultimate outcome had entered his thoughts; not until he was watching Brek recant, in fact, had he admitted to himself that there might be truths from which he had hidden. Yet underneath he'd been aware that they existed. They'd emerged gradually from his increasing knowledge of science, and only concentration on its technical aspects had kept them back. The worries they'd raised could hardly be unfounded...

"Forgive me," Stefred said. "That was brutally abrupt, but it told me something I had to be sure of: you don't wish to use science as a shield. If you did, I couldn't have opened your eyes so quickly. Some Scholars take years to recognize what you just grasped." There was no reassurance in his tone, though the usual warmth came through; Stefred's honesty was what inspired people's confidence in him.

Straightforwardly he continued, "We have no time to go into this problem right now; you must grapple with it alone. And it's only the beginning, Noren. I'm leading up to more upsetting things."

"I—I hope you're not going to ask how I feel about wearing the robe," Noren faltered, sensing the direction events seemed to be taking. He was to be offered some challenging new task, one for which full commitment was undoubtedly a prerequisite...and much as he might want to accept, he could not yet become a High Priest—not when deeper reservations were mingling with his original ones.

"I must, Noren. You need give me no decision—you will never be pressed for that—but if you have strong leanings one way or the other, I've got to know."

"I honestly don't know myself, Stefred. If that's what you meant when you said I'd choose involvement—"

"It is not what I meant. I wouldn't presume to influence you in regard to commitment; it isn't a step to be taken lightly." As relief spread through Noren, Stefred went on, "Don't answer this next question if you don't want to; I have valid reasons for asking it, but not ones that entitle me to invade your privacy. Do you attend Orison, Noren?"

Turning away, Noren felt his face redden. "Not often."

"You've no need to look so guilty. Attendance isn't required of you, and surely you know that none of us thinks less of you for not going, as villagers and Technicians would. There are committed Scholars who serve as High Priests before the people but take no part in our private religious rituals."

"I don't feel guilty," said Noren. "I never felt any guilt for not having faith in religion, and I don't now." He paused, deciding what had caused the flush of shame; with Stefred there was no alternative to complete candor. "I'm embarrassed, I guess," he continued slowly, "because the private rituals like Orison are the one thing I've encountered here that makes no sense to me. I just don't see what they accomplish. The symbolism of religion was designed by the Founders to give hope to those who couldn't be told our secrets, to express truths that couldn't be stated in plain language. Yet as Scholars, we've learned the truth; our hope is in science. To the people we must speak of the Mother Star in symbolic words, but we who know the facts about it—what use have we for such symbols?"

"That's a perfectly legitimate question, and not one to be ashamed of."

"But look—I'm supposed to be so intelligent; I should be able to figure it out! There's got to be something I'm missing. *You* go to

Orison. Every time I've been, I've seen you there, and I—I've seen you enter while I stayed outside."

"Have you lost any respect for me because I do go?"

"Of course not. Why should I?"

Stefred smiled. "You might, if you were staying away merely to assert your independence."

Startled, Noren confessed, "It was that way in the beginning… though I don't think I knew it. But not any more." He had found that among Scholars, the right to independence was so plainly acknowledged that one had no need to assert it, and his boyhood antagonism toward religion had given way to genuine puzzlement. Though he'd been too busy to devote much thought to the problem, it was apparent not only that the villagers and Technicians expected more of the Mother Star than fulfillment of the Prophecy's promises, but that the High Priests endorsed this view. Were it not so incredible, he might even have concluded that they shared it.

"You've come further than you realize," Stefred commented. "Last year you wouldn't have believed that there were any mysteries you couldn't comprehend." Then, with a penetrating look that warned of disquieting words to come, he once more broached a painful topic. "Do you think it possible, Noren, that if you don't wholly understand my attitude toward the Mother Star, you also missed something in Talyra's?"

At the sound of the name Noren winced. First Brek and now Stefred, when for so long he'd repressed all thought of her! "There's no comparison," he asserted.

"If you see none, I won't pursue it. But there are other things you don't understand about Talyra, and in fairness to you I can't let them pass."

"What use is there in discussing them?" Noren burst out, a bit too sharply.

Quietly Stefred declared, "I called you here this morning to find out if you still love her. Your face tells me that you do."

Astonished, Noren abandoned all defenses. "I'll always love her," he agreed miserably.

"Enough to take on the burden of a relationship that would never be truly open—that would require you to conceal much of your inner life, respecting her beliefs without explaining yours?"

"It doesn't matter, really. You know I'll never see Talyra again; she'd have to take the initiative—"

"Which you've been sure she would not do. But she has."

"Talyra...requested audience?" Noren whispered, suddenly cold. "When?"

"Shortly after you recanted. I did not grant it then; I had to be sure that your feelings for each other would not be changed by separation. She was told merely that I would see her before she left the training center to return to her village as a nurse-midwife. However, something's developed that makes it necessary for me to act at once."

"And you—you want me to decide whether she's to stay here as a Technician? It's too soon, Stefred! I can't say whether we'd ever be able to marry." Such a marriage would not be permitted unless he revealed his true status by assuming the robe, for no Scholar could take a wife who was unaware of his obligation to keep major secrets from her. Yet not all the secrets could be kept. Once admitted to the Inner City, Talyra would know too much to leave; Technicians who entered were, like the Scholars themselves, subject to lifelong confinement. And they too had to give up their children for adoption by village families, since a child who grew up knowing that Scholar rank wasn't hereditary would have been doomed to a confinement not of his own choosing. These sacrifices were made gladly by those who considered Inner City work a high honor—but to let Talyra make them for the sake of a love that might remain hopeless...

"The final decision will be mine, based on her wishes as well as yours," Stefred told him, "but I cannot admit her without your consent. The problems are difficult and complicated. With Talyra there's a special complication, since she was present at your recantation and therefore knows that you were not only a heretic, but impenitent. That knowledge will make her ineligible for Scholar status once she learns you have attained it, even if she becomes a heretic herself."

"Talyra would never do that!" Noren exclaimed.

"No, probably not. Though she is braver than you realize, I don't think she has that particular sort of mind. Nevertheless, the opportunity is every citizen's birthright, and it would be unjust to bar her prematurely from it. Your marriage must therefore be postponed. You must promise to delay any revelation of your rank until we're sure that adjustment to City life won't cause her to develop heretical views."

"I see that," Noren concurred, "though in her case it's just a formality." Inner City Technicians did not witness recantations and naturally assumed that any heretic who was made a Scholar had been penitent. The few who'd accidentally learned otherwise before entering the Inner City were necessarily excluded from candidacy because they alone, of all non-Scholars, were aware that unrepented defiance of the system could result in personal gain; the tests of incorruptibility were for them not valid. It was right that care should be taken to ensure that no potential heretic gained such awareness. But as far as Talyra was concerned, he was more worried about another injustice. "There'll be no difficulty about postponement," he continued, "because if I do decide to assume the robe, it won't be soon. That's the trouble; it's so unfair to her—"

"She has no expectation of marrying you, Noren, and if she loves you and has continued to grieve for you, she'll be happier here than outside, believing you a prisoner. She can serve as a nurse-midwife as well here as in the village, after all. She might even study to become a doctor."

"I—I'm not sure she could adapt. She's so unwilling to change the way she looks at things."

"Is she? That doesn't follow from the fact that she wouldn't give up her faith on your say-so. I suspect that Talyra can adapt quite well; the question is whether you can. The stress on you will be very great—too great, Grenald thinks." In an impassive voice Stefred added, "In his opinion I'd be a fool to let you involve yourself with a girl."

Indignantly Noren protested, "Look, I have every respect for Grenald, but—well, he's old enough to be my great-grandfather."

"Yes. He is an old man who has devoted most of his life to research that he won't live to see completed, and who gave up his children as infants. He may have grandchildren and great-grandchildren, but he knows neither their names nor the villages where they live. Now you've come—and you are his heir, Noren. Of all the young people he has taught, you are the one most likely to advance the work that his generation cannot finish. Can you blame him if he doesn't want you distracted from it?"

Again Noren flushed. Stefred was the most compassionate man he had ever known, but he could be harsh at times when he had to be, and he'd implied from the outset that this was one of those times. Didn't the priority of the research override all other considerations? "You're telling me I have no alternative," Noren said, striving to keep the emotion out of his own voice. "If I'm really dedicated—if I'm sincere in what I've always claimed about my willingness to sacrifice anything necessary to make the Prophecy come true—I should forget Talyra and commit myself to the job, whether or not I go so far as to accept the role of High Priest."

Surprisingly, Stefred frowned. "That would be the easiest way," he said after a short silence.

"Easy?" Noren echoed in bewilderment. Stefred was usually so perceptive...

"It would be easiest," Stefred repeated, "but if you elect that course, I'll thank you not to do so under the illusion that I advised it. I thought you knew me better by now, but if you don't, at least bear in mind what we established a few minutes ago. The work, vital though it is, remains part of a larger whole."

"But if I've used study as a shield against...problems," protested Noren, "they're problems related to our work! They're connected with—with fulfillment of the Prophecy; if I face them, I'll be more absorbed by that than ever. I don't see the comparison you're drawing."

"I don't suppose you do," Stefred conceded. "You are very young, and martyrdom still has its appeal." He leaned forward, saying gently, "Under other circumstances I would not go into this when you're unready to work it out on your own. In one brief talk I'm having to cover ground that should be explored over a period of weeks, perhaps years—and it's unfair to demand a decision that you are not mature enough to make with full understanding. Yet in the real world I'm bound not by what should be, but by what is, and the events of the moment force us to decide Talyra's future today."

Noren, thoroughly baffled, gave up the attempt to resolve the issue and asked humbly, "Will you help me, Stefred?"

"If you mean will I choose the shape of your life for you, no. But I'll tell you my own view of it." He turned toward the window, looking out beyond the City to the open land that he himself had not walked upon since youth. Slowly he said, "I've been quite frank about our hope for you as a scientist, a hope that was born during your childhood when Technicians under our direction watched you and subtly encouraged you in the path of heresy. Grenald is not the only one who believes you'll someday be instrumental in achieving the breakthrough that's been sought since the First Scholar's time. But you were not brought here to be an extension of the computer complex. You are a human being with the right and the responsibility to become enmeshed in human problems, personal problems. You must make sacrifices, yes—we all must, for we are stewards of our people's heritage, and the ultimate survival of the human race rests upon us. But we do not sacrifice our humanity. We do not give up the thoughts and feelings and relationships of our individual lives. If we did, our dedication would in the end be self-defeating; we would have no more chance of fulfilling the Prophecy than computers alone would have."

Staring at him, Noren saw the Chief Inquisitor in a way he never had before, despite their months of friendship. Stefred himself had once been married. His wife had been a Scholar, one of the few village women to seek knowledge beyond the station in which custom had placed her. She had been killed accidentally during a nuclear research experiment. There had no doubt been children who'd become craftsworkers or farmers somewhere, proud of their status as adopted sons or daughters without dreaming that their true father still lived. Or perhaps they had become heretics; perhaps they were now Scholars themselves! Stefred would not know. Even if he had presided at their inquisitions, he would not know, for though babies were placed only with good and loving families, no records of parentage were kept. Chagrined, Noren began, "What you said about Grenald—"

"Was meant merely to remind you that he too is human."

"I—I've oversimplified things, I guess."

"Sometimes one must in order to keep one's balance."

"I don't really want to, though. And I do want Talyra here if she wants to come."

"So I thought." Stefred rose, "I'm sure you've guessed that I'm concerned about more today than you and Talyra, that this issue is related to a larger one. At tonight's meeting you will learn the facts. Noren, there are two things you must go through before you learn. I would not subject you to them in quick succession if it were not an emergency."

"That's all right," Noren assured him, though inwardly he was already more deeply shaken than he cared to admit. The day was apparently to be as demanding for him as for Brek.

* * *

Several hours later, after introducing Brek to the computer room where Scholars were free to call forth any information they cared to about the Six Worlds, Noren met Stefred in the courtyard beside the inner gates that led to the City's exit dome. "It's best for you to be present when I interview Talyra," Stefred had told him. "It will not be an easy thing to witness, and you won't be allowed to speak; but she will need you, Noren. Merely seeing you will give her confidence."

Noren shuddered. It would be necessary, he knew, to determine not only Talyra's willingness to enter the Inner City, but her ability to adapt to customs totally unlike those under which she'd been reared; and neither issue could be approached directly. "If I'm not convinced that she'll be happy here, I shall send her away," Stefred warned. "You will have to watch her go, knowing that you won't see each other again, and she'll be unaware that it might have been otherwise. Do you love her enough to endure that?"

"Yes," Noren said steadily. "But Stefred, she can't be given enough information for her to decide whether she'll be happy until it's too late for her to go back."

"She won't need information; she will judge and be judged by her feelings and her sense of values, just like a Scholar candidate, during my talk with her."

Noren frowned; Stefred's talks with people were apt to be grueling. "Will you—test her, then?" he asked worriedly.

"Yes, briefly, but there's no danger in it; I promise you she won't be hurt in any lasting way."

As they walked down the wide corridor that stretched toward the main Gates and outer platform where public ceremonies were held, Noren's pulse accelerated. He had not been in this dome, nor indeed in any other, since the day of his recantation; the huge domes that ringed the area of closely spaced towers were Outer City, off limits to Scholars and Inner City Technicians. Exceptions were made when it was necessary for a Scholar to appear publicly, to interview someone, or to investigate trouble with equipment such as the nuclear power plant, which was normally maintained by ordinary Technicians who lived in the domes and were free to go outside. But Noren had as yet done none of these things. The research laboratories, where he'd sometimes assisted, were located in the towers themselves.

Walking beside Stefred, Noren thought back to the last time he'd passed through the corridor, recalling how clear-cut the Founders' decision had seemed to him then. Prone though he'd always been to question, he had not questioned their conviction that the sealing of the City would result in discovery of a way to change the world. He had known too little of science to guess that the essential research might fail. He'd acknowledged the Prophecy's truth only because he'd believed that it *was* true, literally, despite its symbolic form—nothing could have induced him to recant on any other basis. Nothing else could have justified his acceptance of a rigid caste system under which most people were deprived both of technology and of all but the most rudimentary education.

When, in recanting, Noren had endorsed that system, he had done so in the belief that synthesization of metal was only a matter of time. He had assumed that if the Scholars went on doing their job, there could be no doubt about cities and machines someday becoming available to everyone. Once he'd begun to study, however, he had found that research didn't work that way. If scientists didn't know how to do something, then they had no real proof that it could ever be done. And so far the Scholars hadn't learned how to achieve nuclear fusion of heavy elements. Their progress over the years had consisted mainly of eliminating once-promising possibilities. To be sure, the current experimentation offered hope of another possibility; but hope was not the same as assurance. Would he have proclaimed the Prophecy to be "true in its entirety" if he had realized that? Noren wondered. Would he have freely renounced his opposition to the Scholars' authority as "false, misconceived and wholly pernicious?"

Those statements echoed in Noren's mind as he and Stefred continued along the corridor leading toward the platform where he had made them. The memory was all the more vivid because Stefred was robed; as a known Scholar, he could not show himself to Talyra—or in fact to any villager or Outer City Technician—without covering his ordinary clothes. And even so, such face-to-face discussions were few. Routine business was carried on by radiophone, for only thus could the air of mystery surrounding the Scholars be preserved.

The small windowless room they entered contained a desk and several chairs, all made of the white plastic material with which the starships had been outfitted. Most City furnishings were similar and had been in continuous use throughout the generations since the Founding. That would have been thought strange on the Six Worlds, Noren had been told; there, people had recycled things long before they wore out simply for the sake of variety. Variety was one of the luxuries the City could not afford. Even the homes of the villagers, who made their own furniture from softstone, wicker and the hides of work-beasts, were less monotonous. For that reason Outer City Technicians sometimes bought village-made furniture although it was relatively uncomfortable; their quarters were more spacious than those of Inner City people, and unlike the Scholars—who, as stewards, were not permitted to own anything—they had money.

Waiting, Noren turned his mind to Talyra, trying to quell the hope that had risen within him. Even if she wanted to join him, she might not measure up. She was so very devout, so unwilling to question the superiority of the Technician caste, that she could easily give a wrong impression. Stefred would not accept anyone who believed that being a Technician meant having the right to look down on the villagers.

She is braver than you realize, Stefred had said. She must be, Noren reflected, if she had requested the audience. Any villager would feel terror at personal contact with the awesome High Priests who, under ordinary circumstances, were seen only at a distance. And Talyra had additional cause to be afraid. Supposing them omniscient, she would fear that they were aware that she'd once helped him elude their custody.

"You won't let on that you know about her part in my escape from the village, will you?" he asked anxiously.

"I shall have to," Stefred told him. "She'll expect it. Since those who request audience are informed that their past lives will be investigated, her coming here is tantamount to an open confession. And though a villager normally can't be accused by Technicians or Scholars unless first convicted by his peers, a student at the training center is under our jurisdiction."

"She took the risk deliberately," mused Noren. "Why?"

"Why did you take the ones you took? You wanted something, wanted it so much that you ignored everything reason told you and followed your heart instead."

"But she has no hope of even seeing me."

"She hopes to help you through intercession on your behalf. Also, though you may find it hard to fathom, it's likely that she's torn by guilt over what she did—which is not the same as regretting it—and is seeking to declare herself and take the consequences. That is a form of honesty, Noren."

Maybe it was, Noren thought, recalling the suggestion that he might have misinterpreted Talyra's attitude. In the village they'd argued from opposite premises—she, that Scholars could do no wrong; he, that they could do no right—and neither view had been based on any real knowledge of the situation. Yet of the two, his had been the more dogmatic. There had been no doubt in his mind that it explained everything. Talyra, on the other hand, had believed both in the goodness of the Scholars and in the injustice of his imprisonment. Honesty was simple when one's convictions didn't conflict; now that he was facing doubts and conflicts of his own, he was beginning to see why she had seemed so bound by unexamined assumptions.

"She'll accept your reassurance," he said, "but as for the rest, it may be hard to get across. The very idea of becoming a Technician may—well, shock her. Talyra's awed by Technicians; she won't admit to herself that she's as smart as they are."

"She will admit it to me," Stefred said. "I've dealt with many candidates, Noren, and I know how to find out what they really want." He paused. "I'll have to frighten her a little in order to be sure of her true feelings; and to make her aware of them herself, I'll need to be a bit cruel. You must be silent and let me handle it; you must not offer any encouragement, for if you do, her choice will not be wholly free."

Nodding, Noren strove to master his turbulent thoughts. Not since their parting had he dared to envision Talyra deliberately: her face; her long dark curls; her slim figure clad in a tunic and underskirt of the light green worn for holidays and other religious affairs, adorned by blue glass beads of spiritual devotion and today, perhaps, by the red love-beads he'd once given her…

The door opened; she stood there between two uniformed Technicians, pale but with her head held high. At the sight of him her face was illumined with a brief, astonished joy that turned quickly to anguish. She thought him a prisoner, Noren realized miserably; she would feel terror for him as well as for herself. He longed to go to her, comfort her, but he knew he must not. Talyra must have a fair chance to withdraw.

Stefred dismissed the Technicians, motioning Talyra forward, and she knelt at his feet. "That is not necessary," he said brusquely. "It is done only on formal occasions. Sit beside me, Talyra."

"Yes, Reverend Sir," she replied, using the form of address employed in public ritual. She rose and took the chair offered her.

"'Sir' alone is sufficient." Glancing at Noren, Stefred added reflectively, "It would be well, Talyra, for you to become somewhat less worshipful in regard to Scholars."

Noren gulped. If Talyra were ever to address *him* as 'Reverend Sir,' he would be too embarrassed to speak.

"You have requested audience with us," Stefred went on, "ostensibly to plead clemency for someone you love. Yet we think perhaps you may also seek our pardon on your own behalf. Surely you know what has come to our attention in our review of your past."

"I—I think so, sir." Though her voice wavered, she appeared less dismayed than Noren himself by the directness of Stefred's approach and his use of the cold, ceremonious *we.*

"We must accuse you of having once helped this man, a self-proclaimed heretic, to escape. You cannot be required to confess to us; it is your right to demand a civil trial. If you waive that right, however, you must swear to answer my questions truthfully and to accept my judgment."

"I do waive it, sir. I have no wish to deny the charge."

"Swear, then."

"I swear by the Mother Star that I will tell you the truth." Talyra drew a breath and added hastily, "But I wouldn't sir, if it were not that Noren is already condemned! I'd never tell anything that would hurt him; I only hope I can make you see that he doesn't deserve such a terrible punishment as—as was announced."

"You must pledge also to accept my judgment, Talyra."

"I so swear, as far as my own case is concerned—but not for Noren's!"

Stefred leaned forward across the desk, fixing his gaze on her. "You must care deeply for him to feel yourself a better judge of his heresy than I. Or are you too an unbeliever? Do you perhaps consider denial of the Prophecy no crime at all?"

Talyra looked horrified. "Sir, I believe the Prophecy! I have never questioned it! Upon my oath—"

"Your oath by the Mother Star is worthless as a defense," the Scholar said dryly, "since if you were indeed an unbeliever, it would have no meaning for you." He frowned. "Talyra, heresy is a very grave charge. You say you do not think Noren deserves life imprisonment, yet have you ever heard of any heretic who was seen again after his recantation? And not all heretics recant. Some are not even charged publicly, for if they waive civil trial, as you have just done, their cases are not made known in the villages."

Talyra met his eyes. "I did not waive a heresy trial," she declared firmly. "I am not a heretic, and no court would convict me. You told me merely that I am accused of helping Noren, and that is the only crime I've admitted."

"That's quite true," Stefred agreed. "I wasn't trying to trap you, Talyra, but I had to assure myself that you have the wit not to incriminate yourself falsely. If you didn't have, it would be improper for me to continue this interview without appointing someone to defend you, for though you are not yet formally charged with heresy, it's possible that I will find grounds for such a charge in your responses."

"What reason could you have for even suspecting me?" cried Talyra indignantly. "I helped Noren because I love him, but I never agreed with what he said—he'll tell you so himself!"

The Scholar eyed her intently. "What would you say if I were to tell you that he has said the exact opposite: that he has not only reported your part in his escape, but has claimed that you shared and encouraged the false beliefs that he has now abjured?"

By great effort, Noren avoided her incredulous stare. One look from him, and she would know what to say; he must not give her any clue. Stefred, he realized, was testing them both by these tactics, for if he feared her answer enough to influence it, it would be proof that he was unwilling to accept a decision based on Talyra's feelings alone.

In a cold dull voice Talyra declared, "I would say that you were lying. I didn't think Scholars could lie, but if you tell me *that,* I'll have to believe they can. You are setting a trap for me after all, sir. To accuse a Scholar of lying would indeed be heresy."

"You have nothing to fear from me as long as you are honest," Stefred assured her. "The point at issue here is your motive for helping Noren. To have helped him simply because you love him is one thing, but to have done it because you held heretical beliefs yourself would be something else. So you see I must determine whether you really do love him. If you do, it would be impossible for you ever to believe that he'd done what I suggested. He hasn't, of course. I did not say he had; I merely said *if.*"

Talyra's tense face relaxed into a faint smile. "You're very wise, sir. I just can't think you'll really lock Noren up for the rest of his life! He—he was always honest, too; doesn't that count for something? He was wrong, and he's admitted it—but he believed what he said. Would you have wanted him to lie? Would you have wanted him to repent not having lied?"

"Certain things have inescapable consequences," Stefred said quietly. "Noren is to be confined within the City permanently and nothing can change that; it is the consequence of heresy. But you don't really know much about the City, after all. Has it occurred to you that life inside may not be so terrible? The Technicians live here; I live here myself."

"But not as a prisoner, sir!"

"No? Have you ever seen a Scholar outside the City?"

She shook her head, confused. "Yet you could go outside if you wanted to. You could do anything you wanted to."

"Why is it," said Stefred, sighing, "that people so often think that those above them can do anything they want? It works the other way, Talyra. I have a good deal less choice than you do. If Scholars did whatever they liked, Noren's suspicion would have been all too accurate; they would be unworthy guardians."

To Noren's relief, Talyra's expression showed that she was thinking, and the new thoughts didn't seem unduly disturbing. His concern had been groundless, maybe; he'd feared that the process would be more painful.

There was a short silence; then Stefred began an innocuous line of questioning quite evidently designed to lead directly to the decision. "Is there anyone outside the City for whom you care more than for Noren?"

"No, sir."

"Not even anyone in your family?"

"I love my family, but I was planning to marry Noren. Now I'll never marry anyone."

"What are you going to do, then? Do you really want to be a nurse-midwife?"

"Yes, I like the work at the training center."

"Yet you turned down the appointment when it was first offered."

"That was because it meant delaying our marriage."

"Why was getting married right away so important? Were you eager to have children?"

Noren held his breath. He and Talyra had never discussed that, for it had been assumed as a matter of course; in the villages a woman who bore few babies was scorned. The rearing of large families was considered a religious virtue. He did not know whether a family was important to her for its own sake, but if it was, she should not enter the Inner City, and Stefred would undoubtedly send her away.

"You don't understand," Talyra said. "Noren and I were in *love.*"

Slowly Stefred continued, "I do understand. Suppose, Talyra, that you had to choose again whether or not to help him; would you do the same thing?"

"Yes."

"What if it meant that you would suffer the consequences of heresy even though you yourself had not incurred them? What if it meant that your family and friends might never learn what had become of you?"

Talyra met his eyes bravely. "I'd do it."

"Then you're as unrepentant as he is? You still love him, and you won't ever be sorry?"

"That's right, sir."

It was going to work out, thought Noren joyously. In a moment Stefred would tell her, and the ordeal would be over...

And then he saw that the true ordeal had not yet even begun.

With Stefred's next words, Noren knew what the Chief Inquisitor was going to do; and he was appalled. Talyra's wits were sharp, but she would be defenseless against an expert assault on her misconception of herself. He wished heartily that he had never agreed to let her be questioned.

"When a person loves someone that much," Stefred was saying, "it's only natural for her to be influenced by his opinions. Surely you did not disagree with all of Noren's ideas."

"Of course not, only with the heretical ones," Talyra said confidently, too naive to sense her peril.

"He must often have told you that the things here in the City should be available to everyone, and not just to Technicians and Scholars. Did you agree with that?"

"It is not in accordance with the High Law."

"I know the High Law, Talyra. I am asking whether you agreed with that particular idea of Noren's, and you are bound to answer truthfully."

She dropped her eyes. "I—I agreed that it would be good for everyone to have things," she admitted in a low voice. "But they will have them after the Mother Star appears."

Oh, Talyra, thought Noren hopelessly, *the orthodox answer won't do for Stefred! For the village council that would be a clever reply, but Stefred will hang you with it.*

"Yet what if when it appears," the Scholar went on, "the Technicians decide to keep everything for themselves?"

Shocked, Talyra protested, "That couldn't happen."

"How do you know it couldn't? Have you never met a person who might want to?"

"Yes, but such people aren't Technicians."

"Noren believed otherwise. He believed that Technicians were ordinary men and women like the villagers. Suppose, for instance, that you yourself were a Technician—"

"Don't mock me, sir," she pleaded.

"I am not mocking you. Suppose you woke up one day to find yourself a Technician. Would you feel glad to have things that other people don't, or would you wish that the Mother Star would appear sooner so that you could share them?"

Talyra was almost in tears. "How can I answer? I'd want to share, of course, yet if I picture myself in that position, I'm committing blasphemy by thinking of myself as Noren used to."

Ruthlessly Stefred drove the point home. "Come now, Talyra—do you really, deep inside, believe that you'd be unable to do the work of a Technician, or that you would not enjoy it?"

She buried her face in her hands. Noren's grip tightened on the arms of his chair and he half-rose, but Stefred shook his head, going himself to Talyra and laying a firm hand on her shoulder. "You have sworn by the Mother Star that you'll tell me the truth," he said impassively. "To break such an oath is a worse offense than the other."

"I am guilty, then," she sobbed. "I didn't even know it before, but you were right about me!"

"You acknowledge these ideas? Think, Talyra! Your answer may determine the whole course of your future."

"I can't deny them. My guilt's greater than Noren's, for he at least was not a hypocrite."

Her despair was more than Noren could bear. He would never forgive himself, he thought; he should have known that Stefred's relentless approach to truth, so exhilarating to himself, would destroy Talyra. She'd been happy with her illusions; why had he let himself be convinced that she could remain happy after those illusions were gone?

"No!" he burst out. "I'll not let you do this to her!"

"Be silent! If she's to face what's ahead, she must see herself for what she really is."

"Let her go free," Noren begged, his lips dry. "Don't make her face it for my sake."

"Having gone this far, Noren, I must proceed for her own sake; to stop now would be misplaced mercy."

Raising her head, Talyra faltered, "I—I never asked for mercy, sir. Even for Noren I asked only justice."

"And you seemed convinced that in the end I would be just. I promise you that I shall be."

"I believe that. You have exposed my impiety, which I most heartily repent; I don't expect to escape—consequences."

Noren cringed. To him, the kindness in Stefred's tone was evident, but to Talyra, who had been forced to confess what she thought was an unforgivable crime, it would not be; and he knew that Stefred would probe her further. Underneath she could not actually feel she'd done any wrong; she must be compelled to admit that, too. Otherwise she'd remain forever unconvinced of her worthiness to be a Technician.

"So be it, Talyra," the Scholar said decisively. He returned to the desk and faced her. "Because you have helped and defended Noren and have even accepted some of his ideas, you must share his fate. You shall be confined within the City, as he is; you will never see the village of your birth again."

She swayed, staring at him, obviously overwhelmed by the seeming severity of the sentence. She had expected punishment, but not the punishment she'd considered too great, even for Noren. In panic, Noren clenched his hands. Stefred had promised that there would be no danger! Yet he had gambled and made a pronouncement from which there could be no turning back—what would happen if she failed to rise to the challenge? As long as she was contrite, she could not qualify.

"Do you want to retract anything you've said?" Stefred asked.

"N—no, sir." Talyra whispered.

"Do you think the verdict too harsh?"

"I—I deserve it, I guess."

The Scholar shook his head. "Talyra, you're being dishonest either with me or with yourself. You know in your heart that you've never harmed anyone and that your inner thoughts are not evil; you can't possibly feel that you deserve life imprisonment any more than Noren does. Tell me what you do feel, not what you think I want to hear."

"I feel such a penalty's heavy in proportion to the offense," she admitted, "but if it must be Noren's, I'm willing to share it. You've shown me that I'm no less presumptuous than he."

"And is presumption to be punished equally with crimes of violence? For that matter, is any form of heresy? Here in the City even a murderer would receive no worse! Really, Talyra—is that fair?"

Talyra stood up, flushed, at last jolted into questioning the shaky premises of the villagers' brand of orthodoxy. "No," she said, "it's not fair. My thoughts may be blasphemous, but they are my own, as Noren's were his; and as you've said, they never hurt anybody. I came here believing myself innocent of all heresy, but your effort to find it in me has fanned its flame. There's no need to goad me into any more incriminating statements. I will give you one freely: I hereby abjure my penitence, for you have made me see that Noren's doubts about the High Law were justified."

Good for you, Talyra! Noren cried inwardly. A mere indication that she was no longer sorry would have been enough, but by stating it formally, she had shown her true courage. In her view, if there was anything worse than a heretic it was a relapsed heretic—one who returned to heretical beliefs after having retracted them—and she had laid herself open to that charge.

She trembled a little, awaiting retribution, and then bewilderment crossed her face as Stefred answered, "I did so deliberately, Talyra. Later you will understand why." To Noren he said. "All right. It's finished; go to her now. The rest will come better from you than from me."

Noren, with pounding heart, came forward to take Talyra in his arms. She clung to him, her eyes glistening. "I'm glad it turned out this way," she said softly, giving him no chance to speak. "I could never have been happy in the village thinking of you here in prison; now at least I'll be close by. And I—I see things clearer, Noren. Some of what you used to say makes more sense. Underneath I must have known it did; the Scholar judged me rightly."

"He wasn't mistaken, then, in deciding you'd rather be here with me than return to the village where we'd never see each other again?"

"Be with you? You mean I'll be allowed to see you—often?"

"As often as you like," Noren told her, smiling. "We're not going to be punished, Talyra. I didn't understand either when I was sentenced—we weren't meant to—but the Scholar Stefred never said we'd be put in prison; he simply forbade us to leave the City."

"But—but only Scholars and Technicians live in the City! And besides, we've broken the High Law—"

"I broke it, but I've recanted and been pardoned. You never broke it at all. In the Scholars' eyes you're completely innocent."

"How could I be, Noren? Helping you to escape may have been just a civil offense, but I'm still guilty of blasphemy."

"No," said Noren gently. "I was right about some things; it's not blasphemous to think you'd like to be a Technician. Talyra, you are a Technician now! Stefred had to make sure you wanted it before he passed judgment, because no one who's aware that not all Technicians are born to their status can be released."

She stared, wide-eyed. "Are *you* a Technician, too?"

Noren had learned long before that one could conceal without lying. "As you said, only Scholars and Technicians live in the City," he told her. "A heretic who recants is confined here because of the secrets he knows, but he lives and works like the others."

Talyra, for the moment speechless, turned to Stefred in a mute appeal for confirmation. His smile was warm, yet solemn. "There is nothing in the High Law that prevents a villager who is qualified from becoming a Technician or even a Scholar," he said. "There can never be anything wrong in a person's wanting to know more than he knows, or be more than he has been; the Law specifies only that those who do choose that course can never go back."

He rose and walked to the door. Freeing herself from Noren's embrace, Talyra followed, holding out her hands in the ritual plea for blessing. As Stefred extended his, she knelt, and this time he did not forbid her; she would have felt crushed, rejected, if he had, for she sought not to pay homage but to receive. But before the words could be pronounced, she looked anxiously over her shoulder. "Noren?"

In dismay, Noren watched her new glow of confidence fade to troubled confusion at his failure to kneel beside her. He moved to do so, but with a barely perceptible shake of the head Stefred stopped him. No pretense would be permitted. Not yet High Priest, he was nevertheless a Scholar, and one Scholar could neither kneel to another nor receive from his hands what faith alone could bestow; Talyra's distress could not alter that. And this would not be the last time he would have to hurt her.

The flowing sleeves of Stefred's blue robe hid her face as he intoned the formal benediction: *"May the spirit of the Mother Star abide with you, and with your children, and your children's children; may you gain strength from its presence, trusting in the surety of its power."* Surety? thought Noren bitterly. But there was no surety! One could not trust that the Star's heritage of knowledge would lead to a transformation of the world, for it was quite possible that it would not. That was the truth he'd hidden from, the thing he was learning from science, and there was indeed no going back. He wondered how Stefred could sound so sincere.

Chapter Three

Alone together, Noren and Talyra forgot all doubts and fears in the joy of their reunion. Then, later, he took her through the corridor into the Inner City that was to be her whole world; and though it was strange and awesome to her, she did not seem to mind. To Noren the high spires of the towers that had once been starships were beautiful because of all that was preserved there. He'd thought that Talyra, who must remain ignorant of their origin and who had never craved more knowledge than was useful in the village, would find them disturbingly alien. She did not. She found them holy. In her own way, she too considered them the abode of truth.

They stood hand in hand, with the sun streaming down between the lustrous towers to the incongruously rough pavement of the courtyard, while he told her all he could about the life in store for her, amazed by the serenity with which she confronted it. Talyra had always thought it proper for the Scholars to have secrets, so the fact that anyone who learned some of those secrets must be kept permanently within the walls was in her view very logical. That among Technicians Inner City work was an honor seemed natural to her; that she herself should be so honored filled her with gladness. Slowly, Noren began to see that he'd underestimated Talyra. She had never been unwilling to accept new ideas. Her convictions were entirely sincere, and the discovery that the exaggerated teachings of the prevalent religion weren't officially endorsed merely strengthened those convictions. "I've said all along that our sacred duty is to the spirit of the Mother Star." she declared. "If some of what people think about it is mistaken, so what? Do you suppose I'd take my *family's* word over a *Scholar's?"*

She was surprised, of course, to learn that Scholars were not born, but appointed; yet this did not shock her either. "How are people chosen?" she asked curiously.

"That is a deep secret," Noren replied gravely. "Only the Scholars themselves are allowed to know that." It was an answer that satisfied her completely.

All the things he had expected to have trouble in presenting—that Scholars wore robes only for ceremonies and audiences; that one did not kneel to them on other occasions; that Inner City people, whether Scholars or Technicians, commonly ate together, shared leisure time, and even intermarried—proved easy for Talyra to accept. There was just one point that was awkward. "Noren," she asked hesitantly, "can former heretics marry, too?"

He was prepared; he'd known well enough that the matter must be discussed. "A heretic must have the permission of the Scholars," he told her, "but in time, it is often granted." He drew her toward him, fingering the red necklace she wore, the betrothal gift he had bought in the village with coins hoarded throughout his boyhood. "You know, don't you, that we'd get married right away if I were free to?"

"Of course."

"There are reasons why I am not free, and I—I don't know when I will be. There may be a long wait. It may never be possible at all." Painfully he added, "You are not bound by such restrictions. If someone else were to ask you, you could marry him whenever you wished."

"Oh, Noren! As if I would!"

"It's likely that you'll have suitors," he said frankly. It was all too likely, since because of the way girls were reared in the villages, far fewer women than men became heretics. Although unmarried Technician women who requested Inner City work were frequently brought in, they did not stay unmarried long. He could hardly ask Talyra to wait for him. Yet neither could he pretend that he had left her free, he thought miserably, for obviously she *would* wait, whether he asked it or not. He'd known that when he'd consented to her admission, and he had also known that she might wait in vain. Perhaps he'd been selfish...but much as he loved her, he could not assume the robe on that basis.

She regarded him with concern, sensing his anguish. "You couldn't receive the Scholar Stefred's blessing, nor can you yet marry—is the penance so harsh, Noren? I thought at first, when you said you'd been pardoned—"

"There is no penance. The Scholar Stefred has conferred more upon me than you can imagine; underneath he's as kind as he is wise."

"But he told me that even he is not free to do as he likes."

"Not if it would interfere with his duties as a guardian of the Mother Star's mysteries," Noren agreed. "He wouldn't want to be; no Scholar would. Sometimes he has to do things he hates doing, things that seem cruel."

He was referring to the interview just past, but Talyra grasped more than he'd meant to reveal. "You've been hurt," she observed sadly.

"No," Noren insisted, but she was not convinced; he had never been a good liar. "I haven't been hurt in the way I feared once," he assured her. "Not the way you must have thought when I recanted."

"Physically? I never thought that! I knew they'd done something that showed you how wrong you'd been. Why, I told you long ago that the Scholars wouldn't want anyone to recant unless he really meant it."

She had, and he'd considered her naive; yet her guesses had come closer to the truth than his own. *Perhaps it's like the inoculations Technicians give,* she'd said. *The needle hurts, but without it we'd all get sick and die.*

"When the Scholar Stefred questioned me," Talyra reflected, "I felt awful; he made me say things I'd been afraid even to think. It seemed as if all of the firm ground would crumble away and leave me falling. But afterward—well, I was surer of myself than before. Even though I saw I'd had some false ideas, I liked myself better—" She broke off, watching Noren, realizing how much older he looked than when they'd parted. "What happens to heretics is like that, isn't it? Only it's harder, and goes on longer?"

He nodded. "Something like that. We're not permitted to tell the details."

There were so many details he could not tell, so many areas in which there could be no communication between them. She must not ask about his work; she must not question his absence if for hours or days she did not see him; though she might speculate about the hidden mysteries, she must not do so aloud. That was the Inner City's way, he explained. Technicians did not discuss such things. They didn't seek information about the duties of friends who were assigned jobs inside the Hall of Scholars, or about why some were given such jobs far oftener than others. Neither did they discuss each other's past lives.

"For instance," he cautioned, "you must never describe my recantation to anyone; you mustn't even mention that you saw it. What a heretic has been through is best forgotten."

"I'm glad," she said simply. "I want to forget. I know what you had to do was necessary, and—and you were awfully brave...yet you suffered for something you couldn't help! I couldn't believe you deserved to suffer just for having been mistaken; that's haunted me so long."

"It's over. It needn't haunt you any more, darling."

"Nothing will, now that I'm here with you. The spirit of the Mother Star has blessed us both."

They kissed again, and for a few minutes he felt carefree, light-hearted, as if he too need no longer be haunted by anything. But after he'd left her with the head midwife, who was to find her lodging space and introduce her to the other women with whom she would work, Noren found that his perplexity had grown. If Talyra's belief in the Prophecy and the Mother Star was genuine—if she was not, as he'd always assumed, merely sticking by what she'd been taught—then on what grounds was she basing that belief? He himself had been shown the facts, and knew that she wasn't deceived; at least she wasn't unless the Scholars were also deceived about the Prophecy's eventual fulfillment. It was easy to forget that she had never been given any proof. Without proof, how could anyone be deeply convinced?

Two things you must go through, Stefred had warned: two trying experiences before the mysterious, suddenly-called meeting that evening, and as to the nature of the second, Noren had been given no clue. An hour remained before the time appointed for him to report back to Stefred's office.

He found Brek still in the computer room. "It's—tremendous," Brek said, his eyes shining. "I never conceived of a setup like this, not even after the dreams. You can ask *anything—*"

"The trick is in learning what to ask," said Noren. He entered Brek's console booth and sat down next to him, preparing to key in a question; there was a principle of chemistry he wanted to verify.

"I know; I've been experimenting," Brek agreed. "Most of the time I couldn't understand half of what showed up on the screen. And once I had to press INTERRUPT just to get a chance to rephrase."

"What had you requested?"

Grinning sheepishly, Brek admitted, “I’d asked for a full description of the mother world’s history.”

Noren smiled, knowing that the response to such an inquiry would have gone on for days if uninterrupted. He was past the stage of unrestrained eagerness himself. Yet communication with the computers never lost its fascination for him; study discs were marvels, but the thought of direct access to an infallible repository of all truth thrilled him in a way that nothing else could match.

In theory, he knew, it would be possible for all Scholars to have computer access from their own rooms; aboard the starships, study desks’ screens had indeed functioned as full consoles. But the metal wire of the connecting cables had been diverted by the Founders to more essential uses. Though unlike the computers themselves, the remote screens had been adapted to run on solar-charged batteries, they could not do anything more than display the contents of discs. Only those in the computer room were fully functional.

The computer complex consisted of the separate computers that had served the ships of the fleet, now located adjacent to each other and interlinked. The Founders had planned carefully, distributing the knowledge that had come from the Six Worlds among the various ships in such a way that the most vital portions had backup, and had reprogrammed the system upon assembly to operate as a unified whole. It was self-monitoring and, with regard to its programs, self-maintaining—fully protected against inadvertent erasure of data—and no accident short of power failure could damage it. Such a failure would, of course, make it impossible to access any of the data, and if prolonged would cause all storage media to deteriorate in the planet’s hot, corrosive atmosphere. For that reason as well as for the preservation of life-support, maintenance not only of the computer complex but of the power plant on which it depended was, in the Scholars’ eyes, a task of the highest and most sacred priority.

To be sure, under the High Law all machines were sacred, as was metal itself. Villagers viewed them with reverence and awe, believing them to be of supernatural origin, for they had been told—quite truthfully—that they came from the Mother Star. Noren had doubted this; in the days of his heresy he had held the very unorthodox opinion that machines were made by Technicians and Scholars. To his great surprise, he had found that he was mistaken.

Machines were irreplaceable, except insofar as worn parts could be recycled, a process carried out under the computers' control. It was not just that there was no more metal for making parts; a few, in fact, could be made out of plastics derived from the planet's native vegetation. The problem was more complicated than that. There was also a lack of the machines needed to fabricate new parts. The Founders had brought what equipment they could, but they'd been unable to transport enough to reproduce the industrial facilities of the Six Worlds.

Though villagers stood in awe of machines, they assumed that the Technicians—in their eyes superior beings—must have no such feeling, but this was not so. Villagers did not handle machines at all; Technicians, who bore responsibility for them, were reared to view the mishandling of a machine as a sacrilege. To damage a machine beyond repair was a mortal sin, punishable by deprivation of Technician status. This provision of the High Law was entirely just; the loss of a machine could cause serious harm to generations yet unborn; enough instances of damage would bring about the extinction of humankind. Yet Noren had been startled by the diffidence with which Brek had first approached a computer console. "Are you sure it's fitting for me to touch it without more instruction?" Brek had asked incredulously.

"Fitting? You're a *Scholar,* Brek." Noren had frowned; he too considered the computers sacred, in the sense that all knowledge was sacred to him; but he had never doubted his own worthiness to use them.

"But the Law is more binding than ever now that I know its justifications," Brek had protested.

"The Law…oh, you mean the part about mishandling. Yes, of course, it is; but you don't need a High Law any more—none of us do. We'd be careful anyway, wouldn't we? Besides, you can't hurt a console by pushing keys, and the computers themselves are sealed behind that partition."

With that assurance, Brek had lost his anxiety; but Noren saw that in some ways new training might be harder for a Technician than for a villager. He himself had never hesitated to touch whatever he found in the laboratories.

Now, turning to him, Brek said, "I still can scarcely believe I can come here whenever I want without supervision."

"We're not supervised at all," Noren told him. "We were put through a lot to prove ourselves trustworthy, but now that we have proven it, we're trusted."

"In everything? What happens if we break the rules?"

"There aren't any rules. Well, there are, I suppose, but they're called policies, and they're not arbitrarily imposed—they're simply principles no Scholar would violate." He paused, trying to think of a concrete example. "About ten weeks ago, before your arrest, you were living in the Outer City, I suppose. Was there any water shortage?"

"Water shortage? Of course not; there's always plenty of water."

"There is when the purification plant works. When it doesn't, like the week I'm talking about, most of the pipes to the Inner City are shut off. People too old to have children drink unpurified water, and the rest of us ration ourselves so that there'll be no interruption of the Outer City or village supplies. No one checks up, but would you have drunk enough to keep yourself from being thirsty?"

"I see what you mean," Brek mused. "But Noren, weren't you scared? Knowing what could happen if the breakdown lasted?"

"We were all terrified," Noren admitted, without going into detail about what his feelings had been before he'd heard that breakdowns were periodic occurrences to which the older Scholars, who had seen many repaired, were well inured. "It's the same way with everyday things," he continued. "All goods on this planet are in short supply—at least processed ones are, since there are so few machines for manufacturing them—so we in the Inner City restrict ourselves to the barest minimum. Only what's absolutely essential is bought from the Outer City merchants. As heretics we arrive with nothing, not the smallest token of our former lives, and we never acquire anything, Brek. We have no personal belongings but the clothes we wear."

It was an unnatural way to live, and not, according to what he'd been told of the Six Worlds, one that fostered the progress of a society. But the Inner City wasn't a society; it was an association of people who, for one reason or another, had voluntarily given up normal life to pursue an extraordinary goal. Most were dedicated in a religious sense. Moreover, having grown up with the idea that Scholars belonged to a supreme and privileged caste, most could not have felt comfortable had no austerities been practiced. Noren had found that Inner City privations were not merely tolerable, but welcome.

Outside, there was no privation except what the planet itself imposed. The villagers and Outer City Technicians traded freely in what goods the existing machines could turn out, as well as in the few that could be handmade from the world's limited resources. There were not many such, since no trees grew and wood was unknown—there wasn't even any fuel, other than tallow and dried moss. So glass had to come from the Outer City's domes, as did cloth, paper produced from rags, and other essential commodities. Villagers had plenty of money to purchase these things; the Technicians paid them well in plastic coinage for food. Food was abundant, although, Noren had been told, it was by his forebears' standards even more monotonous than furnishings. The hybrid grain once developed to meet the nutritional needs of the overpopulated mother world was the sole crop, aside from an herb tea, and it was supplemented only by the flesh and eggs of caged fowl. Workbeasts were inedible, having been adapted through controlled mutations to a diet of native fodder.

"The First Scholar often went hungry," reflected Brek, recalling the dreams. "Do we?"

"We would if the harvests were small, as they were in the Founders' time. There's no need nowadays. On Founding Day, though, it's traditional to fast in remembrance." Noren thought of how strange that had seemed to him. In the village where he'd grown up, Founding Day had been a time of feasting.

"All this…assuming hardships to avoid imposing them on the villagers and Technicians…is it what was meant by 'discipline' in the sentencing?" Brek asked.

"In a way. But for those of us who choose to study, the real challenge is mental discipline—learning to use our minds efficiently."

"I don't see," Brek admitted, "how I'm ever to absorb all I'll need to know to become a nuclear physicist, or a scientist of any kind, for that matter. The computers told me that on the Six Worlds people my age had been studying for years and still weren't ready to specialize."

"That was the custom, one started long before anything was known about faster methods. But now it's possible to catch up in a hurry."

Noren went on to explain how it worked. One learned mental discipline through a game played with the computers, a game that demanded logic and fast thinking. "It almost threw me at first," he confessed, "because in the village school I'd never had to think; all we did beyond learning our letters from the Book of the Prophecy was to memorize parts of the High Law, figure a little, and listen to the teacher talk. The computer measures your capacity the first day and holds you to it. You have to score at your level or admit defeat—you aren't given any other type of training, except in non-scientific work, until you've passed that hurdle."

It had been a harsh lesson, but not one Noren had minded. Having based his whole defense during his trial and inquisition on the idea that he was not the Scholars' inferior, his pride hadn't let him quit. Nobody had forced him. He had simply been told that before he could work with tutors or receive study discs he must earn an acceptable score in the game. When first informed that the game was merely a matter of pushing the proper buttons, he had thought it would be ridiculously simple, and indeed, the initial session had been great fun. What was so hard about watching colored lights and following the instructions on a screen?

That had been before the lights multiplied, the instructions grew complex, and the pace increased to the point where he was given only a few seconds to react.

Intense concentration had never been required of him before and he'd been prone to daydream as a defense against the dullness of village activities. In the game one could not afford to let one's mind wander. Noren had been appalled by the lowness of his scores and yet, during the first week or so, he'd been unable to improve them—he would freeze, find himself worrying over the unexpected failures, and the seconds allotted for response would be gone. The computer was infinitely patient; it never got tired of presenting comparable, although somewhat altered, instructions, and in fact would not proceed to the next degree of complexity until the current one had been mastered. Noren himself got exhausted; several times he kept at it all night. Eventually, after passing from despair through anger and grim determination, he'd learned to focus on the task and had begun to make progress. Thereafter, the game was exhilarating.

He still spent considerable time at it, he told Brek, for its scope had been expanded to include rigorous testing of his academic progress. The computers were programmed to keep close track of this and to guide each Scholar's course. Study discs, generated in sequence to meet individual needs and aptitudes, were the foundation of instruction, just as they were for all Technicians. These were generated at a computer console and taken to one's room. Upon return the disc was reused for something else, since the supply of them was limited. But direct questioning of the computers—either on matters unclear on the discs or on any other subject of interest—was permitted whenever there was a console free.

The best way of learning about the Six Worlds' civilization, however, was through dreams. The Founders had recorded a great many memories as a means of passing their heritage on to posterity, and all novice Scholars, scientists and non-scientists alike, experienced controlled dreaming frequently.

"Don't you have books?" Brek asked, puzzled.

"No." Noren laughed. "I was horrified when I discovered that; I'd always longed to own books, and I thought Scholars must have lots of them. But they would have been too heavy to import, of course, and even if there were enough paper, the printing press here couldn't supply many. We don't need them, not when we can request literature discs as well as factual ones."

"Stefred has books in his office."

"Those were written here—on this planet, I mean, by people with literary talent. They're copies of what's sold in the Outer City and by village traders. Stefred keeps them in sight to show new candidates that he's human, but any of us can borrow them, and some are as good as literature from the Six Worlds. Not all the gifted people become heretics, after all. Besides, plenty of Scholars pursue the arts on the side, and work that doesn't involve our secrets is sent to the markets under assumed names. You may well have seen some without guessing it came from the Inner City."

"Scholars must create the music for public ceremonies, too," Brek reflected. "How is that done, Noren? I've always known it wasn't supernatural, as villagers think; still it's completely different from flute music."

"Most of it was recorded on the Six Worlds," Noren explained, "and stored on discs. The sounds originally came from instruments made of metal or wood, instruments we can't have here. But Scholars do compose synthesized music with the computers—and we can listen to music at the consoles."

They talked on for a while, Noren describing the rest of the important training techniques: hypnosis for memorizing technical data that would otherwise require years to absorb; discussions, both formal and informal, with one's tutors; active assistance in the laboratories. Brek listened with avid interest, yet he seemed preoccupied. "Noren," he asked finally, returning to a topic that evidently still troubled him, "about the water plant breakdown...I didn't know things like that could happen. Is our survival on this world so precarious in spite of all the safeguards?"

"The more you learn, the more you'll realize how precarious it is," Noren said, hoping he would not have to elaborate. The conversation was coming all too close to matters he still did not want to ponder.

"I don't see how Scholars cope without—without anything to hold to," confessed Brek. "People on the outside are afraid at times, but they've got faith in the Mother Star; they think there's some mysterious power controlling things. It doesn't seem quite right to give that up."

Noren stared at him. "It's funny you should say that. You're a heretic—"

"Not in the same way you are. I—I never doubted the Mother Star, Noren. I challenged only the Scholars' authority. And now, since I've learned what the Star really is...I'm torn. I feel empty! Something's lost that I can't ever get back again, though I respect the Prophecy for what it is and what it means for the future. I lay awake last night thinking that that might be the hardest part of being a Scholar." Shamefaced, he mumbled, "I guess you think I'm crazy; certainly all the others would."

Slowly Noren replied, "Perhaps not. To most Scholars the Mother Star means more than the Six Worlds' sun. It's become a sort of symbol."

Brek looked up, surprised. "A symbol of what?"

"That's the strange thing...I can't tell you. I don't understand it at all. The private rituals leave me cold."

"What private rituals?"

"Orison, mainly. It's like the Benison held each morning outside the Gates, only there's much more to it than reading from the Book of the Prophecy—references to the Six Worlds' traditions, for instance, and a liturgy that seems to convey something I can't grasp. I've tried to analyze it, but I don't get anywhere."

"Can't Stefred explain?"

"You know Stefred; he likes people to find their own answers, especially about anything serious. And he takes Orison seriously. He goes himself."

"Doesn't everybody?"

"No, and most of the time I don't."

Soberly Brek asked, "Will you go with me, Noren?"

Fighting an odd reluctance, Noren nodded. If Brek felt that he'd lost something, something akin to what ordinary people got from believing the Mother Star was magic, Stefred must know, he realized; the psychiatric examination a candidate underwent was very thorough. Perhaps that was one reason the subject of Orison had been raised that morning. Perhaps Stefred had been hinting that since he'd been given the responsibility of initiating Brek into the Inner City, he should be prepared to enlighten him about its religious observances.

Was it possible, he wondered suddenly, that in this Brek didn't need enlightenment? Inside, was he afraid that Brek would make sense of the symbols and consider him blind? For the first time it occurred to Noren that they might be intended to learn from each other.

The computer room was built into the foundation of the Hall of Scholars; Stefred's study was on an upper level of that tower, which, having been designed as a starship rather than a building, was a baffling maze of compartments, jury-rigged lifts, and passageways leading off at odd angles. Its interior partitioning had been altered by the Founders, of course, since in space the outer walls had been "down" in terms of the artificial gravity.

Noren knew all the shortcuts. Hurrying to keep his appointment, he passed through the narrow corridor off which the Dream Machine was located, and to his surprise, overtook Stefred. "We've no need to go back to the office," Stefred told him, "I'd have asked you to come here in the first place, Noren, but I didn't want you anticipating a dream."

"A dream—now?" Under ordinary circumstances, for controlled dreaming one reported at bedtime and slept through the night. Moreover, Stefred's presence indicated that he had just dismissed another dreamer, and it was rare for him to operate the Dream Machine personally. Routine sessions didn't require the attendance of a skilled psychiatrist.

As he entered the cubicle, Noren smiled, remembering how terrifying it had seemed the first time, when he'd been allowed to give his imagination free reign as to the sinister purpose of the equipment. He would never be afraid in that way again, not of anything!

He settled himself in the reclining chair and leaned back against the padded headrest, awaiting the hypnotic preparation that would send him into receptive sleep. During his dream sessions before recantation, drugs had been used, but these were scarce and precious; a Scholar—who trusted the therapist as an unenlightened heretic could not—had no need of them. Hypnosis was employed for various purposes in training, and one learned early to be a good subject.

But this time Stefred did not proceed in the usual way. "I have reasons for not describing this dream to you in advance," he said evenly, "and also for plunging you directly into it without any type of sedation. It will be rather frightening, in some respects a nightmare, but I think you'll find the experience interesting."

Normally one was unconscious when the Dream Machine's electrodes were applied to one's head. Despite himself, Noren tensed during the process, wondering what new challenge lay in store for him. It was apparent that what was ahead could not be merely educative. Only once before had he been awake at the time the machine was switched on, and that had been a deliberate test of his susceptibility to panic. No doubt he was again to undergo an evaluation of some sort. Yet the surrounding array of wires, control knobs and dials was no longer dismaying to him, nor was he likely to be thrown by the abrupt shift of location and identity that would occur when the sensory inputs to his mind were replaced by electronic ones. The point at issue must be his ability to adapt to the conditions of the dream world itself: to adapt quickly, unassisted by the relaxing effects of a preliminary sleep phase. Then why not get it over with? he thought irritably. Stefred could have started the machine long ago, and the delay was nerve-wearing...

It was meant to be, Noren realized. Reason told him that he had nothing to be apprehensive about, yet an attempt was being made to arouse apprehension through subtle forms of stress. That wouldn't be done without a constructive aim. He willed himself to remain calm, to enter into the game with confidence; and in the next instant he heard the switch close. There was an explosion of colors before his eyes, followed unexpectedly by total blackness.

Everything around him was black—he was adrift in blackness, falling endlessly into a pit that had neither sides nor bottom. In desperation Noren groped for something to catch hold of. Failing to find it, he reached out with his mind, attempting to draw on the knowledge of the person from whose memories the dream had been recorded. To his dismay, he could grasp no such knowledge. He did not share the man's thoughts as he had the First Scholar's, and, to a lesser extent, the thoughts of the recorders of dream visits to the Six Worlds. His personal identity, however, remained stronger than usual, strong enough to reason that the limitations imposed on him must be the result of drastic editing. The recording was composed less of ideas and emotions than of pure physical sensation; his mental reaction to it would be almost entirely his own.

Resolutely he mastered his initial fright. It was impossible that he could be falling; it had gone on too long. There was no such thing as a pit with no bottom. Besides, there wasn't any sense of motion. Yet his body felt very peculiar, as if it had no weight, and his most basic subconscious instincts interpreted that as a fall. Perhaps he was failing to detect motion merely because he had nothing to relate to, not even the rush of air...

No air? But that *was* impossible He was breathing, after all...or was he? The second onslaught of terror was worse than the first; he wondered whether this was death. Could one dream of death—not of dying, but of death itself? Obviously a dead person could not record any thoughts. But this was unlike former dreams, for he had no real alternate identity; maybe it had not been recorded and then edited, but had instead been simulated from the beginning. It was technically possible to do that. Once, some weeks after his recantation, when his growing comprehension of science had led him to conclude that he had no objective grounds for belief in the authenticity of the original dreams, Stefred had let him sample one induced by a faked recording. The difference had been indisputable, and a major part of that difference had been the lack of genuine emotions separate from his own—just what was most noticeable now.

There had been another distinction, however. In the faked dream, the sights and sensations too had seemed unreal. He had been confined to a narrow segment of normal perception, sure that what was apparently taking place could not be happening, could never have happened—yet unable to escape. This was not like that. Unnatural though it was, it *had* happened, somewhere, to someone! It was true...so true that it occurred to him that he might actually have died. Perhaps he was no longer dreaming at all.

The truth isn't to be feared, Noren told himself, clinging to the one principle that to him was beyond question or compromise. Slowly the wave of panic passed. There was no doubt that he was breathing; he inhaled and exhaled naturally enough, although no wind touched any part of his body. And his inability to see was probably caused by blindness. He had supposed that the blind knew a softer dark, more like the closing of one's eyes at night than the jet-black expanse before him, but that evidently had not been the case with whoever had made this recording.

Noren resigned himself, surrendering to the realities of the dream. Suddenly he became aware that he had begun to move—though his fall continued, he was also moving by his own effort. There was purpose in the movement; though he still had no external reference points, his muscles worked and he was going somewhere... A dazzling flash of light hit him. He was not blind; the darkness really existed! In its midst was radiance so bright he could scarcely bear to look upon it. He turned aside and for the first time observed his own body, encased in a thick white garment that covered even his hands. Incredibly, he found himself close to one of the City's massive towers...but the tower lay on its side. It had no ground beneath it, or any sky overhead.

Something had gone wrong, Noren decided. This dream must be natural, not controlled; only in natural dreams could the disorientation be so extreme. Controlled dreams had logic. One met the unknown, the incomprehensible, but never the incongruities that arose spontaneously while one slept. He had been neither drugged nor hypnotized; he could will himself awake if the dream was indeed natural...yet he wasn't sure he wanted to. The weightless feeling, now that he had gotten used to it, was really quite pleasant.

He put out his hand to touch the silvery surface of the horizontal tower, feeling a kind of wonder. Disoriented he might be, but his mind was clear; the impressions he was gathering were sharp, detailed—not hazy as they'd been in dreams where he had struggled with abstractions that were beyond him. He was near the tower's top, at least what would have been the top had it been standing. Seizing a handhold that projected from the wall, he reached for another above and began to pull himself around—"up" in terms of his present position, though there was little of the effort involved in climbing—curious as to what might be visible from greater height. To his astonishment, he got no higher. He passed handhold after handhold, only to see the convex wall stretch on and on above him as if its span had become infinite.

Once again fear stirred in Noren. A black shadow cut sharply across the wall, coming ever closer; if he kept going he would soon re-enter darkness. And he had no choice. He had no volition as far as the actions of his body were concerned; when he tried to control them, he discovered that the Dream Machine was doing so after all. His only freedom was in his personal inner response. To be sure, that had been the case in the previous dreams, but always before there had been the compensation of shared thought. He had not been compelled to proceed into the unknown with no idea of what his alter ego's goal had been. Then too, he had not been so alone. There had been people around, talking to him, listening to words that came from his lips and by their reaction guiding his adjustment. Here he was isolated; it was all taking place in utter silence.

He approached the shadow, thinking how very odd it was that the tower, when first seen from a short distance, had been fully illuminated. Something behind him must be casting that shadow, some monstrous thing that was advancing... If only he could turn his head! His heart thudded painfully and he felt chills permeate his flesh, yet his hands were firm as he moved them from grip to grip. The physical symptoms of fear must be his own, he realized; they were occurring in his sleeping body, while the recording contained only the confident motions of a man who had not trembled. He held to that thought as his right arm disappeared into the dark.

Then, without any foreknowledge of the intent, he did turn for an instant, looking back over his shoulder toward the source of light he was leaving behind; and it so startled Noren that he felt he was not only falling, but spinning. Though the tower was still there, he was sure that he'd lost contact with it, that he would fall forever toward a fire that was worse than darkness. There was no shape to cast a shadow. There was only a vast black sky dominated by a sun, immense and horribly brilliant, that looked much as it had on film and in his first controlled dream and in all too many of his natural ones; but he had no shelter from it now. He was in the presence of the nova…

One glance was enough. It was a relief to creep on into the dark where that intolerable flame could not reach him. Why couldn't it? Noren wondered, momentarily baffled. A sun, when it shone, shone everywhere. Why wasn't it shining on the whole tower? His head and shoulders were by this time enveloped in blackness; he raised his free hand to turn a knob on the helmet he hadn't realized he was wearing. Instantly there was light again: not sunlight, but innumerable swarms of blazing points that could be nothing but stars.

Awestruck, Noren clung to the wall of the tower, facing outward, while comprehension flooded into his mind. It came not from the recorder's thoughts, to which he still had no access, but from his own power of reason; the pieces at last began to fit. He'd been climbing not up, but around—around the circular tower to the side opposite from the sun. And it wasn't really a tower yet; it was still a starship. He was in space!

Noren had seen space from the viewport of the First Scholar's starship during the first controlled dreams he had experienced, but that was not at all the same as being outside such a ship. Aboard the starship there had been artificial gravity; he had encountered neither weightlessness nor the absence of "up" and "down," although he'd since been told of these conditions. He had also been told that stars would appear abnormally bright outside the atmosphere of the planet on which he'd been born, which was even thicker than the Six Worlds' atmospheres, and that the sun, too, would be brighter—but mere words had not prepared him for the actuality.

It was not the nova which he'd just glimpsed, he perceived. The nova had been observed only from the escaping fleet, which had gone into stardrive minutes after the explosion; no one could have been outside a ship then. He must have seen the Mother Star at some time before it went nova. Yet he had never heard of thought recordings having been brought from the Six Worlds, and this dream seemed so real, so immediate, that he felt sure it had been recorded in real time rather than from memory.

The stars…he could not grasp what it meant to be seeing the stars this way! Obscured by the polarization that had protected his eyes from the naked sun, they'd burst into visibility when he, the astronaut, had changed the filter setting of his helmet. The astronaut had no doubt seen them often, but Noren did not share his thoughts and was still overpowered as he clambered further around the ship—and came face to face with the most awesome sight of all.

It was a planet, a huge planet half-filling his field of vision, that except for some yellow splotches was shrouded in grayish-white. Noren turned cold. Not one of the Six Worlds had looked like that! He had seen films showing all of them; most had been predominantly green or blue, with their white areas forming clear, though shifting, patterns. Was this then an alien solar system, one judged unsuitable for use and quickly abandoned? There had been many such. The planet looked inhospitable enough; some deep, racial instinct told him that it was not right for colonizing, that it could not support life of his kind. As a human refuge it would indeed be useless...

No, he thought suddenly. Inhospitable, yes, but not quite useless. It was not an abandoned planet. It was his own.

The waking was as it had frequently been in recent weeks: slowly, naturally, Noren slipped back into the real world, feeling not the relief of escape from nightmare, but a sense of loss, of exile from a place he had not wished to leave. Before he reached full consciousness, there were flashes of memory from other dreams—a surging ocean, a broad green meadow dotted with shade trees, a city without walls where men and women partook freely of wonders past description—but he clung longest to the glory of the unveiled stars.

"You adapted." Stefred's approval seemed tinged, somewhat, by a trace of feeling Noren couldn't identify. Turning from the panel of dials that enabled him to monitor a dreamer's well-being, he continued, "If I asked you to go through that again, with some variations—perhaps to do so repeatedly—would it bother you?"

"No," Noren replied confidently. "It's only a dream, after all. Besides, I understand it now, and there were parts that were—exciting."

Stefred smiled ruefully. "Some people find them so, others don't. I was practically certain that you would."

"Who recorded it?" asked Noren. "The other dreams, except the First Scholar's, were of the Six Worlds, but this was here. I looked down on *this* world."

"We don't know his name. He was one of the shuttlecraft pilots who dismantled the starships and brought them down to be reassembled as towers." With odd hesitancy, as if it was painful to go on, Stefred added, "For him, of course, it was more than a dream."

"It was his job, and he—he must have liked it," Noren commented, making a guess as to Stefred's own immediate job and resolving to face what must be faced squarely.

"Would you like it if it were yours?"

To consider that was frustrating, but Noren made no attempt to evade the question. Part of the discipline of a Scholar's education, he knew, lay in coming to terms with the fact that the vast universe beyond this one deficient planet—the universe accessible to his forefathers—could not be reached outside of dreams. This was necessary. Scholars were not supposed to be content with what they had; they were supposed to long for the unattainable, since only in that way could the goal of restoring the Six Worlds' lost riches be kept constantly in view. People who want what they don't have progress faster than those who are satisfied. The Prophecy itself had been created to ensure that they would never stop wanting the changes it promised.

"You're tantalizing me," he said, determined to take it in stride.

"Not this time," Stefred replied. "This time I'm doing something quite different." He drew breath, then persisted, "How would you feel about going into space not in a dream, but in reality?"

"That's impossible."

"No. A space shuttle still exists. Some of the starships are still in orbit, though in the First Scholar's time they were stripped of all useful equipment."

Yes, awaiting the Time of the Prophecy, when each hull would become the nucleus of a new city; Noren knew that. He tried to make light of the matter by stating the obvious: "I don't know how to bring down a starship."

"You know as much as anyone on this planet, or at least you will after you've been through that dream in its complete and unedited form often enough."

Looking into Stefred's face, Noren exclaimed, "You're...*serious!*"

Stefred nodded soberly. He detached the Dream Machine apparatus, saying, "Save your questions, Noren. I realize that's difficult, but there is no time for them now, and at the meeting tonight they will be answered."

Dazed by the overwhelming implications of what he was hearing, Noren sat up. "One thing more," Stefred cautioned. "I must ask you to say nothing of this dream, particularly not to Brek."

"Can't you let him in on it, too?" protested Noren, thinking that when Brek did find out, he would be justifiably envious.

"I intend to, and the test isn't valid unless a person comes to it unsuspecting, as you did." With a sigh Stefred admitted, "Quite possibly it's not valid even then, but there's a limit to what I can devise on three days' notice."

Noren knew better than to prolong the discussion. He took leave of Stefred and headed downstairs to meet Brek, in such turmoil over the momentous happenings of the day that he found it hard to keep his composure. Only a little while remained before the meeting. There wasn't time to go to the main refectory open to all Inner City residents, where he had hoped to see Talyra; he and Brek must again eat at the one in the Hall of Scholars.

It was crowded, for the coming assembly was on everyone's mind and few had wished to interrupt their speculations about what might take place, as would have been necessary in the presence of Technicians. Steering clear of that topic, Noren talked instead of Talyra. If she had arrived on any other day, he would be sharing supper with her, not with Brek, he thought ruefully. He would never have spent her first evening in the City at the Hall of Scholars, the one tower she was barred from entering unless summoned for specific duties. He was torn; he longed to be with her, yet excitement about what lay ahead outweighed everything else. If the starships were to be retrieved from orbit, that could only mean that a breakthrough in the research was much closer than anyone had guessed!

They went to Orison. For that also, more Scholars were present than usual; even regular attendees did not come every night, since they often worked late, but this evening all work had been stopped. Besides, the room in which Orison was held was the only one large enough for a general assembly and people had already begun to gather.

Noren did not know the liturgy well, except for the parts that were direct quotations from the Book of the Prophecy. He was aware, of course, that in ritual created by the Scholars for their own use, the Mother Star was meant to be viewed neither in the villagers' way, as a magical power in the sky, nor in the scientific way, as a sun that had become a nova. It was representative of something else. The difficulty lay in grasping what the "something else" was. "You told me that some things Scholars do can't be explained in advance, but have to be experienced," Brek reminded him as they went in. "Maybe this is one of them."

"But when I come," Noren objected, "I don't experience anything."

This time he did.

Perhaps it was the larger group, the air of tense expectancy; perhaps, too, it was the fact that he was already thoroughly shaken by the events of the past two days. There was nothing different in the dimly lighted room itself, with its prismatic glass sunburst, larger than the one in the refectory, affixed to the ceiling's center. Nor was there anything unique in the Six Worlds' stirring orchestral music that no longer overwhelmed him as it had when he'd first heard it outside the Gates. There was no apparent difference in the ritual. The presiding Scholars were robed, as was customary, but all the others wore everyday clothes like his own. The words, presumably, were the same ones always used, allowing for a normal amount of daily variation.

He was standing, staring upward at the light glinting from myriad facets of the sunburst, and had allowed his mind to drift. Talyra…some of the words were those Stefred had used to bless Talyra, except for being expressed in first person plural: *"May the spirit of the Mother Star abide with us…may we gain strength from its presence, trusting in the surety of its power."* But there was no surety! That was the truth he'd hidden from…

All day it had lain at the surface of his thoughts; still he had not dared to consider its full significance. *You must grapple with it alone,* Stefred had said, yet he hadn't done so. What was the matter with him? Noren wondered in dismay. He did not want to shrink from the truth! Truth had always been what he cared most about, and though he'd known it could sometimes be painful, he had not ever meant to let that deter him. He had not faltered when confrontation of the facts had required him to give up his most cherished theories and to undergo the ordeal of recanting. He would not falter now. Grimly, Noren forced himself to face the thing his recent doubts implied: it was possible that he would someday find that recanting had been a terrible mistake.

It was not just that he'd unwittingly affirmed a promise that might not be kept. As matters stood, the Scholars intended to keep it; they were struggling toward that end; they were not deceiving the people for any reason but to attain that end. If it was attained, there would have been no deceit. But what if at some time in the future they were to learn that the Prophecy could never be fulfilled? What if the research was to end in utter failure? There would then be no justification for secrecy, no justification for withholding either machines or knowledge from anyone. The First Scholar himself would not have justified such policies on lesser grounds than saving humankind from extinction; he wouldn't have concealed truth from people to uphold a vain hope any more than the Six Worlds' leaders had concealed news of the impending nova. He had assured his companions that he was not asking them to establish a false religion. But the religion he'd created had been the center of people's lives for generations now, and somehow Noren couldn't picture its High Priests abolishing it if it proved invalid, although the restrictions it placed on the villagers would then be unwarranted.

The ritual words went on: *"For there is no surety save in the light that sustained our forebears; no hope but in that which lies beyond our sphere; and our future is vain except as we have faith..."* He had heard them before, but he hadn't grasped them. He had thought them a reference to the necessity for preserving the knowledge of the Six Worlds. Yet they weren't that at all! The Scholars knew such knowledge was insufficient, that research based on it might fail, and that hard work wasn't enough to ensure that the Prophecy would come true. The words were an admission of these things. No wonder even the scientists clung to religious symbolism; it kept them from having to say in plain words that their own hope might be a delusion.

Noren wrenched his mind away from the thought. It didn't matter now, not now, when there had evidently been some unexpected new development, when there were plans to retrieve the starships... And yet, he realized suddenly, Stefred had not acted as if he knew that a breakthrough was close. He'd been clearly aware of what was to be discussed at the meeting, but he had not been happy—he'd been troubled. Even about the starships he'd been troubled. In no way had he behaved like a man who was privy to good news.

As the solemn ritual proceeded, Noren stood transfixed, his eyes uplifted less from custom than from inability to look away. The Mother Star...symbol of a delusion? All at once he swayed giddily, gripped by an intangible terror unlike any he had ever encountered. If there was delusion, it concerned not merely the Prophecy, but survival itself. In theory he had known that survival could not continue unless metal became available. Yet he hadn't followed his fears to their logical conclusion. He had never imagined the death of the human race occurring, not through anyone's lack of effort, but because synthesization of metallic elements turned out to be inherently impossible.

There were more words, but he did not hear them. The sunburst blurred, and in its place the desolate planet, alien and inhospitable as he'd seen it in the dream, swam before his eyes. Trembling, he lowered them and slowly, deliberately, surveyed the people around him. Brek's face was grave, reverent; that was understandable because Brek did not yet know that the nuclear physicists had no proof that their work would ever succeed. But the older Scholars surely knew, whether they were scientists themselves or mere observers. And they did not seem afraid. Some showed no emotion at all; the rest appeared at peace with the world, as if there were indeed something in which they could trust.

"Noren?" At the touch of Brek's hand on his arm, Noren was jolted back from the precipice. He noticed that the lights had brightened and that most of the people were now sitting down, awaiting the start of the meeting. The rite of Orison was over.

A hush fell as the chairman of the executive council rose to speak. "I'll come right to the point," he said quietly. "As some of you already know, we face a crucial decision. The purpose of this meeting is to discuss whether or not we should make an immediate attempt to found a new city on the other side of the Tomorrow Mountains."

Chapter Four

Afterward, whenever he recalled that meeting, Noren found it hard to believe that he could have sat through it so impassively. Yet impassive he was. Already in shock from the impact of the fear that had overpowered him during Orison, he was incapable of feeling the shock that the prospect of another city would otherwise have aroused in him—and did arouse in those of his fellow Scholars who weren't on the committee that had engaged in advance discussion. A new city had not been thought possible prior to the success of the research. They had barely enough equipment to keep the existing one going; how could any be diverted? There was nothing most Scholars would like better than to be in on such a project, but how could it be justified?

"As heretics, you were warned before the secrets were revealed to you that you would be confined here for life," the council chairman reminded them. "It was repeated at your sentencing and again later, when the conditions of your confinement were explained. No release was anticipated. Never since the First Scholar's expedition arrived has a Scholar been farther than the platform outside the Gates: at first because the risk of disclosing the Six Worlds' destruction was too great, and then because for us to mingle with the villagers—even when we wouldn't be recognized as former heretics—would rob us of the remoteness we needed, both for maintaining general respect and for recruiting people with inquiring minds. And those weren't the only reasons."

The traditional sacrifice of physical freedom could not be abandoned lightly, they knew. For one thing, it prevented distraction from the desperate urgency of human dependence on timeworn machines and the vital need to solve basic technological problems. And there had been no constructive purpose in abandoning it. Technicians had been exploring beyond the Tomorrow Mountains since soon after the Founding, using as many of the precious aircars as could be spared from the top-priority task of transporting land treatment machines to the villages. Scholars might have gone along, since no contact with villagers was involved, but they had not done so, not only because of tradition but because they couldn't take time from their own vital work in the City. It was more efficient for Technicians to survey the land, verifying the detailed orbital surveys that had been made prior to the Founding, and bringing back minerals for analysis. Never until now had there been talk of a permanent outpost.

Like anything involving a major policy change, the idea must be put to a vote among all the fully committed. Even relatively small matters, like whether a particular tool should be melted down and its elements allocated to research, were so decided; for such things were of far-reaching significance. The disposition of one kilo of metal might conceivably determine whether future generations lived or died. The disposition of enough materials to set up an outpost could very easily determine it. Yet no one could be sure, Noren thought in horror. How could they dare to vote on an issue when they were not sure? It was fortunate that he, as an uncommitted novice, had neither the right nor the responsibility to do so.

"Normally, so great a decision as this would demand many weeks of deliberation," the chairman said. "For reasons I'll explain presently, we must hold the vote tonight—"

An astonished gasp from the assembled Scholars made him pause. Then, calmly, he continued, "But before I go into that, I think we should consider the less urgent factors, those related to the status of our work."

Noren had not yet acquired the technical background to follow the discussion fully. The emphasis of his study had been on understanding the fundamental basis of the research, for details, when needed, could be quickly memorized under hypnosis. He'd been told that to be creative, one must have a thorough comprehension of a task's nature—and that had to be gained slowly.

At first he had been impatient with the slowness of the way the work had progressed over the years. He hadn't been able to see why the current experimentation was designed not to produce metal, but simply to verify certain aspects of the theory that seemed most promising. Wasn't there some shortcut? he'd demanded. Wouldn't it be quicker to try out the theory by actually attempting fusion of heavy elements?

It would not, Grenald had explained. If they proceeded that way and failed, no one would be able to tell what had gone wrong.

The various ideas involved must be tested separately. Moreover, having no materials to waste, they could not build the equipment for a full-scale experiment until they were sure that the theory was sound. Everything done so far showed that it was, for it had been developed gradually as, one by one, the conflicting theories had been eliminated. All the same, no matter how many things pointed to a theory's accuracy, a single demonstrated fact that didn't fit would be enough to disprove it.

Although Noren did not have a full grasp of the theory itself, he was familiar with the mathematics involved in it; he always absorbed rapidly any math he encountered. And he was well aware of what was at stake in the experimentation in progress. If it verified everything it had been planned to verify, an attempt to achieve fusion might conceivably be made soon. Experiments rarely worked out that well, however. It was likely that more would be needed. To progress directly to the synthesization of usable metal would require a true breakthrough: an outcome even better than could be foreseen, one that revealed facts nobody had guessed. And if by any chance some facet of the theory proved to be not merely unverified, but definitely wrong, then the theory would have to be modified. That could take years of work. No one talked about that.

At least they hadn't talked about it until the meeting.

As he listened to the discussion, Noren soon saw that the Scholars were divided into three factions: one that favored sticking to the Founders' original plan; one that felt a breakthrough might be close enough to justify getting a head start on another city; and one that feared a setback would occur, a setback too serious to be dealt with except by drastic measures. It was this last group that had first proposed that preparation for the establishment of a distant outpost should begin. "We must be ready," its spokesmen declared, "because if our current theory proves inadequate, there is only one way we can turn—toward techniques that will eventually entail experimentation too risky to be tried in an inhabited area."

That nuclear fusion was potentially dangerous was something that had astonished Noren when, soon after beginning his studies, he had been shown a film of something called a "thermonuclear bomb." It had been quite horrifying, especially when the purpose of the bomb—for which nothing in his own world had prepared him—had become clear. He'd been thankful that he had not been introduced to it through a dream. There were no such dreams, since thermonuclear bombs had not existed in the time of the Founders and had in fact been abolished long before thought recording had been invented. But the film had been preserved, for there were lessons in it, and among them one of particular importance to potential experimenters: extreme care must be taken lest in the effort to achieve controlled nuclear reactions they produce an uncontrolled one.

The danger had not been great so far. Long ago the scientists of the Six Worlds had learned to control nuclear fusion and had harnessed it for the generation of power. The City's main power plant was a fusion reactor, as those of the mother world had been after its supply of organic fuel was exhausted. Fusion power was clean and safe; it did not even create radioactive wastes. But nuclear fusion of heavy elements was far more difficult and complex than the type of fusion employed in a power plant. If it could be achieved at all, it would be achieved only through methods unlike the proven ones, and the approaches as yet untried were not without peril.

To men of the Six Worlds, it would have seemed obvious that all nuclear experimentation ought to be done far away from the City. It wasn't that simple, however. The facilities necessary for such experimentation did not exist anywhere but in the City, and they couldn't be moved without dangerous depletion of its reserves. The villagers were dependent upon the City for weather control, purified water to supplement rain catchment, and the periodic soil treatment and seed irradiation—without those things they would perish. The hazards of splitting the City's resources had until now been greater than the chances of a serious accident. Yet if new failures were to affect those odds…

The Founders had expected failures. They had realized that they and their successors were facing a task considered impossible by the science of their own era. This, after all, was why they'd set up a social system that was in most respects morally repugnant to them. It had been the only way to buy time, enough time for the impossible to be accomplished.

Transmutation of the elements…it was an old dream; before the dawn of science, men had tried to transform base metals into gold. Later men had laughed. No one had imagined a situation in which human survival would hinge upon a variation of the alchemists' laughable, impossible goal: the changing of other elements into metals.

The very existence of a planet without usable metals had been a surprise to the Six Worlds' scientists when, after the initial fruitless explorations that had followed the perfection of the stardrive, they had come upon it. They'd been looking for worlds to colonize, and had previously found none with suitable gravity, climate and atmosphere. At first, this one had elated them. Its soil contained poisons, but technology could deal with poisons. There had been no expectation of discovering planets where advanced technology would be unnecessary—it had been assumed that if such planets existed, intelligent life forms would have evolved upon them, making them unavailable for claim. A species that had fully populated its own solar system could continue to survive only by means of technology: the technology to build starships, and the technology to utilize otherwise-uninhabitable worlds. That was the natural way of things. When survival was threatened, technology developed to meet the threat. Even the nova could not have endangered the survival of a starfaring race, had it not been for the unfortunate chance that the sole refuge located before tragedy struck lacked the metal on which all technology depended.

Astronomers had long known that some stars were metal-poor; but whether their planets were also metal-poor—or even whether they had planets—could be determined only by exploration. Some had been found to have planets without solid ground. This world, however, had been a puzzle at the beginning. It was solid, composed primarily of silicon, yet its proportion of metallic elements was even lower than that of its sun. There was no metal ore at all; the orbital surveys, made with sensitive and trustworthy instruments, showed that clearly. Only traces were present, traces too small to be extracted without prohibitively complex equipment. Baffled, the first landing parties had investigated further, and had come to an awesome conclusion: what little usable metal the planet had once had was already exhausted. It had been mined in past ages by visitors from some other solar system who had depleted the ore and gone on.

Nothing was known of these mysterious visitors of the past, for though the signs of their excavations were unmistakable, they had left no artifacts. No one could tell where they'd come from or where they had gone. Since this was the first proof of intelligence elsewhere in the universe, the scientists of the Six Worlds had been excited. Such a find had seemed ample compensation for the fact that the planet could never become a self-supporting colony. But that, of course, had been before the nova wiped out all sources of off-world support.

The Founders had known in advance that the Six Worlds' sun would nova—but only a few weeks in advance. The starfleet had been small, and there were frustrating limits to what it could carry. Life support equipment had first priority; the computers with their irreplaceable store of knowledge second; facilities for conducting research, although also vital, had of necessity been confined to an absolute minimum. No expansion of those facilities was possible without metal.

It was a vicious circle. By scouring the planet, the remaining traces of suitable metal might have been located; but such traces could not be utilized without equipment that wasn't obtainable. Once the breakthrough occurred—once even a small amount of metal had been synthesized—it would become possible to manufacture the equipment. Then the world's limited resources could be tapped. Perhaps metal could then be reached by drilling into the planet's core. But would there ever be any breakthrough when the laboratories weren't adequately outfitted?

Never before had Noren heard pessimism from the scientists, but at the meeting there were some who expressed it openly. "We're fools if we don't recognize that our present line of thought may have to be modified," one of them asserted. "Within weeks—half a year at the most—this series of experiments will be finished, and without better facilities we'll find ourselves facing a dead end..."

"No!" Grenald interrupted, rising to his feet in anger. "It's not a dead end. This time we will succeed."

There was silence. Everyone respected Grenald, and he had been head of the nuclear physics department for many years. Yet he looked old, tired; it was obvious to all that with the culmination of his work close at hand, he himself had become uncertain and afraid. Stefred's words came back to Noren: *He is an old man who has devoted most of his life to research that he won't live to see completed.* Stefred knew, he thought sadly. Stefred knew that Grenald's hope of an imminent breakthrough was based on wishful thinking.

"We will succeed," Grenald repeated, "and because we will, we should take the preliminary steps toward founding a second city. We betray our trust if we delay by a single week the Transition Period's beginning."

The Transition Period was the time during which the groundwork would be laid for the keeping of the Prophecy's promises. They couldn't be fulfilled all at once, of course. The people had been told that when the Mother Star appeared there would be machines and cities for everyone, and most pictured those cities rising out of the ground overnight—but it would not happen that way. Building would be a slow process even after metal was available and factories had been established. Furthermore, villagers who stood in awe of machines would not be ready to move into cities, much less to share the job of construction. During the Transition Period, villagers who so wished would be given the opportunity to become Technicians; they would be free to enter training centers, work on the new cities, and then move there. People who preferred to remain farmers, but were willing to sell their land and start farms near the new cities, would rank as Technicians, too. By the time the Star became visible, the promised things would indeed be available to all.

At Grenald's words, there was a murmur of agreement; all Scholars were anxious for the Transition Period to begin. Moreover, the Inner City was crowded. Though no children were reared there, the population outside had grown rapidly over the years, and that meant the number of people who became heretics steadily increased; before long no more doubling up in quarters would be feasible. Then one of the Outer City's domes would have to be taken—an unthinkable step, for it would mean imposing hardship on the Technicians who would be ousted. Some Scholars felt a new city could be justified on those grounds alone.

Others, however, were cautious. "You speak to bolster your own confidence," they told Grenald. "Do you think acting as if the research has already succeeded will somehow bring it to pass? It won't! If we weaken this City by a premature attempt to establish another, we'll certainly betray our trust. The equipment we've safeguarded so long will be lost."

The proponents of this view outnumbered Grenald's supporters, but the proposal for the new city was also backed by the third faction—the group that believed failure of the current experiments would demand an outpost for more dangerous ones. "We know there's risk in weakening the City's reserves," they maintained, "but it's less than that of nuclear accident if we must turn to the avenues saved for a last resort. So in either case the project makes sense. If we succeed soon, we'll have a head start on the Transition Period, and if we don't, we'll be prepared for what may have to be tried next."

Back and forth went the argument, until at last someone suggested, "Wouldn't it be simpler just to wait and see? It will be no more than half a year until we know the outcome of Grenald's work. Surely we could make a much wiser decision then; I fail to understand why the committee has brought up the matter at this point."

It was then that the chairman rose once more. "I did not wish to reveal this until all sides had been considered," he said, "since if there had been a strong majority either for or against the proposal, it would have outweighed the immediate considerations. But the fact is that if we're going to set up an outpost beyond the Tomorrow Mountains, we should do it now. A new base will require retrieval of a starship from orbit, and the starships can be reached only if the space shuttle homes in on their electronic beacons, beacons that have been monitored by the computers since the time of the Founders. Three days ago there was a signal failure alarm. The solar-powered beacon in one of the starships is no longer functioning at full strength—and the computers have warned us that if we do not retrieve that ship at once, it will be lost to us forever."

In the end, when the meeting was over and Noren and Brek walked back to their lodgings to spend the few hours until morning, there could be little doubt that the outpost would be established. The vote had been cast by secret ballot and was not yet counted; but the prevailing opinion had been clear. The beacon failure alarm had become the deciding factor.

The two looked up at the stars, faint dots speckling the gaps between towers that almost touched overhead. Noren thought of them as they had been in the dream: blazing points of pure, unfiltered light. He would perhaps see them so in reality! But Brek knew nothing of that, and so they could not talk of it.

Elated, Brek began, "To go beyond the Tomorrow Mountains—"

"You don't know that you'll be one to go. They said that except for certain specialists, the choice would be made by lot."

"They also said that the place would be staffed on a rotation basis, that no one would stay there permanently. We're young,

Noren. Sooner or later we'll get there even if we're not among the first! It's life imprisonment against…hope."

"Does it bother you that much—the confinement, I mean?"

"I—I don't know. I haven't had as long as you have to get used to the idea. I'm willing, certainly. But I can't pretend that it doesn't matter to me."

Noren was detached, numb. "I don't think I ever felt that way, even at first," he reflected. "The Inner City has everything I was seeking—"

"It's different for you. You're gifted; someday you'll be a top scientist."

"Where did you hear that?" Noren demanded.

"In the computer room today, when you were off with Stefred. Everyone knows it. If Grenald's work should fail conclusively, it would take years to prepare for a new series of experiments, and you're the best prospect for coming up with some brand-new approach."

But that was awful, Noren thought. They were counting on him for something that might not even exist! He did not doubt his ability to learn; he would surely seek out whatever truth was accessible to him; but suppose the truth was that there were no new approaches? He would not become like Grenald, defending an unproven theory with the idea that sheer stubbornness would *make* it true.

The next morning Brek was summoned to see Stefred, and after supper Noren too was called. He was relieved, for though he'd planned to spend the evening with Talyra, sharing the day's meals with her had been a strain. She had not understood his preoccupation; she'd been confused, thinking him tormented by some lingering result of heresy, and had plied him with questions he could not answer. For more reasons than one, he found himself eager to be involved in the retrieval of the starship.

A small group had gathered in Stefred's office, all young men who had experienced the dream. Brek had been through it and was as excited as the rest; an opportunity for space flight was beyond the wildest hopes any of them had ever cherished.

It was not as fantastic as it seemed, Stefred explained. The space shuttle had an automatic pilot, which, as they'd heard at the meeting, was programmed to dock with the starship's electronic beacon—no piloting skill was needed. The crewmen's task would be to dismantle the ship so that it could be brought down piece by piece. They would, to be sure, have to work in spacesuits under zero gravity conditions. No one living had ever done anything like that. But neither had the first men to walk in space, back in ancient times when five of the Six Worlds had yet to be colonized. And those men hadn't had the advantage of a detailed and accurate introduction to it through dreams.

The Founders had planned well. As Noren had guessed, the shuttlecraft pilot had recorded his thoughts not from memory, but in real time during an actual flight, knowing that those who would make such flights again would have no prior experience even with high-speed aircraft, let alone spaceships. "On the Six Worlds boys of your age would not have been given this job," Stefred said, "since years of training would have been required. We have no trained astronauts. The older Scholars are engaged in other work for which they're vitally needed, and besides, they're not in condition physically. Your youth is an advantage in both those respects; the only other qualification is that you be willing to risk your lives." He eyed them intently. "You must understand from the beginning that it's dangerous. The space shuttle has been unused for generations. It has been maintained according to the instructions left us by the Founders, but we have no guarantee that it will perform. And that's not the only hazard—"

"Do you really think any of us would turn down a chance to fly into space?" someone interrupted indignantly.

"I don't," Stefred admitted. "That's why I'm not happy about offering it." Sighing, he continued, "I will tell you frankly that I voted against the proposed new city both in the executive committee and at last night's meeting. The majority was with me until the matter of the beacon failure arose; I suspect that those who changed their minds on that basis were following emotion, not reason."

"But surely, if an outpost is likely to be needed soon anyway, we shouldn't waste the last chance to get this starship!" Noren exclaimed. There were no materials left for constructing domes like those of the Outer City, and certain vital equipment could not be installed in village-type buildings of rough stone or brick, which couldn't be air-conditioned. A prefabricated "tower" would be needed in every city until the planet's industry was well established. Moreover, to villagers, a city without any of the unique and spectacular towers would not be a City at all. They would not consider the Prophecy fulfilled unless their own area had one. "There'll be barely enough towers for the Transition Period as it is," he argued. "Losing one could affect the outcome of the Founders' plan."

"Some of us," Stefred said soberly, "feel that it may affect it more if we risk six promising young Scholars in attempts to home in on a signal that's known to be unreliable."

Noren drew breath. "You mean it may fail completely...while we're in space."

"It may. In that case the automatic pilot may abort the mission successfully—or it may not. Have you wondered why I made the test dream so rough, Noren? Why I plunged you alone into a blackness you could not comprehend, leading you to think you might be confronting death? If that shuttlecraft fails to dock, it may go into an extrasolar orbit, an endless orbit! Have you any conception of what that means?"

The thought, though sobering, did not alter anyone's enthusiasm. Stefred, convinced that they were genuine volunteers, went on to discuss the details of their preparation, setting up schedules for intensive use of the Dream Machine. But it was plain that he was not really comfortable about the project. Noren was uncomfortable also, but for a different cause; when Brek and the others left, he stayed behind a few minutes.

"Stefred," he asked, "why, when you knew I'd be away erecting the tower at the new outpost, did you bring Talyra in yesterday? Why did you say that the decision could not wait?"

Stefred hesitated for a long time. "Someday I'll tell you, Noren," he said finally. "It's complicated." He made a gesture of dismissal; then, abruptly, burst out, "If you have any reservations about what you said yesterday during our talk, any doubts about preferring to know more than can be learned through exclusive concentration on science, then you should not join the space crew."

Numerous though Noren's doubts had become, there were none on that score. He said nothing, realizing that no reply was expected.

"Grenald begged me to disqualify you arbitrarily, but it wouldn't have been fair to do that. The choice had to be yours. Nevertheless, he does have logic on his side; the risk, in your case, is perhaps excessive—"

Slowly, Noren shook his head. "It won't do, Stefred," he said. "You've been trying to scare me, but you know I won't back out no matter how scared I am. We both know that the Scholars who voted in favor of this project are just as concerned about the risking of life as you are, and that it's basic policy to respect the decisions of volunteers. You've admitted you can't bar me from volunteering. You can't even tell me to consider my potential as a scientist; yesterday you advised the exact opposite! There's some other issue that's worrying you, and you still aren't giving me all the facts."

"Maybe I'm not," Stefred conceded. "But did it ever occur to you that perhaps I don't have them all?" He stared out into the night, where the glowing windows of the adjacent tower obscured the stars. "I don't know why I blame myself," he muttered, more to himself than to Noren. "If I followed Grenald's urgings and my own best judgment, you would hate me for it. You've got too independent a mind to want protection from the perils to which skepticism can lead—and you also have youth. That's a dangerous combination. Yet if salvation of the world lay solely in old men's caution, why would young people be born?"

Noren left the room quietly, pressing the point no further. Though the reply he'd received was cryptic, it was obviously not meant to be otherwise. Always before he had felt secure under Stefred's guidance. Now he sensed that something was wrong, terribly wrong—something Stefred himself was disturbed by. This time the challenge was not a planned lesson. It was real and unavoidable, and Stefred trusted him to find a way to meet it.

From then on the days were too busy for brooding over anything. The training dreams, unlike the edited one Stefred had devised as a test, had no element of nightmare; both Noren and Brek found them fascinating. Dreaming, they experienced not only zero gravity and the techniques of maneuvering in a spacesuit, but the specific process of dismantling starships—which, having been originally assembled in orbit, were designed to come apart. The starships were made not of metal, but of a semi-metal alloy that could not be reshaped by any means available on the planet. Had it been possible to melt them down, the material would have been used long before to make tools and machines. As it was, special tools were needed to separate the sections of airtight shell, and only a few had been kept, enough for two men to use at a time. That meant the job would be a slow one. Many trips would be required to get an entire starship down using a single small shuttle, and since only two men could work, only two would go on each flight. The fact that this also appeared to minimize the risk seemed of little comfort to Stefred.

Noren did not see Stefred often; the Dream Machine was turned over to the young women who normally operated it, and the six prospective astronauts used it in rotation, day and night. In between, they scrutinized the Inner City's towers closely, tried on the carefully preserved spacesuits, and—following the detailed instructions of the computers—checked out the shuttlecraft itself. It was stored in its original bay in a tower that had not been fully converted. The first ascent was to be made under cover of darkness so that the villagers would not observe it. After that, of course, all traffic would be on the other side of the Tomorrow Mountains.

Ten days were allotted to preparation, the maximum number that could elapse, according to the computers' projections, if the starship beacon was to function until all the work was finished. Lots were drawn whereby Scholars not held back by essential duties were designated for the first staff of the outpost; they too began to get ready. Until the tower was assembled, only a few would go; but more would follow, and with them, Inner City Technicians. That was necessary because some of the chosen Scholars were married to Technicians, and also because others, like Noren and Brek, were uncommitted. The secret of the outpost's existence could not be kept from the Inner City Technicians, and once they saw people not known to be Scholars going there, they would want an equal chance for themselves.

Everybody wanted to go beyond the mountains. Yet life in the settlement would be anything but easy. There would be backbreaking work with an absolute minimum of equipment, not only in construction, but in the raising of food. Aircars couldn't be spared to transport food indefinitely; the Scholars would have to spend part of their time farming by the primitive Stone Age methods they'd been taught in the villages as children. Noren was not looking forward to that, though he considered the founding of a new city well worth it.

Meanwhile, whatever free time he had he spent with Talyra. He had thought she would be lonely and frightened in the City, that she would seek not only his love, but his comfort; yet it didn't work out that way. To his astonishment, Talyra did not seem to have any difficulty adjusting to her new situation. She liked it. When she was unhappy it was not for her own sake, but because he could not convince her that he himself was all right.

Talyra had been given a job in the nursery, which horrified Noren when he first heard of it; it seemed unnecessarily cruel. Talyra didn't agree. She informed him that this was the first assignment for all Technician women. They were supposed to be under no illusions as to what they would face if they married: the bearing of children they could not rear. Because Talyra had been trained to deliver babies, she worked mainly as a midwife; but she also took care of the babies as the other nursery attendants did, and she didn't mind at all. "But Noren," she declared, "I *like* babies! Why shouldn't I enjoy the work?"

"Doesn't it bother you to see the mothers come in to nurse their children, loving them, yet knowing they'll have to give them up when they're old enough to be weaned?"

"That is the High Law," she answered soberly. "How else could it be? There is no room for families in the Inner City, and we who are privileged to serve here must accept it. It's hard, but everyone knows that Wards of the City go only to homes where their new parents will love them, too."

Noren could understand that view in the Scholar women—who knew why the sacrifice was necessary—although in one way it was worse for them. They also knew that on the Six Worlds, where it had been possible to get milk from animals, babies whose mothers couldn't keep them had been adopted at birth. It was more difficult for him to see why Talyra took it so calmly. Was she covering up on his account? he wondered. Or did she still trust the High Law blindly? She had remained as devout as ever, certainly; like most Technicians she attended the Inner City's open-air Vespers daily. When he could, Noren went with her, telling himself that he did it to make her happy, yet knowing inside that it was to avoid accompanying Brek to Orison, which was held at the same hour.

As a nurse, Talyra occasionally assisted in the medical research laboratory, a fact that appalled Noren still more until he realized that she was completely unaware of the true nature of what went on there. She did not know that the people she tended had volunteered to be made sick. Technicians, of course, were not permitted to do that. The volunteers were all Scholars. He himself had already been through it once, and it wouldn't be the last time. Medical research was, after all, the only type that could be of benefit to the present generation of villagers, and it would be unthinkable to try things out on *them.* There were no animals with a biological resemblance to human beings, as there had been on the Six Worlds. Some diseases that had been conquered there were no longer curable, because of a lack of drugs and facilities; then too, there were still local ills for which no help existed. Noren had tried to exact a promise that if they ever found an antidote for the poison that had killed his mother, they would test it on him; but since the same one had also killed the First Scholar, his name was far down on the volunteer list.

Inner City customs were so unlike village ones that Noren marveled at Talyra's quick adaptation to them. It was strange to see her dressed in City women's trousers instead of the skirts she had always worn, but she found them comfortable, she told him. She was awed by the quality of garments cut with scissors and stitched with metal needles; villagers had only bone. Because there weren't enough scissors and needles to go around, all City clothes were made by seamstresses, and Talyra declared that she hated sewing anyway. That surprised him, for she had never complained as he had about farm chores. He was also surprised to learn that she disliked cooking and thought the arrangement whereby even married couples lived in tiny rooms, taking all their meals in the refectory, was a fine system. Talyra was not one to rage against the world; she simply went ahead with what had to be done. Yet though she'd seemed satisfied in the village, she found the Inner City more truly satisfying—or would have, Noren saw, had it not been for his own evident turmoil.

He hadn't quite realized how hard it would be to conceal his problems if he and Talyra saw each other every day. And the problems had intensified. His feeble attempts to hide them did little good. Repeatedly he asserted that he had not been punished for his heresy, yet Talyra remained doubtful. Finally, after nearly a week of her desperate probing for reassurance, he said sharply. "Have you ever known me to lie? You broke our betrothal because I wouldn't lie about being a heretic; you defended me before the Scholar Stefred on the grounds that I'd always been honest. Why should you think I'm lying now?"

She raised her eyes to meet his, saying in a low voice. "Will you swear to me by the Mother Star that they have given you no punishment?"

"Yes," he maintained. "By the Mother Star, Talyra." As he said it, he recalled the day long before when they had quarreled over his refusal to hold such an oath sacred, thinking that on that point at least, they no longer differed.

To his amazement, she burst into tears. "Then it's as I feared," she whispered. "You—you still don't believe, Noren, I see it in your face. You're still a heretic; that's why you aren't able to accept all they offer you."

Later, lying sleepless on his bunk, it occurred to Noren that Talyra's keen intuition had again brought her very close to the truth; but at the time he was outraged. "Are you suggesting I lied at my recantation?" he demanded angrily.

"No, you wouldn't do that. You'd been forced to concede that the Scholars are wise; yet in your heart you have no faith."

"You're not being reasonable," he insisted. "Faith? What is that but to be content with ignorance? I *know,* Talyra! I know that the Mother Star exists, that it will someday appear as the Prophecy says—"

"And that we need fear nothing as long as its spirit remains with us?"

He turned away, knowing that although he could scarcely acknowledge such a belief, he was not free to deny it; and suddenly it came to him that perhaps the book of the Prophecy would not be "true in its entirety" even if the research succeeded. "*So long as we believe in it, no force shall destroy us, though the heavens themselves be consumed…*" He had not lied. He had believed it; he had supposed that human survival was certain. The First Scholar had been certain! If he hadn't been, he could never had done what he did, nor could he possibly have borne what he had to bear. Moreover, the feeling of certainty had been strong in the dreams. Had the First Scholar, a scientist who must surely have known that, himself been deluded?

"You still can't be happy," Talyra said sorrowfully, "because you aren't whole. Before, you were sure what you believed, so sure…and I used to think that once you saw how mistaken you were, that would fix everything. I—I've been stupid, Noren. Heresy isn't a sin, it's something you're born with, and recanting can't give you faith you just don't have. The Scholars don't punish; that's not their way—you simply have to live with the consequences of what you are."

Noren did not try to talk about it again. Although more than once after that night Talyra sought statements from him to allay her fears, he found that his own fears led him invariably to anger. That was not her fault and he had only a few days left to be with her, so he stifled it, kissing her instead of speaking. And when they kissed he could not regret her entrance to the City, unlikely though it seemed that the barrier to their marriage would ever fall. He now felt that the revelation of his Scholar status must be postponed indefinitely; nothing short of concrete proof that the Prophecy's promises were fulfillable would make him willing to assume the robe. How could he have imagined that his misgivings would lessen with time?

Rooming with Brek did not help, for although Noren welcomed his friendship, shared problems couldn't be pushed into the back of one's mind as easily as those not constantly discussed. "This is good, what we're doing now," Brek declared. "To build a new city, one that will eventually be open to everybody—that's fine, and rank won't make much difference there. But as far as commitment to priesthood's concerned, we're just evading the issue. When our shift at the outpost is finished, we'll have to come back...and probably the Transition Period can't begin that soon."

That it might never begin was something Noren had not mentioned to Brek; he could not bring himself to mention it to anyone, for once he did, he'd feel compelled to take some stand. He did not know what stand to take. As a result, he shared little more openness with Brek than with Talyra, and to be less than frank had always been painful for him. Day by day the pressure built up until he found himself counting the hours until the shuttlecraft's ascent. In space, at least, he would be free!

The space crew had been divided into teams by Stefred. Noren and Brek were paired, and when the lots were cast to decide who would make the first trip, they won. The computers monitored the starship's orbit and set the time of departure at three hours past midnight. No announcement was to be made to the Technicians before the tower was assembled, since its source couldn't be explained; they would later assume that it had been "called down from the sky," as the Book of the Prophecy described. So when

Noren bid Talyra goodbye he told her only that he'd been chosen for special service that would prevent him from seeing her for some time. The possibility that he might not return he refused even to consider. The perils of the undertaking seemed unreal beside his desire to escape to a place where there'd be no abstract problems.

Talyra had no reason to suspect that he was leaving the Inner City, of course. "You look more cheerful than usual," she observed. "I know I mustn't ask about the things people do when they serve inside the Hall of Scholars, but if what you've been called to do makes you look this way, it must be good." Her voice faltered briefly. "It—it must be worth another separation, even though we've just found each other—"

"It's good, darling," he agreed quickly. "It can't bring anything but good." Then, because he knew it would please her, he sought words that fit the formal religion she cherished. "The Scholar Stefred does me honor in judging me qualified," he added. "You must think of it as—as a journey, though the service to which I go is not like any journey in the world. I shall glimpse mysteries that few ever see, Talyra."

"Then I'll say farewell as for a journey," she told him, her face lighting with joy. "May the spirit of the Mother Star go with you!"

"And may its blessings be spread through my service," he replied gravely. He took her in his arms then, and they said less solemn things. Not until he'd left her did he realize that for a few minutes he had spoken sincerely and naturally in the language a priest would use.

He'd been advised to get a few hours of sleep, but he could not imagine doing so. Instead he went on up to his lodging tower's top level, where, in a small compartment that had been the observation deck of the starship, windows looked out on all sides. Each tower had such an area, used as a lounge and normally crowded; but at midnight he had it to himself. He sat gazing out at the stars, tingling with the thought that he would soon be seeing them from an identical compartment that floated free in space.

A quiet voice broke in on his growing exhilaration. "Since you weren't in your room, I thought I'd find you here," Stefred said.

Noren turned, startled. If Stefred had any last-minute instructions, why hadn't he sent for him earlier? Often enough they'd talked informally at meals and in the recreation areas, but never before had the Chief Inquisitor sought him out in his own quarters.

Stefred's face was worn, almost harrowed, though in the dim light of the observation lounge it couldn't be seen clearly. "You go to hazards of which you know nothing," he said with evident distress. "I can't explain them; yet you trust me, and I owe you honest warning."

"Look, you don't need to say anything else," protested Noren. "I've already been told how hazardous it is, and even if I hadn't, the hazards are pretty obvious."

"Not all of them."

"I've risked my life before, Stefred," Noren exclaimed impatiently. "At least I thought I was risking it, as we all did when we became heretics. Haven't I proved that I'm not going to panic?"

Stefred sat on the molded white seat that encircled the room, leaning against the window next to Noren; for a while neither of them spoke. This tower was not central like the Hall of Scholars, and nothing stood between it and the stars. None of the moons were up, not even Little Moon, so the silhouette of the Tomorrow Mountains wasn't discernible. The world was empty, Noren thought suddenly...empty except for the City and the cluster of villages surrounding it. He had never pictured it that way, but from space he would see how empty it really was.

"You've proved your courage," Stefred said slowly. "You've shown more than one kind: the courage to risk death, to face unknown horrors, to stand up for what you believe against various sorts of opposition—I could list quite a few others. You know them. But there are kinds of courage you don't know, Noren." He paused, groping for words that he apparently could not find. "The demands of this job may be greater than they seem at first."

They could hardly, Noren felt, be greater than those of coping with the problems that had descended on him in the past two weeks, from which any diversion—even danger—would be a relief. "Must we keep on talking about it?" he burst out.

"No," said Stefred, sounding oddly apologetic. "You've made your decision, and I've made mine; I shouldn't have come. As long as I'm here, though, I'll say one thing more." He faced Noren, declaring decisively, "In the past I've tested you sometimes, taught you a good deal, and I've never led you into anything beyond your ability to handle; you've learned to rely on that. You must not rely on it now. I believe you'll come through this all right, yet it's possible that you'll meet experiences you're unready for. If the going gets rough, you will need more than courage."

Puzzled, Noren asked, "What? Further knowledge?"

"In a sense."

Hot anger flashed through Noren, overriding the apprehension that had begun to grow in him. "You're deliberately withholding information that would help me? Stefred, you've no right—"

"I'm withholding information," Stefred admitted. "It would not help you; at this stage it would do the reverse. The kind of knowledge that will help is one you must gain for yourself. It exists, and you will have access to it—whatever else happens, Noren, don't let yourself forget that."

They had been through it so often in dreams that it seemed they were dreaming still: donning their spacesuits, settling into the padded seats of the shuttlecraft, strapping themselves down, and then the waiting…

It would be soundless, they knew, and they would hardly feel the motion. The shuttlecraft was not a rocket; Noren and Brek had read of the rockets used in ancient times, but the nuclear-powered shuttles that had been carried aboard starships were far more advanced. The craft would simply move out of the tower's bay and rise vertically into the dark. The liftoff would be totally out of their control. They would be in the hands of the automatic pilot and of the City's computers, which for countless years had held the program for this maneuver in unchanging memory. To the computers the passage of generations had no meaning; the last docking with an orbiting starship might have been yesterday.

Noren trusted the computers implicitly, for they were, after all, the repository of all knowledge, and if they were fallible in anything, the whole cause of human survival might as well be given up. Brek too was confident, although the role of passive crewman seemed less natural to him than to Noren because as a Technician he'd occasionally flown aircars. Neither of them had any real doubt as to their safety; the computers had checked the failing beacon signal and had pronounced it strong enough to home in on. In preprogrammed sequence, they had tested every circuit in the shuttlecraft and had certified its functioning. There was nothing tangible to worry about.

Nevertheless, as he waited through the automatic countdown, Noren was more terrified than ever before in his life.

He had not been seriously alarmed by Stefred's warning. When they'd taken leave of each other, he'd been angry, and he still was; if Stefred had purposely tried to infuriate him, he could scarcely have done a better job of it, Noren thought bitterly. To be challenged was one thing, a thing he'd always enjoyed, but to be told that this was not mere challenge and then to be denied full knowledge of the facts—it wasn't fair! He'd arrived at the shuttlecraft hot with the desire to get on with the job.

There had been a sizable group gathered to see them off—the other space teams, their tutors and closest acquaintances, Scholars with whom they'd be working at the outpost—and at first Noren had felt a sense of belonging that he'd never had occasion to experience. Having been a loner throughout boyhood, he hadn't formed many relationships in the City, despite people's friendliness. He found the warmth of their send-off surprisingly moving. But then had come a bad moment: a small incident, unimportant, yet somehow of sufficient impact to change his enthusiasm to dread.

The council chairman had been present, clad, strangely, in his blue robe, which seemed inappropriate since it was the middle of the night and not a ceremonial occasion. At least Noren hadn't anticipated any ceremony. But just before he and Brek entered the space shuttle, the group had fallen silent. People had stood, eyes lifted, and the chairman—a down-to-earth man who a short while before had been talking casually to Noren about the aircar expedition that had previously been dispatched to pinpoint the landing site—had suddenly become all priest. "We embark this night on a mission of utmost gravity," he'd said. "May the Star's spirit abide with us, and in committing ourselves to its guidance, may we be mindful that only in trusting have we any hope of success. We have made all preparations that are within our power to make. We have calculated the risks and herewith incur them, though there has been honest division among us as to whether they are justified. It is possible that only our descendants will be able to judge. We can do no more than act in the light of such knowledge as is accessible to us..."

They were frightening words, yet Noren sensed that in some way they were meant to comfort. If so, it was cold comfort, certainly. The robed priest continued into ritual: "*...There is no surety save in the light that sustained our forefathers...our future is vain except as we have faith...*" followed by some of the Prophecy.

The memory of that last Orison engulfed Noren, and he recalled with vivid clarity the dream-image that had shaken him so. In the training dreams he'd concentrated on the ship, not the view of the desolate planet, and he had shared enough of the original astronaut's thoughts to be unaffected by the sight of it. Confronting that sight in reality would be less easy.

"...May the spirit of the Mother Star safeguard you," the High Priest had concluded, clasping Noren's hands and then Brek's. Now, strapped down inside the sealed cabin, Noren was kept from panic only by determined pride. This was the most thrilling opportunity he would ever have, he told himself. Space...zero gravity...the stars...all the things he'd been looking forward to with such eagerness—was he losing his sanity? How could he be chilled, shaking, unmanned not by fear of death but by some nameless foreboding he could not even define?

Unable to endure the silence, he said the first thing that came to mind, hoping that his voice revealed no tremor. "Did Stefred talk to you tonight, Brek? Alone, I mean?"

"Yes," Brek said. "He came by our room; he wanted to see us both. I'm sure he was sorry to miss you, though the ceremony just now was much the same as what he said."

That was an odd comparison, Noren reflected, for the ceremony had been mostly ritual, and he'd never known Stefred to use ritual terms in private conversation. "How do you mean?" he questioned.

"Why, he wished me the Mother Star's protection—that sort of thing."

"Stefred spoke to you privately...as a priest?" Noren asked incredulously.

"Not exactly; it was more like any two people saying a formal goodbye."

"But he used the symbolic phrasing."

"Of course. Didn't you and Talyra use it?"

"Talyra doesn't know any other kind," Noren pointed out.

"Noren, there isn't any other kind, not for this. Would you have expected him to say just 'good luck, and I hope the shuttle works'? To invoke nothing greater than his personal friendship for me?"

He'd have expected Stefred to be honest, Noren thought in bafflement; one couldn't conceive of his being anything else. The protection of the Mother Star...well, that could be translated as the protection of the Founders' knowledge in building the shuttlecraft and programming the computers, or perhaps as the protection of their own knowledge passed down from the Six Worlds. But Brek hadn't interpreted it that way; like Talyra, Brek had read in some sort of magic. And Stefred knew Brek's mind too well not to have foreseen that he would do so.

A vibration, noiseless but powerful enough to penetrate their bones, spread through the craft, passing into their firmly restrained bodies. "We're moving," Brek whispered. They looked at each other, and Noren's terror receded, replaced by excitement.

Yet as the vibration intensified a new thought struck him. He was leaving the City—the City, the citadel of knowledge he'd sought so long and finally reached. He would be in the wilderness for many weeks to come, and though he wanted to go, he found himself once again torn. The City had never seemed a prison to him. He would miss it.

To rendezvous with the starship did not take long. As in the dreams, Noren and Brek felt the abrupt shift to weightlessness when the engines cut off; they saw the series of colored lights that told them they were docking; they felt the bump that meant the shuttlecraft had come to rest in a bay like the one it had recently left. They put on their helmets, marveling at the sensation of moving under their own volition in a realm without gravity, a realm where up and down did not exist. They threw the switch to start cabin depressurization, waited for the large green light, unfastened the hatch…and emerged into a "tower" vestibule whose outer doors stood open to a vast black sky.

No stars were visible, for the faceplates of their helmets had been darkened lest on exiting, they confront the sun. It was like the test dream, where he'd fallen blindly and in utter silence. To Noren it was silent, anyway, for there was only one radiophone for communication with the City, and Brek—whose job as a Technician had been the servicing of radiophone equipment—was carrying it. There had been no real justification for allocating two, although Stefred had seemed to feel that two were needed. He'd been overruled, since radiophones were vital for intervillage communication and like everything else had to last until the Time of the Prophecy. Noren did not mind. He could talk to Brek when necessary by touching helmets with him, and anything he might wish to say to the ground team could be relayed.

He was no longer afraid. He felt free, euphoric, just as he'd expected he would. To float in limitless vacuum, restricted only by the thin tether that anchored him to the ship; to move almost without effort by means of a skill that had become familiar to him in dreams; to take up the tools and use them upon a Machine more awesome than any from which village taboos had once barred him—that these things were possible filled him with elation. He and Brek, grasping the handholds, made their way out to the tail of the starship where dismantling was to begin. The sun at their backs, they worked without speaking. There was no need for speech. Absorbed by the task and by the wonders of their situation, secure in their trust of each other and of the technology that enabled them to do what no one had done since the Founding, they encountered no difficulty in performing the job assigned to them.

They had been told to work steadily but unhurriedly; Brek was to report their progress at intervals over the radiophone. Noren could hear neither the reports nor the replies, but he knew that if any exchange of significance took place, Brek would tell him. Each section of hull, once unjoined, was to be fastened to a line and pulled into the shuttlecraft bay. The plan was to stow them all aboard later, when there were enough to fill the hold. Brek motioned that he would take the first one in. The thing wasn't heavy, of course, since it too lacked weight, and a slight push from Noren was enough to give it momentum.

While Brek was gone Noren paused to rest. He was not really tired, but he'd never been one to stick unceasingly to a task when there was something interesting to think about—and in space there certainly was. He pulled himself around the ship to the side away from the sun, not wanting to miss this chance to adjust his helmet's filters for one quick look at the stars.

They were overwhelming. He had seen them in the dream, but not like this, not immediate, tangible, many of them brighter and more splendid than Little Moon. He was no longer dreaming. The stars were *real.*

And all at once everything else became unreal. The villages...the City...the Six Worlds that were now mere space dust...those were no part of reality! He was detached from them. It was they that were dreams; he, Noren, was alone in space, unshielded from the boundless void and the stars that burned with a beauty he could not bear. Suns...all of them suns...how many of them had worlds where peoples beyond contact lived and worked and sought knowledge? How many still had worlds? They were light-years away; some, like the Mother Star itself, might have gone nova long ago...he might be seeing only their ghosts...but if so, was anything in the universe less illusory?

He turned cold, for it was an appalling thought. Always he had trusted in the existence of truth that was firm and absolute. He had searched for it unceasingly, and had supposed he was on his way to finding it. Yet if all was illusion, if the uncertainty he'd found so dismaying involved not only human survival but the very nature of things, then he had no more of an anchor to true reality than to the planet from which he was adrift. He could not even depend on the workings of his own mind.

Once again Noren was engulfed by terror he could not understand. He wanted to cry out, to call and be answered by Brek or by someone, but there was no means of doing so. He wanted to run, to feel air touch his face, to feel life surge through his weightless body; but that was impossible too. He was paralyzed. He was cut off from life. In desperation, knowing himself powerless to combat what was happening to him, he reached out for the next handhold. At first he could not make his arm move. But in time—he was not sure whether it was a long time or a short one—he was floating in a place where he saw not only stars, but the immense rim of the gray, mist-shrouded world.

It was, as he had known it would be, empty. He had always known that no one lived anywhere but in the one small settlement maintained through the Founders' wisdom, but he had not sensed it as he did now, isolated from all contact with that settlement—that island in a huge expanse of emptiness. And there might well come a time when there would be no island! The human race would have no refuge once the City's equipment gave out. Somewhere in the immeasurably great region of dark, Noren thought, were the rays of light from the nova—the Mother Star—traveling at inconceivable speed but not yet close to him. He would die before they came close; soon after their arrival, his people might all be dead. If there was no scientific breakthrough...

Had other human races perished also? Abruptly, as he looked out into the depths, new horror assailed him; he questioned in a different way from before. Those blazing suns...uncounted billions, he had been told, in the whole universe...why did some become novas? He had heard the facts in terms of astrophysics; he knew what triggered the change physically—but that was not the answer he sought now. Why did such facts exist? Why should a star consume its worlds, its people, exiling the escapees to an alien land where the attempt to survive might be futile? For that matter, why did either stars or people come into being at all?

For the first time since learning the truth about the Mother Star, it occurred to Noren to ask not *how* things happened, but *why.*

His mind could not cope with such questions. Yet it had never failed him in the past! He'd relied on it to reason things out, to find meanings... Maybe there were no meanings. Or maybe no effort of his mind was valid. He had broken away from the world; he was drifting, falling, into a black starlit cosmos he could not comprehend. There was nothing solid or concrete to hold to. In the grip of panic, Noren lost touch with the starship itself. A remote part of him knew that if he could clutch the safety tether, he could pull himself back; at least, he knew, he should shut out the view that was so unnerving.

But this time his hand would not obey his will. This time he was truly paralyzed and could not turn the knob to remove the stars from his sight. He could not even close his eyes. He remained staring, no longer in command of either his body or his thoughts, while his panic overmastered him.

Chapter Five

It was Brek who got him back into the shuttlecraft, Brek who activated the automatic control sequence that took them down to solid, but hitherto unexplored, ground. Noren had no memory of it afterward. He was told that Brek had contacted the City by radiophone and had been advised to return at once without cargo.

The ship landed according to plan at the site of the new outpost, to which a guide-beacon had been transported by aircar, since descent to the city by daylight was undesirable and Brek was not judged competent to reset the automatic pilot in any case. A vague impression of gray rolling mossland under an even grayer sky was all Noren recalled of his first steps beyond the Tomorrow Mountains. Yet the sky seemed studded with flaming suns. Later, in the night, he was not sure whether this had been dream or hallucination; but he found his mind clear enough to know the circumstances and feel the shame.

Waking in the dark to the dry oppressive heat of the planet's natural climate, he at first thought himself back in the village; but there were no buildings. He lay on a blanket spread upon moss, and overhead was open sky. Open sky! Noren turned onto his stomach and buried his head in his arms, for he knew that if the clouds should disperse he could not bear even a glimpse of starlight. He remained still, paralyzed once more, conscious that men slept nearby and that he did not want to be seen by them. After a while he became aware that his face was wet with tears.

He had not experienced failure before, at least not of a kind caused by any personal inadequacy, and certainly not in a venture that affected the welfare of others. Tears stung and sobs wracked him, though he made no sound. The trip useless...precious hours of the beacon's functioning wasted...some later crew might well he endangered by his loss of nerve, and completion of the tower might prove impossible. He could not live with that knowledge! He could not face those who had trusted him. He could not face anyone, least of all Brek, who had witnessed his weakness. But it was worse than that. He could not face the world itself. Fear swept through him again as he saw that to him, the world was not the same place as it had been; it still seemed unreal, without meaning, like some of the ancient films he'd been shown that bore no relationship to anything he could interpret. This had nothing to do with space flight, Noren realized. Space had merely opened his eyes to a less substantial view of reality.

He had thought he could not rise and move and speak, but when morning came he found otherwise. It proved possible to go through the motions. An image came into his mind: a creature he'd heard of, a tiny mother-world creature that had over a hundred legs...he'd wondered how it knew which to move next. Had it stopped to ponder the matter it couldn't have known, yet it walked. He too would proceed without pondering. To do so was better than to reveal that what had happened to him was more than a temporary spell of panic; in any case, he could scarcely lie there and let people assume he was sick. He got up, washed his face in the basin that stood on a stone table at the edge of camp, and joined the group clustered around the breakfast fire, marveling that his muscles seemed to function just as they always had. Men greeted him cordially, with studied matter-of-factness; and when he opened his mouth to reply, words came out, despite his conviction that he would find himself mute.

The camp's leaders wanted him to go back to the City at once by aircar. Noren flatly refused. "I'm all right," he maintained, feeling inside that he was not all right, that very probably he would never be, but determined to let no one suspect it.

They frowned and shook their heads, but Noren was so insistent—and outwardly so composed—that they agreed to let Stefred decide. He shrank from talking to Stefred even by radiophone, but since he was gently informed that if he didn't, he would be sent back without his consent, there was little choice. They went away and allowed him to make the call in private.

"Don't you want to come for a day or two, at least?" Stefred asked. "You can go out again with the next supply car—"

"No," Noren declared. It was not merely that he wasn't willing to admit any need to consult a psychiatrist, for he was sure that once he met Stefred face to face and confessed the whole truth, as he would feel compelled to do, he would not be allowed to go out again. He would not be trusted to do anything. And furthermore, he could not endure the thought of confronting Talyra.

"I won't force you, Noren," Stefred said slowly. "If you need help, I'm here—we're all here, and we'll stand by you. But quite possibly this is something you have to resolve alone. Perhaps work at the outpost is the best thing for you right now." There was a long pause, so long that Noren wondered whether the radiophone was malfunctioning. Finally Stefred's voice continued, "There's a good deal I could say, but I don't think you're ready to understand it. Just remember what I told you the other night."

Noren was too numb to be angry, and though his impulse was toward rage when he recalled their talk in the observation lounge, he was too honest not to know that it was mostly rage against himself. There had been plain suspicion of his vulnerability to panic. Stefred had been troubled from the beginning, and had offered warnings that he, Noren, had chosen to ignore. Still, it was unlike Stefred to take an "I told you so" attitude.

Avoiding Brek, Noren went to the camp leaders and asked for work. There was plenty to be done. The camp was in wilderness, and not all the allocated equipment had yet arrived. Little would be provided in any case; the occupants would live under conditions of extreme difficulty, much as the first-generation villagers had, but with the added hardships of the Founders. They would receive nothing but what was necessary to sustain life.

The first priority was construction of a foundation for the tower. It was being built of stone and mortar without the aid of either machines or metal tools. The hardiest men among the Scholars had arrived some days earlier to start it, but the job was not finished, and Noren's strong back was welcomed. He in turn welcomed heavy physical labor that left him no time to think.

He worked ceaselessly, finding that hands that had learned masonry in boyhood did not forget their skill. In the villages stonesetting was not a trade, but a measure of manliness, for whenever a new house was raised all the neighbors came to help. Most Scholars had been reared as villagers; they'd known well the ancestral methods of building that had been passed down from father to son. Like all of the other unchanging village ways, the methods were effective. They were not subject to improvement, for the engineers of the first generation had been ingenious people quite competent to devise the most effective uses of stone.

It was more laborious in camp than in the villages, since there were as yet no work-beasts. Getting a work-beast into an aircar would have been an utterly impractical undertaking. Aircars were not very large, and work-beasts were not very cooperative; their adaptation to unpurified water and native fodder had, of course, been detrimental to their intelligence. Moreover, there were more vital things than beasts of burden to be carried aboard the few aircars available. Nor was it feasible to herd any beasts by land, for aside from the length and difficulty of the journey—which would necessitate climbing to high altitudes and packing enough food and water to last many weeks—there were savages in the mountains, the now subhuman mutants whose ancestors had fled there after heedlessly incurring genetic damage. They too had lost their intelligence, but they were fierce and dangerous. So work-beasts could be brought only in embryonic form after the laboratories were ready, and until they arrived and matured, the wicker sledges on which stones were moved must be pulled by hand.

Wheels would have been a tremendous advantage; villagers, having never heard of them, did not miss them, but the Scholars never ceased regretting that the one invention most basic to the civilization of the old worlds had proved impossible in the new. Each and every person who learned anything of the Six Worlds found it hard to believe that there wasn't some way a wheel could be fabricated. On the Six Worlds they were made of wood, but the new world had no trees. It was simple to cut one from softstone, as sledge runners, furniture, and the like were cut; but softstone wore away quickly from friction, and besides, stone wheels would not turn properly on stone axles. They just weren't efficient enough to be worth the trouble. It was equally impractical to manufacture plastic wheels, for though plastics of the required hardness had been developed from native vegetation, there was no metal to build the high-pressure equipment needed to mold them. Villagers had potters' wheels and millstones, but for transport the primitive sledges were indispensable.

Sledges were meant to be drawn over sanded roads, but in the camp there were no roads at all. The road-grading machine—there was only one in existence—was being used by Technicians in the establishment of a new village. Under the High Law whenever forty families petitioned for a village of their own, they had a right to hire the Technicians' services: road-building, clearing of farmland, initial fertilization and treatment of the soil, purification of the clay for a pipeline to connect another common cistern to the

City water supply—all the necessary jobs that could be done only through the use of the sacred Machines, climaxed by the installation of a Radiophone Machine in the new village center as a symbol of religious sanction. That took precedence over the Scholars' needs. Until the obligation to the villagers had been met, the camp would do without machinery.

The site of the settlement was anything but attractive. Noren, once he became clear-headed enough to survey it, observed that it was very much like the land he had known all his life: undulating gray country, in this case unrelieved by the fresh green of quickened fields. There were fewer knolls, perhaps, and fewer of the purple shrubs that grew mainly on high ground. Then too, the mountains were closer, and their crags of white and yellow rock rose further above the horizon. But somehow he had expected "beyond the Tomorrow Mountains" to be a more novel region.

Maybe it was, he thought ruefully. He was really in no condition to judge. He was still detached from the world; it was flat, unreachable, as if an invisible screen stood between him and what he saw. It was more dreamlike than any of the controlled dreams had been, and far more frightening...

Grimly he turned to the work, swinging his stone pick with a strength he'd not known he possessed. He was thankful the sun was not out, and not merely because of the heat—the sun was too vivid a reminder of those other suns that had overwhelmed him. Could it be possible that he was insane? he wondered in terror. Should he have told Stefred the whole story? He was repelled by the idea; his mind, the sharpness of his mind, had always been what he most valued. Unable to keep his thoughts blank, he allowed them to drift, feeling a strange astonishment that despite the seeming unreality of his surroundings, he'd lost none of the knowledge he had acquired.

He thought of the mother world. Impressions from controlled dreams returned, arousing sudden longing. One dream in particular had taught him much about the lacks of his planet; a dream in which he'd immersed himself in cool water...immersed himself fully, so that he was floating in it! Both the City and the new outpost had been purposely located far from deep bodies of water. Maps made from orbital surveys showed many big lakes, yet no lake could be approached safely until such time as synthesization of metal made large-scale purification feasible. Although the High

Law was an adequate deterrent to drinking impure water, a taboo against all swimming would be impossible to enforce. As he labored in the dry outdoor heat for the first time since his enlightenment, Noren understood that, and he raged anew at the cruelty of his race's exile. Before, he had simply accepted it. Now every turn of his mind led to the unanswerable *why...why...*

At midday everyone paused to eat. Noren had no appetite; he scarcely noticed the meagerness of the meal, though he knew that the plan was for the expedition to subsist on as short rations as possible. While there was plenty of food to spare in the settled area of the planet, room for transporting it aboard the aircars was very limited, and until a local harvest could be produced, hunger would be the rule. Hunger—and also thirst. So far all pure water, too, had to be transported, and the likelihood of rain was small. The general overcast that had made the planet look predominantly white from space rarely produced rain, and the equipment for weather control could not be duplicated. The purification plant, when installed, would have to serve for irrigation of crops as well as for drinking and bathing; strict water rationing was destined to continue.

These discomforts were not discussed. No one complained; no one reminded anyone else to be abstemious. The rations for the day were set out on a crude softstone table and each man helped himself. People sat around in informal groups to eat, talking and laughing, with inward resolve to accept the demanding conditions of camp life as a personal challenge; their morale was high. After all, everybody had wanted to come. The thrill of the venture was ample compensation for the drawbacks.

Noren stood apart, reflecting with bitter dismay that the thrill could no longer reach him. He ate because one must eat to work, but the bread seemed tasteless and his mouth was so dry that it was hard to swallow, although he took his fair share of water. The fear in him grew steadily: fear not of any external threat, but of a self he had not met before and did not wholly trust. His normal confidence in himself was gone. If only, he thought numbly, there was some way to reverse time...to get back what he'd had before confronting the naked stars!

Yet if there was a way to reverse time, it would also be possible to get back all that had existed before the nova. Why must time be as it was? Why, for that matter, must any laws of the universe be as they were? The science he'd studied explained them, but it did not explain their reason for being. It did not explain why six worlds should be destroyed by a nova, nor, in fact, did it tell why even one world should exist in the first place...

Seeing Brek approaching, Noren gulped the last of his bread and went back to work. He spoke to no one, and, once he'd rebuffed them, the others let him be, respecting his desire for privacy. Toward evening the clouds broke, and he avoided glancing at the sun that burned down on him, confining his thought to the effort of handling stone.

He stopped for supper with reluctance. Everyone else was exhausted, since even the former villagers were not yet reconditioned to heavy labor, and those born as Technicians, like Brek, had never performed it before. Noren welcomed the pain of his muscles as a sign that he was still in bodily touch with the world. Ordinary things—the smoke of cook-fires, the spongy feel of the moss on which he sat, the sound of people's voices—seemed like random bits of a cup smashed beyond restoration.

Brek came toward him again, and this time Noren could not escape. "Look," Brek began, "we don't have to talk about it if you'd rather not. But I want you to know that I—I understand, and—well, that I don't blame you—"

Understand? thought Noren wretchedly. Brek couldn't possibly understand what had happened; nobody could. It would be impossible to describe even if he wanted to confide in someone. "I'm all right now," he said sharply. "I just want to be left alone."

"Aren't you coming to Orison?"

"Orison—here?"

"Well, not the formal kind, but everybody's getting together around the fire. You can't just sit here in the dark by yourself."

Noren got up and strode away, his back to the flickering glow of the bonfire on which, now that the cooking was done, more moss was being heaped. He could not, he felt, maintain his composure at such a gathering. The idea filled him with panic.

But as darkness deepened across a clear sweep of sky, the panic became worse; and resignedly Noren turned toward the light that outshone the distant, disquieting stars.

* * *

One day was much like another. The stone foundation was finished and erection of the tower began; its sections were brought down from orbit in the proper order for reassembly. Noren had little aptitude for work requiring manual dexterity, but he had been taught the use of the special tools and was thoroughly familiar with the starship hull's design—moreover, he was determined to perform flawlessly. It was the only way to stave off the solicitousness of well-meaning fellow Scholars. He did not want their pity. He knew that they sincerely wished to help, but there was no help for what had befallen him.

At first he didn't think he could possibly find the courage to walk in space again, but when the other two teams had made trips, so that it was rightfully his turn—and Brek's—Noren knew there was only one course. Steeling himself for the most blatant lie he had ever attempted, he approached the camp leaders and begged for another chance, insisting that he was not afraid. "I panicked before," he confessed grimly, "but by the Mother Star, I won't let it happen again." He had met panic repeatedly since the flight, panic just as severe although even more groundless in terms of tangible cause, and he'd managed to keep it under control. He hoped no one guessed how much weakness he was hiding.

It was no use. His request for further space flights was denied. That was scarcely surprising in view of all that hinged on the success of each one, but it was a blow to his faltering self-esteem. He went away hating himself because inside he felt more relief than resentment.

Though he was sure Brek must despise him, there were no outward signs of it; Brek tried to go on as if nothing had changed. Noren, to whom the whole world had changed, was irritated by this and sometimes hot-tempered, for he could not endure any friendly gestures of sympathy. Before long a new space partner for Brek was sent out from the City, and the flights proceeded on schedule. Brek never spoke of anything that occurred during those flights within Noren's hearing, but he talked incessantly of other subjects. He went out of his way to ask advice, and although Noren was brusque, his pretense of normalcy demanded that he offer what he could. It proved to be a strain even when the queries concerned science.

For the prospective scientists in the group, training was soon resumed. Gradually the camp started to take on some semblance of a civilized community. Though no effort could yet be expended to build shelters, which were not required by the climate, people chose personal living areas and began to spend some of their evenings away from the community bonfire. A few of the City's study-desk screens were sent out, and new discs for them, along with recharged power cells, came aboard every aircar. At first Noren was pleased, since his practice in disciplined concentration enabled him to shut out the world through study whenever he was not working. But the experiences he'd undergone had left their mark. Science was not the joyous pursuit it once had been; its lack of certainty had robbed it of weight, and the basic questions that were tormenting him had raised doubts as to how much of it could be considered valid. Brek did not know that. To Brek it was all new and exciting and authoritative. As his tutor, Noren found himself more and more a hypocrite.

He had never expected to be one of Brek's permanent tutors, and in fact the appointment was not official; but everything was informal in camp, and since no one else assumed the role, it fell to him by default. The Scholars who would normally have held the responsibility, specialists fully trained in nuclear physics, were not at the outpost; they were all in the City devoting themselves to the culminating experiments. Brek did not need their guidance, for he was still at an elementary level and his immediate job left little leisure for study. There was no possibility of his progressing beyond Noren's ability to instruct.

Insofar as he could, Noren kept their sessions strictly technical, and there were plenty of safe topics to occupy Brek's attention. First, there was the matter of why the natural resources of the planet could not be utilized for the building of machines. That they could not was something a new Scholar accepted uncritically, for no villager or even Technician had the background to realize that certain metallic and semi-metallic elements did exist in the native rock; but once a trainee's study of chemistry began, simple explanations became inadequate. It quite naturally appeared that since the Six Worlds' scientists had been so knowledgeable, they ought to have been able to find substitutes for the metals they'd used at home. But in this, at least, Noren was on firm ground. He could assure Brek categorically that it was impossible to obtain usable metal by mechanical or chemical processes. Metals with the properties needed for machines—strength, durability, and so forth—had never been present in large quantities, and what deposits there once were had been taken by the mysterious alien visitors of the past, whose technology had apparently surpassed that of the Six Worlds.

Plastics couldn't serve as a substitute, either, any more than they could be used for wheels. The large-scale manufacture of plastics would require more than the raw materials; it would demand high heat or high pressure, neither of which could be obtained without metal machinery. The same was true of glass and ceramics, which like plastics were limited to the small amounts that could be produced with the City's existing equipment. The planet offered no fuel that would burn hot enough to melt such materials. Without heat or, for that matter, metal cauldrons, there could be no progress beyond unfired pottery.

Thus the Founders had pinned all humanity's hope on transmutation of specific elements through nuclear fusion, in full knowledge of their audacity in setting such a goal. Only recently had Noren come to see how audacious they had been. Foolishly so, perhaps. Still, they'd had no alternative. The orbital surveys had shown the entire solar system to be metal-poor; if there had been a chance of getting metal from any of the moons or other planets, the Founders would have tried it—but there'd been no such chance. The Visitors who'd preceded them had done a thorough job.

Speculation about the Visitors had never ceased among the Scholars, although without more data no conclusions could be reached. In the City the topic was mentioned occasionally, but in camp, around the evening fires, it was attacked with renewed interest. In the back of everyone's mind was the wild hope, "What if we should *find* something? What if we should uncover evidence not only of their presence, but of their origin, or of how long ago they came?"

Noren sat frozen during these discussions, unnaturally silent, cold with an apprehension he could neither analyze nor push aside. His people were not the only sentient beings; they had absolute proof that they were not...yet they could make no contact with their predecessors or even determine whether any of them still lived. What sort of a universe was it where such barriers prevailed? Were all human races isolated, condemned to perpetual ignorance of the rest? Did others, too, rise to greatness and then, through senseless, futile tragedy, die out, like grain shoots crushed beneath the hoofs of work-beasts loosed into a field? Perhaps the Visitors' sun had also ceased to exist except in the form of light rays out somewhere between the stars, invisible because no one was there to see. Were stars, like men, inescapably doomed to death?

He had never thought much about death except in an abstract way. He'd believed himself beyond reprieve during his trial and inquisition and had been afraid; he had felt vague surprise while sharing the dying thoughts of the First Scholar, who as an old man had given up life without fear; he had, earlier, grieved over the deaths of his mother and of a boyhood friend. He had been horrified by the concept of racial extinction and had pledged himself unhesitatingly to its prevention. But he had barely begun to face the implications of prevention being impossible, and somehow, doing so raised the awareness that he himself would someday really die. Alone in the darkness of the outdoor nights, Noren let himself consider death not merely as an abstraction but as a future certainty, feeling terror such as he had never imagined. He, to whom knowledge was all-important, confronted the depths of the unknown, and was overpowered. Had this been buried in him all along? he wondered in dismay. Had his panic in space been based on physical fear after all? The idea added both to his inner shame and to his determination to show no further weakness, but the memory of that paralyzing moment continued to haunt him; though he drove himself to exhaustion in an attempt to suppress it, it followed him into his dreams.

Exhaustion was the common lot of the entire team, of course; strenuous work on short rations had its effect on everyone. Yet all the men had their pride. Moreover, as village youths many had taken pleasure in competition, and camp life brought back remembrance if not full prowess. Stewards and High Priests they might be, but there was nothing somber about them; before long somebody suggested a stonesetting contest, a proposal adopted with great enthusiasm. Though the accompanying festivities could not take place without women and children to watch, to reward the victor, and to prepare the traditional feast, it seemed a good way to initiate work on the water purification plant, which in the absence of domes would have to be installed in an ordinary stone structure.

The stonework of such structures was crude, since without metal tools it was necessary to rely mainly on rocks small enough not to require cutting. Fortunately these were abundant in the area;

the men not engaged in erecting the tower had been able to gather them without too much difficulty. Everybody wanted to take part in the contest, so on the day chosen, tower construction was temporarily suspended, and only the current space crew had to miss out. As was usual in the villages on such occasions, people rose and ate before daybreak, and by the time the sun appeared the workers were in place around the square marked off in the gray earth where the building's walls were to be. Sunrise came late beyond the Tomorrow Mountains. The nearby ridges to the east blocked all rays long past the normal hour of dawn. Noren stood facing them, wondering as he waited how they could look so tall when from space, they'd been merely a yellowish blotch. He felt no excitement; the high spirits of his companions lowered his own by contrast—but he was resolved that as far as stonesetting was concerned, he was not going to make a poor showing.

At sunup the men began a song, taking stones into their hands in readiness. It was the folk hymn prescribed by custom, passed on from one generation to the next as the building skills themselves had been passed on:

May our strength be everlasting,
May our skill be sure.
Till the Star's light shines upon it
May the stone endure.

Noren did not join in, not even when the work started and the songs became livelier and, before long, bawdier. He was kept from it by more than the new depression; his boyhood had not been happy enough to be brought back willingly. Some of the others, apparently, had had fun in the villages, heretics though they were. They were enjoying this chance to relive bygone years. Or was it simply that they were hoping to forget what they knew of the future?

Not once in camp had Noren heard anyone express doubt about the successful outcome of Grenald's experiments. The issue had been argued at the meeting in the City, but after the vote, even the skeptics seemed to have convinced themselves that they, here beyond the mountains, were the pioneers of the Transition Period. Had not another city in fact begun to rise? Was not real evidence of the Prophecy's fulfillment at last before them? Surely the breakthrough would come soon, people declared; surely the vision they saw when they surveyed the drab and desolate camp would be transformed into reality! Noren had always felt that villagers were prone to believe in things because they wanted to, but it was disillusioning to find that Scholars were no different.

He attacked the work that day as never before, conscious only of the stones he handled, not bothering to count them or to notice the rate at which his own section of wall grew in comparison to others; not even noticing when fresh mortar was brought by one of the men who'd chosen not to compete. As the sun rose higher and the day's heat increased, he stripped to the waist, throwing aside his tunic without a glance. Sweat poured from his body and ran into his eyes so that he could scarcely see. He could not see anyway; he was giddy; but it did not seem to matter. Vaguely he perceived that the pain in his arms and back was more severe than any he could remember, yet that did not matter either. He did not pause except during the rest periods called at intervals, when he waited apathetically for the signal to resume work. His body moved of its own accord. It was as though it were no part of him.

Eventually the light began to fade, and Noren decided that he was on the verge of passing out. He did not mind; it might, he thought, be a good thing. Not until men surrounded him, thrusting a mug of ale into his hands, did he become aware that the sun had dropped below the horizon and that the contest was over. And even then he could not take in the fact that he had won.

Dazed, he looked around at the stone walls that had not been there that morning. Stone was real, stone was tangible; it would indeed last until the Mother Star's light shone upon it...but what did that mean? The stone might well outlast the men, and perhaps, in some dim future age, other Visitors would come and wonder who the builders had been. Such things ought to fit together in a pattern, Noren felt, but he could see no pattern at all. He let his fellows carry him to the bonfire, and he drank the ale that, in lieu of a feast, was to supplement the usual food ration; but he knew no joy of victory. The best he could manage was grim satisfaction in not having disgraced himself.

Sparks from the blazing moss flew upward, mingling with the stars. Noren's eyes did not follow them; he had avoided looking up of late. But a recollection of other campfires came to him: fires in the village square, where he and Talyra had sat together in the first season of their betrothal. "If she were here—" Brek began, congratulating him, and Noren turned away. If she were here, she would place the victor's string of polished pebbles around his neck, and she would kiss him while the people watched and cheered; but later, when they were alone, it would be no good at all. She would sense his emptiness, and Talyra's pity was one thing he could not bear.

He drooped with a weariness that was as much of spirit as of body. The singing, which had not continued past early morning, was taken up again: not only the bawdy songs, but slow, sad ones, love songs and laments for nameless things lost in the haze of legend. One after another men recalled ballads they had not heard since boyhood, marveling that those from different villages knew them. It was not really surprising, considering their common ancestry and the fact that the traders who traveled from place to place spent their nights in taverns; yet somehow the provincial attitude of their youth was hard to shake.

"You know, we have one great advantage in this world," someone remarked during a lull. "Despite the reversion, despite all that was taken from us, we still have the part of our heritage our forebears struggled longest and hardest for. We have unity."

"What do you mean?" asked Brek, who had not yet studied much of the Six Worlds' history.

"We have a single culture that's expanding instead of many that must eventually merge. That wouldn't be good, of course, if it hadn't been based on a combination of the mother world's cultures. Diversity is valuable. But it means we won't have to go through the painful business of resolving cultural conflicts all over again."

"The Founders spared us that," another man agreed. "Think what we'd have faced if people had reverted to more primitive customs without keeping any sense of common identity! All the villagers' frustration over their inability to progress would have been turned into disputes between separate villages."

"I'm still confused," Brek admitted. "We're united by the Prophecy and the High Law; we couldn't survive without them. But those of us who know the secrets don't like the system. We're working to get rid of it. So how can you call such unification an advantage?"

"We're working toward the time when we can reveal the secrets, relinquish our control of the City, and abolish stratified castes. We're not trying to get rid of the High Law, though. That will always be necessary here."

"Well, yes. People won't ever be able to drink unpurified water, or cook in pots made from unpurified clay. And religion's certainly not going to become obsolete."

Wasn't it? Noren thought. What good would it do, once its promises had been kept? And if keeping them should prove impossible, it would become a hoax, an inexcusable deception—the Founders themselves had been horrified by the idea of upholding a *false* religion. "Brek," he protested, "surely you don't think heresy should be a crime after the Prophecy's fulfillment is…settled."

"I didn't say that."

"Heresy is not a crime under the High Law," someone else reminded them. "Only village laws forbid it, and those laws aren't going to be changed overnight; it will take time for intolerance to be outgrown."

"But can't we issue some kind of proclamation?"

"Certainly not. We mustn't interfere with democratic government then any more than we do now."

"The point I was making about unity," explained the first man, "is that in the culture that's grown up on this planet, religious tradition will never be a cause of strife. Individual heretics may be persecuted—although we as priests will always offer them sanctuary—but groups of people with different symbols for the same idea will never go to war over it, as happened on the mother world when intolerance prevailed."

"They went to war over the *symbols?"* Noren burst out incredulously. He had learned enough about the mother world to know what war was, and he could understand why it had occurred when dictatorships had tried to rule by force. But over religion…

"Think of how the people among whom you grew up felt about heresy," the man suggested, "and then imagine them deciding that all the citizens of the next village were heretics. Or picture a case where quite a few of them agreed with some new interpretation of the Prophecy, and were condemned as a group, including their families—"

A sharp cry interrupted him. On the opposite side of the bonfire, one of the older men had collapsed.

* * *

It was Derin, the camp's Chief Mason. A heart attack, the doctors called it, an attack brought on by the exertion of the contest, in which he had won third place. No one could have predicted it, for he'd been pronounced fit upon examination in the City; still, because of his age, his friends had tried to persuade him to be content with designing the structure. Derin had laughed at them. Stonework was his pride, and he had won setting contests before. Unlike most Scholars, he had lived in his village until middle life, and had been a highly respected craftsman. City confinement had been a real sacrifice for him, though his natural engineering talent had been put to good use in the drawing of plans for the building to be done during the Transition Period.

People clustered around. "It is good construction," Derin whispered. "The stone will endure—"

"The stone will endure," his friends agreed. Two or three of them knelt beside him, clasping his hands. There was nothing the doctors could do. On the Six Worlds, physicians had been able to replace failing hearts, but on this one the equipment for such surgery was unavailable. Even therapeutic drugs were lacking. As in so many other ways, things had moved backward.

Noren watched in horror as Derin, half-conscious, went on, lapsing into the viewpoint of his youth. "My great-grandfather built the arch of the meeting hall; his name's over it still. This will stand as long; it will stand until the Star appears, and the Cities rise to replace it."

"It will stand far longer," people assured him. "It is part of a City; the Prophecy's fulfillment has begun."

"Yes...yes, I forget..." He sighed, and Noren saw from his face that he was still in pain, though he was trying to conceal it. "In the village we thought Scholars were immortal. We thought they knew all the answers. I...I think I wish it were true."

"The answers exist, Derin."

Although the City was contacted by radiophone, all knew that return could not save Derin even if he lived until an aircar came. The outpost's chief brought a blue robe, which he laid over Derin's helpless form. "May the spirit of the Star abide with you," he said gently, as one of the doctors began induction of hypnotic anesthesia.

Abide with him? thought Noren, aghast. Abide with him *where?* The man knew he was dying, and there were no non-Scholars present; surely this was not a time for pretense.

But the words seemed a solace, somehow, for when Derin closed his eyes he was smiling.

In the morning, when the aircar arrived and everyone gathered for the formal ritual of sending the body to the City, it took all Noren's self-control to attend. He had been to such ceremonies before, not only his mother's but those held for other people of his village—but that had been before he knew what was done with bodies. The idea of one's mortal remains being sent to the mysterious City, where they were given into the custody of revered High Priests, was accepted by villagers as entirely fitting. Even Technicians viewed it so; they were unaware of the necessity for recycling all chemical elements and had no information about the converters that had once been standard equipment aboard the starfleet. Yet to Noren the use of corpses for the same purpose as other human wastes, however well disguised, did not seem dignified. And the recitation of words designed to mask deception ought not, certainly, to be practiced among Scholars who knew the facts.

"Now to the future we commit him, our beloved friend, knowing that in death he will continue to serve the hidden end he served in life, as shall we all, being eternally heirs to that which has been promised us through the spirit of the Mother Star..." Staring dizzily at Derin's body, wrapped in its blue robe as a villager's would be wrapped in white, Noren feared that he was going to be sick before the ceremony concluded. How could these men listen to such words? Many of them had been close to Derin, had loved him!

Yet the words went on. *"For as this spirit abides with us, so shall it with him; it will be made manifest in ways beyond our vision..."* That, Noren perceived, did not appear to fit the case. That kind of statement was applicable less to one's body than to one's mind. He frowned, puzzled; all the symbolism of public ritual was supposed to be translatable by the enlightened. He must be overlooking something.

As a child, when he had asked what happened to people's minds when they died, he had received the usual reply. "That is a mystery," his mother had said serenely. "People cannot understand such things as that; only the Scholars know them." It was a matter in the same category as how Machines worked, why soil must be quickened before crops would grow, and by what means the Prophecy had been transmitted from an invisible star to the hand of whoever had first written it down. About these other things he'd gone on wondering, and his curiosity had in due course been satisfied; to the first he had not given much attention—not, that is, until recently.

The Scholars around him did not seem perplexed. What if he was to ask someone what those words were meant to signify? His pride, of course, was too great for that, since it would mean confessing that the issue troubled him; yet a Scholar would reply honestly... *"He is forever of humankind, holding a share in human destiny; his place is assured among those who lived before him and those who will come after, those by whom the Star is seen and their children's children's children, even unto infinite and unending time..."* That was all right for villagers...or was it? Would that particular bit of poetry contribute to humankind's permanent survival, or had the High Priests, in this at least, exceeded their bounds?

The rites ended, the aircar rose and hovered silently over the circle of people whose faces were still turned devoutly upward toward the sky, the original source of human knowledge and the domain of all secrets. He had seen that sky more clearly than most, Noren thought; he could still see fierce blazing stars beyond the soft blanket of life-sustaining air, which from above was not blue, but gray and foul-looking. So had the Founders, however. How had they endured such a view? Had they closed their eyes to the question of meaning, of whether there was any logic at all to life, to death, to the evolution and destruction of worlds?

All his life Noren had questioned, but never so deeply as this; he had never encountered problems that seemed to make less and less sense as he continued to ponder them. He had assumed that the City held all the answers. And it did! he thought suddenly while he watched the aircar start toward it, ascending to cross the Tomorrow Mountains. It must! Realization struck him forcefully, bursting the bonds of his terror. Was not the computer complex the repository of all truth? In the City he was free to ask the computers anything he wished, and though he had not previously framed such queries as were now torturing him, there was no bar to his doing so. His fellow Scholars had perhaps done it long ago. Neither they nor the Founders could have closed their eyes completely;

yet they could scarcely be at peace with themselves—and even, at times, laugh about things—unless they had information that he did not. To get the information, he had merely to go back, as he'd been advised.

But he could not go so soon. That would look as if he had decided to seek Stefred's help; it would be an admission that he felt unfit to finish the job at the outpost. He was unwilling to concede anything of the sort, and not only because of what others would think, for he knew that without proving his capability he could not live with himself. He could never rely on himself again.

So in the weeks that followed, he went on working; he went on studying; he went on tutoring Brek; and though these pursuits gave him no pleasure, neither did he find them intolerable. From time to time he was struck with amazement at his ability to follow them while doubting their real significance, but for the most part, he kept doubt from his thoughts. He no longer let himself worry, nor did he have spells of unaccountable fear. Life in camp was simply neutral—gray, like the surrounding wilderness of unquickened land. He was suspended from the world. He had not yet returned from space. Yet in the depths of his mind he knew there would be a re-entry, a resumption of the search for truth; and for that he began to plan. The planning was a light in the grayness.

He had come to understand, Noren felt, what Stefred had meant when they'd talked over the radiophone. The reminder about their last discussion had referred not to the ignored warnings, but to the final part. *You will need more than courage,* Stefred had told him the night he left the City. *The kind of knowledge that will help is one you must find for yourself. It exists, and you will have access to it.* That was typical of Stefred's subtle guidance. Though he couldn't have known what would happen in space, Stefred might well have guessed that sooner or later certain questions would arise. He would not provide answers in advance. He would expect a person of intelligence to know where to look for the answers.

Eagerly, desperately, Noren planned his questions: the questions he would ask the computers when the opportunity came.

The final space flight was completed safely, with the shuttle bringing back the portion of starship that contained the weak and faltering beacon. Slowly the tower took shape, rising ever higher as level after level was added to it. The work was fantastically difficult, for without any materials with which to build scaffolding, the builders had to attach each section while standing on the one below, assisted only by ropes and lightweight plastic pulleys. Noren and the members of the space teams did the actual rejoining of the starship, but many Scholars helped get pieces into place, and one fell to his death from a great height. There were several lesser accidents. Meanwhile, other men began the job of interior compartmentalization, which was to be far less extensive than in the City's towers since relatively little of the limited plastic material could be transported.

Noren found it hard to work high above the ground, not because he feared falling, but because it reminded him of the way he had clung helplessly to the starship in space. He suspected that others had the same thought; during supper of the evening before the attachment of the tower's top, Emet, one of the outpost administrators, sat down beside him. "I'm going for supplies tomorrow," he said, "and we thought you might like to come along. There's to be a conference in the City—"

"I have work to do," Noren said stubbornly.

"You can be spared for a day. We heard this afternoon that a conference is being held to discuss some results of the experimentation. You and Brek are the only people here specializing in nuclear physics, and one of you should attend. You will learn by listening."

Noren's spirits lifted. This was the chance he'd been waiting for! What Emet was proposing might not be a mere excuse; they might really think it of some value for him to go. Obviously, the experiments had not yet been completed successfully, for if they had, it would have been announced and everyone would be jubilant. However, there could well be new data of importance. The thought didn't excite him as it once would have, but he was elated for another cause: in the City he might have time to spare...enough time to consult the computers.

Since Derin's death an aircar had been kept in camp at night, so that in an emergency it could set out for the City at dawn. This also made it possible for people to go after supplies, take care of other necessary business, and return before dark the same day. It was not safe to cross the mountains after dark; carrying irreplaceable equipment over them was risky enough in broad daylight.

The outpost had been located where it was only because of the need to have it well separated from the City in case of future nuclear accident, yet at the same time within easy range of the aircars. This outweighed the inherent danger of flying back and forth across a tall ridge. Still, at times when vital metal things, such as components of the new power and water purification plants, were being brought, everybody was nervous lest there be a crash. Aircars were not hard to pilot, but they had been used almost exclusively at low altitudes, and the mountain country was hazardous.

It was also strange and forbidding, Noren thought, as he looked down on it the next morning. Little grew there, and many of the rocks were a garish yellow instead of gray or white like most stone of the lowlands. No one knew much about the mountains. They had not been explored except through occasional aerial surveys that had added nothing to the data obtained by the Founders from orbit, other than to verify that the mutant "savages" did exist there. Expeditions on foot were, of course, impossible, since not enough pure water could be carried.

Noren had never been in an aircar before. As a small boy he had once touched one that had come to his father's farm, and ever since, he had longed to fly in one; now, like so many things, it had come to him too late. There was no thrill left. He had lost the capacity to feel. Emet looked at him worriedly, and Noren sensed that the camp's leaders had hoped attendance at the conference might cheer him up. He knew they were still deeply concerned about him, although they concealed it just as he concealed his own feelings. Determined to forestall any suggestion that his free time in the City might well be spent in a visit to Stefred, Noren asked quickly, "Could I try the controls, Emet?"

The man nodded. "Yes, as soon as we're past the mountains." He seemed to relax a little, and Noren found that although he himself was becoming more and more tense, it was not the tenseness of despair. Rather, expectancy was rising in him. He was about to obtain answers! The computers had answers to everything except the research problems yet to be solved. He was not so naive as to suppose that the answers would be easy to comprehend; but tonight, at least, he would have facts to ponder.

Above the rolling land between mountains and City, he took over the aircar's direction lever, which could be used from either of the two front seats, and Emet showed him how to maintain level flight. There was nothing difficult about it; Noren was almost sorry when Emet resumed control for the descent into the open top of the huge entrance dome. But his eagerness to gain access to the City's repository of truth outweighed all other thoughts. He shivered with anticipation as he stepped onto the landing deck.

"The conference is set for an hour past noon," Emet told him, "and I'll meet you here afterward." He smiled. "Until it starts, you're free to do as you like."

Walking down the stairs and into the main corridor, Noren realized why Emet had not inquired into his plans. He'd assumed he would look for Talyra! Yet the last thing he wanted was to encounter her at this point. Perhaps later, if what he learned proved heartening... He went swiftly to the computer room, hoping fervently that he would not have to wait for a free console; after weeks of waiting, he did not believe he could endure even a quarter-hour more.

He needn't have worried; the computer room was strangely deserted. Its dim light seemed somehow eerie when not a single person was in sight. Luck was with him, Noren thought thankfully. Even his privacy was assured; no one would be watching over his shoulder, wanting him to hurry. He settled himself in the booth farthest from the door and with trembling hands prepared to key in the first of his carefully planned queries.

Noren had conversed with the computer complex often enough to know better than to make the questions too general. He knew that to ask, "What is the meaning of life?" would very likely produce the same result as Brek's initial request for a full description of the mother world's history; the computer would offer more information than could be presented in a reasonable length of time. He had planned ahead because he'd been aware that the issue must be approached systematically, logically, if he was not to waste any of the precious moments available to him. Computers, he'd learned, gave precisely what was asked for—that much, and no more. He had found that it paid to be equally precise.

Nevertheless, his fingers were shaking so that on the very first sentence he miskeyed. WHY DID AN UNPREVENTABLE TRAGDEY STRIKE THE HUMAN RACE? he asked, and the computer responded, NO REFERENT. His heart contracted; then he saw that he had spelled it "tragdey" and tried again, telling himself that this nervousness was foolish.

The question might involve deep feelings on his part, but the computer, which had none, would treat it just like any other inquiry. The answer would appear as quickly and as clearly as if he had requested a mathematical formula.

But it did not. Noren watched the screen expectantly and although the spelling of TRAGEDY changed, NO REFERENT remained there.

He scowled, wondering what error he was overlooking. Computers, once properly programmed, did not make errors; operators did. That was something he had discovered his first week in the City. No referent? Surely "tragedy" must be in the computers' vocabulary; it was a perfectly ordinary word. He had no time to lose, however, so he would come back to it after trying another approach.

The specific matter of why the Six Worlds had been destroyed was hard to lead up to, and after devoting a good deal of thought to the problem of how to do it, Noren had decided that the direct way would be best. Although he could predict the first few responses, it would in the end be quicker than attempting to tell the computer what information he already had. WHY WERE THE SIX WORLDS DESTROYED? he began; and, as expected, the answer was, BECAUSE THEIR SUN BECAME A NOVA. At that point he had merely to ask WHY? again, so that when the astrophysical data concerning elements, temperatures and pressures started to appear, he could press INTERRUPT. Then, with the computer on the right subject and waiting for clarification, it was time to ask what he really wanted to know: WHY DID THESE CONDITIONS OCCUR IN THAT STAR AND NOT SOME OTHER OF THE SAME TYPE?

The computer did not hesitate; its internal processes were, in terms of human time-perception, instantaneous. Flatly, finally, it responded, THAT IS NOT KNOWN.

Noren was momentarily dismayed, but then he cursed himself for his own stupidity. Of course it was not known. If it had been, the Founders would have had more than a few weeks' warning. He still wasn't touching the heart of the issue. WHY IS IT THAT INHABITED WORLDS ARE EVER DESTROYED? he persisted.

PLEASE REPHRASE, replied the computer.

Frowning, Noren sought another way to put it. This would be even more difficult than he'd anticipated, he saw, and he could not afford the time to fumble. WHY DID HUMANKIND EVOLVE ONLY TO BE NEARLY WIPED OUT? he ventured.

The computer responded tersely, INSUFFICIENT DATA.

HAS THIS HAPPENED TO OTHER HUMAN RACES ELSEWHERE?

THAT IS NOT KNOWN.

Well, he'd again queried foolishly; the computer, after all, knew nothing more than what had been entered into it by the Founders and by Scholars since. His plan of attack was already so upset that he could not get back to it. In desperation Noren asked the thing he'd originally thought would yield too much information: WHAT IS THE MEANING OF LIFE?

PLEASE REPHRASE.

FOR WHAT PURPOSE DO HUMAN BEINGS LIVE?

INSUFFICIENT DATA.

Not so much as a clue to suggest what questions might be more fruitful, Noren thought irritably. That was surprising; it did not work that way with science, where inadequate phrasing usually produced a reply from which one could deduce the correct approach. With an apprehensive glance at the console clock he tried frantically, FOR WHAT PURPOSE IS HUMANKIND IN DANGER?

INSUFFICIENT DATA.

IS THERE ANY PURPOSE AT ALL IN THE UNIVERSE?

INSUFFICIENT DATA.

Noren fought down the panic that was growing with his frustration. It was evident that he was not going to get what he'd expected. He simply did not know how to communicate with the computer on a subject of this kind, for it must certainly have more data than it had given out. He was beaten. Yet before he left for the conference, he would make one final try.

He looked around him, seeing that the room was still empty, and he was too overwrought to think about how peculiar that was; he was conscious only of relief. The last question, the one he had scarcely dared hope he might ask, knowing that he would never do so if there were a possibility of anyone's coming before he could clear the screen...He drew in his breath and, rapidly, keyed: WHAT HAPPENS TO THE MIND AFTER DEATH?

Without delay, data appeared on the screen, detailed data about the cessation of brain waves. Impatiently, Noren stabbed INTERRUPT again. OMIT THE BRAIN, he instructed. OMIT ALL PHYSIOLOGICAL CONSIDERATIONS; DISCUSS THE CONSCIOUS MIND.

The screen went blank, and remained blank—except for the simple statement, THERE IS NO NON-PHYSIOLOGICAL DATA ABOUT DEATH.

Noren stared, incredulous. This was the cause and summation of his failure to elicit answers to his other questions; the problems were all closely tied. If the computer did not know anything about death, then it could not know why the thirty billion inhabitants of the Six Worlds had died in a single instant. If it did not know what death was, it could not know what life was either; no skill in questioning could make it explain why planets full of people should exist or cease to exist. Yet with these basic issues unresolved, on what could knowledge of the universe be founded? What meaning was there to "truth" that did not encompass the whole?

That is a mystery, his mother had said when Noren had first asked such things. *Only the Scholars know that.* But the Scholars did not know, and the shock of that left him wondering whether the search for knowledge might not be entirely futile.

Chapter Six

Leaving the computers, Noren found his way to the assembly room without conscious thought. It was not crowded, and in fact even Stefred was absent; apparently only the specialists in nuclear physics had been invited to attend. Noren was so dazed that he scarcely noticed that others also looked troubled, or that none of his acquaintances tried to talk to him. He sat in a sort of stupor, void of all feeling, waiting for the conference to begin. There are no answers, his mind kept repeating. The City does not contain all truth, and if it does not, is there any real truth to be found? How can there be sense to such a universe? How can these others live in it?

He had assumed that the older Scholars must know something he did not; now he felt that such questions as he'd framed must never have occurred to them. They had discussed the limits of their scientific knowledge often enough, and surprising though it had been to find that even apart from the problem of how to synthesize metal, the Founders had not been omniscient about material things, he had accepted the fact. He had seen how knowledge of that kind increased gradually, through observation and experimentation. Yet never had anyone mentioned a general ignorance of other important matters—deep matters that, having once been thought about, could not possibly be ignored. If people had been perplexed, they would surely have said so! Why had he been singled out to endure this burden? Noren wondered despairingly. The rest had once seemed so much like him in their concern for truth...

At the front of the room a Scholar was speaking quietly. "Grenald cannot be with us," he said, "although as I'm sure you all realize, he would not stay away by choice. Two hours ago he collapsed and has been taken to the infirmary. For more than a year the doctors have warned him about overwork, yet he drove himself until there was nothing left to be done. May the Star's spirit now restore the strength..."

As the eyes of the people turned upward toward the overhead sunburst, Noren saw that many glistened with tears, and bafflement penetrated his numbness. Grenald was greatly respected, but he was a reserved and distant man for whom few felt warm affection. "...that he spent on our behalf," the speaker continued, "for while he cannot live to see the day he strove for, the darkness of this one will nevertheless diminish. We who go on would have him see that we are not vanquished."

Several of the women were by this time crying openly, and Noren perceived that some unexpectedly serious failure had been encountered in the work. Terror spread in a cold wave through his body. He felt paralyzed, unreal, as he had on the morning after the space flight. The voice of Grenald's chief assistant, who had taken the floor, seemed dim and far away.

"Those of you who've worked with Grenald during the past few weeks already know the worst," the man declared soberly, "but to the rest it will come as a shock. I cannot soften it. You must understand that the obstacle these experiments uncovered is not in our technique, but in our basic theory. The results have been entered into the computers a thousand times in different forms; always the output is the same. The ultimate equations yield no solution. Last night Grenald and I ran them through again, and at dawn, when we left the console, NO SOLUTION had been before our eyes so often that it seemed not to fade. That is a portent, so to speak, of the significance of this failure. It will not fade; it will not be quickly overcome. The creation of metallic elements by nuclear fusion has been proven impossible at the theoretical level—"

Horrified, Noren focused his mind abruptly. *Proven* impossible? For all his doubts, he had not anticipated a defeat so final. "Impossible at the theoretical level" was quite different from "impossible by present methods." The latter said merely that other methods must be sought. The former included such impossibilities as rocks falling up instead of down, direct communication between people's minds, and the rising of the sun in the west.

"At the theoretical level," the physicist repeated, "and you're all aware of what that means."

Death, thought Noren with bitterness. The death of the human race. NO SOLUTION...NO REFERENT...INSUFFICIENT DATA. There were no answers...

"It means we must find a new theory. It means we must expand our most fundamental ideas of natural law, as the science of the Six Worlds did over and over again during the course of its history. The pressure was not so great then, but with hindsight we see that the stakes were equally high. Let us not forget that. Let us not be dismayed by the years of groping we must face before further experiments can begin."

"A new theory?" someone protested. "We have no grounds for discarding the present one, or even for modifying it! It has not been invalidated; on the contrary, every aspect of it checks out. The fact that it tells us we cannot do what we would like to do is not the theory's fault. It would be nice if men could fly without the aid of machines, but the law of gravitation tells us they can't—and synthesization of metal has now been placed in the same category."

"We must have faith that this theory is merely a special case of some larger, more comprehensive principle," Grenald's assistant said gravely. "There was a time when the law of gravitation told men that they could not fly by any means."

Yes, but there nevertheless remained things that were beyond the realm of possibility, Noren thought; and there was no good reason for supposing that transmutation of elements wasn't one of them. Confidence that a verified theory would be overridden was unfounded. Cold logic told him that it was no less an illusion than the villagers' trust that "the spirit of the Mother Star" could protect them from danger. Words Stefred had once said suddenly came back to him: *People have always looked toward something above and beyond them; they always will. They've called it by different names. You, I think, would call it Truth.* Sick at heart, he realized that this too must have been a warning. Everybody clung to illusions, even himself. He'd perceived that the whole universe might be illusory, yet he had not really given up hope until the computers had drained all vestiges of it from him. Now he saw the hopelessness of his lifelong search. That which he had named Truth did not exist.

He sat motionless, benumbed, as the scientists went over the results of their work, analyzed the inexorable equations, showed that the research was in vain. He was split in two. With half his mind he grasped what was being said clearly, while with the other he reflected that details no longer mattered. The mathematics proved conclusively that success could never be achieved. Despite his preoccupation Noren followed the math without effort; one did not need to be an advanced physicist to understand what had already been formulated, not if one's mathematical aptitude was high. To Noren, math was far more telling than words. Certain parameters yielded by the experimentation, when inserted into the equations, made those equations insoluble. One could no more get around that than one could deny that two and two would never equal five.

The physicists did not try to deny it; yet astonishingly few seemed willing to accept its full import. "Tonight there will be a general meeting," the conference chairman said. "Our fellow Scholars will ask what this discovery means in terms of the Prophecy's fulfillment, and as scientists we must say that there now appears to be no chance. We can mitigate that statement only by pointing out that the apparent certainties of past eras often proved to be naive misconceptions—"

"But there is no time to wait for a new era!" one of the men interrupted. "We have ample cause for certainty that ours will be the last, that the Star will be the herald not of renaissance, but of extinction. In the meantime, we cannot in good conscience continue to affirm the Prophecy, nor can we maintain a caste system that has lost its justification."

"We must maintain it. To do otherwise would destroy all hope of a future breakthrough by our successors."

"How could it destroy what does not exist? You yourself just admitted that as scientists, we see no reasonable hope of breakthrough."

Slowly the chairman replied, "Though we are scientists, we are also priests. And as priests we see that human beings cannot rely solely on reason. Reason deals with data we already possess, whereas a breakthrough involves concepts we don't possess and have no way of predicting."

"I can no longer serve as High Priest, knowing what I now know of the odds," persisted the objector. "I'll declare myself a relapsed heretic before I'll say again to the people that their descendants will have what we're withholding from this generation."

Noren flushed; the room was so hot, suddenly, that he could not breathe. Trembling, he got to his feet and somehow reached the door. He dared not stay. He lacked strength to face the test he sensed was coming. If someone made formal declaration of relapse...

It was an extreme step, although not without precedent. Unlike the Inner City Technicians who had once been heretics and who had recanted under pressure, Scholars could not be charged with relapse by anyone but themselves. An unenlightened person who regretted submission was treated like others "guilty" of heresy; candidacy for Scholar rank was restored. The trials of steadfastness were more stringent, but the basic issue remained the same. Relapse on the part of a Scholar was a very different matter. In effect, it was an announcement that he or she could not be trusted to keep the secrets, and that person was thereafter isolated from all contact with non-Scholars—confined not merely to the Inner City, but to the Hall of Scholars itself. Since the time of the Founding only a very few people had chosen that course, and while their right to do so was respected, on the whole they were considered rather eccentric. Most Scholars felt that relapse was an unforgivable evasion of responsibility.

Would the attitude change now? Noren asked himself, as he walked blindly toward the dome where he was to meet Emet. Would many agree that it was wrong to keep things from the villagers when there was no real expectation of saving the human race by it? No…it was inconceivable that those who thought like the conference chairman would disclaim the Prophecy, and the majority did think that way. Having recanted in honesty, they had become trapped in fraud. That was one circumstance for which the First Scholar's wisdom had not provided.

Emet was waiting by the aircar. "Noren," he said awkwardly, "we had no idea—we knew nothing about the conference beyond what I told you, and though I came today for an emergency meeting of the executive council as well as for supplies, there was no advance notice of the subject."

"You wouldn't have brought me along if you'd known?"

"Of course not. Do you think us heartless?"

"Do you think I'm not strong enough to hear bad news?" Noren retorted.

"I didn't mean that. For the Star's sake, Noren, can't you see—" Emet broke off, sighing. "We'll all need our strength; let's not waste it fighting each other. I know you don't want help. Things would be easier if you could accept friendship, though."

Noren did not trust himself to speak. After studying him intently for a moment, Emet continued, "You have more friends than you realize, friends who—well, who'll go to great lengths on your behalf. If I asked you, as a favor to your friends, to find Stefred right now and tell him that you prefer not to return to the outpost—"

"I can't, Emet."

They got into the aircar and took it up in silence. As they rose above the City's shining towers, Noren bit down hard on his tongue to keep the pain inside him from exploding. Those towers would never again look the same. As far back as he could remember, they had been the focus of all he valued, but there was no beauty left in them. The patchwork of farmland, villages, and unquickened wilderness blurred beneath him; he blinked his eyes and stared straight ahead at the barren mountains.

"Noren," Emet began when they cleared the last range and plunged swiftly toward the stark new spire of the outpost, "I won't say that you shouldn't be discouraged. We're all discouraged. The significance of what's happened can't be minimized. But just remember that some things in life aren't expressible in terms of mathematics. You're a gifted mathematician, and so far you've studied little else—but there is more."

With difficulty, Noren restrained a mad impulse to laugh. Emet did not know how much more he'd expected to find that morning.

"You're young," Emet reflected. "For you there is a chance. The Transition Period may yet come in your lifetime. From what I've heard of you, it's possible that you'll lead the way. Don't let yourself be daunted by the gloom we feel, we who've learned today that we will not live to see it."

At the camp, to which word had preceded them by radiophone, Noren's stricken appearance was attributed to the despair shared by everybody. He did not mention that there was anything else involved. He scarcely spoke at all. Brek asked for details of the failure, and Noren rebuffed him irritably; after that he was left alone. But he found himself obliged to go to Orison, for he knew he would be conspicuous if he did not. Although normally the ritual wasn't attended by everyone, on this night all gathered as if drawn by some invisible force.

It was very informal in camp, held as it was outdoors, around a fire; usually not even the presiding Scholars wore robes. Few had robes with them, since nothing extra had been transported, and when no villagers or Technicians were present, the symbol of priesthood was indispensable only at services for the dead. *We are all dead,* Noren mused, as he saw that the available robes were in evidence, *but for a while we live on, knowing.*

Yet those conducting the service did not speak of death. And stunned though people were by the unanticipated blow, their spirits seemed somehow lifted as the liturgy progressed. "...*We are strong in the faith that as those of the past were sustained, so shall we be also...and though our peril be great even unto the last generation of our endurance, in the end humankind shall prevail...*"

That was hypocrisy! thought Noren in dismay. How could anyone who knew the facts say those things and mean them? He certainly could not. He was indeed a relapsed heretic, despite having fled from the conference to avoid declaring himself. He was not sure why he had fled; he was puzzled as well as mortified to learn that he'd lost the courage of his convictions. By the Star, he must regain it soon, he told himself grimly—for he could no longer accept a Scholar's role in the system he'd condoned only for the sake of human survival.

As time passed, however, Noren found that he played the role, went through the motions, just as he had kept going after the space flight. He did what he'd been accustomed to doing simply because there was no way to stop.

He had work, for one thing—not only Scholar's work, but the farm work he'd done as a boy. It would soon be harvest season. Before the tower was finished, land-clearing and soil-treatment equipment had been brought in, for the raising of a crop had high priority. Relatively few people had been needed to clear the ring of fields that was to enclose the living area, to "quicken" it by inactivating the soil's poisons, and to perform the initial enrichment with metallic trace elements from the dwindling store brought long ago by the starfleet. These were mechanized functions, the basic ones for which preservation of off-world equipment was essential. But when it came to planting, refertilizing and cultivating, everybody pitched in for a few hours each day. It was backbreaking work, since there were neither metal tools nor even handles for the stone ones.

Planting season had been determined solely by the availability of the land-treatment machines; the unchanging climate had no more to do with it than with the various villages' seasons, which, though by now traditional, had been scheduled for most efficient rotation of equipment. On most of the Six Worlds, Noren knew, seasons had had a physical basis—people had planted in mild weather, harvested in the heat, and then, during a long period of inconceivable cold, had actually allowed the land to lie dormant.

"They let *quickened* land go to waste?" Brek protested unbelievingly. "No wonder they started to run out of food."

"All their land was quickened," Noren pointed out. "It stayed that way naturally. Besides, the seed wouldn't sprout when it was too cold."

"What made it colder at some times than at others?"

Noren explained how the axis of a planet was frequently tilted to the plane of its orbit, a mathematical concept that was far clearer to him than the thought of weather being so cold that people could not go outdoors without heavy clothing. Science had taught him that water solidified and formed crystals at low temperatures, just as it had taught him countless other facts about the behavior of chemical elements; but though he'd been exposed to intense cold in a laboratory once, it was hard to imagine such a state prevailing throughout large areas.

Harvest time ended the outpost's dependence on grain brought by aircar, but with harvest came not larger rations but more people. There had been a vote to decide whether the founding of another city should continue and the project had been approved by a large majority. Its advocates included not only Scholars who believed that any future experimentation was more likely than ever to be hazardous, but those who felt that an optimistic defiance of fate was more fitting under the circumstances than a perhaps-futile attempt to husband the City's reserves. So expansion proceeded, and the policy of scant meals remained in effect. Hunger was less noticeable than at first; the original group had become inured to it. Moreover, enough fowl had been raised to provide eggs for eating as well as hatching. Before, there had been nothing but bread and water.

Water, of course, had been—and still was—the most difficult problem. At first it had all been imported from the City. Even to wash one's hands in impure water was an unwarranted risk, since the element causing chromosome damage would, over a period of time, be absorbed through the skin. Not one drop of the precious cistern supply could be spilled. What rainfall there was increased it, but only twice had there been rain. Both storms had been in the evening, and everyone had marveled to see water come from the sky at any hour but the pre-noon one, when it fell four days out of six in the region of controlled weather. It had been exciting, for the unpredicted deluge seemed a gift from above; men had stripped off most of their clothes to revel in it. But not enough free water could be counted on to provide for crops, and before planting had begun it had been necessary to complete both a purification plant and the power plant on which it depended, as well as the purified clay pipes of the irrigation system.

The water-processing and power plants were much smaller than their City counterparts, and had been put together from barely adequate materials obtained by sacrificing reserves. The job had been tricky. At the time Noren had been working on the tower's upper levels and had not participated; but now, besides his shift of farm labor, he was on duty alternate nights at the fusion reactor, which was located in its original compartment within the former starship. Although not yet knowledgeable enough to deal with any emergency, he could call the head engineer in case of problems, and it was vital that a continuous vigil be kept. Maintenance of nuclear power was the Scholars' most critical duty, for without that power none of the other essentials could function. Once Noren would have considered his a post of honor, yet he found the long watch hours dark; they left all too much time for thinking.

Brek's non-farm job was the one he'd held as a Technician: the servicing of radiophone and other electronic equipment. In their spare time, he and Noren continued to study together. This had become a torment for Noren, since it seemed wholly futile, and in his private studies he ignored nuclear physics to concentrate on pure mathematics; still he could not turn Brek's questions aside. Wearily, he explained the vast difference between the kind of nuclear fusion that occurred in the power plant and the kind that would be needed to synthesize metal. Power generation involved fusion of hydrogen isotopes, the lightest atoms in existence. Because the repulsive force between elements was proportional to the product of their atomic numbers, the fusing of heavier elements would demand great amounts of energy—so great that in nature, such elements were created only in the interiors of stars, where there were temperatures and pressures beyond imagination. Metal-rich stars and planets formed in regions of space where other stars had previously exploded...

As he said this to Brek, Noren faltered and broke off, overwhelmed suddenly by the implications of a thing he'd originally learned by rote. An exploding star was a nova. Were some types of novas necessary to the evolution of habitable planets? Brek, looking at him, grasped the point and quickly switched the subject. That was the difference between other Scholars and himself, Noren thought ruefully. The others could turn from such enigmas; he could not...but neither could he solve them.

Every aircar now brought passengers as well as supplies, and many of the passengers were women. Some wives of the original staff members came first, then more couples and a few unmarried girls, those who possessed needed skills or were betrothed to men already in camp. Noren assumed that this was arranged by mutual consent until one afternoon when, without warning, he was called in from the grain fields to meet Talyra.

In the first surge of astonished joy he ran to her and held her tight, not thinking past the loosed emotions that almost overcame him. That did not last, however. "Noren, what's the matter?" Talyra protested, sensing his deliberate effort to check his feelings.

"It—it's just that life's hard here," he declared, "and I don't want you to know hardship." That was true enough, though the main difficulty was that he did not see how he could bear to be near her, knowing as he did that he could not take the step that was prerequisite to their marriage. He knew too that although to allow her to hope would be cruel, he could no more be frank in that regard than with respect to his ignominious failure to complete the task with which he'd told her he had been honored. Talyra had been proud, happy; what would she think if she knew that he'd succumbed to panic?

"You said City life would he hard for me," she reminded gently, "and it wasn't. I was content there except for missing you. When they announced that those who served in secret had gone to build a new City and that their loved ones could follow, of course I chose to come."

"But Talyra," Noren said, "since the day of my arrest we've not been formally betrothed; how is it that they let you?"

"The Scholar Stefred sent for me," she explained. "He asked whether it was by my choice that there has been no formal renewal of our betrothal. I told him that you did not wish to bind me since you weren't sure when you could marry, but that I consider myself bound anyway and accept no other suitors. And oh, Noren, he said that in that case, the betrothal is fact! He wouldn't have if he did not plan to bless our marriage, surely—"

"Permission for our marriage does not depend on the Scholar Stefred alone," Noren replied, thinking that Stefred, in sending Talyra without consulting him, had employed unfair tactics. But he saw that she could not be discouraged and that if he argued further, she might doubt his love and be hurt; so that evening he stood up with her at Vespers and made again the promises of fidelity they'd exchanged before the village council, which were not really lies because he certainly didn't intend to marry anybody else.

Since the Technicians had begun to arrive, the Inner City's custom had been adopted; Orison was held in the tower, and the outdoor service, now called Vespers, became formal. The committed Scholars took turns conducting it, wearing borrowed robes if they had not brought their own. Talyra, as usual, attended regularly; her implicit faith in the promises of the Prophecy nearly broke Noren's heart. "Darling," he said to her, "you've met many Scholars now; you know that they're human. Hasn't it occurred to you that they might mislead us without meaning to, simply by being mistaken?"

"In little things, of course," she agreed. "In big things like the Prophecy—how could they? They're *guided,* Noren."

"How do you know that?"

"I just *do.* Anyway, they said so, just a little while before I left the City. It was the night they all came to Vespers wearing their robes."

Noren frowned; he had heard of no such occasion. "We'd known for several days that something must be the matter," Talyra continued. "The Scholars had been looking terribly solemn, and they'd stayed inside their special tower most of the time. A woman I know who's married to one told me her husband cried in his sleep. Then at Vespers, the Scholar Stefred spoke; he explained that new mysteries had been made manifest to them, mysteries that even they found frightening at first, but that the spirit of the Mother Star would guide them to understanding. And he said we must be patient if our friends and loved ones seemed troubled for a while. During the ritual, though, they didn't look troubled; they looked—well, *brave,*" She added reflectively, "I didn't know before it was so hard to be a Scholar."

Brave? thought Noren. Was it brave to pretend that some mystical spirit, a mere symbol, would offer answers that rational effort could not uncover? It struck him as far more courageous to admit that one's life had been built upon delusion. Yet Stefred, who was the most honest man he'd ever met...

He wondered what Stefred would say if he were to confront him with the issue. Remembering their talks, Noren longed sometimes to sit down in the study where, despite demanding challenges, he had always felt capable and secure, and to go through the whole wretched series of problems; but there was now a greater obstacle than his pride. From Stefred he could hide nothing, and he still felt unable to declare his relapse openly. He was not strong enough to break the pattern through which his shaky balance was being maintained. He might despise himself for not stating aloud that there was no longer any excuse for maintaining the castes or for failing to share the City's contents with the villagers, but he could not bring himself to abjure his recantation. Several others had done so; they'd accepted voluntary isolation in protest against the majority's insistence that the system must be preserved. Something held Noren back. He could not understand it. Perhaps, he thought miserably, it was merely that having lost his self-assurance, he was not sure of anything else either—not even of his own conscience.

On the surface, at least, the majority opinion seemed sincere. As time passed it became increasingly evident that most Scholars really believed there was some remote chance of the system's fulfilling its purpose. They discussed it at length, of course; when away from the Technicians, either in the tower's restricted sections or beside one of the small mossfires around which friends met privately in the evenings, they talked of nothing else. Noren avoided these gatherings when possible, joining instead groups that included Talyra, but occasionally he was unable to escape.

"What we face is really the same dilemma that confronted our forebears more than once on the Six Worlds," the head engineer said on one such night. "It's harder for us because we know what we're facing. The time span is shorter. Our personal responsibility is greater, and we've been forced by a unique emergency to use stopgap measures that would have been unjustifiable in the normal course of evolution. But otherwise, we are in an identical position: the exhaustion of our world's resources is predictable, no sure solution is apparent, and the survival of our species depends on a breakthrough we can't foresee."

"That's a dangerous argument," someone observed. "Look at history that way, and you could make a case for half the schemes that were proposed by well-intentioned men who thought humanity couldn't survive without a controlled society."

"False analogy. In the first place, we don't have a controlled society here; we have control of resources, which is something else entirely. The people of the Six Worlds had to control certain resources too, eventually, and they found ways to do it without abridging individual freedoms, just as we have. They had no moral grounds for controlling what we must control—machines and knowledge—because those weren't irreplaceable resources there. But what's more, the whole notion of a controlled society is founded on the supposition that people can foresee all the paths through which progress will come, and we are aware that we can't."

"I know that," Brek said thoughtfully, "but I don't understand the analogy you do want to draw. On the Six Worlds evolution was working as it's supposed to work. Over the years people just naturally went on learning and developing and solving problems as they arose—whereas here, since resources are so limited that they can't, we're dealing with reversion. If it weren't that the Prophecy makes them look ahead, I'm told, the villagers would be worshipping their ancestors—or maybe even idols—as well as Scholars! So how is there any comparison between the situations now and before the nova?"

"Human nature hasn't changed," explained Emet. "Yes, there's been reversion here, because progress is inextricably tied to technological innovation, which is not possible in the villages. The regression of village culture to earlier ways has been held in check only by the outlook the Prophecy fosters. Without that, people would have become wholly superstitious about machines, for instance, just as primitive tribes once venerated forces of nature they could neither understand nor control. If there were no High Priests, there would be witch doctors. If there were no public recantations, there would be ritualized blood sacrifice. And if it weren't for the adoption of Scholars' children, banishing all heretics would cause the villagers to revert genetically as well. But when we speak of humanity as a whole, we're including ourselves, through whom it is still evolving, and we're as helpless and blind as men and women of the past. We have no choice but to learn what we can and then gamble."

"Gamble?" questioned Noren. "At the conference in the City, Grenald's assistant said that whenever the Six Worlds' scientists had to expand their ideas of natural law, the stakes were as high as they are here, though without hindsight they didn't know it. I don't see that. When has there been a case in which gambling accomplished anything?"

"Well, take population growth," suggested the head engineer, "since that issue is directly parallel. When the people of the mother world first realized that their world's resources weren't inexhaustible, some believed population growth ought to stop entirely. The idea had a good many fallacies, not the least of which was that it would merely have postponed the problem until it was too late to get enough of a head start on space exploration. Fortunately human instinct, the inborn will to survive, saw to it that growth slowed down without halting. But you can't blame people of that age for being fearful. They *knew* the resources couldn't last, and they didn't know what was going to save them; it was too far ahead of their time."

"Couldn't they foresee interstellar travel?" inquired Brek.

"Not with any degree of certainty. For a great many years their experts believed that to travel faster than light was theoretically impossible. It was contrary to some basic principles of their science; the very mathematics of that science proved that no invention could ever circumvent the limitation, just as our mathematics now indicates that we can't synthesize metal. Only when additional principles were discovered did the way open—and at the last minute, too."

"We're going to have to make a comparable breakthrough," Brek agreed. "Basic scientific theory, not mere technology."

"Yes, and our population situation is also comparable. Obviously our resources would last longer if the High Law did not encourage large families. But we're still very few on this planet, too few to limit growth if we're to survive plagues or other disasters and to reestablish widespread technology at the Time of the Prophecy. And besides, if the Founders hadn't decided to foster rapid expansion, there would have been less chance of having enough people with the creative genius needed to produce the breakthrough. So they glorified childbearing, even at the price of the sexism that developed in the villages—which is something women of the Six Worlds wouldn't have tolerated."

"How could they have limited growth if they'd wanted to?" Noren asked. "I thought the contraceptive drugs used on the Six Worlds couldn't be made here, and surely they wouldn't have put anything into the High Law restricting love."

"There are other means of lowering the birth rate, which the High Law forbids in language so archaic that few today grasp its meaning. By now, there's no longer any need for it to do so—after all, you and Talyra wouldn't want *not* to have children, would you, even though you can't keep them?"

"To make love, and not wish for our love to be fruitful?" Repelled, Noren declared, "The idea's unthinkable."

"Yes, in our culture. On a crowded world it would not be. The Founders came from planets that were running out of food; they'd grown up feeling it was unthinkable for a couple to bring more than two children into the world. It wasn't tradition that made them frame the High Law as they did; they had to alter their own fundamental attitude, although they knew they were deliberately cutting short the time the survival equipment and the chemicals for initial land treatment could last. With humankind so nearly wiped out, that was the lesser risk—but it was a risk all the same. There's always risk in human affairs. We can never know exactly what the future will bring; we know only that things cannot and will not remain the same."

"They've stayed the same here for a long time," Noren contended.

"Unnaturally long, after the initial abrupt reversion of the villagers. That couldn't happen if there were the resources to make normal innovation possible, and without the Prophecy, which makes even the villagers *want* change, we couldn't survive it. If people can't go forward they go backward; they don't stand still."

Quite true, thought Noren, but also quite irrelevant. The men—Emet, the head engineer, all of them—spoke as if there were just two alternatives. They were ignoring what happened when the promise proved false: when people could not go forward, and were thereby doomed to inevitable, though belated, extinction.

Talyra adjusted to the camp just as she had to the Inner City: with serenity. There was no work for a midwife, since because of the outpost's short rations pregnant women had not been allowed to come; but minor injuries occurred frequently and as a nurse she was kept busy tending them. She also took her turn at meal preparation as cheerfully as the men accepted the farm work, though cooking was not a task she enjoyed. Hunger, which she had never known before, did not faze her. "We were warned before we came that it would not be comfortable here," she declared, "but Noren, what does that matter when we're actually helping to fulfill the Prophecy?" She gazed up at the towering spire and added, "When I was a schoolgirl I used to look at the mountains and wish I could live till the Cities rose beyond them. I never thought such wishes could come true."

"And I always supposed you liked things as they were in the village," Noren said, realizing how little he'd actually known her then.

"Nobody who believes the Prophecy could be content with things as they are!" she protested. "Oh, I know there are some who only pretend to be devout, and want life to stay the same forever; but it's as much a sacred duty to prepare for the Time of the Prophecy as to obey the High Law. I was silly once; I imagined all the changes were going to come on the day the Star appears. I didn't stop to think of how much work it would take."

They were sitting alone by their own small fire, while dozens of other fires, stone-encircled, made glowing dots in the mossland that surrounded the moonlit tower. "Talyra," Noren began hesitantly, "do you ever want to know more about the work than you've been told? Where the Scholars got the tower, for instance?"

"Of course I do," she admitted, "but there's much, after all, that's beyond knowing."

"I mean…do you still believe it's right for the Scholars to have mysteries they don't share?"

Talyra regarded him seriously, her face illumined by firelight. "Yes," she declared. "The world is full of mysteries we can't expect to understand. You still do expect it, darling, and I think that's why you're not happy—though I know it's not a thing you should be blamed for."

Stefred had been right about her, Noren saw. Talyra did not have the sort of mind for heresy. She was brave; she was intelligent; but though she would never want arbitrary power for herself, she perceived no evil in its being given to others, and that made her unfit to exercise the responsibility of a Scholar.

If he'd wanted to assume the robe, there'd have been no need to postpone commitment longer for her sake. She would lose nothing by becoming technically ineligible for a status she'd neither seek nor earn. Yet he was still pretending that no final decision could he made about their marriage...

The fire had burned down to smoldering ashes; Noren made no move to rekindle it. Drawing Talyra close, he kissed her, and for a little while his mind was far from the dark reaches of that which he could not know. The warmth of the moment was all that mattered... And then, abruptly, she pulled away, and he saw that she was crying.

"Talyra, what is it? What did I do?" he demanded.

"You—you haven't done anything," she faltered.

"Then what happened?"

"Nothing, except I realized that you don't really want to be betrothed to me."

Astonished, he burst out, "I've always wanted to be betrothed to you! Why should you question that now?"

She flushed and did not answer. "Darling," Noren persisted, "haven't I told you over and over again—"

Not facing him, Talyra murmured, "If you wanted me, you'd do more than talk about it."

"But you know I'm not yet free to marry."

"Are you also forbidden to love?" she demanded fiercely.

He sat up, not trusting himself to touch her, much less to admit how often his thoughts had turned in that direction. "That wouldn't be fair to you," he declared with pain.

"Why wouldn't it? It isn't the same now as in the village; when an Inner City woman has a child, she must give it up for adoption whether she's married or not. I would not be dishonored, for our betrothal is public and everyone knows that I let no one else pay court to me. What more would marriage be except sharing quarters?"

"It would be permanent," replied Noren.

"Are you suggesting that someday you'll want some other girl?"

"Of course not! But suppose I can never marry you, Talyra?" He dropped his head, adding wretchedly, "There may come a time...soon...when I will know positively that I cannot; and you must then forget me, Talyra...and choose some other suitor."

"I couldn't! I never could! Do you think I won't love you forever because I've not yet sworn it by the Mother Star in a marriage ceremony?"

"I haven't the right to bind you, Talyra—that's why the ceremony can't be held. And I—I can't bind myself either, in certain ways."

"How can you say such things?" She began to cry again, quietly. "If you loved me, you couldn't say them."

"I say what I must," Noren replied brusquely, knowing that he dared not let himself go further. So many of his once-firm principles had crumbled—already he'd delayed declaration of renewed heresy despite knowledge that the Prophecy was false. He could not count on himself to stand fast about anything.

What Talyra had said was true: there was no real reason why a betrothed couple should not make love, not when the rearing of families was impossible in any case, and when the bearing of offspring for adoption was, under the High Law, a virtue. Though in the villages it was shameful to father a child one was not willing to support, among Inner City people that did not apply. Yet he could not love Talyra casually; his feeling for her went too deep. Once she was wholly his he would be unable to endure the thought of her marrying someone else. Might not priesthood then seem merely one more step in the path of hypocrisy he had taken, and might he not assume the robe for the sake of freedom to seal their union?

In the days that followed, such thoughts worried him more and more. Maybe Talyra was the cause of his reluctance to speak out, he reflected. After all, once he announced formally that he was no longer willing to uphold the system, he would be isolated from the Technicians and would never see her again. Originally, in the village, he had not been stopped by that, but perhaps he was incapable of making the sacrifice a second time. As far as he knew there was no other reason for hesitancy.

The pressure within him built up. He was guilt-ridden by the rankling memory of the space flight, and equally so by his conflicting impulses. He could not trust his judgment any more. At times he hated himself because he had ceased to live by the code of honesty that had once meant everything to him; at others he thought honesty meaningless in a world devoid of ultimate truth; and it was hard to tell which torment was the worst. Inaction became unbearable—and so, with bitterness that masked his shame, he spoke at last to the one person in whom it was possible to confide. He confessed his hypocrisy to Brek.

Brek listened to the whole story, from the source of the panic in space to the facts presented at the conference, and he did not dispute Noren's assertions, though it was apparent that he did not share the terror Noren had felt on discovering areas the computers could not deal with. It was not in Brek to probe the universe that deeply. What he did share was hot anger at the betrayal, at the idea that he'd been led to endorse a system that could not deliver what it promised. He too had recanted solely on the basis of that promise, and Noren's statements about the scientific impossibility of fulfilling it were persuasive.

"I wasn't sure," Brek admitted. "Everyone goes on hoping, and I don't have the math background to judge. But if *you* say the proof's conclusive—"

"Absolutely conclusive." Noren told him. "I—I've been weak, Brek, and I'm confused about a lot of things, but not about math. Mathematical truth does exist. It's the only kind that's really definite."

"Good and evil are definite, aren't they?"

"Yes," Noren agreed, that being one conviction he'd never thought of doubting. "And all of us—all the heretics who've ever become Scholars—believe that this system is evil! We accepted it only because extinction of the human race would be a worse evil, and we thought it could prevent extinction."

"If it can't—" Brek paused, torn by indecision. Finally he said, "Noren, if it can't, it should be abolished; there's no question about that. But declaring ourselves relapsed heretics wouldn't abolish it, any more than the work we're doing now sustains it. We're not priests, and here, we live much as the villagers do. We haven't any City comforts. We don't have access to the computers or to dreams. Actually, we've got fewer privileges than we'd have if we were confined to the Hall of Scholars."

Noren's heart lightened; he had not looked at it that way. "The only privilege for us here is study," he said slowly, "and that, we can give up."

"Even the math?" inquired Brek, scrutinizing Noren closely. "Are you positive that when you're so gifted—"

"The advanced fields would not be open to me if it weren't for my rank," Noren said firmly. It was a small price to pay for peace of conscience, though math was the one pursuit that had offered him temporary mental distraction.

Week followed week. The Day of the Prophecy, observed annually on the date of the Mother Star's predicted appearance, came and went; Noren was appalled to find that the Scholars went right ahead with the usual celebration. In the villages this was the most joyous festival of the year, surpassing even Founding Day, and in the Inner City it was also customary to make merry. It seemed monstrous to do so under these circumstances. All the same, people followed the traditions. Though no one had green holiday clothes in camp, the women baked Festival Buns for supper instead of ordinary bread, and after an exceptionally solemn and elaborate Vespers, there was dancing. Noren was obliged to participate for Talyra's sake, but he loathed such pretense.

Upon abandoning his studies he had volunteered for an additional shift in the grain fields, where he labored far more industriously than he ever had in his father's. The work was still hateful to him, a fact that brought him satisfaction of sorts. Crawling on his hands and knees along a furrow, stone cultivating tool in hand, he could almost forget that he had ever recanted. He could almost forget that he had become a Scholar, thereby implicating himself in a fraud that was none the less real for being unintentional.

Almost, but not quite. He *was* a Scholar, and moreover, his fellow Scholars' attitude toward him seemed to be changing. Although at the time of his disastrous space flight, they'd shown no signs of the contempt he was sure they must feel, he now noticed that their friendliness had cooled. Why? Noren wondered. No Scholar looked down on farm work. It had always been emphasized that one was free to do whatever available work one chose, though one could hardly expect to receive one's living if one did none at all. Could it be that the others despised themselves too, underneath, for not having the honesty to acknowledge the pointlessness of research even to the extent that he had acknowledged it?

He mentioned this to Brek one evening; but surprisingly, Brek was dubious. "I don't think it's that," he said slowly. "No one was upset when *I* stopped studying. But you—you've too much talent to waste. People feel that you're letting them down by quitting. They'd all hoped the foundation for a new theory might come from you, that you'd develop into some kind of a genius."

"It was a vain hope," Noren declared fiercely. "I wouldn't quit if I thought I had any chance of helping matters; you know that! Years of study and research that can't lead anywhere, though...that's something else. It's self-delusion, and it's deluding others." His throat tightened painfully, for still, inside, he ached at the thought of the scientific career that had once seemed so exciting. It was the only kind of life he'd ever wanted; it would always be, if it were not so meaningless...

All knowledge was meaningless. That was what hurt the most. Knowledge was the one thing he had cared deeply about, and the discovery that its very roots weren't secure was even more disillusioning than the insurmountable problem in the research. When Truth was not to be found, the harsh pronouncement of the physicists' mathematics was reassuring, in a sense. Grim certainty was easier to bear than no certainty at all.

A few at a time, the Scholars who had worked with Grenald in the City began arriving at the outpost, where their main task—in addition to the hours of farm labor that were shortened when shared among more people—was the outfitting of the tower. They were subdued, in some cases obviously crushed, but that did not seem to alter their diligence in readying lab facilities for the future. The equipment brought by the aircars was even less adequate than that used in the City; men devoted endless days to designing schemes whereby portions of it could be made to serve purposes for which they had never been intended. A way to hook up two machines with a featherweight's less wire than had previously been required was cause for major jubilation. These men were, Noren thought, like children playing a game where the winning of pebbles *mattered.*

Life in camp had settled into a routine, a mode of existence that to people of any other time and place would have seemed wholly incredible. The single tower, built of the most remarkable substance ever created by technology, rose out of gray wasteland, bordered, at a short distance, by a narrow ring of green. Inside the tower were sophisticated laboratories, a satellite computer linked by radio to the City, an air-conditioning system built to sustain life in interstellar space—but no plumbing. There were electronic devices but no electric lights; workers carried battery-powered lanterns from room to room because there was no wire for installing permanent fixtures. They sat on the floor because as yet no one had had time to weave wicker furniture. Around the tower were low primitive structures of uncut stone that housed not people, but a nuclear-powered water-processing plant and similar equipment. The people were still sleeping on the open ground.

To be sure, the ground was comfortable, since it was covered with thick, spongy moss; the cubbyholes most had chosen amid the undulating hillocks were private; and the weather was such that sleeping outside was preferable to confinement in a stuffy building. Everybody was too busy to bother with houses. Houses would have been superfluous. In the villages their value lay in permanence, but the camp's inhabitants felt none. They could not make homes outside the City; they could rear no families. They had more hardships than villagers with fewer compensations. They cooked on open campfires, ate from unglazed pottery bowls, and washed infrequently because in the absence of rain, the watering of crops had priority. Yet looking at the tower, they envisioned the new city it might someday grace; and irrational though their optimism seemed, most looked with lifted hearts.

Noren did not enter the laboratories. Except when on duty at the power plant, he kept away from the tower itself, avoiding with bitter determination all contact with memories that had become too great a hurt. But at length, just before supper one evening, he was summoned inside. The Scholar Grenald had come and wanted to talk with him.

Grenald had looked old on the night of the decision to build the outpost; now he looked aged, older even than the doddering graybeard who had sold pots in the village of Noren's birth. He had been ill for some weeks after the unhappy finish of his research, and it was common knowledge that he had little time to live. It had been his wish to see the place where his successors would carry on after him. The wish had been respected, though everyone feared that the strain of leaving the City might prove fatal.

He and Noren faced each other in a cool, cavernous compartment of the unfurnished tower, Noren wondering what Grenald would say. It would be disapproving, no doubt. There would be an attempt to talk him into continuing his studies. The disapproval was mutual, for he felt that Grenald, of all people, should have accepted the finality of the verdict, considering that it was the result of a theory he himself had proven. Still, the old man had been an inspiring tutor, and Noren hoped that it would be possible to reply honestly without revealing that in him, all inspiration was dead. *You are his heir,* Stefred had said...

"You are not what I once thought," Grenald declared, after appraising Noren for some time in silence. In a harsh voice, as if each word was forced out by effort, he added, "It's been the worst blow of all, Noren, to learn that you are a coward."

Despite his stunned surprise, Noren kept his face impassive. At last it had been stated openly. He had supposed that at the time of the space flight Grenald had been too absorbed by the research to pay much attention, but no doubt he'd been talking to people since.

Grenald seemed somewhat taken aback by Noren's failure to respond with hot denial; he continued less brusquely, "I did not expect you to take that from me. I hoped simply to jar you; I assumed you yourself didn't realize—"

"How could I not?" Noren mumbled.

"People deceive themselves sometimes."

True, thought Noren, but Grenald was hardly the man to talk. "You once expected to die for your heresy," Grenald went on, "and you were willing. Has a year so changed you that you now refuse a lesser risk? Perhaps it's for the girl's sake; I warned Stefred that you shouldn't be allowed to become involved."

"Wait a minute," protested Noren, puzzled. "I've refused no risk! Maybe they didn't tell you, but I volunteered—"

"For extra farm work, yes, but you will not be kept here long on that account. You and Talyra will return to the City years before any experimentation is resumed. If this outpost blows up you'll remain quite safe."

"You thought...that I've given up science because I was afraid of being killed in the *experiments?"* For the moment Noren was too astonished to be angry.

"What else can one think when a boy of your gifts suddenly decides not to use them for the world's benefit?" demanded Grenald. "It's not as if you disliked study; if that were so, I would not speak as I do, whatever I might think privately about your lack of responsibility. But I know you too well to believe you'd ever tire of it. I also know that if you were totally without faith in the power of science to save us, you would have opted for dissent long ago;

you've never been one to hide your convictions. That's why I'm sure you have fears you're not aware of. Though you may say I'm not qualified to judge, since the physicists of my generation did not face the perils those of yours will, I cannot believe you'd consciously abandon research for that reason."

Noren met the penetrating eyes that seemed too clear for the thin, wrinkled face before him. "You're right," he said stonily "I would not."

He turned his back on Grenald and strode out of the dim tower into sunlight, heading for the fields automatically because there was nowhere else to go. Was that what everyone thought—that he'd quit from fear? he asked himself. Was that the real cause behind people's growing scorn of him? Enraged though he was, he could scarcely blame them; a man who had panicked in space might logically be expected to panic at the idea of working under constant threat of thermonuclear disaster...

Sickness came over him; he knelt by a freshly fertilized row of grain shoots, pretending to cultivate, and his face burned crimson although he was alone. Was it *true?* No...no, he could honestly say that such a fear had never so much as occurred to him. His preoccupation with death had not taken concrete form.

But cowardice was the root of the trouble, all the same. He had indeed abandoned both his responsibility and his most cherished personal convictions. He had held back from declaring the truth others refused to recognize: that people were alone in a cold, vast universe that had capriciously destroyed their predecessors and would offer no better chance to their descendants. Yet if there was any meaning at all to life, then there was meaning to the dictates of conscience—and conscience decreed that men who were doomed anyway must die free. Since the Scholars' supremacy could not save the human race, all must have equal voice in the affairs of the last era.

Grenald had been right, Noren thought, in spite of the way he'd misinterpreted things. He, Noren, was a coward; and though he'd known that, he had not faced the full extent of it. He had not realized what was keeping him from expressing his belief that the system should no longer stand. Now, as if the idea were entirely new, he guessed why he had hesitated. He guessed that all along he must have perceived the one real path of redemption.

But it was a path he could not take alone. He could not leave camp alone in an aircar he did not know how to fly. Noren frowned, considering it. Brek...Brek was a pilot, and in Brek he had already confided. Brek shared his view and would share the action it demanded.

That evening he ate no supper, for he had no appetite and he did not want to confront Talyra. She would not seek him at his private sleeping place, though she had made plain that she would welcome him to hers. Nor would others intrude on a night when he wasn't on duty. Brek, however, would be concerned if he didn't appear, and would search everywhere.

He was lying face down, as had been his habit since he'd come to fear the sky, when he heard Brek approach. Scrambling to his feet, he announced without preamble, "Refusing to become priests, or even scientists, isn't enough, Brek. That's passive—and if we don't believe that people should be kept in ignorance, we've got to demonstrate how we feel."

"I don't see that there's anything we can do," Brek said.

"There's one thing," replied Noren grimly.

"Didn't we decide that to abjure our recantation would be pointless? Our being isolated from non-Scholars wouldn't abolish the system; we could do no good by it."

"Brek," Noren maintained, "it's the principle that counts. We recanted on false grounds—we affirmed a Prophecy that can't come true and a caste system that the Founders themselves would no longer consider justified! We ought to speak out to the Scholars whether we could do any good or not...but that's not exactly what I have in mind."

Brek studied him. "You wouldn't speak to the Technicians!"

"Here? No, there are too few, and they wouldn't listen; they'd just think we were crazy. But villagers will know us for City dwellers. They may not believe we're Scholars since we'll have to go unrobed, and we haven't Technicians' uniforms either; still, our clothes aren't like any obtainable in the villages. Besides, we know enough to speak in a way no village heretic could. We'll be heard."

Brek sat down, pondering the idea. "Just what will be heard?" he asked slowly. "A proclamation that the end of the world is coming, that the Time of the Prophecy will be a day of doom instead of rejoicing? Somehow, Noren, that doesn't strike me as very constructive."

"Perhaps not, but it's *true.*"

"I suppose it is."

"Think, Brek!" Noren persisted. "The villagers and Technicians are being deceived. Does it make any difference whether the Scholars are maintaining the deception to stay in power, the way we once thought, or because they themselves are deluded?" He paced back and forth, treading the moss to a hard mat. "No!" he exclaimed in answer to his own question. "Truth is truth, and people have a *right* to it! I've always believed that truth is more important than anything else. If human survival could be made possible by hiding it from all but those who care enough to prove themselves, that would be tolerable, but since it can't, everyone ought to know the facts. They ought to know that there's no use in their being denied the tools and machines we're safeguarding for posterity, that the villagers alive now could live better if the City were thrown open—"

"I'm not sure we know all the facts ourselves," Brek interrupted.

"I studied more than you did," Noren said. "I may not know all the details, but I know enough of the basic theory to be sure that creation of metal will always be contrary to it."

"Everybody concedes that; if basic theory weren't involved we'd have no need for a major breakthrough."

"'Breakthrough' is just another word for 'miracle.' It's what you call an event that doesn't fit natural laws, that goes against logic." Groping for a way to express the thing that had confused him since long before his disillusionment, Noren continued, "Actually, an idea like that underlies all the symbolism that's grown up around the Mother Star. People expect something more of it than fulfillment of the Prophecy would give them even if every promise could be kept. You know they do, Brek—sometimes I think you do yourself."

Brek didn't look up. "I used to," he admitted in a low voice.

Slowly, another thought took form in Noren's mind. Brek, who had believed in the Mother Star, had been more cruelly deceived than heretics like himself, he saw; and as for people like Talyra..."For the machines and the knowledge to be sealed away to no good purpose is wrong," he said soberly. "But there's something even worse." The words came with difficulty; he did not know how to describe what he was feeling. "Do you remember how in the dream, when the First Scholar proposed that his successors should become High Priests, his friends protested...and how he reassured them?"

"Of course. They were shocked because they thought he was suggesting the establishment of a false religion, and he had to explain that he didn't mean them to—" Brek stopped, suddenly overcome by indignation. "But the way it's turned out, they *did*—and if we keep silent we're party to it."

"I don't understand religion," Noren said. "I never have. I didn't understand all the First Scholar's thoughts even while I was sharing them. But they involved something...sacred, Brek. I don't know what he called it; maybe you do, since according to Stefred, each person experiences the dreams differently, depending on what comes from his own mind. Anyway, whatever it was, I do know the First Scholar wouldn't have used it to fool people. He wouldn't have employed that kind of falsehood for *any* purpose, not even for saving humanity...and if he'd lived to know that the Prophecy isn't as true as he believed it was, he would have repudiated it, just as we've got to."

Brek nodded. "It's a—a perversion of all he stood for to let the Mother Star represent something false," he agreed painfully. "How can any Scholar not realize that? Noren, I—I think I'm more of a heretic now than I was in the first place."

Noren sat beside him, searching his face; it was too dark by this time to see it clearly. "There's an aircar in camp," he said cautiously, "and someone's got to go for supplies. You're a pilot—"

"Yes, but—"

"If we leave just at dawn, nobody will see us; they won't suspect until it's too late. There'll be nothing they can do once we're gone. The villages in the third season zone harvested this week, and tomorrow people will gather in the squares to celebrate. We can land in the largest one, and coming by aircar, we'll draw a big crowd."

"We'll do that, all right," Brek declared. "Crowds can turn into mobs, Noren, and somehow I don't think people are going to like what we say to them. Village heretics have the nominal protection of village law, but City dwellers who dispute the Prophecy while claiming to be Scholars—well, there's no telling what'll happen."

"They'll kill us," Noren stated calmly. "Did you think I didn't know that?"

Brek himself had known, obviously, and had accepted it as he had the apparent death sentence he'd incurred at his original arrest. "I—I wasn't sure whether you'd thought that far," he said.

"Oh? You assumed that if I had, I'd be afraid?" Noren strove to control himself, realizing that he was being unfair to Brek, and added quietly, "I saw my best friend murdered by a mob when I was small."

"You never told me."

"I've never talked about it to anyone. He was a lot older than I was, and the first heretic I ever knew. They arrested him…and then later that night they burned the jail. With us it will be over faster; once they grasp what we're saying, they'll probably stone us." Noren's voice was hard, bitter. "They'll tell themselves they're destroying wicked ideas, but underneath, at least some of them will believe—and the ones who do will throw the most stones."

"You don't have much faith in anything," Brek observed, "not even in people benefiting from what we offer them."

"I'm a realist. As I told Talyra once, faith is nothing more than being content with ignorance."

"What are you going to tell Talyra now?"

"Nothing," muttered Noren. "What could I?" He would have no chance anyway, he knew. Even if he was not killed, he would be isolated in the City; he would spend what remained of his life inside the Hall of Scholars.

Brek looked uncomfortable. "It—it doesn't seem quite right to do this by stealth," he maintained. "I mean—well, they trust us. There's no rule against my flying the aircar without telling anyone; they'll think it's odd, but they won't object. No Scholar would misuse equipment, so they'll assume we've gone for supplies and that we left early because we wanted a few extra hours in the City."

"I know," Noren said, equally distressed. That was the aspect of it he liked least. "We won't try to escape the consequences," he declared. "If for some reason the crowd's not violent—if Technicians are there, for instance—we'll go back to the City afterward and confess. Besides, it's not as if we were endangering the aircar! Villagers won't damage it no matter what they do to us; it's sacred to them."

"Yet if they all believed us and overthrew the system, a lot of equipment would be damaged. We'd have hastened the end."

"As long as there's going to be an end, what difference does it make how soon it comes?" Noren argued. But underneath he was aware that his concern for the fate of the aircar did seem inconsistent.

Noren did not sleep. What point was there in sleeping the night before one died? Lying still in the dark, he closed his eyes to the stars while the endless, futile questions circled in his mind: why were worlds formed...why were worlds destroyed...what *was* life, and what was death? At that last one, terror spread through him again, but he mastered it grimly. He would not yield to terror; he was through with that! Truth was the only important thing, and though the kind he'd once sought might be nonexistent, he was determined to stand by the principles that were firm.

There was no point in eating or drinking either, he decided when dawn approached, silhouetting the Tomorrow Mountains against pale yellow. Food and water were in short supply and should not be wasted. He was not hungry anyway. His mouth was dry, but he knew that was partly the result of fear and therefore he paid no attention. In any case, to go to the cistern might attract notice.

The camp was quiet; no one was yet awake. No guard was kept in a settlement founded on mutual trust. On his way to the aircar Noren passed the low hillock behind which he knew Talyra's chosen hollow lay. Picturing her there asleep, untouched by any premonition of the grief he could not spare her, he knew he could not leave without seeing her once more.

His feet, sinking into the spongy moss, made no sound. He did not plan to wake her, only to look; she slept fully clothed on a lightweight sheet of brown cloth, as did everyone. Standing there, Noren cried silently, *Oh, Talyra, if only we were back in the village...if only I'd not been a heretic at all...* But he knew he did not mean it. He could not have been other than what he was.

Talyra stirred and then sat up, roused not by noise but by his mere presence. She smiled joyously. Too late, Noren realized what he had done. If he simply walked away, she would be hurt and bewildered. She would suppose he had come, only to decide that he did not want what she was clearly willing to offer. She'd remain forever convinced that he had reaffirmed their betrothal more from duty than from love.

"Darling," he whispered, "there's no time...but I had to see you. I'm—leaving. Brek's waiting in the aircar—"

"Leaving? For how many days, Noren?"

"For good."

Talyra, stunned, gasped, "But *why?* Even yesterday you said nothing of going back—"

"I didn't know yesterday."

Rapidly she began to fold her belongings into the sheet. "I'll be sent back too, in a few days," she declared. "Do you think if I spoke to the Scholars, they'd let me come now?"

"No!" Noren exclaimed, too loudly, and then, whispering again, "No, you mustn't!"

His tone of voice gave him away; Talyra was too keen not to sense the desperation in it. "You don't have permission either." she asserted. "The aircar never leaves till after breakfast; and anyway, if the Scholars had told you last night, you'd have said goodbye then."

He could not say that he did not need permission; she supposed him a Technician like herself. Noren pulled her to him, kissing her, but she wrenched away. "You never kiss me like that," she said, "not as if it was...the last time. What's wrong, Noren?"

It was hard for him to keep back the tears. "We...we won't see each other in the City. By the Star, Talyra, I never wanted things to turn out this way—"

He expected her to be hysterical, but she was not. Very calmly she announced, "If we can't see each other in the City, then we'll at least have the trip. Either you let me come, or I'll wake the Scholars and ask."

"No, darling, it's wrong for you—"

"For me more than for you? I don't think so. No Scholar has forbidden me; I break no provision of the Law. They are good and just and sometimes more human than you are! *They* would not expect me to say goodbye like this."

Noren was in no shape to think rationally; he knew only that though any Scholar she might wake would tell him to go and her to stay, he could not face a Scholar with so bald a deceit, nor could he watch her sorrow. Incapable of reply, he started for the aircar, with Talyra walking beside him. He avoided Brek's eyes when they climbed in, and there was nothing Brek dared say in her presence. He did not know how much Noren had revealed to her. "Let's get going," Noren urged, and the aircar lifted. Only as the outpost fell away beneath did he realize that he could not possibly reveal anything.

It was of course unthinkable that Talyra should witness what was likely to take place in the village; and besides, he could not bear that she should know of his relapse. She would grieve over that even without guessing his peril. There was nothing to do but go on into the City, get supplies, and land in the village on their way back.

They climbed into the brightening sky and leveled off over the mountains. "Take over for a few minutes," Brek said. "I didn't check much, leaving the way we did." He turned to the dials on the control panel.

Noren held the direction lever as he had done when flying with Emet, but his mind whirled so that he could not keep it steady. Brek's face was tense, drawn; plainly the change of plan dismayed him. Talyra, who sat behind, was silent. How were they to endure the hours of delay? Noren thought. To leave the City before late afternoon might arouse suspicion; they would have to occupy themselves, perhaps talk to people, all day long. They might even encounter Stefred!

He stared down at the mountains, deeply shadowed in the early light, and it was as if they were no part of the earth. A touch of the same paralyzing detachment he'd felt in space hit him, whereupon his fear burst into panic. He must *move*... Without conscious intent he gripped the lever and pressed it forward until the ridges swung closer, tipping at odd angles like things viewed while one was weightless. Their bulk was appalling, yet still they seemed flat, not solid...

"Noren!" Brek shouted. "Noren, what are you trying to do? We're losing altitude—"

Noren came to himself and in horror jerked the lever back. The aircar rose abruptly—too abruptly. It began to lose power. In flat country that would not have been serious, for even a disabled car sank relatively slowly, drawing on reserves; but the terrain below was not flat, and Noren had no experience with air currents. In the effort to regain control, he veered off course and the rising sun shone full into his eyes through the domed canopy, blinding him; it was the nova once more...

Brek made a grab for the lever. But it was too late; even before the jagged peaks closed in and he heard Talyra's scream, Noren knew that they were going to crash.

Chapter Seven

Noren opened his eyes to sunlight and a sky that was abnormally blue. He was lying amid the wreckage of the aircar; there was a sharp yellow rock within a hand's span of his body, driven through what had once been floor, but he did not seem to be injured. The padded seat had cushioned the jolt of falling. As for the others...

"Talyra!" he shouted, struggling to free himself from the straps. "Talyra, where are you?"

"Here," she answered from behind him. "I think I'm all right; I don't hurt anywhere. But I can't get loose."

Part of the aircar's domed top had collapsed on her, pinning her to her seat. It was not heavy enough to have caused injury, but because of its bulk Noren could not lift it alone. He scrambled back to where he had left Brek, who, although also apparently unhurt, was not yet conscious. "Pour some water on his face," Talyra suggested.

"There isn't any water," Noren replied, noticing that the front section of the aircar, which contained the small emergency supply tank, had been smashed into rubble against the outcropping of rock into which they had plowed. Not until he stood up, surveying the landscape around them, did he realize the implications of what he had said.

They were somewhere in the higher reaches of the Tomorrow Mountains; tall crags closed them in on every side. Beyond those crags, should there be a passage through, would be only more rock, interspersed with gravelly patches containing occasional clumps of wholly inedible vegetation. He did not know if there would be any water, but if there was, it would be impure water, and they could not drink it.

Or perhaps they could. It would not really matter whether they did or not, since they would not live long enough to have children.

There was not the slightest possibility that they could survive; he knew that. The radiophone had been in the smashed portion of the aircar, and it did not take Brek's knowledge of radiophones to see that this one was beyond repair. Nor was there any possibility of repairing the propulsive mechanism, pieces of which were strewn here and there among the rocks. It was pure luck that the force of the crash had been absorbed by the impact of that section, thus sparing the cabin…though on second thought, Noren decided, the luck was bad rather than good. A quick death would have been easier than what lay ahead of them.

He crouched beside Brek, first feeling his pulse and checking for broken bones, and then, when he was reasonably sure that there were no serious injuries, shaking him into consciousness. Brek sat up painfully, holding his hand to his side. "Have you contacted anyone?" he gasped.

Noren shook his head silently. "We'll do that later," he said. "Let's get Talyra out first."

Brek glanced at the wreckage, stifled his cry of dismay, and with Noren's aid got to his feet. Together they moved the pieces of canopy under which Talyra was pinned and unfastened her seat straps so that she too could rise. All three of them were dazed, bruised and shaken, but they could walk; supporting each other, they made their way to a level piece of ground and stared back at the shattered aircar.

"It—it's not going to fly again," Talyra stated unnecessarily.

"No."

"Can we talk to the City by radiophone? Or to the outpost?"

"Noren and I will go and see," Brek told her. "You stay here."

"Wait," Talyra said, seeing him wince as he drew breath. "You're hurt, Brek."

"It's nothing."

"It's a broken rib," she declared, investigating with a nurse's practiced skill. She looked around her, searching for something that could be used to cut bandages; the fabric of their clothing was too strong to tear. "If only I were a doctor and knew the words that ease pain—"

She had come a long way since the days when she had considered an aspiration to be a Technician blasphemous, Noren thought; village nurses did not dream that those words—sacred ones reserved for the induction of hypnotic anesthesia—could be learned, much less pronounced, by an ordinary person. "I'll hunt for a piece of sharp metal," he said, "so you can make bandages when we get back. Come on, Brek."

They returned to the aircar, the search for a cutting tool giving them an excuse to remain there while they discussed the situation out of Talyra's hearing. Brek had no need to examine the radio-phone; there wasn't that much left of it. "I couldn't salvage enough to transmit any signal, let alone a voice," he said sadly. "What are we going to tell her?"

"The truth."

"Are you sure—" He broke off. "That's a stupid question; I know you too well to ask it. But Noren, we've got to offer some kind of plan."

"A plan for what? For walking out of the mountains? It would take weeks even if we had provisions."

"For signaling, then."

"Brek," Noren protested, "you know as well as I do that they haven't enough aircars for a search. If we could contact them, they'd come, but otherwise they'll simply fly the regular route."

"We're not far off it. Maybe we can attract their attention. We could start a fire, for instance."

"In the first place, it wouldn't show except at night, and they won't fly at night; in the second place, there isn't anything here that will burn." That was all too true; there was no moss in the area, and certainly not straw or tallow. The components of the aircar were incombustible, though its batteries could perhaps be used to provide a spark.

Wretchedly, Noren confronted cold fact. For himself he did not care, but by his actions Brek and Talyra had been doomed. He looked back over the long chain of events that had led to this moment, thinking that there could be no more fitting retribution for his earlier weaknesses. The aircar destroyed; his own death wasted; Talyra's meaningless and unnecessary...

And painful. It was not quite as hot in the mountains as in the low country, but there was heat enough to make thirst a torment past bearing. Starvation, if they should find water enough to last until they starved, would be still slower. Then too, Brek's injuries might be less trivial than he was making them out to be. Watching him, Noren said quietly, "I think I could induce anesthesia if you want me to try. You've had practice in going under."

"No" said Brek. "Hypnosis wouldn't be a very good idea; I'll need my wits, and you couldn't make it selective enough."

What good would wits do? Noren thought. In some cases, one's wits merely confirmed the futility of further effort. Brek went on, "I'll be all right once Talyra bandages my ribs. Look, Noren—if you're going to tell her how things stand, you'd better do it privately. Go back to her now, while I find something that will cut cloth."

Reluctantly, Noren headed back to the place where Talyra waited, sitting down beside her on the sun-warmed pebbles. "The radiophone's smashed," he said frankly, "and we can't fix it."

"Then we can't call for help?"

"There isn't any way to."

Talyra met his eyes. "I'm not scared, Noren," she said in a not-quite-steady voice.

Not scared? Then she was closing her mind to the obvious, Noren thought; he himself was terrified. He had, to be sure, started out that morning in the belief that he would not live until sundown...but death had somehow seemed a less real and immediate prospect than it did now, when it was to be slow, certain, and shared by the only person he had ever loved deeply. Of course, he was not going to let Talyra see how afraid he was, and perhaps she felt the same way. She too had pride.

"We mustn't panic," he agreed, putting his arm around her.

"What are we going to do first—after I fix the bandages, I mean?"

"There's not anything we can do, Talyra."

She stared at him, shocked, "You mean we're just going to sit here and wait to be rescued? I don't think that will work! Without the radiophone they can't possibly find us in all this wilderness."

His first impression had been correct, then; she did not realize that it was hopeless. With sorrow, a more stirring sorrow than he had felt during the past weeks of lethargy and bitterness, he admitted, "No, darling, they can't."

"You're talking as if you're ready to *give up.*"

Noren faced her, knowing that decency demanded it, whatever the cost in personal anguish. "Talyra," he began, "it's my fault this is happening; you're here because of me, and I was even flying the aircar—"

"Don't blame yourself," Talyra said gently. "It was an accident, and after all, you didn't ask me to come. I was the one who insisted."

"That doesn't change the fact that I'll be responsible when we die."

"You mustn't say that!" she burst out. "We may be in danger, but that doesn't mean we can't live through it. The spirit of the Mother Star will protect us."

Horrified, Noren realized that this reaction was what he should have expected; it was entirely consistent with Talyra's whole outlook. Yet it was based on a delusion. She must not cling to any such false hope. "You've said yourself no one can find us," he pointed out, "and there's no food, Talyra. We can't escape from the mountains without food; it's much too far to the nearest village."

"I—I know. I don't see a way out either…but it's *wrong* not to search for one! It's wrong to assume we're going to die when we're not sure."

"If I weren't sure—if there could be any means at all of saving you—do you think I wouldn't try it?" Noren demanded.

"No one can be sure of such things," insisted Talyra. "There are mysteries beyond our imagining; the Star's spirit is more powerful than we guess. Doesn't the Prophecy say, *'We affirm life in the face of annihilation, we shall reaffirm it though death be in view; and the affirmation will be our strength'?* It's heresy to deny that, and to give up is a denial."

Yes, thought Noren, and he was again a heretic; had it not been for the crash, within hours he would have proclaimed himself a relapsed heretic before the people. He was unwilling to hurt Talyra by telling her that, but he should at least enlighten her about the Mother Star. To believe literally in symbols of an underlying truth might be all right, but he could not bear that she, like his mother, should die trusting in something that did not exist.

"I've been told more of the mysteries than you have," he said slowly, "and they are not as you think. The Mother Star can't change the laws of nature."

"Of course it can't," she agreed. "But we don't know all the laws of nature, do we? Sometimes…sometimes, lately, I've wondered whether even the Scholars do."

"They do not," declared Noren grimly.

In a confident tone Talyra proclaimed, "Then the Scholars themselves could not say that nothing can save us."

"The Scholars," Noren continued with pain, "know much about the Mother Star that is not in the Prophecy. They know, for instance, that it has killed more people than it will ever save."

She reached for his hand, saying soberly, "Noren, don't speak of this now. It's not that I can't bear it, it's just that you've suffered over it too long, and here we've got enough else to worry about." At his astonished stare she went on, "Do you suppose I can't guess what sorts of things have been torturing you all this time? You needn't answer; I know you're not free to tell—but I'm not stupid, darling. In the beginning I thought they were punishing you, but when you swore they weren't, I began to figure it out."

"Figure what out?" he asked, wondering how much he had given away.

"Not any deep secrets," she assured him. "But you said at your trial that you preferred truth to comfort, and I don't doubt that the Scholars took you at your word. There really isn't any other way they could have persuaded you to recant, is there? They showed you mysteries, and naturally not all the mysteries are pleasant ones. People *do* die. Everybody dies sooner or later, and the Mother Star doesn't prevent it; we all know that. Only we don't think about it very much. The Scholars must have to, and someone like you, who starts out by thinking, has to, too."

At a loss for words, Noren turned aside. It was uncanny how close Talyra could come to facts she lacked the background to interpret. Yet in spite of that she still believed what she wanted to believe! She was still convinced that some miraculous force could deliver her from danger! Would it really hurt anything for her to go on believing a while longer? he thought suddenly. It would be days before they died, and hope, even groundless hope, would make the waiting less dreadful. With weariness, he confessed to himself that he had not the heart to destroy her illusions.

"We won't talk about it," he said; then, because he saw that she expected it, he took her into his arms. And when they kissed, he realized that although he should be strong, he should give comfort, it was she who was comforting him.

Later, when a portion of Brek's tunic had been cut into bandages with a fragment of metal he'd found in the wreck and Talyra had bound his ribs securely, they decided to climb out of the canyon. "We've a much better chance of being seen from higher ground,"

Brek insisted; and Noren, knowing that only action could maintain Talyra's optimism, concurred without argument. If they were to go, they must do so at once, for they'd neither eaten nor drunk that day and their stamina would not last.

They were hardened to some degree, of course, by the weeks of camp life; the self-discipline of voluntary rationing had inured them to hunger and thirst. But by the same token, that discipline had taught them to recognize and meet their bodies' needs. Fasting to the point of malnutrition was not permitted in camp, and dehydration was even more closely watched. They'd learned to know the warnings; to pay no heed would be harder than to ignore what might be dismissed as mere discomfort. Moreover, having no excess reserves, they would face starvation sooner than well-fed villagers would have—that is, if they did not succumb to thirst before finding a stream.

The question of drinking stream water was discussed before they set out. Talyra raised it herself by observing matter-of-factly that rescue would be of little benefit unless it came soon, and Noren seized the opportunity to introduce what was bound to be a difficult topic. "Talyra," he said bluntly, "do you remember how at my trial I admitted having drunk impure water?"

Nodding, she protested, "But it's a sin against the High Law to do that!"

"Yes. Still, there is no other water in the mountains, and the High Law does not demand that we die for lack of it."

"We'd be transformed into idiots—" She stopped, realizing that the villagers' tale that had come automatically to her lips must be untrue. Though originally she'd told herself that others were right in thinking Noren's admission an idle boast, she knew him better now. In horror she whispered, "The other story…the one mentioned in the courtroom—"

"About a man who drinks impure water fathering idiot children?"

His face confirmed its truth; for the first time since the crash she was moved to tears. "That's the reason you can't marry," she faltered miserably, "and you—you couldn't bear to tell me. Oh, Noren—"

"It's not the reason. One can drink a limited amount, and I didn't exceed my limit; the Scholar Stefred has assured me of that." There had also been confirming medical tests. He had been warned, however, that he could drink very little more.

Taking him aside, Brek protested, "Are you really going to run the risk, Noren?"

"What risk? There won't be any child, that's certain."

Reddening, Brek glanced at Talyra and muttered, "I thought—well, anyway, someday—"

"There won't be any 'someday,' not for any of us."

"Oh. But what if something unforeseen happens; what if we get out?"

"You, too, Brek?" Noren snapped. "I'm keeping up the pretense for her sake, not yours. You're scientist enough to be realistic."

"I suppose so."

There'd be no idiot child anyway, Noren thought. The doctors would see to that, if further medical tests showed any chromosome damage, for in such cases the High Law permitted sterilization. He would, of course, break off the betrothal at once if he alone was affected, since Talyra would feel disgraced if she bore no babies, and she should marry someone who could give them to her. But what point was there in considering that? Reason told him that under no circumstances could either of them stay alive.

Before leaving the wreckage they combed it thoroughly for materials that might somehow be of use. Though none were found, not even anything shiny enough to reflect sunlight upward as a signal, both Talyra and Brek were adamant about taking along all the metal they possibly could. "It would be sacrilege to leave it!" exclaimed Talyra when Noren objected to the idea of loading themselves down unnecessarily. In this Brek supported her, despite the fact that whatever he carried would add to his pain. Metal was sacred, and to sacrifice any was unthinkable; Noren could produce no argument other than the one he had decided not to use. It would make no difference in the end whether that irreplaceable metal was lost at the site of the crash or elsewhere, but to say so would be defeatism in Talyra's eyes. Moreover, she seemed to look upon it as a sort of talisman. Once, as a village girl, she had possessed a silver wristband—a holy thing passed down to her by an aunt to whom she had been kind. She had sold it for money to aid in his escape and had never expected to touch a metal object again; although as a Technician she'd often done so, she still treated such objects with reverence. Perhaps, Noren thought ruefully, she felt that the spirit of the Mother Star was more likely to protect people who were guarding metal than those who were not.

By the time they were ready, with all detachable wire and other metal parts tied in makeshift packs devised from the material of the seat cushions, it was almost noon and the heat was increasing rapidly. Their thirst was already intense, and as Noren looked up at the whitish cliff to the east that seemed to offer their only chance of ascent, he decided that perhaps the effort, arduous though it would be, would prove wise in that it would hasten the inevitable finish. They would be more likely to find water if they circled the canyon, searching for passages between the cliffs, but they could not be seen from the air there; even Talyra realized that such a course would serve merely to prolong their suffering. He was glad that a more rapid end was in view.

The cliff's surface was rough and steep, and it was hard to find footholds. Their shoes were not designed for traversing country like this, although they were the kind worn by villagers, made from the thicker parts of work-beast hides and bound together with heavy thongs. Again and again Talyra almost slipped and fell, and Noren too had trouble keeping his balance, so that the hand he held out to her was not always firm.

They spoke little, for their dry mouths burned with a fire greater than the scorching sun that struck their shoulders. Brek, forced by the exertion to breathe deeply, swayed and clutched his ribs, his face contorted with agony. It would not be possible to reach the top, Noren felt, not if there were many places where progress required one to cling to protruding rocks. Their strength would give out. He found himself moving not by will, but automatically, simply because to stop would demand a decision he lacked the energy to make.

At last, after five or six hours, they stumbled up the final stretch of sun-baked slope onto a wide plateau, blocked on one side by still higher cliffs but otherwise surrounded by a gaping abyss. Talyra, daunted by its barrenness despite her courage, began to tremble both with physical fatigue and with the fear she had earlier suppressed. "I—I don't know what I expected to see," she murmured.

There was nothing to be seen—nothing but more rocks, more dead ground, and stretching everywhere into the visible distance, more jagged mountains. The plateau was infinitesimal compared to all that wasteland. If a low-flying aircar were to pass directly over it, they might be spotted, but aircars did not fly low over such terrain, not if their pilots' minds were on the job. Already the City had lost one; to risk another would be to risk the sustenance of villagers yet unborn. No car would come without an unmistakable signal, a signal that could not be sent.

Noren dropped his pack and sprawled on the stony ground, heedless of the heat that scorched his skin, not noticing that his feet were raw and blistered and that what remained of his left shoe was stained with blood. After a moment or two the others did likewise. For a long time they lay there, and though in the back of his mind he knew that if he did not rouse himself soon, he might never do so, it did not seem to matter.

The air was very still. It was thinner at this altitude than in the settled lands; that was why the sky was so blue, he thought idly. Blue…and still farther up, it was black. At night it would be black here. He feared the blackness still, and the bright stars, and the other darkness that was death; he feared them because they were past all understanding. Yet he could no longer hope to understand. He was too weary even to try. *No,* something inside him kept protesting, *no, that's a betrayal of truth…truth's the one thing I'll never abandon…* And suddenly it did matter. He was going to die; he could not expect to understand it beforehand—but whatever it was, was *true.* It was wrong to fear the truth, whether one understood it or not. And it was wrong not to care whether one lived…

"Noren!" Talyra was shaking him urgently. "Noren, listen! Don't you hear something?"

He sat up, dazed, analyzing the stillness; and then, as from a long distance, he heard his own voice ask. "Water?"

"Yes! Yes, I'm sure it is—somewhere behind us."

She clutched his hand and he went with her, not stopping to reason, not questioning the instinctive impulses of his body. Brek followed. Instinct led them to the tall cliff behind, where from a small cleft a thin, swift stream cascaded; instinct made them thrust their faces into the cool foam and gulp enough to damp the fire that was consuming them. But something more than instinct made Talyra stop.

"You said there's a limit," she declared, backing away. "We can't drink more than we need; it's sinful—and besides, we don't know how many days we'll be here."

Noren, his thirst far from quenched, drew back also, revived by the moisture and by its extraordinary coldness. He saw no real value in stopping, but he could hardly indulge himself while she remained thirsty, and Talyra still had her irrepressible hope.

"The spirit of the Mother Star is with us," she reflected, tilting her head to gaze up into the deep sky that for her held no terrors. "We have been led to this place; shall we not receive further blessings? It would be a sin to drink impure water without believing that we're doing it to preserve our lives."

He watched her, the love he'd restrained so long suddenly overwhelming him. Deluded, foolish, unreasonable...she might be all those things; but she was untouched by the grim fate awaiting her. The life in her was strong, and he was stirred by it in a way he had not been during the past weeks when so many problems and questions had weighed him down. Those worries were far away now, the burden of them dissolved. Life was what mattered...life, and truth, which were one and the same...and they need not be understood to remain valid. Could love be understood, and was not love a form of truth? He had loved Talyra through all the time when he'd considered truth the only thing of importance to him. Yet he'd been blind.

We are soon to die, he thought, *but now we are alive. As long as we're alive, life will go on.* "Darling," he began, holding out his arms to her. "Talyra, darling—"

They embraced, and he kissed her with more ardor than he'd previously dared to release; but the sun, hovering over the western crags, was glaring down, and though Brek had walked away, the plateau was bare of outcroppings or shrubs. It did not seem decent. Noren and Talyra followed the rivulet that trickled along the base of the cliff from the place where the cascade splashed, seeking shelter.

There was an archway, an opening in the rock wider than the stream, leading through into a shallow canyon. They stooped under, well shaded from sunlight although the sky was bright beyond. Noren's arms tightened around Talyra—and to his dismay the joy in her face gave way to stark terror.

She was looking through the arch, where, some distance down the slope, the stream joined a larger one bordered by clumps of reeds. "Noren," she gasped, "There are *people* there!"

He glanced over his shoulder, disbelieving; then cold terror struck him also. What he saw was no less horrifying because he had greater knowledge of it than she. It was in fact a good deal worse than anyone but a Scholar could realize. "No, darling," he whispered, motioning her to be still. "Those aren't people. Those are savages."

Eight or nine of the creatures squatted by the stream, though they did not appear to have ever washed themselves in it. They were, of course, completely naked. That in itself did not seem shocking, for although they had human form, their brains were not human; Noren knew that they were incapable of speech, much less rational thought. Their ancestry was of the Six Worlds, but they were as drastically changed as the work-beasts, and they were not much brighter.

Talyra knew their origin, for the basic facts were taught in every village school: how at the time of the Founding a few people had defied the High Law, drunk too much impure water, and then fled in fear to the mountains, thereby losing all trace of their heritage. They (in reality their offspring) had become idiots that lived like beasts. These and other gruesome details, such as a story about savages eating slithery things that swam in streams, were commonly used to frighten disobedient children, as was quite necessary if a repetition of the incident was to be avoided. "Were it not for our obedience to the High Law we would be as they are, Talyra," Noren murmured.

"Yes," she agreed soberly. "Once you wouldn't have thought so, though—" She stopped, remembering that it was not proper to speak of his past heresies; and Noren flushed with the recollection of the night he'd tried to convince her that their own remote ancestors had been like the savages. He'd had it backwards. On the mother world human beings had indeed evolved from savagery, but these were not "savages" of that sort. These were mutants, the product of damaged genes rather than evolution, and had no future potential. In them no vestige of human spirit remained.

He cringed as the largest mutant, a male, stood half-erect, revealing the filthiness of its body and the absence of mind behind its vacant stare. If the Founders had not controlled the City—if the Scholars did not continue to do so—all humankind would be like that…and it would be "humankind" no longer. It was as justifiable to prevent such degradation as for a starship captain to take full command of his ship to safeguard its passengers' lives.

Yet if there could be no prevention? If control of people's inheritance was useless because in spite of it, their descendants would inevitably become mutants like these that crouched and gibbered beside the stream?

Talyra pressed close to him. The big male and two smaller ones had snatched up something and moved toward them, upstream. Noren's stomach lurched; they were now close enough for him to see what they carried. "Talyra," he said firmly, "go back to the plateau—"

"Without *you?*"

"Go back and tell Brek to come here—he won't hunt for us, and I don't dare shout. Tell him to come, but don't come with him."

"I won't leave you, Noren!"

"You must," he insisted. If he retreated from the archway, the mutants might follow, whether or not he and Talyra had been seen; only from that vantage point could he hope to defend the plateau. But he could not do it alone, and Brek, unaware, would not approach until morning.

Talyra sensed his desperation, knowing nothing of its cause, and slipped away. Noren gripped the largest rock he could find and held it in readiness, knowing the gesture a feeble one. If the mutants came before Brek did, he had no chance. Still, there were only the three males—the females probably were not dangerous—and at the moment all were well occupied. It would be twilight soon; perhaps they'd sleep.

He could not take his eyes from the loathsome scene before him. *Not this,* he pleaded inwardly. Death he could face, but not this death, certainly not for Talyra. A lingering one, however painful, would be better. It might even be better if they jumped from the cliff.

At a sound behind him, he froze, but it was Brek. Talyra had returned too, as Noren had known she would. "What are they doing?" she asked in a low voice.

There was no point in evading a fact that was clearly evident. "Eating," Noren replied tersely.

Talyra peered ahead into the dusk. "Noren," she exclaimed, "they're eating *flesh!* It's not fowl's flesh, the bones are too big. It must be a work-beast's—"

He had wondered, briefly, that she could be so composed; now he realized that she hadn't noticed the shape of the bones, nor was she aware that there were no work-beasts in the mountains. She had no way of guessing what all Scholars knew about the ghastlier habits of these creatures. "They are animals," he reminded her, "without intelligence or speech. The High Law does not apply to them."

"Impure flesh will make them sick, though."

"No sicker than they already are," said Brek grimly. He was pale, on the verge of getting sick himself.

One of the smaller mutants looked up from the meager portion of raw meat it held and its eyes focused abruptly, not with hostility, but in the manner of a carnivore sighting prey. Giving a loud grunt, it lurched forward.

"It's seen us!" Talyra whispered. "It's coming toward us; it—it looks as if it might want to hurt us. Why, Noren?"

"I don't know," Noren lied, struggling to remain steady.

In strength, he and Brek were no match for the attackers; they wouldn't have been even if Brek had not been crippled by his broken rib. Besides lacking comparable weight, they were weakened by thirst and exhaustion, and the mature male—which was now advancing behind the younger ones—was a huge brute with years of experience in making kills. The mere fact that it had lived past maturity proved that, since among its kind only the victors survived. The mutants had turned to cannibalism because they had no other source of meat, and the eating of meat was deeply ingrained in their biological inheritance. But grown males would have fought to the death in any case. They'd have fought for band dominance and, Noren recalled in dismay, for possession of females, as most animals had done on the Six Worlds—for Talyra, slaughter was not the chief peril. He and Brek had been told these things. They had not, however, been told how to defend themselves, since the possibility that they might have to had never occurred to anyone. Intelligence was their sole armor.

"We can't let them approach," Brek said quietly. "Once they grapple with us we're finished." He seized a rock, preparing to aim it at the oncoming "savage."

"Wait," Noren told him. "They'll not be frightened off, and if you miss his head you'll merely enrage them. We've got to know more about their ways." Though the mutants did not use tools, they might throw rocks themselves, and as to whether they could do it purposefully he was not sure. "Wait, Brek," he said again, "and be ready to aim when they're nearer; with your injury, you may not get many chances. I'm going to try something."

Behind him, Talyra stood shaking, recognizing the immediate danger if not its potential aftermath. "Keep back," Noren ordered, "but gather all the stones you can. Pile them at my feet." Picking up a small rock, he hurled it as far as he could, aiming not for the mutants but well beyond them.

All three of the creatures turned instantly; what they lacked in wit was partially made up for by keen hearing and fast reactions. Quickly Noren grabbed more stones and threw out a barrage. The mutants remained facing the direction in which it landed, and shortly, they too began flinging one rock after another—but theirs were tossed aimlessly and fell wide of the mark, some even landing in the stream.

"It's a good diversion," Brek observed, "but you can't keep it up forever. If we don't kill them now, they'll simply attack again later."

"I know. This was just a test." Stopping, Noren outlined the only strategy that seemed feasible. "We draw their attention back to us. Then we stand fast and let them get close, very close. When we're sure we can't miss, we make them turn again, and while they're facing the other way we aim to hit."

"What's to say they'll keep on facing the other way?" protested Brek. "Two of us can't hit three of them simultaneously."

"No, but we can each disable a small one, then deal with that big one together."

"I can throw rocks too, at least I—I think I can," Talyra ventured, her voice quavering only a little.

Noren frowned. That would add to their chances of success, certainly. She could not throw with sufficient force and accuracy to kill, but she could toss the stones to make the attackers turn, thus allowing him to act faster. "All right," he agreed reluctantly, "but don't do it till I give the word—and aim a long way past them." He drew a deep breath and flung another stone, deliberately directing it to a point only a short distance away. Then he grasped a larger, heavier rock like the one Brek held, and with pounding heart, he waited.

The mutants, confused, advanced slowly. There was ample time to absorb an unforgettable picture of their slouching gait, the filth of their long matted hair, and worst of all, the mindlessness of their faces. This travesty of human life—this housing of animal mentality in men's bodies—was more hideous than anything Noren had ever encountered. He had seen men behave like brutes; some of the ones who'd abused him at his arrest and recantation had been of a low sort. Some would have killed without hesitation when sufficiently inflamed. But they had not revolted him as these mutants did, for despite their faults they'd been human beings still.

He and Brek stood in full view, calculating how long it would be before one lunged at them, knowing that to move too soon—or too late—would mean sure defeat. Finally, when their taut nerves could endure no more, Noren breathed, "Now, Talyra!" and as the mutants whirled toward the sound of a new hail of stones, he heaved his rock with all the force that was in him. It struck the foremost one's skull, felling the creature, but Brek's first throw only grazed its target. Though his second hit true, the largest savage turned and charged before he and Noren could act in unison. Not until it was within instants of seizing Brek were they able to bring it down.

The two of them walked forward, shaking with released tension. The stench of the bodies was overpowering. Noren stared for a moment, realizing that the horror was not quite over, then returned to Talyra. They clung together, her body quivering with sobs. "Darling," he said gently, "go now. Go to the plateau and wait for me."

"No—"

"You mustn't watch the finish, Talyra."

Grasping his meaning, she obeyed. Noren and Brek, suppressing their sickness, went to the felled mutants, two of which were merely unconscious, and did what had to be done. Afterward they dragged the carcasses some distance downstream and dumped them beside the foul and bloody half-consumed one, covering them with reeds. The females had fled. It was unlikely that there would be another band nearby, for the vegetation that was the mainstay of their diet was more plentiful at lower elevations; and in any case revenge was beyond their conception.

"I'll sleep here," Brek said as they returned to the archway, "and guard it, though I doubt that any more will come. There's no need for you to worry, Noren."

It was nearly dark by this time. Noren washed in the clear

shallow water, letting none touch his lips, and went back through the arch onto the barren plateau. The dead stony landscape was softened by the glow of three crescent moons; it looked unearthly and yet less unreal than most things had been since the space flight. The inertia he'd fought against was gone.

Talyra was waiting near the cascade. At night, the emptiness of the plateau gave a sense of privacy, not desolation, and indeed it did not seem that any place could be desolate when she was there. He knelt on the still-warm pebbles, smoothing a hollow with his hands. "There should be moss, at least," he mumbled. "This is not fit for you, Talyra. I've never brought you anything but hardship—"

She flung herself down beside him, chiding softly, "Oh, Noren as if I cared about *that!* We were almost killed, and now we're alive; haven't we cause for joy?"

We cannot stay alive, his mind told him, but the thought was remote; it was a time for feeling, not thinking. Curiously, the imminence of death freed him to feel. There was a point past which one could not reason, could not analyze...maybe Talyra's refusal to despair was not so foolish after all. Her joy enveloped him; he knew fierce joy of his own, and surrendered to it as they joined in the ultimate affirmation of survival.

In the morning, when they woke to brilliant sunlight and bathed briefly in the perilous water of the cascade, Talyra drank a very little; but Noren, being far closer to the safe limit than she, carefully rinsed his parched mouth and did not swallow.

The days that followed were the strangest Noren had ever known. Suspended between life and death, he felt a peculiar lightness, not only from fasting but because burdens were lifted that had been too heavy for him to handle. The whole universe no longer seemed his concern.

Most of the daylight hours they spent at the cliff's archway, for it provided the only nearby shade and their thirst was too great to permit much movement. At night Brek continued to sleep there while Noren and Talyra returned to the plateau. Their joy in each other overrode all fears, all discomforts; it seemed ample compensation for the painful things. Noren stopped worrying about what was past and what was to come, and lived one moment at a time. Though the moments brought suffering, they brought elation, too. He was free for elation, since there were no grave decisions left to be made.

They felt no hunger after the first; although they were weak from it, their stomachs did not torment them. The plants the mutants ate were no temptation. To taste that vegetation was out of the question, for while they might escape poisoning and eventually adapt, as the mutants' ancestors had done, the chance of rescue was too small to warrant such a course. None of them even considered living on indefinitely in the mountains. There was an unspoken agreement between them that death would be preferable, not only because of the subhuman offspring that might come with the years, but because if Noren and Brek should be poisoned or killed, Talyra might be left at the mercy of the bestial creatures that would sooner or later reappear. At her insistence Noren had explained their ways, and she was aware that for a woman there was more to be feared than cannibalism.

So hunger was accepted, then ignored. It was thirst that brought anguish, all the more so because they were within sight and sound of the tantalizing stream. With calm realism, they estimated the maximum length of time it would be possible to survive without food and calculated the amount of water that could be safely consumed each day if the entire limit were spread over that time. Brek and Talyra had to endure nothing worse than a continuous craving that they were obliged to deny. Noren's quota was considerably less, and he suffered intensely, drinking only as much as was essential to prevent high fever. Although moistening his skin provided some relief, it could not be done too often. During the worst hours, the long hot afternoons when he waited with burning forehead and throat afire for the shadow of the crag beyond the arch to tell him that it was time to permit himself a few more drops, be wondered why he had changed his mind about the pointlessness of restraint. To his amazement, he could find no answer. He knew only that something inside him would not let him go to Talyra if the limit were to be passed. The fact that their present situation made this irrational did not seem to alter it.

Brek's injury was increasingly painful; the attack on the mutants had been a strain. Talyra redid the bandages and also bandaged their raw, blistered feet, using the carefully saved metal scrap to cut strips from her own tunic and Noren's. All the metal they'd salvaged was piled neatly near the cliff where, Noren felt privately, it would remain until the light of the Mother Star touched it—by which time, one way or another, its loss would have ceased to count.

He no longer dwelt on such speculations; but while he was turning away from abstract thought, Brek was thinking more deeply than in the past. "Noren," he said the fifth evening, when Talyra had gone on ahead, "we—we were wrong…what we planned, I mean. This may sound crazy to you, but if it weren't for Talyra, and for the aircar being destroyed…I'd almost be glad we crashed. We were going to die anyway, and it's better like this. We aren't harming people by it."

"The truth wouldn't have harmed people," Noren protested indignantly. "Truth *doesn't.*"

"No, not if it doesn't destroy their faith in a greater truth. I agree it's no kindness to deceive people about important things, not even to spare them unhappiness. That's why I let you persuade me. Only now—well, now I'm not sure that what we were going to say is true."

"You're afraid to acknowledge it?" Feverish and irritable from the searing thirst that made speech an effort, Noren replied with rancor. "You know as well as I do that there's no more chance of the human race surviving on this planet than there is of our staying alive here in the mountains."

"We've managed to hold on so far."

"What's that got to do with it? We've had certain resources, resources that won't last indefinitely. That's *fact,* Brek! When they're gone, we'll die. I'm afraid, too, but not so afraid I can't face up to it."

Brek looked at him strangely. "Is that what you set out to prove, Noren?"

With a rage he did not wholly understand, Noren turned his back and started toward the plateau; but Brek was not ready to drop the issue. "I should have seen it sooner," he declared. "I'm sorry for you, Noren, if what you said that last night in camp is what you believe! But I don't really think it is."

"I do believe it." Noren said doggedly. "I've learned too much to believe anything else. There won't be a magical, miraculous breakthrough 'in the last generation of our endurance,' as ritual has it, any more than there'll be a magic rescue for us now. What do you expect, some unpredictable solution that we're led to by the spirit of the Mother Star, the way Talyra does?"

Brek leaned back against the cliff wall, looking up at the section of fading sky framed by the arch. Then, slowly, he asserted, "It's not impossible."

"You're no more honest with yourself than the rest," accused Noren bitterly. "When the going gets rough, the ideas you grew up with come back. You could study all that the Six Worlds knew and still believe that there's some mysterious force in the universe that provides for people's welfare."

"Yes."

Appalled, Noren perceived that Brek meant what he was saying. Against all logic, he had returned to the teachings of the religion in which he'd been reared—not only those the Scholars had planned to substantiate, but the ones that had never had any scientific basis at all. "You wouldn't have gone through with it, would you?" he demanded. "At the last minute you'd have backed out and left me to reveal the facts alone."

"I wouldn't have abandoned you to the mob, Noren."

"Would you have left me in the City? Turned me over to Stefred maybe, to keep me from betraying the sacred trust?" He laughed grimly at the irony of it. Brek, who had once risked himself to save him from the Chief Inquisitor...

"I—I don't quite know," Brek confessed. "I think I'd have gone to the village with you and argued against what you said."

"That would have been dangerous," Noren retorted, "for someone who's decided he wants to live at the price of deception. People wouldn't have stopped to notice which of us they were stoning."

Brek's rigid control gave way, and he too lashed out in anger. "Are you admitting you wanted to die?"

"*Wanted* to? You don't understand much—"

"I understand more than you think. *You* talk to *me* about self-delusion? You've hated yourself ever since that space flight because you've been afraid you were a coward, so afraid that a time came when you had to disprove it—at any cost. Even suicide! What we set out to do was suicidal; I knew that. I was willing to die. But not for as many reasons as you were. You were trying to show yourself and everybody else how heroic you could be."

Noren stumbled forward, fury amplifying his depleted strength, and seized Brek's shoulders; but Brek was past the point of restraint. "What's more, it wasn't a very big sacrifice, was it?" he went on, his voice harsh and unpitying. "Your life wasn't worth much to you or to anyone, the way you were sulking—"

Outraged, unable to control the conflicting feelings the suggestion aroused, Noren swung on Brek and struck his face. Both of them were in bad shape; both fell, Brek letting out an involuntary cry as his injured rib hit stony ground.

In dismay, Noren bent over him, overwhelmed by remorse. *Brek,* he thought, *oh, Brek, I don't blame you for despising me—everything I do ends in disaster...* Aloud he said, "I'm sorry. You look at things differently, but you're entitled to, I guess. Maybe you're even right. I don't know myself any more; I don't understand half of what I think. Yet I can see facts. I can still reason, and reason says there's no hope for us on this planet—"

"Go tell *her* that," Brek said, glancing toward the plateau where Talyra waited. "Tell her that whether she lives to bear your child or not makes no difference."

Noren bowed his head. "I can't, Brek. I can't, and I don't know why. I still believe that truth's the most important thing there is—I'll never deny that—so if I love her, don't I owe her honesty? She doesn't want to be shielded. She's stronger than I used to think."

Brek did not reply. After a while Noren pulled himself to his feet and left the archway. But he saw no beauty in the plateau that night, and though Talyra slept in his arms, he felt no peace.

The next day his fever was worse, yet he drank barely enough to keep it below the danger level. Talyra helped him to the shade and sat silently beside him; none of them wasted energy on talking. The world was unreal again to Noren, this time as the result of near-delirium; he felt the heat, and the air seemed full of bursting suns.

"The spirit of this Star shall abide with us, and with our children, and our children's children..." Neither Talyra nor Brek whispered it aloud, but he knew that both believed it, and were the stronger for their belief; he knew that if they had not believed, all three of them would now lie dead in the canyon where they had crashed. *He* had not insisted that they make the effort to move on. He had not found the water that had staved off death this long. Yet he did not want to die any more; he wanted, desperately, to live! He wanted humankind to live. Though it was hopeless, he wanted to work with all his strength toward the future so many believed in.

He wanted his child—the child that might already be conceived—to continue after him, whether as villager or as Scholar. Why had he begun to feel this way only when it was too late?

If he had believed as Talyra and Brek did, there would have been no crash. But what good did it do to realize that? Wanting to believe was not the same as believing; he could no more force faith on himself than those who'd condemned his heresy could have forced it upon him. He was what he was, and he could not discount the facts he knew.

"Noren," Talyra said softly, "are you awake?"

He nodded, for his mouth was too dry for him to force out words. "I see something up there," Talyra continued, pointing to a portion of cliff wall that was visible beyond the arch. "I was looking, thinking how bare it is, and then the sun struck something shiny. I—I think it's *metal.*"

"Metal...there? But that's not possible," Brek declared, getting painfully to his feet. "No other aircar has ever come down in the mountains." He walked through the arch and shaded his eyes, staring upward.

"Are you sure?" asked Talyra. "Maybe the Scholars once landed here."

Brek frowned; he knew, as did Noren, that the Scholars had not. If the small object glinting in the midday sun was indeed metal, it could only be that one of the people from whom the mutants were descended had penetrated farther into the wilderness than had been supposed; first-generation villagers had possessed whatever articles they'd had with them when they were locked out of the City.

"A Scholar would not have left any metal behind," said Brek, answering Talyra's suggestion without touching on unrevealed secrets.

"That's true," she agreed. "And we must not leave it unprotected, either! However it got there, it is sacred and should be guarded."

How futile, Noren thought miserably. The piece of metal didn't look big enough to make a real difference in the resources of humanity; still every scrap was precious, and if they had been going to get back he'd have been the first to say that it should be recovered. But they weren't. What benefit could there be in retrieving it to eventually corrode in company with the salvage from the aircar?

Corrode…that was odd; if it had lain in a niche in the cliff wall since shortly after the Founding, it should have corroded long ago. Even equipment that did not have to be stored in air-conditioned buildings required occasional protective treatment, for the planet's atmosphere was hard on the alloys that had met the Six Worlds' needs. To be sure, some metals did not corrode at all, but they were rarer than those that did, and far less likely to have been among the personal belongings of the mutants' ancestors. This object shone like silver, yet had too much bulk for any sort of jewelry. His curiosity aroused, he pulled himself up from the half-reclining position in which he'd been resting, but he was too weak to rise and join Brek.

The question of retrieval was academic, he realized. None of them would be able to climb that cliff; it would be dangerous to try it without ropes even if they had their normal strength. As it was, besides being debilitated by hunger and thirst, Talyra had neither the skill nor a long enough reach, Brek was incapacitated by the broken rib, and he himself was giddy with fever. "We can't do anything," he asserted through cracked lips.

"Darling, we must!" insisted Talyra. "It's a sin to let a holy thing like that be lost in the wilderness."

"We're lost ourselves."

"No!" she burst out. "I won't let you give up, Noren! If we die expecting to live, we'll be none the worse for it; but if we stop living because we expect to die, we'll have thrown away our own lives."

Noren looked at her, seeing a confidence that her growing recognition of their doom could not shake, and he knew that for the sake of their love he must make her believe he shared that confidence. Through some flamboyant, mad gesture he must offer proof that he did—for otherwise, in her view, he would be throwing away not only his life and hers, but very possibly that of an unborn child.

A child who belonged to the future…the future that wasn't going to come… He was no longer thinking coherently. Somehow, what he was about to do seemed no less a defiance of wrong than the gesture he'd planned to make in the village.

Crawling to the stream, Noren thrust his face into it and drank deeply, then splashed water over the rest of his body. He lay there, letting the moisture cool him, realizing that this gave him but two more days' leeway and that after that, during the remaining time before they starved, he would stop rationing himself and sleep alone. At length, when he was somewhat restored, he got shakily to his feet and approached the cliff.

Brek accompanied him. "I wish I could help," he said quietly.

"You don't consider this—suicidal?"

"Not in quite the same way."

It was not the same. Surveying the rock wall above him, Noren did not doubt that he would succeed in scaling it, and somehow he did not expect to fall to his death. Strength surged through him, as if he had tapped a resource to which he'd previously had no access, and with cautious movements he began to climb.

There were handholds and footholds, but they were widely spaced and hard to judge. He could not judge them accurately, Noren knew; he must simply make the best estimates he could and then gamble. Surprisingly, he was unafraid, despite the handicaps of faintness and pain from his bandaged feet. He saw everything very clearly: the shades of rock color; the shapes of the crevices; and, over his head, the gleaming piece of metal. It beckoned him, and the closer he got the more peculiar its appearance seemed. It was round! He had never seen a spherical metal object of that size—about as large as his fist—and he could not imagine why it had been placed in such a niche.

Balancing precariously with one foot well supported and the other braced by a mere toehold, Noren clung to an orange-yellow crag and stretched his free arm to grasp the strange ball. "Push it out," called Brek. "There's no need to *carry* it down." Noren ignored the advice; for some reason he felt that he should not risk smashing the thing. It was more than scrap metal, though what its function had been might remain obscure. He inserted it carefully into the open neck of his tunic.

Climbing down was harder than climbing up, since the footholds below could not be seen. Gingerly Noren probed for them, assisted by Brek's guidance from the ground. Fatigue made his muscles tremble. He was sustained only by the touch of the smooth metal sphere against his chest; near the bottom, when at last he slipped, he instinctively clasped his hands over it as he fell.

Talyra rushed to him, Brek at her side. Noren's burst of unnatural energy had faded; he was bruised, one foot was twisted, and even with help he could not stand. He wanted to lie where he'd fallen and never move again. Yet the sphere's fascination was too great for that. Sitting up, he drew it out and examined it thoughtfully. It wasn't uniformly smooth; there were oddly arranged indentations, some of which were almost translucent.

"That isn't just metal," Talyra observed. "It's a Machine."

"Yes, I'm sure it is," Noren agreed. He pressed his finger into the deepest indentation, feeling its texture. Abruptly, to his amazement, one of the translucent ones gave forth a greenish glow.

For a long time he stared, while Brek and Talyra looked on with the respectful awe any unknown machine merited. Then he tried pressing other hollows, obtaining other variations of light and memorizing the scheme whereby the number of glowing points could be increased or decreased. Finally, with the sphere wholly dark again, he raised his eyes. He could not comprehend the thing; he could not be sure that he wasn't taking a terrible risk; yet to reject any potential opportunity…

"Talyra," he asked slowly, "does this machine frighten you?"

"No, Noren."

"It should be put with the other metal on the plateau, but I can't walk, and Brek shouldn't. Will you take it?"

"Of course; I'm not hurt. Do you mean right now?"

"Yes." He placed the sphere into her hands, adding, "Just before you leave it, Talyra, press *here* and *here* and *here*—so that all the lights will glow."

Brek started to speak, but Noren shook his head. "All right, Noren," Talyra said, puzzled, but trusting him and perceiving that he did not want to be questioned. She walked swiftly through the archway and disappeared.

"I suppose you had to send her away," Brek said, "so that we could talk about it. But I'd have liked to look at it more. What was it? I've never heard of any equipment like that."

"I don't think anyone has," Noren declared, "here, or on the Six Worlds either. It's not the product of our technology, Brek. I—I think it must have been left by the Visitors."

"An alien artifact?" demanded Brek incredulously. "How do you know?"

"Well. I can't be positive, but it just doesn't follow the principles of Six Worlds' engineering. And those holes were made for fingers…but not ours; they aren't placed right."

"Noren," Brek objected, "if that's the case, why did you want it taken up to the plateau where we can't study it? And why, for the Star's sake, did you tell her to turn it on? We've no idea what it'll do."

"I think it may give out some kind of radiation."

"That could be dangerous."

"It could also be detectable—from a distance."

"From the City!" Brek breathed excitedly.

"There's a chance. Don't say anything to her; it may not reach that far, and even if it does it may be lethal as far as we're concerned. It could even explode, though I don't think it will while she's activating it, since it didn't when I was experimenting." Noren lay back, gazing at the wild and inhospitable peaks of the Tomorrow Mountains. "We have nothing to lose," he murmured. "If we don't try this, we're dead, so isn't *any* attempt—even one we're not sure of—better than none at all?"

Chapter Eight

The aircar came just before sunset, dropping out of the eastern sky to hover above the plateau. Brek heard it first, and in that instant Noren—who had not really dared to hope—knew from his face that the gamble had paid off.

Raising his head from Talyra's lap, he cried, "Run, darling! Wave, make them see you!" She'd heard it too and scrambled to her feet, racing back through the arch toward the faint but unmistakable humming sound. She did not connect the aircar's arrival with the mysterious metal sphere, yet she showed little surprise; she had felt all along that in the end the spirit of the Mother Star would bring help.

Noren was unable to walk; the two Scholars from the rescue car had to carry him to the flat place where they'd landed. Brek, with assistance, got there on his own. He explained about the sphere while Talyra stayed beside Noren.

It was indeed alien, the Scholars agreed. They had not known what to expect, for the radiation was powerful and unlike any the computer complex had monitored before, although it was not of a hazardous sort. No one had seen how it could be coming from the lost aircar, yet because its source was in the region where the crash was presumed to have occurred, a team had been sent at once. Now, with reluctance, it was decided that the sphere must be left where it was until more could be learned about it; to take it into the City would be an unjustified risk. It could be found again, and indeed would serve to mark the pile of metal that the rescue car, which was already overloaded with passengers, could not carry. After that it would be studied at the outpost.

Hearing that, Noren was stricken with disappointment. For a few minutes he had held with wonder a thing from another solar system…a thing made by a human race unlike his own. He wanted to see it once more, to share in the unraveling of its mysteries. But he could not expect that he'd be allowed to leave the City again. His confinement this time would be final and complete; he had forfeited the trust of those who were guarding the secrets.

It was nearly dark when they reached the City. Looking down from the air as they approached its cluster of lights, he remembered the first time he'd seen it so, driving a trader's sledge up the final hill and halting at the crest to gaze with unbearable longing at the stronghold of all hidden truth. How naive he'd been. Even while he lived in the City he'd not thought it a prison; he'd assumed that everything he sought was there...

Talyra squeezed his hand and smiled. Wan, emaciated, clothed in the tattered remnants of a tunic cut away for bandages, she was nonetheless radiant. To Talyra it had all worked out as it was meant to work. And perhaps, Noren thought sadly, she had again glimpsed the truth more clearly than he had; she'd seen through some window that to him would be forever obscure. They would surely have died if he had not carried through the masquerade for her sake. Still, he could not do that indefinitely. He'd once feared that he might accept priesthood rather than give her up, but when it came to the point of choice, he knew he would never be as great a hypocrite as that. Those who became High Priests were not hypocrites either, yet much as he might wish to believe as they did, he could not alter what he felt.

So, having had her love, he must once again sacrifice it. Since their marriage could never be authorized, he must free her from the betrothal. It would be best if there proved to be no child, for she would be hurt less that way; still he could not regret their brief hours of happiness. Little more lay in store for him, for though he knew that insofar as he was permitted, he would devote his remaining years to the work that had come to seem worthwhile despite its hopelessness, he was aware that neither love nor work would be enough to satisfy him. He would always be searching for something that was not to be found.

He turned to Brek, who did not meet his glance. Like himself, Brek had refused the hypnotic sleep offered by the rescue team. They had assuaged their thirst and hunger and had submitted to preliminary treatment of their injuries, but they had not wished to evade what awaited them on entrance to the City. Or rather, they hadn't been willing to admit that they wished it. They were answerable both for the loss of an irreplaceable aircar and for their unfulfilled intent to betray secrets; neither could be easily dismissed. Perhaps they would be considered relapsed heretics and denied all contact with non-Scholars, Noren realized. Perhaps he would not even see Talyra after he had confessed. To his shame, he was thankful that her presence made immediate confession impossible.

The lights loomed brighter, then vanished as the aircar dropped into the open top of the entrance dome and settled gently. A crowd of faces appeared at the door: solicitous faces, faces that showed not reproof, but relief and welcome. One, Noren saw, was Stefred's, and he looked away, lacking words, while he was carried down from the landing platform and through the maze of corridors leading to the Inner City's courtyard. People didn't yet know the whole story. Curious though they must be, they did not press for details; but they stayed with him until he was laid on a couch in a small private cubicle of the infirmary.

"You must have rest," the doctor said. "If you will not consent to hypnotic sedation, I'll have to use drugs—"

The pride that had kept Noren adamant made him yield. Drugs were scarce; it was not fitting for any to be consumed by a Scholar. He accepted the hypnosis, slipping resignedly, almost gratefully, into oblivion.

When he awoke, he found himself physically recovered, though still quite weak, and realized that days had passed while his body was nourished intravenously. As remembrance hit him, he was overwhelmed by remorse and despair. He no longer knew what was true and what was not; but he was certain that, not knowing, he could have done nothing but harm by destroying the villagers' belief in the Prophecy. To be sure, deceiving people was wrong and they should be given the chance to claim their entire birthright if their descendants were already doomed...but what if humankind was not doomed? If a chance of a scientific breakthrough did exist—a chance as remote and unlikely as his discovery of the alien sphere—his proclamation could have ruined it.

Reason, mathematics, told him that there was no such chance. He still could not feel any hope. But as Talyra had said, if one stopped living because one expected to die, one threw away one's own life. Had he thrown away the significance of his? he wondered. Could he, untrusted, share fully in the research? He knew that he would not be punished for what he had done. Even if he was isolated as a precautionary measure, Stefred and the others would be all too compassionate. Something else Talyra had once said echoed in his mind: *The Scholars don't punish; that's not their way—you simply have to live with the consequences of what you are.*

The doctor entered and examined Noren briefly, pronouncing him fit to have visitors. "Stefred has asked to see you," he said. "Will you receive him, Noren?"

"It's not my place to refuse."

The man regarded him, disturbed. "You are a Scholar," he said, "and Stefred's equal; he would not presume to command except in matters concerning his official duties. Like your other friends, he merely wants to know whether he is welcome."

"I—I'd rather not see anyone." Noren asserted. It was true; he could not bear the thought of talking, not even to Talyra—and least of all to Stefred, whose trust he had betrayed. Besides, he reminded himself, Stefred had deceived him. He'd promised him access to knowledge that would help…

But later, when he was released from the infirmary, it was to Stefred's office that he went; for he owed Brek that, at least. He knew Brek would not denounce him, and would not be able to speak freely until he, Noren, had denounced himself.

Mustering all his poise, he stood erect before Stefred's desk and declared forthrightly what his intentions had been at the time of the crash. Stefred remained impassive, but Noren knew him too well not to recognize that mask; he wondered whether the Chief Inquisitor was concealing contempt, pity, or a mixture of both. Very likely he would never be allowed to find out.

"Brek admitted something similar," Stefred told him, "though he implied that he hadn't discussed his plan with you."

Noren, who had also tried to imply that the plan had been a private one, dropped the formality of guarding his words. "Brek isn't to blame," he said. "It was all my idea, and though he listened to me at first, he regretted it later. He would never have gone through with a public revelation. He—he doesn't deserve to be barred from going back to the outpost, much less to be confined to the Hall of Scholars."

"Do you?"

Wretchedly Noren murmured, "I'm unworthy of trust."

"It's unlike you to feel that way."

"I haven't felt like myself for a long time, Stefred."

"Since the space flight?"

"I guess that's obvious. But there's more to it than you can imagine, and I—well, I'd better give you all the details."

Stefred nodded. "There are ways I could make it easier," he said. "Hypnosis, for instance, or a shot of the drug I used during your initial inquisition."

Noren looked up, tempted. That would certainly be less painful. "Whether I give you such aid is up to you," Stefred added quietly.

"I—I've got to tell it straight, then."

"Do you understand why?"

"Because it's not just what I did or how I felt; I have to make sense of it. Consciously."

"Yes. But it will take more than confession to accomplish that, Noren."

"I have to try."

Pushing buttons on his desk to ensure that they'd be uninterrupted, Stefred said soberly, "We'll try together. I'm more closely involved than you realize; still, I can't offer any simple solution."

"I don't expect you to." Sitting down in the chair near the window where so often in the past he had faced difficult things, Noren started at the beginning, at the moment of searing terror that had paralyzed him in space. He went on to describe it all: all the fears, the doubts, the unanswerable questions that had led to his final disillusionment; all the rage that had followed; all the decisions he had reached. Stefred spared him nothing. Whenever Noren faltered, he was led on with astute, searching inquiries that left no room for equivocation. At first it was agonizing, but as the discussion proceeded, he found himself rising to the challenge and even welcoming it. He was heartened by Stefred's very ruthlessness. To his surprise, though he was confessing to weakness, to cowardice, to failure, the Chief Inquisitor showed him no mercy; rather, he acted as if these self-accusations were untrue.

By the time he had explained the strange reversal of feelings he'd experienced in the mountains, Noren had regained much of his normal composure. How was it possible? he wondered as he spoke. How could he be talking naturally, confidently, as if life could indeed make sense, when he'd seen what a senseless place the universe was? "You can't know what I really felt," he concluded ruefully. "I've told all I can put into words, but—"

"But there were things for which no words exist. I do know about them, Noren." Stefred met his eyes unflinchingly. "I knew beforehand; that was the information I withheld. The responsibility is as much mine as it is yours."

Incredulously Noren burst out, "You knew what would happen to me in space?"

"I feared it. Noren, on the Six Worlds no competent psychiatrist would have let you become an astronaut; you are too introspective, too imaginative, too prone to think deeply instead of concentrating on the task at hand. But most people who become heretics are like that. The risk applied to nearly all the eligible Scholars." He sighed, continuing, "Brek and one or two of the others were less vulnerable; I assigned pairs accordingly. And I did what I could to prepare you. I gave you so much else to worry about that I hoped you'd be distracted—by your love for Talyra, by the physical danger, and finally, in case that wasn't enough, by anger at my admission that I was not telling you everything. I dared not warn you of your real peril because that would only have turned your mind into the wrong channel."

Indignation rose in Noren, but he curbed it, sensing that Stefred too must have suffered during the past weeks, that the decision he'd made had been difficult and costly. "You warned me that there were hazards I wasn't aware of," he said, "and I chose freely. I wouldn't have chosen to evade them even if I had known."

"No. That was your strength, Noren. That was why I believed that if the worst happened, in the end you'd come through."

"But I didn't," Noren said miserably. "I failed you, and if it hadn't been for the crash, I'd have done even worse damage."

There was a short silence; Stefred, on the verge of a reply, seemed to think better of it. Steeling himself to the inevitable, Noren asked, "What's to become of me now? I can't ever make amends—"

"For the loss of the aircar? No, all you can do is work toward a time when the building of more aircars will become possible."

A gesture, reflected Noren—yet a more positive one than his attempted martyrdom, which would not have accomplished its purpose either. Stefred had undoubtedly realized that no act of his could endanger the system; otherwise he'd have taken steps to confine him sooner. "Will I be isolated from the Technicians?" he inquired, wondering whether the chance of their believing a renegade would be thought great enough to matter.

"Certainly not, not unless you choose now to formally retract your recantation. And I don't think that can solve your problem."

"Can anything?"

"It depends on how much courage you have."

Bending his head, Noren mumbled, "Not as much as you gave me credit for; we've proved *that,* anyway."

"Really?" Levelly, as if control of his own feelings required effort, Stefred said, "The day you disappeared, Grenald spoke to me with more self-reproach than I have ever heard from anyone. He hadn't known you had cause to take his accusation seriously; he thought it so preposterous that you'd recognize it for what it was: a calculated challenge to your pride."

Astonished, Noren looked up as Stefred continued, "This may surprise you, but I think you've displayed a good deal of courage all the way along. I think you have enough to go on with what's been started. It will mean confronting some things that frighten you, but you've never wanted to escape that."

"Yes, I have," protested Noren shamefacedly. "I volunteered for another space flight, but when they turned me down I was—relieved. And besides, the space work is finished. We can hardly send the shuttle out again just on my account."

"Of course not. That isn't what I'm talking about."

Noren's skin prickled as he ventured, "There is one way, isn't there? A—a dream—" He found himself shaking, though he kept the tremor from his voice. "You could make it like that last one, without letting me share the recorder's thoughts."

"I could," Stefred agreed, "but I'm not sure it would be wise."

"You were lying, then. You don't think I'd be equal to it."

"I think you would be. As a matter of fact, you'd probably find it an anticlimax; you'd feel worse than ever about having once let space bother you. Controlled dreaming is a very useful technique, Noren, but it's not a substitute for life, and in real life one can't go back. One must come to terms with the past without reliving it."

"You mean I've got to learn to trust myself...without proof."

"Yourself—and other things." Stefred smiled. "Since you're perceptive enough to see that, you don't need my help. Sometimes psychiatrists do use dreams as therapy, but in your case no therapy is called for. You're not mentally ill and you never have been. You simply have a mind daring enough to explore questions many people never face up to."

"Have you ever heard of anyone else being panicked by them?" Noren inquired grimly.

"If I say no," Stefred observed slowly, "you'll have the satisfaction of considering yourself a martyr to a unique concern for ultimate truth; and if I say yes, you may find comfort in the thought that you are not alone. Which way do you want it?"

"I want the facts, just as I always have," Noren asserted, caught off balance. "Are you asking whether I'd rather have you lie?"

"I'm suggesting that you think the situation through a little more objectively, Noren. Do you really suppose you're the only one of us to whom such questions have occurred?"

With startled chagrin, Noren read the facts from Stefred's face. "I can't be," he admitted in a low voice. "You knew; you must have been tormented by them yourself! Oh, Stefred, how could I have been so weak as to be thrown by it, and then to—to feel that the martyrdom of a public relapse would absolve me?"

"Think deeper," said Stefred relentlessly. "You couldn't control your feelings; to reproach yourself for them now is self-abasement. That's no solution either, and it doesn't become you, Noren."

After a long pause, Noren declared, "You're telling me that panic isn't uncommon. I was justifiably afraid, and trying to cover it up was false pride."

Nodding, Stefred agreed, "The questions you framed are unanswerable, and to be terrified by that is a sign not of weakness but of strength. A weak person wouldn't have opened his mind to such terror. It hit you young, and hard, under circumstances in which you had nothing to hold to—that's the only difference between your experience and the one most Scholars eventually undergo."

"But then why—"

"Why didn't I enlighten you earlier? I couldn't have, Noren. It wouldn't have done any good; in this particular adventure one has to proceed at one's own risk, at one's own pace."

A trace of uncontrollable fear brushed Noren's mind again as he grasped what he was being asked to confront. "Questions that have no answers...Stefred, I don't see how I can ever face that! Before this happened—well, it was hard not knowing all I wanted to know, but I expected to learn it all in time; at least I thought the answers existed *somewhere—*"

"They do," Stefred said gently. "The fact that neither you nor any other human being can obtain all the answers doesn't mean they don't exist, any more than the fact that we can't see all the stars in the universe means those stars aren't there."

"And someday I'll just get used to being condemned to ignorance?" Noren demanded bitterly.

"Yes, one way or another. The easy way is to stop searching."

"I can't," retorted Noren with growing anger. "I—well, I still care about truth; I always have, and I'm not going to change."

"I'm glad to hear it," said Stefred dryly. "For a while the reports I was getting from the outpost had me worried."

Noren flushed, knowing he should have spotted the trap before falling into it. "We know more than the people of the mother world once did," he mused, "yet if they'd just quit— Did they wonder about the sorts of things I do, too?" Even as he spoke, he realized that it was a foolish question. Of course they had. They must have, if they'd been intelligent enough to discover as much knowledge as they'd accumulated.

"The wisest had thoughts worth preserving about those things," Stefred told him, "thoughts you can study if you query the computers properly." Regretfully he admitted, "If I'd known that you visited the computers the day of the conference, I would not have let you go away unsatisfied. I was negligent there, Noren."

"You had enough to worry about that day without keeping track of me," Noren said. "Besides, the computers weren't telling me anything."

"That was because they are programmed to teach lessons that can't be learned in one short session," replied Stefred, "lessons that in your case proved more painful than was intended." He went on to explain, "The Founders knew that young Scholars would think of the computer complex as the repository of all truth, and must sooner or later be made aware of the distinction between *truth* and *fact.* They also knew that since the beginning of time the key to advancement of human knowledge has lain not in discovering the right answers, but in discovering the right questions to ask. So in certain areas of inquiry—areas that a person doesn't explore until he is mature enough to grasp such ideas—they deliberately refrained from programming leading responses. They didn't expect any Scholar to leave the City, of course; and given time, you would have persisted until you caught on."

"Is that what you meant when you said I'd have access to a kind of knowledge that would help?"

"No," Stefred declared. "I wasn't referring to the computers then. You won't understand what I meant until you attain such knowledge for yourself."

Noren went to the computer room; he sat at a console and calmly, carefully, phrased his questions: not WHAT IS LIFE'S MEANING? but WHAT HAVE PEOPLE THOUGHT ABOUT LIFE'S MEANING?...not WHY WERE THE SIX WORLDS DESTROYED? but TO WHAT CAUSE DID PEOPLE OF THE PAST ATTRIBUTE UNPREVENTABLE DESTRUCTION? He stayed there until long past the hour of Orison, and by then he realized that the study of what had been written on these subjects would absorb not mere days, but years. Yet he had seen enough to know certain things.

He knew that others had suffered as he had, and that there was no way to escape it except by giving up the search.

He knew that there were two paths one could follow if one were willing to give up: one could decide it was all too futile to bother with, or one could fool oneself into thinking that one had already found the answers. Some people had done that. Some, in fact, had felt such a great need to convince themselves of what they'd found that whenever anybody appeared whose answers were different, they'd fought over it. If they'd been powerful men with many followers, the fights had, at times, turned into wars.

But Noren also knew that there'd been some who had not given up. They had recognized mysteries that they could not resolve and had borne it; they'd gone on gathering the bits and pieces of truth available, in full knowledge that they would fail to assemble the whole pattern.

And he knew that these people had been sustained only by faith.

Their faith hadn't always been called a religion. Sometimes it had; but many, particularly the later ones, had simply trusted that there *was* a pattern without using any symbols for the elements beyond their grasp. For the most part, such people had not been in a predicament as difficult as the Scholars'. Those facing adversity had tended to find symbols indispensable.

Noren thought back to the dreams in which he had become the First Scholar, remembering the painful yet triumphant time while he lay dying. For years the First Scholar had sought symbols; he had, Noren realized abruptly, sought them not only for his people's comfort but for his own. WHAT WAS THE FIRST SCHOLAR'S PERSONAL RELIGION? he keyed in, perplexed.

THE FIRST SCHOLAR WROTE NOTHING ABOUT THAT, responded the computer. IT IS BEST UNDERSTOOD FROM HIS RECORDED MEMORIES.

But aside from the idea for the Prophecy, the recordings had contained nothing of this, at least not unless one counted the First Scholar's sureness that a way for humankind to survive permanently would be found. Noren perceived that this surety, which had been so puzzling in the light of his scientific knowledge, must indeed be counted as faith—yet that wasn't enough. If questions about *why* instead of *how* occurred to all wise and courageous people, they must certainly have occurred to the First Scholar. No such questions had troubled him during the dreams.

He returned to Stefred. "The dreams I had before my recantation were edited," he declared, "to conceal the First Scholar's plan for choosing successors. Later I experienced them in a more complete form. Was that edited, too? Is there a third version?"

"Yes," Stefred admitted, "for those who request it; and it's a more constructive thing to go through than another dream of space would be. But if I were you, Noren, I'd wait a while. Wait until you understand what happened to you more thoroughly, because something quite similar will happen in those dreams."

"You mean it happened to *him?"* There had been a gap of many years in the dreams, Noren recalled, and he had never been told exactly what the First Scholar had undergone during the interim.

"I've said before that his mind was very like yours," Stefred replied simply, "and after all, he had witnessed the destruction of the worlds he knew."

"But he went on to create the Prophecy…and it—it meant more to him than a way to give people hope. It symbolized his whole attitude toward the universe! If anyone had faith in the future, he had."

"Did you suppose he was born with it? Some people are—people like Talyra, for instance—and their faith is entirely valid. Those who are born to question must find it through experience."

Noren swallowed. "Is there any chance, do you think, that I—" He broke off, embarrassed by the strange, compassionate look Stefred gave him. *There isn't,* he thought, *and he doesn't want to hurt me.* "Only you can be the judge of that," Stefred answered, and Noren left without asking whether one could live without faith indefinitely.

He found Brek waiting for him in their old room, and it was apparent that he wanted to talk. "I—I messed things up pretty thoroughly," Noren said after an awkward silence, knowing that any attempt at specific apology would be too weak. "I don't expect you to understand—"

"It's not that," Brek said quickly. "We've both done things we're sorry for, and they're past. Only there's something else." He paced nervously from one side of the compartment to the other. "I wish we could go back to sharing the same ideas, but—well, there's something I've got to tell you, something *you* won't understand, and that you'll probably despise me for. I can't help it. In this I've got to make my own decision."

Puzzled, Noren stood patiently while Brek paused with his back turned and then, with quiet determination, announced straightforwardly. "I'm assuming the robe tomorrow."

Noren's initial amazement gave way to surprise at his obtuseness. Of course. Brek had not been born to question; though he'd defied injustice and had balked at accepting the seemingly privileged status of a Scholar, once those obstacles proved unreal, there was no barrier to his becoming a priest. He would be a good one. "I don't despise you," Noren declared. "I—I think I envy you, Brek."

"Envy me—you?" Brek burst out. "But Noren, that's crazy! If you no longer feel that commitment's wrong, why don't you wear the robe yourself?"

Why didn't he? Because there was more to it than right or wrong, Noren thought unhappily. Priesthood was not merely a matter of committing oneself to certain ethics and certain actions. A priest must know more than science could teach him. Brek could represent that other knowledge—the kind one must attain for oneself—without hypocrisy; he himself could not.

"I'm unfit," he said in a low voice, "and anyway, as a relapsed heretic, I've forfeited the right."

"Did Stefred tell you that?"

"He didn't have to."

"It's not true," Brek contended. "Commitment concerns only the future, and you're no more a relapsed heretic now than I am." He spoke with cool assurance, and for the first time, except during that one exchange made in anger, he'd contradicted Noren directly. Their roles had been reversed, Noren realized. Brek did not need his guidance any more.

"Noren," Brek went on slowly, "there's another thing I think you ought to know. It's none of my business what's passed between you and Stefred—"

"No," declared Noren firmly. "It isn't."

"But he risked a lot for you, and since he's not likely to mention it, I've got to. The man I heard it from must have had that in mind when he didn't pledge me to silence."

"Risked?" Noren inquired in bafflement. "How?"

"By not ordering you recalled from the outpost."

It was true, Noren thought, that except for the promise not to force him, such a move would have been natural; Stefred had known what was troubling him and must have had a fairly good idea of how he would react. "I suppose so," he admitted despondently. "I might not have gotten people to fight the system, but if I'd been killed trying, the scientific talent everyone's had such fine hopes for would have been lost."

"Don't belittle it. It's important to others if not to you, and he took a big gamble. But more than that, he staked his own career; the issue was raised in the executive council, and he told them that if they reversed his decision, he'd resign as department head."

"But *why?*" Noren gasped.

"That was his only recourse; he could see he was about to be outvoted."

"I mean why should he go to such lengths to keep his word? I'd have released him; I'd have come back voluntarily if I'd known." With chagrin, he remembered how Emet, just after an executive council meeting, had asked him to remain in the City for his friends' sake.

"I'm in no position to judge," Brek said, "but I think there was more to it than the fact that he'd promised. The others all wanted to help you, but Stefred felt you should be let alone. And he thought you were better off outside—that if you stayed, you'd redeem yourself."

Then he miscalculated, Noren reflected, and such a great miscalculation was scarcely to be believed of Stefred. Yet it was either that...or Stefred still knew more than he was telling.

He did not want to see Talyra, for he knew that when he did he must break their betrothal. He would not do so publicly until the child was born, if there was to be a child; but he could no longer let her think there was hope of their marrying. Nor could they go on as they had begun in the mountains. The joy of it could not last. His burdens had been set aside then; now they were back, and in time those burdens would crush their love, for he could not keep up a convincing pretense of happiness. Talyra had put up with his dark moods too long already, and she deserved better. He would not have her stay with him out of sympathy.

All the next day he avoided her by remaining inside the Hall of Scholars, but he had to attend Vespers since Brek was to preside, as it was customary for the newly committed to do. There was little ceremony attached to commitment; one simply signed the official roll book and then, the same evening, donned the blue robe and appeared to Technicians as a priest. The service was no different than it was when conducted by a Scholar who had been doing it regularly for years. No special notice was taken, except by one's friends.

Noren purposely delayed his arrival until the last moment, so that when he approached Talyra the hymn had started and she had no chance to speak. He did not intend to touch her, but as Brek mounted the platform he found himself reaching for her hand. She would be astonished, of course, and perhaps flustered; he must not add to her bewilderment by failing to greet her with affection, though his throat ached so that he could not sing.

The others' voices resounded through the courtyard; then, in the hush that followed, Brek began the invocation. "*...The Mother Star is our source and our destiny, the wellspring of our heritage...*" Talyra's eyes were raised devoutly, so she had not noticed yet; but at the familiar voice she turned to look, lips parted in awe. Noren pressed her fingers. "*...it is our life's bulwark...*" Brek spoke with utmost sincerity, and he was not talking about the Six Worlds' sun alone. He had seen life in a way that he himself could not, Noren thought wistfully. It would be nice to go on believing that he could not take that view because he was too honest to accept false comfort, but real honesty told him that doing so would be a greater self-delusion. What Brek had attained was the result not of blindness, but of vision.

"I'm so glad for him," Talyra said when the service was over and they walked hand in hand across the dusky courtyard under three orange moons. "I sometimes wondered if he was a candidate—I mean, his having been a Technician outside and all. You must have suspected, too. Oh, I know we mustn't speak of people's backgrounds," she added hastily at Noren's frown. "But aren't you curious about how they chose him?"

Talyra did not know that Brek had been a heretic, of course; though everyone in the Inner City was aware that some of the Scholars were former heretics, the Technicians had no reason to suspect that they all were. Past lives were not mentioned, and she wouldn't even have known that he was a Technician by birth if she hadn't seen him at Noren's trial. Nor would she ever learn that he'd been a Scholar before he assumed the robe. "The choice does not lie with the Scholars alone," Noren told her. "The role of High Priest must be earned, but it must also be chosen by the candidate himself; that much is no secret."

"Did you know when we were in the mountains that he wanted it?"

"No," Noren declared, "I didn't."

They sat on a low stone bench in the shadowy triangle between three towers, and Talyra caressed his face fondly, expectantly. Noren kissed her, but he dared not do so with passion, and he knew that she was baffled. With sorrow he began, "Darling, I have to tell you…I've learned that permission for me to marry can't be granted. There was…well, the aircar, you see—"

"But that was an accident! Surely they wouldn't punish you for it!"

"No…but I shouldn't have been in that aircar at all, you know. It's not a matter of punishment, but of—consequences. There's more to it that I can't explain—"

"You needn't," Talyra said reassuringly. "In time they'll absolve you, and meanwhile, we'll just go on being betrothed."

He should have known that it would not work, Noren thought. He must be cruel to spare her the greater hurt of seeing their love wither from his failure to find contentment. "Talyra," he said painfully, "we shouldn't have done what we did…those nights. Now that we have, you see, there's no stopping, no going back to the way we were before—"

She shrank away, wounded. "Do you want to stop?"

"Of course I don't, but you—well, you should, because you'd be better off with someone like Brek than with me."

"I'm not in love with Brek!" she exclaimed, shocked.

"I don't mean him specifically. He's not in love with you, either; do you think I'd give you up for his sake? What I'm trying to say is…he has the same outlook you do, and there are plenty of others who have. I'm not one of them. You've told me that yourself. I—I can't make you happy, Talyra."

"Can I make *you* happy?"

"If you can't, no girl ever can. But it's just the same now as when we said goodbye in the village. 'You are what you are,' you said, 'and our loving each other wouldn't make any difference.'"

She was silent; then, turning back to him and taking his hands between hers, she murmured, "I also said that someday you'd find the spirit of the Mother Star had been with you."

"Someday may be a long way off, Talyra."

"It's already here! Do you think I could watch you week after week, loving you, and not notice when it came?" At his confusion, she shook her head, laughing softly. "Darling, you're blind. You're still off in the sky somewhere, dreaming; you haven't looked at the world since it happened!"

"Since what happened?"

"Do you really not know that during those days in the mountains you stopped being afraid?"

"I resigned myself to dying, that's all."

"No," she told him. "Not to dying—to living! You were never afraid of death, and I think that when we crashed, you…you almost wanted to die. I won't ask why. That doesn't matter any more, because all of a sudden you were aware of the Mother Star's protection. You knew that however things turned out, it wouldn't fail us, and then, when you stopped worrying, you were at peace with the world. You were whole and free."

"I wish that were true," he said sincerely. "It's not, though. I didn't have any hope of our being saved, the way you and Brek did."

"But Noren," she protested, "you *did,* underneath. All along you did. Why else wouldn't you have drunk more water?"

He stared at her, his mind reeling. He'd asked himself why he should abstain and had obtained no answer. Nevertheless, he had refrained from exceeding the safe limit; could he have done so without any underlying purpose? The water would not have harmed him; it would have been damaging only to any children he might subsequently father. If he had been totally without hope—if he'd been sure that Talyra would not live long enough to bear a child, nor he to love again—he would have had no reason to suffer thirst. He would have had no more qualms about drinking than in the days when he had believed the High Law was groundless.

Yet he had known positively that there was no logical chance of survival. He had climbed the cliff where the sphere lay only to please Talyra; he'd not thought it could possibly be of any use. That it might lead to rescue had not occurred to any of them. If underneath he'd had knowledge not born of logic, knowledge that had driven him to struggle against such odds, wasn't it conceivable that the wish to continue his work rose from the same source? And wasn't it valid to hope that the research might also succeed against all logic?

Through experience, Stefred had said. Those who are born to question can attain faith only through experience.

Talyra sat looking at him, waiting; and all at once Noren knew that the gulf between them no longer existed. Perhaps it had never been as unbridgeable as he'd believed. "You saw what I lacked before I did," he whispered, "and you saw what I'd gained before I did, too." He took her in his arms and there was no need for either of them to say anything more.

"I'm still awfully confused," he admitted to Stefred the next morning, not yet able to acknowledge, even in his own mind, the reason he'd sought him out. "How could she have known something I didn't know about myself, when so much has been kept secret from her?"

"You've no doubt that she was right?"

"None."

"Then be thankful that she had the wit and the spirit to tell you what you would not have accepted from me." With warmth, Stefred went on, "I could have given you the key when we talked two days ago. You were so bewildered, so torn by problems you weren't able to resolve, that it was hard to remain silent. But a lecture wouldn't have helped. You needed to fit the pieces together—which you can do now, if you try."

There was a long pause; then Noren said thoughtfully, "All that time…when I held back from declaring myself a relapsed heretic…was it not cowardice after all? Was it that I still believed the Prophecy without knowing I did? How *could* I—"

"Noren," Stefred interrupted, "have you ever wondered why you and Talyra love each other?"

"Why—why we just *do!* A thing like that isn't something to be analyzed, Stefred."

"Certain feelings can't be," Stefred observed dryly. "A scientist's ability to analyze is a priceless gift, Noren, but it sometimes gets in the way. However, in this case my question wasn't meant as an object lesson."

Smiling, he continued, "You and Talyra share something deeper than a casual love affair. Why? Back in the village you were little more than children, and you didn't know each other any better than villagers usually do at the time of betrothal; it wasn't surprising that you were in love then. But when you parted, you considered yourselves unalterably opposed on an issue very basic to your view of life. You expected to be separated permanently, and you both had opportunity to meet others whose beliefs were more compatible. Isn't it rather strange that your love endured?"

"You mean how could she go on caring for someone who scorned what she values most? I—I don't know, Stefred."

"I'd have thought you'd be asking how you could go on caring for someone who valued what you scorned."

Noren contemplated it. "There's just one answer," he said wonderingly. "I didn't scorn it as much as I thought I did, and—and she sensed that. Perhaps I sensed it, too, underneath; perhaps I wanted it all along."

"You had it all along."

"Yet I was so sure I valued only the truth," Noren declared ruefully.

"And you were right. Not all truth can be expressed in scientific terms, Noren, not even by us; and from the beginning you valued the whole truth, including the parts unavailable to you. At your trial and inquisition you said so specifically."

"I assumed you could make it available if you chose," Noren reflected, "and then when you gave me access to your own sources of knowledge—" He broke off, realizing with chagrin that although as a boy he had questioned what he'd been taught about the Scholars' supernatural supremacy, he'd never doubted that they possessed the answers to all mysteries. To find that they did not—and could not—had shaken him in a way he hadn't thoroughly understood, for despite himself, he had clung to a naive picture in which they and their City symbolized the knowledge he craved. When the City's computers failed him, he had held all the harder to the one thing left that was sure: mathematics. He'd been afraid to believe the Prophecy after mathematics discredited it! That would have meant admitting that math itself was not absolute...

"I couldn't give up my symbol any more than Talyra could give up hers," he concluded. "I needed one."

"So do we all," Stefred replied.

Startled, Noren stared at him, then turned slowly to survey the room, the tower's view, the far-off outline of the Tomorrow Mountains where for a time he had abandoned despair and fear. Countless things meshed into a previously invisible pattern, a pattern that made unexpected sense of them. "I—I think I see now," he said at last. "The Mother Star is a symbol of...the unknowable. Not just to villagers and Technicians who can't know our secret, but to us, too, because there's so much *we* can't know."

Stefred nodded. "There is no magical virtue in that particular symbol, and some Scholars prefer to adopt their own, or one of those used on the Six Worlds. But symbolism is most powerful when it is shared, and on the whole, those of us who have inherited that of the Prophecy find it more meaningful than anything else we could employ."

"And priesthood is more than receiving people's homage—"

"A High Priest does not receive. He gives. He gives hope and faith to people who might otherwise have neither."

"But in order to do that," Noren mused, "he has to find those things himself. I never thought I would, but now...oh, Stefred, if it weren't that I set out to destroy them—"

"You wouldn't have destroyed anyone's faith, Noren."

"I suppose nobody would have listened, but if it hadn't been for the crash I'd have tried. At any rate, I'd have destroyed the prospect of my accomplishing something important in the research. Why should a chance accident like that determine the course of a person's life—perhaps even of...a world's history?"

"Look at it the other way around," Stefred suggested, "and ask yourself why the accident occurred."

Noren frowned. If anything was unanswerable, that was, yet he had been at the controls..."You mean—I didn't really want to do what I was planning to?"

"That's one possibility. There are others, none of which depend upon chance. Neither of us will ever know what forces were operative, Noren. This much is certain, though: when brought to the test, you would not have chosen the destruction of hope over a gamble on the truth that lies beyond your vision."

"How can you be sure?"

"You had the power to destroy Talyra's," Stefred pointed out, "and you didn't use it."

Stunned once again, Noren sat motionless while the implications grew clear in his mind. He'd known he owed Talyra honesty, known she did not want false comfort, yet he hadn't been able to speak truth as he saw it. This too had been the result of inward knowledge! This too had been not a betrayal of truth, but an expression of his real belief.

He had not seen the analogy. He had not stopped to think that it was all or nothing: the affirmation of life, of survival, for the world of the future as well as for Talyra and himself—or the denial of his deepest feelings. Had his view of "truth" been so narrow as to permit him to repudiate the Prophecy publicly, *it* would have crushed his buried hope for their lives and for that of their child.

"You were sure beforehand," he said in wonder.

"Of course. During your inquisition I studied your subconscious feelings; could I have done that without seeing your underlying faith? Would I have exposed you to emotional peril if I had not seen it? For that matter, I wouldn't have judged you a potentially gifted scientist if I hadn't believed that in due time you would plunge beyond our knowledge, just as you plunged beyond the villagers'—and to take such a plunge, one must sense that there's something ahead."

"You—you had faith in *me*. And you knew that sooner or later, as long as I was outside the City, some kind of test would arise; that's why you insisted on letting me stay."

"It was the only way for you to regain your self-trust," Stefred agreed. "Once you'd begun to doubt, the thing had to be carried through to the end."

All or nothing... Very softly Noren declared, "Commitment's not something you decide on...you just find you're already committed. And when you put on the robe you're merely offering to share what you've found."

"Are you ready to offer that, Noren?"

"Yes," Noren replied, overcome by emotions for which no speech seemed adequate. "Yes, I guess I am."

Alone, he stood in the dim assembly room under the glittering sunburst, looking up with reverence he had not felt before; and the once-frightening words echoed in his mind as words of comfort. "*...There is no surety save in the light that sustained our forebears; no hope but in that which lies beyond our sphere; and our future is vain except as we have faith. Yet we are strong in the faith that, as those of the past were sustained, so shall we be also. What must be sought shall be found; what was lost shall be regained; what is needful to life will not be denied us. And though our peril be great even unto the last generation of our endurance, in the end humankind shall prevail; and the doors of the universe shall once again be thrown open...*"

Noren's eyes blurred with tears. He had never been so moved. There had been excitement and sometimes pleasure in things he had done during his first term in the City, but never this particular kind of happiness. Lately he had felt that for him no happiness was possible. How incredible, he thought, that in the space of a few hours he could be so changed.

The new peace of mind was not permanent, he knew. There would still be bad times. Yet there would be satisfactions, too—in his studies; his work; his growing comprehension of all he must absorb if he was to contribute significantly to the research upon his return to the outpost beyond the mountains; in the love he shared with Talyra; in the children they would give to a world that would someday be transformed. Wasn't that how it had always been, for everyone?

Humankind will survive, he thought, because people *do* survive: not all of them, under all conditions, but some at least to carry forward the heritage that is ours. In our natural environment instinct ensures that—the instinct that enabled us to evolve from mere animals into human beings with the mind and spirit to advance—and in an alien world where evolution can't progress normally, our instinct guides us in different ways. We do what we must. Hating it, knowing it involves evil and injustice that ought not to exist, the human race lives on in the only way it can; but we who recognize the evils go on working to abolish them, just as our forebears did. It is all part of the same pattern.

Crossing the room to the small closed alcove he'd never before entered, he knelt at the low shelf where, beneath a miniature sunburst, a thick, well-worn book rested: the roll book of the committed. Noren leafed through it with awe, for on the first page, under the faded legend, "We the undersigned do hereby hold ourselves answerable for the preservation of human life on this alien planet and for the restoration of our people's birthright," was inscribed the seldom-pronounced name of the First Scholar himself. And below it were other strange names with even stranger dates: birthdates in four figures—Six Worlds' reckoning—with the Year One listed as date of commitment. That had been before the Prophecy was conceived; further on was written a formal pledge to work toward the keeping of its promises and to fulfill the solemn obligations of priesthood. And then came page after page of two- and three-digit dates opposite the names of those who had upheld the trust through all the years since the Founding.

At the last, on a still half-empty sheet, Brek's signature stood out, clear and fresh and decisive, showing no trace of hesitancy. Noren signed below it with a firm hand, wondering how many others would do so before the need for such commitment was past.

There would never be an end, he realized as he rose and left the alcove. The book would be filled and a new one begun; the Time of the Prophecy would come and go; but there would always be priests because no matter how much future Scholars might learn, some things would remain unknowable. It would not be the same once the Prophecy was brought to fulfillment. Scholar status would carry neither rank nor privilege, and heresy would cease to be regarded as a crime; people who wished to offer themselves would apply voluntarily for acceptance. They would no longer be the only ones engaged in scientific investigation.

Yet the search for truth—all truth—being the proper function of a priest, such work would naturally remain one of their prime concerns. They would begin to look ahead to the time when interstellar travel must be resumed, for the world would never have rich resources, and once people learned what their forebears of the Six Worlds had possessed, they would look to their religion for a new promise. And would not the Scholars give them one, one less specific than the Prophecy, yet just as sure in the sense that if it was not fulfilled, humankind would someday die? No race could endure forever confined to a single world—knowing that, the Scholars would be committed to the discovery and mastery of still another alien environment. Someday they themselves might crew the exploratory starships. Someday, perhaps, they might meet face to face the Visitors who'd made the mysterious sphere...

That evening, as the hour of Vespers approached, Noren drew the blue robe from the storage compartment beneath his bunk and unfolded it, remembering the day it had been given to him, the day of his recantation; and he was suddenly conscious of the distance he'd come since then. He would stand before people now not as a despised rebel, a hero in his own eyes if not in theirs, but as an avowed representative of their most cherished traditions. It was odd, Noren thought, that he no longer seemed to mind.

Carrying the robe with him, he went back to the Hall of Scholars, for though he had neither time nor desire to eat anything, he hoped he might speak to Brek. He encountered him coming out of the refectory; they gripped hands wordlessly, and both were aware that the temporary rift between them need never be mentioned. "I'll find Talyra," Brek said, "and tell her you want to see her before the service."

Noren nodded gratefully. He was barred from disclosing his status before he appeared robed, which by tradition he must not do until Vespers, and the sight of him so attired would stun Talyra; it would be best if they could exchange a few private words as he emerged from the Hall of Scholars. Returning to the tower's vestibule, he stood just inside its door until he saw her approaching. Then he flung the robe over his shoulders and, feeling its full weight for the first time, he walked forward to meet her.

She inclined her head in the automatic gesture of respect, not yet recognizing him; then as he drew near, she froze in startled disbelief. Noren waited, stricken by fear that this revelation would turn her love to deference. But the face she raised to him was radiant, and when he opened his arms she came unhesitatingly.

"Talyra," he said, "I'm free now! The waiting's over—" His heart lifted at the thought that soon, perhaps within a few days, she would come to him in the festive red skirts of a bride.

Nestling close to him, enveloped by the blue folds of the robe, she whispered, "It was this all the time? Not the heresy, but—this?"

"It was both," he admitted, saying all he would ever be able to say. "They were—well, mixed up."

"And the things you suffered, the ones you couldn't tell me about, were...preparation?"

"You might put it that way."

"I should have guessed," Talyra murmured. "I should have guessed when I first heard that villagers could become Scholars. You wanted so much to learn everything they knew, I should have known that once they saw what kind of person you are, they'd let you."

"You had no cause, since I wasn't permitted to reveal any of it. There will always be secrets I can't reveal. That's why our wedding had to be postponed; it wouldn't be fair for a wife to suddenly find herself married to someone who is bound by such great secrecy."

"Did you think I'd object, darling?"

"Not really. But it was your right to be warned before choosing."

"As if I'd choose to leave you! But that you've chosen *me*...I'm honored. After the way I doubted your faith—"

"I doubted it, too," he told her. "If it weren't for you, Talyra, I'd still be doubting. They taught me secrets; they are teaching me to do a Scholar's work; to that I was sealed long ago. But I wasn't ready for priesthood until you opened my eyes."

They embraced quickly; then she walked by his side to the semicircular platform around which Technicians and Scholars were gathering. The dusk was clear, and the stars that sparkled overhead seemed uncommonly bright. He could gaze at them undismayed, Noren realized with gladness. Their image would not haunt him any more.

Around him, the assembled people had begun the vesper hymn. Just before he released her hand Talyra asked softly, "Will you bless me, Noren?"

"The blessing is our heritage from the Mother Star," he replied gravely, "and is not mine to bestow. It falls upon all of us; I merely proclaim what I've found to be true."

Mounting the steps, Noren looked out at familiar upturned faces: Brek's, Stefred's, those of many whom he could always count as friends. To his surprise he felt no nervousness; and though he held the Book of the Prophecy, he had no need to consult it, for the words came readily to his lips. "*...So long as we believe in it, no force can destroy us, though the heavens* *themselves be consumed...*" He glanced up at the surrounding towers, envisioning the starships that would someday be rebuilt, as he extended his hands to pronounce the sacerdotal blessing: "*May the spirit of the Mother Star abide with you...*" And with me, he thought reverently. May I hold fast to that upon which we all must draw. Talyra smiled at him, glowing with love and pride; and Noren knew joy that his faith was no less genuine than hers.

The Doors of the Universe

Chapter One

The day, like all days, had been hot; the clouds had dispersed promptly after the morning's scheduled rain. As the hours went by the sun had parched the villages, penetrating the thatch roofs of their stone buildings. Now low, its light filtered by thick air, it subdued the sharp contrast between machine-processed farmland and the surrounding wilderness of native growth, a rolling expanse of purple-notched grayness that stretched to the Tomorrow Mountains. Sunlight was seldom noticed within the City, for the domes, and most rooms of the clustered towers they ringed, were windowless. But since long before dawn Noren had watched the landscape from the topmost level of a tower he'd rarely entered. Like the other converted starships that served as Inner City living quarters, it had a view lounge at its pinnacle. And it was there that he awaited the birth of his child.

He'd been barred from the birthing room—part of the nursery area where infants were tended until, at the age of weaning, they must be sent out for adoption by village families. That was off limits to all but the mothers and attendants. By tradition, Scholars could not see their children. Even the women did not, except when no wet nurse was available among Technician women. Talyra, as a Technician, would nurse her own baby. Whether that would make it easier or harder when the time came for her to give it up, he was not sure. The knowledge that she could not keep the child hadn't lessened her gladness in pregnancy any more than it had tarnished his own elation. It would not affect their desire for many offspring in the years to come. Yet it did not seem fair—she'd given up so much for his sake...

For the world's sake, she would say, and it was truer than she imagined. *"In our children shall be our hope, and for them we shall labor, generation upon generation until the Star's light comes to us,"* she'd quoted softly the night before, when her pains began. Unlike himself, Talyra had found the symbolic language of the Prophecy meaningful even during her childhood in the village. He too now used it, not just to please her but with sincerity.

"And the land shall remain fruitful, and the people shall multiply across the face of the earth," he'd replied, smiling. Then, more soberly, *"For the City shall serve the people; those within have been consecrated to that service."* He knew that Talyra indeed felt consecrated, no less than he, though in a different way. Still, it troubled him that she could not know the truth behind the ritual phrases. She could not know that the City and its dependent villages contained but a remnant of the race that had once inhabited six vaporized worlds of the remote Mother Star, that to bring forth babies was not only an honor and sacred duty, but a necessity if humanity was to survive. Nor could she be told the main reason why Inner City people were not free to rear families, though it was obvious enough to her that the space enclosed by the Outer City's encircling domes was limited.

She'd clung to his arm as they left their tiny room and walked across the inter-tower courtyard. At the door to the nursery area, she'd leaned against him with her dark curls damp against his shoulder. The pains were coming often; he knew they could not linger over the parting. And there was no cause to linger. Childbirth roused no apprehension in Talyra; she was, after all, a nurse-midwife by profession.

"It's nothing to worry about, Noren," she assured him happily. "Haven't I been working in the nursery ever since I entered the City? Haven't I wished for the day I could come here as a mother instead of just an attendant? Men always get nervous—that's why we keep them out. We'll send word when the child comes, you know that."

"I'll wait at the top of the tower," he told her, "where I can look at the mountains, Talyra. Ours is the only child in the world to have begun life in the mountains. Maybe it means something that the wilderness gave us life instead of death."

"It gave you your faith," she murmured, kissing him. "We were blessed there from the start, darling—not simply when we were rescued. Let's always be glad our baby's beginning was so special." She drew away; reluctantly, he let her go. They'd be separated only a few days, after all. Past separations, before their marriage, had been far longer and potentially permanent; he wondered why he felt so shaken by this brief one.

"May the spirit of the Star be with you, Talyra," he said fervently, knowing these words were what she'd most wish to hear from him. The traditional farewell had become more than a formality between them, for Talyra took joy in the fact that he, once an unbeliever, had come to speak of the Star not only with reverence, but with a priest's authority.

Now the long night had passed and also the day, and still no word had come. Far beyond the City, sunset was turning the yellow peaks of the Tomorrow Mountains to gold. Noren stared at the jagged range, the place where during the darkest crisis of his life, their child had been conceived. It was there that his outlook had changed. He did not share Talyra's belief in the Star as some sort of supernatural force, yet he had felt underneath that the world's doom was not as sure as it seemed. Perhaps that was why the aircar had crashed—perhaps there'd been more involved than bad piloting on his part; only that, and their unlooked-for survival, had kept him from his rash plan to publicly repudiate the Prophecy...

After the crash, thinking himself beyond rescue, he had felt free, for once, of his search for peace of mind; he'd shaken off the depression that had burdened his previous weeks as a Scholar. He had at last stopped doubting himself enough to accept Talyra's love. It had been a joyous union despite his assumption that they were soon to die, and afterward, he'd known she was right to maintain hope. Talyra, who knew none of the Scholars' secrets, was almost always right about the things that mattered.

On just one issue was she blind—she saw nothing bad in the fact that Scholars kept secrets. Though she'd learned that they were not superhuman, she never questioned their supremacy as High Priests and City guardians; she perceived no evil in the existence of castes that villagers thought were hereditary. And she was therefore ineligible to attain Scholar rank. Talyra simply hadn't been born to question things, Noren thought ruefully.

He could not communicate fully with Talyra. He couldn't have done so even if no obligatory secrecy had bound him. She'd come to respect the honesty that had condemned him in the village of their birth. She had protested his confinement within the walls and had been admitted to the Inner City, given Technician rank, because she loved him enough to share it. The explanations she'd received contented her. It mattered little that she did not know, could never be allowed to know, that he'd ranked as a Scholar before committing himself to priesthood; the true nature of Scholar standing was past her comprehension.

While his status was concealed from her they could not marry; and though there'd have been no objection to their becoming lovers, he had held back while their future was uncertain. Talyra had been puzzled and hurt. Already she'd longed for a baby, Noren realized with chagrin, although she was as yet too young to be pitied for childlessness. In the City she wouldn't be scorned as barren women were in the villages. He had assumed that since she could not rear a family, a delay in childbearing wouldn't disturb her, or that if it did, she would break off her betrothal to him. At least that was what he liked to tell himself, though he knew he'd been too absorbed by his own problems to give enough thought to hers. There had been a time when he'd not cared to live, much less to love.

Then, in the mountains, everything had changed. He'd thrown problems to the wind and followed his instincts, and instinct led him not only to love, but to strive beyond reason for their survival and their child's. They'd had no sure knowledge, of course, that there was a child—yet what couple would believe their first union unfruitful?

He couldn't remind Talyra that she would not live long enough to give birth; certainly he couldn't remind her that perhaps she had failed to conceive. More significantly, he found he could not tell her that it made no difference to the world one way or the other. Science had proven the Prophecy vain—according to all logic, the human race was doomed by the alien world's lack of resources. But he could not destroy Talyra's faith. This too had been instinct, and through this, he'd discovered to his surprise that he could serve as a priest without hypocrisy. The role of a Scholar was to work toward a scientific breakthrough that could fulfill the Prophecy's promises; the role of a priest was to affirm the Prophecy without evidence. He no longer felt the two were inconsistent.

He owed much to the child he would never be permitted to see, Noren thought: the child who would grow up as a villager—where, and under what name, he would not be told—and who, knowing nothing of his or her parentage, might someday in turn fight the High Law's apparent injustice...

"Noren—"

He looked up, expecting news from the nursery, but it was his friend Brek who stood in the doorway. "I guess you're wondering why I didn't come to the refectory," Noren said. It was their habit to take their noon meal together in the Hall of Scholars, the central tower where as advanced students, they normally worked. "I wasn't hungry, I'm as nervous as all fathers—just wait till it's your turn." Brek, quite recently, had married a fellow-Scholar; their delight in their own coming child had been plain.

Brek hesitated. "By the Star, Brek," Noren went on, "it's taking a long time, isn't it? Should it take this long?"

"Noren, Beris asked me to tell you. They've sent for a doctor." Brek's tone was even, too even.

A *doctor?* Noren went white. Rarely had he heard of a doctor being called to attend a birth. The villages had no resident doctors; babies were delivered by nurse-midwives, trained, as Talyra had been trained in adolescence, for a vocation accorded semi-religious status. In the City there was no cause to usurp their prerogatives. Besides, it was improper to intervene in the process of bringing forth life. Only if the child were in danger…

Vaguely, from his boyhood, he recalled that babies sometimes died. So too, in the village, had mothers who were frail. It was not a thing discussed often, unless perhaps among women—though he had never known a woman whose eagerness for another child wouldn't have overshadowed such thoughts.

"I think you'd better come," Brek was saying.

As they descended in the lift, other boyhood memories pushed into Noren's mind. The child might be past saving…against many ills doctors were powerless. They'd failed to save his mother. Though at the time he'd been outraged, he now knew she couldn't have been helped; the poison in the briars she'd touched had no antidote. But some things without current remedies had been curable with Six Worlds' technology.

Had the Six Worlds had ways of ensuring safe births? The computer complex could answer that, of course; he wondered, suddenly, if any past Scholar had been moved to ask. He himself was prone to ask futile questions as well as practical ones, a tendency not widely shared when it could lead only to frustration.

Brek was silent. That in itself was eloquent—Brek, Noren reflected, knew him much too well to offer false reassurances.

It had never occurred to Noren that the baby might die. He could face that himself, he supposed; he was inured to grim circumstances. The seasons since his marriage had been the happiest of his life, too good, he'd sometimes felt, to last. But Talyra's sorrow he might find past bearing. It was so unjust that she should suffer...after all the grief and hardship he'd brought her in the past, he'd wanted to make her content. He'd vowed not to let her see that a priest could have doubts, or that even when closest to her he knew loneliness.

Was it only because of her pregnancy that he'd succeeded? If the child died, if she was desolate over what she'd surely perceive as a failure as well as a sorrow, would her intuition again lead her to sense that his own desolation went deeper? "You are what you are," she had told him long ago, "and our loving each other wouldn't make any difference." It hadn't; for a time this had seemed unimportant, yet throughout that time, the child had bridged the gulf between them...

Talyra would blame herself if it wasn't healthy; village women always did, and she'd been reared as a villager. It wouldn't matter that no one in the City would consider her blameworthy. Noren cursed inwardly. Village society, backward in all ways because of its technological stagnation, was both sexist and intolerant; and while Talyra might be openminded enough to be talked out of most prejudices, she wouldn't listen to him on a subject viewed as the province of women. Among Technicians there was less stigma attached to the loss of a child. Brek's wife Beris had been born a Technician, in the Outer City, as had Brek himself. Maybe later on Beris would be able to help.

Yet Brek had said Beris sent the message—that was odd, since she was neither midwife nor nursery attendant. As a Scholar, Beris had work of her own in water purification control, vital life-support work she could not leave except in an emergency. As they reached the nursery level, Noren faced Brek, asking abruptly, "What's Beris doing here?"

"She—she was called as a priest, Noren. I don't know the details."

The door where he and Talyra had parted was in front of them; Noren pushed and found it locked. He felt disoriented, as if he were undergoing a controlled dream like those used in Scholars' training. Beris called as a priest? To be sure, no male priest would be summoned to the birthing room, and Talyra knew Beris well. But why should any priest be needed? At the service for the dead, yes, if the baby didn't survive...but that would be held later, and elsewhere. He would be expected to preside himself, at least Talyra would expect it, and for her sake he would find the courage, disturbing though that particular service had always been to him. What other solace could a priest offer? Had they felt only a robed Scholar could break the news of her baby's danger? That didn't make sense—Talyra would know! She was a midwife; if the delivery didn't go well, she would know what was happening.

She'd rarely spoken to him of her work. He knew only that she liked it, liked helping to bring new life into the world. Yet there had been times when she'd come to their room troubled, her usual vitality dimmed by sadness she would not explain. It struck him now that she might have seen babies die before. Perhaps she had seen more than one kind of pain.

That women suffered physically during childbirth was something everyone knew and no one mentioned. It was taken for granted that the lasting joy outweighed the temporary discomfort. Midwives were taught to employ a modified form of hypnosis that lessened pain without affecting consciousness, or so he'd been told, though Talyra wasn't aware that the ritual procedures she followed served such a purpose. Doctors—and often priests—could induce full hypnotic anesthesia. Had Beris been summoned for that reason? Had Talyra's pain been abnormally severe, could that be why they'd sought a doctor's aid? Anguish rose in Noren; her confidence had been so great that he had not guessed she might be undergoing a real ordeal.

"I've got to go in there," he told Brek. Having never been one to let custom stand in his way, he felt no hesitancy.

"You can't do any good now. When you can, they'll call you—"

"For the Star's sake, she may need me! The doctor may not be here yet, she may be suffering—she's not been trained to accept hypnosis as we have, and she's not awed enough by a blue robe to let just any priest put her under."

"Beris said something about drugs."

"Drugs for childbirth?" Drugs were scarce and precious, not to be used where hypnosis would serve and surely not on anyone who wasn't ill; Talyra would not accept them during the biggest moment of her life. Unless her baby had already died...but no, not even then; Talyra was no coward.

"I don't understand," he protested.

"Neither do I," Brek said. "We don't know enough about these things; sometimes I think women keep too much to themselves. I'd never have thought it could be risky for Talyra. She's young and strong—"

Stunned, Noren burst out, "You mean there's danger to *Talyra?* Not just to the child?" In sudden panic he threw his weight against the door, but it would not yield.

Brek grasped his arm, pulling him aside. "The child was stillborn, I think," he admitted.

The door slid back and Beris emerged, still wearing the ceremonial blue robe of priesthood over her work clothes. She blocked Noren's way.

"Let's go down," she said quietly. "I know a room that's empty where we can go."

"I've got to see Talyra."

"You can't, not here."

"Where, then?" He wondered if they would move her to the infirmary; he knew nothing of what illness might strike during a delivery.

"Noren." Beris kept her voice steady. "It was over faster than anyone expected. Talyra is dead."

Later, he wondered how Brek and Beris had gotten him to the lift. They took him to a room on the next level that was temporarily unused. Once there, he collapsed on the narrow couch and gave way to tears. For a long time they said nothing, but simply let him weep.

When he was able to talk, there was little Beris could tell him. "It happens," she said. "Usually with older women, or those who've never been strong; but occasionally it happens with a girl who seems healthy. Talyra knew that. She knew better than most of us; all midwives do."

"She never said—"

"Of course not. You would be the last person to whom she'd have said such a thing."

"Did it happen on the Six Worlds, too?" Noren asked bitterly. "Or could she have been saved there?"

"I don't know. At least I don't know if she could have been saved at this stage. It's possible—they had equipment we haven't the metal to produce, and they could tell beforehand if there were complications, so that their doctors could be prepared. Sometimes they delivered babies surgically before labor even began."

Beris paused, glancing uncomfortably at Brek; her own pregnancy, though not yet apparent, could scarcely be far from their thoughts. "Talyra wasn't a Scholar—she didn't know how it was on the Six Worlds. But I do. I suppose men don't absorb all that I did from the dreams the Founders recorded…but you do know it wasn't the same as here. I mean, people didn't have the same feelings—"

Noren nodded. The Six Worlds had been overpopulated; women hadn't been allowed more than two children, and they'd had drugs to prevent unplanned pregnancies. Hard though it was to imagine, people hadn't minded—at any rate, that was what all the records said. Sterility hadn't been considered a curse. Some couples had purposely chosen to have no offspring at all; they had made love without wishing for their love to outlast their lifetime.

"Well," Beris went on, "it was the custom there for women to be seen by doctors, not just during delivery, but all through pregnancy. They knew a long time ahead if things weren't going right. And so pregnancies that were judged dangerous were—terminated."

Noren was speechless. Brek, aghast, murmured, "You mean deliberately? They killed unborn children?"

"Their society didn't look on it as killing. And it wasn't done often once they had sure contraceptives—only when the child would die anyway, or when the mother's health was at stake."

"Talyra would not have done it at all," declared Noren.

"No. That's what I'm trying to say, Noren. She wouldn't have, even if the option had been open, because in our culture we just can't feel the way our ancestors did. Our situation is different. So unless the Six Worlds' medical equipment could have saved her without hurting the baby, our having that equipment wouldn't have changed anything."

But the baby died too, Noren thought. She'd given her life for nothing. Perhaps these things happened, but why—why to Talyra? It was the sort of useless question that had always plagued him, yet he could not let it rest.

"She was so strong, she loved life so much…there's got to be a *reason,*" he said slowly. He recalled how in the aftermath of the crash, Talyra's indomitable spirit had kindled his own will to live. She had refused to let him give in. All the hardships—the terror of the attack by subhuman mutants, the heat, the exhaustion, the hunger and above all the thirst—had left Talyra untouched. How could she have come through all that, only to die as a result of the love that had led to their near-miraculous rescue?

"She believed the Star would protect her," he persisted, "even in the mountains where we *knew* we were dying, she kept believing! You were there, Brek—you saw. I couldn't disillusion her. That was what pulled us through. It's so ironic for her faith to let her down in the end."

"Talyra was a realist," Brek declared, "I remember she said, 'If we die expecting to live, we'll be none the worse for it; but if we stop living because we expect to die, we'll have thrown away our own lives.'"

"She didn't feel faith had let her down," Beris added. "It comforted her! She knew she'd lost too much blood, she'd seen such cases before—and she wanted the ritual blessing. That's why I was sent for."

"You gave it to her, Beris? You said those words to a dying person as if they were true?" Noren frowned. *May the spirit of the Mother Star abide with you, and with your children, and your children's children; may you gain strength from its presence, trusting in the surety of its power.* He had conceded the words were valid when said to the living, who were concerned for the welfare of future generations. But in the context of death—death not only of oneself but of one's only child—they took on a whole new meaning.

"I've never used ritual phrases lightly, not as a priest, anyway," Beris answered. "The words do express truth, just as much as the ones you say every time you preside at Vespers. Of course I said them, and part of the service for the child, too, because she wanted to hear it."

He turned away, realizing that though he himself could not have denied Talyra's wish, he'd have been choking back more than tears. "A priest gives hope," he said softly, "that's what Stefred told me when I agreed to assume the robe. It's a—a mockery to use the symbols where there's nothing left to hope for."

"But Noren—" Beris broke off, seeing Brek's face; she did not know Noren's mind as Brek did. "Talyra hoped for *you,*" she continued quietly. "The last thing she said to me was, 'Tell Noren I love him.'"

Noren sat motionless, already feeling the return of the emptiness that had paralyzed him during his weeks at the research outpost. Brek and Beris seemed far away, their voices echoes of a world he no longer inhabited.

"This isn't the time to tell you this," Beris was saying, "but Talyra made me promise. She said you must have more children, that it's important, because otherwise the world will lose twice as much—"

"She knew I wouldn't want anyone's children but hers."

"That's why she said it—she did know. She knew you don't hold with custom and might not choose someone else just for duty's sake. And there was something about what happened in the mountains that I didn't understand, she said it would become pointless, what you suffered there."

"I suppose she meant your drinking so little water," Brek said. To Beris he added, "I never told you the whole story. Noren nearly died of dehydration; he couldn't drink as much impure water as Talyra and I could because he'd already drunk some as a boy in the village."

"You'd drunk impure water without need?" Beris was shocked.

"Just for a few days before I was taken into the City," Noren assured her. "I didn't believe in the High Law then, not any of it—it wasn't only the injustice that made me a heretic. And I'd decided I'd outgrown nursery tales about stream water turning people into idiots."

"But then how could you dare to—"

"I was tested for genetic damage, just as Brek was after we got back from the mountains. He must have explained about that, or else you wouldn't have married him. Anyway, I'd been told how much more I could safely drink, and in the wilderness I kept within that limit for Talyra's sake. We'd *seen* the mutants, you know. Talyra hadn't heard of genetics, but she knew they were subhuman because their ancestors drank the water…and, well, even though I thought we'd die there, I couldn't let her fear, while we were sleeping together—" He broke off and concluded miserably, "She was right; it's turned out to have been pointless. I'm not likely to want another child."

"If you say that, it's like telling Talyra your love for her made you stop caring about the future. That it was hurtful to you."

"To *me?*" Wretchedly he mumbled, "If it weren't for me, Talyra might have lived a long, happy life in the village."

"How could she have? She'd surely have tried to have children, so the same thing would have happened."

"Would it?" Noren burst out, "Beris, my child may have killed Talyra! You've learned all these things about pregnancy, things they knew on the Six Worlds—hasn't it occurred to you it may not always be the woman's fault when things go wrong? How much do you know about genetics?"

"Not much," she admitted. "I don't think anyone does, beyond the fact that technology's needed for survival here because something in the water and soil damages genes if it's not removed."

"There must be more detail than that in the computers—they preserve all the Six Worlds' science, and more must have been known in the Founders' time." The idea came slowly; as it formed, Noren wondered why no one had ever spoken of it. "In the dreams, the Founders knew the genetic damage was unavoidable without soil and water processing. Yet there weren't any subhuman mutants then. The mutants came later, as the offspring of rebels who fled to the mountains rather than accept the First Scholar's rule. That means the First Scholar *predicted* the mutation, and he couldn't have done that without understanding what genes are! What's more, there must have been cases of genetic damage on the Six Worlds themselves, because the concept wasn't a new one. Perhaps there were mutations that didn't destroy the mind."

"Genetic diseases, yes," Beris agreed. "I did get that much from one dream. But not necessarily mutations. A lot of people had defective genes to begin with, only not all the genes a person has affect that person, or all her offspring."

"Why aren't some of our offspring still affected, then?"

"The Founders—women and men both—passed genetic tests," Brek reflected. "Don't you remember, Noren? When they knew their sun was going to nova, how they chose the people eligible to draw lots for the starships?"

"And there was something about genetics in the First Scholar's plan, too," Noren recalled. "It was one of the reasons he wouldn't let Scholars' children be reared in the City, even the Outer City. Their being sent to the villages had something to do with what he called the gene pool."

"You're right, there's got to be a lot of stored information," said Brek. "I suppose no one's ever taken time to study it because it's so irrelevant to our work now. 'Til we find a way to synthesize metal, so that soil and water processing can continue indefinitely, it doesn't make any difference whether we understand genes or not. Understanding can't prevent the damage, only technology can."

True, thought Noren grimly. Still, he'd always wanted to understand things—and to him, this was no longer irrelevant.

It was near midnight when he returned to his own quarters. At Brek's insistence he had accepted bread and a hot drink, knowing that one should not go more than a full day without nourishment. "Or without sleep," Brek said worriedly. Tactfully, he avoided any direct suggestion about hypnotic sedation.

"I'll sleep," Noren said quickly. He did not see how he could do so in the bed he'd shared with Talyra, but the Inner City was crowded; barring the infirmary, there was nowhere else to sleep. And after all, rooms were nearly identical, having once been cabins aboard the Founders' starships. There were no personal furnishings, for such materials as could be manufactured were allocated to the Outer City, while the Inner City practiced an austerity that even to villagers, who had wicker and colored cloth, would have seemed strange. Talyra had kept her few belongings neatly stored in a compartment beneath the bunk; none would be in evidence to torment him.

"Noren," Brek continued hesitantly, "the service tomorrow—"

"I'll be all right."

"Will you preside?"

"I—I can't, Brek."

"I understand, of course. So will everyone. But it's your right, so I had to ask."

"You don't understand at all," Noren told him. "I wouldn't crack up. I'd like to be the one to speak about Talyra, what she was, what her life meant to us. It's the ritual part I can't do."

He thought back to the first such service he had ever attended, the one for his mother, and how awful he'd felt hearing the Technicians, who in the villages performed priests' functions by proxy, read the false, hollow phrases over her body. His mother had *believed* those things. She'd believed her life and death served some mystical power, the power of a star not yet even visible in the sky.

He had since learned it was not all a lie. But the service for the dead was not a part of the Prophecy that science might fulfill. Nor did it deal only with the Mother Star. It was one thing to accept the Star as a symbol of the unknowable—as he'd done when he assumed priesthood—as well as of the heritage from the Six Worlds. Symbols no longer bothered him. But in this ceremony alone, the Founders had gone further. "I'm not like you and Beris," he told Brek. "I can't feel the words about death symbolize truth."

The night dragged on. Noren could not cry any more, even when alone; he did not believe any emotion would return to him. He'd been right, perhaps, when despair had first gripped him, the year before at the outpost. His marriage had been only a brief reprieve.

Toward dawn he drifted into sleep and was immediately caught up in nightmare, the old nightmare induced by the controlled dreams through which Scholar candidates learned of the Founding. He was the First Scholar, yet at the same time, himself; the woman dying in his arms had Talyra's face, Talyra's voice...He surfaced, telling himself as always that it was just a dream, Talyra still lived, in experiencing the First Scholar's emotions he had drawn images from his own memory. But when fully conscious, he knew that never again would it be a dream from which he could wake up.

The First Scholar too had lost his wife. She had killed herself because she could not bear the knowledge that the Six Worlds were destroyed. That had been what convinced the First Scholar that the secret of the nova must be kept; it was a key episode, so despite its pain it was one new Scholars had to go through. What kind of woman would prefer death to serving the future? Noren wondered. Talyra wouldn't have! Why then had Talyra died? There was no sense in any of it...the First Scholar's wife had served the future after all, for her husband's decision had hinged on hers, the symbolic interpretation of the Mother Star itself had hinged on it. How could the future be served by senseless tragedy?

In the morning he viewed the bodies privately, dry-eyed, before they were shrouded and moved to the open courtyard. Because Talyra had been a Technician, the service was not held within the Hall of Scholars. Except for the absence of kinfolk, with whom all Inner City people sacrificed contact, it was more like a village ceremony; and for this Noren was thankful. Ritual of one sort or another could be more easily dismissed as routine in mixed groups than when only Scholars were present.

Alone, for Brek had quietly assumed the presiding priest's place, Noren joined the gathered mourners as they began the traditional hymn. He was too much a loner to want others' sympathy, though there were many present who would offer it. The ceremony was a thing to live through. So, perhaps, would be all his days to come. Reason told him his work in nuclear physics was futile, and without Talyra to bolster his faith…

How proud she'd been when he first put on the blue robe, and how needless his fear that it would turn her love to a deference he would abhor. Not until he was much older would he be required to assume the burden of appearing at public ceremonies outside the Gates, where villagers and Technicians would kneel to him. In the Inner City such customs were not observed; the robes, in fact, were rarely worn except for formal officiation. But like the other acknowledged Scholars in attendance, he wore his now, as befitted the solemnity of the occasion.

He had steeled himself to the words of committal; the shock of understanding them had worn off since he'd first heard them as a Scholar. Recycling of bodies with the ancient converters from the starships was necessary to future generations in an alien world that did not provide enough of the trace elements on which biological existence depended. In any case, he had never shared the villagers' reverent awe at the thought that when one's body was taken into the City, one somehow became part of the life cycle only Scholars could comprehend. He'd long since resigned himself to the fact that the physical side of this holy mystery was all too earthly.

It was the other part that still disturbed him. *"For as this spirit abides with us, so shall it with her; it will be made manifest in ways beyond our vision…"* Sunlight beat down between the glistening towers onto Noren's uplifted face; he closed his eyes, marveling at the sincerity in Brek's voice.

Villagers and Technicians believed that Scholars were omniscient, that they *knew* what happened after death. Did not the Scholars know the answers to all other mysteries: why crops would not grew in unquickened soil, how impure water could turn sane men into idiots, and even how Machines had come into the world? Having been enlightened as to these latter things, Noren himself had not, at first, doubted that the former was equally explicable. He grew hot at the memory of his naivete when he'd queried the computer complex about death, and of his stunned disillusionment at its inability to provide any information. He'd been a mere adolescent then, of course. The past year had taught him much. His emotions had become less involved, at least as far as his own fate was concerned. But now, Talyra...

"Her place is assured among those who lived before her and those who will come after, those by whom the Star is seen and their children's children's children, even unto infinite and unending time. And not in memory alone does she survive, for the universe is vast. Were the doors now closed to us reopened, as in time they shall be, still there would remain that wall through which there is no door save that through which she has passed..."

Somehow, said of Talyra, it seemed less incredible than it always had to him. Surely Talyra wasn't just...extinguished. He could not imagine a universe in which Talyra had ceased to exist.

He had studied the computers' records of the Six Worlds' religions, and he'd learned that belief in continuance after death had been common though not, by the time of the Founders, widely accepted among scientists. He had wondered why the Founders—all trained as scientists—had put it into the liturgy; for in establishing themselves as priests, they had been scrupulous about proclaiming only those ideas in which they sincerely believed. To the First Scholar, who had planned this, the test of a false religion was not whether someone had made up its symbols on purpose, but whether that person had been aiming to defraud. The Founders had been required to cloak certain facts in symbolism, but they had not practiced deception. They had meant everything they said. How, Noren had asked himself, could they have meant what they seemed to be saying in the service for the dead, especially after they'd seen thirty billion people die in the vaporization of the Six Worlds?

Now, suddenly, he understood. It had been the First Scholar's influence, the dreams' influence! They'd all experienced the death of the First Scholar's wife: experienced it in personal terms—just as he, Noren, had—as a result of the dual identity one assumed in controlled dreaming. The dream material, even in its most complete version, was edited. The Founders had recorded memories for posterity, knowing that only thus could they convey the reality of the Six Worlds' tragic end to those in whose hands survival of their race must rest. But they'd had a right to some privacy; the

First Scholar had edited his thoughts to remove such personal ones as would contribute nothing to comprehension of future problems. Thus his image of his wife's personality had not been preserved. But he had loved her. No doubt he'd indeed felt that somewhere in the universe she must, in some way, live—such a feeling might even remain in the recordings. Each dreamer drew different things from them, according to his or her own background. The Founders, having lost loved ones to the nova, might well have clung to emotion as if it were the First Scholar's actual conviction. After his martyrdom they had revered him, as all Scholars still did, striving to emulate him in everything.

It was ironic. To the First Scholar himself, faith not based on evidence hadn't come easily. "Did you suppose he was born with it?" the Scholar Stefred had said when Noren, on his return from the mountains, had begun to perceive the real nature of commitment to the Prophecy. Stefred had always maintained that Noren's mind was very like the First Scholar's.

From his place in the inner circle Noren glanced around, expecting to see Stefred among the blue-robed figures closest to him. Astonishingly, he was absent. It was unthinkable that he wouldn't attend this service if aware of it; unthinkable, too, that Brek would have neglected to tell him of Talyra's death.

Noren himself had not sought out Stefred, nor did he intend to do so. There was no help for this sort of pain. As head of recruitment and a skilled psychiatrist, Stefred knew all young Scholars' deepest feelings; he had guided them through the ordeals of inquisition, enlightenment and recantation. He had aided their adjustment to the status they'd neither sought nor welcomed. He'd been their first friend in the Inner City and remained, to all, a warm one. But though he'd want to help, he was uncompromisingly honest—he would not try to argue away grief.

Yet neither would he ignore it. Could he be tied up with urgent Council business? Noren had not entered the Hall of Scholars for two days; he had heard none of the current rumors about the City's affairs. Abruptly, it occurred to him that these affairs had not halted, that little as they now mattered to him, they would go right on. The effort to fulfill the Prophecy would go on, hopeless though it was. He had committed himself to participation. For a time he'd had faith that it was worthwhile. Had that been only for the child's sake?

He'd thought such faith, once discovered, would be permanent. But perhaps it had never been valid at all; perhaps it had been a mere feeling, no better founded than this unexpected feeling that Talyra's true self still lived on.

"...so may the spirit of the Star be with her, and with us all." Brek stopped speaking; there was a long silence. Gradually Noren became aware that men stood ready to lift the shroud, that they were waiting for his signal.

Stepping forward, he dropped his eyes. There was nothing to be seen, of course, but dazzling white cloth; wherever Talyra was, she could not be there. Nor could the child—the boy, he'd been told—in whom they'd taken such joy. *Oh, Talyra,* he thought, *it wasn't the way we imagined. The wilderness gave us death after all.*

When it was over, Brek took him to the refectory, persuaded him to eat. "Stefred sent a message," he said. "He'd like you to stop by his study—"

"I don't need to do that."

"You and your starcursed pride," murmured Brek. "I should have known better than to say it that way. I know you don't need therapy from Stefred. So does he. But after all, his own wife died—and he still mourns her; he's never looked at anyone else. It's no wonder if he's sorry he couldn't be at the service and wants to tell you so personally. You owe him the chance, when he's so troubled right now himself."

"Troubled? Why?"

"You haven't heard? Everyone's mystified. We don't know what the problem is, except that he's working with a heretic who's been reacting badly to the dreams. Apparently he doesn't dare leave her."

"Not at all?" The testing and enlightenment of a Scholar candidate took several weeks of intensive therapy, but not all phases demanded Stefred's presence. There were rest periods, and some of the machine-induced dreams could be controlled by assistants.

"Well, he won't leave his suite at all; he's having his meals brought to him. And he's monitoring the entire dream sequence personally. As far as that goes, he handled the inquisition personally after the first hour or so—the observers were sent out. I don't suppose we'll ever hear what happened."

"No," agreed Noren, "but it must have been rough for them both." Any candidate experiencing the dreams had been judged trustworthy. That meant she had stood up to Stefred despite real terror, which in Technicians—and most female heretics had been born to that caste—could sometimes be hard to induce. Technicians weren't overwhelmed by City surroundings, as villagers were; stress had to be artificially applied. Stefred knew how to do it harmlessly, and when necessary he could be ruthless. It was for the candidate's own benefit: no one unsure of his or her inner strength could endure the outwardly degrading recantation ceremony, or accept the "rewards" that came after. One must be certain in one's own mind that one hadn't sold out. If that certainty could be engendered only through extreme measures, Stefred would use them; but he would not enjoy the process.

"The odd thing," Brek went on, "is that she's a village woman. Yet at first, I'm told, she was fearless. Everyone who saw her noticed—she was as self-composed as an experienced initiate. It was almost unnatural."

Slowly, Noren nodded. It was indeed odd that a villager, brought straight from a Stone Age environment into the awesome City—believing she'd be put to death there for her convictions—could be so cool under questioning that Stefred would have to employ unusual tactics. But they would learn nothing of her background. Not only were closed-door sessions with Stefred treated as confidential, but no questions were asked in the Inner City about newcomers' past lives. This convention had been established because the true significance of heresy must be concealed from the uninitiated, but it was also a matter of courtesy. Former heretics, who were by nature nonconformists, had not always behaved admirably in youth; it would be tactless to risk embarrassing anyone, or to stir up memories better left to fade.

"What's strangest," Noren reflected, "is that someone strong-willed enough to need special handling would be endangered by the dreams. They're hard for everybody at first. A person who wasn't bothered by what the Founders did wouldn't be a fit successor. But close monitoring—that's used only for the most terrifying ones, the ones that could induce physical shock. I never heard of monitoring the whole series."

"Could he have put her under too much stress beforehand, maybe?"

"Stefred? He's never miscalculated; you know that!"

"I do know," Brek replied. "Yet now he's worried. No one's seen him since Orison the night before last, and then he looked—well, as if he needed that kind of reassurance. Since he's willing to talk to you—"

"I'll find out what I can." It was true enough, Noren realized, that only pride had made him resolve not to go to Stefred, the one person in the City to whom he could speak freely of sorrow.

But there was another encounter that had priority. On the verge of taking the lift up to the tower suite in which he'd met so many past crises, Noren moved his hand instead to the button for "down."

At the foundation of the Hall of Scholars was the computer complex, most sacred of all places in the City because there alone the accumulated knowledge of the Six Worlds was preserved. To Noren, knowledge had seemed sacred from his earliest boyhood; to all Scholars, its guardianship was a holy responsibility. The information stored in the computers was irreplaceable. If lost, it could not be regained, and without that information, human survival would become impossible. Unrestricted access to it was the right of every Scholar. Priesthood wasn't a condition—but it was in contact with the computer complex that Noren felt most nearly as he supposed a priest ought to feel. The computers held such truth as was knowable. He knew better, now, than to think that they held *all* truth, but they held all his human race had uncovered, all he was likely to find in his own world.

In this only, there was happiness he had not shared with Talyra. It was the single aspect of his life her loss would not diminish. But he could not accept the joys of learning without also accepting the demands. *I care more for truth than for comfort,* he'd declared at his trial. He'd been a mere boy, fresh from the village school; it sounded naively melodramatic now. He had known even then that most people would think it foolish. The village councilmen who condemned him had been appalled by his blasphemous presumption. During the subsequent inquisition, however, Stefred had not thought it foolish; he'd called it the key point in his defense. Stefred, who knew more than any village council about uncomfortable truths, had challenged him to choose. He could not now revoke the choice he had made.

Noren sat at a console, not yet touching the keys, glad that in the dim light of the computer room no one would notice his hesitancy.

He had never been afraid of knowledge. He'd learned early that it could be painful to possess as well as to acquire; he had shut it out at times; still he could not consciously deny that knowing was better than not knowing. Somewhere in the computers was information that could tell him: had actions of his killed Talyra?

Quite possibly they had. If so, it was fitting retribution for the mistakes on his part that had led to the crash in the mountains…yet how could things work like that? *She* had been guiltless!

He himself was not. He had by his rashness destroyed one of the world's few aircars; its loss might affect the well-being of generations yet unborn. He'd thought himself willing to destroy people's hope at the cost of his own life. These events were behind him now. Stefred had said he must look forward, not back. Yet considering the death of the child…

Could the child have been harmed by the mountain water after all? Though Noren's genes hadn't been affected by it, Talyra had not been tested. They'd said it was more complicated with a woman, that it would demand surgery for which they had no proper equipment and which would in any case be risky during her pregnancy. Talyra had drunk no more of the water than Brek, whose test result showed no harm—not nearly as much as the officially established limit. Still, if genetics hadn't been studied since the Founders' time, did anyone really know how exact the limit was?

All the science of the Six Worlds was in computer memory. He had access to all of it if he could frame the right questions. Since becoming a Scholar, he'd acquired skill in questioning, a process that demanded deep thought. It would not be possible simply to ask why Talyra had died, or even why the baby had; the program couldn't respond to a query of that kind. His questions must be specific. He must analyze the issues, however hard they were to face.

Suppose there had been damage to Talyra's genes, suppose the limit was not the same for everyone—even so, the mutation caused by impure water wasn't lethal. The mutants in the mountains, despite subhuman brains, were all too healthy. Besides, the baby most likely had been conceived the first night. Impure water was harmful only to reproductive cells, not to embryos…wasn't it? He frowned, struggling with concepts unfamiliar to him, as a new thought came into his mind.

He knew little about pregnancy. Such things were not studied—babies came and were welcomed; one did not ponder how they grew. Beris had said that on the Six Worlds doctors had known more. Had they known what could harm an embryo during the first days of its existence?

A child newly conceived was alive; like all living things it needed water; it must get this through its mother's blood. But it was surely very small. So could a small amount of some damaging substance hurt it, even if the mother herself was not damaged?

This, he knew, was the kind of question that was answerable. Whether or not anyone had asked it before in the City, the program would reply as promptly as if the query concerned recent experiments. His hands trembling, Noren keyed, CAN AN UNBORN CHILD BE HARMED BY WHAT ITS MOTHER CONSUMES EARLY IN PREGNANCY?

Instantly the screen before him displayed, YES.

EVEN IF SHE HERSELF IS NOT MADE ILL?

YES. SUCH DAMAGE IS CALLED TERATOGENIC.

IS THAT THE SAME AS MUTATION?

NO, IT IS A DIFFERENT TYPE OF GENETIC ERROR. TERATOGENIC DAMAGE IS NOT INHERITED BY THE CHILD'S OFFSPRING.

SUCH A CHILD SOMETIMES LIVES, THEN?

USUALLY IT LIVES, BUT IS DISEASED OR DEFORMED.

CAN TERATOGENIC DAMAGE CAUSE IT TO BE STILLBORN?

OCCASIONALLY. MORE OFTEN, LETHAL DAMAGE WOULD RESULT IN EARLY MISCARRIAGE.

Noren gripped the edge of the console keyboard, fighting sick despair. If it could happen, it was reasonable to assume that it *had* happened, given the fact that the impurities of the water had been in Talyra's bloodstream throughout her first week of pregnancy.

He drew deep breaths; then, with effort, continued, IF SUCH A CHILD IS STILLBORN, CAN THIS CAUSE THE DEATH OF THE MOTHER?

NOT DIRECTLY. IN RARE CASES TERATOGENIC DAMAGE MIGHT LEAD TO COMPLICATIONS IN DELIVERY. CAN YOU SUPPLY SPECIFIC DATA?

WHAT SORT OF DATA?

GENETIC DATA THAT WOULD PERMIT THE PROBABILITY TO BE CALCULATED.

No, thought Noren in dismay. He could not supply that. But the Founders could have—otherwise the computer wouldn't be programmed to ask for it.

He knew nothing about biology, but he was well-trained in higher mathematics; the calculation of probabilities was something he understood. HOW MANY INPUT VARIABLES ARE INVOLVED? he ventured.

THE ENTIRE GENOTYPE OF BOTH PARENTS MAY BE RELEVANT. THE PROGRAM CAN DETERMINE SIGNIFICANT VARIABLES FROM THAT, PLUS CHEMICAL ANALYSIS OF THE SUBSTANCE IN QUESTION AND ITS TIME OF CONSUMPTION. THERE MAY BE OTHER ENVIRONMENTAL VARIABLES ALSO.

Genotype? He did not know the word; fortunately computer programs were patient with stupid questions. DEFINE GENOTYPE, he commanded.

GENOTYPE IS THE GENETIC MAKEUP OF AN INDIVIDUAL ORGANISM, THE SPECIFIC SET OF GENES IN ITS CELLS.

HOW LARGE IS THE SET IN HUMANS? Noren inquired, thinking that perhaps some doctor would help him list his own genes in a form suitable for input. Incredibly, he found himself staring at a six-digit figure.

THAT IS THE NUMBER OF GENES THAT MAY VARY? he asked in disbelief.

IT IS THE NUMBER WITH WHICH THE PROGRAM DEALS. THE SET IS LARGER, BUT SOME GENES ARE REDUNDANT OR OF UNKNOWN FUNCTION.

No wonder the Scholars hadn't devoted time to studying the field, thought Noren. Genetics must be as complicated as nuclear physics. And surely even a knowledgeable person couldn't key in that many separate bits of data; it would tie up a console for weeks.

WHAT IS THE INPUT FORMAT FOR GENOTYPE? he queried.

THE ANALYSIS CAN BE MADE DIRECTLY FROM A BLOOD SAMPLE THROUGH THE USE OF AUXILIARY INPUT EQUIPMENT.

Did such equipment still exist? It must; the Founders had been careful to write the program in a way compatible with the facilities preserved for their descendants. So his own genotype could evidently be analyzed. For Talyra's, it was too late. If he had known before her body was sent to the converters... Perhaps it was best that he had not, that he could obtain no real estimate of the odds, for they would not be zero, and they might prove conclusively that having a child under other circumstances wouldn't have been fatal.

Yet he could not just drop the matter. *It happens,* Beris had said. *Occasionally it happens with a girl who seems healthy.* Generations of women had accepted that, when all along the computers had been able to calculate probabilities in specific cases! Why had the Founders made no mention of this in the High Law, which explicitly mandated use of all other existing life-support technologies?

Because, he saw, it would not fit the High Law's purpose. The original population of the colony had been dangerously small, so small that maximum increase had been deemed desirable even though it would hasten the depletion of resources. Thus for survival's sake the High Law encouraged childbearing; it forbade all contraception, not only the drugs that couldn't be manufactured with available resources. There was no longer need for such a prohibition—any decent couple would be outraged at the mere thought of the things Scholars knew about from the old records. He himself had been more shocked by them than by the literal meaning behind the phrases referring to disposition of bodies. But this hadn't been true in the Founders' time. The Founders had grown up in a society where overpopulation was a serious problem; they had considered it natural and even admirable to limit births. They'd assumed that if people went on computing the odds of trouble when medical facilities were inadequate, no one would take any risk at all.

Yet...there were nevertheless perplexities. Why, for instance, had he come upon this knowledge only through purposeful inquiry? Basic information about human reproduction was not obscure, and the sexual customs of the Six Worlds were known to any Scholar familiar with material about the vanished culture; there were allusions to them even in dreams. Scientific details, on the other hand—and especially those related to genetics—received practically no mention. It was almost as if references to the topic had been deliberately omitted from the reading matter of the Scholars themselves. And that was strange. Not only was access to knowledge supposed to be unrestricted, but genetics was the very thing most pertinent to understanding of the alien world's limitations.

Guardianship of the City was justifiable only because it was the sole alternative to genetic damage: so the Founders had believed, so all Scholars since had agreed. There was no question about this fact. But why was it thought sufficient to know that it was true, if the computers had detailed information about why it was true, about the biological mechanism that produced the damage? And why hadn't the First Scholar's recorded thoughts dealt with the subject more fully?

Having raised these issues, Noren could not fail to pursue them; it was not in him to let such things ride. CAN THE PROBABLE CAUSE OF THE MOTHER'S DEATH BE ESTIMATED WITHOUT HER GENOTYPE? he asked.

NOT ACCURATELY. A ROUGH APPROXIMATION CAN BE MADE.

That was better than nothing. SHE CONSUMED UNPURIFIED WATER, he keyed. FOR CHEMICAL ANALYSIS REFER TO MEMORY. The computers had more information about what was in it than he did, after all.

AMOUNT AND TIME OF CONSUMPTION?

MINIMUM DAILY RATION, FIRST SIX DAYS OF PREGNANCY OR LESS.

FOOD DURING THIS PERIOD?

NONE AT ALL. They had agreed to starve—there'd been no safe food, so he, Brek and Talyra had calmly discussed it and decided that starvation would be preferable to an adaptation that would lead to production of subhuman offspring. Had she even then been carrying a defective baby?

QUALITY OF PRENATAL MEDICAL CARE?

Again, NONE.

ANY EXPOSURE TO RADIATION?

No, Talyra hadn't entered the power plant; and though he himself had worked both there and in nuclear research labs, any failure of the shielding would have been detected. No case of radiation exposure had occurred since the accident that had killed Stefred's wife. But wait...*radiation?*

There had been the mystifying radiation given off by the alien sphere.

It had brought about their rescue. They'd found the little sphere in the mountains, an artifact from some other solar system, long ago abandoned by the mysterious Visitors who'd mined and depleted this planet's scant metal resources before humans from the Six Worlds had arrived. He had manipulated it, made it radiate—an alarm had been triggered in the monitoring section of the computer complex. Thus an aircar had been sent out from the City and had located them. But he'd been unable to walk after retrieving the sphere from the rock niche where it had lain; it had been Talyra who, at his instructions, had carried it to the open plateau and turned it on.

Since then, the sphere had been studied at the research outpost. It had been pronounced harmless; the radiation it emitted was of a previously unknown sort and no one could tell what it was for, but it didn't seem to hurt anybody. It caused no mutations in fowl, the only creatures available to test it on. There were no facilities for taking it apart or attempting its duplication, but as the only artifact of the Visitors ever discovered, it had been observed with great fascination by the few Scholars fortunate enough to draw duty at the newly built outpost. Were any of those Scholars pregnant? One thing was sure—no woman who'd touched the sphere as early in pregnancy as Talyra could yet have given birth, for Talyra had been the first.

CAN TERATOGENIC DAMAGE BE CAUSED BY RADIATION HARMLESS TO ADULTS? Noren asked.

YES.

BY THE UNKNOWN RADIATION THAT LAST YEAR TRIGGERED AN ALARM?

INSUFFICIENT DATA, replied the screen tersely. That was what it always said when one asked a question for which the programmers hadn't had an answer.

Noren dropped his head, burying his face in his folded arms. He was indeed responsible, he thought despairingly—for the child's death and no doubt Talyra's also, for would it not be too great a coincidence if she'd died of some other cause? As a scientist, he could see that there was no conclusive proof. But how could he ever, in the face of so many suspicious factors, believe otherwise?

And for how many more deaths might he become responsible, if women at the outpost now carried unborn children damaged by the sphere?

It would have been better not to have found it. It would have been better if they had died in the mountains, as they'd expected they would. Yet Talyra had viewed its discovery as a confirmation of her faith. She'd believed the spirit of the Mother Star would guard them, and in her eyes it *had*—they had been led to an utterly unpredictable deliverance, as the Prophecy proclaimed would someday happen for their whole race. *Though our peril be great even unto the last generation of our endurance, in the end humankind shall prevail; and the doors of the universe shall once again be thrown open…* On the basis of the analogy, he had accepted priesthood. So great an irony as that was past bearing…

No. The whole chain of events had begun with his unwillingness to live with his own failings; he would not make the same mistake twice. Wearily, Noren sat upright once more and went on questioning.

Chapter Two

As dusk came on, Noren waited alone in Stefred's secluded study high in the Hall of Scholars. Beyond the window three waning moons hung between the lighted pinnacles of adjacent towers. There had been moonlight on the plateau in the mountains, too, he found himself thinking, the harsh, desolate wasteland that to him and Talyra had been a place of beauty. And long before, the same three crescents had shone on the village square where they'd made their first pledge of love. Life had been simple then, despite his dissatisfaction with its injustice and his inner knowledge that he might someday face punishment for heresy. He hadn't imagined how much things could change.

What was left for him now? he thought numbly. It would be better if he had some constructive job to turn to. He didn't expect happiness—without Talyra, how could he know happiness again? Nor did he still look for peace of mind. But tomorrow morning would come, and the next, and the next...he would have to do something, since no one was idle in the City, and how could he go back to work—futile work—when all hope for its success was dead in him?

This was not a question to ask Stefred, or for that matter, anyone else. Even from Brek, he knew, he would receive an all-too-ready answer. It would be said that if his actions had caused deaths, that was all the more reason why he was obligated to work toward the ultimate preservation of lives. By many of his fellow-priests, in fact, he would be told that if he'd survived last year's events at high cost, it was because he might be destined to preserve humanity; that was the basis on which they'd justified the loss of the aircar. He must therefore avoid letting the issue be raised in the light of what he'd learned about the baby, for he could not endure the thought of its life, and Talyra's, being figured into the balance. The proffered answers would no doubt be the same.

No price would be thought too high for his salvation. He, Noren, was regarded by most as a genius who, in his later years, would bring about the advance in physics needed to realize the

Founders' hope of synthesizing metal through nuclear fusion. All efforts of past generations to achieve this had been proven vain by last year's experiments; a flaw had appeared at the level of basic scientific theory. The computers now said the task was impossible. The priests, however, maintained that it could not be impossible—that since nothing else could enable their species to survive, an unforeseen breakthrough would occur if they kept working. Noren was viewed as the most likely person to make it.

He did not share this confidence. He himself had never been deluded about the chances of his talent producing such an outcome. His very gift for the work showed him, with a clarity not apparent to others, that the limits imposed by available facilities were absolute. More and more, since his return from the outpost where future experimentation was to be tried, he had seen that the research would be fruitless. Study, like priesthood, was for him a gesture—a gesture that sustained people's hope, unlike the destructive one through which he'd sought to deny life by declaring all hope fraudulent. He had acknowledged the value of faith and had even felt its power, but he'd found it couldn't alter his scientific pessimism.

At times, with Talyra, he had forgotten all this. The end would not come in his lifetime, and he'd lived as if long-term survival of his people were indeed assured. He'd been on his way to becoming like everyone else. But he couldn't have gone on with that forever, he thought, suddenly overcome by a sadness that was more than grief. He was not like everyone else; he never had been…

The door slid aside, and Stefred stood for a moment in the lighted opening. Noren rose to greet him, and they gripped hands. "Noren," he said quietly. "I—I've no words."

"They aren't needed," Noren replied. With Stefred this was true; he had an uncanny ability to convey the warmth of his feelings even when forced to speak words not easy to hear.

"I can't tell you it will stop hurting. I've been through it, and I know better. But in time—"

"You've never remarried."

"That's different."

"How?" demanded Noren. Stefred wasn't an old man—more than old enough to be his father, no doubt, but in a world where most married in adolescence, that did not make him old in years. Furthermore, everyone who knew Stefred liked and admired him; he'd scarcely have had trouble finding another wife.

"My position's awkward," he replied painfully. "There is a—a bond that develops between me and each candidate I examine; you know that. With the men it means lasting friendship. With the women it could mean more; ethics require me to suppress all such thoughts while acting in my professional role. Later…there've been several women I might have approached later, but by then they'd chosen others."

"You could marry a Technician, though."

"Could I? Noren, every Technician who enters the Inner City kneels to me in a formal audience during application for admission, seeks my blessing, thinking me of supernatural stature! I can't hide my rank while getting acquainted with the newcomers, as the rest of you can." His voice dropped as he added with bitterness, "No Technician woman would refuse me; she would feel awed by the thought of bearing my child. It goes without saying that I don't want love on that basis."

Of course not, Noren realized. In the villages most heretics were men. The balance between sexes would not be equal in the Inner City if Technician women weren't brought in; but the religious devotion of these girls, who considered it a high honor to be accepted for lifelong confinement within the walls, was not exploited. They assumed they were to be courted by their peers. Stefred, who must appear robed at the admission interview and accept the near-worship accorded High Priests, was doomed to a unique sort of loneliness.

And loneliness wasn't his heaviest burden. Meeting his eyes, Noren noticed the shadows beneath them, the lines of fatigue and worry in his face. Only a real emergency would have kept Stefred from the service for Talyra; he'd just now returned from a dream-monitoring session with a candidate whom he must consider in peril of cracking up. "This is a bad time for me to have come," Noren apologized. "I know you can't tell me the details, but people have heard rumors."

Stefred crossed to his desk and slumped wearily into its chair, not bothering to turn on the lamp. "I'll tell you this," he said after a short pause. "I'm—afraid, Noren. For the first time, I'm dealing with someone I'm afraid I can't bring through."

"She's not strong enough?" Noren sat down again, sensing that Stefred really wanted to talk about it. Detached though he felt, the situation puzzled him. If the girl lacked courage, that judgment would have been made earlier, before it was too late to pursue the heresy charge less rigorously and give her Technician rank. Once secrets had been revealed to her, she must be isolated from Technicians for the rest of her life if she proved unable to withstand the full sequence of ordeals that led to Scholar status. Since this would mean not mere confinement to the Inner City but true imprisonment, it was indeed a dismaying prospect—but surely a remote one. Stefred knew how to bring out the best in people.

"Oh, she's strong," he was saying, "she's more than strong enough; she's the most promising candidate I've seen in a long time. If I fail, the tragedy won't be just hers and mine. It will affect all of us."

"But then if it's just some personal reaction to the dreams, can't you help her deal with it?" Stefred, Noren knew, would never violate anyone's confidence, let alone reveal a confession made under the drugs, which, in a private inquisition, he must have used. However, it was no secret that things in a candidate's background could make particular aspects of the dreams unduly trying, and in such cases, hypnotic aid was normally given.

"She's concealing too much from me," Stefred said. "There's a wall in her mind I can't get past, and I wouldn't be justified in breaching it even if I could. I'm already sure she meets the qualifications—she hates the caste system as much as we all do and will gladly work toward its abolishment if she finds herself on top. I've no warrant to invade her privacy except to determine that. You know I can't probe her subconscious merely to spare her suffering."

"Not unless she consents," Noren agreed. "Still, if you'll risk killing her otherwise..." It was possible, in theory, for someone who'd identified closely with the First Scholar to literally share his death in the last dream, the crucial one that dealt with the Prophecy's origin.

"The last dream's not the problem. If it were, I could handle it; she'd need temporary isolation, perhaps, but given time, I could prepare her. What seems to be happening is that she's too intuitive. The recruiting scheme wasn't designed to deal with someone who grasps things outside any conceivable past experience." He leaned forward, frowning. "Noren, what if you'd guessed the extent of the editing in the candidates' version of the dreams? Could you have gone through with voluntary recantation?"

"No," Noren said. "No, I based my decision on first-hand knowledge of the First Scholar's motives. When you told me afterward about the editing I was furious—I thought for a moment you'd manipulated things to deceive me."

"Lianne," Stefred reflected, "underwent more anguish than any person I have ever monitored in the first dream. It's not enjoyable for anyone—it can't be; watching a sun nova and consume its planets isn't an easy experience. But most candidates are detached at that stage; it's nightmare, not reality. Not till later does the reality sink in. Lianne got it all. From what she said after she regained consciousness, I know she got everything the First Scholar felt—but of course, without his foreknowledge."

"Everything? But she couldn't have known what populated worlds are like," protested Noren, remembering his own slow absorption of the idea that not just one City but thousands had been wiped out in that single surge of intolerable fire.

"I wasn't sure she could take another session," Stefred went on, "but she was willing, and I went ahead with close monitoring. Her physiological responses showed she was coping; I thought we'd passed the crisis. And then, when she woke, the first thing she said to me was, 'Why have you edited it so much?'"

"Oh, Stefred."

"You see what's going to happen. She'll stick to her refusal to recant even after finishing the sequence—precisely because she *is* strong, is perceptive, she'll hold out on the grounds that I've kept part of the truth from her. Her very fitness to become one of us will force her into a position that deprives her of the chance."

"That's awful. It's one thing to make that choice out of real disagreement with the First Scholar's decision, but to have to live with its consequences because of a false suspicion that you're cheating—"

"I know," Stefred sighed, "especially since I have cause to believe she doesn't disagree. The dreams wouldn't affect her so deeply if she didn't share his convictions. For that matter, she wouldn't be unsatisfied by the explanation I've given her about the editing."

"Stefred," Noren mused, "why wasn't I unsatisfied? You told me thoughts beyond my comprehension had been removed from the recording, and I took your word."

"It was true in your case," replied Stefred grimly. "With Lianne I've come close to lying."

Noren stared at him in bafflement. Stefred never lied to anyone; that was why even candidates under stress learned to trust him. "I don't see," he admitted, "how the partial truth can be less valid in her case than in mine."

"Neither do I, really. Even mature candidates don't notice what's absent from the First Scholar's thoughts at first; his world is too strange and distracting. As for you, though, you were very young, Noren. You didn't miss the deleted emotions because you'd never imagined such feelings, and they'd have been truly beyond you. That's one reason we see to it that known heretics are brought to trial in adolescence."

"Is she an older woman?" Noren asked, surprised. The majority of people with heretical tendencies did reveal them early, though since opportunity to earn Scholar status was every citizen's birthright, older candidates occasionally appeared.

"Well, not adolescent, certainly. Oddly enough, her age is one of the things she won't tell me. She was a stranger in the village where she was arrested, so we don't know her real identity, and all she'll say is that she has no children—which, barring some medical cause, means she's unconventional in more than her opinions. She can't have lacked suitors; she's quite pretty, in an unusual sort of way." He shook his head, obviously perplexed. "Her face looks young, but her mind seems as old as any I've encountered. The full version of the dreams would not be incomprehensible to her, and she's well aware of that."

"The full version...wait a minute! Are you saying she's concerned about things in the *full* version, the one I haven't been through myself yet, not just the second version that contains the plan for the succession scheme?" Shaken from his stupor, Noren realized that he'd nearly forgotten that such a version existed. He had been told about it when, in deciding to accept priesthood, he'd inquired about the First Scholar's personal religious beliefs. But it covered much more than religion. Though its ultimate effect on most dreamers was heartening, the First Scholar's trust in the future had been hard-won. His recorded memories were said to involve agonizing periods of doubt and near-suicidal depression. Ordinarily only experienced Scholars chose to grapple with these feelings; Noren, who'd tasted them in his own life, had nevertheless been advised to wait awhile.

That advice had been given just after the return from the wilderness, he reflected. Stefred had known then that Talyra might have conceived a child there; had he also known there was risk of a disastrous outcome? Was there something related to such an outcome in the full version of the First Scholar's memories, something there'd have been no use in worrying about while awaiting the birth? It was all too likely. The First Scholar had been absolutely positive that genetic damage was unavoidable without technology to compensate for the alien environment—the edited recordings emphasized this certainty, for nothing else could justify guardianship of the City. But, Noren thought suddenly, it was not a fact he'd have accepted without strong proof...

"Yes," Stefred was saying, "she sees the questions you recognized last year as things he must have thought about. Life, death, why novas wipe out worlds—you know what I mean. And the despair, Noren. She perceives he'd have experienced despair, not just horror and regret."

"Does she also sense that he rose out of it?" inquired Noren. In the end the First Scholar had met death fearlessly, with genuine conviction that the world was to be saved—but could a person who knew about despair guess that? Perhaps he'd not guessed it himself during the bad times. And perhaps it wouldn't have happened that way at all if he'd known what had since been discovered about the impossibility of synthesizing metal.

"I think she does," Stefred replied, "though I admit I don't know just why. I haven't even hinted; my only recourse has been to hope she'll assume I'm withholding the worst parts out of misguided kindness. Actually, of course, to use the full recording would be a mercy in her case. She—she has begged for it, Noren; it is very hard to subject her to as much torment as I must." Incredibly, his voice faltered as if he were struggling to hold back emotion he could not share even with a fellow-Scholar.

"Torment? But why is it any worse than what came before, when she knew Scholars weren't telling her all she wanted to know?" Noren asked. Obviously the full recording could not be used; it included references to the secret of the succession. But if the feelings it contained were so painful, to keep it from candidates not yet informed about the hopeful ending seemed indeed kind as well as essential.

Stefred, once more in full command of himself, explained, "Right now she's suffering in a way that should never be necessary: she reaches for thoughts that won't come, knowing full well what sort *should* come. You know how hard it is to reach out that way in the dreams; you had courage enough to reach further than most—but you were too inexperienced in life to absorb all the data you received. The real gaps you accepted as mystery. If I put you through the candidates' version now, you'd find it intolerable to be held within its limits."

Limits…yes, the City, too, had once seemed limitless, thought Noren, looking out from the dim room to the closely grouped towers that blocked most of the night sky. He had thought he could never exhaust the well of knowledge preserved here in the City. He'd thought there could be no need to seek beyond. Even when he'd found that limits did exist, he had told himself he could live within them. He had resolved to play the game because there was no other; he had stopped reaching for what he knew would never come.

Was this strange village woman, who by her reaching took on torment even Stefred felt was excessive, less of a realist than he?

He'd changed so much since his own initiation…but in what direction? How many directions? He knew more, and yet perhaps he'd lost something, too, something besides Talyra. He did not feel like the same person; perhaps he'd lost part of himself. Confused, cold with apprehension he did not understand, he heard his own voice ask, "What if you put me through the full version now? I—I think the time's come when I need to know what's in it."

"Not when you're burdened by grief, you don't," Stefred said gently. "Maybe in a year or two."

"No," declared Noren, suddenly very sure of what he was looking for. "Not in a year or two—now."

He had thought Stefred would be unwilling even to discuss it at a time when he was preoccupied, a time when the Dream Machine was obviously not available in any case. Candidates always had priority for controlled dreaming, and there was always a waiting list of Scholars who'd signed up to experience library dreams through which they could learn more about the Six Worlds. Yet surprisingly, Stefred seemed eager to dissuade him from a decision that could simply have been delayed.

"The part about his wife," he said. "That would hurt, now, more than you expect; you'd experience it in a very personal way."

"But he did come to terms with it."

"Are you thinking you might be helped to do the same?"

"Well, yes, that too," Noren said, realizing this was true. "But I have something else in mind." No doubt Stefred assumed that he hadn't guessed, that he still needed protection from knowledge of his own blameworthiness in what had happened; maybe that was why he'd suddenly averted his eyes, as if stricken by remembrance of something better left unspoken. But if so—if Stefred knew portions of the First Scholar's memories did deal with the problem of genetic damage—that was all the more reason for proceeding as soon as the equipment was free.

It was unlike Stefred to avoid anyone's gaze. Normally he was brutally straightforward about harsh reality, thereby inspiring people to rise to the challenge. To be sure, he was expert in masking his feelings for good purpose; but Noren knew all those games and had always found them exhilarating. Now his tone was oddly uncertain. "Noren, it's not like the first times through," he said. "You don't just relive nightmare and wake up with new knowledge. What you gain from the full version is more subtle: emotions, value judgments, that take a lifetime to interpret even after you've shared the First Scholar's view of them. In fact it contains some feelings none of his successors have ever managed to interpret. It's a harrowing experience. Ideally it should be spread out over many weeks, one step at a time."

"But you say this village woman, this Lianne, wouldn't be harmed by getting the whole thing fast, under stress of heresy proceedings."

"I'm balancing perils. To her, we are liars if we make it seem too simple; and since that may lead her to choose permanent imprisonment through misunderstanding of our aims, she has nothing to lose."

"Neither have I," Noren muttered. Then, because Stefred had heard and reacted, he added quickly, "I mean, would I suffer more than I'm already suffering? I'm not going to feel *good,* whatever I do now."

"No—and I wouldn't have you believe I'd try to distract you from sorrow that's natural and unavoidable."

"I don't want distraction," said Noren, thinking that no such aim on Stefred's part had been implied by any of his comments. "It's just that I—I have to move on, Stefred. I can't slip back into the mold, or I'll end up paralyzed, the way I was at the outpost."

"There's risk of something worse than that," Stefred said with artificial, measured coldness. "You might be thrown into a depression more serious than last year's, and the recovery could be a good deal slower."

Perhaps, but last year too Stefred had cautioned him, and had assumed responsibility before the Council when things seemed to be turning out wrong. Yet he had not felt it was wrong for either of them to take risks. Looking at him now, Noren could see plainly that he was deeply troubled. He would consider it his fault if Lianne got hurt, however unavoidable his actions had been in the case. He was not judging objectively in this separate matter—he simply didn't want another crackup on his conscience.

"You know me better than to warn me away from the truth," Noren said levelly.

Stefred nodded without answering, and Noren saw, suddenly, that it was unfair to let him bear any part of the accountability for his own future undertakings. "The decision's mine," he went on. "As a committed priest I have the right of access to the entire heritage left us by the First Scholar; that's the rule."

"It is," Stefred replied reluctantly, "though I never expected to hear you claim the prerogatives of the priesthood in opposition to me." He lowered his head, so that his face was hidden, but the pain in his voice was unmistakable.

In confusion and remorse, Noren went to him and touched his shoulder. "Stefred, I'm sorry. We're both under strain; I shouldn't even be here tonight. Certainly I shouldn't be talking about my problems when you've got a big one of your own to deal with. But—but I can't play it both ways. I can't go on acting a priest's role without taking full responsibility for what I do. You're my friend, you always will be. I'm grateful for the way you've helped me—and I know what you gambled for my sake when I was too proud to seek help—but I'm not a candidate any more, not even a trainee. You can decide what's best for Lianne, but not for me. Not any longer."

For a time Stefred was silent. Then he said, barely audibly. "Do you mean that, Noren? You're willing to go counter to my advice in this?"

"Yes. I'm sorry if I've hurt you—I never wanted to. It—it just didn't come out the way I meant it to." Like so much else, he thought in misery. Stefred's friendship had been the one firm thing left to count on.

With evident effort, Stefred smiled. "You haven't hurt me," he said. "Did you imagine I'd think less of you for having a mind of your own? It's what we demand of heretics in the first place, after all."

"Oh, of course you wanted me to stand out against you while you seemed to be supporting injustice. But—"

"But it's harder to do when you're aware my job's to support *you*."

"This isn't just a matter of pride, this time."

"No. It's more a matter of growth."

Startled, Noren felt his face redden. "What a fool I've been," he murmured. "You've known that it is, all along."

"Well, I've known you're a promising innovator."

"For the Star's sake, are we back to that?" exclaimed Noren impatiently. "That's part of the trouble; I'm sick of hearing about my so-called promise! I'm sick of having everyone expect something of me that I'll never be able to deliver. I know you think I'll achieve great things someday, but I just can't take your word for it."

"I realize you can't," Stefred admitted sadly. "That's part of the pattern; one sign of your promise is your inability to take anyone's word for something you've reached the point of doubting."

"That's the same thing you see in Lianne," Noren observed.

"One of the things, yes."

"Then you're manipulating me again, and I'm letting you! It's why you've told me as much about her reaction to the dreams as you have; you knew I'd see the comparison—"

"No!" Stefred burst out, wrenching his chair around to face Noren directly. "By the Star, Noren, I never anticipated this. It didn't occur to me it could help till you proposed it yourself. Eventually, yes; we both knew you'd choose it eventually—you're too much like him not to want awareness of all he went through. But no wish of mine led you to suggest it now, not—not unless you can read my mind."

"You do think it may help me, then."

"I don't presume to judge; you've taken the decision into your own hands." At Noren's look he added, "I guess that sounded sarcastic. Forgive me; I'm slow tonight. As you said, we're both under strain. I honestly don't know if it will help you. My thought was—elsewhere."

On Lianne, yes, as it should be. "I'd better go," Noren said.

As he reached the door, Stefred stood up. "Noren…wait," he said softly.

"I've already said more than enough I'm sorry for."

"You've changed your mind?"

"About the full version of the dreams? No, of course not, but I shouldn't have bothered you with it. I'll sign up for the first open time slot on the regular schedule sheet."

"They're not like library recordings. They have to be monitored."

"Oh, come on, Stefred—they won't send me into physical shock or anything. Not at this stage."

"I trust not. Nevertheless monitoring's standard procedure. Does that alter your enthusiasm?" Restlessly, Stefred paced back and forth between the desk and the window, his indecision more evident than ever.

"What it alters," said Noren sharply, "is my optimism about how soon my theoretical right of access is going to take effect. You can always give me a medical disqualification, and since you're the only one in the City qualified to monitor controlled dreaming—"

"Don't reproach me for a circumstance I've spent the past two nights regretting," said Stefred wearily. "Just sit down again and listen."

Noren sat. "Since I can't read your mind," he said, "I think it's time you told me what's going on in it."

With resignation, as if conceding defeat in some inner battle, Stefred said, "There's one way I could help Lianne, a way I've not let myself consider. If I could use the full recording—"

"You'd waive the requirement that she can't know in advance what recantation will lead to?" exclaimed Noren, astonished. Stefred wasn't one to go by the rule book, but to violate that particular policy would be unthinkable. The key to the succession was that Scholar rank could be attained only by those who did not want it, who most certainly would not accept it as payment for submission to necessary evils. "It would be self-defeating, if you want my opinion," he went on. "She'll never recant if she knows what she stands to gain; none of the rest of us would have."

"The recording could be re-edited, the secret parts taken out."

"If that's feasible, why haven't you done it?" asked Noren in bewilderment.

"Because as you say, I'm the only person in the City qualified to monitor controlled dreaming at all, let alone the form of monitoring used in the editing process." He met Noren's eyes for the first time since the dreams had been mentioned. "Did you think I could sit down at a computer console and push keys, as if I were editing a study disc? The computers can't read thought recordings, you know—they've got to be processed by sleeping human minds."

Abruptly, Noren understood. "You need a volunteer to work with."

"Unfortunately, yes. I'd prefer to take the dreamer's role myself."

"That would be a waste of machine time," said Noren, keeping his voice light, "considering that I'm going through those dreams as soon as possible anyway."

"I suppose you are," Stefred said, his voice low, "and I can't deny that I'm tempted to take advantage of that. I—I did manipulate you, perhaps. Not purposely, and not by plan, yet I won't pretend I didn't know underneath that you'd force my hand if I argued."

"You also knew all that argument wasn't necessary. If you'd explained what was at stake in the first place—"

"If I'd done that, I wouldn't have been sure you wanted this experience for its own sake. And I couldn't weigh her welfare against yours."

"Then you're slipping," Noren said. "I'm a priest—and she is a prisoner in our hands. There's no question about whose welfare comes first; any one of us would offer, wouldn't we?"

"But I couldn't use just anyone, and the very things that make you a suitable subject will make it more grueling for you than for others."

"What things?" asked Noren, beginning to realize that he was not quite sure what he'd volunteered for.

"Your likeness to the First Scholar—and your willingness to reach for his entire thought. I couldn't rely on someone whose mind would retreat from the rough parts; there'd be danger of missing something significant."

"I don't understand the technique," Noren admitted. "I thought the monitors showed only physiological responses. Is there a way they can indicate content, too?"

"Not directly. It has to be done with hypnotic suggestion—in this case, commands to respond physiologically in some unmistakable way whenever a thought we must delete comes into your mind. You'll be unconscious, of course; you won't feel anything."

"You—you stop each time?"

"The master recording? Not with this kind of material; to keep stopping and starting would drive you insane. No, it's possible to synchronize the timing so that I can make the actual edited copy later, by feeding small sections into my own mind while I'm awake, as if I were working with a recording of my own thoughts, or with something briefer and less emotional." He smiled, seeming more like himself, like the Stefred in whom it was impossible to lack confidence. "It's a safe procedure; that much I can promise."

"I'm not worried."

"That's because you know little of what's involved. Under some conditions such hypnosis can be extremely dangerous; I wouldn't dare to try it on a person whose mind I hadn't previously explored—which rules out older Scholars originally examined by my predecessor. You, however, I know. Your peril lies not in what I'm going to do to you, but in your reaction to the dreams themselves."

"That's a chance I have to take," Noren said firmly.

"You realize this must be begun now, tonight, and the whole series must be completed in quick succession without proper rest breaks?"

Noren nodded. They could afford no delay; having once started the dreams, a candidate could not be permitted long conscious intervals in which to notice discrepancies caused by the necessary omission of the secrets, nor could she be kept under sedation indefinitely.

"You aren't in fit shape for it," Stefred said unhappily. "Only this morning you held rites for your wife—"

I killed my wife, Noren thought, *and if I can do anything toward salvaging some other woman's future, that may help even the score.* Aloud he said, "If I back out now, how will I feel if Lianne is lost to us? If I must see her isolated, knowing I might have prevented it? Will that heal me, Stefred?"

"It's too late for either of us to back out," Stefred conceded. Silhouetted against the window, his face in shadow, he went on, "You're right, I'm slipping—but I'm human; I saw you suffer last year in a way I don't want to see again. I staked my conscience and my career on my conviction that you'd take no harm from it, and my belief in you was justified. You took not harm, but strength. I know perfectly well that if you run into problems with this, the same thing will happen. You've always been strong. You'll withstand it."

"I should hope I'll withstand it as well as an uninitiated village woman," replied Noren, indignant. But he was aware that sorrow and exhaustion had made him reckless, that if he were not already half dreaming, he would be afraid.

He came to his senses in the Dream Machine's small cubicle. When he opened his eyes, he could see at first only the pattern of dials, switches and colored lights that covered its walls. He was still reclining, and became aware that electrodes were taped not only to his head but to other parts of his body. Dimly, he recalled Stefred's telling him to remove his tunic before beginning the ritual of hypnotic sedation that, during his time in the City, had become familiar to him. Stefred bent over him now, the concern in his manner all too plain.

"Is it over?" Noren asked. "I—I don't remember anything!"

"It hasn't started yet." Stefred sat on a stool close to the reclining chair, his eyes on Noren's. "I had to wake you; there's something troubling you that you haven't told me about."

"What makes you think so?"

"I did some routine checking in preparation for giving you hypnotic commands and found evidence of psychological trauma that's never been there before. It's too risky for me to proceed without understanding it, yet I'm not willing to probe your mind without your permission."

"What sort of evidence?" Noren asked slowly.

"Basically, Noren, you respect yourself," Stefred said. "You've never felt guilty about being *you,* or about not seeing things just as other people do. That's one of the things we go into quite deeply with heretics; the self-confidence that results in defiance of conventions has to be genuine. Yours was extraordinarily so. Now it is—shaken."

"Well, after what happened last year—"

"I know you doubted yourself then. But it was never a deep-seated doubt; though it caused you pain, what lay underneath was more powerful than your conscious feelings. That was how I knew you'd come through. What I find now is a bit more serious." Sighing, he declared, "You have the right of privacy, but not the right to force me to work in unknown territory. I must have your consent to probe, or we call this off."

Noren turned his face aside. "It's nothing so complicated," he said. "I'd rather not talk about it, but if you really need to know, I'll tell you outright. I guess it's true I don't respect myself much now; I guess I never will, because I—I killed Talyra."

Stefred shook his head. "To feel guilt after the death of a loved one is a normal thing. Especially when a man's wife dies in childbirth, he can't help thinking he's partly to blame. I would be much surprised if I found no such feelings in you. What I do find is more than that. It's as if you are torn by a belief that you've done some real and avoidable wrong."

"Oh, it's real enough. I did kill her, Stefred. Not just by getting her pregnant—by getting her into a situation that caused genetic damage to the child."

"You know better than that," said Stefred, surprised. "You've been tested; your reproductive cells are undamaged. She drank far less unpurified water than you've drunk, and anyway, the mutation doesn't kill."

"I've been through all this with the computers! There's a lot of information no one ever talks about. Isn't it in the dreams?"

"These dreams? I'm not sure what you mean."

Briefly, Noren summarized what he had learned. "The Founders knew, they must have," he concluded. "I thought you did too, that it was why you were afraid I could get hurt by knowing all the First Scholar's thoughts."

For a long time Stefred was silent. "No," he said finally, "no, the First Scholar didn't record any thoughts about mutation beyond the basic facts in the edited recordings. That does seem strange, now that you raise the issue—you're right that he must have known much more. As to this teratogenic damage, the danger's never occurred to anyone. There's nothing edible here that could cause it, after all."

No, thought Noren, nothing to eat but products of caged fowl and grain grown in machine-treated fields; nothing to drink but tea and ale, both of which were, of course, made with purified water. And the few drugs kept for emergencies had rarely been used on anyone who happened to be pregnant.

"Even if the child did suffer such damage," Stefred went on, "you've no cause to assume that was the reason Talyra herself died."

"But it might have been. Could my knowing this account for what you found in my mind?"

"Yes, it could. Guilt based on rational grounds, as if, for instance, she'd died in the crash of the aircar—there are people who wouldn't feel to blame, but you're not one of them." He sighed and continued soberly, "I won't try to tell you that because you meant no harm, had no way of predicting any harm, it shouldn't bother you; that's unrealistic. It does bother you. I—I haven't an answer for you, Noren."

"Well, I didn't expect you would have," Noren said, relieved that Stefred hadn't attempted to offer empty consolation. "That's why I wasn't going to mention it. Can we go on, now?"

"I'm not sure. With a trauma I can't remove, a relevant one—"

"Relevant? The First Scholar had no part in his wife's death."

"No," Stefred agreed. "Not in that—but there are some perplexing feelings in these dreams, guilt feelings that are quite strong; and you see, Noren, I can't give you hypnotic suggestions to remain detached from them. That would set up a conflict your subconscious mind couldn't resolve."

"Guilt—in the First Scholar's thoughts? Besides the guilt he acknowledged about sealing the City and establishing the caste system?" Noren was incredulous. "Surely he never did anything else bad enough to suffer over."

"Hard as it is to believe, he seems to have—we don't know what. You realize that what we call the full version isn't actually unedited; he did some editing himself to remove private things. The cause of his submerged suffering is one of the things he deleted."

"But he wouldn't—I mean, he wasn't self-righteous; if he'd done anything he was sorry for, he wouldn't hide it," Noren protested. "And if he did want to hide it, why didn't he remove all record of his emotions about it at the same time?"

"Those are questions no one has ever been able to answer. After he died, the Founders wondered, too. Even his contemporaries couldn't believe he'd had grounds for the feelings in these recordings." Stefred frowned. "Nevertheless, they are there. Which means, Noren, that when you experience them, you'll transfer them to your own situation—not getting a cause from his mind, you'll draw it from your own, just as you'll still see Talyra's face instead of his wife's."

"If that's true," Noren said, "then there's no way around it. I can't live my whole life without going through these dreams—you said a while ago we both know I've got to do it eventually."

"Yes. But if you've chosen to undertake it now because of a hope that you'll gain more understanding of genetic damage, I can't let you proceed on that basis. Though people do draw different things from the recordings, that's too big an area for all of us to have missed."

"Which in itself is a mystery I can't back away from. Besides this guilt you say he felt...there are two ways to look at it. He came to terms with that, too, evidently."

"You're wise beyond your years," Stefred murmured. "I can't contradict you—just so you realize that the real thing won't be as easy to deal with as the theory."

"Is it ever? Look, Stefred, I hope you don't think I'm so stupid as not to feel any fear of this, especially if we're going straight through to—to the end." Lying back against the padding of the chair, relaxing his body only by effort of will, Noren could not suppress the chill spreading through him; the end—the facing of the mob, the pain of the wounds, the dying—was very hard.

"Actually, the danger in the last dream is negligible for you now," Stefred told him, "far less than during your first subjection to it, when you were less mature and when you had no foreknowledge of the outcome. We'll go right on through, though of course I'll monitor for your safety as well as for the editing." He turned to check a panel of dials; as he did so, Noren caught sight of motion in the doorway to the corridor.

A woman stood there, dressed in the beige tunic and trousers all Inner City people wore, yet looking somehow strange in them. She was too tall, for one thing; her skin was too pale; and her hair...

"I woke," she said simply. "So I thought it must be time to go on. Probably I should not have come here—but then, my door wasn't locked, and I suppose you're not surprised if a heretic doesn't stick to the rules of proper behavior."

Noren stared. Cool, self-composed, strong—yes, she was all that, and more. He had never seen a woman with so much poise. Nor had he seen one with piercing blue eyes and hair near-white in youth…

Her hair! That was what was wrong—her hair had already been cut short. Stefred had not mentioned that; but of course he wouldn't have, for the indignities she'd suffered before entering the City need never be generally known. The cropping of one's hair was among the humiliations to which one submitted voluntarily on the day of one's public recantation; short hair was therefore common, and in no way mortifying, among young Scholars. No one who'd not seen her during her candidacy would suspect that Lianne had borne such a badge of shame beforehand.

How had it happened? The High Law stated specifically that convicted heretics must be turned over to the Scholars unharmed; no village official would have dared to cut this woman's hair after her trial. Only earlier, during the night in jail, perhaps, as the best friend of his childhood had been murdered by an enraged mob, as he himself, while in bonds, had been beaten senseless by drunken bullies—but even they had not gone so far as to crop his hair. If that had been done to Lianne, what more had she undergone? Had she hidden the rest from Stefred, unable to speak of it, not yet guessing, of course, the depth of understanding and compassion he would ultimately offer her? How painful it must have been for him to put her through an inquisition harsh enough to buoy her self-esteem.

Whatever he'd done, it had been successful. Despite the shorn curls, she held her head high, as if she were already on the platform outside the Gates, already grasping the symbolic significance of that ritual exposure to an abusive crowd. Small wonder he considered her promising.

Only a moment had passed since she'd spoken; Stefred, his back to the doorway, had not seen her enter. As he swung around, startled, Noren glimpsed his eyes, and for an instant there was more in them than professional concern. *Of course,* Noren thought. *She's a match for him, certainly!* And then, *No wonder he feared his decision to let me do this wasn't objective enough.*

He hoped fervently that Lianne wouldn't choose a suitor before Stefred was free to seek her love.

She stepped forward into the cubicle. “It was stupid of me not to realize that I must wait my turn,” she said. Then, to Noren, “Are you a heretic, too?”

He could not give her any clue, of course; he said shortly, “I’m a Scholar.”

“But you’re as afraid as I am!” Her blue eyes penetrated him. Then suddenly she lowered them, regretting, apparently, that she’d revealed such intuition of his thought.

“It’s frightening for everyone, sometimes,” Noren told her. “Still we choose to dream.”

“To learn, as I’m learning?”

“Yes—or to reach beyond what can be learned.” He had not expressed this even to Stefred; he was not quite sure that it made sense.

Lianne’s eyes met his again. “You’re afraid of something past what will happen in the dreams,” she declared, as if her mind and his could somehow touch.

“Of what will happen in the world, perhaps.”

She said softly, with soberness that was not fear, “I think you and I have much in common.”

“We both have ordeals ahead,” he agreed.

“May the spirit of the Star be with you in yours.” The conventional words, as she spoke them, sounded rehearsed and yet deeply sincere; it was odd, he thought, that a heretic not yet fully enlightened could impart so much meaning to them. Noren was still wondering at it when Stefred took his hand, and at his silent nod of assent, put him into deep trance. Afterward, Lianne’s voice was the last he remembered hearing.

Chapter Three

The nightmare was unlike anything one might imagine; he knew of no words that could convey its content. There were no thoughts: not his, not the First Scholar's, not anyone's. There was only horror and revulsion. This horror...nameless, shapeless...was part of him, or he of it; the scope of it had no boundaries. He knew it not from sight or sound but as pure emotion. It was as if he'd fallen into another dimension...no, as if he'd created such a dimension and had been trapped there. Its evil was of his own making, yet he'd meant no evil; he had tried to achieve something good. He must not stop trying, though he knew he would be punished for it by this unbearable deprivation of all rational connection to the universe he knew, to the form of life he knew...

There were no concrete images in the nightmare itself, but just before waking he saw the mutant—not an adult mutant such as he'd killed in the mountains, but a hideous mutant child. Its body was like that of a human child just able to walk, but it was not human. It was mindless. There was only emptiness behind its eyes. Noren came to himself with long gasps, not sure if he'd been sobbing or retching. *By the Star,* he thought, *not again! I can't take it again...*

Gradually his head cleared. He sat up, finding himself as always in his own quarters, his own bed, knowing that many weeks had passed since his first waking from this agony. Knowing, too, that more weeks—perhaps years—might go by before he'd be free of it, if indeed he ever would be. He wondered how long his courage would last.

It was not a recollection of anything in the controlled dreams. Those had been all right: terrible at times, of course, but also uplifting. Though he'd shared depths of the First Scholar's feelings that surpassed anything in the edited versions, the heights, too, had been correspondingly more intense. He had begun to grasp what it meant to come to terms with depression and fear that couldn't be banished, evil that was part of a world from which no escape existed. He'd felt the rising of a faith that was more than escape, and pondering it, he knew why the full version of the recording was considered worth going through. It would be a long time, he realized, before he could consciously understand all he had learned from the First Scholar.

About the controlled dreams he had no regrets, except for disappointment at the fact that they'd indeed contained no additional ideas on the subject of genetic damage. But the ensuing nightmare was another matter.

Even Stefred was puzzled. It wasn't the kind of problem he'd anticipated; and at first, during the long, deep follow-up discussions they'd had after the completion of the machine-induced dream sequence, he had said Noren had reacted remarkably well to the ordeal. There had been no signs of trouble then. Even the inexplicable guilt feelings of the First Scholar's later years—which Noren perceived less as remorse than as a grief too dark and too personal for any dreamer's comprehension—had not been unduly disturbing.

He had gone back to his own quarters, resigned to a return to study. In the days that followed, his grief for Talyra, though still painful, had gradually receded. He found himself not thinking about her until some small, sharp reminder—the sight of a Technician woman's red bead necklace, for instance—brought back a temporary wave of engulfing sorrow. He'd quelled his rage at the way of things, recalling acceptance he'd drawn from the First Scholar's mind; and once he had even presided at Vespers. He'd said the ritual phrases of hope with renewed confidence that they might, in the end, prove true.

Then the nightmare had begun.

The first time, he'd discounted it as fatigue mixed with too much ale. The second night he was more shaken, yet during the day he'd carried on and had relaxed with Brek and Beris in the evening. He'd been only a little apprehensive when he left them at bedtime; but that night, the third, had been the worst of all. After that, he'd been unable to eat, and as darkness came, he'd gone in helpless, shamefaced panic to Stefred for formal consultation.

"It's nothing to worry about," Stefred had said calmly, though his eyes were troubled. "First we'll check to see if it's my fault."

"Stefred, that's nonsense—"

"Possibly not. There shouldn't have been risk in what I did to you, but I was so tired that week I may have botched it, left you with some posthypnotic suggestion that's creating a problem. If so, I can remove it; you must let me explore, Noren."

Seeing the logic, Noren had agreed to further hypnosis, but it had solved nothing. "If a person were to have recurrent nightmares of this sort without cause, we would call him ill," Stefred said, "but in your case we know the cause. It hit you harder than I believed it could, despite all my misgivings; you're handling it better than you realize."

"But other people who go through the full version of the dreams don't react this way. Even Lianne—"

"Lianne owes a great deal to you, Noren. She has said so."

"You told her about me?" That surprised him; he did not want her assuming he'd done it for her sake when that hadn't been his main motive.

"Not specifically. After her recantation, though, when I had to explain the edited secrets, she guessed a good deal more than I'd have expected she could about why I'd finally yielded to her request for less editing of other things. Lianne's adapted to the Inner City fast, and she's remarkably good at putting two and two together."

Although she was now a Scholar, Noren had not seen Lianne often, for her work shift was at night. Surprisingly, despite obvious scientific aptitude, she had not chosen to study nuclear physics. Instead, she was working as a technical assistant in the controlled dreaming lab. Ordinary dream material, not the First Scholar's thoughts but memories other Founders had recorded of the Six Worlds, required no monitoring; those who wished to experience such dreams did so during normal sleep hours. Someone must be on duty to operate the equipment, but this was not skilled work, and the job was often given to young, new Scholars who had not yet chosen permanent vocations: those most eager to dream of the Six Worlds themselves when the Dream Machine wasn't being used for anything of higher priority.

"Why did Lianne withstand the full version better than I did, when she has so much less experience?" Noren persisted.

Stefred's look was grave, yet a little perplexed. "Perhaps because you haven't forgiven yourself for what happened to Talyra."

Noren frowned. "You said I might transfer the First Scholar's guilt to my own situation—but that's not how it is in the nightmare;

Talyra isn't in it. None of the personal things are involved. I do still feel guilty about them, but I've...accepted that."

"I know," Stefred agreed. "You acknowledge it consciously, which in theory should keep it from causing you subconscious trouble. Yet there's the image of the mutant." He continued thoughtfully, "That might have appeared anyway in your natural dreams; you and Brek are the only people living who've actually seen mutants, and now that you fear your stillborn child might have been damaged—well, we may be dealing with a separate problem. It's not the sort of thing the First Scholar's memories could have triggered in you."

"I'm sure it's not," Noren declared. Certainly there'd been no thoughts about mutants in the recording; he had been alert for them. "Besides, the focus of the nightmare is something else, something I can't put a name to, not an image at all—something I can't face because I can't even define what it is."

Stefred appraised him searchingly. "Noren, posthypnotic suggestion could free you of this nightmare, let you sleep peacefully. Do you want that kind of help?"

"No!" Noren burst out.

"Why not?"

"Because—because it wouldn't solve anything. I'd still not know *why.*"

"Given a choice, you prefer to go on suffering?"

"I—I deserve it, I guess. Or it wouldn't be happening."

Soberly, Stefred reflected, "That could be true."

"That it's punishment? Oh, Stefred, you don't really believe the spirit of the Mother Star can reach down and strike me, the way villagers would think!" No such preposterous idea was implied by official liturgy; only the villagers' corrupted notions of blasphemy endowed the Star with power to punish.

"Of course I don't," Stefred assured him. "But you are quite capable of punishing yourself; your subconscious mind can do more than you realize, and you are strong enough to take a good deal of voluntary punishment."

"You mean that's really what's happening?"

"It's one of the things that can happen. But it's not a healthy response, and with you I think the situation's more complex. You don't despise yourself enough to abandon all constructive aims for destructive ones, any more than you did last year."

"By the Star, Stefred, I *want* to do something constructive! Only I—I feel so helpless, because there's nothing to do." He remembered just in time not to mention the uselessness of his work specifically.

"You're still searching for something."

"Yes, I suppose so. It was why I insisted on the dreams...but I seem to have hit a dead end."

"I'm not so sure," Stefred said slowly. He was silent for a while, then went on. "You want to get to the bottom of this. You don't want me to stop it for you artificially—which, incidentally, I was counting on when I offered to, because suppression of such a dream might do you real harm. So we're going to have to wait and see what happens."

"You mean I've got to just—live with it?" Noren faltered. Talyra's sad voice echoed in his memory: *You simply have to live with the consequences of what you are.* She had not blamed him for being different, but she'd always felt it would doom him to suffering, and for that, she had wept.

"For the time being. I'm not callous; I know how bad it is, and I'm too much of a realist to tell you not to let it frighten you. In fact the best advice I can give you is not to fight that—fighting will only make it worse." Pressing Noren's hand, he added, "Come back to me in a week or two if the nightmare doesn't stop; there are some other things I can do if necessary."

It had not stopped. It hadn't come every night, but Noren had learned to fear sleep. At first he'd thrown himself into his work in the daytime; that was a strategy that had brought him through bad times before. It was no longer one that worked. He found it wholly impossible to fix his mind on the mathematical problems he had once found engrossing. The image of the mutant child haunted him, looming between the study screen and his eyes.

One day in desperation, unable to work, unable to face Brek's well-meant solicitude or to confess that he had not eaten, he'd hidden in the computer room. Idly, without conscious plan, he had asked, IS THERE A TRAINING PROGRAM IN GENETICS? The computers were programmed to give systematic training in sciences relevant to the Scholars' work, training designed to enable young people with no schooling beyond that offered in the villages—the mere rudiments of reading, writing and arithmetic—to rapidly master material that on the Six Worlds would have required years to absorb. It was done through individually generated study discs, intensive quizzing, and memorization of details under hypnosis: a fast-paced, demanding process, yet enjoyable if one wished to learn. Noren had been through such programs in math, physics and chemistry; he knew there were certain others, but he did not expect genetics to be among them. Surprisingly, it was.

Feeling uncomfortable about so blatant a departure from the job to which he was committed, he told himself that a short break could do no harm; he was only going through the motions with regard to nuclear physics anyhow. He embarked on the genetics program—and soon found why the Founders had provided it for the benefit of posterity. No one could possibly be expected to assemble such a program from scratch after fulfillment of the Prophecy, for no non-specialist would be able to ask the right questions. The basic vocabulary and concepts alone took him days to acquire even with hypnotic aid. He had not known what genetics involved; he'd assumed it just had something to do with reproduction and biological inheritance. He hadn't imagined every cell in every organism's body was continuously controlled by the interactions of countless genes. In fact he'd had no real idea of what a gene was. That it consisted of a chemical code so complex as to demand computer analysis amazed and fascinated him. No wonder the First Scholar's memories contained no details about genetics. They contained no details about the mathematics of nuclear reactions, either.

The short break from physics stretched on, week after week. Noren's days became bearable; often they extended from one to the next—it was a good excuse for not sleeping. It was customary for Scholars pursuing specific training programs to work far into the night. Among the young initiates, this was viewed as a game, a challenge. To force one's mind to the point of exhaustion was a gesture of protest against living a life one had looked upon as privileged. Noren was past that stage. He'd long since learned that the so-called "privilege" of Scholar rank entailed hardship and deprivation beyond the imagination of the relatively prosperous villagers. But his long hours in the computer room were not thought strange; even Brek accepted a new study program as a legitimate retreat from grief. That it was also a retreat from terror, Noren confided to no one.

Now, however, waking again from the nightmare, he knew that he could retreat no more. He'd completed the formal training sequence and had reached the point where in other sciences one could progress further only with the aid of a tutor. No one was qualified to tutor him in genetics—he himself already knew more about it than anyone had learned for generations. In any case, what a tutor did was to introduce trainees to applications of the knowledge they'd acquired. Genetics had no applications, not in this world, anyway.

On the Six Worlds, which had had a tremendous variety of plant and animal life, genetic engineering had been used for agriculture—it had been, during the last centuries of the civilization's existence, a major weapon in the battle against hunger. The Six Worlds had been overpopulated and short of food. Genetic alteration of crops and livestock had increased the supply. But there was no food shortage on this alien planet, and no edible life forms either, other than the few imported ones already fully utilized. No genetic alteration of native life forms could overcome the fact that they were based on alien, damaging chemistry, incompatible with human life. That was the reason human life wasn't going to be possible after the irreplaceable soil and water purification equipment gave out…

Everything led back to that one inescapable fact.

Noren, sitting on the side of his bunk, found himself literally, physically sick—sick from fatigue, from frustration, from terror and despair. He had honestly tried to act constructively. He'd put fear out of his mind while learning, and what he'd learned was *important*—all preserved knowledge was important, it all reflected the Six Worlds' rise. The Six Worlds' people, his people, had penetrated so far into the mysteries of the universe…how much further might they have gone? It was too late, now. He had learned something worth learning, but he could not pass it on. Someday he would die. Eventually his whole species would die—not in some dim, unforeseeable future, but by a known date, not many generations ahead. All the effort would prove useless. He'd learned a whole new complex of ideas, ideas that should be exciting, and they could be of no use whatsoever. He felt worse despair than that with which he'd begun.

The First Scholar had felt despair too; by sharing it in the dreams, one was supposed to learn the way out. One suffered, but one got past that. In real life, Noren realized suddenly, he wasn't going to get past it. The way out was through action. The First Scholar's life had been full of action: hard action, action sometimes justifiable only as the lesser of evils, yet action he believed would save his people. He had not faced a situation where the more knowledge he gained, the more clearly he saw that no such action was open to him. *It's no wonder,* Noren thought, *that I feel trapped in the nightmare…*

He reached for the washbasin, a white plastic basin since, without metal for pump parts, adequate plumbing was a luxury the City's towers did without. His sickness was no mere feeling. He hadn't thought he had eaten enough to be so sick; perhaps the cup of tea he'd forced down had been a mistake.

At length, when he was able to stand, he mustered his courage and returned to Stefred, knowing that no alternative remained.

He consented to deep probing not only under hypnosis, but under drugs. A time came when he found himself conscious; Stefred was saying to him, "I'd like to monitor the nightmare itself, Noren."

"I'm not sure I can go to sleep. I'm not even tired any more." Saying this, Noren realized he'd undergone prolonged sedation.

"I can induce it, if you'll let me. It can't be done against your will."

Thinking that it had happened against his will all too many times, but ashamed to admit he did not feel he could endure it one time more, Noren agreed. The session was grueling despite Stefred's calm support, and he came to himself shivering, soaked with sweat.

"What's wrong with me?" he murmured, for the first time dreading the relentless honesty on which his trust in Stefred was founded. "I could always cope before. Even during my first days at the outpost, when I'd panicked in space and thought I was losing my sanity, I *didn't* lose it—"

"That thought's what scares you most," Stefred observed, "much more than the nightmare does."

"Yes," Noren confessed in a low voice. He had never seen insanity, but he'd learned enough from the computers to know it existed. "They told us when we were little, in the village, that we'd turn into idiots if we drank impure water," he reflected. "I laughed then because I didn't believe it. And now, of course, I know better, I know it can't happen that way to me. I even know it wasn't just like that with my child—" This was true; he had learned from his study of genetics that Talyra's baby could not have been like the mutants after all. It had perhaps suffered teratogenic damage, but not the same sort of damage that had produced the subhuman creatures in the mountains.

"Is the child in the nightmare some kind of symbol not only of what did happen, but of what I'm afraid is happening to my mind?" he continued. "Things are so…so mixed up…but all tied together somehow. The First Scholar's feelings, too! When I'm awake, I remember his good feelings; why do only bad ones, indescribable ones, come in my sleep?"

"This is hard to say to you," Stefred admitted, "but I don't know. And I've no means of finding out."

"You can't cure me?" whispered Noren, appalled. He had not wanted to seek help, but he'd never doubted Stefred's ability to provide it.

"There's nothing to cure, Noren. You are not sick; you've in no way lost touch with reality. Difficult though it is for you to accept my estimation of you, I am professionally qualified to diagnose mental illness." He smiled, though it was obviously an effort for him. "If you can't take my word, you're accusing me either of incompetence or of dishonesty."

Noren raised his head. Put that way, the judgment was indisputable. "You're telling me the nightmare may not stop," he said shakily.

"I wish I could tell you otherwise." replied Stefred gently. "But you want the truth, and the truth is that we're faced with something beyond my skill to analyze. Your sanity is not in question, and the monitoring has shown that the nightmare's harmless to you. That's as far as I'm able to see; you will have to find your own way."

"I'm willing to try," Noren said, "but I—I don't think I'm equal to it."

"With that, I'm on firmer ground," said Stefred, his smile genuine now. "There are ways of proving to you that you are. At least there would be if you were a candidate and still afraid of me so that I could demonstrate how much you can endure of your own free will."

"But this isn't like what you do to candidates; no one could bear it voluntarily—"

"No? Suppose when you'd come to me as a heretic, convinced that my aim was to pressure you into submission, I had induced such terror in you—I could, you know—and demanded your recantation as the price of freeing you of it. Would you have knelt to me and begged my mercy?"

"Well, of course not," declared Noren. "What a silly question, Stefred."

"To you, it is. To someone to whom it wasn't, I would never pose it."

"I see your point," Noren conceded. "Why doesn't it make me feel any better?"

"Because you don't yet see that you're in a comparable situation." Seriously, Stefred went on, "Noren, the mind is strange, and there's much about it we can't comprehend. Of this much I'm sure, though: what is happening to you is happening by your own inner choice. Strength, not weakness, has brought the ordeal upon you."

"I don't understand."

"I've told you in the past," Stefred reminded him, "that a strong person can open his mind to things a weaker one wouldn't be willing to confront. The subconscious mind gives you whatever protection you need—there are psychoses and drugs that can circumvent that, but in you I find no trace of interference with normal functioning. Therefore you are experiencing something you're able to handle and that is in some way purposeful."

"But what constructive purpose could it serve?"

"That, I can't answer."

"I suppose the fact that it's unpleasant doesn't rule out inner choice," Noren said slowly. "After all, we do suffer voluntarily when we reach out in the controlled dreams. You know, what you said about Lianne, when she was being subjected to the candidates' version of the recordings…it—it's a little like that, I think. As if I'm trapped by intolerable limits, reaching for something that isn't there. In the nightmare it's always just beyond the edge, where I can't touch it. Is that a reasonable analogy?"

Stefred leaned forward. "It could be more than analogy," he said, his voice edged with excitement. "Think: did you feel this at all in the controlled dreams?"

"Well, I was definitely reaching for something I didn't find. Only the rest was so overwhelming that I didn't mind much, any more than I minded the limits of the candidates' version when I was younger."

"We don't understand just how controlled dreaming works," Stefred mused. "We're sure only that the dreamer has a certain degree of freedom. The more courage you have to reach out, the more you gain—"

"You told me that the very first time I was subjected to it," Noren recalled.

"Yes. You've always had that kind of courage—from your earliest childhood you've sought knowledge, and even from the first dream you took more than was forced on you. And your identification with the First Scholar is exceptionally strong. I can't guess what you drew from the full version of his thoughts—but conceivably, it was more than the rest of us have gotten. We've always known the editing he did for privacy left gaps we can't fill."

"Could that cause nightmares, the way the gaps in the partial recording were agony for Lianne?"

"Yes," said Stefred thoughtfully. "Yes, it could. The unanswerable questions he pondered aren't disturbing you, not in the sense of giving you nightmares, anyway. But something he *knew,* yet deleted...if it was an emotional thing, a significant one—"

"But why would he delete anything significant? His goal was to pass on all his knowledge; surely he took out only personal details that were no one's business but his own."

"That's the puzzle," Stefred agreed. "He wouldn't have removed anything his successors would care about. And he was skilled in the editing process; he wouldn't have left gaps that could cause a dreamer to suffer."

"I wonder. He wouldn't have left any that would cause harm—but you say that what's happening to me is not harmful. You say I've chosen to experience more than was forced on me. He made a lot of plans that depend on people being willing to do that."

"For fulfilling the Prophecy, yes—but we know those plans."

True, thought Noren, and yet..."What if I were to stop shrinking from the nightmare, enter it as I would a controlled dream?" he asked.

"That would be a very wise approach," Stefred answered soberly, "but I can't tell you where it would lead. Noren, if you have taken something unprecedented from the First Scholar's memories, you are already past the point where I can counsel you." He smiled and added, "But then, I've always believed you'll move beyond me one way or another in time."

Of course, as the world's most promising nuclear physicist, Noren thought bitterly—but on the verge of an exasperated reply, he became aware that Stefred was no longer trying to reassure him. On the contrary, he had just presented him with the most frightening challenge of all.

Lying sleepless, Noren courted nightmare, wishing with full sincerity that it would overtake him. Seldom had it come, lately, and when it had, he'd been able to draw nothing more from it. Though it was still acutely painful, he no longer found it terrifying, for he was increasingly convinced that its emotions had originated not with him but with the First Scholar—and it was something he wanted desperately to understand.

Stefred had been speculating about direct transfer from a recorder's subconscious mind to a dreamer's; he had reread all the information in the computers about the thought recording process and had even reexperienced the First Scholar's recordings himself in the hope that he'd get from them whatever Noren had gotten. That hadn't happened. Noren, embarrassed, realized that now more than ever, Stefred regarded him as having some special rapport with the First Scholar that set him apart from everyone else. He was torn; he did not want such a position—yet could Stefred conceivably be right? Was there something buried in his mind, perhaps, which could explain why he felt unlike other people, even the people who shared his concern for knowledge, the Scholars with whom he'd once thought he wouldn't be a misfit?

He had been a misfit as a boy in the village. He'd never gotten on well with his father and brothers, who had not cared about any of the things that mattered to him. Once he had despised them, as he'd despised the village life they had found satisfying. He was no longer so callous; for all their rough ways, they had been honest men who'd worked hard and who would leave many descendants. He wondered sometimes what had happened to them. Did they still feel shame at his having been convicted of heresy? The severance of family ties demanded of Inner City residents had been no sacrifice for him, though for most others he knew, it was. It bothered him a little to realize that he'd had nothing to lose.

Except, of course, Talyra. And he had not lost her because of his heretical ideas after all. Ironically, he had lost her for no purpose whatsoever; and worse, she'd lost her own life...

The First Scholar had come to terms with grief. But his wife had chosen to die—chosen tragically and mistakenly, to be sure, but nevertheless she had made her own decision. Talyra hadn't. He could never reconcile himself to that! If some end had been served by it, something she would have chosen had she known...but it had achieved nothing.

He could endure his own guilt. He knew, from the dreams, that the First Scholar had lived with some terrible and mysterious horror for which he'd felt to blame, and had endured it—he could never have been at peace in the end if he had not. The end, the deathbed recording, contained no traces of any horror. There was sadness in it, and physical pain, but otherwise only hope: the exultant hope that had engendered the Prophecy. For himself, Noren thought, there would never be hope again. Talyra had died uselessly, and the things she'd believed in, the things the Prophecy said, were never going to come true in any case.

It always came back to that.

Turning over in the dark, the total darkness of a windowless room in which, for lack of metal wire, there could be no illumination when no battery-powered lamp was in use, he found himself thinking again about genetics. It was strange he could not put that out of his mind. He'd long since learned all he could about it, lacking practical applications to focus on. He had satisfied his curiosity as to the specific way in which unprocessed soil and water damaged human reproductive cells. It was an incredibly complex process requiring understanding of both chemistry and biology at the molecular level; he'd spent weeks wholly immersed in it, and even so, only the mental discipline acquired from his past study of nuclear physics had enabled him to master the concepts. He was by now, he supposed, the greatest authority on useless information who'd ever lived in the City. The greatest shirker of responsibility, too, people would say, had he not gone back to an outward pretense of devotion to the unattainable goal of metal synthesization.

Yet he could not let his new knowledge drop. He did not know why. It wasn't escape from terror any longer, nor was it still escape from the futility of his official work—for was not genetics equally futile?

How frustrating that he couldn't justify devoting more time to it. He would like to experiment. He might genetically modify some native plant to grow in treated soil, and that would give people relief from the monotony of a diet based on a single crop. But the cost would be too high, not only in his time, but in the time the land-treatment machines would last. A second crop would be welcomed by village farmers; they would want extra fields to grow it in. The Founders had been wise to provide only one kind of food. They had also been wise, perhaps, not to encourage even the Scholars to learn that if it were not for the limitation imposed by the machines' durability span—which had been calculated on the basis of necessary population increase—more variety would be possible.

The Founders had made just one practical use of genetic knowledge: they had developed the work-beasts. Everyone knew that, of course; even the villagers said that the work-beasts had been created by the Scholars at the time of the Founding. It was one of the notions he had scorned during his boyhood, but from the dreams of his enlightenment as a Scholar candidate, he had learned to his astonishment that it was true. Animal embryos had been brought from the Six Worlds and had been genetically altered so that they could eat native vegetation and drink from streams. They were essential to the villagers as beasts of burden as well as for hides, tallow and bone...what a pity that there wasn't a way to make the meat usable, too. But genetic alteration couldn't accomplish that. Work-beast flesh, like any creature's, contained chemical traces of the food and water that had nourished it; the High Law decreed that it must be burned or buried. You couldn't deal with the damaging substance in the soil and water by biological modification of what people consumed. The problem—the biological problem—was not in the food sources, but in people themselves...

Noren sat upright, his heart pounding. Why wasn't it possible to make biological modifications to *people?*

It was all too possible in nature. That was the trouble. The mutants were biologically changed. They ate native vegetation and drank from streams as work-beasts did; what had been accomplished with the work-beasts was called controlled mutation. It had been detrimental to their intelligence—not as seriously as in the case of the mutants descended from humans, since the beasts hadn't been very intelligent to begin with, but a similar type of brain damage had been involved. *Only it needn't have been.* He had studied the research done by the Founders, and he knew—with hindsight it had been recognized that the brain damage could have been avoided. The world had needed strong work-beasts, fast, more than it had needed smart ones. The researchers had been working against time and they had not tried to deal with the complexities of the genes that regulated brain development. Later on, they could not retrace their steps, for the inherited brain damage was irreversible.

But if that damage had been needless, if it could be averted if controlled mutation were done in the right way, why couldn't mutation in people also be controlled? Biologically, genetically, people were animals…

He fumbled for the lamp, suddenly unable to bear the darkness. He knew he would not sleep until he had discovered the answer.

There must be an answer, of course. The Founders were not stupid; they could scarcely have failed to perceive what he had just perceived. They would hardly have established a system they loathed, a caste system they knew to be evil, if there had been any alternate means of human survival—they had maintained over and over again that they would not. They'd experienced heartbreak during their decision and its implementation. The factors in the decision had been considered in full and painful detail by the First Scholar, who had suffered most agonizingly over it. Noren knew, beyond any possible question, that the First Scholar would not have done the things he did if there had been any choice. Nor would he have overlooked any conceivable future way of saving humanity from extinction.

But it was surely very strange that his recorded memories hadn't included any regret about whatever it was that precluded controlled genetic alteration of humans.

Noren pulled on his clothes, his hands shaking, and took a small lantern; it was so late that the corridor lamps had been turned off. Outside, only the lights at the tower pinnacles still burned. He strode across the courtyard to the Hall of Scholars. The computers could tell him what he needed to know. They preserved all knowledge, and the answers he now sought had once been known. They must have been.

He looked up at the dazzling tower lights and the faint stars that showed between them. Off to his left was the red-gold glow of Little Moon, now rising. *As bright as Little Moon,* said the Prophecy; the Mother Star, when it appeared in the sky, would outshine any other. He would not live to see that, but his people must...his descendants must. Talyra had been right, he knew—he must eventually have other children. He did not feel he would want love again, not for itself, but he did want to believe that his offspring would live after him. She'd understood that, and her last thought for him had been to send word that she understood.

The towers...the City...to him they had always been a symbol. Of the future. Of the knowledge he craved. Outside, as a heretic, he'd gazed at them with more longing than he could bear. Had he offered his life for conviction's sake alone, or only because without access to knowledge it had meant little to him? City confinement had been no more a hardship for him than separation from his family had. In his very arrest he'd had nothing to lose, though he'd believed himself soon to die. Had it been right to accept priesthood when he'd made no real sacrifice?

Approaching the computer room, he knew again that it had been. The essence of priesthood, for him at least, was guardianship of knowledge and extension of it—only by that means could knowledge ultimately be made free to all people. Only through its use could metal become available. Yes, that aim might fail, probably would fail; in the end everything would be lost...but the human race must die striving for life.

Suppose, just suppose, it had been possible to alter humans genetically so that the species need not die. Noren realized, with his hand poised above a console keyboard, that he did not want to crush this fantasy yet. The replies to his questions were going to crush it. But suppose that option *had* been open to the Founders—the Prophecy's promises would already have been fulfilled! He would be living in the era all Scholars wished to see. The City would long since have been thrown open, knowledge and machines would be available to everyone...

Or would they?

No! There would be no more metal than there already was. Its synthesization wouldn't have been achieved, and in fact it wouldn't need to be achieved—people wouldn't even have kept working toward it. If people could drink unpurified water and eat plants grown in untreated soil, they could survive *without* metal, *without* machines!

But the knowledge in the computers could not.

Computers depended on metal parts and on a supply of nuclear power. The knowledge in them could not be accessed without those essentials. If the power failed, if the electronically stored data could never again be retrieved, then that knowledge would be lost. The Founders had known this; it had been one of their main reasons for sealing the City, for if the knowledge were to be lost, the machines essential to survival would be lost too, along with any chance of ever obtaining the metal for more machines.

It was a circle. If it was broken, humanity would die. Yet if it had been broken in another way, a way that had enabled humans to live without the City...then the City would no longer exist. He would be living the Stone Age life of the villagers, and without metal resources, without people trained to preserve even the remnants of a metal-based technology, there would be no possibility of regaining such a technology in the future.

The universe would be closed to his race. Forever.

The accumulated knowledge of the Six Worlds would be lost forever.

And the First Scholar must have foreseen that outcome.

Numb, paralyzed, Noren closed his eyes; the room had begun to swim dizzily around him. The nightmare that had eluded him earlier was assailing him now—though he was still conscious, he began to feel the familiar horror. He no longer wanted to understand its basis. He knew he could not face such understanding. He knew what significant facts the First Scholar had edited from his memories; he wished he could edit them from his own.

He should go now, walk away from the computers, forget genetics and return to his study of physics. Life would go on, as it had gone on throughout the generations since the Founding. As it would go on for a few more after him. No one else would learn what he had learned. People would be content. The villagers and Technicians would be content because they believed the Prophecy, and the Scholars would be content because they had faith in their power to bring about the Prophecy's fulfillment. *There shall come a time of great exultation...and at that time, when the Mother Star appears in the sky, the ancient knowledge shall be free to all people, and shall be spread forth over the whole earth. And Cities shall rise beyond the Tomorrow Mountains, and shall have Power, and Machines; and the Scholars will no longer be their guardians.* Everyone believed that. Would they be happier knowing that it was false? Had he not faced exactly the same decision last year, when he'd first lost confidence in the nuclear research, and had Talyra not died because of his mistaken attempt to offer truth in place of illusion?

But it was not the same. Then, truth as he'd seen it had been a destructive truth. He could not have saved anyone by exposing the Prophecy's emptiness. He could not, by sacrificing all he personally valued, have enabled future generations to live.

Could he now?

Could the Founders have done so? The First Scholar?

They had not, certainly, been insincere in what they did. Their suffering had been real. They had made a choice, a hard one, too hard to impose on their successors, and they had made it for humanity's benefit. They had chosen a relatively short era of social evil to attain a long era of future advance, evidently. He did not have to judge whether they'd been right or wrong; the option was no longer open. For him, knowing that synthesization of metal had been proven impossible, the choice was simply between preservation of knowledge and a chance for permanent preservation of life...if in fact there was now any choice at all.

He had better start finding out, Noren told himself grimly. If he left the computers without knowing, he might lack the courage to come again.

Afterward, he did not remember his whole line of questioning. He was dazed and couldn't be sure which of his words triggered a long-hidden branch in the control program. For a time, quite a long time, he was conversing normally; then all of a sudden he found himself waiting, the light at the top of his console glowing orange, as auxiliary memory was searched.

A wait in itself was not unusual; information about subjects not of immediate concern to the world was kept in auxiliary storage to be called up only on request. The computer complex, he'd been told, was not really well designed for its role as a central library. It had been put together from the separate smaller computer systems of the dismantled ships of the starfleet, a task the Founders had accomplished under the extreme handicap of having no unit with adequate capacity for a central server and no materials or equipment for the manufacture of extra parts. The resulting system was therefore inefficient and slow by Six Worlds' standards. It was no great problem; rarely did anyone need data such as he'd just requested. Yet he had already waited once upon his initial request for the genetics file, which he'd supposed was a single entity...evidently, that wasn't the case.

There had been a contingency plan, then. The Founders had not burned their bridges; they had known metal synthesization might fail. He was, he supposed, going to be given specific instruction in the process of modifying human genes. How excited he'd have been if this had happened earlier tonight, before he'd perceived the implications! He wondered if the program would spell them out. Probably not, he thought bitterly; no doubt the Founders hoped the implementer of the contingency plan would work as an unwitting tool. So much for the sacred principle of access to knowledge for the priesthood, and the even more sacred one of equal share in the burdens...

That was what hurt worst, Noren saw. He had never wanted to be a priest, but he had come to feel it was wrong to refuse the responsibility. He had become convinced that the priests' worldview was genuine, that the role involved no sham or delusion. Now it seemed that the whole edifice had been built on sham after all. When in recantation, one went through symbolic reenactment of the First Scholar's death, one believed one had shared the full burden of the Founders' moral dilemma—but if they had made the hardest choice of all and then hidden the fact that such choice existed, their successors had been duped! The Scholars were all tools. Right from the beginning it had been that way. How could the First Scholar have been a party to that? How could he have founded a religion on such a basis, a religion he'd believed valid? In the dreams he *had* believed; those feelings couldn't have been faked...

Words appeared on the console screen. YOU HAVE ASKED QUESTIONS THAT PROVE YOU ARE NOT OF THE FIRST GENERATION. HOW MANY PLANET YEARS HAVE PASSED SINCE THE ARRIVAL OF THE FINAL EXPEDITION?

But the computer knew that! thought Noren in amazement. It was the computer that had kept track of the time since the Founding; the Scholars relied on its internal clock. *It* told *them,* not the other way around. Odd, too, that the word "Founding" had not been used in the question. "The final expedition" was an obsolete phrase, one he knew only because the First Scholar had used it in the dreams.

He was not a trained programmer, but he'd learned enough since becoming a Scholar to realize that the normal executive program was no longer operating; the information he was to receive had been so well protected that it was not to be processed by the integrated system at all. Some vestige of a first-generation master routine had assumed control. Slowly he keyed in the requested number of years.

HAS METAL YET BEEN SYNTHESIZED? the program asked.

NO. THAT IS NOW KNOWN TO BE IMPOSSIBLE. He might not be given the full truth unless he made clear from the outset that there was no remaining hope in the original plan.

YOUR INQUIRIES CONCERN GENETICS. HAVE YOU COMPLETED THE TRAINING PROGRAM IN THAT SCIENCE?

YES.

YOU MUST BE EXAMINED WITH REGARD TO YOUR READINESS TO RECEIVE FURTHER INFORMATION. THE TEST IS EXTREMELY DIFFICULT AND WILL REQUIRE SEVERAL HOURS. ARE YOU WILLING TO UNDERTAKE IT NOW?

YES, replied Noren. He was a fool, probably; the night was far gone and he was giddy with fatigue and emotion. Common sense told him that he would do better on such a test if he took it when fresh. But having come this far, he could not back away.

He had been tested many times before by the computer system, though never as a prerequisite to obtaining answers to his questions. Usually information was simply presented—if one couldn't understand it, one had to study up on background material and then ask again. Testing was reserved for the formal training programs, and it was made very arduous. One was pushed to the limits of one's individual capacity and a little beyond; computer programs excelled at that. Noren had learned not to mind it. Once he'd discovered that tolerance of one's failures was a carefully calculated factor in the scoring, he had even learned to enjoy the challenge. But no previous test had come close to the one to which he was now subjected.

At first it was simply a matter of understanding basic concepts of genetics, not too different from the tests in the training program he'd recently completed. Then, when he thought he was nearing the end, a new phase began. It turned into a fast-response exercise. This was similar to the computer game in which, as a new Scholar, he'd been trained in the mental discipline needed for advanced study. He knew how to deal with it. He was aware that he was not expected to respond within the allotted time to every question; the aim was to see how well he could cope with confusion. But in this case, the confusion was compounded. Not only did the questions demand thought, being full of technical details often over his head, but irrelevant inquiries were interspersed, presumably to throw him off the track. He was asked about his personal life. He was asked his opinion of various Inner City policies. Noren tried ignoring these superfluous matters, but that did not suit the testers' strategy; he found that if he neglected to respond to *any* demand, however foolish, he would be forced to restart the current series of technical problems from the beginning. And to make things even rougher, he was given no feedback whatsoever concerning his scores.

This went on literally for hours.

Eventually, when he was trembling with exhaustion, the screen cleared, and a nine-digit figure appeared upon it. MEMORIZE THIS ACCESS CODE, he was told. OTHERWISE, IF YOU SEEK INFORMATION FROM THIS FILE IN THE FUTURE, YOU WILL BE REQUIRED TO REPEAT THE TEST.

Too overcome to protest, Noren committed the digits to memory. What, for the Star's sake, was wrong with his name? The computer system kept track of everyone's test scores, but name was the only identification needed to refer to them.

UNDER NO CIRCUMSTANCES PUT THE CODE IN WRITING, the instructions continued. IT HAS BEEN RANDOMLY GENERATED AND IS RECORDED ONLY WITH YOUR TEST RESULTS. EVERY PRECAUTION MUST BE TAKEN TO ENSURE THAT WHAT I AM ABOUT TO TELL YOU IS NOT COMMUNICATED TO ANYONE I'VE HAD NO OPPORTUNITY TO JUDGE.

Noren stared incredulously. The reason for using an access code had become clear enough, but the word "I" created a greater mystery.

FORGIVE ME FOR TESTING YOU SO RIGOROUSLY, the displayed wording went on. IT WAS NECESSARY. SURVIVAL ON THIS PLANET MAY DEPEND ON MY SECRET BEING PASSED TO A PERSON WHO WILL USE IT WISELY. I DO NOT KNOW HOW THE WORLD'S CULTURE WILL CHANGE AFTER I AM GONE. I KNOW ONLY THAT I CANNOT LET THIS KNOWLEDGE PERISH, AS MY FRIENDS WOULD WISH.

Who had programmed this? The computer complex never referred to itself by personal pronouns; he was reading the words of some past Scholar who'd chosen to speak to posterity as an individual—who had, moreover, carefully chosen to whom he would speak. The Founders had not done things that way. Everything, even the separate control routine, indicated that the file had been added to the system not as an official contingency plan, but secretly.

DO YOUR CONTEMPORARIES STILL HAVE HOPE OF SYNTHESIZING METAL?

YES, Noren replied. I MYSELF HAVE NONE.

IS YOUR INTEREST IN GENETICS SHARED BY OTHERS?

I HAVE TOLD THEM NOTHING OF SIGNIFICANCE. THEY THINK IT A MERE PASTIME.

YOU ARE IN A DIFFICULT POSITION, THEN, MUCH MORE DIFFICULT THAN YOU KNOW. I HAD HOPED IT WOULD BE OTHERWISE.

It gave him an uncanny feeling to see such phrasing; it was as if he were conversing with a conscious being, though he knew his responses would merely determine which of various preprogrammed statements would be presented to him. In the same way as in a programmed text, the writer had provided comments to fit differing circumstances. I HAVE GUESSED A GREAT DEAL ABOUT THE DIFFICULTIES, Noren confessed. I HAVE GUESSED WHY INFORMATION ABOUT HUMAN GENETICS WAS CONCEALED BY THE FOUNDERS.

YOUR GUESS IS UNLIKELY TO BE CORRECT, FOR IF YOU KNEW THE REASON, YOU WOULD NOT HAVE HAD TO GUESS—IT WOULD HAVE SEEMED OBVIOUS. POSSIBLY YOU THINK WE WERE UNWILLING TO LOSE THE CHANCE OF PRESERVING THE SIX WORLDS' KNOWLEDGE. DO YOU APPROVE OF CONCEALMENT FOR THAT PURPOSE?

Noren hesitated. Finally he responded, I HAVE NEVER APPROVED OF DECEIT.

THAT IS TO YOUR CREDIT. BUT YOU ARE EMBARKING ON A COURSE INVOLVING FAR MORE COMPLEX ISSUES THAN THE ONE YOU HAVE IMAGINED.

This was like what Stefred had said to him long ago, Noren recalled, during his candidacy, when he'd objected to the withholding of the truth about the nova from non-Scholars. Was it really so much worse for the Scholars themselves to have been kept in partial ignorance? No…but the Founders had *lied!* The First Scholar had lied! They had said specifically to their successors that there was *no means of human survival* apart from guardianship of the City. To be sure, the First Scholar had lied to the villagers of his own time by pretending to be an insane tyrant; he had told open falsehoods about his motives. Yet that was different. He had not led them to make moral choices on false grounds.

The programmer of this file had been very clever. By using the personal pronouns he had created an illusion that encouraged trust. Perhaps he'd been one of the Founders after all; he had said "we" at one point. There might, of course, have been a rebel among the Founders—but what basis was there for judging such a person's credibility? He, Noren, had been judged, and he saw now he had been judged on more than his knowledge of genetics; the seemingly irrelevant personal questions had been the most significant of all. He had undergone a thorough psychological examination. How was he to evaluate whoever had devised that? How much of the programmed sympathy could he believe?

WHOSE WORDS ARE THESE? he inquired, not really hoping for a meaningful answer. Few of the Founders were remembered by name, since when they'd assumed priesthood they had chosen anonymity in fear of worship.

Promptly, as if the statement had no greater import than any other computerized response, an answer was displayed. YOU KNOW ME. I WAS LEADER OF THE FINAL EXPEDITION FROM THE SIX WORLDS, AND SO FAR, I HAVE LED THE CITY. SOON, WITHIN A FEW WEEKS AT MOST, I MUST DIE; IF IT DOES NOT SO HAPPEN I SHALL DESTROY THIS FILE, FOR I CANNOT RISK ITS DISCOVERY DURING MY LIFETIME.

The First Scholar himself? Utterly bewildered, Noren sat motionless, trying to quiet the racing of his heart.

ARE MY RECORDED MEMORIES FAMILIAR TO YOU?

YES, Noren keyed, glad that no fuller reply was needed; his hands were unsteady.

IN THEIR FULLEST FORM?

YES. BUT EVEN THAT WAS EDITED BY...YOURSELF.

THAT IS TRUE. AND IF YOU NOW KNOW ENOUGH TO ASK THE QUESTIONS YOU'VE ASKED AND TO RESPOND AS YOU'VE RESPONDED, YOU HAVE GROUNDS TO DISTRUST ME.

Noren paused; how could one possibly tell the First Scholar that one distrusted him? Perhaps this whole night's experience was unreal, not a thing truly happening. Perhaps he was still in his own bed...

He was aware, suddenly, that it was *not* happening—not distrust. Though logic did give him grounds for it, logic wasn't what mattered. He had shared this man's inner thoughts and emotions, had done so repeatedly. He could not help trusting him! He would always trust him, just as after experiencing the candidates' version of the dreams, he had trusted enough to recant on that basis. Logic had told him then that the Scholars might deceive him; but in controlled dreaming there could be no deceit. Editing, yes. Since the First Scholar could not possibly have done what the evidence indicated he'd done, perhaps someone had tampered with the recordings later, reedited them as Stefred had prepared the version for Lianne. That, in fact, might explain the incomplete cuts that had caused his nightmare. Things could indeed be cut from thought recordings—but the thoughts that weren't cut could not be altered. Having shared the First Scholar's mind, Noren knew positively that he was trustworthy.

I STILL TRUST YOU, he declared. BUT THERE IS MUCH I WISH TO KNOW. He hoped this secret file had been designed as a crosscheck; since tampering was technically feasible, the First Scholar might have foreseen that it could occur.

YOUR QUESTIONS WILL BE ANSWERED. BUT BEFORE I CAN TELL YOU ANYTHING CRUCIAL I MUST ASK YOU FOR A COMMITMENT. WILL YOU PROMISE TO PURSUE FULL ENLIGHTENMENT WITH REGARD TO THE ISSUES THAT HAVE BEEN CONCEALED, NO MATTER HOW MUCH YOU MAY SUFFER FROM IT?

YES! The First Scholar too had been forced to trust, Noren perceived. No promise keyed into a computer could be binding except in the mind of the person who made it—yet he would feel bound. Had the psychological examination predicted that he would?

I MUST SUBJECT YOU TO A GRIM ORDEAL. I AM DEEPLY SORRY, BUT IT IS UNAVOIDABLE. I CAN GIVE YOU NO ASSURANCE THAT IT WILL BE HARMLESS TO YOU; IT MAY PROVE SERIOUSLY DISTURBING—YET OUR PEOPLE'S FUTURE WELFARE IS AT STAKE, AND YOU HAVE THE RIGHT TO KNOW THE FACTS IT WILL REVEAL.

I AM NOT AFRAID TO KNOW, Noren replied, aware that although this was not wholly true, any other response would be unthinkable.

OF THAT, I HAVE MADE SURE: YOU HAVE BEEN TESTED IN MORE WAYS THAN YOU REALIZE. THE STATEMENT NEXT IN SEQUENCE IN THIS PROGRAM WOULD NOT BE PRESENTED TO YOU IF YOU WERE NOT BOTH QUALIFIED AND COMMITTED TO ACT UPON IT. ITS MERE EXISTENCE IN COMPUTER MEMORY IS DANGEROUS.

The screen went blank for an instant, and Noren drew breath. Then more words appeared. THE KNOWLEDGE YOU SEEK CANNOT BE EXPLAINED VERBALLY. YOU MUST ACQUIRE IT THROUGH A DREAM. THERE IS A HIDDEN RECORDING; I HAVE PUT IT WHERE IT CANNOT BE FOUND BY ACCIDENT. I AM RELYING ON YOU TO EXPERIENCE THAT RECORDING, AND TO LET NO ONE ELSE KNOW OF IT UNTIL YOU HAVE DONE SO.

A dream, an *unknown* dream, hidden for generations? The shock of the idea wasn't unwelcome; Noren's mood began to rise. There was some tremendous secret here, something far more complex than he'd imagined, and perhaps even...hope! Valid hope for the world! He felt ashamed to have doubted the First Scholar even briefly.

ARE YOU WILLING TO FOLLOW THESE INSTRUCTIONS?

YES. The hardest part would be keeping it from Stefred...

I WARN YOU THAT THE DREAM WILL NOT BE PLEASANT.

NONE OF THEM ARE, Noren acknowledged. Not the First Scholar's, anyway.

THIS CONTAINS ELEMENTS NOT PRESENT IN THE OTHERS, BOTH IN RECORDING TECHNIQUE AND IN CONTENT. YOU WILL UNDERGO CONSIDERABLE STRESS.

More than in the deathbed recording? But of course, when the First Scholar had programmed these words, he hadn't expected to make that one. It had been the result of the last-minute inspiration he'd had about the Prophecy. He had planned his martyrdom—to prevent widespread violence, he'd purposely incited the villagers to kill him—but he had not known when he made those plans that all future Scholar candidates would experience his death, or be required to ceremonially reenact it. He had not yet conceived of viewing the Mother Star as a symbol, even.

So one could hardly swear by the Star to do as he asked. Feeling foolish at the thought that he'd been about to do just that, Noren keyed simply, WHERE WILL I FIND THE RECORDING?

IN THE OLDEST DOME, BEHIND THE MAIN RADIOPHONE CONTROL BOARD. THERE IS A SMALL LOCKED PANEL. The lock's combination followed; Noren memorized it.

Putting the recording in a dome rather than a tower had been a brilliant tactic, he saw. If it had been concealed anywhere in the Inner City, Scholars might easily have come across it. But the Technicians of the Outer City, bound by the High Law to avoid touching machines they hadn't been personally trained to handle, would never disturb its hiding place. A combination lock would be a "machine" in their eyes, and to tamper with it would be sacrilege.

ONCE YOU HAVE EXPERIENCED THE DREAM YOU MUST BE THE SOLE JUDGE OF WHETHER IT SHOULD BE SHARED WITH YOUR CONTEMPORARIES. YOU MUST ALSO MAKE CERTAIN OTHER JUDGMENTS. THEY WILL NOT BE EASY.

WILL I RECEIVE FURTHER INSTRUCTION?

THIS FILE CONTAINS DATA YOU MAY CHOOSE TO RETRIEVE. I HAVE LEFT YOU NO MORE WORDS. I CAN OFFER YOU NO COUNSEL, FOR CIRCUMSTANCES IN YOUR TIME WILL NOT BE THE SAME AS IN MINE. MAY THE INFINITE SPIRIT GUIDE AND PROTECT YOU; AS I DIE, YOU WILL BE IN MY THOUGHTS.

Stunned, Noren absorbed the significance of this final message, written mere weeks before the First Scholar's death, the death he himself, dreaming, had come near to sharing. The full version of that particular recording was, of course, wholly unedited. And there was a mystery about it. "There's a sense of deliberate effort to channel his mind away from something that haunted him," Stefred had said. "The self-control needed for that would have been staggering, especially for someone in as much pain as he was. And it seems so unnecessary. No one would have thought less of him for failing to hide his private worries."

He had not intended to make such a recording. Faced with an impelling reason to make it, he'd been obliged to guard this secret.

At that time, had he indeed thought of the successor to whom the secret would be passed? In the deathbed dream one's thoughts were framed in the symbolic language of the Prophecy, since one had known those words all one's life. But they had not been written until after the First Scholar's time; the recording itself contained only the concepts, later translated into poetic phrasing. There was controversy over the interpretation of some passages. *We are strong in the faith that as those of the past were sustained, so shall we be also: what must be sought shall be found, what was lost shall be regained, what is needful to life will not be denied us…* That was usually taken to mean that the First Scholar had been absolutely positive that somehow or other, the synthesization of metal would be achieved. But could the underlying idea have been a less specific one?

Had the First Scholar, dying, believed that some future priest might find a different solution?

Chapter Four

The outer city, except for the dome containing the power plant, was normally off limits to Scholars, certainly to Scholars young enough to be recognized by Technicians as former heretics. For those who'd grown up there and were known, like Brek and Beris, there could be no exceptions; it was lucky, Noren thought, that the task of finding the secret recording hadn't fallen to one of them. He himself took little risk. In the oldest dome, which was partitioned into areas for what few pieces of manufacturing equipment existed in the world, he would not even attract much attention. To go there was a violation of policy, but priests were expected to evaluate policy in the light of circumstances. He did not need to ask anyone's permission.

But he would have to go robed. That fundamental rule couldn't he set aside. Only Inner City Technicians knew that Scholars were ordinary mortals; the Outer City ones viewed them as villagers did. As a small boy, Noren had assumed they wore *only* robes, with no clothes underneath! Thinking them ageless and sexless, it had not occurred to him to wonder if they ever took them off. He'd devoted some thought to this later, to be sure, but it was one of his more heretical speculations—his mother would have labeled it blasphemy.

He carried the blue robe, folded, from his room to the gates of the exit dome. Then, passing through them into the corridor that led to the City's main Gates, he slipped it on and secured the fastenings. Never before had he appeared robed to anyone but Inner City people, and it was not a milestone he looked forward to. Ceremonial appearances, on the platform outside the Gates or in audience chambers, were demanded only of older Scholars. He'd rather hoped, as did many young initiates, that a research breakthrough would make it possible to eliminate the caste system before he got that old. Was this now conceivable, perhaps, if research in genetics could bring about long-term survival?

Though he hadn't explored the Outer City, he had studied a map. A corridor intersecting the one to the Gates connected the domes in the ring, which had no openings to the Inner City courtyard they enclosed. The oldest dome, the one built before the Founding, was adjacent to the one he'd first entered. It was silent there; work did not begin this soon after dawn. But Technicians were on duty in the radiophone room. All the villages had radiophone links to the City, not only for the transaction of routine business, but for requesting emergency medical aid. Noren thought back to the night when he himself had been viewed with awe by a village radiophonist simply for managing, to his own surprise, to replace a dead power cell. How long ago that seemed!

He stepped into the compartment and resolutely approached the main control board. The man and woman sitting there rose from their chairs and, turning to him in deference, they knelt.

Noren froze. He had known, of course, that it would happen, but he'd not let himself remember. It was so *wrong*...

Wrong, but necessary—as his abhorrence of it, too, was necessary. He was not supposed to enjoy it. Anybody who might enjoy it would have been screened out during the inquisition Scholar candidates underwent. The blue robe helped, at least. The robes were identical; they, not their wearers, inspired reverence. To these Technicians he was not a man, but a symbol. He was not receiving personal homage. *A High Priest does not receive,* Stefred had assured him. *He gives*...

"May the spirit of the Star be with you," he said quietly. "Please return to your duties; I only wish to inspect the equipment."

He walked around the control board, which was set out from the wall; behind it were cabinets, and one did indeed have a combination lock. Rapidly he opened it, feeling awe at the thought that the last fingers to touch it had been those of the First Scholar, generations ago. There was no dust in the domes, for prolonged exposure to the planet's atmosphere was corrosive to most Six Worlds alloys and the air was therefore filtered. No Technician would have questioned the strange device, any more than the two now present questioned his need to inspect it. The panel swung open. Noren removed a sealed plastic container and relocked the cache.

As he returned to the corridor, he found he was shaking less from possession of a sacred relic than from the turmoil that the kneeling of the Technicians had stirred in him. Necessary, yes...but it should not have to be! The First Scholar would *not* have designed it, given choice! If by genetic change people could be enabled to live without the City, he would not have perpetuated the caste system any longer than was necessary to effect such change—even if it meant the City's ultimate destruction. Even if it meant loss of the computers' knowledge. And he, Noren, could not do so either, he thought in agony. Would the recording he now carried give him power to abolish the castes, power that for some reason hadn't been available to the First Scholar?

He had been psychologically tested. He had been warned of difficulties past imagining. And it had been made clear that for the recording to fall into the wrong hands would be disastrous. Abruptly, Noren saw what might lie beneath these measures.

All Scholars were trustworthy; the selection process ensured that. All were honest. But they did not all agree on matters of policy...and to eliminate need for the City would not only cause knowledge to be lost, but would leave the Prophecy unfulfilled. Priesthood meant affirmation of the Prophecy. If its promises came into conflict with the more basic issue of human survival...

He held the recording under the folds of his robe, wishing there were a duplicate copy back in the cache.

For the present, the big problem was how to experience the dream secretly. Thought recordings weren't private property, and they were not carried around; he couldn't simply walk into the dream room and hand it to the person on duty. Nor did he know how to operate the Dream Machine himself, even if it should be unattended long enough. And it wouldn't be. He might have to wait weeks for a time slot without priority authorization from Stefred—yet he could not tell Stefred, excited though Stefred would be by an ancient recording's discovery.

It was still early; the past night's scheduled dreamer might just be waking. Right now would be best! The prospect of prolonged delay was more than Noren could stand. Stefred wouldn't be around at this hour when he wasn't working with a candidate. Who would be?

Lianne, probably. All at once he recalled Stefred's words: *Lianne owes a great deal to you, Noren. She has said so.* And Lianne was so new at the job that she might not know that such a request was unprecedented. Even if she did realize, somehow he knew she wouldn't feel bound by the rule book...not Lianne. She was too mysterious a person to refuse involvement in further mystery.

His pace quickened as he crossed the Inner City courtyard, his priest's robe once again folded over his arm. The upper level of the Hall of Scholars was deserted; most people were at breakfast. Noren had no appetite, nor did he feel lethargic from lack of sleep—which was fortunate, he thought with detachment, since the coming sleep of controlled dreaming would be anything but restful.

Lianne was in the dreamer's chair, the headband nearly covering her cropped curls. At first, thinking her unconscious, he turned away in disappointment. Then to his astonishment she sat upright, smiling not only with recognition but with welcome. She reached out for the switch on the panel beside her; a blue light turned to yellow.

Noren stared at her. "You were getting input while you were awake?" Stefred could do that; it was a step in the editing process and must also have been done by his professional predecessors. Not by other people, however.

"Just sampling the library. There are so many dreams I want to experience, and not nearly enough time—I was trying to choose one."

"For your next scheduled session, you mean?"

"It's this morning. There's no one else due until noon."

Then he must take a quick plunge. "Lianne," he asked bluntly, "can you keep a secret?"

Her smile became unreadable. "I'm rather good at that, actually."

"Even from Stefred?" Too late, he recalled that Stefred was attracted to this woman and that weeks had passed since his professional relationship to her had ended; conceivably they were already lovers.

No hint of that showed in her expression. "Especially from Stefred," she told him. "Because I've had practice." She raised the reclining chair and removed the wired band from her head. "It's hard, isn't it, with Stefred—once you know him well, you want to tell him everything. But when you've an earlier commitment to keep quiet—"

"A commitment to other heretics?" It was the only thing he could imagine a candidate being obliged to conceal, and he had been told she'd concealed a great deal during her inquisition. "Stefred doesn't probe for that. He wouldn't want you to betray anyone's confidence. At the beginning, though, when he's testing you, he lets you worry about it."

"Stefred and I understand each other," Lianne agreed. "He knows I've kept something from him, yet he's never tried to pry it out of me. I'm told past lives aren't mentioned in the City. I suppose everyone must be curious about mine."

"Well, we're human. And there were rumors about your reaction to the dreams, so that when you chose to work here, despite how bad it had been for you at first—"

"But you've all experienced them; you know...oh, maybe you don't. *You,* though, Noren—" She broke off, embarrassed. "I guess I've heard rumors, too."

"What rumors?"

"That you're a lot like the First Scholar."

"You mean because I'm supposed to turn into some sort of scientific genius? That isn't going to happen, Lianne. Oh, I'll work toward it, but I'm not going to come up with any radical new nuclear theory; it's not possible." This was the sort of thing he'd resolved not to say to people, but with the situation now about to change...

Surprisingly, Lianne didn't argue. "I'm not talking about what you'll accomplish. I meant outlook, strength—knowing life's not as simple as most people try to make it. That sort of likeness."

"I didn't realize there were any rumors about that. Stefred knows, but he wouldn't talk about me that way."

She didn't meet his eyes. "He wouldn't—he hasn't! I suppose it...it must be what he calls my gift of empathy."

"Empathy?"

"Sensing people's feelings. That's why he's training me in psychiatry." She caught his wordless surprise and went on, "You didn't know? Of course not, most of the women who take shifts in the dream room aren't his personal students, they're just temporary assistants. I'm to study medicine and psychology, help with interviewing and so forth."

"I didn't know Stefred wanted any help."

"Noren—I'm a lot younger than he is. Someday he'll have to choose a successor. He's waited—"

"For someone with the right talents. I see." I see more than she's saying, he thought.

Though he had not spoken this aloud, she blushed. "Maybe you've heard—other things. They're not true. It's not that I don't like Stefred, I do! He's one of the most admirable men I've ever known. I'm truly sorry I can't feel as he wishes I did. When he asked me to marry him, though, I had to say no. I don't plan ever to marry."

How sad, Noren thought, for both of them. She must have loved someone in the village, someone she'd never see again. "You're being trained as Stefred's heir," he said slowly, "and you know he wants to marry you—yet still you keep secrets from him?"

"I told you, he's aware of that."

"All the same, I shouldn't have come to you with mine."

"Is it against Stefred's best interests?"

"No. No, it's more like what you said—a prior commitment. A—a higher loyalty, if you like. But he'd give almost anything, personally, to know it."

"He'd feel that way about some of my secrets, too. That's why it hurts to keep them." Beyond doubt she was sincere; Noren perceived that it hurt her with an intensity he couldn't account for.

"I can't tell you everything," he began, wondering why he dared tell her anything at all. "I never planned to; I thought you'd be too inexperienced to realize how much I was holding back. I see you aren't. But if you're willing to be stuck with something else that'll be hard to hide—"

"For you, I'm willing," she said softly, again averting her eyes.

He pulled the recording from his tunic. "I'm not free to say where I got this," he declared, "and I can't pretend it's normal for me to be carrying it around. But it's a dream I have to go through. Soon."

She took the container and broke the seal to examine the cylinder within. "How long is it?"

"I've no idea."

"You haven't experienced it before, then."

"I'm not even sure what's in it, except that it's—significant."

She studied him, once more seeming to grasp thoughts he hadn't expressed. "You've got mixed feelings. Is there any chance it needs monitoring?" At his hesitation she added firmly, "I have to know."

"I suppose you do. It's not fair not to warn you that we could run into trouble. It—it's probably pretty nightmarish, Lianne. Theoretically I guess it should be monitored. That's one reason I can't let Stefred find out; he knows me so well that if he was monitoring, he'd see it's too important a thing for me to keep to myself. In fact under hypnosis I might talk freely to him—it's something I've no deep determination to hide."

"So you were going to just give it to one of the untrained assistants, have her put you under and close the door on you as if it were a sightseeing tour of the Six Worlds?"

"I hadn't any choice."

Lianne frowned. "Are you sure this was prepared by someone qualified, that it's not raw thoughts of a person who might have been emotionally disturbed?"

"Absolutely. Whatever strong emotions are in it are there for a purpose." In desperation he added, "Look, I wish I could explain more, but I'm bound, and I—I *have* to do this."

"I believe you. But you don't have to do it without monitoring." As he drew breath to protest, she rose from the chair and inserted the cylinder into the machine. Her back to him, she said, "Noren, you're trusting me awfully far. I could do more than tell Stefred, you know. I could copy this while it's running and experience it later myself."

Appalled, he could do no more than stand silent. He had not known the equipment well enough to foresee that possibility.

Lianne turned to face him. "I won't, of course—which you realize, or you'd be calling this session off. So get into the chair."

He obeyed, discovering that now that the moment was upon him, he was terrified. The First Scholar had warned that this dream might not be harmless.

"We're going to have to trust each other," Lianne said quietly. "I won't tell Stefred—and you mustn't tell him that I know more skills than he's taught me." She tilted the chair all the way back and then with quick, deft fingers she unfastened Noren's tunic and began taping monitor electrodes to his chest.

"Lianne, how can you possibly—"

"Know how to monitor? That's like asking you how you got hold of a recording with a seal that's been intact since before your grandparents were born."

He remained silent as she adjusted the band to his head. "I didn't have to be so honest with you," she pointed out. "I could have attached the monitors after you were asleep. But you're too tired to be plunged into this without deep sedation; I'll bet you haven't closed your eyes since the night before last. I'm going to put you into trance, and for that, you've got to trust me completely. You've got to know I'm hiding no more than I'm required to hide—and that I'm competent."

"Stefred hasn't taught you deep trance techniques yet, either."

"Hardly." Her voice was even, yet somehow reassuring. "Nevertheless, this isn't the first time I've used them. And there's something else we need to consider. If you fear you might speak openly to Stefred under hypnosis, you might to me. I won't probe, but if you talk freely—"

"You wouldn't understand enough of it to matter." He looked up into her face and then murmured, "Or would you?"

"It depends on what you mean by 'matter.' You say you've no underlying determination to hide the dream content, yet you were ready to risk physical shock rather than confide in Stefred."

"Well...Lianne, it's not just a—a personal thing. Stefred couldn't treat it as a medical confidence. It may be relevant to fulfilling the Prophecy, so he'd be obligated to tell the whole Council."

"I'm not bound to that yet. I haven't assumed priesthood." She appraised him thoughtfully. "But *you* have."

"Yes." He saw that he would have to say more. "If a person's been given cause to suspect a conflict could arise between fulfilling the Prophecy and following the First Scholar's plans, what should he do?"

"In your place," she declared, "I'd be sure I knew all the facts before getting the Council involved. And Stefred is one of its senior members."

Noren didn't answer her. Lying still for the first time since last night's inspiration, he found his mind beginning to drift. It touched questions he'd overlooked before. Genetic alteration of humans...but *how?* The analysis and modification of genetic material itself was something he'd studied; it would surely work with human cells as well as animal ones. But how would that help? The work-beast modification had been done on embryos. There'd been no room aboard the starships for animals; the embryos had been transported in test tubes. They had in fact been conceived in test tubes on the Six Worlds: an agricultural technique he had read about. Such a thing could hardly be arranged with humans, even if people would tolerate the idea of it, which of course they would not. There was only one way of conceiving babies, after all; the mere suggestion of interference would be indecent…and besides, there just wasn't any means by which…

He felt his face grow hot. Lianne was bending over him; he caught sight of a monitor light flashing red. It was a good thing her "gift of empathy" didn't extend to the actual reading of minds.

"I'll put you in trance, now," Lianne said. "I won't use quite the routine you're used to, but it'll work the same if you want it to." As her hand closed on his she added seriously, "Being scared of the dream is all right. But you mustn't be nervous about *me.* I understand all kinds of feelings. I suppose you don't expect that from women, even Scholar women."

"Old ones, maybe, who've been priests for a long time."

"But the young ones, scientists or not, are still influenced by village customs. Noren, I've never thought the way the villagers do."

"Of course not. You became a heretic."

"I don't mean just that."

An idea came to him. "Were you accused of witchcraft?" That could explain a lot. Most alleged witches, village women reputed to have strange powers, were innocent of real heresy and were given Technician status if condemned and delivered to the City; but there were occasional exceptions. And according to Stefred, some witch-women did use hypnosis.

Lianne laughed. "Witchcraft? No, but I probably would have been if people had known more about me. I'm—different. I can't pretend not to be."

"I used to feel that way myself, sometimes. As if I belonged in some other world."

Very quietly she said, "That's a good way to describe it."

"I think if I'd heard then about the Visitors, the aliens who left the sphere we found in the mountains…Do you know about that, yet?"

"Yes," Lianne said. "I do. I'd like you to tell me more, though, Noren…only first you need to sleep…

She was skillful; he didn't have time for apprehension.

As in the other dreams, he was the First Scholar, but retained consciousness of his own identity. He was standing in a wide space within the inner courtyard of the City—it was a time when not all the towers had been erected, so he knew it was some years before the end of the First Scholar's life. The images of the dream, having been recorded as a long-ago memory, were less clear than in most. But the emotions were strong. Though he could not yet comprehend them, Noren was immediately aware that these were the undefined emotions of his nightmare.

Reaching out as he'd learned to do, he found he could gain no quick understanding of his situation. It was like his first experience in controlled dreaming, when he'd lacked the background to interpret what came into his mind, when he had sensed only that the First Scholar's underlying thoughts were acutely painful. He would not grasp what was happening until he heard words spoken by himself and people around him; he must confront it one step at a time.

And the feelings were worse than those in the earlier controlled dreams. There was horror of a different sort from the horror he'd felt while watching the nova, or during the Founders' reluctant seizure of power. Then, he had been horrified by things outside himself. Even while letting the village people think him a dictator, he'd known that he was not what he was forced to seem and that he was not going to hurt anybody. Now he knew the course he planned might bring someone harm. Indeed, it might bring harm to one intimately close to him…

"It is unthinkable," said the man who stood beside him.

"So was our sealing of the City," Noren replied. "That went against all our ethical principles, too."

"Yes, but we had no choice. There was no other chance for human survival," the man replied. The personalities of the First Scholar's companions were dim in the dreams, for he'd focused not on them, but on issues, in recording his memories for posterity. Noren was aware, however, that this man was one of his best friends—they were discussing something that to the Founders as a group would he unmentionable. "We supported you," the friend continued, "because you convinced us that without preservation of the City, our grandchildren's generation would be subhuman. It's presumptuous to tell you that my conscience bears a heavy load. I know yours bears more than mine, and that you suffer from it. I will simply say I cannot bear a heavier load than I now carry—nor can any of us. We could not violate ourselves as you ask even if we saw justification."

"Do you not see it? Death of our human race will be just as bad generations from now as it would be for our grandchildren."

"*Will* be? Generations from now, a way to synthesize metal will have been found! The technology can be maintained indefinitely then. The City will be thrown open, and more cities will be built. That's your own plan; you've made us believe in it—"

"It is my hope," said Noren in a low voice. "And I have planned for its fulfillment. But it is not sure." With dismay he realized, as himself, that the First Scholar had never been sure! In the full version of the officially-preserved dreams, he had experienced these doubts and the despair to which they led; but there had been editing, the First Scholar's own editing, still. What he was feeling now had been removed. This was not just discouragement, not just lack of proof that synthesization of metal could be achieved. It was rationally based pessimism akin to what he, Noren, had developed later, when there'd been many years of unsuccessful experiments. From the beginning the true odds against success had been concealed.

"Think," he found himself saying as the First Scholar. "There are avenues our descendants can try; nuclear fusion may indeed prove the key to artificial production of metallic elements. But what if it's inherently impossible to do it that way? No doubt metal can be synthesized, but a likelier route to that goal would be a unified field theory—a way to transform energy directly into matter. You know that as well as I do."

"If nuclear fusion won't work, the unified field theory will be developed. Past physicists have failed, yes, but they never gave it top priority, as our successors will."

"There won't be the facilities to develop a unified field theory, let alone test it," stated Noren bluntly. "If that weren't so, I'd have taken that route to begin with. But it would demand an accelerator larger than the City's circumference, containing more metal than we've got tied up in the life-support equipment. You'd know that, too, if you weren't afraid to think it through."

"You're treading on dangerous ground," replied his companion, after a short pause. "You're coming close to telling me that we have sacrificed peace of conscience in a futile cause, that those who died aboard the starships—your wife, for instance—were perhaps wiser than we were."

"No! There is a chance for survival in what we're doing; otherwise there'd be no chance at all."

"That's not good enough. Most of us couldn't live under this much stress without full belief in the goal."

"I know," agreed Noren. "That's why I'm approaching people individually with the alternate one."

"Oh? I assumed it was because you have the decency not to discuss obscenities in front of the women."

"I have approached some women," he replied quietly. "This thing is not obscene. You are too blinded by tradition to be objective. The Six Worlds are gone, now. A taboo on human genetic research should never have existed even there—but here, it is as meaningless and fatal as our taboo against drinking unpurified water would have been on our native planet."

"That may be true. Yet I tell you I'd risk extinction rather than experiment with the genes of my unborn children, and I don't think you'll get any different reaction from the others."

"I know that, too," Noren confessed. "You are the last person on my list, and it's true that the rest reacted as you did. All except…one."

He, the First Scholar, allowed the memory to surface, and as Noren he accepted it, letting the despair engulf him. Only one supporter…just one whose intelligence, whose natural faith in the future, overrode the conditioning of her rearing—and perhaps it was for his sake that she'd opened her mind. Why should she bear the whole burden, she for whom he cared more than anyone else in the whole City?

Dimly, in the part of himself that was Noren, he felt surprise. The First Scholar had not remarried in all the years he'd lived after the death of his wife. There were no thoughts of love in any of the other dreams. It was a thing many Scholars had found strange—no grief for his wife remained in the later recordings, and his own plans for the new culture encouraged the production of offspring. It was odd that he had not set an example, for in all other ways he had lived by the precepts of the High Law he'd designed. Now, the thoughts coming into his mind made plain that far more editing had been done in the official record than anyone had guessed.

But though they were thoughts of love, they were not happy thoughts. The recording, of course, had been made many years after the events with which it dealt. The mental discipline required to make such a recording, keeping later emotions below the surface, must have been tremendous. Noren perceived that the First Scholar had not wholly succeeded—the horror of his feelings was not all apprehension; there was recollection involved also. In the dream it was like precognition. Terror began to rise in him. He was doomed to proceed step by step toward disaster.

"You acknowledge, then, that we must continue as we've started?" asked his friend.

"Yes," he agreed shortly. He had approached only the people he felt might be receptive to an even more drastic plan than the one he'd originally set in motion. They had rejected it. He'd foreseen that they would, but he had been obliged to try. There was no further step he could take to win open support. He must pursue the alternate course in secret, since he was unwilling to let future survival rest on the nuclear fusion work alone.

Yet there was risk. If anyone found out what he was doing, he would lose his place of leadership. His companions had accepted much from him, but for this, they would despise him and would vote him down. Even the original plan would then be doomed, for there were steps in it he had not confided to the others. There was the matter of his calculated martyrdom, which would ultimately be necessary in order to win the enduring allegiance both of the villagers and of the City's future stewards. Without it, there would eventually be fighting. Those who told him no such system as he'd established could last without bloodshed were right; they did not guess that he knew this, and that he expected the blood to be his own. But it would not work unless he retained leadership until the time for it was ripe.

Was he to die for nothing in the end? He was willing to die, but not without the belief that future generations would live. Synthesization of metal would save them, but it was by no means the most promising way to do so. He'd realized that from the start, though he'd edited this realization from the thought recordings. The recordings weren't for posterity alone. They were experienced as dreams by his fellow Founders, and there was too much peril in confronting his contemporaries either with doubt about metal synthesization or with its alternative.

Genetic engineering…the mere mention of it was branded as obscenity! The taboo was so strong that the way out of the survival problem had not even occurred to the biologists who'd worked on the animal embryos brought for beasts of burden. They'd genetically modified them to accept a diet of native vegetation, yet had never reasoned that the same principle might work on human beings.

As things stood, the human race could never adapt biologically to the native environment. The damaging substance in the water and soil would result in offspring of subhuman mentality; within a generation there would be no human beings left. But it was so needless! A simple genetic alteration to permit the alien substance to be metabolized, and the damage would no longer occur. It would not have to be done in any generation but the present one, for the alteration, once made, would be inherited. Water and soil purification would never again be necessary.

There would be a price, oh, yes—a terrible price. The City's technology would be permanently lost. The technology couldn't be maintained without the caste system, and the caste system was justifiable only because there was no way of surviving without it. Once people could drink unpurified water and eat native plants, the City must be thrown open. Its resources would be used up quickly, for they must be equally shared among members of present generations instead of being preserved for future ones. Some metal must be diverted to farming and craft tools. The research could not continue long; it would be doomed to fail even if metal synthesization was theoretically possible. Once the machines wore out, no more could ever be built.

This prospect, to him, was a grief beyond measure—yet as the price of ultimate human survival, of a free and open society that could survive, it would be endurable. Some might disagree. But so far, they were not even considering that issue. They could not look far enough ahead to confront it, so great was the taboo on human genetic engineering itself.

The Six Worlds, long before the invention of the stardrive, had banned all research into modification of human genes. All forms of interference with procreation, in fact, had become anathema once sure contraceptive drugs had been perfected. Medically assisted conception had been abandoned as contrary to the public interest. It had been declared that human reproduction was not the business of science.

To be sure, there had been legitimate worries about abuse. There had been all too strong a chance that governments would try, by any scientific means that existed, to control people. Agricultural genetic engineering techniques had been discovered while the mother world's governments were still primitive and corrupt. Use of such techniques on humans was indeed a potential that might have been misused.

Ironically, however, justified fears of abuse had been magnified into distorted ones. Genetic engineering would have been no more dangerous than other scientific capabilities that could be used wrongly—but there had been political opposition to it. It was known, for instance, that it might lead not only to misuse, but to elimination of genetic disease and to longer lifespan. Such benefits had been less well publicized than the dangers. The Six Worlds' governments had not wanted to spend money on the research that could lead to starships, and they had not liked the thought of people traveling to other solar systems beyond their control; so they'd encouraged the notion that it was wise to ban anything that might ultimately result in a population increase.

By the time interstellar travel became a reality—just in time, as it turned out, to save one small colony from the nova—human genetic engineering was a forgotten concept. People had been conditioned to believe that application of science to alteration of human genes, unlike all other medical science, was somehow "unnatural." Perhaps, eventually, this might have changed. But the discovery of the impending nova had come...and it was too late to regain the lost ground.

If it had not been for the ban, specific techniques for genetically adapting to the alien world would have been already available, even routine—he had known this when he received the mandate to lead the final expedition. He had known when he made his plans that if his ancestors had not restricted freedom of research, those plans would not have been necessary. *There would have been no need to establish the caste system in the new world at all.*

Noren, absorbing this thought, grew cold with the dismay of it. The Founders and all generations since had upheld a system they knew was evil, supposing that the necessity for it was an unavoidable quirk of fate. No one could have prevented the destruction of the Six Worlds. No one could have made the new world different. But if the Six Worlds had not taken a wrong turning, if people there had been allowed to pursue knowledge freely as he himself had always believed it should be pursued, the evil could have been avoided! And the First Scholar *knew.* No wonder he'd kept this particular recording hidden.

But there were worse things in it than the pain of knowing what might have been. The First Scholar wouldn't have used a dream instead of a computerized text if all he'd had to present was Six Worlds' history. What had happened so far was only background...

The scene shifted, as happens in dreams, and he soon realized that there was a shift of time as well as scene. It came to him that several recordings had been spliced. Episodes that would normally be separate dreams were to be experienced in unbroken sequence, without intervening rest periods, without time to think and adjust. For the first time in controlled dreaming, Noren found himself fighting to be free of an experience he did not wish to share. He had been warned that he would be placed under great stress; still he had not expected to be as afraid as this...not when there was no physical danger. How could he feel such dread, such revulsion, when neither he nor the First Scholar believed genetic change to be wrong?

Resolutely he willed to surrender. His own identity was primary now, and with a corner of his mind he remembered, thankfully, that Lianne was monitoring the safety of his sleeping body. Unaccountably, he saw an image of her face: a pale oval framed with white curls, eyes searching him. Then he was caught up again in the mind and body of the First Scholar.

He was with Talyra. He was happy—he could not think beyond that. The future did not matter while he was with her...

It was not Talyra, of course, but the woman the First Scholar had loved. Sitting on the edge of the bed, he became aware that be had not seen her at all in the dream—he had experienced only feelings. He, Noren, could not associate such feelings with anyone but Talyra, but as the First Scholar they'd been aroused in him by the woman now at his side. Since the recording contained no pictures, her form was dim; but from his thoughts he knew that she was beautiful and good and that she was the most important person in his life.

"We are committed now," she said, her voice trembling a little.

"Are you afraid?"

"Not for myself. Not even for you, though you've risked the most; you chose to take the chance. But the child—"

"I know," he replied grimly. "The child didn't choose. Yet there's no other way."

"It has to be tried," she agreed. "We owe it to the generations who'll come after us."

"To those that might not come after us if we fail to try."

"Yes. Still, I don't feel good about it. I never will."

"We've done the best thing," he said reassuringly, although he did not feel good about it either. Gradually, Noren perceived that "we" referred not to the Founders as a group, as it usually did in the dreams, but to himself and this woman alone. And he knew what they had done.

She was a geneticist, one of those who'd worked on the modification of the work-beast embryos. Secretly, with the aid of the computers, she had determined what alteration of human genes would be needed to enable people to drink unpurified water. But of course, she could not modify human embryos in the same way she'd done the animal ones; that would indeed be unthinkable, and it would not be practical in any case. In humans, the genetic modification must be made in adults, made in such a way that it would be inherited by their children. The concept wasn't new—on the Six Worlds, some genetic work with animals had been done in that way. Genes of adults could indeed be changed.

But it had never been tried on humans before.

So again they must accept an evil that, except for the ban on human genetic research, could have been prevented. On the Six Worlds, far more animal tests would have been done before such a technique was considered ready for human testing. But in the new world no biologically similar animals existed. All medical tests must be done on human volunteers. She had wanted to try it on herself, to alter her own genes. He, the First Scholar, hadn't let her do that. His unwillingness to expose her to such a risk had not been what had convinced her; in the end, he'd argued that she was young enough to have other babies and that the colony needed children. If the test should fail, the person on whom it was done could have no more offspring. It was better for that person to be a man. He had persuaded her to try the genetic alteration on him.

That did not mean she took no personal risk, however, for it was she who would bear the child. And the child might not be normal. They knew that; they knew they were experimenting with a human being who'd been given no choice. They hated themselves for it. The child might be mutant…the horror of that engulfed Noren. He saw again the image of the mutant child that had appeared in his nightmare…

This, of course, must come from his own mind. Reaching for the First Scholar's thought, he was aware that unlike himself, the First Scholar hadn't actually seen any mutants of the sort that later inhabited the mountains. He knew the result of drinking unpurified water only from the record of what had happened to the planet's first explorers. He, too, felt horror, but it did not come from personal experience, at least this recorded memory included no such experience. There was a—a foreboding, somehow…

Perhaps it was only fear. He had drunk the water *on purpose.* He'd had to; there was no other way to test the genetic alteration. That alteration had been made in his body—it had been done with a vaccine—and then he had deliberately drunk more unpurified water than was considered safe. Theoretically, the genetic alteration made it safe: his body should now be able to metabolize the damaging substance in the water. His genes should not have been damaged by drinking. But how had he found the courage to put such a thing to the test?

He wondered. Even as the First Scholar he wondered. Now that it was too late to turn back, he did not feel courageous at all.

"What will we do if…?" the woman questioned, not for the first time.

"We will face that if we must," he told her. "Don't worry now. There's no point in worrying before the child is born."

There was no way of knowing beforehand if the water had damaged his genes; the computer system was not yet programmed for the sperm tests routine in Noren's own time. The two of them must simply wait. For her, he felt, that would be even harder than for him—to know the child she'd conceived might be a mutant seemed past any woman's bearing. Yet she had been willing. She believed, as he did, that it was a lesser evil than to passively accept the odds against survival without genetic change.

He embraced her, trying not to think of the future. It was not only peace of conscience they were prepared to sacrifice, and not only the anguish they might feel about the child that they were risking. Nor was the risk of his position as leader what troubled his emotions. They would lose everything if their child wasn't normal; they would even lose each other. That was why they hadn't married. He wanted to marry her, he planned to do so once they knew the experiment's outcome—surely, he told himself, it would succeed! But if it did not, then she must be free to marry someone else. Only on the grounds that the world needed her future children had he persuaded her to try the genetic change on him instead of on herself. He could have no more children if this test failed. He had drunk the water, and if damage had been done it was irreversible.

They had been lovers before he had drunk it. They'd been careful, since they had not wanted a child until they were ready to make the test, but the worst an unexpected pregnancy could have caused would have been delay. Later, should there prove to be genetic damage, they could take no chance at all. There would be no question of sterilization, for the colony's gene pool was considered a resource and he could not tell any doctor what he had done. He could not marry her, and he could not remain her lover, either, even if she chose to reject all other suitors.

As the dream became hazy and began to shift, Noren understood with dismay why it was that all thoughts of love had been edited from the First Scholar's later memories.

She whom he loved was no longer in his arms; she receded from him, and feeling her go, he knew it was forever. He knew the test had not succeeded. As Noren, he'd known this all along, underneath—if it had been successful, the course of history would have been different—and the First Scholar had known also, for the recording had been made not before the child's birth, but long afterward. This was the submerged horror that had been in the dream from the beginning.

The horror not only of this controlled dream, but of his nightmare. The mutant child had been real…

He knew what he would be required to face, both in the dream and after waking.

The mist cleared; once more he found that time and place had altered. In terror, he perceived that he would be given not knowledge alone, but direct experience. He must not retreat from it. He, Noren, had been chosen—but he had also been permitted to choose. As the First Scholar, he knew that the incomplete editing in the officially preserved recordings had been deliberate, that it was designed as a test and as an invitation. This horror would not be forced on anyone. Only a person willing to confront it consciously would reach the point where he must look into the eyes of his mutant son.

Perhaps the dream had not been intended to be so vivid. Perhaps if he'd not met mutants in the mountains, an event the First Scholar couldn't anticipate, he would see the child no more clearly than the mother. In her he sensed pain and felt it as his own; but her face was still shadowy. The child stood out in sharp contrast, mindless, but with the body of a human. It had light skin and reddish curls and it was old enough to walk.

He clutched the woman's hand. He still loved her, deeply and hopelessly. They no longer lived as lovers, of course, but they let it be assumed that they did; it was the only way they could explain their refusal to take other partners. All the Founders had originally been married, since only married couples had been selected for the starships; but with the passage of years open love affairs occurred among those widowed or separated. That their leader should have such an affair did not bother anyone. That he should neither remarry nor love would, in view of the need for children, be less acceptable.

"There is no more time," she said to him with sorrow. "The child is old enough to be weaned, and I can keep it in my room no longer. You know I can't! By your own rule all others must give up their babies. People will not like it if you make an exception of yours."

"No," he agreed, "but perhaps they will tolerate it. They will not tolerate the truth." So far, no one had gotten a close look at the child's face; she had told them it was sickly and had allowed no one but herself to tend it. Now it should be sent to the dome where the rest of the Founders' offspring were being reared to become the new and essential Technician caste. But that was impossible. This child was not merely retarded, it was of subhuman mentality—and a doctor could determine why. Everyone knew what damage unpurified water caused; without that knowledge they would not have gone along with the sealing of the City. They all knew such water wouldn't be drunk accidentally. She was a geneticist, and to some he'd argued for genetic engineering. If they saw the child, they would guess the truth, and his chance to establish a lasting society would be lost.

Somehow it had not occurred to him beforehand that such a child would live.

He'd assumed that if the test failed, the child would die in infancy. The mutant children of the exploratory team had died;

their brains had been sent to the Six Worlds for autopsy. That was how the nature of the genetic damage had become known. Yet, he now realized, the mutation itself was not lethal. The colonists' descendants, if not saved by future science, would not die but would become subhuman. He really did not know how the other mutant babies had died. He perceived that he hadn't wanted to know.

But he could imagine. *Her* courage had not faltered; for more than a year she had nursed this mutant—one couldn't think of it as one would think of a human baby—and had borne the sight of its empty stare. There was no love in it. She had treated it gently, but it was not a docile creature and he knew, sickened, that when it was older its mindless rages would turn to animal ferocity. Loose in the wilderness, it would survive for that very reason. *The mutants in the mountains were cannibals,* Noren thought, remembering all too well...but as the First Scholar he did not have foreknowledge; he simply doubted that another woman, one who'd not taken a calculated risk with the resolve to bear the consequences, would have nourished such an infant at her breast.

"We can no longer hide it," she told him, "yet the truth must not be known. There is only one thing I can do."

Stunned, appalled, he waited, not daring to answer her. For the first time he feared that perhaps he should not be leader after all. He'd handled countless bad situations and had often been called wise and brave, yet now he felt utterly helpless. He did not see anything they could do, though he knew the welfare of future generations might hinge no less on this decision than on his others.

Calmly, holding back tears, she continued, "I must leave the City. Though it's forbidden, there are no guards, and when I'm gone, no one will guess the reason."

"No! Dearest, you can't!"

"It's the only way. And there's nothing more I can do here in any case. I have analyzed the genotypes; I know where I may have gone wrong—but nothing can be proven without more testing. I'd be willing to try again, I would even take another lover if there were anyone we could trust. But there's no hope of that. I can help you only by going. I've enough medical knowledge to be useful in the village, and you know I won't betray the City's secrets to the people there."

"You don't understand," he protested. "There've been rebels in the village, those unwilling to acknowledge dependence on water piped from the City. They are outcasts. They drink from streams, and most flee to the mountains before they give birth. If you take the child to the village, you may be forced to follow them."

It was more than he could endure. The present inhabitants of the village, colonists who'd been shut out of the City, had been born on the Six Worlds; they knew the danger of the water as well as the Founders did. Their leaders would not permit violation of the already-sacred rule: those who incurred genetic damage, or who bore damaged children, could not live among them. His most painful visions were of the rebels he'd failed to save, those he could not contrive to take into the City as he took other dissidents. They faced worse than peril and hardship in the mountains, worse than the production of subhuman offspring—observing his own child, he knew that when such offspring grew to maturity their parents would be endangered by them.

He could not let her take so great a risk as that. Yet neither could he prevent it. She had nursed the child; it was animal, not human, yet if he killed it to save her, she would not forgive him...nor would he ever forgive himself.

"My darling, I know what may happen," she said steadily. "But what choice have I?"

"You have none," he heard himself whisper. "We made our choice long ago, both of us."

"Do you regret it?"

"No. We did wrong, and we must pay for it—yet what we did was best. Not to try to prevent extinction would have been a greater wrong. For all children to be like this would be the worst form of extinction."

"I've left the genetic data in the computers. Will people of the future try again, perhaps?"

They *must,* he thought. Not only to ensure survival if metal synthesization failed, but so that her suffering would not be vain. "They will," he promised. "I'll see that the knowledge is passed to them. That won't be easy to manage, but neither will the—the rest of my plans. I can arrange it so that things work out."

He had not told her that in the end he himself must die at the hands of the villagers. It was the only secret he had kept from her. Were it not for that, he thought despairingly, he might go with her, as he longed to do—he would rather share her lot than stay behind as leader. He no longer wanted to lead. The burden was too heavy;

without her, he might not be able to bear up under it; others might do a better job of leading than he. But there was no other who would carry through the ultimate phase of his plan.

Resolutely, he lifted the child, held it in his arms, his face for the moment averted.

"Don't torture yourself," she murmured. "That serves no purpose."

"It serves our successors," he said. "This is necessary for the same reason I observed the nova from the starship—there are certain lessons they can learn only from thought recordings. They'll know the evils we established, the closed City and the castes. They must be shown the larger evils with which we had to deal."

"The nova, yes. But how can you record personal contact with a mutant? How can you explain it?"

"To most future dreamers I can't. In time, though, there will be a person who won't shrink from the truth. That person may succeed where we've failed."

He turned the child toward him and, for the first time since its early infancy, fixed his own eyes on its vacant ones.

And now, there could be no question from whose mind the image came. Like the nova, it was burned indelibly into the memory of the First Scholar, and the recollection was sustained during the recording process in such a way as to overwhelm whoever experienced the dream. It would make no difference, Noren knew, if he had never seen other subhuman mutants, never been attacked by them and killed them as in fact he had; he would draw from this moment the full shock of all he'd previously undergone. The mindless creature cloaked in human flesh would be no less revolting to him if he'd never been tormented by fears about Talyra's baby…for as the First Scholar he knew that this was *his* child.

He knew also, while recording the memory, that in the end its mother had been driven with it into the mountains. That the bestial breed established there would carry his genes.

But even that was not the worst. The First Scholar, in subjecting him to this, had meant him to know the agony of personal involvement, yes. But the true evil was not in involvement but in the illustration of what might happen to the whole human race. This was a warning not of the consequences of action, but of those that might follow inaction. The First Scholar had taken the fathering of this child upon himself, as he'd later taken the villagers' wrath at their exclusion from the City, to spare future generations. Better that his genes should be damaged than that everyone's should...

And it was not to justify himself that the First Scholar had made the recording. He had made it for a chosen heir. *That person may succeed where we've failed,* his words echoed. He, Noren, had said them, yet as the dream faded and his own identity emerged from it, he was not sure that he wanted to wake.

Chapter Five

Noren knew, of course, what he must do. The secret file gave him the results of the work done in the Founders' time; the mother of the First Scholar's child had left specific, detailed data and an analysis of what she believed had gone wrong. Though theoretically, it would have been possible to proceed without further preliminaries, the stakes were so high that he must move slowly. He must develop his skills by personally repeating such work as was possible to do with animals. It was necessary to design and carry through experiments like those done on the Six Worlds, using a vaccine to produce genetic changes in adult creatures and verifying that these changes were passed on to the next generation. None of this was original research—the computers contained complete information about it, and in fact were equipped to handle the actual molecular analysis of the genetic material in living cells. But to him, biology was a new field, and he had no one to tutor him. He had to become absolutely sure of his own competence.

He expected the work to be hard, and it was. But it was not nearly as hard as the things he'd thought would be easy.

His first impulse, after waking from the dream, was to tell everyone about it. Surely all Scholars would be elated to hear that a means had been found whereby survival could be assured and the caste system abolished! That they must face personal risks, suffer new conflicts of conscience, would not deter anyone; they'd earned Scholar rank in the first place on the basis of their willingness to make such sacrifices. Noren shrank from the thought of the chance he himself must take—but he didn't intend to let that stop him. Was he to be less courageous than the First Scholar? Besides, it would be easier under the circumstances of his own time. He'd have plenty of support.

Or would he? On reflection, he remembered that even before the dream he had perceived that there would be controversy.

Perhaps the Scholars of his era weren't bound by the taboo that had shaped the Founders' views. But they were dedicated to the Prophecy. If this new work succeeded, the Prophecy would not come true. To be sure, it wasn't going to come true in any case—metal synthesization wasn't going to become possible. But his fellow priests didn't believe that. They believed he, Noren, could *make* it possible! If he were to stand up after Orison some night and suggest abandoning the effort…

No, like the First Scholar, he would have to approach people one at a time.

A few days after the dream, once he'd outlined in his own mind the course he must follow, he sought out Brek. Brek was the only close friend he had, aside from Stefred. Though he was on good terms with everyone in the Inner City, he didn't form friendships easily. He was a loner by nature; he always had been. And since Talyra's death he'd avoided social contacts. He'd not wanted to talk, nor had he wanted to intrude—at meals, for instance—when Brek and Beris were together. Or was it simply that it hurt too much to see them as a couple, to see Beris glowing with happiness about their coming child?

Talyra…waiting for Brek in the refectory where they'd agreed to meet, Noren's thoughts returned to Talyra. If only things had been different. If only…

No, he thought suddenly. No, if Talyra had lived, things would not have worked out well. He could not, of course, have asked Talyra to take the risk.

There would be no risk of producing a mutant like those in the mountains. He could be tested for the genetic damage that would cause that, so if his experiment failed to prevent such damage, he would lose only his ability to father normal children. He could be sterilized and continue a normal married life. Sterility was, to be sure, grounds for divorce; but Talyra would not have divorced him. She'd have borne the disgrace of childlessness rather than do that, and he could have told her in the symbolic language that what had happened was the result of his work as a Scholar.

But the other risk, the risk that would follow success in his trial use of the vaccine, would be one to which he could not have exposed her. He couldn't have done so even if he'd been willing, for that would have been against fundamental policy; medical experimentation was done on Scholars, and Scholars alone. Technicians could not participate. They could not give informed consent, since they could not be informed.

If he successfully altered his own genes so that unpurified water caused no detectable damage to his reproductive cells, that would not prove his children would be normal—it would only mean they wouldn't be subhuman. They might suffer genetic damage of some other sort, which he would have no way of predicting beforehand. To ask a woman to experiment with her baby would be even worse than to ask her to permit medical research on her own body. Such a request could be made only of a Scholar woman. Oh, Talyra, like any Inner City Technician, would have gladly volunteered if told it served the spirit of the Star—but that would not be "informed consent." It would be unthinkable for a priest to exploit religious devotion in that way.

So if Talyra had lived...well, it was pointless to wonder what he'd have done.

And now what? A loveless marriage, he supposed, to some Scholar who like himself cared more about human survival than personal happiness. He could no doubt find a bride easily, for though in the village, where women chose steady men who'd be good providers, he'd been considered a poor match, in the City different qualities were admired.

It was past noon when Brek joined him, and Noren was in no mood to waste words. He filled his meal tray automatically; they were barely seated at their table before he burst out, "What would you do, Brek, if you had a chance to help make sure of human survival on this planet—and it meant changing your ideas about the Prophecy, supporting steps you'd hate?"

Startled, Brek replied, "You know what I'd do. We all made that decision when we recanted. What's the point of going through it again?"

"That's what I want to talk about. We may have to." As quickly as possible he explained, omitting only what had been revealed in the dream. For some reason he'd begun to feel that the First Scholar's role was a secret to be held in reserve.

Brek heard him out. Then, slowly, he said, "Noren, I know you're discouraged about nuclear research. Everybody's discouraged. But it's not hopeless—you decided when you accepted priesthood that it's not. We've been through all this before, too—"

"No, it's different now, Brek! When I assumed the robe, I did it because I'd discovered that I believe a way will be found for us to survive. I didn't know *what* way. Nobody knew—that was the whole point of faith! Well, this is the way; we don't have to rely on faith any longer."

"I've still got faith."

"That's fine, but it's not enough, not when there's a means of action. Just sitting back and having faith was constructive when we had no other choice, but now that there's an alternative, we've got to *act.*"

"I'm studying physics," Brek insisted. "That's action. But you, Noren, you aren't really trying any more, are you?" He hesitated; it was obvious he wished the discussion hadn't gotten started. "I haven't said anything till now," he continued unhappily. "Nobody's wanted to—we all know how hard things have been for you since Talyra died. Only...only people are beginning to wonder how long your mourning's going to interfere with the work that needs doing."

"You don't think I'm serious about what I just told you?"

Brek dropped his eyes. "I—I don't see how you could be. Oh, I know you're honest about it. You're the most honest person I've ever known; you always were. But—but it's not quite the same, you know, to get all this abstract information out of the computer as it would be to do what you're talking about doing. Stop and think what it would mean for a man—" He broke off, embarrassed not by the subject itself but by the sudden realization that it might be tactless to speak of it to a friend whose wife had recently died.

"I've thought," Noren assured him. Grimly, he recalled the dream, which he was now sure he must not mention. Brek had not yet experienced the full version of the First Scholar's official recordings; he wouldn't be qualified for exposure to the secret one until he had done so. Perhaps he wouldn't be qualified even then—the First Scholar had taken care not to impose it on anyone who was unready. He had foreseen that not all his successors would be ruled by reason, any more than his contemporaries had been. With dismay, Noren began to grasp the magnitude of the task he himself had been chosen to take on.

He was not good with people. He had no inborn gift for sensing their emotions, persuading them to see things as he saw them. For a while, when they'd both been younger, he had influenced Brek strongly by his confident expression of heretical opinions; but Brek, who had admired his courage more than his realism, had long ago learned to use his own mind.

"I have thought, Brek," Noren repeated. "Don't try to spare me."

"All right, then—have you pictured how you'd feel if it were you, your wife instead of Beris—"

"Do you suppose I'd ask this of you and Beris without trying it on myself first?" Noren demanded.

"No," said Brek in a low voice. "No, you wouldn't. I'm sorry; it was unfair to assume you haven't considered remarriage. Only that doesn't really change things. One test wouldn't be enough. And you just aren't going to find anybody else with your kind of tough-mindedness."

"What kind?"

"The willingness to sacrifice everything to logic...to—to set aside all human decency, all normal feelings...for an ideal. For a future none of us will live to see. I'd give my life, Noren, but I wouldn't—well, I hate to be so blunt, but I wouldn't sleep with Beris knowing I could beget a genetic freak. You know how I feel! In the mountains you suffered agony rather than drink that water—"

"For Talyra's sake. Talyra couldn't have consented; Beris can. She's not only a Scholar, she's even accepted priesthood. Doesn't she have the right to decide for herself?"

"For herself, but not for me—and not, I think, for the child, who wouldn't be a Scholar, wouldn't even be consulted. I don't believe any of us have that right. If you want the truth, which I know you always do, I'm giving it to you."

That was the beginning. Noren knew, then, that he was indeed going to face more difficulties than he'd imagined.

He spoke, without receiving any encouragement, to several other men, ones he felt he could trust to keep quiet about it—young ones either unmarried or married to Scholars. The older men he avoided in fear they might let some rumor reach the Council; more and more, he saw it was too soon to get the Council involved. For that reason, dishonest though it made him feel, he hid all hint of his new goal from Stefred. Ostensibly out of pride, he let Stefred assume he was still learning to live with the nightmare. It was hard not to enlist his aid, especially since Stefred would surely support the plan. If anyone was tough-minded, he was. But Noren knew that Stefred hadn't enough power to sway the Council alone.

He needed a woman's viewpoint. He'd expected to receive this from Beris, but after what Brek had said, discussing it with Beris was out of the question. So was discussing it with anyone else's wife, and to ask one of the unattached Scholar women might look like—well, like a proposal. He was not ready for that yet. He went, therefore, to Lianne, whom he knew wouldn't take it that way, and who had specifically claimed to understand all kinds of upsetting feelings. It occurred to him that her gift of empathy might be very useful under the circumstances.

Lianne listened, and she wasn't shocked. Noren realized, after they'd talked a while, that her remarks had been very neutral, very noncommittal. "What about it, Lianne?" he demanded finally. "Would you support this if it came up in a general meeting?" Not yet having committed herself to the priesthood, Lianne wouldn't be entitled to vote at a meeting even if there should be one; but he valued her opinion.

"Noren," she said soberly, "I—I don't think you should rely on what I think. I'm different. I told you that. I'm not like other women here; I don't plan to marry—I've never even wanted a baby. So how can I give you an answer that's valid?"

"You've never *wanted* a baby?" He had never heard of a woman being quite that different.

"Well, the rest of my feelings are normal," she said, turning red. "Noren, how can you be so brilliant and yet so blind to what is custom and what isn't? You've dreamed plenty of library dreams. You know lots of women on the Six Worlds didn't want babies. That doesn't mean they didn't want—" she broke off. "Look, I wouldn't be embarrassed if you weren't, but you are, and I—I'm making things worse with every word I say! Go get some other woman's opinion."

"Wait," he said. "You can answer the other question. Do you believe we should do what we have to do to survive, even though it means not fulfilling the whole Prophecy, the part about cities and machines for everyone?" He'd received surprisingly little opposition on those grounds from the people he'd talked to—the discussion had always turned to more emotional channels.

"Yes," Lianne declared. "I believe we should. But that's not what the argument will be about. It will be, among other things, about whether we can survive and fulfill the Prophecy, too." Her composure restored, she gave him a strangely compassionate look.

"You're in a more difficult position than you know," she said, her voice so low that she seemed to be speaking mainly to herself.

That was exactly what the First Scholar had said to him.

Having exhausted the supply of potential allies in whom it seemed safe to confide, Noren turned to the work itself, feeling that once he proved the method practical, people would be easier to convince. But that too involved serious problems. He hadn't anticipated having to keep the animal experimentation secret; he'd thought that before he reached the stage where it was necessary, the project would be officially approved. It was one thing to spend a lot of time in the computer room studying genetics—for all people knew, he might be developing some wonderful new mathematical basis for the synthesization of metal. Nuclear experimentation was at a standstill in any case, since for the past year the existing theory had been recognized as inadequate. It was not hard to explain why he stayed away from the nuclear research lab. Explaining a desire to work in the biology lab was another matter.

Scholars were, to be sure, free to choose their own work. Council approval was required only for things involving allocation of irreplaceable resources; the use of one's time was one's own business, in theory, anyway. In practice, use of it for any nonessential purpose was not a way to win friends.

There was no essential work for a Scholar in biology. Such equipment as existed was used almost exclusively for the training of doctors, most of whom were Technicians—and this meant it was located in the Outer City. The only lab Noren was free to visit easily was a small one for medical research, which was done in the Inner City because of the requirement that all volunteer subjects must be Scholars. There was little such research, as facilities were too limited. Metal instruments, drugs—they just couldn't be manufactured, not the complex ones common on the Six Worlds. Many disorders that had been conquered there were again incurable, and would remain so. The lethal diseases of the new world, against which no one had natural immunity, were controlled by vaccines manufactured in the Outer City and routinely administered to each generation of children by Technicians.

A search did continue for antidotes to the poisons given off by native plants, and better treatments were being developed for illnesses caused by them. This was the only real area of progress, and the one in which volunteer subjects were used. Noren had participated once, shortly after his entry to the Inner City. Then, he'd known nothing about what was going on; he'd been miserably sick and had not paid attention to the equipment, which, for lack of adequate space, was crowded into a compartment adjacent to the room where he lay. Thinking back, it occurred to him that he'd have had easy access to it—and a good excuse for running experiments merely for his amusement.

Bacteria, viruses...he would have to learn to work with them before he could try experiments with animals in any case. He would have to prepare the vaccines. A vaccine to be used for genetic alteration did not work in the same way as one to produce immunity against disease, and it wasn't made in the same way either. But to an observer who'd never heard of genetic engineering, one culture dish would look like another.

Yet there was just no legitimate reason he could offer for spending weeks in that laboratory. Even Stefred might start wondering if he did; Stefred knew that despite the ordeal of the nightmare, he wouldn't abandon all useful endeavors for what could only seem an obsession with a fascinating hobby. Realizing this, Noren evolved a quite desperate plan.

After absorbing everything he could from the First Scholar's records, he thought through every detail of the lab work carefully, transferring essential data to computer-generated study discs. Unobtrusively, he gathered the necessary supplies, even making one trip to an Outer City lab not visited by a Scholar within memory—a whole roomful of Technicians knelt in silence while he took what he needed, none of them questioning, and none ever likely to encounter another Scholar to whom they'd venture to mention the incident. At night, he stored everything in the cabinets of the medical research lab, which like all Inner City facilities was unlocked. Since Scholars had complete trust in each others' integrity, by custom they made no checks either on people or on equipment. One bore full responsibility for one's own acts.

When ready, he went to see the doctor in charge of medical research. "I'm not getting anywhere studying physics," he stated honestly, "and—and right now I can't face any more of it. I've got to have some kind of break, yet I can't just sit around without doing anything useful."

"Have you talked to Stefred?"

"Yes, weeks ago. He says I'm not ill. Yet I haven't been able to get back into my work routine."

The doctor sighed. "What you need is a vacation."

"A what?" Noren had never encountered the word.

"On the Six Worlds people took time off from work, a few weeks out of every year, usually. Took trips just for a change of scene. Sometimes I think we'd be more productive in the long run if we could do that, though it wouldn't be acceptable in our society. The outpost helps; what a pity you've already been there."

"Yes." It was indeed a pity, for he could accomplish a great deal more at the outpost; he could even experiment on workbeasts. The thought of bringing one of the gigantic, clumsy workbeasts into the Inner City was, of course, ludicrous, so his "animal experiments" here would have to be confined to fowl. But the outpost was new, and all Scholars were eager for terms of duty outside the walls that had traditionally imprisoned them. It would be years before he got a second chance. "I need a change of scene, all right," Noren continued. "That's why I thought if I could be of use to you—"

"I'm sorry," replied the doctor, shaking his head. "I won't tell you what you already know, that we all feel you're most useful in physics and would be wasting your talent if you were to switch fields. You're brilliant. I'm sure you'd make a fine medical researcher. But Noren, it takes long study. I can't use an untrained lab assistant."

"Of course you can't. That's not what I mean. I had in mind volunteering for something more—restful." He tried to put a brave face on it.

"There's a long list of volunteers. Besides, a week or so of bed rest wouldn't—"

"Wouldn't solve anything for either of us," Noren agreed. "Look, your project data's in the computers like everyone else's; I have the right of access to it. I know what you haven't any volunteers for, haven't requested any for because it would take too much time away from their own work. You've developed a new treatment for purple fever."

Frowning, the doctor observed, "You're serious! I think maybe you should check back with Stefred."

"What for? So that he can tell me I'm too honest with myself to resolve my subconscious conflicts by coming down with some psychosomatic illness, one that might confine me to the infirmary for weeks without being of practical benefit to anyone?"

"You've got a point, I'll admit. And there's no denying that purple fever's a real problem in the villages." He appraised Noren thoughtfully. "If you've read that report, you know we can't cure it; it has to run its course. The treatment, if it works, will make it somewhat less painful and less apt to produce permanent crippling—that's all."

"There's no significant danger of crippling, is there?"

"Not if you don't overexert yourself. Villagers often do."

"I won't set foot out of this lab," Noren declared fervently.

The next few days were worse than he'd anticipated. He had been warned that he'd be given no hypnotic anesthesia, which after all would defeat the purpose of the experiment; villagers couldn't be kept under hypnosis during long-term illnesses since doctors couldn't be in constant attendance away from the City. There was a hospital to which injured patients could be taken by aircar, but purple fever victims couldn't be moved. Painkilling drugs were unavailable, but now a specific drug had been developed that might partially alleviate the symptoms. To test it, however, the subject must be in a position to describe his symptoms. Noren found them indescribable.

At the onset he had merely a fierce headache and shooting pains throughout his body, which he decided he could tolerate. Not until he tried to sit up on waking did it occur to him to be frightened—he felt sure his spine had fractured. The next thing he knew, he was lying flat, immobile, and the room seemed darker. He realized that he must have passed out.

"How's the headache?" the doctor asked.

"Worse." The point was to provide data, not to display stoicism. With effort, Noren managed to whisper, "I don't think your drug works very well."

"It hasn't had a chance; it's designed to treat the disease, not ward it off. I'll give you the first injection now. By tomorrow night you should start feeling some improvement." Encouragingly, he added, "If you're wondering whether this experiment's worth doing, remember that an untreated villager feels no improvement for at least a week."

He could not move his head without pain so intense he feared he'd cry out with it. He couldn't move his limbs or torso either, and in fact was cautioned that to do so would be "overexertion" at this stage. He lay motionless, dreading every muscular twitch, for three full days. After that, he was asked to try lifting his head slightly, or an arm or leg, to judge whether it was getting easier. "Easier" wasn't exactly the word, but it became possible. "The real benefits are in the convalescent phase," the doctor told him. "Without treatment a victim of purple fever is bedridden for six weeks or more and may never regain full use of the muscles if they're taxed too soon. But you're recovering nicely. Before long you'll be moving around the lab." Noren wasn't in shape to believe this confirmation of what he'd counted on.

The fifth morning, Lianne appeared instead of the doctor. "I'm glad to see you haven't turned purple, anyway," she said. From her smile he could not quite tell if she was joking.

"Didn't you ever hear about purple fever in your village?" he asked her. "It's the *plant* that's purple, the plant with the spores that cause it."

"My mother must have forgotten to warn me."

"I guess she didn't warn you that it's contagious, either. I thought they weren't going to let anyone in here."

"I'm a medical student, remember? Stefred won't require me to be a full-fledged physician as Six Worlds psychiatrists were; he isn't one himself, because his work's with healthy people instead of mental patients. But we do have to know the basics." She stood calmly at the edge of the cot, looking down at him with emotion he couldn't define. "You can sit up now, but don't make any rapid movements. I'll help."

"Seriously, Lianne, you could catch this—"

"If I do, there's a proven treatment—but I'm not going to. Lift yourself slowly and don't turn your head. The motion's going to hurt, but you need to begin getting used to it."

He started to speak, but as he raised his back the pain knocked the breath out of him. Lianne laid her hand lightly on his shoulder. Gradually his fear ebbed, leaving a purely physical agony that didn't seem to bother him as much as its severity warranted. Noren's spirits rose. Maybe the plan was going to work after all. For a while, he'd wondered whether he might have overestimated his own stamina.

"In a couple of days you'll be ready to sit at the lab bench," Lianne said. "I'll be around a good deal if you need anything."

"You mean you've been assigned to work in here?" he burst out, dismayed. No other experiments were in progress, and he'd assumed the chance of contagion would ensure his privacy.

"Let's just say I've chosen this week to start my student lab projects," she said evenly. "That way, no one will touch what's on the bench; you don't want somebody else to barge in here and mess up your test tubes, do you? It would be an awful waste of heroic fortitude."

And so, for the next six weeks, the work proceeded more smoothly than he'd imagined it would. He did not even have to invent a story about needing a pastime to keep his mind off the continuous ache of his muscles, for the doctor assumed all the paraphernalia was Lianne's. Actually, she did very little on her own. When present she watched him gravely, quietly; sometimes he got the feeling that she knew more about what he was doing than her comments revealed. She had guessed his purpose through uncanny intuition combined with her knowledge of his ultimate aim—but how could she possibly know that he'd progressed to the point of splicing genes?

His physical weakness, the pain of motion and the persistent headache failed to handicap him greatly. He was not sure just why. Though to concentrate on his task took effort and to steady his hands throughout the hours of intricate lab work was a bigger challenge than he'd foreseen, he found that he was enjoying it. He was truly accomplishing something, after so many seasons of futile study—that must be the reason. Yet he felt something more was involved. Confidence, perhaps, confidence not only in his mind but in his control over his body? As a village boy he'd considered himself too awkward even to make a good craftsman. Now, though, things seemed to be happening to him that extended beyond the ability to cope with the effects of the disease. Lianne taught him to allocate his strength, to relax totally except when his movements demanded tension; then later, when the doctor pronounced it safe, she taught him exercises to recondition his muscles. Evidently her medical training was including physical therapy techniques. Or, he reflected, perhaps she'd been a village witch after all. People did go to witch-women with ailments such as purple fever, for which the Technicians could provide no help; the fact that she hadn't been charged with witchcraft didn't mean she'd never practiced any of the healing methods associated with it.

He found himself wishing that he could confide more fully in Lianne, perhaps even let her experience the dream—but that would be too unfair to Stefred. It would be, even if it weren't for Stefred's personal interest in her; and in view of that factor, the mere prospect of a close friendship made him uncomfortable. There were times when he saw something in her face that made him turn away. Only the recency of Talyra's death allowed him to accept Lianne's companionship, Noren realized. He was doing enough behind Stefred's back without creating a false impression that he was a rival for the one woman whose love Stefred wanted.

After some weeks in the lab, Lianne brought him fertilized fowl's eggs, and he proceeded from gene splicing in bacteria to the manipulation of genes of higher organisms. Some of the eggs hatched, and he went further. Finally she managed to smuggle in a grown hen, which he successfully injected with a gene-altering vaccine. She took a sample of the hen's blood to the computers and brought back a disc proving that its genotype had indeed been modified. Thereafter, the hen laid more eggs, the analysis of which proved that the modification had affected reproductive cells. Lianne took the hen away and returned, in due time, with chicks. Analysis of their blood was unnecessary; they had blue tail feathers. "Did you know what you were doing," she inquired, "or did it just happen?"

"I knew." He frowned and added, "But I didn't know they were going to hatch early."

"I hope not. I have enough trouble hiding a poultry coop on the aircar deck without having to explain blue-tailed fowl! I was going to bring them in here before they hatched. And I'm going to have to get rid of the rooster pretty soon; you have no idea what a noise it makes."

What an odd thing to say, Noren thought. He'd grown up on a farm and so, presumably, had she—or at least she'd lived near one; no village dwelling was beyond the noise of cockcrow. "It's not only the idea of someone seeing them that worries me," he said. "I was working with a regulatory gene, one that affects timing of development. They wouldn't normally have tail feathers at all so soon after hatching; I used the blue coloring just for a marker. Well, I speeded up the appearance of tail feathers all right, but evidently I speeded up hatching, too. Either the computer's gene mapping for fowl isn't accurate or else I fumbled."

"No complex experiment works perfectly the first time it's tried," Lianne said, sounding as if she'd been a Scholar for decades.

"Lianne," Noren declared grimly, "the big one has *got* to."

"From your standpoint, yes. But if it should fail, if you can have no more children, you'll still have a chance to—"

"I'll have no chance, and you know it! People won't accept the idea even now; what chance would they give me after a failure?"

"I can't answer that," she admitted in a low voice. "One step at a time, I guess. What comes next?"

"I find out what went wrong here and try a few other alterations. Till that's done, I'm afraid you'll have to hang onto the rooster." He wondered where he'd be now under his original plan, which hadn't included steps demanding outside aid. As she turned to go he went on, "Lianne? What are they saying about me? In the refectory, I mean, not officially."

"They're upset," she told him frankly. "Oh, they admire courage, Noren—but any Scholar would have been willing to undergo purple fever if there'd been a request for volunteers; I talked to one young man whose father was crippled by it, and he thinks you usurped his rightful role. The rest see the dark half of your motive. They interpret your being here as a retreat from working toward metal synthesization. And they know that you wouldn't retreat if you didn't feel hopeless, so they're depressed."

"Then maybe they'll be readier to consider an alternative, knowing they can't rely on me the way they've been doing."

"Don't count on it. The goal was set by the First Scholar, not by you—and if they decide they can't rely on you, they'll blame you rather than the goal itself." Gently she added, "Retreat from hope isn't appropriate conduct for a priest."

"You say that as if you were quoting it."

"Not the words. But it's what all the older people are thinking."

Slowly, he observed, "You also say it as if you agree with it, even now that you know human survival and the other hopes aren't necessarily tied together. Yet you've not accepted priesthood yourself—and you've helped me get away with neglecting 'appropriate conduct.' Could it be that you're slipping back into heresy, Lianne?"

"If you mean am I questioning the validity of the official religion," she told him, "then no, I'm not. My reasons for not becoming a priest are…personal. I support the aims of the priesthood and share the underlying faith. So do you, Noren."

"For a while I was convinced I did. But it's tangled up with so many things that aren't true, won't be true if humanity does survive."

Faith was a way of dealing with unanswerable questions. Yet now, Noren thought miserably, some of those questions could be answered—and the answer was *no.* Cities and machines for everyone. Knowledge free to everyone, all human knowledge, past and future, being expanded "even unto infinite and unending time," as the poet had expressed it. *Knowledge shall be kept safe within the City; it shall be held in trust until the Mother Star itself becomes visible to us.* The Mother Star, symbol of the unknowable…until the unknowable becomes clear, then? He had believed that. He'd been sure there would still be priests, as searchers for truth though not as a social caste, after the Prophecy was fulfilled. He'd believed they would explore the universe. *There shall come a time of great exultation, when the doors of the universe shall be thrown open and everyone shall rejoice…*What was priesthood without that goal? What was faith without it? Faith in survival wasn't enough.

"Of course it's tangled," Lianne declared. "Religions usually are. *Were,* I mean, on the Six Worlds," she added hastily. "But Noren, you aren't going to get very far with people just by proving chicks can be given blue tail feathers. So maybe you'll have to try to untangle it."

By the time he was fully recovered and discharged from the medical lab, Noren had taken the experimentation as far as he could with fowl and had even started work with human blood serum. His results with the latter had been confirmed by computer analysis but were not, of course, ready for actual testing. He'd spliced human genes in test tubes, but to prepare a live-virus vaccine for human use would have been far too dangerous without the Outer City's facilities, even if he'd had the time. And he had no more time. He considered faking a relapse, but that would have negated the success of the purple fever treatment, which had been declared ready for village use. Or else, if the doctor had caught on, his malingering would have put an end to what little sympathy his fellow Scholars still had for him.

They were cool enough as it was. They didn't show it openly—they went out of their way not to, in fact—but he could tell how they felt. During his past bad times, they'd been sympathetic; yet he'd refused all sympathy, rebuffed every offer of help, not because he disliked people but because he had never known how to respond to them. Perhaps he'd indeed been guilty of what Brek had termed "starcursed pride." In any case, Noren reflected ruefully, he'd provided more than enough excuse for them to stop trying and let their real feelings surface.

There was nothing personal in these feelings. Lianne told him that, and he believed her. He could see the logic: he had become a symbol. He was the ordained heir, the youth destined to achieve the long-sought breakthrough and, by synthesizing metal, fulfill the Prophecy! He had been viewed as heir even by his first tutor Grenald, an aged man whose own lifework had failed, and who, last Founding Day, had died whispering Noren's name. That had seemed significant to people, for the failure of Grenald's research had frightened them. Fear, not moralism, prompted their current disapproval; for if Noren could not advance the work, could anyone? And he was refusing the role in which he'd been cast.

How very ironic, he thought, when he'd indeed been chosen heir to a different task—and by the First Scholar himself.

Would people support the new goal if they knew the full truth about the First Scholar? Logically, they should; the reverence now felt for him should guarantee its acceptance. He probably hadn't foreseen such veneration when he wrote the programmed cautions...still, he'd already planned his martyrdom, already taken steps to ensure that it wouldn't lead to his worship outside the City. And he'd nevertheless hidden the secret not only from his contemporary opponents, but from most successors. Something about that made Noren uneasy.

Yet he himself couldn't delay indefinitely. He felt weak and helpless not so much from the lingering effects of illness as from the fact that as long as his goal remained secret, he was blocked from any action.

He could not return to physics, yet he couldn't study genetics, either. He could do no more with human genes without better lab facilities, and he could get them only with Council approval. There was other necessary work, many years of it, which during the hours he'd been bedridden he had analyzed. Grain must be enabled to grow in untreated soil and to recover trace elements from organic fertilizers, which could in the future include work-beast manure, more efficiently than at present. Irradiation of seed must be made unnecessary. The need for weather control must be eliminated. Immunity against disease must be made heritable. There were feasible genetic solutions to these problems; the secret file dealt with some of them. But they all depended on the basic alteration of human metabolism being implemented. That alteration had to be tried first, and soon—for it couldn't be made in the whole species until it was proven in a third generation. Only if his grandchildren were normal could implementation of the change safely proceed in the villages!

He could afford no more lost time. Even without support among the younger Scholars, he must risk telling Stefred.

"I'm glad you've finally come," Stefred said when Noren appeared at his study door three nights after leaving the medical lab.

"You don't know why I'm here yet." Noren was sure of this; Lianne had sworn she'd revealed nothing.

Stefred, his smile warm and unsuspecting, pulled another chair close to his. "I thought I did," he said, "but now—" He broke off, sensing that this wasn't to be like their previous talks. "You're—older, Noren."

"You thought I went into retreat, I suppose, and that I've come out to find myself still in need of help." Noren hoped his own smile was warm; he wanted desperately to preserve this friendship despite the strains he'd been forced to put on it. "I do need help, Stefred, but not the kind you think."

"Right now I'm not sure what to think," Stefred admitted. "Your face gives the lie to all the rumors I've been hearing. Obviously you're not here to consult me in my professional capacity."

"More in your executive capacity. I couldn't come to you sooner; I've learned something I wasn't ready to bring to the Council. Now I've got to. But it's going to shake people up—even you, Stefred." Painfully he added, "Especially you, because you're going to hate me for having concealed it from you."

Stefred waited silently. Noren continued, finding it hard to frame the words, "You remember what we suspected about my nightmare? We were right."

"That you got something the rest of us missed from the First Scholar's memories?" Obviously Stefred was wounded, though he tried to keep his tone even.

"Something he purposely concealed. He arranged things so that I'd uncover it, or that somebody would, anyway. There were—tests, not just what's buried in the official dreams, but some in the computer system that he programmed personally."

"Secretly?" Stefred burst out incredulously.

"Yes. With elaborate precautions. I couldn't get at the file again easily if I ever forgot my access code."

The delaying action didn't work; Stefred had caught the key word. "What," he asked in distress, "do you mean by the *official* dreams?"

"You've just guessed, I think." Unhappily, Noren held out the recording, which until now had been hidden in his own room, wrapped in the blue robe no other Scholar would touch during his lifetime. Belatedly it occurred to him that this would have been a poor place for it if by some unforeseen chance he'd died of purple fever. "By the Star, Stefred," he went on, "I wish I didn't have to hurt you so much, but you're going to figure out the answer to the next logical question too, and I can't help matters by trying to avoid it. I've been through this dream, and you know I couldn't have done that without Lianne's help."

"Has she been through it, too?" Stefred's voice was very low.

"No. She doesn't know who made it or what it contains, though she and a few others have heard some related facts. The First Scholar told me in plain words that I've got to be sole judge of whether to share it."

"That gives you a great deal of power," Stefred said slowly.

"I never asked for it. But I've come to see I may need it—so though I can't expect you not to inform the Council, I need a promise that you'll go through this yourself first and that you won't copy it when you do."

"You have my word." Holding the container carefully between cupped hands, Stefred asked, "Am I to assume it's on the same level as the full version of the others?"

"Not exactly," Noren said. "It's got the things he edited out of the others. It's…rough. Very rough. You won't enjoy it."

"I suppose I should count myself fortunate that you're not telling me it should be monitored, which would make me ineligible till Lianne's trained."

"Don't laugh. For anyone but you, it does demand monitoring—and for some people we'll need an edited version." How unreal it seemed, Noren thought, for him to be offering Stefred advice on such a matter. He rose to go, knowing that before he reached the turn of the corridor, tonight's scheduled user of the Dream Machine would be bumped by a priority requisition. He hoped Lianne was on duty; perhaps he should have checked and waited for a night when she was sure to be. It was hard to imagine Stefred needing monitoring, yet with no advance preparation...well, it wouldn't hurt, and she could start it after he was unconscious.

"Stefred," he warned, realizing that perhaps he hadn't been explicit enough, "this isn't just a private memory, though parts of it are—well, personal. It's the most important thing any of us have learned since his era. Till now we haven't been given the whole plan, you see."

Startled, Stefred demanded, "It affects the future? The Prophecy?"

"I told you it's Council business."

"I thought you meant simply because of the right-of-access rule. If it's relevant to his plan, then why—"

"I'll explain if you want. But it might be better to see what someone without preconceptions draws from the recording."

"You're right. Come back, say, around midnight."

"No. You can do without monitoring, but not without sedation before and after. Surely there's somebody qualified in hypnosis you can call on." He didn't know whether Lianne had yet disclosed her talent in that area. "I was psychologically tested before receiving this. I assume your training means you can cope with it. All the same, it'll be stress."

When Noren returned the next morning, Stefred looked even more shaken than he'd expected him to be. His face was ashen. "What were you doing these past weeks in the medical lab?" he began without preamble.

"You know, or else you wouldn't be asking."

"And Lianne?"

"She watched, mostly, and helped me get supplies. It was her own idea," he added hastily. "You know how intuitive she is; she guessed why I'd gone in, just from my having gotten her opinion of the basic concept."

"Is she committed?"

"To what?" Noren hesitated; at first he'd assumed "committed" was a reference to priesthood, as it normally was.

"To this—experiment." For the first time in the years they'd known each other, Stefred lashed out in anger. "The Star curse you, Noren—you know what I mean."

Noren turned white. "Lianne—with *me?* What do you think I am?"

There was a long silence. Finally, in control of himself, Stefred said levelly, "I think you're the most dangerous man in the City, because you believe you've inherited a sacred charge and you're strong enough to let nothing stand in your way. If I was wrong about the extent of Lianne's involvement, I apologize. But she visited you daily while you lived in that lab; she made excuses to go there—I could see she looked forward to it. And she is the only unmarried woman you know well who might wholeheartedly support what you're trying to do."

Bowing his head, Noren mumbled, "She's the only supporter I've found, all right. We were working with fowl; she kept a coop for me on the aircar deck. I got as far as modified chicks."

Stefred didn't respond at first. When he did, he sounded no happier. "Please forgive the emotional outburst," he said, "but you know better than I do what going through that dream is like. Last night I thought you must be exaggerating; I was wrong. Only there's so much you don't yet see." He got up and came to Noren, who was still standing. "Noren, about Lianne—she has refused me. She's made plain that she won't change her mind. If you and she were to love each other, I wouldn't begrudge your happiness. Did you think I was accusing you of taking her from me?"

"Weren't you? I wouldn't blame you; I can see how it must have looked."

"You misunderstand. She's refused me; whoever she chooses will have my blessing. What I feared was that she might have accepted a sacrificial role in this genetic scheme, as apparently she has." At Noren's protest he went on, "Oh, I realize it hasn't gone that far yet. But if she encourages preliminary lab work, she will go further, if not with you then with someone else."

"And you can't endure the thought of her babies being genetically modified?" Noren burst out, astonished. "Stefred, you're a psychiatrist! You're training her to be a psychiatrist! Surely you don't feel the way the Founders did, with their taboo, I mean—you couldn't call it obscene just because it might involve Lianne."

"No," Stefred agreed, "though you'll find people today who will feel it's an obscenity. Traditions like that don't disappear in a static society. But as to Lianne, I am human, Noren, and I love her too much to see her hurt in a futile cause."

The implication of the last phrase didn't strike Noren immediately; he was absorbed with the sudden realization that for Stefred, the woman in the dream would have been Lianne. It was just as well if she hadn't been present to monitor after all. "I'd hoped," he said frankly, "that in time, if it works with me, you and she—"

"You thought I'd support this goal?"

"Why yes, in the Council for now, but later personally, too." The evident reluctance bewildered him; it had never occurred to him that Stefred would be anything but a strong ally.

"I'd better make clear from the start," Stefred said, "that it won't get my support in the Council or in any other way—and in general meeting I will vote against it. I will fight you by every means at my disposal, Noren. When I said you are now dangerous, I meant that."

Noren, stunned, was unable to reply. Not evading his eyes, Stefred continued, "If I'd had the courage of my convictions, I would have destroyed that recording this morning. I didn't. I couldn't take it upon myself to do that. It's part of the heritage to which all priests have a right—or perhaps the right is only yours. A man's memories are his own, to bequeath as he sees fit; I'd need to see what he told you in words to know for whom he recorded them. I know only this: the situation has changed since he did so, and if you use them as he intended, may the Star help us all. We will lose everything that's been achieved on this world, and in the end our descendants will die."

"Oh, no, Stefred. The genetic change is feasible—do you think I won't test enough to be sure? I know I can do it, do it safely."

Grimly, Stefred conceded, "No doubt you can. That's precisely what worries me."

"Then when you say we'll lose everything—"

"We don't live in the world the First Scholar knew. We have a culture built on the Prophecy."

"Do you suppose I haven't thought about that? I know there'll be a fight in the Council over it. To some of the older priests, the Prophecy is more than it was ever designed to be—more important than survival, even, because they're not realists. Well, you know how I feel about the City, about the preservation of knowledge! About fulfilling the promise to give machines and knowledge to everyone. About...reopening the universe. You can't possibly believe I'd find it easy to give up those things, or that I haven't been through every aspect of what we'll be sacrificing, over and over—" Noren's eyes stung; it was incredible that Stefred, of all people, would fail to understand.

Stefred sighed. "Sit down, Noren. I've been harsh, I'm afraid. You have lived for many weeks with the conviction that you can save future generations by working toward the end of all that you most value; it's cruel to crush your hopes. Yet I must. The whole issue's vastly more complicated than it seems on the surface."

"The *surface?"* Noren protested, declining to sit.

"Of course you have gone deeper in many ways: into all the emotions the First Scholar felt, and worse, because you've seen what came after—the mutants, the—the descendants, perhaps, of his own child."

"I may have killed one of those in the direct line," Noren mumbled.

"And so for you, the horror is even greater than what he intended you to bear—yet you are bearing it. He chose his successor well. The tragedy is that you were born too late."

"A priest," said Noren dryly, "is not supposed to say it's too late for hope."

"Or to tolerate unnecessary evils?" Stefred took his arm, drew him toward the window. They looked down between the towers to the outer circle of domes. Though they could not see the Gates or the broad platform beyond, that place was vivid in every Scholar's memory. "You have been there only once, outside of the dream in which you faced death there as the First Scholar," Stefred said. "You took abuse at your recantation feeling very much a hero. But I have appeared on that platform countless times as presiding priest—at Benison; at the blessing of seed after harvest; at more recantations than I like to recall; even, one year, as chief celebrant on the Day of the Prophecy. On all those occasions I have stood impassive while crowds knelt to me and paid me homage, which is something neither you nor he ever had to endure. The evil of the caste system, to me and to the others old enough for ceremonial responsibility, is hardly an abstract one. Do you think for one minute that in a choice between life without this system and the City's preservation, I'd hesitate to sacrifice the City?"

"I didn't," Noren said. "Yet now you're hesitating."

"No, there is nothing hesitant about what I'm doing. I am telling you there is no such choice. For the First Scholar, there was, and I imagine you've made yours as he did—but he could not foresee what changes would occur after his time. If he had envisioned a society like ours, he'd have warned you. I think, Noren, he must have hoped for the secret to be found within a generation or two. And in any case, remember, he hadn't gotten the idea for the Prophecy when he made the hidden recording. That inspiration came to him only as he lay dying."

"What would he have warned me about?" Noren questioned, inwardly aware that the First Scholar had indeed said he could not know how the world's culture would change, and had mentioned that difficult judgments would be necessary.

"That the physical ability to survive might not be enough to keep humanity from perishing."

"I see why that was true when he made the decision to keep the destruction of the Six Worlds secret—people would have been so hopeless that they wouldn't have defied their instincts enough to avoid unpurified water. You're going to say, I suppose, that they'll be hopeless again without the Prophecy, that they rely on it as their ancestors relied on being part of the Six Worlds' civilization. It will be different now, though. They won't have to defy instinct; they can live off the land."

"Noren," Stefred said sadly, "after all these generations, there's no such instinct left. The land is alien. Life, now, comes from the City, and the City alone. The instinct to live is embodied in the High Law. Can you imagine people breaking it willingly?"

"But if we tell them—"

"Tell them what? If the next time I speak from the platform outside the Gates, I were to tell people they can now drink impure water and eat food not grown in quickened fields, would they go home and do it?"

"It wouldn't be that simple," Noren acknowledged. He hadn't thought about it before, but of course villagers would not do that. "We'd have to be ruthless, I guess," he said slowly, "as the Founders were when they established the City in the first place. We might have to cut off the piped water supply, and certainly we'd have to stop treating land. But we could do it without harming anyone."

"Could we?" Stefred turned to him. "If the day comes when you figure out how to do it without harming anyone—or even without setting off enough violence to seriously threaten the long-term survival of our species—then perhaps I'll back you after all. Until then, consider me an opponent. And I am not just challenging you; I mean it. I will fight this idea all the way."

Dismayed, Noren saw that he did mean it. He would not merely withhold support, but would lead active opposition against which the goal of changing people genetically could not possibly win approval. And yet, he thought, Stefred had called him dangerous, considered the recording itself dangerous…and therefore must feel he could succeed.

That there was no chance of getting the Council to sanction genetic research became more and more apparent as, one after another, its members experienced the dream. Noren knew he couldn't prevent their doing so. He had been free to return it to the cache from which he'd obtained it, but having revealed it to Stefred, he could not keep it from other priests, all of whom had equal right to the truth. Realizing this, he felt at first there should be a general announcement of what had been learned. Yet to his own surprise he held back, some inner sense in conflict with his normal desire for full openness.

Stefred and his fellow Council members concurred. "We've got a delicately balanced society in the Inner City," he said, "and our reverence for the First Scholar is its focal point. If you stand up in a meeting and declare that the mutants in the mountains are descended from him, you'll deal a blow not only to your own aims, but to the rest of his plans—which he himself knew."

It was true enough, Noren saw, that even to enlightened priests such a statement would be akin to blasphemy. Only by experiencing the dream itself could they understand. It was therefore made available to those who chose to go through what was described as a difficult and unnecessary ordeal. Since the experiencing of the full version of the other dreams was made a condition for exposure to the new one, few younger Scholars sought it. How, and by whom, a previously unknown recording had been discovered was told only to the Council; and the Council said that it contained private memories irrelevant to life in the present era.

Noren did not contest this judgment. He knew that if he joined battle too soon, he would lose. He allowed even Stefred to believe that for the time being at least, he was willing to let the matter drop.

He could see that Stefred's arguments were valid. After discussing them for hours, he was forced to agree that people couldn't survive the sudden loss of all they believed in. Even for the Prophecy's fulfillment, the making of cities and machines available to all, there was an elaborate plan for a transition period. Though most non-Scholars assumed everything would happen on the day of the Star's first appearance, of course that wasn't how it would be. The Founders' plan for the transition did ensure that no one would get hurt by the changes. The trouble was that it assumed survival would demand continued observance of most provisions of the High Law. It made no allowance for abolishing the whole Law along with the castes. And of course, the transition plan was also based on people being given what the Prophecy promised them.

"If genetic change had been initiated in the First Scholar's time or soon after," Stefred said, "there'd have been a chance for a culture based on the conditions in this world to develop. But now, if people's established values should fail them, they wouldn't be able to develop anything new. Innovation has been repressed too long. Without adequate natural resources, it can't start again, not with a population as small as ours is."

"But we've grown since the Founders' time—"

"Those gains would be lost. There would be fighting, Noren. Bad as our world is, we've at least kept it free of mass violence. But if its culture disintegrated, the survivors would kill each other off. They'd fight over the pure water in the rain-catchment cisterns, over the last remaining land-treatment machines..."

Yes, thought Noren—they would. He knew only too well that they would. But the First Scholar's companions aboard the starship had told him his plan for the Founding would lead to violence, too.

Besides, there was no alternative. Without synthesization of metal everyone was going to die anyway when the machines wore out—and metal synthesization was a lost cause. That was the thing no one but himself seemed willing to face. Eventually, no doubt, others would reach the point of facing it; but by then it might indeed be too late. The genetic change couldn't be considered proven until it had been inherited by its developers' grandchildren.

Without quite knowing why, Noren began going to Orison, a religious observance open only to Scholars. He had previously avoided this; he'd gone instead to Vespers with Talyra, and after her death he'd rarely attended either service. Orison had always disturbed him—there'd been a period when it had even frightened him. So many unanswerables, so many fine words that might not come true...

*There is no surety save in the light that sustained our forebears; no hope but in that which lies beyond our sphere; and our future is vain except as we have faith. Yet though our peril be great even unto the last generation of our endurance, in the end humankind shall prevail; and the doors of the universe shall once again be thrown open. Not on this world only, but on myriad worlds of innumerable suns shall the spirit of the Star abide...*To him, at the time of his earliest awareness of the Prophecy's futility, this sort of liturgy had been more a terror than a comfort. Now it became piercing anguish. And yet he was drawn, somehow.

One evening, as he stood silently with eyes raised to the prismatic glass sunburst, symbolic of the Mother Star, that emblazoned the ceiling of the Hall of Scholars assembly room, comprehension came to him. It struck him so forcibly that he grew dizzy. How blind he'd been! He had thought he'd learned something of faith. He'd known its emotional impact before; on the day of his commitment to the priesthood he'd been deeply moved by these very symbols. It had not lasted, not the emotion...but that had been faith in which he'd had *no choice.* No choice but to die, anyway, as they'd all have died in the mountains if his subconscious faith had not sustained them. That was one kind, a necessary kind: simply to go on because there was nothing else to do. But it demanded no real action. Faith and action weren't opposites; all at once Noren perceived what an act of faith involved. There had to be choice in it, a decision that might go either way; one must *choose* a road that might lead nowhere.

"...so, therefore, we consecrate ourselves to stewardship, to the ensuring of human survival; and may the spirit of the Star be our guide." Into the familiar words Noren put for the first time a commitment to risk of failure; and he knew he would never be quite the same person as before.

Late that night, robed, he went to the Outer City lab where vaccines were manufactured. Because equipment was limited, the work there was done in shifts; there were always Technicians present. They were trained microbiologists, far older and more experienced than he—still they knelt to him, addressing him as "Reverend Sir." Noren thought ruefully that he'd have preferred another siege of purple fever. One did what one must, however. He gave orders, and since the High Law commanded obedience, he was asked for no explanations. It was unheard of for a Scholar to visit Technicians instead of sending for them, still more so for him to require a virulent virus strain and use of one of the few existing biological safety cabinets so that he could work with it personally. But people didn't question the ways of Scholars. If it occurred to them that it was ludicrous and downright hazardous for him to put a lab coat over a flowing blue robe, they refrained from saying so.

Noren returned to the lab many nights, carrying sealed test tubes to the computers for analysis in the hour before dawn. At length, after a passage of weeks, he carefully but matter-of-factly injected himself with his new vaccine.

As he prepared to leave, he told the lab chief he wouldn't return in the near future, receiving the usual courteous acknowledgment. He started toward the door, feeling lightheaded with a mixture of relief and fear; but the Technician's voice stopped him. "Reverend Sir—we would be honored by your blessing."

Noren turned. He owed them that. It had been a breach of etiquette to necessitate their working in a "superior being's" presence night after night, one for which he'd have been severely criticized by fellow priests. Furthermore he had delayed their own work by preempting scarce equipment. These people were entitled to all he could give them. Holding out his hands in the formal gesture of benediction, he nodded, and the lab workers clustered around him. He'd used the words often enough at Vespers, but never in personal audience, never to people kneeling, awaiting his touch. *"May the spirit of the Mother Star abide with you, and with your children, and your children's children…*

Your children's children. He hoped so; he hoped it would be a more tangible blessing than he could offer in mere words.

For three weeks after that he waited, his dread growing. He did not expect the injection to harm him—although in any experimental work there was that possibility—for he'd modified the virus to remove its toxic effects as well as to give it genes for the capabilities he wanted it to have. Nor did he worry about whether it would spread throughout the cells of his body; that could be, and was, confirmed by computer analysis of blood and tissue samples. Whether the added genes would work as expected was another matter entirely. To test that, he'd have only one chance. Once he'd drunk unpurified water, there would be no turning back.

And the next step? A marriage of convenience, he had thought. Well, he'd be willing. What he'd had with Talyra could never be duplicated, and it was respectable, even customary, for a man to marry without being in love. Yet who was there to marry? There were very few unmarried Scholar women, and all of those young enough to bear children had plenty of suitors. Though he might successfully court someone, he didn't want to do that. It wasn't just that most women wouldn't support the genetic research—he could probably find one who would share his belief in its necessity. But she would want him to love her in a way he could not; and what if later, she met someone who did?

No, it would not be right for him to bind anyone. It would be fairer if there was no expectation of permanence on either side.

For couples to be lovers was not unusual; in the Inner City, where families couldn't be reared, it was not frowned upon. Still, a woman could be hurt that way. She could fall in love and be heartbroken over a breakup even if there had been no promises. Asking someone to bear a genetically altered child was bad enough without that. Now that the time was at hand, Noren knew he was unwilling to let it happen.

To be sure, there were women among the Scholars who loved casually. In the case of most such women, he feared, birth of a normal child would not prove much about any particular man's genes. However, there were exceptions. There was Veldry, for example. Veldry had been faithful to her lovers; she was a decent enough person. It was just that she couldn't seem to be happy with anyone for more than a year or two. To swear by the Star to be faithful forever wasn't her sort of commitment.

Veldry was always doing unexpected things, Noren reflected. She was, for instance, one of the few younger women who'd chosen to experience the newly discovered dream. Admittedly, she liked newness. But there was more to it than that; she'd been through the full version of the First Scholar's memories earlier, and one didn't undergo that ordeal merely for love of novelty. Perhaps he was unfair to her in considering her shallow because of her short-term personal relationships. She might be just the person to commit herself to an experiment in genetics; she'd already had several babies, and she was, after all, a Scholar who had passed all the tests of dedication to the welfare of future generations. Yet he could not help the way he felt. He wanted a child, a child to live after him—and he did not want Veldry to be that child's mother.

So if he could not marry, and could not bring himself to start a casual love affair either, what was left? He knew underneath that just one course was left; he'd known even before Stefred had spoken of it. Looking back on those days of recovery from purple fever, he saw that Stefred had been right. Lianne would wholeheartedly support the goal. But there had been more in her friendship than desire to work toward ensuring human survival. She had refused Stefred, as she would no doubt refuse any man for whom she had no deep feelings, and had declared she did not want marriage. Yet Noren knew, from the way she'd looked at him, that Lianne would not refuse his love.

He did not love her as he'd loved Talyra. He wouldn't pretend to, wouldn't want to pretend even if he could. But if it must be someone—and Talyra herself had said he must have children—he could not honestly tell himself that he didn't want it to be Lianne.

More than a half a year had passed since his discovery of the First Scholar's secret when Noren, knowing the vaccine had had more than enough time to act on him, took the irrevocable step. Under cover of darkness he unflinchingly violated the High Law's most sacred precept.

On the east side of the Inner City courtyard was a sort of garden. It was just outside the dome containing the water purification plant—in the triangular area between that dome's wall and the adjacent one were rocks, some native shrubs, and a waterfall. The water poured out of a spout in the wall, draining back into the dome after splashing into a stone basin. This water was, of course, unpurified; and it had practical functions as well as aesthetic ones. Its main use came when the purification plant underwent one of its periodic partial breakdowns. On those occasions people too old to have children drank there, since most of the pipes to the Inner City, which always bore the brunt of resource shortages, were cut off. Also, if one wore long plastic gloves, the impure water could be used for washing articles that weren't absorbent. Perhaps the chief reason for the waterfall, however, was psychological. Villagers lived within sight and sound of cool water they were forbidden to touch, despite year-round blistering heat. For Scholars to do the same was a poignant reminder of the alien planet's restrictions.

Staring at the moonlit glimmer of the plunging water, Noren thought back to the day he'd first quenched his thirst in a forbidden stream. How triumphant he'd felt, how sure that by defying the High Law he was asserting his trust in his own mind, his independence from foolish taboos! He'd turned out to be wrong, that time.

Then there was the other time, the time in the mountains, the days when in agony of thirst and fever, he'd barely moistened his lips. Had that restraint indeed been meaningless? No, for if he'd suffered genetic damage then, he could not be doing this work now; and if no one else was willing to do it, the future of the world would be grim. But there was still no sense in what had happened to Talyra. If he were now married to her, he'd have no choice but to be faithless, at least during this first experiment. Yet her death and their child's had been too high a price for avoiding that.

No! All of a sudden, he saw...*even her death wasn't meaningless!* If she and the child hadn't died, he would never have begun to study genetics. The secret might never have been found. The means of human survival might never have been imagined by anyone.

Holding to this thought, inspired by it, Noren thrust his cupped hands into the waterfall and, over and over again, he drank.

Chapter Six

The weeks of waiting were hard, as Noren had known they would be. And he also knew that this was just the beginning. If the water he'd drunk had damaged his genes, the obstacles to continuing the work might prove insurmountable, a prospect he refused to think about. But if it hadn't, he would nevertheless face a long period during which his self-discipline would be severely tested. For that, he began to prepare himself.

He could do nothing active toward the goal until enough time had elapsed for the water's effect on him to become detectable. To spend that time in pointless reanalysis of the genetic work was a temptation, yet he would only be putting off his return to physics. He realized that he had to return. Once a child was conceived, seasons must pass before the experiment's outcome was known, and during those seasons, when no progress could be made in genetic research, he must pretend to have abandoned his interest in it. He must earn the other Scholars' respect again, so that later, armed with proof that the genetic change worked, he would have hope of winning support. Furthermore, he must provide evidence that metal synthesization was a lost cause. He owed people that, he felt.

And he owed it to his child-to-be.

At night, alone in the dark, he worried about the child. What he'd resolved to do was wrong; he could not deny that. Though the mother would consent, the child could not. And it was wrong to experiment on any unconsenting human being!

Yet the choice was between risk to a few babies and the sure extinction of the entire human race. He *was* sure—as sure as it was humanly possible to be—that metal could not be synthesized in any way short of a Unified Field Theory, which, as the First Scholar had known, could not be developed and tested without large-scale equipment that was unobtainable. Wrong as it was to experiment with his child, to let humankind die when the life-support machines wore out would be a greater wrong.

If he could find a mathematical basis for a Unified Field Theory, Noren thought—show how metal had to be synthesized in principle—people might admit that their faith was misplaced. This, then would be his task. It was an impossible one; the greatest physicists of the Six Worlds had sought a Unified Field Theory for centuries, and the chances of his coming up with it within his lifetime, let alone within the next year, were therefore effectively zero. Yet he had to do something with the year! And it wasn't an entirely unpleasant prospect, even knowing himself foredoomed to failure. It would help keep fear of a worse failure from his mind.

The day after reaching this decision, he mentioned it to Lianne. He'd been seeking her company casually, in the refectory and in other gathering places, since modifying his genes. She did not know about the vaccine; he had not yet told her how far he'd gone in genetics, or how far he planned to go. That must wait 'til he had checked the impure water's effect on him. But considering what he planned to ask of her, he must strengthen their friendship. Though he would not court her as if he loved her, he could scarcely ignore her until it was time to broach the subject. And he discovered, with some surprise, that he did not want to ignore her. That troubled him; it seemed disloyal to Talyra. Having pledged himself to Talyra in mid-adolescence, he'd never paid attention to any other girl. Now to his dismay he found himself enjoying Lianne's companionship—even, on occasion, looking forward to the time when they would share more than companionship.

Lianne knew how he still felt about Talyra. He was sure she did, for though she quite evidently welcomed his company, she was as careful as he to shy away from anything suggesting courtship. She was on guard, he felt, against displaying her feelings, and sometimes the joy in her eyes turned to pain. Yet it was not his lack of ardor that was hurting her. Lianne's pain went deeper. Whatever her secrets, they seemed to weigh heavily upon her, and Noren sensed that he could not have helped even if his heart had been free to give.

Nor did Lianne need help. She was...self-sufficient. He could not doubt her ability to handle problems. For some reason, however, her self-sufficiency was unlike his own—she was not a loner, as he was, and nobody thought her cold or unapproachable. Lianne radiated warmth. He felt comfortable in her presence, despite the fact that her mind was inscrutable. Her wisdom was baffling at times, but never irritating. The Unified Field Theory, for instance...

"It's not a thing I can explain," Noren told her, "not to someone who hasn't studied physics. But matter and energy are—well, two aspects of the same thing. The power plant converts matter to energy. If we really understood the relationship, completely understood it, we might reverse the process, convert energy to matter, to metal, perhaps—"

"But you don't have the facilities you'd need to do that," Lianne replied promptly. "They didn't fully understand it on the Six Worlds, even studying particles with far higher energies than we can produce here."

Noren gaped, incredulous. To be sure, Lianne had experienced the secret dream by now, and the First Scholar had spoken of the Unified Field Theory in that dream. But had he thought specifically about subnuclear particles? Even if he had, how could a village woman—one now studying psychiatry, not physics—have drawn their significance from the recording?

"Some of the mathematical foundation might be laid," she went on, "only I think it's beyond you, Noren."

"Of course it's beyond me," he agreed. "That's the point! It's beyond all of us; that's what I've got to prove before I can make people accept the alternative."

"Can you really work with math at that level, or are you going to fake it?"

"Fakery," he replied quietly, "is something I've never been willing to stand for."

"So I thought," she murmured, troubled. She seemed about to say more, yet held back. "It's so hot," she burst out, "let's find someplace cooler! I don't see how people bear this endless heat."

The heat was, to be sure, scorching, as it always was outside and had been every day within Noren's memory; the cool interiors of the towers and domes had been startling to him on his initial entry to the City. Lianne had been in the City less than a year. "We'll go indoors if you like," he said, wondering if her white hair and extraordinarily pale skin made her sensitive to sunlight.

"I guess that's our only choice. Don't you wish, though, that we could walk somewhere in the shade, under trees?"

"You've been spending too much time with library dreams," he told her, smiling. He knew what trees were; five of the Six Worlds had had them.

"Dreams?" Lianne, who made incredibly complex connections between abstract things, was often dense about simple ones.

"Yes—hasn't Stefred explained about them? The pleasant ones aren't just recreation; they're designed to show us what this world hasn't got, to make us feel the lacks in a way non-Scholars don't. So that we'll never be satisfied, always keep struggling. And maybe someday, once we have metal, we can find a better planet—" He broke off, aware with renewed anguish that this goal was among those that must be renounced.

"I didn't mean to stir that up," Lianne said hastily. "I'm not quite sure how I managed to."

"What you said about trees, of course. Why not ask for an ocean?"

She turned even paler than her normal coloring, as if the casual remark had been an unpardonable slip of some kind. Noren took her arm. "Lianne—don't be sorry! I have to learn to bear this; we all do. It's just that when we've believed in the Prophecy so long, believed not only in survival but in a better future—"

"Yes," she agreed; but she was still trembling. "Yet a—a simple thing like trees—"

"We could have them, maybe!" Noren cried excitedly. "That might be done with genetic engineering after the essential jobs are finished. There are plants with thick stems, they just aren't strong enough to stand upright. I never thought before, but in principle I could alter them. There's a lot I could do! Oh, I know we're going to lose the City—the power and the computers—in time, but as long as I'm alive I can keep them going; I can keep the genetic technology long enough to make this world better for our descendants. And though we don't have oceans, there are big lakes. Villages could be built near them once it's safe for people to touch the water. Do you know what swimming is?"

"Well, of course—" she broke off. "I have experienced a dream of swimming," she said slowly. "And boats. If there were trees, and wood, we could build some. Even Stone Age peoples have boats."

Noren stared at her. "You've studied the Six Worlds more than most of us," he observed thoughtfully. "Not only the dreams, but facts stored in the computers. It's not just what you know, but how you think, as if—as if you came from the Six Worlds, like the Founders."

"That's one way to look at it," she confessed. "I—I'm different, I've always told you that…and there's the empathy Stefred talks about…and I—well, I identify in the dreams, not just the First Scholar's, but the library dreams, too. I mix them too much with reality, perhaps. I suppose that sounds like a retreat, a coward's course."

"No," Noren said. "No, it takes courage—don't you see? Because you're here, in the real world, and you're not deluding yourself, not even with the Prophecy. You experience those dreams fully, think about them while you're awake, knowing all the time you'll never get out of this prison we're in, not the City but our whole planet—"

"Please don't! You're giving me credit I don't deserve."

"You do deserve it. I know it hurts to talk about this—but Lianne, you *choose* to. Most people don't. They enjoy the library dreams, but in the daytime they can't bear to remember them. I'm like that myself—I push them out of my mind because awareness of our limits here is just too painful. Oh, I can take it; I force myself to think it through sometimes just to make sure I can. But you seem to live with it naturally."

"I—I wish I were what you believe." Lianne's eyes glistened with tears.

"I'll bet I can prove you are." He had led her to a spot in the courtyard shaded by the shadow of a tower, where they could look up into the blueness of the sky. "You remember you said once you'd like me to tell you more about the alien sphere I found in the mountains?"

Abruptly Lianne pulled back, withdrawing her arm from his; she stiffened. Noren smiled. "I'm testing you; already you see that. Which is part of the test, because most people aren't even perceptive enough to shrink. They look at the sphere and it fascinates them, and they talk endlessly about what sort of beings the Visitors must have been, and they speculate about what function the thing might have had—and their emotions aren't involved at all."

"But yours are?"

"What do you think about the sphere, Lianne?"

"I'd rather hear what you think," she said levelly.

"I think there's a good chance that the civilization that once came to this world and left the sphere still exists somewhere. That things that used to be real on the Six Worlds are still real, other places. Maybe millions of places. Has that idea ever come into your mind?"

"Yes," she admitted, "it has."

"Do you believe it's true?"

"Certainly. I mean—well, of course they couldn't all have been wiped out by novas, all the civilizations in the universe."

"But you've never heard anybody else in the City mention that."

"I guess I haven't. It's so obvious—"

"No, it isn't, not to the people who don't have what it take to face the thought that we're cut off from them. Lianne, that sphere is physical proof of what used to be only theory. Oh, the Founders knew this planet had been mined, but that could have been a billion years ago. The sphere isn't that old. Right after I found it, I used to try to talk to people about the implications, only they didn't see any implications. They didn't want to see. Somebody told me once that if I'm hoping we'll be rescued—"

"That's impossible!" Lianne broke in sharply. "You mustn't have any such hope."

"I don't. The odds against it are fantastically high; people know that, all right. So they'd rather not think of other civilizations as really existing, existing at this very moment—because once you think of them that way, you know we're in a worse prison here than the First Scholar imagined. We lost more than the Six Worlds; we lost our starships. And since we aren't going to succeed in synthesizing metal, we aren't ever going to get them back. I know *I'm* behind bars; I'm not brave enough to imagine what that means very often, but I do know. I also know what it means for our human race to be maybe the only one in this whole galaxy that's never going to get in touch with the rest. And the look in your eyes right now tells me you know, too."

Lianne didn't answer; the emotion in her seemed beyond words, beyond even what he himself had felt whenever he'd allowed himself to ponder these things. "I'm not trying to be cruel," he said. "I'm trying to show you how much I admire you, how much stronger you are than you think."

She managed a smile. "Stefred's tactics? I'm the one who's supposed to become the expert in encouraging people."

"You have a talent for it. Not only in what you do and say, but in what you don't need to ask. Nobody else, not even Stefred, has been able to grasp how I feel about the sphere." He hesitated. "There's another thing. The Council ruled that it can never again be turned on, but the reason wasn't publicized. It's something I learned when I started studying genetics—there's a chance the radiation might be what harmed Talyra's child."

"Oh, no, Noren." Lianne's face showed not shock, but certainty.

"Don't try to spare me. If it was the cause, the fault's mine; Talyra wouldn't have been near it if it weren't for me. Now that I'm sure no other pregnant women came in contact with it, I can't say I'm sorry we found it, because if we hadn't, Brek and I would have died, too, and Talyra would have died sooner—we'd all have died of starvation. But before I learned the radiation may have done harm, I was *glad* we found it. Underneath, it almost seemed like compensation for losing the aircar. Even though I know it can't ever help us, even though it makes me feel worse than before about being stuck on this world—just knowing seemed better than not knowing. Talyra believed the Mother Star led us to it. Well, my ideas about its meaning weren't any more realistic." He searched Lianne's face. "Was I a fool, do you think?"

Her hand touched his. "No. Go on being glad; knowing *is* better. And the radiation did not harm the baby, I—well, I can't explain why, call it my crazy intuition, but I'm sure it didn't."

"There's no way you could be sure of a thing like that."

"I suppose not, only what could a portable radiation device be except a communicator of some kind? And they wouldn't have used communicators that could be harmful."

There was a strange intensity in her voice, so strong that he found himself believing her. Her argument was reasonable, yet hardly conclusive; who knew what might or might not be harmful to an alien species? Still...Lianne's knowledge of things beyond her experience was often truly uncanny.

Twice in the past his reproductive cells had been tested for genetic damage; doctors had handled it. But there was no need to involve a doctor if one knew how to use the computer input equipment and ask the right questions about the data. At least for a man there wasn't. Since to test a woman's reproductive cells demanded surgery, the vaccine, if it worked on men, must be presumed to work on women without this intermediate check. The really crucial trial would be the health of the baby. But before daring to father a baby, he himself must make sure that impure water hadn't affected him as it would have before his vaccination.

He did the test at night, as he'd done the blood tests, when the computer room was deserted. Handling the apparatus, entering preliminary analysis commands, he worked steadily and impassively without permitting his mind to stray. Only when he keyed the final query did his fingers fumble and his eyes drop from the screen. Cursing himself for his cowardice, he forced himself to look. The report read, FERTILITY UNIMPAIRED. NO INDICATION OF GENETIC DAMAGE. NO KNOWN CAUSE TO EXPECT DEFECTIVE PROGENY.

Noren's clenched hands let go, and he felt weak, reeling with the release of pent-up tension. To his astonishment he found that he was weeping. He had not let himself know how terrified he'd been.

As he emerged from the Hall of Scholars into the brightening dawn, Noren knew elation for the first time since Talyra's death. That was behind him now. The memory would always hurt; he could never feel for anyone what he'd felt for Talyra. But the children he'd have had with Talyra would not have helped humanity to survive. His future children would! They would be the first of a new race, the first born able to live without aid in the only world now accessible to them. *What is needful to life will not be denied us*...that was true! If the genetic code of life could be changed, surely the problem of getting people to do it could be overcome also. By the Star, Noren vowed, he'd make a *good* world for his children!

His and Lianne's. He was not sure why it had become so important that they be Lianne's—perhaps, he thought, because she, above all women he'd known, would understand the meaning. She saw nothing unnatural in using knowledge to alter life. With eagerness, he turned back into the tower.

He found her in the dream room; she still worked there some nights, and her shift was just ending. "Let's go for a walk," he said. "Now, while it's cool out in the courtyard."

She looked so openly pleased that he was ashamed. His impatience to make plans, more than consideration for her comfort, had prompted this suggestion—and he realized that he cared how she felt about trivial things as well as serious ones. Maybe sunlight really was hard on her. He'd learned Talyra's feelings, all of them, but never anyone else's. Had he tried? Could he become close in that way to Lianne?

"We haven't talked about the secret dream," he said as they crossed the deserted courtyard, their footsteps loud in the hush of daybreak.

"You never seemed to want to." This was true; he'd carefully stayed clear of the topic while unready to pursue it fully. "I understand how it must have been for you, Noren," Lianne went on. "Personal, too personal to speak of. I monitored you, of course—"

"What did that show?" he asked, wondering.

"Only that it affected you deeply…in lots of ways. Later, when you asked me what I thought about genetic change, I guessed the dream was involved. And then when I went through it myself and learned how the First Scholar's experience fits in, I knew you must feel—chosen."

"Stefred thinks that makes me dangerous. I'm not quite sure why. I see his point about how hard it'll be to get people to abandon the High Law willingly, but if he's right that it's too late, I couldn't cause any harm by myself. Any implementation is far in the future anyway. So why does he oppose even the research?"

"You don't know?" Lianne asked, surprised. "Noren, of course you couldn't do anything alone that would threaten village culture—and you wouldn't; Stefred's aware of that. But think what it would do to *us,* to the priesthood, if we stopped believing the Prophecy."

"I stopped a long time ago," Noren confessed bitterly. "And it hurts. Stefred isn't a man who'd back away from that."

"Not from the despair," she agreed. "Suppose, though, that you were to win official support for genetic alteration, Council support—and we gave up metal synthesization as hopeless. Gave up the plan to fulfill the Prophecy's promises. No priest, least of all Stefred, could ever again speak those words about knowledge and cities and machines with a clear conscience. Starting now, in our generation, not in our grandchildren's! We'd reinterpret the symbolism among ourselves, but nobody would be able to preside at public ceremonies."

Noren drew breath, horrified by his own blindness. "It would become a real fraud after all, just as I thought when I was a heretic—"

"Yes, that's another thing. Recantation depends on a heretic's being honestly convinced that the whole Prophecy is true, doesn't it? If we revised the official plans, Stefred couldn't recruit any more Scholars. The system would turn into a sham that would no longer work."

Appalled, Noren mumbled, "You don't know how ironic it is, my not seeing it like that in the first place. After the way I took off in that aircar, ready to throw away my life and Brek's proclaiming that the Prophecy is a false hope—" He broke off. "Lianne, I wondered then why all the others didn't feel as Brek and I did. Now…they would, wouldn't they, if they accepted the alternative to hoping."

"Of course. And if they did, we couldn't last even till the genetic change could be put into effect. Stefred has to oppose you! He has to keep you from gaining wide support, no matter whether you're right or wrong. That's the only way the priesthood can remain genuine."

"But if I'm right, I've got to have support. It's a paradox."

"Yes. One you'll someday have to resolve. Meanwhile, you and Stefred both have vital parts to play."

"And you, Lianne?"

"I—I can only be an observer," she said sadly.

"More than that, I hope." Noren put his arm around her shoulders, feeling less shy than he'd expected he would. "In the dream—what the First Scholar did, what *she* did—do you believe it was ethical?"

"Not in itself; they knew it wasn't, because the child had no choice and suffered harm. But it was the lesser of the evils they had to choose between."

"Would you make the same decision?"

"In her place, yes, I would."

"I don't mean that—I mean in yours."

"The situation's not going to arise."

"Because of Stefred's opposition? You didn't think I was going to let that hold me up."

"No—no, of course I knew better," Lianne said. "But to prepare a live-virus vaccine—"

"I've already passed that stage. I bent a few policies by using the Technicians' lab, but there just wasn't any other way. And—" he faced her. "It works. I've tested it."

"Altered your own genotype?" She smiled. "I guess if I'd stopped to think, I'd have realized you had kept on working. I suppose you're going to say you're ready to risk drinking from the waterfall, and I—well, I can't argue. We're walking in that direction. I won't stop you, Noren; I'll stand by and wish you the Star's blessing."

They were indeed approaching the waterfall, though he hadn't planned it. The ring of domes stood dark against a yellow sky; the sun hadn't yet risen above them, but overhead the towers shone with its reflected rays. Noren didn't speak until they reached the garden. Then, barely audible over the splash of the water, he said, "I drank weeks ago. There's been no damage. I thought you might want to do more than stand by."

She drew back, to his surprise suddenly wary. "Noren, I—I don't think I want to hear what you're about to say."

"I won't lie to you. I won't tell you I'm in love with you the way I was with Talyra."

"I know that," she said, hiding her face from him.

"I'll just say I admire you more than any woman I've ever known," Noren went on, realizing this was true. "The research has to go forward; you understand why. But I don't want just that. I want a child, the first child who really belongs to this world—and I care about that child's mother being someone to be proud of. I don't suppose you'd want to marry me, not after turning down a proposal from Stefred; you told me you don't plan to marry at all. If you'd like us to be married, though, we can be. I'll be honored. And if you'd rather we were together for only a while, I'll understand."

Lianne raised her eyes, and they were filled with tears. "You don't understand! Noren, I admire you, too, and I'm flattered that you'd choose me—please don't think I'm not. But you're asking for something I can't give. The first child who really belongs to this world—oh, that's ironic—"

Noren watched helplessly, puzzled by this lapse in Lianne's usual composure. It wasn't like her to give way to emotion. If she did not want him as a lover, she could simply refuse, as she'd refused Stefred and many other suitors. Yet…surely he hadn't been mistaken about her feeling toward him, her effort to suppress it had been too plain.

It must be, then, a matter of some past commitment. She might well have been married outside the City, but conviction of heresy meant automatic annulment; under the High Law her wedding vows were no longer binding. Still, she might feel that to break them would be a betrayal of the man from whom she'd been parted.

"Talyra wanted me to have children," he said gently. "If there's someone back in your village you'll never see again, wouldn't he feel the same? He wouldn't want you to remain childless just to be faithful to a memory. We both cherish our memories—and if we're both in the same situation, we won't risk hurting each other."

"Oh, Noren," Lianne whispered, "I never want to hurt you—"

"You won't. You don't have to promise me anything. You'll be better off if you don't—if there was some problem with the vaccine my tests didn't show, I won't be able to have more children after the first, and you've got to be free to have babies with someone else. I accept that."

The words seemed cold. Lianne didn't respond, and Noren moved to take her in his arms, realizing suddenly that she might fear that because he wasn't in love with her, he would offer her no tenderness. "I can't make promises either, I haven't the right," he went on. "But don't you know that while we're together, it'll be real for me? I mean, not like an experiment or anything—"

She wrenched away, almost on the verge of hysteria. "Tell me the truth," Noren pleaded. "Is it the experiment itself? You're not a geneticist like the woman in the dream; you didn't do the lab work personally. I won't be hurt if you believe I'm not competent to have done it safely—"

"No! No, it's not that, I trust your genetic work—you've got to test or there's no hope for this world's future!" Lianne burst out. She struggled to choke back sobs, then resolutely continued, "I can't let you think I don't have confidence in you. Too much depends on this. I'd have your child if I could help that way, only—only I *can't,* Noren. I—I can't bear you a child. I mean...that is, I wouldn't get pregnant."

He stared at her, overcome with appalled sympathy. This was the answer to many of her secrets; no wonder she'd declared she would never marry. "Are you sure?" he asked gravely.

Lianne nodded, still weeping.

But she couldn't be, Noren thought. In the villages women always got the blame for childlessness, but genetics had taught him that it could be the man's fault. Lianne wasn't the sort who'd have had enough experience to be sure.

Then too, some types of female infertility were curable. "More's known in the City than in the villages," he reminded her. "It may be that a doctor could help you."

"A doctor—oh, no!" Her eyes widened with genuine dismay. "That's out of the question, Noren."

How odd, he thought—Lianne wasn't easily embarrassed, and besides, she was a medical student. "Haven't you thought of consulting a doctor now that you're a Scholar?" he inquired.

"There's no need—I am already absolutely sure." Her composure restored, she was again speaking with the intensity of total conviction. "Please, let's forget it, shall we? I haven't told anyone else here—I shouldn't have told you, even, only I had to convince you to ask some other woman. You aren't in love with me, after all. It wouldn't have been fair to let you waste time hoping I could have your baby."

That was true, of course. Noren wondered why he was so disappointed.

She had told him to forget it, but he could not. He was distressed for Lianne's sake. *I never wanted a baby,* she had said once long ago—poor Lianne, she had convinced herself she did not even want what she could not have. It wasn't fair that someone so deserving of happiness should be deprived of one of the few joys not prohibited by life in the alien world. And perhaps it was unnecessary! If only she were willing to get a medical opinion...strange, how that suggestion had seemed to horrify her even more than the belief that she was infertile.

To be sure, doctors could not always help. There were, he knew, techniques for conceiving babies mentioned only in the secret genetics file, techniques banned as "obscene" under the Six Worlds' rigid taboo against medically-assisted conception. In theory, it was possible to conceive a baby by laboratory methods and then implant it in its mother's womb. Though it had shocked Noren to learn this, by now he had become objective. Yet for him it was not a valid scientific option. Even if people would tolerate the idea, even if he convinced some doctor to support his goal, the surgical and lab procedures were untried; there would be too many variables. If a child conceived by such means wasn't normal, there'd be no knowing whether the genes or the medical techniques were to blame. He was already taking enough risks without departing from the time-proven way of fathering children.

So he must choose someone else. Some woman who wouldn't be hurt—more than ever, after seeing Lianne's emotions, he was resolved upon that. Who, then—Veldry? She was the only one he could think of, and she was unattached at present; her last lover had moved out of her room some weeks back. Inner City rumors being what they were, he'd have heard if anybody else had moved in, as would everyone. For that reason he could hardly move in himself. People knew him too well not to guess his motive; certainly Stefred did. But Veldry would realize that and would be discreet. She wasn't one to let anyone's secrets reach the Council.

Veldry had experienced the dream; he should at least get in touch with her to find out how she felt about it. Yet somehow he put off doing so. He could not get Lianne out of his mind.

What if Lianne was not infertile, what if it had been her husband's problem all along? Even analysis of her genotype would tell something…and he could test that himself. All he'd need would be a blood sample—which, of course, he could not get without upsetting her terribly again. Village-reared women were like that; they felt worthless if they were barren. As if that would matter to a man who truly loved a woman! To Stefred, for instance…

All of a sudden Noren guessed what kept on troubling him. Lianne evidently hadn't told Stefred; she'd said she had told no one but himself—yet it was probably why she'd refused Stefred's proposal. She had felt unworthy! And that was tragic, for though a village man might consider her so, Stefred would not. Surely he, Noren, would be justified in clearing up the misunderstanding. He had not promised Lianne to keep what she'd said confidential.

"Look," he said, confronting Stefred in his study, "I know this is none of my business, but I can't stand by and see two people I care about kept apart when it may be needless. Has Lianne given you any idea why she won't marry you?"

"Not in words," Stefred replied painfully.

"You're not one to give up easily without understanding the reason," Noren observed, probing with the hope that Stefred might already suspect, that it might not be necessary to mention his own discussion with her.

"I know when it's best not to pry," Stefred said. "She has rejected all of her suitors. She—she seems to feel she couldn't make anyone happy, which is of course untrue; but it's something she believes, something from deep in her past, behind the mind barrier I found during her inquisition. I had no warrant to breach that barrier then. I've even less right now."

"Yet you feared she might get involved in a genetic experiment."

"It's natural, in our culture anyway, for a woman to want a baby. If Lianne could have one without facing whatever buried emotions keep her from believing she's desirable for her own sake—"

"Only she can't," declared Noren, aware that Stefred's happiness—and Lianne's—mattered more to him than the risk he was taking by revealing that genetic research still interested him. "Stefred, I—I talked to her about such experiments; I need to know people's views. I asked her how she'd feel personally. She didn't want to discourage me, she favors genetic change—so she was frank. She said she can't have babies at all."

Stefred's eyes lit. "That explains a lot."

"So I thought. She was emotionally upset, extremely so."

"By the Star," Stefred burst out, "I try to make allowances. I know village culture couldn't have been kept from reverting in all ways when it had to regress technologically. I see heretics abused, sometimes murdered, and I resign myself to it—observing that kind of intolerance is part of my job. But the other kinds, like sexism—" With bitterness he continued, "Girls are treated like outcasts if they're childless; I suppose Lianne's family was fanatic about it. Her husband may have divorced her for sterility. No wonder she wouldn't talk about her background."

"And the whole thing could be a mistake," Noren said unhappily. "I told her she could be tested, but she refused to consider it. Which is strange, when she's studying medicine herself."

"Not necessarily. It's a painful topic to stir up—if she weren't emotionally scarred, it would have come out naturally when I did the initial psychiatric exam." Sighing, Stefred said, "Now that I know, I can convince her in time that I think no less of her for it. Yet as you say, it could be a mistaken idea; it's too bad that she can't be checked without raising her hopes."

"I could find out from a blood sample if she's genetically sterile," Noren told him. "And if she's not, either there's no problem or it's one that might be correctable."

"She may not consent even to a blood test," Stefred said, frowning.

"Need she? What possible violation of privacy would a simple blood test be now that she's disclosed the only secret we could uncover by it?"

Thoughtfully, Stefred asked, "You can handle this test alone?"

"The computers do the analysis; it's routine. I've already studied my own genotype a lot. I'd have gone ahead with hers, but I've no way to get a blood sample without her knowledge."

"It would be easy enough for me to get it while she's under hypnotic sedation," admitted Stefred. "Tonight, even."

"Is she still undergoing dreams in deep trance?" Noren asked, surprised. "I thought only the First Scholar's recordings require that."

"There are some specialized ones I'm using in her training—a psychiatrist has to understand the dark side of human nature, and in our circumstances here, dreams are the only means of learning. They're rather nightmarish, but she wants to learn, and she can handle it." Vehemently Stefred added, "Not one Scholar in a hundred could handle the stress at the rate she's accepting it—yet she feels deficient because she's never gotten pregnant! I can't endure that, Noren—I can stand losing her to someone else if I must, but not seeing her underrate herself."

"That bothers me, too," Noren admitted. "I think a lot of Lianne."

Late that night he got the sample of Lianne's blood from Stefred and took it to the computer room. Carefully he put the test tube into position and, at the adjacent console, ordered a general genetic breakdown while framing in his mind the specific queries he would enter. The entire genotype would be analyzed in short-term memory, but there would be time to get output only on portions directly relevant to his concerns. INPUT ACCEPTED—HUMAN MALE, he was accustomed to seeing as the signal to begin questioning. He expected, this time, to see HUMAN FEMALE.

The delay seemed unusually long. He turned to check the input equipment; it seemed to be functioning. Glancing back at the screen, he saw INPUT UNIDENTIFIED. PLEASE ENTER SPECIES SO THAT GENE MAP CAN BE OBTAINED FROM AUXILIARY FILES.

Noren frowned. There were only three animal species on this planet: humans, fowl and work-beasts—these, plus common plants and microorganisms, could be identified and dealt with by the files already obtained. Auxiliary files stored information only on extinct species of the Six Worlds. In any case, the blood was human and should have been recognized as such. The computer system, programmed generations ago by the Founders, was infallible; if it were not, all science would have long since come to a standstill. But could the input device be out of order?

He had divided the blood sample into two tubes, having learned early in his work that tubes were all too easily dropped, especially when brought in concealed under his clothes. He had also learned that it was wise to carry a syringe and extra tubes when working with his own blood; from habit he had brought these with him. He put the contents of short-term memory into temporary storage, drew blood from an often-punctured vein, and proceeded to verify the input operation.

With his blood it worked perfectly, just as it always had.

He cleared short-term memory again and started over with the second sample of Lianne's blood. INPUT UNIDENTIFIED, the screen announced. PLEASE ENTER SPECIES...

HUMAN, Noren keyed impatiently.

THE INPUT GENOME IS NOT HUMAN, the program responded promptly.

This was ridiculous; he had watched Stefred take the sample from Lianne's arm. HOW MUCH DOES IT DIFFER? he asked, scowling in perplexity.

APPROXIMATE SIZE AND COMPLEXITY OF GENOME IS COMPARABLE, BUT BANDING PATTERN OF CHROMOSOMES IS DISSIMILAR. MORE EXTRA CHROMOSOMES ARE PRESENT THAN CAN BE ACCOUNTED FOR BY ANY KNOWN DISORDER.

HOW MUCH DIFFERENCE AT THE MOLECULAR LEVEL?

THAT CANNOT BE COMPUTED WITHOUT A GENE MAP FOR THE INPUT SPECIES. THERE IS NO INDICATION OF COMMON ANCESTRY; DIRECT MOLECULAR COMPARISON YIELDS NO GREATER SIMILARITY THAN WOULD RESULT FROM CHANCE.

Then somehow the data had been randomly garbled. CAN SEX BE DETERMINED? Noren inquired, groping.

ON THE BASIS OF MATCHING CHROMOSOME PAIRS, SEX IS FEMALE.

What kind of garbling would leave the pairs intact? It just wasn't reasonable, even if one assumed that the computer program could garble input data, which it never had in any other field of science.

Noren, nonplused, recalled the original data from temporary storage and ran a comparison. The two samples were identical; whatever the problem, it wasn't sporadic. He asked specific questions about physical characteristics, most of which were answered with the comment INSUFFICIENT DATA—and this, had the sample really not been human, would be logical, since lacking a map for the species being analyzed, the program would be unable to locate the particular genes involved. There was just no characteristic he could pinpoint.

Or was there? He had used the blood sample only for genetic data, but short-term memory still contained other data about the blood itself. Personally, he knew little about blood proteins, but he realized that the program could analyze them in much the same way that it could analyze the genes that coded for them. And it could compare them against norms. Slowly he entered appropriate commands.

The blood was *nearly* human. There were, he was told, abnormalities, but none so great as to make the program insist it had come from some nonhuman species. Yet the genetic content of the same blood was undecipherable! It was as if the hundreds of thousands of genes that made up Lianne's genotype had been shuffled; not even those that coded for proteins found in the sample could be located on their chromosomes.

COULD THE INPUT BE FROM A MUTANT HUMAN? Noren asked doubtfully.

NO MUTATION OF SUCH MAGNITUDE COULD PRODUCE A VIABLE ORGANISM. THE EVOLUTION OF THIS GENOME WOULD REQUIRE MILLIONS OF YEARS.

Transfixed, Noren stared at the words while a stunning thought surged into his mind. On impulse be keyed, WHAT WOULD BE THE RESULT OF CROSSBREEDING BETWEEN THIS FEMALE AND A HUMAN MALE?

CROSSBREEDING WOULD BE IMPOSSIBLE, the screen declared. CONCEPTION COULD NOT OCCUR.

She had not said, "I can't bear a child," he remembered suddenly. She'd said, "I can't bear *you* a child."

And she had told him from the beginning that she was different.

This different? A different *species?* But there weren't any other human species, not here, not anywhere the Six Worlds' starships had traveled. The only proof alien civilizations existed was the sphere left on this planet by the Visitors who'd come and gone long before the arrival of his own people's first exploratory team.

The alien sphere...a communicator, Lianne had guessed—she'd been sure it hadn't harmed Talyra's baby. Might she not have been guessing at all? Could Lianne herself be alien, an emissary of some off-world civilization brought here by the sphere's activation?

Incredible as that was, it would explain a lot.

She had been arrested in a village where no one knew her. There'd been a barrier in her mind Stefred could not get through; she'd admitted frankly that she was keeping secrets from him. The City had not awed her, and she had understood the dreams fully from the very first, suffered as if she'd grasped what destruction of populated worlds would be like.

She knew techniques Stefred hadn't taught her. She had incredible insight into things, and into people's feelings...

But she'd been surprised by the crowing of a rooster. She found hot sunlight hard to bear and had spoken wistfully of trees as if she had seen real ones.

Over and over again she'd shown she did not think as village women did...or, for that matter, as anyone else did.

Noren's heartbeat quickened as the implications bit him. Lianne—not of his species, born into an alien civilization? But she'd come here on a starship, then! He wouldn't have thought the radiation from the sphere able to cross interstellar space, but there might have been emanations the computer system couldn't detect. There must have been. If the sphere was a communicator, it must be a faster-than-light communicator; he'd turned it on less than a year before her entry to the City, and there were no other solar systems less than a light-year away.

The Six Worlds hadn't had such communicators. Only their ships had traveled faster than light; that was why no news of the nova had reached this world except through the Founders. But there might be a civilization with faster-than-light communication capability, a more advanced civilization. It might respond to unexpected signals.

Such a civilization would have metal...it could *help!*

Why Lianne alone and not a whole team of aliens? Why the secrecy? Why hadn't the help yet been offered, and why, when Lianne understood how he felt about isolation from the universe, had she not let him know that he would not be cut off forever?

There must be answers. He could not bear to wait until she revealed the truth in her own time. He was, Noren told himself, quite possibly hallucinating in any case; it was too fantastic, too good—literally too good—to be true. Yet everything fit! The more he thought, the more pieces he found that did fit. He would have to confront her with the evidence.

Methodically, suppressing excitement he feared would consume him, he set about transferring the evidence from computer memory to a disc.

To sleep the rest of the night was impossible, though Noren knew he should get some sleep. Stefred had told him that when Lianne woke from the training dream, they would spend all morning discussing it, might even have their noon meal brought to Stefred's study. He'd been warned not to appear with the results of the blood test until later in the day. Now, he didn't want to take the results to Stefred in any case, not until he'd seen Lianne alone. The delay he must endure before seeing her stretched endlessly ahead.

He sat in his room, going over the evidence on his study screen, and watched sand dribble slowly through his time-glass. Surely, he thought, more hours had gone by than it indicated—perhaps it had gotten stuck. Yet as always when tense, he craved solitude, so he could go nowhere to check the time. Aside from the courtyard's stone sundials there were only a few clocks in the entire City. Time-glasses must serve to measure passage of hours in personal quarters, for small though the traces of metal in electronic or mechanical timepieces would be, the world did not have even small traces to spare. Or rather, it *had* not…now, all at once, there was going to be metal! Each random thought heightened the thrill of it. Noren clenched icy hands and willed the sand to run faster. He could not see people, make casual conversation, with a secret like this on his mind. He could not act as if nothing had happened, as if the world were not about to be transformed.

It was as if the Mother Star itself had indeed sent supernatural aid. There was nothing supernatural about an alien communicator, of course. And yet the fact that he'd crashed at just the right place in the mountains, that Talyra had spotted the sphere and that he'd climbed the cliff to retrieve it simply as a gesture for her sake…

Had she died to summon help for the world?

To be sure, the sphere's radiation evidently hadn't harmed her. Still, the mountain water might have caused teratogenic damage—if not, what had been accomplished by the deaths? He had thought he'd found an answer. Those deaths had led him to study genetics. But genetic change wouldn't be necessary now! Not if an alien civilization, a civilization with metal, had come.

Strange...Lianne had encouraged his genetic work. Why, when she'd known all along that it was needless? The acquisition of knowledge was never a waste, he supposed; since for some mysterious reason she must postpone the revelation of her identity, she'd undoubtedly thought genetics a more constructive occupation for him than futile worry about synthesizing metal that could be supplied in its natural form.

But why had she wanted him to risk having a child with altered genes? She'd given herself away over that, admitted a physical abnormality, when she could simply have said she didn't believe human experimentation was justified. Under the circumstances, it *wasn't!* Her urging him to go ahead didn't make sense, unless...could it be that there was no real risk involved? A person from an advanced civilization probably knew enough about genetics to gain access to the secret file. She must have studied not only its original content, but what he himself had stored in it—she must know his work was accurate and would be successful.

Was there anything Lianne's people didn't know?

All his life he'd sought knowledge. As a boy he'd been taught that the Scholars knew everything; he'd assumed, on becoming one of them, that he could learn. And he'd indeed learned, Noren thought ruefully—he had learned that too much was unknowable. Though he'd faced this limit when necessary, he had often repressed the thought of it, living day by day without stopping to envy peoples elsewhere in the universe who really did possess the knowledge his own civilization lacked. Could he have gone on that way for a lifetime?

No, he thought as he lay back on the bed, shaking with the release of feelings he'd kept below the surface. He could never have borne it. In time it would have destroyed him, just as living in the village, shut out of the City, would have destroyed him. How could anyone aware of the universe live with closed doors?

*The doors of the universe shall once again be thrown open...*Not 'til now could he fully acknowledge how much he cared. He had said it mattered only for future generations' sake. For one's own sake it was adolescent to care, or so he'd told himself. Growing up was learning not to let oneself long for the unattainable. At least it was called "growing up," but wasn't that merely an excuse for hiding from the pain of longing?

The open universe...he'd waited years, hopelessly. Now he did not see how he could wait through another half-day.

At noon he went to the refectory on the chance she would appear, but she didn't, though he waited until no more food was being served. She might, he supposed, have eaten in the commons open to Technicians, though that wasn't her habit. Or she might be still with Stefred. What could she discuss with Stefred during all those hours of "training"—Lianne, who knew far more, probably, than Stefred himself? To be sure, her own culture's psychology might be very different from this one's. Perhaps that was why she'd chosen psychiatric training; perhaps her people felt they must understand his thoroughly before any open contact could be made. In any case, she'd been right when she'd remarked that Stefred would give anything to know her secrets. How stunned Stefred was going to be.

Noren looked for her in the computer room, where he now suspected she must spend most of her free time. There was no sign of her. He resisted the temptation to try Stefred's study, for if she was there he could say nothing, and if she wasn't, Stefred would ask about the blood test. Instead he tried the medical lab; he tried the gym and other recreation centers; finally, in desperation, he went to Lianne's own room, discourteous as it was to visit someone's quarters uninvited. He knocked, but there was no response.

All afternoon, as he combed the Inner City, his tension grew. By suppertime it had become intolerable. He returned to the refectory early, to be sure not to miss her, and ate less from hunger than for a reason to linger inconspicuously. When he was finished with his food, he got back into line and refilled his mug with ale. It took the edge off his nervousness. There was nothing else to do while waiting—more than ever he shrank from the idea of talking to anyone, particularly to Brek and Beris, who, fortunately, were on the far side of the room and had not noticed him. He took pains, after refilling his mug the second time, to sit in a corner where they would not.

When at last he gave up expecting Lianne to come, it was past time for Orison, which she rarely missed. That was the only place left to look. Entering the room late with the service already in progress, Noren stood in the back. He felt giddy, partly with extra ale but partly, too, because Orison still stirred him uncomfortably in a way he could not fathom. He wondered why Lianne, who hadn't been reared by people who believed in its symbols, found it meaningful.

His heart jumped; she was standing only a few rows ahead of him. Her face, raised reverently toward the symbolic sunburst, was more than solemn; he saw to his astonishment that there was worry in it, almost sadness. That made no sense at all. Lianne, above all others present, knew the Prophecy was to be fulfilled. He could understand if she were unmoved by the ritual phrasing. He could also understand joy, the joy believers felt, enlightened ones as well as the unenlightened—yet when he stopped to think about it, he could not recall ever having seen that kind of elation in Lianne. He had supposed she was simply too mature to start out with illusions, that she must sense what the experienced Scholars knew about the odds against survival. How could she not feel joy if survival was certain?

The Mother Star is our source and our destiny, the wellspring of our heritage; and the spirit of this Star shall abide forever in our hearts... And so long as we believe in it, no force can destroy us, though the heavens themselves be consumed! Through the time of waiting we will follow the Law; but its mysteries will be made plain when the Star appears, and the children of the Star will find their own wisdom and choose their own Law." No more waiting, Noren thought. No more mysteries. We will not have to find our own wisdom.

The ritual dragged to a close. Noren pushed his way forward to Lianne's side; at the sight of him, the shadow of sorrow in her eyes gave way to brightness. "There's something I want to show you," he said, keeping his voice as level as possible.

On the way to his room they said little, for he could think of no way to express it. How did one tell somebody that one had found out she'd come from another world? He couldn't possibly be mistaken, yet she seemed so—so normal. Her spirits were rising; it occurred to him she might have feared she'd lost his friendship by her refusal to have his child. He couldn't guess how she'd react to his discovery. Would she look on it as a betrayal? With the confrontation at hand, Noren became aware that it mattered to him—how *she* felt mattered. He couldn't think of her as alien.

Wordlessly he pointed to the study desk, where the first screen of the disc he'd prepared was already displayed. Lianne sat down and began to read.

Gradually, she whitened; her pale skin turned nearly colorless. Though she was obviously stunned, she didn't seem angry and certainly was not bewildered—the data she was scanning surprised her only by being in his possession. She read through to the end without speaking, her very silence confirming his interpretation of her origin. Suddenly the silence terrified him. He'd hoped, underneath, that she would be glad she need no longer keep up the pretense. But the face she finally turned to him was a mask of pain and despair.

"How did you get the blood sample?" she asked in a low voice.

Noren told her. "We weren't trying to pry," he added. "We meant it for your good, Lianne. We never guessed we'd learn anything except whether you could be cured of barrenness."

"I know. The fault's not yours, it's mine. I said the wrong thing. I got—emotional. If I'd remembered how people in your world feel about sterility, I wouldn't have blundered. I'd have told you I drank too much impure water as a village girl; you'd never have questioned that." As she rose from the study desk Noren saw to his dismay that she was crying, not hysterically this time but silently, as if she were facing some profound and private grief.

Puzzled, he guided her to the bunk and sat on its edge beside her, putting his arm around her trembling shoulders. "I know you must have some reason for not wanting to tell us yet," he said, "but is it really so terrible that we've found out?"

"We?" she inquired anxiously. "You haven't told Stefred, I was with him almost all day—"

"No. I wanted to talk to you first. I guess I felt I needed verification of anything so—tremendous. Lianne, you surely don't believe I think less of you for it, do you? That I think of you as inhuman or something? Why do you mind so much having me know?"

"Because it's you who will suffer for my mistake," she whispered.

"Suffer? Oh, no, Lianne! I suppose you mean you need to keep the secret awhile longer. If that's important I'll go along, and you're right that it'll be hard for me—but I'd still rather know than not know. Even just the knowledge that we're to be saved—" He broke off, perplexed. "Why did you say before that rescue's impossible, that I mustn't hope?"

Lianne met his eyes. "I told you how things are."

"I don't understand."

"There is a great deal you're not going to understand. And you will be hurt by that, as well as in other ways you can't imagine so far. I'd have done anything to prevent it, Noren, because I—I care about you. I wanted your love, I wished I could have your child—that's why I wasn't thinking clearly. I betrayed my responsibilities, and I betrayed you, too, without meaning to. Now it's too late; nothing can undo the damage."

"But Lianne, just because I know a little ahead of time—"

"You weren't ever meant to know."

"That you're alien? But why not?"

"You weren't ever to know aliens came." She drew away from him, pausing as if she needed time to collect herself; when she faced him again she was very calm, composed not just as she usually was, but in a way that made her seem indeed the daughter of a different world.

"We would have to know eventually," he pointed out, "I mean, when it comes to replenishing our world's metal—"

"Noren," Lianne interrupted, "I've got to set you straight, and it's best if I don't put it off. You want the truth, I think, even if it's not pleasant to hear."

"I've always wanted the truth."

"And today—all the hours you couldn't find me—you've been building your hopes on the idea that you're about to receive it, all of it, from my people. That we're here to give you metal, restore the Six Worlds' lost civilization and more." He had the odd feeling that she was drawing this directly from his mind, though she knew him well enough, he supposed, to have guessed that he personally expected more than the Prophecy's fulfillment, that it was her people's knowledge that excited him most.

"Those hopes won't be satisfied," Lianne continued steadily. "We are here to observe—that's all. Nothing in your world will change because of us. It's necessary for you to realize that from the beginning."

Horrified, Noren protested, "You're saying you'd stand by and observe evils you could put an end to? Lianne, I don't believe it!" And yet something in her look frightened him; it was almost as if her words were true.

"You *must* believe it. I don't expect you to comprehend it yet. In time, if you have courage enough, you'll begin to perceive what's involved. But meanwhile you must take my word—if you refuse, if you cling to the illusion that we will save your people, you'll lose your own chance to do it. And then nothing can save them."

"Your civilization wouldn't let us die."

"That's a complicated issue. There's more to it than survival—after all, your descendants could survive as subhuman mutants. You want more than life for them, Noren. You want them to regain their rightful heritage. It may be in your power to ensure that. It is not in mine."

"It *is,* it must be if you've got starships," he began; but then a new thought came to him. He had assumed Lianne represented her people—yet it was strange that she was here alone, that she'd been arrested and convicted of heresy, brought into the City without any means of communicating with the others. Could they possibly have abandoned her? Was she herself in fact powerless?

"What are they, your people?" he asked slowly. "Why did they come?"

"We are anthropologists. We have more knowledge than you can envision, Noren, but at the same time less; we visit young civilizations to learn. We aren't the ones who left the sphere on this world, but we did pick up its signals. They were—incongruous. We came to investigate. Not to interfere, only to watch."

"To watch us struggle against hopeless odds?" Noren exclaimed bitterly.

"If you want to put it bluntly, yes."

"You're—inhuman, then, after all, at least your people are."

"From your standpoint, now, perhaps so. There are sides to it you can't see."

"And are you on our side, Lianne," Noren demanded, "or on your cold-blooded observation team's?"

She hesitated. "I'm on both. I wish I could explain more, but I'm bound by a commitment; there's nothing I can do to help you."

Anger rose in Noren; he seized her by the shoulders, pulling her toward him. "Nothing you can do, or nothing you will?" he questioned. "You're not insensitive, Lianne. You've been playing a role all this time, yes, but you do care what happens to us. You couldn't have gotten past Stefred if our people's future didn't matter to you; no Scholar candidate can. And there've been other things you couldn't have faked."

"You're right," she confessed, "I couldn't fake how I felt about you. I couldn't even hide it—you knew when you spoke of the child that it wasn't just that I supported your experiments. Only I couldn't stand in the way of those experiments; they're too important! They're the one chance you have of saving your people, and if they succeed—"

"If? Lianne, you must know the work I'm doing's going to succeed. You wouldn't let me risk harming a baby."

"There's risk in all scientific progress. You're aware of that."

"But you've got advanced knowledge of genetics, surely—"

"I'm an anthropologist, not a geneticist. I know what you're doing is feasible, but I'm in no position to judge the details."

"Not personally, perhaps, but your people…I can't keep working by trial and error, knowing there are people around who've already passed this stage!"

"That's one reason you weren't supposed to know," Lianne admitted miserably. "It's going to make what you have to do much harder."

"I can't take risks that are unnecessary. There's got to be another way."

"There is no other way! What can I do to convince you?" She drew a resolute breath, then continued with deliberate coldness, "My civilization's further above the Six Worlds than you can conceive, and we don't share our knowledge with primitives."

Before Noren could reply she dropped her head; the next thing he knew she was leaning against him. He was dazed—with the ale he'd drunk, with ups and downs of emotion, with the conviction that Lianne could not be as coldhearted as she seemed; instinctively he embraced her. She was warm, not cold at all…

"You're so alone," she murmured. "I can't spare you what you'll suffer from knowing about us. But I might—comfort you sometimes, offer the only thing I'm free to offer—" Though she said no more, abruptly her thought blazed clear in his mind, and outraged, he thrust her away.

"Sex?" he burst out in fury. "Am I on no higher level than that in your view—a primitive who'd be satisfied with sex when you could give me the *stars?"*

Lianne sprawled motionless on the bunk where she had fallen, her face set with anguish and resignation. She did not answer.

"I don't need anything from you," Noren said. "Or from your people, either. If they're hoping to observe a so-called primitive civilization's reaction to foreknowledge of certain doom, they'll be disappointed—because we're not going under. I'm going to have children, and I'm going to see to it that others do, too, children who can live on this world without the metal you see fit to deny us."

For a moment a light flared in Lianne's eyes; then, as he went on speaking, their brilliant blue darkened. "That's not all," Noren told her. "We respect each other here, and we respect privacy—but since you don't rank us on your level, you've forfeited all right to be treated as human by our standards. Stefred could have had all your secrets during your inquisition if he'd chosen to take them without consent; he will take them now. Whatever knowledge we can get from your mind, we'll get. It may be you know the key to metal synthesization after all, maybe even to the Unified Field Theory—"

"You aren't going to tell Stefred or anyone else who I am, Noren," Lianne declared with clear assurance. "Not ever."

"What's to stop me? I've got proof you can't deny."

"No one will believe the disc; it will only discredit your genetic work."

"They'll believe the computers if the blood test is repeated by experts."

"There will be no opportunity to repeat it. If you tell, I will kill myself, as I would have if Stefred had pursued the inquisition too far in the first place—there's no way he can forestall that. Did you think I came unprepared?"

Noren stared at her in astonishment, sensing beyond doubt that this was no empty threat. She meant it. "Why?" he asked, baffled. "Why is secrecy worth giving your life for?"

"Think about it sometime," she replied quietly. "You won't like the answer, but you're capable of figuring it out, part of it, anyway."

He was too aroused by rage and frustration to think anything out at the moment. He wanted no more of Lianne, not now, not ever except as an information source—yet she remained unmoving, showing no sign that she intended to leave his room. Turning his back on her, Noren strode out the door, realizing only dimly that he'd been left no choice, that he was on his way to find Veldry.

Chapter Seven

Noren awoke in a bed not his own, unsure of whether or not it was morning. In the windowless rooms of the towers one couldn't tell, and his inner time sense seemed hazy. The lamp was on; he could see the tall time-glass in the corner. Its sand had run all the way through—but would Veldry have turned it over as people usually did on retiring? Under the circumstances, that seemed unlikely.

He found to his dismay that he had little recollection of what he and Veldry had said to each other. He'd intended only to ask her...somehow it had gone further than that. He ought, he supposed, to be glad. Instead he felt as if something very special had been devalued.

Veldry sat at the foot of the bed, her back to him, brushing her hair. It was long and dark, like Talyra's. He had, he remembered, imagined he was with Talyra, much as he had during the secret dream: Veldry's own identity had been vague, like that of the woman the First Scholar had loved. Only this had not been a dream. He hadn't been wholly himself—he'd been so hot with anger that he'd not thought beyond his vow that he *would* bring about his people's survival—yet he could not say he had not known what he was doing. He'd had too much ale earlier in the evening, perhaps; he'd raged at Lianne's refusal to bring help to the world, and yes, she had roused other feelings too; all those things might explain his impulsiveness. But they did not make what had happened any less real.

He sat up, reaching for his clothes. "Veldry—" he began, wondering what he could possibly say. He had assumed she wouldn't get hurt. He'd supposed making love was something she took lightly. It hadn't been that way; her welcome had been genuine, and her emotions as he'd explained the risk had been deep, though unreadable. That much he did recall.

She turned to him. Her face, of course, was not Talyra's. It was older and lined with past sadness, though now it was alight with joy. It was also, by ordinary standards, more beautiful; Veldry was considered strikingly lovely. But there was more to her than that, Noren realized, trying to guess her thoughts. He sensed more intellect than rumor credited her with. If only he were better at understanding people…

"Veldry," he said stiffly. "I—used you. I'm sorry."

"Don't worry," she answered, "I've never let anyone use me. One thing I always do is make up my own mind." Then, watching his eyes, she suddenly exclaimed, "Noren, you don't believe me! You really think you came here last night and got me to give something you're sorry you asked for, when it wasn't that way at all. You were the one who gave! You've given me the only chance I've ever had to *be* somebody."

"I don't see what you mean."

"I'm—beautiful," she said slowly, not in a boastful way, but as if it were some sort of burden. "I'm acclaimed for my beauty, and that's as far as anyone's looked. When I was a girl, they called me wild; I guess I was, by their scale of values. I had a lover in the village before I was married, and there, that was a disgrace. But I really loved him. Then I found out that all he saw in me was—physical. That was all my husband saw, too. After a while I left him and started telling people what I thought about the world, only no one listened." With a bitter laugh she added, "They didn't even listen to heresy! If a girl's pretty enough, it's assumed she hasn't any thoughts, let alone heretical ones. Do you know what I was finally arrested for? Blasphemy—the blasphemy of claiming to have made love with a Technician."

"Why did you tell a lie like that?" Noren asked, appalled. It could not possibly have been a true claim; Technicians were forbidden by the High Law to take advantage of village women, who, assuming them to be superior beings, would obey any request without question.

"Didn't you ever want to convince people Technicians were human, and that you were their equal?"

Yes, of course he had. All village heretics defied the caste concept; Veldry's form of rebellion had been imaginative if not prudent.

"Maybe I wanted to see the inside of the City," she went on, "or maybe I just wanted to die trying to be more than the object of men's desire. I knew the Scholars were wise. I thought they'd see what I was, even though they'd kill me for it."

"But Stefred did see, surely. He judged you qualified for Scholar rank."

"Yes. At first I was overwhelmed, it was so inspiring—the dreams, I mean. I wouldn't have accepted rank as payment for recanting; I've never sold myself in any way. But the Prophecy...well, I was never a heretic about that; I liked the ritual even as a little girl. I liked the thought of a changing future. I was so dedicated in the beginning, Noren. Only...there hasn't been anything I could do here, to help change things, I mean. I'm not a scientist, my mind isn't that sort. I know officially the work I do rates just as much respect. But—but men still single me out for my starcursed *beauty!"* She reached out for his hand, clutched it. "You're the first one who's wanted anything more important."

"You've had babies before. That's important."

"Yes, of course, but the men who fathered them weren't thinking about future generations, they just—well, you know. I don't mean they didn't love me, I've never had a lover who didn't claim he was in love...only there was never anything lasting."

"Veldry," Noren said painfully, "I'm not sure what I said about us, and that bothers me, because what's between us can't last, either."

"It will! Not you and me, no, of course I know that. Do you think I wouldn't have known even if you'd tried to pretend?" She stood up, began fastening the front of her tunic. "You'd never been with anyone but Talyra before, had you?"

He didn't reply. "I knew that, too," Veldry went on. "You were still with Talyra last night, in your mind, anyway."

"I suppose I was. And it wasn't fair to you," he confessed in misery. "You're *you,* and I didn't respect you enough. It wasn't right."

"How can you say you didn't respect me? You told me future generations will live because of us! That our child will be the first person truly adapted to this world, that from him and others like him will come a race that can survive after the machines break down, and maybe someday, somehow, will get back to the stars. No one ever talks to me about things like that. You did. You asked my opinion of what the woman did in the dream. And when I said I've always wanted to be the kind of person she was, do something really significant and daring, I meant it."

"Even knowing how it turned out for her?"

"Even so—because someone's got to try, somebody's got to take the risks. I admire you for taking them, even going against the Council to take them. You paid me the biggest compliment anyone ever has by guessing I'd be willing to take them, too. That's what matters, not the fact you can't fall in love with me."

"I wish I could, Veldry," Noren told her. "But I'm not ever going to fall in love again."

"Yes, you are," she said gently. "In time, you are. I'm not the right person for you, but in time there'll be someone—not to replace Talyra, no one ever could—but someone different, someone you'll share a whole new life with. And she will be a very fortunate woman."

"I hope you'll find someone to share with, too."

"Maybe it'll happen. I try—every time, I believe it will, only there just aren't many men who look at things the way I do. I—I'll always be happy to know there's one, and that I'm having his child."

"We can't really be sure yet," Noren pointed out, "and much as I'd like to promise I'll be back—"

"You won't be back," Veldry acknowledged. "What happened last night couldn't happen twice, not between you and me. But I wouldn't have asked you to stay if the timing had been wrong. I wouldn't have presumed to take Talyra's place without expecting to conceive. You mustn't worry yet—I'm pretty sure there's going to be a baby."

Back in his own room, alone, Noren began facing the fact that there was nothing further he could do until the baby was born. Nothing…and he did not see how he could live with his own thoughts, let alone carry on normal relationships with people, considering the magnitude of the secrets he now bore.

He did have to keep Lianne's secret. He was absolutely convinced, as if she'd somehow communicated it directly to his inner mind, that Lianne would kill herself if he told anyone about her. To be sure, he might tell Stefred in confidence—but no, Lianne would sense that Stefred knew. She was too intuitive not to. And if she carried out her threat, Stefred would suffer terribly.

Think about it sometime, Lianne had said when he'd asked why secrecy was worth her life. She'd said it was one mystery he might solve. He'd never approved of secrets. No Scholar did; the guardianship of knowledge was condoned only as a necessary evil.

How could Lianne have gotten through the tests of candidacy if she accepted an equivalent form of secrecy as right?

For that matter, how had she gotten through them at all?

Stefred had not invaded her privacy. But he must certainly have tested her in all relevant ways. If she did not truly care about the survival of future generations, she would have been disqualified. If she considered herself superior to people, even subconsciously, she'd have been screened out, too; that was one thing for which prospective Scholars were probed very thoroughly. Anyway, it just wasn't possible to believe Lianne's view was as heartless as she'd claimed. He, Noren, had long known how she felt toward him, and the kind of love she'd been hiding could not exist in someone whose inner feelings were inhuman.

The other kind, the outward physical expression...Lianne had not offered that before; she'd understood too well about Talyra. How could she have been so inconsistent in the end? It wasn't just that she wanted his love—she'd had her chance, she could have lived with him for weeks without confessing there'd be no child. What he'd discovered shouldn't have altered anything, for she knew better than to think he'd accept that sort of "comfort" from her. The pieces didn't fit. She'd risked a secret she'd give her life to keep by refusing him, then at the last minute, had insulted him by suggesting...

Oh, Noren thought suddenly, oh, what a fool he'd been! Both times, she had been thinking of the child she couldn't give him. When his discovery had made him balk at the risk of the experiment, she'd insulted him purposely to drive him in anger to Veldry.

She'd taken terrible chances. In his rage he might have gone straight to Stefred if it hadn't been that she was his only link to more information about the aliens. Why must she keep their presence secret? For the same reason the Founders' secrets had been kept—people in general simply could not live with the frustration of knowing themselves to be cut off from the wider universe. Noren was not sure he would be able to live with it, even temporarily. He wasn't sorry for his discovery, not when he'd felt deeply since childhood that it was always preferable to know the truth. But few others felt that way. He and Lianne had agreed on that, the day they'd talked about the alien sphere. *He* had told *her* that most Scholars refused to acknowledge its implications! No wonder she'd realized he could figure out the need for secrecy.

To hide knowledge was evil, yes. But necessary in this case, too, if his genetic work was the only hope. Yet how could it be, when there was an alien starship standing by?

Lianne was on his side, but on her own people's, too. She had not said she was in conflict with them; she was their agent, their observer. How could they justify letting the caste system stand another two generations when they could end it by supplying metal? Lianne considered it evil, she couldn't have qualified for Scholar status otherwise, still she wasn't condemning her people's inaction. Besides, after the genetic change was put into effect, the world would lose its metal-based technology, lose the Six Worlds' heritage of knowledge—surely she could not let that happen. And if the aliens must intervene eventually, why not now?

In time, if you have courage enough, you'll begin to perceive what's involved, she'd said. In his anger Noren hadn't stopped to ponder that. He'd indeed been a fool, he now realized. He had expected understanding their ways to be *easy!* He had been picturing a starship like the Six Worlds' ships, "advanced" in the sense of having faster-than-light communicators, but not the vessel of a truly alien culture. He'd imagined no disquieting mysteries—yet at the same time he'd anticipated being immediately given all the answers to the secrets of the universe. Enlightenment didn't work like that, not even for heretics who entered the City as Scholar candidates. One could hardly expect education by aliens to be less difficult than learning about the heritage of the Six Worlds. How blind he'd been not to see the comparison.

Stefred, too, had warned him that he would suffer, that there would be a price for knowledge. No doubt this was also the case with alien knowledge. Noren's spirits lifted. He must face an ordeal, perhaps, but it would be the sort of challenge he'd long ago found he enjoyed.

He must not judge Lianne's people prematurely, he thought as he put on fresh clothes. After all, he'd judged the Scholars throughout boyhood on the basis of false premises and had learned that motives couldn't be guessed from the outside. He would not make that mistake again.

Sulking in his room would get him nowhere. He must prove himself worthy to be enlightened by proceeding with the research they considered essential. Though he couldn't do any more with human genetics until his child's birth, it would be possible to design the genetic changes needed to enable grain to grow in untreated soil. Low priority as that was, it would be constructive. Even if metal became available in time, ability to live off the land would be desirable. Of course! The genetic change would be needed in any case for his human race to be self-sufficient; knowing that, the aliens would see how far he could go without aid. In the meantime, they'd be evaluating his readiness to receive what would ultimately be offered. Heartened, Noren went to the refectory for a meal.

Later that day he saw Stefred. "I ran the blood test," he told him impassively. "It showed Lianne's right; genetically there's no chance of her getting pregnant."

"I'm sorry, of course, for her sake," Stefred said, "but someday I'll make her see that she's worth as much as any other woman."

"That shouldn't be too big of a problem," Noren agreed. He did not say, however, that he hoped she and Stefred would become lovers; he discovered to his surprise that this was no longer quite true.

Noren tried, honestly, to work. He sat at a computer console long past suppertime reading technical genetic data about grain. But he could not keep his mind from wandering.

He'd resolved to question Lianne no further until he had proven he could conquer impatience. So that evening after Orison it was she who came seeking *him*—he glanced up from the console and saw her standing there, looking so stricken that he was overcome by remorse. It hadn't occurred to him that she might need reassurance.

"Lianne, you didn't think I'd stay angry, did you?" he asked.

"I wasn't sure," she replied in a low voice. "I was afraid you'd hate me, but I see you already understand what I was doing—"

How could she? Noren wondered. Intuition couldn't possibly be that specific—and for some reason he guessed she knew about Veldry, too, although he was positive that Veldry would have told no one. Perhaps this was his own wishful thinking; he found he was relieved at the idea of not having to tell Lianne.

"Anyway, that's not why I came," she was saying. "There are things I've got to tell you."

They went upstairs and out into the starlit courtyard. Seeing the sky, Noren felt more awe of it than he'd experienced since his trip into space to retrieve the orbiting starship hull used at the outpost. But now his awe was elevating, not terrifying. Now he need not worry about the meaning of that vast universe; he was with someone who *knew.* Perhaps someday he might be allowed to board her people's ship...

"How many of those stars have you been to?" he whispered, wonder-stricken.

"Orbited? I don't know, I've never kept count. This is the tenth planet I've landed on."

"Counting the one where you were born?"

"I wasn't born on a planet. Only relatively immature human species live that way. We live in orbiting cities, most of us, and keep our home planets as parks."

"Why were the Six Worlds so crowded after the civilization matured, then?" Noren asked. "They had orbiting labs, but not cities in orbit."

"Noren," Lianne said levelly, "the Six Worlds' civilization wasn't mature, that is, your species wasn't—isn't. Inventing space travel's near the *beginning* of the evolutionary timescale." Before he could say anything she went on, "The Six Worlds were unusual in not having orbiting cities at the stage they had reached, though. It was because the solar system had so many planets similar to the mother world. In most systems, colonizing in orbit is more practical than settling neighboring planets."

He turned to her, eager to hear more; but the sight of her eyes cut short his questions. It was as if she'd been crushed by personal tragedy—evidently something far more important than his curiosity was at issue. "Lianne, what's the matter?" he asked. "What's happened?"

"You don't know what it means, my having given myself away," she murmured. "I'm not blaming you for what you did, only—"

"Only what?" Suddenly it occurred to him that her own people might be angered. "They won't punish you, will they?" he demanded, appalled.

"No. All the same, there will be consequences."

"That's what I used to tell Talyra," he recalled sadly, "before I assumed priesthood, when she could see I was unhappy and thought the Scholars must be punishing me for my heresy. Finally she realized the consequences just followed of themselves."

"Yes," Lianne agreed. "But your heresy wasn't a mistake. You had no load on your conscience. The position I'm in is more like when you crashed the aircar, except worse—possibly much worse. I may have upset the future evolution of your species, you see."

"I don't, quite. I guess I see that if I'd refused to keep working on genetics because I don't understand the need, that might be your fault. But I'm not going to refuse. Even without understanding, I'm going to play the game."

"It's more than a game. And it'll be harder for you, knowing about us, than it would have been otherwise. If—if that affects the course of your life, Noren, I'll be responsible."

"Don't worry on my account," Noren told her. "I'll take full responsibility for my own fate, Lianne. And if it does turn out worse than I imagine, I still won't be sorry, any more than I was sorry for becoming a heretic and learning the truth about the nova."

"I realize that," she said soberly. "One part of me grieves because you're going to suffer, yet another part knows you'll think it's worth it. That's not the thing that scares me."

"Then what is?"

"I told you I'm bound by a commitment," Lianne said. "It's—well, formal, like commitment to the priesthood as for you, except it's not just sharing accountability, it's personal. When we're alone or in small teams on primitive worlds, our actions can change those worlds' histories unless we're awfully careful. We swear to put the native people's best interests above everything else, and their best interests normally demand that we not influence them at all. We swear specifically, for instance, to die rather than let them find out about our existence. I'd have killed myself to prevent your knowing, Noren, just as I still would to prevent the secret from going any further—not because you'll suffer from knowing, but because of what it may do to your people's future."

"Our future isn't very bright," Noren observed grimly, "unless you do help us. You could hardly make it worse."

"Yes, I could. I may have already, unwittingly. There are scenarios you don't know about."

"I think it's my right to know, Lianne."

"No, it isn't," she said with sorrow, "but of course you aren't going to take my word for that. And now, since you already know more than you should, you do have to be told enough to give you a basis for the decisions you'll be forced to make. I—I lay awake all last night deciding to be frank with you, even though that means breaking my oath not to disclose anything."

"I don't expect you to give me more knowledge than I've earned," Noren protested. "I've thought a lot, too, and I've figured out a good deal. You'd have refused to support your people's policies in the first place if you'd believed they were wrong! You've got the instincts of a heretic in spite of having only pretended to be one during your inquisition. And that means—"

"Wait a minute! What makes you think I was pretending? I was masquerading as a village woman, of course, but everything else was *real.*"

"The qualities Stefred judged you on, yes; that's what I'm saying. But the defiance of the High Law, the risks and the enlightenment and the initiation, that couldn't have been real in the same way as for the rest of us—you knew our secrets from the start. That bothered me till I realized that because you weren't gaining anything personally, it couldn't have affected Stefred's evaluation of your motives."

"The risk was real enough," Lianne said. "After all, I thought I might have to kill myself. I would have, if he'd probed too deeply."

"Maybe so," Noren conceded. "I—I believe you really would give your life to save us from something you're convinced would harm us. But a convicted heretic expects to die without hope of saving anyone. It's a matter of principle, of standing out against evil. You knew at the beginning the evil was necessary."

"No, I didn't."

"You must have known our life support equipment's irreplaceable."

"I didn't; none of us did when we landed here. We only knew something strange was going on. And what we saw, we didn't like. We thought what you thought when you were a boy, that the Scholars were dictators. There was just one thing that didn't fit: we couldn't understand why the villagers had so much freedom."

"Freedom? Freedom to live in the Stone Age, shut out of the City?"

"Noren," Lianne said gently, "in every similar culture that we've observed, the outsiders would have been slaves of the City—or else equipment wouldn't have been expended on them. We couldn't guess why they were permitted to live, dependent on City aid, yet free to govern themselves, not exploited, not even taxed. It was the strangest setup we'd ever encountered."

"But still a bad one."

"Of course. Not as bad as it could have been, but bad; I was a real heretic in the sense that I believed that. I also believed the Prophecy was a myth the Scholars had invented to maintain power."

"Didn't the references to the Mother Star make it clear? You knew we were colonists, and you surely knew what a nova is."

"Yes," she agreed. "Only I didn't know the entire Prophecy. Nobody sat down and recited the whole thing, after all. Everyone in the village assumed it was common knowledge. We'd heard just scattered passages—and we didn't hear the High Law at all till I got caught breaking it."

Noren stared at her, startled. "You didn't plan your arrest?"

She shook her head. "I filled a drinking jug from a stream right before the eyes of a group of women gathering reeds to weave baskets. It never occurred to me it could be wrong. We're trained to respect local taboos, but drinking the water isn't taboo anywhere, unless it's radioactive or something. We'd only been on the surface a couple of days; we hadn't had a chance to observe the restrictions on food and drink." With a rueful smile she added, "The village women surrounded me, taunted me about what would happen when the Scholars got hold of me. Scared? Noren, the night I spent in the village jail was the worst I'd ever been through, ttil then, anyway."

"Couldn't your people have helped you escape?"

"Yes, but I chose to see it through. We realized we'd have to get someone into the City sooner or later to learn the facts about this world."

"The villagers must have told you that no one's ever been released from the Inner City," reflected Noren, puzzled. "You couldn't have known then that you'll be free to simply walk out when your job's finished, not if you didn't suspect the truth about the Scholars. So you were risking possible death and almost certain imprisonment—for *information?* Information that not only wouldn't benefit your own people, but that you probably couldn't ever pass on to them?"

"It's a bit more complicated than that," she admitted slowly.

"I'm sure it is," Noren said. "What you've just told me makes me surer than ever. We don't rate your help automatically—all right, I won't argue with that. We have to prove ourselves, pass some kind of test. And maybe for me, because I've found out too soon, the testing will be harder than it was meant to be. I'll—cooperate, Lianne. I don't want you to bypass anything for my sake. Whatever I have to go through to earn us a place in your interstellar society, I'm willing to take on."

She sighed. "You have no idea of what you're saying. And I'm tempted to let it pass; you've phrased it so that I could do that without lying."

"If my statement of it is true, we can let it pass for now," Noren declared resolutely. "You came to judge us. I don't fear your judgment."

"Did you fear Stefred's?"

"When I was first brought into the City, you mean? That was different; I had misconceptions about what I'd be judged on."

"So do you now," Lianne said. "That's why I have to warn you."

"What I said *is* true, isn't it?"

"In a sense. It's true as far as it goes, just as the Prophecy's words are true. I'm here to evaluate circumstances, and they're such that you, personally, will have to take on a great deal. Ultimately, if you succeed, your people will attain their rightful place. But it will not happen as you envision, any more than cities will rise out of the ground on the day the Star appears."

"I'm not naive," Noren assured her. "I know I can't imagine exactly what will happen. Later, when I've done whatever's expected of me—"

"That will be the bad time for you, Noren," Lianne said, squeezing his hand. "As if the City had shut you out for your heresy instead of in. It might be kinder of me not to tell you this, but cruel, I think, in the long run. I can't let you build false hopes."

"You've acknowledged we can earn a place among you."

"Yes, in time—your species can—but…it's a *long* time…long after the Star's light has reached this world."

"Not—in my lifetime?" Noren went cold, beginning to see where she was leading. "Lianne, I can't accept that!"

"Perhaps not. It's asking far too much of you; I never wanted you to bear so great a burden." She was once more close to tears, though her voice was well controlled. And again, he could sense more than she'd said, as if he had become as intuitive as she. Very, very quietly her words continued…

Noren blinked his eyes, finding himself giddy; his mind was reeling. This wasn't just his own emotion, or even his perception of hers—there were concepts he could not integrate with the words Lianne was saying…or was she still speaking at all? Abruptly he became aware of silence. Had she said he must accept the burden for his people's sake, that nothing but his voluntary acquiescence could save them? That didn't make sense! *Lianne,* he thought despairingly, *you don't know! You can't, no one who's been to ten planets could know what it is to be confined forever to this one.*

Lianne's hand tightened on his. "Let's sit down," she whispered.

The paving stones of the courtyard were still warm from the day's heat. Noren leaned back, gazing up at the stars. *It's not wrong to want the whole universe!* he persisted. *It's not wrong to keep searching for the truth, no more so to demand it of your people than it was to demand it of the Scholars when I was a heretic. I'm willing to earn access to knowledge, but not to renounce it.*

Lianne pressed close to him, not in a sensual way but in a gesture of complete and genuine sympathy. In her eyes was understanding as well as sadness. Somehow she did know. Could this be part of the test? Noren wondered. Was he expected to defy her people's edict, as Scholar candidates were required to defy the teaching that it was wrong to aspire to the High Priests' secrets? *Yes,* he thought dizzily, *she admires strength of will. She no more wants passive acceptance than Stefred wants heretics to recant!*

He faced her. "Look at me," he said, "and tell me that there is no way for me to win your people's aid during my lifetime."

"I won't lie to you—even if I were willing to, you'd realize in due course and stop trusting me." *Full trust between us is the only chance we have of getting through what's ahead,* she seemed to be saying. "There is one way," Lianne continued. "But don't found your hope on that; it's one I don't believe you'll ever use."

"By the Mother Star, I will!" Noren swore.

"Hardly in that name, if you hold it sacred." She tried to smile. "I'm speaking in riddles, as Stefred does to candidates, because I shouldn't be speaking of this at all. And you're not ready; there's a lot you need to know before you can begin to grasp the situation we're in."

Noren was silent. *I won't plead with you,* he was thinking, *but if you're going to tell me some of it, what's wrong with right now?*

"Are you up to that tonight?"

"Yes, of course," he declared, his head spinning so that he scarcely noticed that she had answered his unspoken thought.

"I mean physically—or doesn't the disorientation bother you?"

"Does it show?" Noren burst out, mortified. The odd giddiness did seem to have become physical, and his mind wasn't quite clear; looking back over the conversation he found it hard to recall all Lianne's words. *Am I going crazy?* he thought in sudden panic. *It's not as if I haven't been through plenty of stress in the past; I should be able to handle it by this time.*

"This is something you're not equipped to handle," Lianne said. "It doesn't show from the outside, but I get your sensations."

With forced levity he said, "Sometimes I think you're a witch after all, and can read people's minds."

"I admitted long ago the villagers would have accused me of witchcraft if they'd known more about me," Lianne replied, not laughing.

Why laugh? an inner voice told him. *Mind-to-mind communication's natural enough—* Horrified, he cut off the thought. He must indeed be going crazy. Mind reading was only a superstition; he had heard of it in Six Worlds' folklore, but never from any other source. Desperately, his thinking now under firm control, he reflected, *If it were real, Stefred would have mentioned it, surely.*

"Stefred would be even more upset by it than you are," Lianne said dryly, "because he's read everything in the computers about psychology, and he believes the same theories of the human mind the Founders did."

Lianne, what are you doing to me? Noren cried out silently, aware at last that this was not mere imagination, and that it terrified him.

"Nothing I haven't done before with both you and Stefred when I had need," she answered calmly. "I'm simply doing it now on a level at which you're conscious of it. You must know about it to understand my role here, and you wouldn't have believed in it without a demonstration."

"You've been reading our minds all along?" he protested, appalled. "This is what we've been calling intuition?"

"Well, yes, but 'reading minds' isn't an accurate way to describe it. I can't invade anyone's private thoughts—I get only emotions, plus ideas people want to communicate to me. If you want to tell me something, consciously or unconsciously, I know without being told; but nothing you want to conceal is accessible."

"I guess I shouldn't be surprised that you have abilities we don't," Noren said slowly. "You're a different species, after all. But your getting my thoughts wasn't all that happened. I—I think I got some of your thoughts, too."

"Yes. That was the frightening part. I induced you to knowingly accept mental input in a form that's unfamiliar to you and beyond your control. I knew it would scare you, but I had to seize the opportunity that came to do it in a way that wasn't dangerous."

"Opportunity?"

"Strong emotion. That enhances everyone's psychic power. For a person in a culture like yours where the existence of telepathy isn't acknowledged, it's essential, barring some artificial techniques I'd rather not try."

Noren frowned. "Are you saying inhabitants of all worlds have this power?"

"This and some rather more spectacular ones I'm not even going to demonstrate. They are latent in all species. Full conscious control of them is possible only to those further evolved than yours, though people with exceptional talent sometimes have spontaneous psychic experiences when the circumstances are right." She added, after a pause, "A few individuals, like Stefred, use telepathy unconsciously with their close associates."

"Stefred? He does what you do?"

"Not to the same degree, and he's not aware that he's doing it. You know, though, that he's unusually skilled in understanding people and in winning their trust." She did laugh at Noren's expression. "You needn't be so shocked; there's nothing sinister about it. It's a gift like any other, and you've recognized all along that you don't have the same gifts Stefred has. Yours are different."

"I can't learn to develop such skills, then." The thought pained him.

"No," Lianne said gently. "I could teach you to converse with me silently without feeling dizzy, but there are perils along that road. What comes naturally is harmless. Tonight I forced a level of rapport that was...well, let's say a calculated risk. I won't do that again because there's no justification for it. I'll stick to the sort of thing I've done with you in the past—for instance, last night when I convinced you I was serious about killing myself if you didn't keep my secret."

"I wondered why I believed you," Noren reflected.

"It was because I communicated more than words or the idea the words expressed, I also communicated feelings. That level's safe; it's when telepathy is allowed to disrupt your thinking processes that we could run into trouble."

"With your own people...you use even higher levels?"

"I have passed on all I've learned of the Six Worlds to the members of my team outside the City," Lianne admitted. "That's one reason you need to know I'm telepathic."

Trying to seem unshaken, he asked, "Have you told them about me?"

"Not that you've learned my identity—they're no longer within range. I've told them other things about you."

"What?" inquired Noren, curious as to why she would have singled him out to be mentioned in what sounded like her official report.

"That the welfare of your species depends solely on you."

He drew back, stunned. Lianne continued, "You've been assuming that only your knowledge of us has put you in a key position. But the position's been yours all along, Noren. The Scholars who've been considering you the best hope for the future are right."

"Lianne, it can't be like that! The fate of a whole human race can't depend on one person—it couldn't even if no alien starship was around."

"Normally it couldn't," she agreed. "We've had occasion before to judge a species' chance of survival, and we've never been able to identify the person on whom it depended, or even say it was dependent on some unknown person. But this is a very abnormal case. There are so few of you, and you have such limited resources, that we know positively that no one else has the potential to do what needs doing—and there isn't time to wait for another such person to be born."

"But I'm not what people think," Noren protested. "I'm not the genius they've been hoping for; if you're telepathic you must know that! I'll try to change things so we can survive here, but I may fail."

"Yes. And your discovering who I am has increased your chance of failure, which is why I'm so worried about my mistakes," Lianne confessed.

"You've no right to be so highhanded with us, to set me up as a game piece forced to win or lose this world according to your arbitrary rules," Noren said bitterly. "You can't take it on yourselves—"

"That's just the point," said Lianne. "We can't. We're not wise enough; our intervention could do more harm than good."

"Yet you think *I'm* wise enough?"

"Perhaps not. But you do have the right to act on behalf of your own people." She got to her feet. "There's more to it than this, Noren. First, though, you'd better hear some background—and if we're going to talk all night, let's sit someplace that's private."

She was an agent of what she called the Anthropological Service, the representative not of a single species, but of an organization made up of volunteers from many worlds united in an interstellar federation. The Service was not easy to get into; candidates, it seemed, were tested even more arduously than Scholar candidates and must prove themselves trustworthy during a long and difficult course of training. That was hardly surprising, Noren thought, considering that these people had to be ready to die for their convictions at any time it became necessary on any planet where they happened to land. They also, he gathered, had to undergo hardships other members of their civilization never encountered. Planets were uncomfortable compared to orbiting cities. And the planets visited by observing teams not only had living conditions that were primitive by Federation standards, they were also too apt to be the scenes of disease, violence and wars.

The worst of visiting such planets, Lianne said, was not the danger. It was the horror of seeing evils one was powerless to prevent. People who didn't find that painful, who didn't care what happened to other species, were not accepted into the Service. One was required to have empathy.

It sounded like a strange life to volunteer for, yet still, it was the only way to truly explore the universe, see more than the orbiting cities and the planets kept like parks beneath them. Federation citizens outside the Service were not permitted to land on the worlds of species not yet mature; there was too much danger of their doing inadvertent harm. Furthermore, Service life was challenging. Lianne was a person who enjoyed that. Other challenges had been open to her—she was rather vague about their nature, and he had the uncomfortable feeling that she considered it over his head—

but the Service was the one she had chosen. It was an irrevocable choice; the commitment she'd made was permanently binding, an arrangement that eliminated people who merely wanted a few years of adventure.

She had come to his world as one of three agents dispatched to investigate the undecipherable signal of a faster-than-light communicator in a solar system where no such communicator should be. "Only three?" Noren asked, surprised.

"We were among the few aboard who happened to look enough like your people to pass among you. A service ship carries agents of many species, since we never know till we orbit what sort of natives we'll find."

"But to commit a whole starship all this time, if only three of you could take action—"

"It orbited for a few weeks, then went elsewhere."

"And *stranded* you here? With just two others?"

"No. Just me; the others went on. The ship will be back to contact me, don't worry. I've been stranded on alien worlds before." She smiled. "It's not done just for efficiency—it's a good strategy for preventing field agents from getting illusions of power."

Their tangible support varied with circumstances, she told him. On some planets they did keep whole teams for the duration of the mission, and often even offworld equipment. On this one they realized, from having examined the Six Worlds' stripped starship hulls they found in orbit, that they dared not possess any equipment a starfaring people could recognize as alien. Their shuttle abandoned them with nothing but native-style clothes and one concealed signaling device with which they could recall it. Being telepathic, they got the meaning of remarks villagers addressed to them, and since one of them was a skilled linguist they quickly learned the language. They knew from the Service's vast experience how to be inconspicuous in the first village they entered and inquisitive in the second. It was a routine mission except for the presence of the mysterious City and the fact that the faster-than-light communicator, which had since been identified as an ancient artifact of a Federation species, was not in the City but in the outpost beyond the mountains—routine, at least, until Lianne's unexpected arrest.

She'd communicated telepathically with the others during her night in the village jail. The team leader had advised her that she wasn't obliged to accept the risk of entering the City—apparently there were situations in which she might have been, but in this case she was free to choose. She'd decided to take the chance. Not just to learn what was going on, though it had become obvious that they were dealing with something that didn't fit known patterns; and not, evidently, to do anything against the Scholars if they turned out to be dictators, since that too would be interference. "There was a reason, Noren," Lianne said, "and what I found here proved the risk was warranted. That's something you'll see later." Having learned he must let her tell it her own way, he nodded and did not interrupt.

She had been thoroughly trained to deal with stress, and at the beginning, even within the City, she had the telepathic support of her teammates. When she was first brought before the Scholars, her only serious fear was that they would probe her mind forcibly by methods against which she'd be powerless. She had means to suicide if that seemed imminent, but the decision would be a hard one, for she could resist most drugs and might not be able to predict what sort they'd use. Fortunately, the inquisition turned out to be quite different from what she'd expected. A few minutes with Stefred and she knew her secret was safe from him, that even under the relatively mild drugs he did give her, he would not attempt to make her betray information she wanted to conceal.

But at the same time, she knew she was facing an experience unlike any that agents had previously encountered in fieldwork. She was being judged by the Service's own criteria of worthiness—Stefred approached it as her instructors had, and as an individual he was equally expert. Yet it was not mere instruction. She was aware from his emotions that it was deadly serious, and that by her own code as well as his, it would be unethical as well as impossible to get through such a test by faking.

"According to what you've said about the training you had, you must have known you'd be able to pass it honestly," Noren protested.

"That was the trouble," Lianne said. "I did know, so I wasn't scared—it was fear I'd have had to fake, and I couldn't have, even if I'd wanted to; he's too perceptive to be fooled. You know why he uses stress tactics even with candidates he's sure of. They've got to be genuinely afraid of cracking up before he can proceed with the enlightenment, or else they'll never be certain afterward that they couldn't have been made to recant by terror. I was already certain; I'd been through similar experiences in my training, designed to give me that kind of confidence. But Stefred naturally assumed I simply didn't know what real terror is like. He kept looking for ways to show me, and none of them worked since I'd picked up enough telepathically to realize he wasn't going to subject me to any harm."

"How much more did you pick up?" asked Noren, frowning.

"Not anything enlightening," Lianne assured him. "I had no more access to his secrets than he had to mine. But of course, emotionally, he does want candidates to trust him—I knew the pressures he was using were for my benefit. And I knew he wanted me to resist them."

"Is that why you didn't recant in the first place? I've wondered, because from your standpoint, since you were there just to get information and weren't part of our society, pretending to play along with the Scholars wouldn't have been wrong. Especially not if you were offered knowledge in exchange for submission, as I was."

"Stefred didn't use that strategy with me. He never does in cases where he sees the candidate's hoping to learn something that might be passed on to others who oppose the system. The bribe was a valid test of motivation for you only because you were convinced that if you accepted it, you'd be the only one to gain." She stopped for a moment; when she continued it was with telepathic overtones of intense feeling. "I didn't know whether or not resisting recantation would be to my advantage, Noren. That wasn't the basis on which I was acting. When we take on this sort of role, we act as we personally would if we'd been born into it. I truly opposed what the Scholars seemed to stand for. If I'd really been a village woman, I'd have refused to endorse the caste system, the Prophecy or the High Law; so that was how I had to play it—otherwise I'd have been lying instead of just concealing things."

"I guess I see," Noren admitted. "There's a difference; *he* conceals without lying, and in fact we all do, as priests. I did with Talyra."

"Yes. The scale of values in the Inner City is much like ours—on most worlds we don't fit in as well, and sometimes we're forced to lie. Here I've lived as if I were one of you. I want you to know that; it's important."

To her, Noren perceived, *important not just because she values honesty or because she needs my trust...it's important because of how she feels about me.* "I owe you honesty, too," he said. "I don't doubt you mean all you're saying, but there's one thing you seem to have overlooked. The initial risk, the stress you let Stefred impose on you, your opposition to the caste system—all that may have been real. The ordeals of enlightenment and recantation may have been as rough for you as for any of us. But the sentencing, *that* was sham, Lianne."

She didn't reply. Noren went on painfully, "When we kneel in that ceremony and hear ourselves sentenced to life imprisonment within the City, we believe it. We don't know what's going to happen to us here, either the good or the bad; but we know it's permanent, a real price, not something we can get out of when we're through playing the game—"

"Game? Do you suppose that's all it is to me?"

"I'd like to believe it's not. I guess I do believe, now, that you're sincere about wanting to help us even though you've been taught not to interfere. But you aren't stuck here, as we are. Lianne, the City isn't our real prison—this planet is! All of us who've been through the dreams know that we and our people have been deprived of our rightful heritage. You're pretending to share that sentence when you're really free. That's the deceit I can't ignore, not that your genes are different or that you concealed your origin from Stefred. It doesn't matter that you believe the same things as a real heretic, that you're willing to suffer or even die for them. When you submitted to the sentencing, you were lying, and so you're not a real Scholar—you're acting the part without paying the price."

He could feel her surge of emotion, not anger at his accusation, but a mixture of sorrow and guilt. "I haven't overlooked that," she said quietly. "It's why I haven't assumed the robe."

Noren was speechless; it had not occurred to him that Lianne would see more in religion than a mask for secrets. He'd been assuming she wasn't a priest because she supported the genetic change that would make fulfillment of the Prophecy's promises impossible.

"Stefred doesn't understand, of course," she continued. "He's eager for me to do it because I can't appear at inquisitions unrobed, and he feels that by now I could help new candidates more than the Scholars he's been using as assistants during the open questioning. That's true; and I'd like to take part in ritual, too...I'd like to give hope if nothing else. But you are right, Noren—I am not wholly committed. There are roles I can accept here, but not priesthood."

"For you it wouldn't be a religious kind of priesthood anyway, even if your ship never came back," Noren argued, "so why does it matter ethically whether or not you wear the robe?"

"Why wouldn't it be religious? That's what priesthood *is.*"

"Well, you don't believe in the Star—"

"Do you?"

"Not the way some do. I don't believe there are any supernatural powers out there for it to symbolize. But it's come to mean something to me, it stands for truth I can't reach—I need that. You don't."

"Oh, Noren." She did not have to use words; attuned now to the emotional channel of communication, he perceived for the first time what Lianne had been trying all evening to convey. *No one can reach all truth. Even people who've visited many stars can't, people whose resources aren't restricted. But the more one does know of the universe, the more one longs to reach further...and the harder it is to accept one's limitations.*

"Lianne, I—I take it back," he said awkwardly. "I think it could all be real for you. Even priesthood could."

"No. When a priest speaks the ritual, he or she acts as spokesman for the people; that's universally true. I have no right to be your people's spokesman. I am limited, but not by the same set of barriers." She smiled and touched his hand. "Don't think I lack sources of faith. I have my own symbols, after all."

"You do?" Almost before the words were uttered Noren was thinking, *Sorry—that's a stupid question.*

"It's not stupid. You associate the need for them with your own world's unique problems—you've never been in a position to generalize."

He absorbed not only her reply, but the feeling behind it. "Are the problems of other worlds...hard, Lianne? As hard to face as ours?"

"For individuals, often a great many individuals, they are worse. You'd know that if you'd ever had to fight in a war."

"I've been more naive that I thought, I guess. I've read what the computers say about the Six Worlds' wars, yet I can't picture them as—reality."

"Reading doesn't tell you enough. In the Service we are taught such things through controlled dreaming," Lianne replied grimly.

"Dreaming? But then when Stefred began it with you—"

"I was afraid," she acknowledged. "You've got to hear the rest of the story. But since you asked a question, I'll answer it first; I'll warn you where the story's heading. For individuals, Noren, life can be worse on many worlds than on this one, and the more immature the civilization, the more suffering people undergo. For whole species, though, the problems are soluble. The suffering leads somewhere; it's part of evolution. Your species is experiencing an interruption of evolution—perhaps an end to its progress. That is far more serious than problems of other kinds. It's terrible in ways you've not yet conceived. Alone, you would not become aware of them."

"I want to be aware of them," Noren declared, inwardly dismayed by the cold terror he'd begun to feel. *I've always wanted the whole truth; why am I afraid now, almost as if I were undergoing another dream?*

He needed no answer—he knew the fear was hers as well as his, that telepathically he was sharing her emotions, much as in controlled dreaming one shared the feelings of the person from whose mind the recording had been made. Lianne was truly afraid for his people. She was not forcing this rapport—he had freedom to reach for it or shut it out, and as always in the dreams, he chose to reach.

Stefred had been unable to scare Lianne during her inquisition; they had reached an impasse, for measures extreme by his standards could not frighten her. She had been taught more than he could guess: not only self-assurance, but methods of controlling her physical reactions. He suffered far more than she did, both from the seemingly harsh tactics he was forced to employ and from his knowledge of the tragedy that might ensue if they failed to challenge her sufficiently.

Ironically, that was the turning point. When Lianne sensed Stefred's growing fear for her, she herself began to feel terror.

She could draw no facts from his mind; she knew only that he was an inwardly compassionate person whose ostensible cruelty was designed to protect her best interests. She'd understood all along that he was testing her rather than attempting to break her, but she had assumed it was to satisfy himself of her sincerity. Now she perceived that he'd been satisfied for quite a while, that the point still at issue was her own awareness of strength; he was preparing her for some mysterious ordeal from which he could not save her. He pitied her even as he strove to ensure that she would meet it with confidence. Lianne could not tell whether Stefred's view was shared by all Scholars or whether he was simply one admirable man playing a dangerous game within a society of tyrants, but she knew he was powerless to spare her the suffering that lay ahead. No hint of its nature came through to her except that in his eyes, the fate in store for her would be permanent, and bravery would be her sole defense.

Until this point, she'd expected she could learn the City's secret and then be rescued in some way. Stefred's feelings made her realize it would be more complicated. There might be no chance of rescue; she might face ceaseless, futile punishment; worst of all, she might learn nothing to justify her sacrifice. But she did not falter. The unanticipated terror hit swiftly, and it took only an instant for her to pass from fearlessness to courage.

Though she showed no outward sign, Stefred was sensitive enough to her emotions to be immediately aware of the difference and to see that she could now be safely enlightened. Thus her fear was compounded, for his inner relief was mixed with worry. He could not guess why she'd slipped suddenly to the verge of panic; could the foregoing stress she'd withstood too well have brought on a delayed reaction? For the first time he found himself dealing with someone he could not understand—someone he must subject to the dream sequence without anticipating what unusual problems she might face in it.

If he had foreseen how great those problems would be, or if he'd been aware that had he shown her the Dream Machine in the first place there'd have been no need to bother with any other stresses, he might never have dared to begin the dreams at all.

At the moment he judged her ready for enlightenment, they were not in his study, where the initial steps were to take place. As he escorted her through the corridor, they passed the dream room, the door of which stood open with complex equipment, sinister in appearance to the inexperienced, plainly visible. "Take a good look," Stefred said casually. "If you persist in your refusal to recant, you will spend a great deal of time strapped into that chair." The remark wasn't meant to be cruel; it was a routine instance of the tactics he used with everyone: a true statement that was unnerving when heard as an implied threat, but heartening when remembered later as one successfully withstood. In the light of Lianne's proven fortitude, he expected her to gain an immediate sense of triumph. To his astonishment and dismay she nearly stumbled against him, her face ashen, and in that moment their fear fed each other's.

"I'm glad he'll never have any suspicion of how rough he made my last hours of ignorance," she told Noren, "because he'd be horror-stricken by what was in my mind."

"You recognized the function of the equipment, I suppose," Noren reasoned, "and if they train you to understand things like wars that way, no wonder you were nervous. That's nothing to be ashamed of."

"We're conditioned to fear controlled dreaming, yes," she agreed, "and not just because it's the only means of showing us evils that don't exist in our own civilization. It's through dreams that we're taught to meet fear itself—after all, we couldn't be seriously afraid of our own instructors. I'm used to training dreams, I don't mind them however scary they are. But there were worse possibilities." She turned to him, her eyes large with remembered terror. "Some cultures use controlled dreaming in ways Stefred is too innocent to imagine."

"I'd be surprised if there's much that Stefred is naive about," observed Noren. "He's read a lot of things he doesn't speak of, evils that sometimes occurred on the Six Worlds. If you mean controlled dreaming could be used for torture, well, even I've imagined that. But you knew he wouldn't do it."

"I wasn't sure how much power he held; I thought I might be taken over by some higher authority—he was afraid of something bad happening to me, certainly, and I realized that what he'd said was less a threat than a true warning. I could deal with torture, though, if it were temporary—"

"It couldn't very well be permanent."

"Yes, it could. A body can be maintained indefinitely with life support equipment and dream input. Only that's not the worst, because if the mental input is pure nightmare, the brain dies relatively soon, and I did know that wasn't going to happen to me. He was thinking in terms of wasted life, not lingering death. The other thing sometimes done isn't called torture; there are worlds where people actually choose it. A person can be kept alive year after year on a machine like that with *pleasant* dreams."

Noren struggled with sudden nausea. "Lianne—that's *horrible.*"

"Of course. To you and to Stefred and to me, to anyone who values consciousness. But it matched the pattern of what I knew at that point. There are societies where it would be considered fitting punishment for heretics, and others where it would be viewed as a merciful alternative to imprisonment in close quarters. I had visions of a compartment somewhere in the City with row after row of encapsuled dreamers, like frozen sleep quarters on a slow, primitive starship except with no oblivion and no promised awakening."

"Oh, Lianne." Noren put his arm around her, found she was trembling.

"I'm not looking for sympathy, you know that," she said quietly. "But understanding how I'm vulnerable is related to the rest of what you need to understand. The next part's even more so, only you won't like what you hear."

"I have to hear it. I want to. But—but Lianne, it's hard because I've always thought of the universe as, well, *good,* somehow. In spite of freak disasters like the nova, I've believed there are more than enough wonderful things out there to balance."

She was radiant for a moment; he sensed an emotion new to him. "There are!" she burst out. Then, slowly, "There are wonders past your imagination. But if I were to show them to you at this stage, you would only feel more bitter. Right now you believe that I am heir to all the glories while you are doomed by fate to a dark prison world. You must see that darkness, too, is universal—then later you'll find that you do have access to some of the light."

Of course, Noren thought as the surge of elation ebbed. *You've got to have seen more good than I have, or else you couldn't possibly bear to confront all you're telling me about.* Aloud he said, "If I've shown any courage in my life, it's been only because I've had no choice. But you, you *chose*—not only here, but at the start, when you chose to be exposed to evils you would never have had to know exist. I admire your strength more than ever; don't think my finding out who you are has changed that."

"You chose, too, by becoming a heretic," she answered.

"I couldn't have been anything else on this world."

"No, because you wouldn't have been content not to look at all sides of things. But it was a choice all the same. Elsewhere you'd have had more options, and you'd have picked the one that let you see farthest. Which on any world would have meant looking at darkness, just as my choice did." With a wry smile she added, "That's why you share my horror at the idea of perpetual sweet dreams."

He shuddered. "Lianne—when you were hooked up to the Dream Machine for your first session, did you really think that was what would happen?"

"No, I knew better by then. I'd been shown the films of the Six Worlds and the Mother Star before that point, and I recognized a nova when I saw one. I'd begun to piece things together—and it was more of a shock than you've guessed, worse than the other, much worse."

The hardest act she'd put on had been concealing the fact that she understood the film of the nova. There was no actual revelation of the Six Worlds' destruction in that film, but for Lianne, of course, its mere identification as the Mother Star was the key to the colony's situation—it would have been even if she hadn't received Stefred's powerful emotions.

The Service had known from the beginning that the people of the planet were not only colonists but lost colonists, out of touch with their world of origin. That had been evident from the converted starships used as living quarters in the City, which like the orbiting hulls were made of an alloy that couldn't be melted and used for other purposes with the facilities available. Lost colonies, however, were not particularly uncommon. In the early phases of every civilization's interstellar expansion, some starships failed to get home. Descendants of their passengers weren't necessarily in danger—they often survived successfully enough, and in due course, were contacted by other explorers of their own species. In any case they were not the sole representatives of their species. The Service did not worry about the welfare of lost colonies.

Novas were another matter entirely. And when Lianne perceived that she would be forced to dream of the nova, she wasn't at all sure she would be able to endure it.

Her experience in controlled dreaming, in voluntary acceptance of nightmare, made it harder rather than easier. She knew in advance that this would be so. She realized that the dreams were ordinarily used with people who did not have any foreknowledge about novas, or even about worlds unlike their own. For them, there would be terror and emotional pain—but there would not be complete grasp of significance. They would not absorb anywhere near all the feelings of the person who'd made the recording, while she would share those feelings fully. And she would suffer other feelings beyond that. One experienced a dream according to one's own background, and her background was such that to her, destruction of an entire human species was an ultimate, intolerable evil. Lesser evils she'd been taught to bear on the basis of evidence that they occurred in all species and were thus apparently part of the evolutionary process. But what answer was there for an evil that robbed all the rest of meaning?

The Service was, of course, aware that novas sometimes destroyed populated solar systems. But never before had such a case been observed—once a nova was detected, there was no way to determine whether the planets of the star had been populated or not. If the star of a Federation solar system novaed, the event was predictable and the population was evacuated. The same was true when a known immature species was similarly endangered…

"Wait a minute!" Noren broke in. "You're saying that if your Service had been observing the Six Worlds before the nova, it would have saved the people?"

"Not all of them; that would have been impossible. But enough to make sure your species was safe."

"But then you're admitting you do intervene sometimes."

"If nothing else can prevent extinction, yes. There is no evil worse than extinction of a whole human species. The Founders were right about that; every Scholar who recants is right about it. I know what you're going to ask next, Noren—but don't ask it, not yet. Hear me out."

Deeply though she feared the dreams, having grasped what they would contain, Lianne had been obliged to undergo them willingly. That was required of her not only by the role she was playing with Stefred, but by her own oath to the Service. Her awareness of the nova changed everything. She now knew that the colonists might be the sole survivors of their home system; it was her responsibility to find out for sure. And if they were indeed the only survivors it was her responsibility to determine whether or not they had the resources to go on surviving.

The dream sequence proved even more taxing than she'd anticipated, for she identified in a close personal way with the First Scholar. She hadn't expected recordings made by anyone with insight so far ahead of most of the people of his civilization. The agony was somewhat tempered by his courage, yet on the other hand, she knew his specific hope for survival to be groundless. It was evident to Lianne that the nuclear research goal was unattainable with the City's facilities—she drew more detail from his thoughts about these than less knowledgeable dreamers could—and she knew from the start what Noren had learned gradually, what most other Scholars, even Stefred, still could not bring themselves to believe. If they relied on synthesization of metal, the colony was doomed.

Furthermore, there was the edited state of the recordings to cope with. "It was bad in the way Stefred explained it to you," she told Noren, "more of a torment than he realized, in fact, to have my mind held within unrealistic limits, because I was so accustomed to full recordings. If you hadn't done what you did to spare me that, there's no telling what would have happened. Even knowing the editing was drastic, I trusted Stefred enough to believe it hadn't been done for deception. But I might have cracked up during the later part of the dream sequence."

She had not been in touch with her teammates at that point; when she'd first grasped the nature of her inquisition, she had broken off with them so as to have no unfair advantage. She had asked them not to resume telepathic communication until she initiated contact herself, and she'd resolutely refrained from doing so not only during the intervals between dreams, but throughout the ceremony of recantation. They had witnessed that ordeal without understanding it. Afterward, however, she had passed on the whole story, and she'd told them what they already saw from the discoveries she reported: there was no question of her leaving the City until she had learned whether anyone had found the route to permanent survival of the colony.

"Genetic engineering, you mean? But I didn't find out about it till weeks after you recanted," Noren objected. "Why did you stay so long?"

"You'd begun to be interested in genetics—I'd learned that much."

"Telepathically?" he inquired uncomfortably.

"No, at least not till you came to me with the secret recording. I sensed your goal then because I already knew you'd studied the field, and because I'd been looking for the same thing you had in the full version of the First Scholar's memories."

Did it give you nightmares, too? he wondered. He'd never told her of his own.

"I have skills for gaining access to my subconscious mind," Lianne said, "so I perceived the clues he left without being disturbed by them. I didn't follow them through; I waited to see what you'd come up with."

"What would you have done if I hadn't found the secret file? The timing was quite a coincidence, after all—generations passing, and then its being discovered the year you got here."

"Not really a coincidence. Your finding the sphere in the mountains triggered both my arrival and the thoughts that led you to pursue genetics. As to what I'd have done if you hadn't pursued it, well, after a while I'd have used telepathy to steer you in that direction."

Noren frowned. "You mean you can control people that way?"

"Definitely not. They must choose to respond, but I sensed that you would. I had you identified as the potential leader even before I knew you were on the right path."

Keeping himself under rigid control, Noren ventured, "What if there'd been no potential leader?" He would not ask the more fundamental question directly; Lianne was aware that the inconsistencies in what she'd revealed were obvious to him. *You were trained by the same principles Stefred follows,* he thought, *and like Stefred, you expect people to work out the answers on their own…*

"I could have told you the answers hours ago," she agreed, "but you'd simply have rejected them. I had to give you the emotions, the conflicts, make you feel the paradox for yourself. I've tried to state enough of the facts for you to resolve it."

Slowly, Noren said, "You're sure in your mind that if there'd been no potential leader, the outlook wouldn't be bright. In that case your people would save us, as they would have from the nova, because nothing else could prevent our extinction."

"Save you from extinction, yes, since there's no greater evil."

"But some other evil would follow that they couldn't save us from," he went on painfully, "one of those scenarios I don't know about." *That's got to be how it is—I've had proof that you feel as strongly as I do about what happens to us: Stefred's judgment, and now direct communication from your mind to mine. What's more, your feeling is tied in with how you feel about the Service! The conflict's not between two loyalties, and you're not so timid as to stand back just for fear your action might miscarry…*

"The results of intervention are well known from the Federation's past history," said Lianne, her voice remote and sad. "In the early days some species were brought in too soon. It was thought mature civilizations could help young ones, that if an effort was made to respect their cultures, it would work like the merging of ethnic groups on a single mother world. But that's not comparable."

"Why isn't it?"

"Different cultures on a mother world are made up of people of the *same* species. There's no difference in length of evolutionary history involved. But with separate species that have evolved on separate worlds, a certain level has to be reached before contact is fruitful, before it's safe, even. If a species hasn't yet attained that level, all the struggle of its past evolution goes for nothing."

"You mean because the struggle turns out to have been unnecessary? But that's saying still earlier contact would have been better."

"No! The struggle *is* necessary; no species can evolve without it—the struggle to solve its own problems, I mean. Its people can't hold their own among biologically older peoples without that background. And their potential contribution to galactic civilization can't develop, either. If a species turns to absorbing knowledge from others before gaining enough on its own, its unique outlook is lost. It has nothing to give, and the spirit of its people dies, Noren. No more progress is possible for them."

"But they can mingle with the rest of you, surely—"

"Not in any permanent sense. Since it's genetically impossible for species that evolve on different worlds to interbreed, they will always retain a separate identity. What's more, the majority of individuals in a young species can't develop their latent telepathic powers or any other abilities they consider paranormal. So if their own culture isn't viable and they lack the psychic skills basic to ours, their descendants are doomed to be like retarded children in the eyes of the Federation. The Service is dedicated to making sure that never happens where there's an alternative."

Noren pondered it. Finally he said, "Lianne, I can't argue with the goal, but…it's not as clear-cut as it sounds. There are more factors to weigh—"

"Of course there are. That's why I'm still here."

"To judge not our worthiness, but the odds against us?"

"To obtain data so that judgment can be made." She reached out to him, fear surfacing once more. "Don't you see, I'm just one person, quite a young person, and we're talking about a decision that demands the collective wisdom of all the mature species in the galaxy! The Service will make it—but they will not tell me while I'm here, Noren. As long as I'm among you, I'll be given no more power than you have. They won't tell me the odds, or what's best for your world, any more than they will tell you."

Chapter Eight

It was astonishing, Noren thought, what one could adjust to when one had no other option. He wouldn't have believed he could behave just as he always had since his entrance to the City—rise, dress, eat, work hour after hour at a computer console, even mingle naturally with people—knowing that the world was being observed by an alien civilization. Yet he did it. Weeks passed, and it became habit to push thoughts of that civilization from his mind and get on with the demands of routine living. He learned to treat Lianne almost exactly as he had before, and incredible though it seemed that the existence of secrets between them could go unnoticed, she assured him those secrets were safe.

"The most anyone might wonder," she declared matter-of-factly, "is whether we are lovers. And since they wouldn't mind if we were, it makes no difference if they guess wrong."

"What about Stefred?" Noren inquired miserably. Despite the value he'd always placed on honesty, he was now hiding the genetic experimentation, hiding the existence of the aliens, hiding the true nature of his relationship with Lianne. For Stefred to have a false impression about that relationship would be one thing more than he could endure.

"Stefred can see you don't love me," Lianne said with pain. "Do you think I'd let him believe you do, when I'm forced to deceive him so many other ways?"

The deception was a deep grief to her. Though Stefred would never know the full extent of it, it wasn't failure to win her love that was going to hurt him most. He was counting on her as the heir to his work, yet in time, when she disappeared from the City—something no Scholar had ever done—he'd assume that she was a deserter. Nor was that the only misapprehension she was fostering. "It's not just that you won't carry on after him," Noren observed sadly, "but you already know more about the job than he does—"

"Not more about the techniques he uses, but I'm trained in some he's never dreamed of. I wouldn't be qualified to teach him such skills even if it were permissible; I can tell myself it's a kindness not to let him suspect what he's missing."

"But Stefred wouldn't look at it that way," Noren protested, "any more than I do."

Lianne sighed. "I know. But Noren, he would choose to reject access to knowledge for the sake of the principles he believes in. As you would. As you both did, in fact, when you were candidates."

"Then, I thought the Scholars were going to kill me," Noren reflected grimly. "The prospect of having to live with the choice wasn't something I considered."

Day by day, he learned to live with it—though in this case, he'd really been offered no choice. He told himself that if he were, he would of course choose to act in the long-term best interests of his species. He took pride in schooling himself to seem impassive, and that skill came back, for throughout boyhood he'd been obliged to conceal his feelings from his family. He'd been a heretic for years when they'd supposed him simply a muddle-headed dreamer. Now he was again a rebel: against the Scholars' opposition to genetic research, and on another level, in the privacy of his deepest mind, against the relentless hands-off policy of Lianne's people. By day, he turned from this second rebellion to devote his attention to the first. He proceeded with preliminary computer work so that if a chance ever came to test genetically altered crops, he would be ready.

At night it was harder. Nights had been hard in any case since Talyra's death. Now, lying sleepless too long in the dark of his lonely quarters, he could not help imagining the wide universe that was Lianne's heritage—that, if things were different, might well have been his. It *should* be his! He accepted the fate that barred him from it no more gracefully than in boyhood he'd accepted the idea of being forever barred from the City. Inwardly he raged just as he had then. And despite himself, despite his sureness that Lianne was truthful, he began to hope for a similar outcome. She'd admitted she did not know what her people would decide about his chances, that in fact there was much involved that was beyond the grasp of younger field agents. So was it sure that he would be offered no aid? There could be no open contact between cultures if that had proven invariably harmful, but in secret...what harm could be done if they enlightened a few individuals in secret, accepted a few, perhaps, into their own ranks?

This vision built up gradually, so that he was scarcely conscious of its formation. The Service to which Lianne belonged was mysterious in a way that excited him, drew him, as in his adolescence he'd been drawn to the mysteries of the City. Its senior members took on qualities he'd once attributed to Scholars, untarnished by the assumptions he'd then had about the Scholars' motives. Knowing that Lianne trusted these elders implicitly, he let reverence displace the resentment he found intolerable. They were immensely powerful and wise, surely, beyond his furthest conceptions; their minds, their culture, their technology were infinitely advanced—and they could give him answers if they chose.

He did not expect them to make it easy for him; he did not even want them to. His growing dream-scenario included unimaginable trials, which surpassed the stress of Stefred's challenges as those had surpassed his boyhood guesses about what Scholars might do to a steadfast heretic. The attempt to picture them was rather pleasantly terrifying. Inside, he longed to feel as he had during his earliest days as a Scholar, confident of his ability to handle himself in any situation that might arise. The ordeals of his candidacy had built that confidence, and he would be happy to endure further ones to get it back. The awesome Service grew in his mind as the one agency that might do for him what Stefred no longer could.

That he must first prove himself was only fair. Yet since Lianne's people would not let his species die, they would not ask him to achieve the impossible—therefore what he was striving for must be possible. They might not come right out and say so, even to her; but neither she nor he himself, much less this planet's inhabitants, would be allowed to come to harm. Had not her fellow agents taken a solemn oath to put the best interests of the worlds they visited above all other considerations?

The elation he'd first felt about the success of the genetic experiments began to return. Seen as a test of his abilities, the work no longer seemed futile, and he realized the Service was indeed wise—he would not want aliens to take over a task he himself could accomplish. With rising spirits, he looked forward to the birth of Veldry's child.

She had not told him in words that she was pregnant, for they could not talk privately without fear of gossip. But one evening, after the appropriate interval of weeks, she had paused by the table where he was sharing a meal with Brek and, imperceptibly, nodded.

Her face had shone with something deeper than its beauty; and in that moment he became aware that he too had crossed the line from bitterness to acceptance—even, at times, to joy. A child, *his* child, first of the new race that would someday regain its place in the universe...

There was, to be sure, the fact that without metal the City's technology couldn't be maintained. Once it was gone, people couldn't rise back out of the Stone Age. Without metal they'd have no chance of reaching the stripped starship hulls orbiting the world to which they'd be forever confined. So logic told him.

But now there was another logic. It couldn't happen that way! The permanent loss of technology would mean the end of his civilization's evolution just as surely as extinction would, and far more surely than would premature contact with the Federation. Thus there had to be a way out of the trap, though neither he nor anyone else in the City could yet perceive it—there *had* to be, or else Lianne's people would consider intervention justified. There could be no point in withholding aid for the sake of not interfering with evolution if evolution was going to stop anyway.

He did not question Lianne directly about this. He guessed that one of the trials he, and no doubt she herself, must meet was despair over the Prophecy's eventual failure. If he were given the answer to that despair, there'd indeed be outside influence on the course of the world's history, for armed with an answer, he could easily win majority support. Besides, he was sure Lianne would not be told anything specific she would be obliged to keep from him.

Yet she evidently had faith in the Prophecy. She'd affirmed it at her own recantation, after all, knowing the attempt to synthesize metal was doomed to fail, and she insisted her only pretense concerned her background. Lianne never laughed at faith. "You have to believe in something," she told him once, "and the more worlds you visit, the truer that is. Terrible things do happen. I've seen them everywhere—and here, the nova, I couldn't bear that if I didn't trust the universe further than I can see."

"How did you learn to trust it?" he asked, genuinely puzzled.

"Well...at the Service Academy, I suppose I started there; I never saw any of the bad things when I was little. At the Academy we have rituals, like Orison only far more complex, with telepathy in them, deep levels you can't imagine. The old, experienced people, who've seen hundreds of worlds, participate. They show you the dark side, they make you feel horrible at some points, but then they show the good...and it seems you'll never be afraid of *anything* after that. You are, of course. In the real world, you are. But you can't ever forget that there are forces stronger than fear."

Noren caught a hint of her emotion, though it was communicated on a level he didn't know how to receive. For an instant he grasped the key concept: evil that couldn't be banished could be transcended... *It all fits,* he thought...but the perception quickly faded, and he could hold no more than the memory of a state in which he'd have given a great deal to remain.

Dazedly, as his surroundings became solid and familiar once more, he said, "I've—felt something like that before, I think."

"Yes, in the last dream, when the First Scholar was dying."

"He knew? But how? And why don't I remember better?"

"Such knowledge can be attained by all humans," Lianne told him, "but without expert teaching it usually comes only at times of crisis—and then only to those ready to open their minds. It's not based on logic, it's truly intuitive, a matter of sensing how the universe *is.*" Compassionately she added, "You don't understand me. I could force rapport but you'd fight it, as you did even while you shared the First Scholar's dying thoughts. He was an old man who'd reconciled the two sides of his nature, while in you there's still conflict. That's why you remember mostly terrifying feelings from the deathbed dream."

"I remember his faith for the future."

"His future, or the world's?"

"The world's, of course—the Prophecy. The ideas that became the Prophecy, anyway, that we now know were deluded hopes. He never had delusions about himself. Despite what's been put into the liturgy, he knew perfectly well there wasn't any future for *him.*"

Shaking her head, Lianne said, "What one draws from a controlled dream is limited by one's preconceptions, I know that in principle. All the same, it's hard to believe you missed so much."

"What? Lianne, did I miss something significant?"

"Only to you. And perhaps," she amended thoughtfully, "to your effectiveness in the role you'll have to fill. Don't expect to handle all the problems ahead with logic."

Noren frowned. "I know the value of faith. I admit we can't keep going without it. But on the other hand, we can't solve our problems with it, and the trouble is that most Scholars are trying to! I thought it was because I do follow logic instead of clinging to the Founders' illusions that you believe I'm the one destined to make survival possible."

"Yes, but logic alone won't be enough." For a moment she seemed on the verge of adding something illuminating, then hastily she declared, "I mustn't speak of this; it's too soon."

Did she know the details of what the Service would demand of him? Noren wondered. That he must trust its elders was clear, and perhaps...perhaps she was saying he must go further, place faith in them of the sort his fellow-priests vested in the admittedly symbolic Star. That was reasonable...that was the logical answer to a lot of questions for which he could see no other. It explained how Lianne could find meaning in religious ritual, for instance. He had never fully understood religion. Its symbols were uplifting only when he managed to view them as an affirmation that the unanswerables would be answered, by his descendants if not by himself. But the Service already had answers. If one were to say the words with that in mind, not some vague future acquisition of knowledge, but contact with beings who possessed it...

He tried it the next time he attended Orison. *What is needful to life will not be denied us*...not if the Service is watching out for our welfare. *The children of the Star shall find their own wisdom*...of course, if the Service knows all human species ultimately do so and that when they do, they become ready to join the Federation. *There is no hope but in that which lies beyond our sphere*...yes, and it existed! Now that he'd met proof that it existed, things made sense, more than they ever had while he'd thought such assurances must be accepted blindly. The Founders, to be sure, had been blind; if they'd been right about those promises it had been for the wrong reasons. Possibly that was what Lianne meant by true intuition. Or perhaps it was fortunate chance—but in any case, she herself was in a position to know, and so, now, was he. He need only trust her people.

For the first time, Noren began not only attending Orison regularly but assuming the rotating role of presiding priest. He'd presided at Vespers occasionally for Talyra's sake, but never at the services open to Scholars alone. The mere fact of his priesthood did not require it of him; the placing of one's name on the roster was strictly voluntary. Somewhat to his own surprise he found it exhilarating. Was this merely because he knew secrets others didn't? he asked himself in dismay. No—he still hated the secrecy. He longed to tell what he knew. And the only words in which he was free to tell it were those of the poetic liturgy. It was the knowledge itself that buoyed him, convinced him at last that those words were justified.

No one commented at first on his new assurance; the extent to which one took on priestly functions was something never mentioned except by one's closest friends. Noren noticed, however, that people seemed pleased—perhaps they thought his active endorsement of religion signified a return to the specific goals of the Founders. Almost certainly this was Stefred's assumption. Lianne, who knew better, was strangely silent.

Veldry also knew he hadn't returned to orthodoxy, yet she came to every service at which he presided and was clearly elated by his public commitment. Her face, watching him, was at times as rapt as Talyra's had been. It was probably a matter of traditional faith, Noren realized. Not being a scientist, Veldry hadn't quite grasped that his abandonment of metal synthesization meant that without outside aid, the Prophecy could not come true. She knew only that he rejoiced in the child she carried, that his hope for the future was genuine. She seemed not to need to know why.

Brek, however, had known Noren too well not to wonder. They were no longer as close as they once had been. Their companionship had been strained by the dark seasons after Talyra's death when Noren had found it hard to watch the bliss with which Brek and Beris awaited the birth of their own baby. Then, after that baby was born, the disagreement about genetic experimentation had become a barrier to much conversation. He knew Brek would be shocked by what he had done. And he couldn't have confided in him anyway, for Brek had not sought to experience the secret dream—by which, Noren felt, he would very likely be even more shocked. The love between Brek and Beris was too bound up with conventional values to permit any thought of risking its fruitfulness. Beris was by now again pregnant and they were both ecstatic; Noren found it hard to meet their eyes.

But having shared his past crises of conscience, Brek was well aware of what full honesty had always meant to him. So it was Brek who cornered him one evening and demanded, "What's going on, Noren? I've seen people change, but not this much! You swore to me that it's impossible to synthesize metal, yet if you believed that, you wouldn't be still affirming the Prophecy at all, let alone going out of your way to do it formally in priest's robes. What do you know that the rest of us don't?"

"Stefred doesn't feel a need to ask me that," Noren temporized.

"Stefred hasn't been hearing you argue that we should hedge our bets by creating biological freaks," replied Brek grimly. "He has no grounds for suspecting you've given up on the Prophecy's promises."

This was partially true; since the Council had rejected the idea of genetic change, Noren had stopped expressing his opinions on the subject in front of its members. He stood helpless, inwardly debating how to answer Brek. He did not think he could get away with a direct lie even if that tactic weren't repugnant to him, and besides, there was no lie that would serve to explain away Brek's bewilderment. Best, then, to use half-truths to forestall further questioning, even at the cost of deliberately breaking their remaining ties of friendship.

"I do know things the rest of you don't," Noren admitted flatly. "I know we have just one chance to survive and that only as an active priest will I have any chance of winning leadership away from narrow-minded diehards. I'm sorry if what I'm doing violates your principles."

Brek paled. "It violates yours," he said incredulously. "It's a betrayal of everything you've always stood for."

Miserably, Noren turned away in silence. Not until afterward did he reflect that the First Scholar himself had been obliged both to betray many of his principles and to purposely let his motives be misunderstood. Of course, things wouldn't be as bad for him as for the First Scholar. Though he might be very much alone against opposition from even the few formerly close to him, he would not face the loneliness of total responsibility. He had the support of Lianne and her people. Strange, he thought; for years he'd felt alien in the world, and now aliens were the only friends he had.

* * *

Lianne was not quite his only friend; there was also Veldry. But it wasn't safe to let that friendship become known to anyone. That he was the father of her unborn child was perhaps the only such secret in the City about which no rumors existed, and a secret it must remain until he was ready to confront the Council with the proven success of genetic engineering. People wouldn't need much insight to see that if he'd chosen to have a child by Veldry there must be more involved than an ordinary love affair. So, aside from customary courtesy to her when they met publicly, he was forced to be content with seeing her during the services where he acted as presiding priest. She always stood in the front row on such occasions. Time passed, and he watched the child grow. Women, being proud of pregnancy, did not wear clothes of a style that masked it, as Lianne had told him they did in some cultures; he didn't have to count weeks to be aware of the baby's approaching birth.

The prospect both thrilled and terrified him. He dreaded the hours he must wait while Veldry was in the birthing room and half-hoped he wouldn't know when her labor began. But one evening when he went to the dais to begin Orison, she was not in her usual place. Under the blue robe Noren's flesh turned to ice. She never failed to appear when he presided; there could be only one cause for her absence. She had given birth without trouble in the past, he thought—surely there was no danger, and yet with this special child for whose genes he was dually responsible…

Somehow he got through the ritual, his voice unfaltering, his hands steady as he raised them. *"May the spirit of the Star abide with us, and with our children…"* No one would send him word—they would ask Veldry if anyone was to be informed, and she would say no. He might hear no news until long after the child was safely delivered, perhaps not until the formal announcement was posted. There would be a festive meal, for all births were celebrated, but probably no private party; Veldry's beauty had won her few friends among the women. He wished he could have been with her when she entered the birthing room, could have said something encouraging. Maybe she too was now frightened by the risk they'd taken. Maybe she was afraid to see the baby.

Would they even let her see it? No, under the stern tradition of sacrifice that permitted Scholars no contact with their children, she would see it only if no wet-nurse was available. But if it was not healthy, she would be told. She could handle that, Noren realized.

Veldry had plenty of strength; she did not need to draw on his...unless, perhaps, that was what she'd been doing all this time during the services. Was that why she'd been eager to hear the words of faith proclaimed in his voice?

After Orison Lianne spoke to him. He'd never told her who had conceived his child, but no doubt she'd sensed it telepathically. "Go to the computer room," she said quietly. "I'll bring you news as soon as there is any."

"You? But what excuse—"

"I'm a medical student, and since fortunately I'm a female one, the midwives won't think it strange if I ask to attend a birth. Who did you think was going to get a sample of the baby's blood for genetic analysis?"

He hadn't thought. What went on in the nursery was not for men to ponder. "While you wait, you'd better start examining this world's customs," Lianne advised, only halfway amused. "I really don't know how you'd get that blood sample without me, though no doubt you'd come up with some scheme as you did in the case of my blood. And I don't know how you're going to check on the child's health after it's adopted by villagers, either."

Nor did he, Noren thought ruefully. He'd been aware that he must test the genetic health of his grandchildren, but how was he to know who they were? No Scholar knew! No records of parentage were kept when babies were adopted; the Technician women who placed Wards of the City—presumed by the adoptive parents to be village-born orphans—made sure only that they went to good homes. Originally he had supposed that once genetic experimentation started, record keeping would become possible. Particular children could be placed under surveillance, for Technicians who visited the villages routinely reported to Stefred on those identified as potential heretics. Noren himself had been watched from early childhood. But without Stefred's cooperation, this would be impossible to arrange. And after the child had been given out for adoption, it would be too late to trace where it had gone. That wouldn't happen until it was old enough to be weaned, of course. Perhaps by then, the need for secrecy would be past.

Check on its health, Lianne had said. He'd somehow assumed that either it would be born healthy or it would not, and that if it was all right, the only further step would be verifying passage of the altered genes to the next generation. Now, waiting for word,

Noren began to consider factors he'd thrust from his mind during Veldry's pregnancy.

The child's health must be continuously monitored. In the population as a whole, genetic disease was virtually nonexistent, for all who'd come from the Six Worlds had passed genetic tests. However, it was theoretically possible that the genetic alteration he'd done could have affected genes besides the ones he'd changed purposely, affected them in some way not detectable at birth or by computer analysis. And of course one test wasn't enough—he must monitor many children. How was he to find enough volunteers? Noren wondered despairingly. For a long time he'd pictured himself displaying with triumph a normal son or daughter whose very existence would make the objections melt away. Now with the time at hand, he realized that no matter how healthy the baby was, there was nobody he yet dared confide in.

Hours crept by. He was too agitated to think clearly. *Tomorrow,* he thought, *if the child's all right...and of course it* is *all right, the Service wouldn't have let me go through with this otherwise...*

He looked up, suddenly sensing Lianne's presence. Simultaneously, with sickening fear, he sensed that in her mind was shock, horror—more than she'd displayed since the night he'd confronted her with his discovery of her identity. Her face was dead white. Noren found himself paralyzed; he could not even speak. *The baby?* he pleaded mutely, knowing that she was reading his thoughts although her own were shielded from him.

A trace of color came back to her, and she smiled. "You have a strong son." Hastily she added, "He's fine, Noren—no problems I can see."

"What's the trouble, then? Is Veldry—"

"She's fine, too. It was an easy birth. I—well, they were using hypnosis to ease her pains and that made her receptive, so I couldn't resist helping a bit." At his evident bewilderment Lianne explained, "The way I helped you deal with the effects of purple fever. By communicating wordlessly, giving her skills that can't be taught with words."

Weak not with fear now but with relief, Noren was unable to piece things together. "Do you feel guilty about using telepathy that way?" he asked slowly.

"No, certainly not. There's no harm in my helping people as individuals. Veldry doesn't know why the birth was easier than usual any more than you knew why your convalescence wasn't as bad as you expected, and in both cases I prevented needless suffering."

"But when you came just now, your face—"

Lianne's smile faded. "Noren," she said cryptically, "you've a long way to go. The road's rougher than you've let yourself think, rougher in some ways than you've any grounds for anticipating. Let's not talk about it now! Let's just be happy because the baby's so healthy."

"You're certain he's perfectly normal?" Noren persisted, striving to attain the state of elation he'd assumed would come naturally.

"As certain as anyone can be by looking at him. But I'm not omniscient, Noren, and I'm not as competent to judge his genetic makeup as you are."

She hadn't brought the blood sample with her; she declared he was too tired to handle it effectively and insisted that he get some sleep. It being impossible to visit the birthing room, Noren followed this advice. He woke exultant, so exultant that as he ran the tests he was not even nervous.

The standard programmed analysis of the baby's genotype, completed rapidly by the computer system, revealed no genetic defects of types known to the Founders. Noren's own painstaking work, the many hours at a console during which he examined the coded data in detail, proved that the change he'd made to his own genotype had indeed been inherited by his son. The genes involved were, of course, dominant; it had been designed that way so only one parent's genes need be altered in the first experiment. This meant the boy could metabolize the normally-damaging substance in native vegetation and water without ill effects, though verification would be needed after he was mature. Not all his descendants would inherit the same capability, however. The changed genes were unavoidably paired with the unaltered recessives that had come from Veldry, and chance alone would determine which would be passed to particular offspring. From now on, since the vaccine was no longer untried, the genes of both parents must be altered.

And yet, Noren thought, this wouldn't be the case in the next generation unless experimental children paired with each other. How was he to arrange that? To deprive them of free choice would be unthinkable; Scholars saw to it that heretics were subtly encouraged, but no other interference in villagers' lives was permitted. Even if he managed to keep track of the babies, there would have to be a lot of them before enough data could be obtained to prove it was safe to inoculate the whole population.

So what next? "What's your next step?" Lianne challenged when they met late that evening—and Noren became uncomfortably aware that underneath, he'd hoped she would tell him. Had he not gone as far as it was possible to go without Service guidance? What constructive end would be served by letting him waste time in further groping, considering they must already have analyzed what he ought to do?

"I don't know what to do now," he said, thinking that perhaps this direct admission was required of him. "But you, Lianne—" He stopped; he still could not speak openly of his conviction that he'd be ultimately enlightened. "You know the people in the City better than I do," Noren went on slowly. "I'm not good with people. You are, and you've some degree of access to their minds. Who can you name that might be open to the idea of volunteering?"

"I can't name anyone," she replied soberly. "Oh, I would, Noren—I am permitted to help you in any way I could if I were truly of your people, even by using psychic powers abnormal among you. But if you have any potential supporters, they're keeping their thoughts to themselves."

"How can everyone be so shortsighted?" Noren burst out angrily.

"They aren't in a position to judge metal synthesization," Lianne pointed out, "and they'd rather believe you are wrong about it than that the Founders were."

And they have no grounds for believing the Prophecy can come true without it, Noren remembered. If he had not learned Lianne's identity, neither would he. And to go on affirming religion's promises under those conditions would have been impossible.

"There's more involved," Lianne said. "Not all of them feel that losing technology would be intolerable—they don't all see, as you do, that it would mean the end of your civilization's evolution. But as long as they believe there's hope of synthesizing metal, they can't endorse an alternate plan. They're afraid the caste system might be maintained longer than is necessary for mere survival."

"But we wouldn't maintain it if the alternate could be implemented!"

"No? For a while you suspected even the Founders had done so."

"It would be a—a hard decision," he conceded. "There'd be a fight over it. Some would say that as long as there was any chance of bringing the Prophecy to fulfillment, we should keep the capability even though it would mean keeping the castes. I haven't faced that because I knew, even before you told me, that the Founders' plan offers no chance."

Lianne's eyes weren't visible in the darkness of the courtyard. "You must face what you're asking your followers to face," she said levelly.

Yes. I can't be spared anything merely because I know the point's a moot one, he perceived. Knowing nothing of the Service, what would he say? After a long time he ventured, "There might be a compromise. The research outpost's set up for the nuclear work; we could move the essentials there so they wouldn't be lost when the City's opened to everyone and its resources are quickly exhausted. Each Scholar could choose personally whether or not to go there. But oh, Lianne, the aircar traffic would stop, and the people who went would be exiled futilely—"

"*You* know that."

"And knowing, I should try to talk them into it?"

"It may be the only arguing point you have. But it won't be enough. To win out, you'll have to—to act, Noren."

He pondered the implications. "In the end, when the genetic change is accomplished and I'm old, I'd have to go there myself and continue nuclear research. Die there as leader of that lost cause."

Her calm tone gave way to hesitancy. "Perhaps."

He would have to promise that, certainly, and he would have to mean it. He couldn't go to the outpost until his work was finished, since the computer complex was indispensable to analysis of genotypes. But afterward...wasn't it what he'd have wanted if he hadn't known the truth about Lianne? To preserve technology—some remnant of knowledge at least—after sharing of metal with the Villagers made maintenance of the City impossible, simply as a monument to what the Six Worlds had once accomplished? The gesture would be empty now; this must be why Lianne had told him he'd suffer for his discovery. Whatever the Service offered him, he must return to play out the charade, unless the real route to restoring technology appeared during his lifetime.

"I'll do whatever's necessary," he declared, wondering if he was as sincere as he wished to be, and if she could assure her seniors that he was.

"I believe you will," Lianne agreed, not happily. "But even action won't be enough; people need—inspiration. You'll have to give them that."

As a priest gives hope. In the past he'd given little of anything. When he'd offered the truth, which was what he most valued, it had often been rejected.

"Noren," Lianne said suddenly. "You're willing to give, I know that, yet I—I think you also must learn to receive. You're—you're more isolated here than I am, even. You don't know how to interact."

His heart ached for her. She, warm and loving by nature, had made her feeling toward him plain, and in this he'd been the one to reject the offering. "You do understand, don't you—" he began, knowing that with her, there was no need to complete the thought in words.

"About Talyra? Yes, very well—more than you do, maybe."

He didn't probe her meaning; he knew only that although it had been nearly two years since Talyra's death, he could not love Lianne in the same way. There were times when he wanted to. He certainly wasn't held back by the fact that she was alien—and although that made marriage impossible, since it precluded an honest commitment to permanence, there was no rational reason for not turning what City gossip now held to be fact into the truth. Perhaps he hesitated only because Talyra had said simply that he must have children, not that he should love for love's own sake. Yet he sensed that there was more to it than loyalty.

Besides, he must indeed have more children. With Veldry? She was as dedicated to the future as the rest of the Scholars, and less narrow-minded. Maybe he should marry her. She would accept him; he could make her happy; on his side, it would be no worse than any other marriage of convenience. Veldry had taken no lover since the night their child was conceived, and if for his second genetically-changed baby he turned to someone else, she would be hurt as he'd never expected her to be. He did not want to seek another bride. Why, then, did he not want to marry Veldry, either?

It did not matter what he wanted. If he married her, he could acknowledge their son publicly without implying anything extraordinary. Most Scholars would be surprised but not suspicious—yet on the other hand, if any did support his proposal, they would recognize that he had acted upon it. Lianne would let it be known that she was barren; that was no shame among her own people and would not bother her. With rumor as it stood, he would appear to be giving her up on that account, which would show potential allies that his talk of genetic change was more than talk, more even than cold science. It would be seen as a human commitment. A gesture, a symbol, yes—but in such things lay power. Only so could he inspire anybody to follow him.

But he did not look forward to the end of Veldry's confinement, knowing what he must say to her when he told her of his joy about the child.

Women stayed in the birthing room three days, then rejoined friends and loved ones at the noon meal in the commons. Everyone came forward to congratulate new mothers; Noren had no chance to speak to Veldry privately. No one saw anything odd in the warmth of his felicitations, or even in the fact that he took the chair next to hers—Lianne was on his other side, and it was assumed they were simply being friendly. Veldry was radiant. "You've given a great gift to the world," said Noren, and his intensity was noticed only by her; the people present thought it merely a conventional phrase. But Veldry took his true meaning without need of further words.

"I am fortunate," she replied; and that too had double meaning. It struck him that when they married, many would be less surprised by his choice than by hers. Desiring her for her beauty, they would be envious. There was envy in their looks as they waited for the unnamed father to appear. It embarrassed him; he should not acknowledge the child, perhaps, until the interest had died down. So he told himself.

To see her alone, he would have to go to her room, which he felt himself obligated to do. But that evening when he joined the group gathering for Orison, she stood in the front row. Only then did it dawn on him that he—never attentive to religious observances—had overlooked a more obvious duty: she'd assumed he would arrange the roster so as to preside at the ritual Thanksgiving for Birth. Hastily he found the priest scheduled to officiate and with the excuse that he wouldn't be free for his regular turn, asked to switch, donning a borrowed robe in lieu of his own. There was no time to review the service. He had heard it, naturally, but had never read it through, and almost stumbled over the substitution of "this mother" for "these parents" which he should have been prepared to manage smoothly. Otherwise he found the experience strangely moving.

Veldry came forward—without kneeling, of course, since it was not fitting for one Scholar to kneel to another—and met his gaze with high spirits as he placed his hands on her head in the formal gesture. *"The blessing of the Star's spirit has been bestowed upon her, for she has given herself freely in love and in concern for the generations on which its light will fall. Now in their name we acknowledge their debt to her, and wish her joy in the knowledge that her child will live among those whose heritage we guard as stewards."* Her child, and his! Ever after, he'd know that somewhere a part of him lived on.

She expected no private talk, Noren perceived as she stepped back. It was too soon for her to start another pregnancy; without conscious decision, he put off making any move. Days passed. And then early one morning, awakened by a knock at his own door, he opened it in dismay to Veldry.

He hardly knew her; there were lines in her face he'd never noticed before, and she was red-eyed from weeping. "What's wrong?" he demanded, his voice rough with anger not at her, but at whoever had found out and now scorned her. It was the only explanation he could think of—and marriage would not mend matters, not if she with her pride had been reduced to this by someone's branding of the experimentation as "obscene."

"I—I don't know how to tell you," she faltered. "You don't deserve so much tragedy in your life. It's not fair, when you meant to do good."

"Look, Veldry," Noren said, gripping her shoulders, "I'm ready to face up to anything that happens—don't worry about *me.* But I won't stand for it if people are blaming you for trying to do good yourself. I'll take full responsibility, I'll lie if I have to, say I didn't tell you till afterward—"

"Noren," she broke in, "no one's found out. No one ever will. But the baby's—dead."

"What?" His legs buckled; he reached out for support, and Veldry clung to him, led him to the bunk where they sat side by side. "How—*how*?" Noren whispered.

"The nursery attendants don't know. He was just—weak, as if he hadn't had enough to eat, though he'd been nursing well. He...he was never strong after the first, Noren, only I didn't want to see it, I kept thinking he'd gain weight soon...I didn't nurse my others personally, you know, I didn't have anything to compare with. The women who took care of him between feedings didn't tell me because there wasn't anything to do except hope. But when I went in yesterday morning, I knew something was wrong. I held him all day, but finally in the night he stopped breathing."

"Didn't they call a doctor?"

"Yes, near the end, but he wasn't sick in any of the ways doctors can help with."

"The doctor must have said something," Noren protested.

Veldry was silent. "You can't hide it from me," he urged. "He was my son; I have to know what the doctor thought he died from."

"Well, at first she said malnutrition, but we knew he'd had plenty of milk." She didn't meet his eyes.

"Would you rather I talked to the doctor myself?" he asked gently.

"No! If you're going to crack up, it had better be here instead of in front of people." She turned to him fearfully; he wondered if she thought that like a traditional village father, he might blame her for failure to produce a perfect infant. "She said," Veldry continued, "that apparently this baby's body couldn't get the right nourishment from milk, couldn't—metabolize it properly."

"That's crazy! All babies live on milk."

"Of course, but she said there could be something wrong, some congenital problem—"

Congenital. The room spun around Noren. "A genetic defect, you mean."

"The doctor didn't know if there could be a defect just like this, she said she'd have to ask the computers."

"It doesn't matter what the computers say." Noren's voice was cold, remote; in his own ears it didn't sound like his own. "Don't you see, Veldry, whether such a disease has occurred before or not—and the blood test I did shows it hasn't—in this case I *created* it. I altered the genetic pattern of metabolism. I brought a baby to life who was foredoomed to starve."

"You couldn't have known ahead of time," she said in a carefully rehearsed tone, "and you tried the metabolic change on yourself, you told me—the baby's metabolism was like yours."

"Yes, I tested it on myself first. But I don't drink milk, after all; there isn't any milk on this planet except human milk. Probably I can't metabolize it any more, either." He wondered how he could have been so stupidly, tragically blind as to believe he'd checked everything.

After a long pause Veldry said steadily, "We knew there was risk. We wouldn't have done what we did if it hadn't been a choice between that and letting all our descendants die. We'll grieve, we can't ask not to suffer—but you mustn't blame yourself."

"I can't not blame myself," Noren declared.

"I—I suppose that's true. I guess that's part of the burden you've taken on. And I still admire you for taking it, Noren."

Hazily, he was aware that he should comfort her, should turn from his own guilt and despair long enough to give her the support that was her due. He did not know how. He couldn't marry her, of course; he would never be able to remarry, since to attempt a second alteration of his genes would not test the change to be used on other people. To father a child for his own sole benefit would not be a justifiable form of human experimentation. So there was nothing he could offer Veldry.

Not until she was gone did he reflect that he might have offered the solace of ritual words. With Talyra he'd used such words to mask secrets; Veldry, who knew those secrets, also viewed them as a source of strength. Though she had long ago accepted accountability for the Scholars' stewardship by assuming the robe, she never functioned as a priest, perhaps less from scorn of convention than from lack of self-respect. She honored his active priesthood and must have wished him to exercise it in sorrow as in joy. But he couldn't have done so even for her sake—not when his newfound grounds for faith had proven hollow.

How could they, Lianne's people, have let it happen?

Strangely, he felt no resentment against Lianne herself, nor did he shrink from companionship as he normally did in times of anguish. It was to her quarters that he went, following an urge he did not stop to question.

He was not sure how much he told her verbally. Lianne held him, and wept. Noren too shed hot tears, not only of grief and remorse, but of outrage. "How could they?" he demanded. "I expected trials, defeats—but how could they let an innocent baby—"

"It wasn't a question of letting; they had no way to know. We aren't gods, Noren."

"Gods?" He did not know the term.

"I forget," Lianne said, "that concept's not in your world's religion, and I don't suppose you've read much about the cultural history of the Six Worlds. In many cultures the power symbolized here by the Star is personified, attributed to supernatural beings. Primitive cultures worship whole groups of gods, but civilizations advanced enough to know there's only one Power often conceive of it as a Being, too. The Founders didn't happen to have that tradition. Some Federation worlds do."

"They believe there's a *being* off in the sky like the Star, controlling things?"

"Well, not in a physical sense. It's simply a different symbol." She sighed. "It's hard to explain when you don't understand the Star either; you're so literal-minded, Noren. The point is that we acknowledge a power beyond our own power. We're not gods in the Service, and we don't play at being gods! To see ourselves that way would be blasphemy."

Forcing himself to speak levelly, Noren reflected, "It would be making light of the truth, you mean. In the village people called me blasphemous—yet they cared less about truth than I did, or so I thought. I knew the power's not in a magic star. You're saying it's not in the Service, either."

"No more than in the Scholars," Lianne said gently, "who would be gods to the villagers had not the Founders very wisely used an impersonal star as the symbol of something higher. You don't want to be worshipped; do you suppose my people do, or that we merit it?"

"Oh, Lianne." As understanding flooded his mind, he was overcome by a sense of sin unlike any he'd experienced before. "I—created my own false symbol; I've been imagining them as gods, all right. You don't know—" He broke off, unable to confess that he had done so consciously even when performing the offices of priesthood.

"I do know," she admitted miserably. "When I came to tell you about the baby and found you thinking such thoughts, I was horrified. I saw then why acting as a priest had been getting easier for you, and I knew that sooner or later I'd have to set you straight."

"Don't worry about it," Noren said grimly. "I can see for myself. I knew in the beginning there was risk, only I didn't want the responsibility—after I found somebody to pass it on to, I refused to believe it was real. But it has to be real if it's to accomplish anything. If your people were gods, what I'm doing would be futile after all."

"You'd be merely a puppet—your whole race would become puppets—if we could protect you from error," she agreed, "or even if we could ensure your ultimate success."

He sat hunched over on Lianne's bunk, his head buried in his hands, unable to think of the future. Going out to face people, bearing the secret not only of the baby's existence but of his accountability for its death, was past contemplation. He could not endure that even privately. Starvation...the baby had *suffered.* Even the subhuman mutants like the First Scholar's son didn't suffer...

Lianne's arm was warm across his shoulders. "I prayed you wouldn't have to learn through disillusionment," she was saying, "and I evaded my job. I should have been prepared. Though I couldn't have saved the baby, I should have kept going to see him—but I was a coward. I knew if he wasn't thriving I wouldn't be strong enough to tell you. Yet now in the space of a few hours you've got to make a very difficult adjustment, when I could have bought you more time."

"A few hours—I don't understand." He was not sure he'd be able to accept the consequences of his failure in weeks, let alone hours.

"You've got to preside at the service for the baby," Lianne said.

"Lianne, I can't!" he burst out, appalled. "I couldn't do that even for Talyra, and now, after my—my blasphemy, I can't ever preside as a priest again. I couldn't anyway in this case. I couldn't stand up and declare it'll turn out for the best, knowing the death was my fault."

"It's going to be hard. But you are obligated."

"You're right, of course," he conceded. "Veldry will expect it, and I owe it to her."

"Noren," Lianne questioned after a short silence, "Do you intend to go forward with the work?"

He didn't answer; she, being telepathic, ought to know he wasn't ready to talk about that. "If you do," she continued, "you're obligated not just for Veldry's sake but for everyone's. When you tell future volunteers about this baby, they'll know whether or not you were the one who spoke at his death rite."

Yes, and if he was not, they'd feel he was either too weak to accept the responsibility or not convinced that the experiment had been justifiable. There would then be no volunteers. Furthermore, there might not even be opportunity to seek any, for the secret would be out. It was a father's place to arrange the service for a dead child. If he himself presided, it would be assumed that the father was unwilling to reveal his identity and that Veldry had simply gone to the priest who'd officiated at the earlier Thanksgiving for Birth. But if he sought a substitute, there could be no hiding the reason for his involvement.

"There's something more," Lianne went on. "Now's a bad time to stir up an issue I've held off raising, yet it's only fair to warn you." Her arm tightened around him, and he sensed, beneath her sorrow, the ache of a deeper one—pain not merely for the present tragedy, but for some other that lay ahead of him. "You've no conception yet of where you're going," she said. "You're thinking that if you can get through this one service it will be the last act of your priesthood. Don't look at it that way. Make it a beginning, not an end; it's as a priest that you must lead your people later on."

Noren raised his face, startled into anger. "I told Brek that," he recalled bitterly. "To protect your secret I led him to believe I'd turned hypocrite. But I'm not a hypocrite, and I won't use priesthood as a route to power."

"Do you think I'd want you to do it hypocritically?"

"No more than you want me to create congenitally defective babies," he replied, his voice harsh, "but I suppose hypocrisy too can be justified in the name of survival. Reason tells me it can. Well, you've sometimes said I rely too much on reason. About this, I'll follow my feelings."

"And your feelings don't include faith right now. But they used to, before you found out who I am."

"In survival of my race, yes. Not in the Prophecy's promises, not after I became sure that genetic engineering is our only chance to survive. If the Service isn't backing those promises, I can't affirm them any more than the rest of the Scholars can give them up."

Hesitantly, Lianne said, "I've affirmed them, knowing the Service hasn't the power to make them come true."

"On what grounds?" Noren challenged, thinking with regret of how logical his speculations about her motive had seemed.

"Your reasoning wasn't all wrong," Lianne told him. "I'm sure that some way does exist for your descendants to regain the technology that will be lost here, so that the Prophecy can ultimately be fulfilled. If that weren't true, open intervention by the Service would be judged essential—because without it, the evolution of your species would reach an end worse than the consequences of artificial interruption. And you are right that we wouldn't let you engage in human experimentation to no purpose if such intervention were considered inevitable. We'd intervene now, not as gods but simply as human beings abiding by ethics, balancing lesser evils against greater, just as you do."

"But then your people know the way!"

"Yes, they must—but that doesn't mean they can make sure it'll be implemented. They're dealing in probabilities, not certainties. They too need faith; but we have evidence that they do have grounds for it."

Noren's head swam. "If you hadn't come, I wouldn't know that. I couldn't act as a priest, yet you say it's in that role I must lead—"

"So by speaking like this, I've altered the odds," she admitted. "I haven't an answer. We are...agents, Noren, not only as representatives of the Service, but in the sense that once we interact at all, we influence histories to an extent we're not able to compute. It goes back to what I said about trusting the universe. Things we can't explain do happen, things like your finding the sphere that brought us here, for instance—they are not mere coincidences. We've observed such things on enough worlds to know that they follow statistical laws other than laws of random chance. But we can't predict which problems synchronicity of that kind will solve."

"Lianne, don't hold out on me," he pressed. "Will I receive help in finding the solution once I've gone as far as I can alone?"

"As much as I'm able to give you," she replied, her voice low.

"I mean the part you don't know. Does the Service tell individuals facts that can't be announced openly to their cultures?"

"Occasionally, if there's urgent need. It must be done very subtly. In this case, to prevent the harm that would result from disclosure of our existence, it would have to be managed in some way that would make your possession of advanced knowledge seem natural both to your fellow Scholars and to this world's future historians. That may not be feasible. And the time may not be ripe for it in your era—it may be that the genetic change must be thoroughly established before the next step is taken."

Resentment flared in him again. "They'd let me live my whole life in ignorance of what they foresee? It's not fair."

"Life's never fair to people who set out to change things. In the normal course of progress, strength to strive can hinge on not knowing the future. They won't tamper with that course unnecessarily."

"What if I'm not strong enough to keep striving?" Noren began—but then, in a stunning flash of insight, he knew. All Lianne had told him in the past meshed as with a kind of awe he stated slowly, "The decision is mine. It has been, all along. If I quit, they'll step in and give us aid."

"Of course." Lianne's eyes glistened. "I never denied that it's in your power to make them do it."

"I—got things backwards. I believed if I proved deserving enough, I could gain help. I thought they were testing me."

"You mean you wished they were." She tried to smile, adding, "Not being tested is harder. I know; I've lived both ways, just as you have."

He'd been living, since his discovery, for the day when he would pass their test and feel triumphant. Now, uncertain not only of his strength but of his talents, would he be right to go on gambling with infants? It wasn't as if he had no option… He savored a bright vision: open contact with the alien culture; ships landing, unloading more metal than anyone had seen since the Founders' time; the Prophecy fulfilled in his generation, cities rising almost literally overnight in accord with the villagers' naive expectations. The caste system abolished forever. Knowledge freely available to him and to everyone, not merely the Six Worlds' stored heritage, but greater wisdom than the Scholars dreamed could exist. If open contact was deemed unavoidable, there'd be no point in further delay. One word from him, and he could have all he'd ever longed for; his contemporaries could have it too…and there would be no more defective babies.

But it would mean the loss of his people's potential. Overshadowed by older species, they would never evolve to Federation level. Future generations would pay the price.

"You have the power to decide," Lianne repeated. "At the start, I had it. I could have lied in my initial reports, said there was no one here fit to carry your people forward. But I judged that you and Stefred and others I'd met would want to be the ones to say."

There was nothing else to be said. After a while, when he felt able to talk without weeping, Noren went to arrange the rite for his dead son.

Chapter Nine

In the days that followed, Noren immersed himself totally in analyzing what had gone wrong with the genetic change. His error could not have been avoided, he found—it had not been a stupid mistake or even a careless one. And it had been made initially by the geneticist of the First Scholar's time, whose design he had followed. She, like himself, had been forced into human experimentation long before it would have been tried if test animals had been available. Success at so early a stage would have been almost miraculous.

With painstaking care, he redesigned the change and went back to the Outer City's labs to prepare a new vaccine. He injected himself with it to make sure it wasn't virulent, but that, of course, proved nothing about its genetic adequacy. It must be tested on someone whose genes hadn't been previously altered. His agonized doubt over whether he'd have the courage to perform such a test was mitigated, somewhat, by the fact that he saw no immediate chance of finding a volunteer to perform it on. As long as he was busy, he pushed that problem from his mind.

He continued to preside at religious services whenever his turn came. Lianne insisted that a sincere commitment to priesthood was indispensable to his task, rather than simply a means of gaining power among the Scholars; but she would not explain further. She seemed deeply troubled by the issue. "The knowledge of your course must grow from within you," she told him. "It's not beyond your reach, not something you need outside help to discover. To give you specific advice wouldn't do you any good—while you're unready to face it, I'd only cause you more pain."

"Lianne," he protested, "I'm ready to face *anything*. I've never backed off from the truth, not knowingly, and I won't start now." Which she ought to realize, he thought indignantly.

"It's because I do realize it that I believe you have a chance of achieving the goal," she replied, grasping more than he'd said, as always.

"I can tell you're not happy about what you're concealing," he said forthrightly, "and I wish you wouldn't try to spare me. I'd feel better knowing the worst." Actually, he was sure nothing could be worse than the things to which he'd already resigned himself. The prospect of more pain did not seem to matter.

"There'll be time enough to worry about it later," Lianne declared. "I'll say only that winning the villagers over will demand greater sacrifices than you've considered."

Greater than the sacrifice of contact with her civilization? She did not know his mind as well as she seemed to, Noren thought in misery. Even so, he'd lost peace of conscience, the ability to have children, all hope that the Six Worlds' technology could be preserved. He'd accepted the likelihood that he would end his days in exile at the now valueless research outpost beyond the mountains. "I've considered becoming a martyr like the First Scholar," he said dryly, "but giving up my life wouldn't do any good—and barring that, I don't think there's anything left for me to give up."

"That's because you don't see how much you have to lose," she observed sadly.

Contemplating this night after night, Noren confessed inwardly that it did dismay him, not so much because he minded being hurt—he felt past minding, numb—but because of his evident blindness. Why could he not perceive what Lianne foresaw? He tried, yet it eluded him. The fact that the means of gaining village support for a change in the High Law eluded Stefred also, and that she apparently expected no insight into it on Stefred's part, didn't cure him of self-doubt.

He saw little of Stefred these days, but Lianne was, of course, a go-between. Stefred allowed Noren to go his way without interference, presumably because he did not guess how far he had gone. Not guessing, he must feel that he, Noren, had turned his back on constructive science, that his youthful promise had gone sour; the thought of this was hard to bear. Some said such things openly of him. He now argued for genetic research and was viewed less as a threat to the established order than as the City eccentric. It had happened before, he'd heard: Scholars disillusioned in youth had become fanatic champions of impractical schemes, and while their right of free speech had been respected, the quality of their judgment had not. He must list the admiration of his peers among his losses, Noren knew, although never having cared much what others thought of him, he did not count it a great sacrifice. The loss of his closeness to Stefred was something else again. He missed that, and like Lianne he hated the deceit he was forced to practice upon the one man in the City most worthy of confidence.

He was free to study genetics; any Scholar was free to study anything—but to devote years to it, abandoning all pretense of research into metal synthesization, was out of the question. Genetic research fell in the avocation class, like art and music. Inner City people were expected to perform essential work, if not out of sheer dedication, then merely because they received food and lodging. Noren, as a trained nuclear physicist, volunteered for a shift in the power plant; and thereafter, since he spent even longer hours on the genetic work, he had a bare minimum of time left to eat and sleep. Fatigue added to his numbness, and for that he was grateful. Only work could insulate him from despair.

Veldry continued to attend Orison whenever he presided. One evening she approached him after the service and asked to talk in private. Too much time had passed for that to start gossip, he decided, and in any case he could refuse no request of Veldry's. He went with her to her room, suppressing with effort the memories it stirred in him.

"Noren," Veldry said, "the risk has to be taken again, doesn't it?"

"Yes," he agreed in a low voice. "I've—reconciled myself to that. Only there's no one I can ask."

"You could use a volunteer who doesn't need to be asked."

"I don't expect to be let off that easily. Who'd offer, when there's no support for genetic change even in principle?"

"I'm offering," she told him simply.

"You—what?"

"I'm willing to try again whenever you're ready."

"Veldry," Noren protested, reddening, "I thought you understood. You and I can't try again; my genes are damaged, and if I tried to repair them it wouldn't be a valid test—the risk to the child wouldn't be warranted. The new vaccine has to be used before the man drinks unpurified water."

"I do understand. The man doesn't have to drink it, the woman can. Genetically it doesn't make any difference which parent gets the vaccine, so I'm volunteering to be inoculated."

"Oh, Veldry," he burst out, deeply moved. "It's brave of you, but you mustn't have a baby who might die, not twice—"

"I lost my special baby," she said softly. "I want another to take his place—and anyway, why should more people than necessary get involved before we know it's safe? I'm already committed. It's better this way, really."

Perhaps it would be, Noren thought. It had meant a lot to her; perhaps the chance of a happy ending was worth the danger. He paused, embarrassed, wondering if she'd really grasped the extent of the risk she was taking. "What if I fail again?" he asked.

"You won't."

"I may. I refused to accept that, the first time; I told you the change I'd made might not work right, but I never actually believed it. Now I do, and it has to be considered."

"I wouldn't be the only woman in the world to have lost two children."

"You'd lose a good deal more," he reminded her. "You'd lose your ability to have normal ones."

"I've had my share in the past."

"That's not the only thing," Noren said bluntly. "There are only a couple of doctors in the City qualified to sterilize a woman, both of them senior people we don't dare to confide in—"

"I've had my share of lovers in the past, too," Veldry broke in. "I thought I'd made clear that I want to do something more with my life."

"But—if you should ever find the man you've been looking for, the one who'll see beneath your beauty and whose love for you will last—"

"Then it will last until I'm past the age to have babies, and if he sees beneath my beauty, Noren, he'll know that's not such a lifetime away as you think." She smiled ruefully. "You'd be surprised, I suppose, if you knew just how old I am—but didn't you ever wonder how it happened that I'd experienced the full version of the First Scholar's dream recordings long before the secret one was found?"

He drew breath; he had indeed wondered, for he'd assumed she'd arrived in the City only a few years ahead of him, and young people rarely sought the full version. It hadn't occurred to him that being beautiful might mask the usual effects of age.

"I ask just two things," Veldry went on levelly. "First, I've got to have your permission to tell someone the truth about the first baby."

"Well, of course. I wouldn't do this unless the father of the second one was informed. May I—ask who it's to be, Veldry?"

"No, you can't," she replied. "That's the second thing; I may never be able to name him to you, though I'll get you a blood sample." After a short pause she added slowly, "I may have to tell more than one person, and I can't consult you about who. Do you trust me to choose?"

"You mean you're just going to...persuade somebody?"

"I'm in a better position to do that than you are, after all." Bitterly she continued, "I've got one asset, which has never done either me or the world any good. Is it wrong for me to take advantage of it the one time I might accomplish something worthwhile that way?"

"No," he said. "No, maybe this will make up for all the grief it's caused you. I trust you, Veldry. Tell whoever you need to, just so the facts don't reach anyone who'd put a stop to the birth of genetically altered children."

"If I have a healthy one," Veldry declared, "nobody can stop it. Under the High Law I have a right to get pregnant as often as I want, and my genes will be changed for good."

With grim determination, Noren injected Veldry with the corrected vaccine. When the alteration of her genes had been confirmed, he and Lianne stood by her while she drank from the courtyard waterfall. Veldry, having been told that Lianne was barren, not only shared the widespread assumption that she and Noren were lovers but rejoiced that they could remain lovers despite the necessity that he father no more children—in her eyes, Lianne's apparent curse had become a blessing. He could not yet be sterilized; there was no doctor at all in whom he could confide, and the High Law prohibited sterilization except in cases of proven genetic damage. Unlike the First Scholar, who had been in the same position, he was young, and he was realistic enough to know that a time might come when this aspect of his personal sacrifice would become more burdensome than it was in his present state of depression. He might someday want love, and Lianne would not be in the City forever...but at that thought he turned, wounded, from all such reflection.

He drew back from a deep relationship with Lianne, even from the friendship that had grown strong between them. She knew him better than any human being ever had; she understood his dreams, his longings—his whole outlook on the world—in a way that hadn't been possible for Talyra. It was due not only to her telepathic gift, but to the compatibility of their minds. With Lianne he knew, for the first time in his life, what it was not to be lonely. Yet this kinship of spirit had become a searing agony. He wanted desperately to glimpse the universe as she had seen it, to share the ideas she was now willing to discuss, but at the same time he could not bear to talk of them. What he could not have, he must forget, or lose his grip on the routine of everyday living. To his dismay he found himself avoiding his sole chance to exchange thoughts about the things that mattered most to him, shunning all reminders of the realms he had renounced.

There was little time to talk to Lianne anyway, considering his double workload; when he saw her, he fell into casual comments on daily happenings or technical points of the work. He was not fully aware of the extent to which this was deliberate. Looking back, however, he knew his one opportunity for real communication was slipping away. Lianne obviously knew, too, and was saddened. It occurred to him that she, left alone in his world for an indefinite number of years, was desperately in need of his companionship though she was resigned to not having his love. If she was the only person in the City he'd found who *cared* about the universe, the reverse was even more true. He was nevertheless powerless to help himself. Inwardly aching, he let their moments of contact run out in empty conversation.

Some weeks after Veldry had begun drinking unpurified water, she told him, radiantly, that she was pregnant. She seemed even more elated than she'd been the first time; Noren thought with chagrin that her courage outmatched his own. He was pleased by the news, but he could scarcely feel good about it—he knew that as time went on his terror would grow in pace with the growing child. Did joy in a new love override her fear? "I don't suppose—" he began awkwardly.

"That I can say who the father is? No, he made me swear not to tell even you."

With discouragement, Noren reflected that he would never be able to sway people, as a priest or otherwise. He just wasn't the kind of person they confided in. Did someone think, after all the risks he'd taken privately, that he'd betray a supporter who desired secrecy, much less spread rumors about one brief and probably extramarital relationship?

"I'll say, though, that you'd approve of him," Veldry added, her eyes alight with fierce pride.

"He's made you happy, then. I'm glad."

"In the way you did, yes, he made me happy. He offered me respect, and he'll share my feeling about the child whatever happens. But I meant you'd approve of him as—well, since you can't be the biological father of the new race yourself—"

So the man was admirable, not a casual lover but someone who truly cared about future generations. For that he was thankful. Yet he was not sure he'd wholly approve of someone unwilling to declare his convictions openly. To conceal the experimentation was one thing, and necessary—but experimentation would serve no purpose unless the idea of genetic change eventually gained defenders.

Since he seemed unable to progress toward finding any, he finally broached the topic with Lianne. "No amount of sacrifice on my part will help matters if the majority can't be won over," he complained.

Lianne was silent, thoughtful, for a long moment. "What was the hardest part of what the First Scholar achieved?" she asked slowly.

Noren pondered it. Not martyrdom; that had been only the climax. Not the secret genetic experiment, which had achieved nothing in his time. "The worst was having to endorse a system he knew was evil," he said. "We all know that, and we all relive it."

"Yes, you reconcile yourselves to it, to the pattern of hardship his plan demands. But he himself had to do more. He had to break away from his society's pattern. The truly difficult step was accepting the fact that a social structure like the one the Six Worlds had—the one he was used to and believed worked best—would not work in this colony. You probably got so wrapped up in the ethical issues that you haven't grasped what a tremendous innovation it was for him to think of making any change at all."

"I guess I haven't."

"I have," Lianne told him. "Because I've studied lots of societies, I can make comparisons. People normally want to hang onto what they're used to. The villagers' feeling about the High Law is simply an exaggerated form of a tendency that exists in every culture, and what's more, so is the Scholars' outlook. It affects even your own thinking. You're resigned to the necessary evils, therefore you haven't separated the customs that are still necessary from those that aren't."

"Are you saying I've condoned evils that needn't exist?" he protested, shocked.

"No, but you haven't examined what's essential as opposed to what's merely traditional. For the Founders, changing their old system was hard not just because it meant condoning wrongs, but because it involved abandoning traditions. The First Scholar was the only one among them who questioned those traditions enough to see that some could be altered."

"And if I were his equal, I could do that here?"

"Because you *are* his equal, you *will* do it."

"That doesn't sound—sacrificial," Noren said. "If I'm not expected to lose my life in the process, where can I go but up?"

Soberly Lianne said, "Giving up the pattern of customs you've come to depend on is harder than you may think. I know! When we join the Service, we renounce allegiance to our native worlds, and we're required to analyze thoroughly what it is we're putting behind us."

"That's different," he reflected. "You do it because you want the new pattern the Service offers; you don't have to strike out on your own without one."

"I never claimed *I'm* the equal of the First Scholar," said Lianne.

Startled, Noren shielded his thoughts from her, unwilling to let her sense the dismay in them. "I...think I just got the point," he said.

It was disconcerting to realize he had not questioned all his premises. As a heretic, had he not always been a questioner? Had he not, since, challenged the Founders' plan itself? He'd never hesitated to break rules when he saw purpose in it; now, during the next weeks, Noren began looking for rules to break. None seemed relevant to his cause.

He could, to be sure, devise plans that went against tradition. For instance, it would help tremendously if the outpost were turned into a center for genetic research instead of nuclear research. Genetically altered crops could then be grown there by Scholars, who, beyond the mountains, did their own farming in any case. He'd by now nearly completed his computer work on the design of the changes necessary for growing food without soil treatment, weather control or irradiation of seed; at the outpost he could test them personally. By an even more radical breach of custom, parents of genetically altered children might rear their own families at the outpost, which would eliminate the large problem of keeping watch on those children and arranging intermarriages between them. But there was no way he could take over the outpost in the face of majority opposition. Besides, such a course would be useless for bringing about eventual genetic change in the villages, and that, rather than the research, was his main problem.

The seasons passed. Veldry once more became great with child, and it was Noren who felt the sickness by which she herself seemed untouched. "What did you do to her during that last birthing?" he asked Lianne. He had read that posthypnotic suggestion could be employed in powerful ways, though neither she nor Stefred had ever insulted him by offering it as alleviation of anxiety.

"Nothing lasting," Lianne assured him, following his thought. "I only helped with the delivery. Now, I think, she's got a real sense of destiny. But you are right that hypnosis can do more than anyone here uses it for. I was appalled when I first saw how commonplace it is in the City. Many societies misuse it before they understand the powers of the mind."

Noren waited, hoping to hear more. He still knew little of those powers, and it was a subject she usually steered away from. "I needn't have worried," she went on. "Stefred is competent; he knows what not to try, and the others trained in induction don't go beyond hypnotic sedation and anesthesia for physical pain. I stay within comparable limits, though I'm tempted sometimes to use my own training."

"I wouldn't want—anesthesia, not for mental things," he told her.

"Of course not. But hypnosis can increase awareness, too. I could open whole areas of your mind that you've shut off—" She stopped, sorry, evidently, to have said something that might tantalize him.

"I suppose that isn't permitted," he said, unable to keep bitterness front his voice.

"Technically it isn't, but that's not what holds me back. It would be…disorienting, Noren. You'd be badly scared at first."

"Well, I wouldn't let that matter," he declared with sudden hope.

"All the same it would interfere with your functioning as a scientist. You'd have to adjust to new states of consciousness; you wouldn't be able to work till you'd regained confidence in your own sanity."

"Like—like after my space flight," he reflected. *Like what?* Lianne's thought echoed, and he recalled that she could not know. He'd never told anyone but Stefred what had underlain his panic in space, where he'd been literally paralyzed not by physical fear but by what was happening in his mind. He rarely thought of it himself any more, having learned to put such things aside and get on with life. Now, at Lianne's silent insistence, he let it well into memory: the detachment from ordinary reality, the horror of feeling that nothing had meaning in a universe too immense for rational comprehension…

Lianne was speaking, urgently and aloud. "Those are feelings you connect with religion?"

He shook himself back. "I felt them first at Orison," he admitted, "though not as strongly as later on. I know they don't make sense. I doubt if they did even to Stefred, despite what he said about its being normal to get upset by unanswerable questions."

"They make sense," Lianne stated positively, surprisingly undisturbed by this most painful recollection of his past. "The fact that you've experienced them is—significant."

"Stefred called it a sign of strength." Noren had never fully understood that, though he'd tried to take Stefred's word for it.

"He was right, as he usually is within the limits of his knowledge. What's puzzled me is how anyone as strong as you could have shied away from them entirely, both the dark side and the bright. Now I see. You went part way on your own, young, in circumstances of great stress; and you got burned."

"Part way to what?" Noren whispered. *What bright side?*

"To another state of consciousness where perception is not tied to reasoning. If you want a physical explanation, such a state involves separate areas of the brain; but it's more than that, and more complicated. People react differently. Some find it pleasant—euphoric, even—but it can be terrifying, too, especially to anyone who values reason as much as you do."

But it's a way to see more of the truth, he thought, sensing from her emotion that the abyss that had haunted him was merely a stage on the road to the sort of mental power her own people possessed.

"I've been concerned," Lianne said, "because your culture has no real mystic tradition. The Founders were scientists and preserved little of what they could not analyze. The computer record glosses over what other values were cherished on the Six Worlds. Normally, you see, a planetary civilization at your level has both science and mysticism; and both are needed to reach the levels ahead."

Perplexed, Noren considered this. "Are you saying we'll never learn the meanings of things, no matter how far advanced our science gets?"

"Through science alone you won't. But there is a state of—of *knowing* the meaning, knowing in a way beyond faith that everything fits together." Sighing, she added, "I can't describe it any more than you can describe the bad part. There are no words."

"You could show me...telepathically, couldn't you?" *Please, Lianne, please don't withhold this from me!* he pleaded silently.

"I have tried," she said gently. "At Orison I've tried to reach you, but you shut me out. I know why, now. You were burned once; underneath you're afraid to enter those regions again."

"Never mind that. Use deep trance if you need to; I'm willing."

She pressed his hand between hers, meeting his eyes. "Noren, to get there artificially, through hypnosis or drugs, is extremely dangerous. I'm trained to some extent, I could keep you from permanent harm, yet even if there weren't that past panic to be overcome, it would interrupt your working life. I'm not a psychiatrist in my own culture, you know—I can do more than Stefred only because a standard Service education covers more information about the mind than Six Worlds psychiatrists possessed. I am no better qualified to heal you quickly than he was."

And in the future when his work was completed, Noren thought in anguish, she would be gone. What would it be like to know that Lianne was out among the stars somewhere, seeing worlds he could never see, probing spheres of consciousness he could not attain?

She shivered, as if the sorrow were more hers than his own; he found himself wanting to hold her. But on the point of embrace, they both stood back. There was nowhere that could lead except to tragedy.

"At least it helps to know a bright side exists," he said resolutely.

"It exists, and someday, if you hold your mind open to whatever inner experiences may come, you can reach it spontaneously. You have the proven capacity. To pursue that way actively simply isn't your role."

No, and to turn back from it was merely another sacrifice his role demanded. He wondered how many more there were going to be.

Somehow he got through the suspense of Veldry's pregnancy; through her confinement; through the Thanksgiving for Birth that followed the delivery of a healthy baby boy. He'd privately hoped he might learn the father's identity from that service, but Veldry forestalled him. "It would give away his secret, to you at least, if he arranged to preside," she said. So the regular roster was evidently followed. As it happened, ironically, it was Stefred who officiated. Noren wondered how Lianne hid her feelings from him, and what he would say if he knew what he'd inadvertently blessed.

Veldry wasn't permitted to nurse her own child this time, since there was no lack of wet nurses; but Lianne visited the nursery often enough to provide assurance that nothing was amiss. Gradually Noren's dread gave way to elation. The ensuing relief, however, was shadowed by the realization that his grace period was over—he must delay no longer in finding volunteers to produce other children.

The solution dawned on him unexpectedly. One evening in the refectory a new Scholar, a man named Denrul, joined the table where he was sitting with several friends. Noren, rather amused at first, watched him rest his eyes on Veldry with something akin to adoration. Denrul, though older than most novices, was too recently admitted to have lost his awe of City women, and he'd as yet heard none of the long-standing gossip. Her beauty, for him, overwhelmed all else. Or did it? There was more in Denrul's gaze than desire; Veldry's own eyes lit with response, and Noren perceived that hope had wakened in her once more. Telepathy? he thought wryly. Maybe it was; maybe that was what love at first sight always was. In any case the two seemed well on the way to becoming love-stricken.

A new Scholar, Noren thought with sudden excitement—one whose ties with City tradition weren't yet formed. As a recruit barely a week past recantation, Denrul's idealism would be at its peak. That did not seem quite fair, and yet why not, except because he was just the sort of person who might be swayed? If to try to sway such people was wrong, then so was everything else he, Noren, had done. His instinct to avoid taking advantage of immature consciences was, perhaps, merely a sign of conflict in his own.

"Yes," Lianne told him, "Denrul would be receptive. So would most candidates I've worked with, if approached early. I wondered when you would think of it."

She now worked with them—he hadn't stopped to consider that, for her discussions with candidates were as confidential as Stefred's own. Unrobed assistants had always monitored some phases of the enlightenment dreams; Lianne was by this time fully trained to do so routinely. Thus the novice Scholars, their first few days after recanting, knew her better than anyone in the City aside from Stefred. Most of them were adolescent; all were elated by their triumph as heretics; all expected to adapt to new ways. Even more crucially, fresh from initial exposure to the dream sequence, they were loyal to the First Scholar alone.

The secret dream, by Council decision, had thus far been made available only to people who'd experienced the full version of the First Scholar's other dream recordings: a policy Noren now saw was aimed toward restricting it to those with long-standing commitments to the Scholars' traditional goals. He had been charged by the First Scholar's words with full authority to decide who should be given access, and he recalled that at first, Stefred had feared the power this gave him. Power, yes! Novices would emerge from that dream ready to support what they'd see as an underground movement within the still-mysterious Inner City society. There were not enough of them to affect policy decisions, but as volunteer parents they would suffice.

During the days he pondered this, Veldry and Denrul spent much time openly in each other's company. It reached the point where Noren wondered if she'd already explained about her genes; she'd have to, of course, if they became lovers, and in inoculating her he'd authorized her to reveal his own role as she saw fit. But when he brought up the subject, she seemed surprisingly embarrassed. "No," she said. "He'd agree, but it shouldn't come from me. That would be—seduction. You tell him, Noren. Tell him the truth about me, the whole truth. And then—" she blinked back tears "—then whatever he wants to do is up to him."

Noren sought out Denrul, and they had a long talk. "You understand," he said at the end of it, "that I'm asking you to perjure yourself as far as the Prophecy's concerned. That's what the others won't do, and you've recanted on that basis of believing they won't. To become a Scholar, at the same time realizing that what you affirmed in the ceremony's false after all, won't be easy. Especially when you'll, well, gain personally—"

"Veldry? Noren, that's not how I feel about her," Denrul protested, shocked. "I'd never involve her in anything I had doubts over."

"I've told you frankly that you'll be far from her first lover."

"I will not," Denrul declared. "I'll be her husband if she'll have me at all."

"That's the village way," agreed Noren, wondering uneasily whether Denrul's fervent words reflected true devotion to Veldry or merely his inexperience with the Inner City's less-strict conventions.

"It's the only way right for her," insisted Denrul. "Look, here's a woman you say has had her choice of men—yet she thinks more about what's best for her descendants than who she chooses? I say she wants more than love. I say she deserves a partner committed to more."

"So do I," Noren admitted with relief. "But you see, people not in on this secret have no way of knowing what she really cares about."

Although Denrul had been won to the cause of genetic change without the secret dream, Noren was unwilling to alter the genes of anyone who hadn't experienced it. It was too harrowing in some respects for anyone unready for the full version of the others; but it could be edited—Lianne was as skilled in that process as Stefred. During one long, agonizing night he went through it again, serving as monitored dreamer while she prepared a version suitable for those who'd recently completed the enlightenment dreams. This she kept in her personal possession. Denrul was told to sign up for library dream time, and on his scheduled night, she arranged to be on duty. Shortly thereafter, pale but resolute, he returned to Noren for inoculation.

A few weeks later, Denrul and Veldry stood up at Orison and to everyone's amazement exchanged marriage vows. Veldry wore everyday beige trousers instead of a traditional red bridal skirt, and there were no officially designated attendants—Noren, who couldn't publicly have assumed that role without arousing comment, found himself in the less welcome one of presiding priest. It was his regular turn, Veldry having carefully checked the roster, so when the newlywed couple stood before him to receive formal benediction, it was assumed they had no special friend to perform the office. The blessing was taken for a routine one. To Noren, however, it was a turning point: his own confirmation of total responsibility for other people's risks.

He joined them afterward for a private feast in Veldry's room, at which Lianne was the only other person present. She poured from a large jug she had brought, and Noren proposed the conventional toast: "To this union—may it be fruitful and bring lasting joy."

They drank. At the first taste Veldry seemed ebullient and Denrul perplexed. Noren, in bewilderment, burst out, "By the Star, Lianne, this stuff's like water! Couldn't you find any better ale?"

"Under the circumstances I thought watered ale might be more appropriate," she said pointedly, "considering where the water came from."

Denrul's puzzled frown gave way to bravado; with shaking hands he drained his cup without pausing. Indignantly Noren protested, "Lianne, that was cruel. At a marriage feast, a time for celebration—"

"No, Lianne's right," Veldry interrupted. "It's melodramatic, maybe, but not cruel. It's got to be like this. I mean, if we believe in what we're doing, believe strongly enough to overthrow the old traditions, we've got to establish new ones. We need to dramatize! Life's not all abstract science and ethics."

Lianne was brimming with exhilaration; it was as if the ale had been more potent than usual instead of less so. "I propose a second toast," she said, "to the day when stream water will be drunk sacramentally at village weddings."

In high spirits they finished the contents of the jug. Denrul—who like many heretics had sampled impure water before his arrest—passed the safe limit in a single evening. Only for him was it a crucial step, since the others had consumed plenty of such water before. The symbolic significance in the act was nevertheless strong. For Noren in particular it was a poignant reminder of what he had lost, what he had yet to hazard before the gamble could pay off.

Later, walking back to his own lodging tower with Lianne, he mused, "I couldn't see for myself what Veldry saw. Is that why I'm not getting anywhere, why I'm blind to the path ahead?"

"Partly." Lianne seemed troubled; the elation she'd shown earlier had faded. "I—I gave you a clue, Noren, in my toast. I don't think I overstepped my role because both Veldry and Denrul got what I was driving at. You…for several reasons you'll find that harder."

"I've never liked ceremony, that's one, I suppose—though what happened in there was *good.* Were you doing something to us with your mind?"

"Nothing more than people usually do with their minds under such circumstances. That's one of the things you don't grasp about ceremony."

"Well, nobody here knows about psychic undercurrents." She could hardly be expecting him to act on the basis of knowledge she'd insisted was beyond him, Noren thought in frustration.

"Not consciously. But they sense what's going on, as Veldry did—and as Stefred would. He'd deny the existence of telepathy, but he could predict exactly what the effects of the symbolic action would be."

"Why doesn't he, then? You say the clue's in your suggestion about watering the ale at village weddings, but he maintains villagers wouldn't be willing to drink unpurified water at all. And I should think a wedding would be the last occasion they'd pick to do it."

"There's a gap between existing tradition and what must replace it," she agreed. "Stefred can't bridge that gap; he's too bound to the conventions the Founders established. You are freer—precisely because you've stood off from religious symbolism, you are free to reinterpret it as the Founders reinterpreted their own."

"I already tried that once, trying to make gods of your people. I'll not repeat that mistake."

"Have you analyzed it, though?"

Not as well as he should have, Noren thought with chagrin. His mistake, as with his earlier errors concerning religion, had been in trying to name the ultimate. He was willing now to call it the Star and let that go. But Lianne was talking not about ultimates but about concrete things: the provisions of the High Law, for instance. The things that not only could change, but must. The Law forbade drinking impure water; she foresaw not merely the breaking of that Law but its reversal, for people would never ignore religion on a formal occasion like a wedding. He'd imagined their hoarding what little purified water was left simply to serve wedding guests...

"Oh, Lianne," he murmured. "I'm beginning to guess where you're leading—but if symbols can be manipulated like that, turned around and given whatever significance someone wants them to have—"

"It is dangerous," she admitted. "Like everything else, it's a principle that can be put to ill use, and on most worlds both unscrupulous people and deluded ones have misused it. Here there are exceptional safeguards, which you will have to override."

It was true, he reflected, that the Founders had deliberately created the symbols and ritual of a new religion in the first place; what they had done could in principle be redone. Yet conditions had not been the same. "I don't think Scholars would ever revise the basic symbols," he declared. "That's not as simple as creating a little ceremony to express our own feelings about defying a taboo we've already decided to ignore at our own risk. There'd be—well, no *authority* for it. People don't just make up their minds to change what things mean. The Scholars won't take my word for scientific facts; how can we expect that I can alter their religious views?"

"We can't," Lianne acknowledged. "The kind of thing we did tonight will help form a small group of dedicated volunteers to produce genetically altered children. What I proposed in the toast was something altogether apart. It concerned not the Scholars' religion but the villagers'."

"But one's got to lead to the other."

"Really? Who believed in the symbols first when the Founders established them?"

The villagers did, Noren realized, confused. The Founders gave them the Prophecy and High Law believing in the ideas behind the symbols, but it was the villagers who took them at literal face value. Only later, when village-born heretics were brought into the City, did those symbols acquire true religious significance within the walls. "We can't alter people's views by a proclamation from the Gates," he protested. "How can the interpretation in the villages change before it's changed here?"

Lianne stopped and faced him, reaching for his hand. "You're beginning to ask the right questions," she said, almost with sadness. "Noren, we are coming perilously close to things I must not say to you. If that last question is answered, it must be by you and you alone—not so much because I shouldn't intervene as for your own sake. I—I couldn't bear to have you change the shape of your life on my word."

She gave his cheek a light kiss, then turned quickly and hurried across the courtyard toward the tower where she lodged. Noren was left listening to the echo of her footsteps.

It was not long before Veldry was pregnant again. By that time, the group of volunteers had grown by another couple and several young men—novices still in adolescence—who were willing to be genetically altered as soon as they could find brides. Once a man's genes were altered, he would never be free to love Technician women, who could not participate in human experimentation. For this reason Noren decided to accept couples only, and their number was necessarily limited by the number of female novices who entered the City. It seemed a bit unfeeling to tell these women that if they wished to serve the cause of human survival, they must choose husbands immediately from among the eligible men on the waiting list—yet after all, in the villages most marriages were arranged by families. Few girls grew up expecting to marry for love.

Though men and women alike were free to refuse the dream Lianne offered them, none did so, and none, having experienced the dream, refused to support the First Scholar's secret goal. They were not yet priests and had been told by Stefred that they need never assume the robe; the conflict between endorsement of the Prophecy and advocacy of genetic change was not severe with them. More significant, Noren suspected, was the fact that in working for the latter they were continuing to oppose authority. A new Scholar's biggest problem was generally turning from heresy to support of the established order.

The risk to the children was no longer a great worry, with Veldry's baby thriving well. The worst part of the whole business, for Noren and Lianne, was the extent to which they were deceiving Stefred.

He had always been close to each Scholar he'd brought through candidacy; now all the new ones, within days of recantation, were being sworn to stop confiding in him. Noren feared some might break this oath, but Lianne seemed to see no danger. "It's not as if he's going to suffer any harm," she pointed out. "Oh, he'll feel hurt if he finds out about the conspiracy, but they don't realize that. He's still Chief Inquisitor to them. Though they trust his integrity, they don't know he's vulnerable to personal feelings."

"You and I know." Noren bit his tongue; he was sorry that had slipped out, for Lianne was in a far worse situation than he was. She worked with Stefred, saw him daily and discussed the progress of these same novices with him. Furthermore, Stefred was still in love with her, though he'd long ago given up hope of her returning that love, and there was now small chance of his finding happiness with anyone else. Were he to be attracted to some newcomer, that woman would be committed to genetic experimentation before he was free to speak.

Denrul had chosen medical and surgical training, realizing that a physician who knew of the experimentation was desperately needed. On the side, he completed the computer training program in genetics, and Noren began tutoring him privately in the details of his own more advanced work. He himself must have a successor, in case...in case of emergency, he told himself firmly. The Service was not going to take him away aboard the starship, not ever. But the work was too vital to depend on a single person's presence. And besides, Denrul, who was to specialize in medical research, had more access to lab facilities than Lianne. There was even the possibility that after he was no longer being supervised, they could produce the genetic vaccine in the Inner City instead of having to make clandestine excursions to the officially off-limits domes.

Noren rarely saw Brek any more except at large gatherings, but when he did, Brek's troubled look was haunting. It was not only that Brek now thought the worst of him. Nuclear physics, for Brek, was finally producing the disillusionment Noren's greater talent had found there earlier. Even his happiness with Beris seemed affected. One evening, when she wasn't present, he approached Noren and said miserably, "You were...right. It's hopeless. I want you to know that I—I understand, better, why you gave it up. I think I even forgive the hypocrisy now. I can't seem to renounce priesthood myself, and you—you never felt as I did about the Star in the first place. You at least believe we have *some* way of surviving."

"Are you sure my way's wrong?" Noren asked slowly.

"Maybe not. Maybe I'm simply a coward—only Beris…I couldn't let Beris—"

"Even if there were healthy babies before hers?" Telling Brek would do no harm now. He would never betray anyone, and though he might be shocked, sickened, by the now-available dream of the First Scholar's involvement, it would lend weight to what he'd viewed as an indefensible position. Things were not the same as before the birth of Veldry's son.

"That's a hypothetical question," Brek declared, "to which there's no honorable answer. I couldn't ask others to do the dirty part."

"Nor could I," agreed Noren; "but the issue's not hypothetical any more." He went ahead with the whole story, omitting only the truth about Lianne.

"There's no excuse for me, for the way I doubted you," Brek said when he'd heard it all. "I've known you too long and too well. I'm not saying I could have done what you did—I've never been as strong as you—but I should have known things weren't as they seemed. I'll talk to Beris. I'll go through this dream; I owe you that much. Only…about the Prophecy…I'm not sure. Even if we keep working at the outpost, we'll know that cause is lost—"

"We know now," said Noren sadly.

Hypocrisy about it wasn't a solution—not for him, not for Brek, not for anyone. Yet neither was abandonment of the symbols. They must be reinterpreted, not abandoned; he'd known that since the night of Veldry's wedding…but how? How?

"I've been going at it backwards," he said to Lianne. "Destruction of symbols doesn't work, I know that! I tried it in the village when I was condemned for heresy, and then later I crashed the aircar on the way to trying it again; Stefred permitted it both times because he knew there was no danger of my succeeding. Yet I've still been thinking in those terms, and so has he. We can't ever get people to break the High Law by destroying their belief in it—"

"No more than the First Scholar could have overcome people's attachment to the Six Worlds by revealing those worlds were gone," she agreed.

"He gave them something *constructive,*" reflected Noren, "turned a symbol of tragedy into one of hope."

"That wasn't unprecedented," Lianne said. "Successful religions of many worlds have been centered on symbols with transformed significance."

"Then what we do with watered ale at wedding feasts is more than dramatization of our defiance?"

"Well, it represents defiance, but not just of the Law. We defy our fear of destruction, Noren, and our confinement within the limits this world's environment imposes. It's a small thing, of course, not the equivalent of the Star and not nearly so powerful. Yet many religions do incorporate rites that involve food or drink with symbolic meaning—that's a missing element in what you've got here, where there are only negative taboos. It would fit naturally."

"But nobody not already willing to drink impure water would accept it, or get any lift out of it if they did."

"No. By itself it's not the answer."

"What is?"

"Read up on the Six Worlds' religions, how they originated, how they changed," Lianne suggested, evading a direct answer.

He'd come to the end of the genetic design work and had found no way to experiment with plants past the sprouting stage, so he followed this advice—and was soon absorbed in a field of inquiry wholly new to him. In the past, he'd questioned the computers about beliefs; now he sought detail about the histories of those beliefs. It fascinated him and at the same time disturbed him...so many of the beliefs were manifestly untrue. And yet, it was not true that a miraculous star controlled the destiny of this world, either. Had the symbols of the ancients, even those taken literally, been less valid?

To be sure, evil as well as good had been done in the name of religion. There had been hideous episodes in which whole opposing populations had slaughtered each other in the belief that their causes were holy. Manipulation of symbols could, as Lianne had acknowledged, be dangerous. But the danger lay in the character of the manipulators. *Anything* could be twisted, perverted, used to destroy people's freedom, their minds, even their lives; still a man of integrity could lead without destroying. The First Scholar had done it. Before him, there had been others. An appalling number of them had died as martyrs. Unlike him, some had been openly worshipped after their deaths. Yet, Noren realized, the worthy ones never sought this, would never have wanted it personally—it was a price to be paid for the victory of the truths they'd lived for.

Time went on. Noren resigned himself to an interval of inaction. The pain of past losses had dulled, and while he could not call himself happy, his appreciation of the Inner City—of his access to the computer complex and the Six Worlds' accumulated wisdom—began to return. It was anguish to know that Lianne's people had far more knowledge than the computers, knowledge he could not attain. Still, he had by no means exhausted the resources available to him. *More than you can absorb in a lifetime,* Stefred had promised him long ago; and that was true. Lianne herself knew only a fraction of what the Service knew.

Lianne too was unhappy. Increasingly, she shielded even her emotions. He wondered if she missed her people despite her insistence that she did not. "It's normal in the Service to spend long periods alone," she declared, "that is, apart from our own kind. I'm not really alone. Here, I'm among people equal to my own—with individuals, the evolutionary distance doesn't count. That's significant only for cultures."

Another child was born to Veldry, a girl, Denrul's daughter. Soon afterward, a son was born to the second genetically altered couple, premature but otherwise healthy. That made three healthy children, two of whom had the altered genes from both parents, and since several other couples had been recruited—including Brek and Beris—more were already on the way. It was almost time for the first child's weaning. He would be sent out for adoption soon; a plan for keeping track of his whereabouts must be made.

"Is this the tradition I must somehow overthrow?" Noren asked. "We can't rear families in the City, both because there isn't room and because the castes mustn't become hereditary. But I suppose the custom of losing track of our children isn't essential. It was set up merely because the Founders felt Scholars should sacrifice normal kinship ties."

To his surprise, Lianne shook her head. "It's far more important than that; the system couldn't work without it. If Scholars' children weren't reared as villagers, indistinguishable from the others, a question would arise that no one here's ever raised: the question of how much more survival time could be bought if some villages' life support were cut off. There'd be a kind of division even the castes don't create."

Horrified, Noren protested, "We're stewards! We couldn't possibly prolong life on this planet by not spreading the resources equally."

"That's what a starship captain does in an emergency," Lianne pointed out, "where it's a choice between death for some and ultimate death for all. And that's what it would come to when the time ran out here with no metal synthesization in sight. The Founders foresaw it. They barred specific records of adoptions because they knew Scholars wouldn't cut off their own offspring as long as there was any alternative."

"It's a tradition I can't tamper with, then."

"You can't abolish it," she agreed, "but you'd be justified in modifying it because with genetic changes, the villages will be self-sufficient. It won't matter if the advocates know where their children are…

She went on talking, but Noren was deep in thought. As always, it came back to the problem of how to withdraw City aid without bloodshed. Religious sanction…but he was no closer to knowing how to provide that than he'd been seasons ago. "You told me to study how the Six Worlds' religious traditions changed," he said reflectively, "but things were different there. The leaders with new ideas, the prophets, weren't shut away in a City, and usually they weren't the official priests. They were often considered heretics, as far as that goes. They lived among common people and interacted with them."

There was an abrupt silence; Lianne cut off what she'd been saying in mid-sentence. "Priests here begin as heretics," she said, her blue eyes focused on his. "And they do grow up among the people."

"But as heretics they can't persuade anybody to change. I know; I tried it! And after they get in a position to speak with authority, they're isolated."

Lianne kept on looking at him. "Must they be?" she asked quietly.

"Well, of course; the most basic tradition we have is our confinement to the City—" He broke off, struck suddenly, horribly, by the implications of what he had said. *Tradition.* By tradition, Scholars did not mingle with villagers. When he and Brek had planned to defy that tradition, they'd gone as relapsed heretics, not as priests, and would not have been recognized as Scholars. But if a robed Scholar were to walk into a village square, people would listen to what he told them, listen in a way different from the way they listened at formal ceremonies. On the platform before the Gates, Scholars were anonymous figures; in a village they'd be seen as individually human.

Or superhuman.

Faintness came on him as the blood drained from his face. "Set out to become a prophet, you mean? Lianne, I couldn't!"

She remained silent, waiting; he sensed her sympathy, but not whether the thing he was now thinking was what she'd foreseen all along. "I couldn't," he repeated. "You didn't grow up here yourself; maybe you don't know how villagers feel about us. They'd worship me! It would be everything the First Scholar wanted to avoid when he set up our anonymity—why, they'd follow me around, treat every word I uttered as holy."

"Well, yes, that would be the idea," she agreed. "They would accept what you said in personal contact with them when they'd never tolerate it as a sudden ceremonial proclamation. They'd get used to the idea of a coming change, over the years—"

"Years!"

"Oh…I assumed, that is, I was thinking in terms of the preparation years being the main point. The genetic testing of crops will take a long time, too, and you could handle it yourself—" She bit her lip, hesitant, unsure how far he had gone in the perception of something obviously well-developed in her own mind.

"We won't be able to delay more years after we prove the change is safe to implement," Noren protested. "It's bad enough having to wait for the first generation of babies to grow up."

"You don't have to wait shut inside the City."

"Start talking to villagers *now,* not knowing for certain that implementation's going to become possible?"

"You're confident of the vaccine now."

"Three normal babies, yes, I'm confident enough to use it on as many Scholars as will accept it. But I'm not ready to risk the entire species. And—and if I promised such a change, people would want a demonstration. That would mean human experimentation on villagers, which is unthinkable."

"If it's unthinkable, Noren," Lianne said bluntly, "you had best say so before Veldry's baby is adopted. When that boy matures, you will have human experimentation among villagers whether you like it or not, with the first child he begets. The gene pool of the species will be permanently affected. Surely you weren't counting on his being convicted of heresy before ever touching a girl."

He had been. Without thinking it through, he'd pictured the children becoming heretical enough to reach the City before they married, while remaining conventional enough to abstain from earlier involvements—which was of course an unreasonable assumption. It was true that with their adoption he'd be committed to tests involving non-Scholars. Perhaps a small-scale experiment with village volunteers would be no worse.

That paled, however, beside the other issue. To personally visit the villages...but of course, it would be impossible. "Stefred wouldn't let me go outside the City," he said, ashamed of the inward relief that swept through him at remembrance of the obstacle.

"Stefred can't keep you from going," Lianne argued, "any more than he can stop me when I go."

"Not from walking out the Gates, no—but if I spoke to villagers he'd have me brought back and lock me up from then on." The Technicians who reported to Stefred kept in touch by radiophone and aircar. Village affairs were quickly known in the City, and Stefred would not hesitate to use force if he believed the people's welfare was at stake.

"I think you're mistaken," said Lianne slowly. "Noren—Stefred knows human experimentation has gone on."

"Knows? You told him?"

"Of course not, but do you think anyone as perceptive as he could remain blind so long, when we recruit all the novices?"

"But if he knew, he'd have put a stop to it."

"No. Interference would be an even worse threat to the Inner City than supporting you would be—social interaction here is founded on the right of each Scholar to make his or her own decisions. Stefred can't override that when the experimentation does no harm to people not involved in it. If he felt that there was danger of children with defective genes being sent to the villages, he'd act, but he trusts your scientific competence."

"Have you—discussed it with him?" Noren asked, appalled.

"No! Never—and I haven't picked up much from his mind, either; he shields more than when I first knew him, as if he has secrets of his own. But he's an excellent psychologist, after all. On that basis I can predict his reactions, even his reaction to the idea of your speaking out publicly."

"He left me free to do that before because he judged me bound to fail," Noren said. "If he kept his hands off again—well, I wouldn't be willing to do such a thing as a mere gesture. I'd have to believe I could succeed. Yet if in principle I could, he'd be duty-bound to prevent it. The Council would force him to."

"You underestimate Stefred. He has more independence than you give him credit for—and more courage." Lianne's eyes filled with tears. "More courage than I have, Noren."

"I don't understand—"

"Because there's so much you don't yet see, and I—I'm not brave enough to tell you. Stefred will be. Since he can stop you anyway if he wants, you have nothing to lose by talking it over with him. As a favor to me, will you do that?"

"Yes," Noren promised, putting his arm around her, realizing from her trembling that she was even more upset than he himself. "If a time comes when I feel I should talk to villagers, I'll talk to Stefred first."

He tried to drive the idea from his mind, but it would not let him be. The more he thought of it, the more he knew it could work. It would demand unprecedented personal sacrifice, as Lianne had foreseen—the idea of receiving homage was repugnant to him. The prospect of doing so in official ceremonies when he got older was bad enough; this other would be infinitely worse. He had never liked villages in any case and would despise whatever time he spent there, all the more so because his role would encompass all the most difficult aspects of priesthood. Yet several ends would be served by it: not only alteration of the villagers' attitude, but the crop testing—which he could accomplish with the aid of Technicians under his orders—and continuous observation of the children through successive visits.

The one thing he did not see was how Stefred could let it happen. But he had never known Lianne to be wrong. And he'd promised her to discuss it with Stefred, rash though that seemed. She avoided him during his days of deliberation; she seemed afraid to confront him, afraid even to meet his eyes. Noren knew he must get the decision over with.

"Yes," Stefred admitted when Noren asked, "I've known for some time you are experimenting. I don't know exactly who's involved, and I don't want to. It's a matter for individual consciences."

They were alone in the study, in the old way, the old atmosphere of trust strong between them; it was as if there had never been any rift. Never again, Noren thought, would he stay away from the one person with whom he felt free to express his deepest thoughts. Even with Lianne he was not as free as he was with Stefred. Between Lianne and himself, on both sides, was the tension of holding back feelings. And he feared hurting Lianne, whereas Stefred, as she'd perceived, had unlimited strength to face whatever needing facing.

"I've hated deceiving you," Noren said, knowing the words weren't necessary, knowing too that one deceit must continue. He could never reveal Lianne's identity or the fact of her people's existence—but with the reasons for that restriction, Stefred would concur.

"You've had to deceive me," Stefred acknowledged. "As I've deceived you, pretending not to know."

"I'll spare us both and tell you the next step outright." He did so, finding the words came easily. Stefred's face, listening, was unreadable.

For a long time after Noren finished he was silent. Then, wonderingly, he said, "It…might work. It's bolder than anything that's occurred to me, further from the principles I've spent my life upholding. Strict isolation from the villagers is indispensable to their freedom under our system, yet while we hold to it, the High Law can't be altered. In contact with villagers…there would be a chance. We'd have a chance, while otherwise there is none."

"You're saying you'd *support* me?" Noren asked, incredulous. To his chagrin, he felt more dread at the thought than elation.

"No," Stefred told him. "If we should commit ourselves to your plan and fail, the morale of the Inner City would be destroyed just as surely as if I had supported you all along—and without the Inner City's stability, the villages would be doomed. I can't risk that, even knowing this change may be the only means of saving our remote descendants. I have a responsibility to the intervening generations."

Noren found himself tongue-tied, unable, somehow, to argue. Had he come to Stefred hoping that he'd be overruled and would thus escape the burden of carrying out a plan he hated?

There was another pause. Then in a low voice Stefred said, "It's impossible for me to support you. But if you take it upon yourself to act, I will look the other way, Noren."

"I—thought you might. The idea depends on your treating it as you have the experimentation. Yet in this case, how can you get away with that?"

"The Gates are unlocked; we are held here only by our freely accepted obligation to follow the First Scholar's rules. If you decide your conscience leads you elsewhere, no one will hear that the issue was discussed between us."

"But wouldn't tolerance on your part be the same as support as far as most Scholars are concerned? If I'm allowed to come and go, they'll see you're letting me do it."

Stefred's eyes widened with surprise that faded into evident pain. "By the Star," he murmured, "I've been wondering how you of all people could propose this scheme so calmly. I assumed you understood what you'd be taking on." He rose and came to Noren, laying a steady hand on his shoulder. "I didn't say I could permit you to come and go," he said quietly. "Only to go once, with the assurance that as long as you incite no violence you won't be brought back by force."

Stunned, Noren formed words with difficulty; his mouth was so dry he wondered if they were audible. "Leave the City—permanently?"

"You'd best think in those terms. Many years from now, after the genetic change has been accomplished, you might be able to return. But our society will be so altered that neither you nor I can make sure predictions."

It hardly mattered. Years…enough years for the babies to grow up and have babies of their own, then for inoculation of the whole population…and then the cutoff of the purified water supply; if he made people accept that through their trust in him, he would have to stay with them while it was happening. Yes, to be exiled that long would be the same as permanence.

He had never imagined that kind of exile. From the morning he'd first seen the City, its bright towers dazzling with reflected sunrise, he had believed he would live and die within its walls. That thought had uplifted him even while he'd assumed he would die soon. He'd invited capture for the sake of one brief glimpse of such existence! There had been disillusionment; the City was not the Citadel of All Truth he'd envisioned, shouting his heresy before the Gates in defiance of the Law that barred them. It did not hold all he'd expected to find—not, he now knew, all he might find elsewhere in the universe. It was nevertheless the sole repository of knowledge in his world, and its contents had been ample compensation for what was formally termed "perpetual confinement." How could he give up that sustenance? Access to knowledge was his life's core. He'd contemplated eventual exile at the research outpost, but only with the supposition that stored knowledge would be transferred there, that it would become the last bastion of knowledge when the City's technology wore out. To leave the City now, to live in a Stone Age culture among people with whom he could never speak of matters not taught in the village schools, without the computer complex, without discs or even books apart from village tales and the Book of the Prophecy…

This was the step to which he'd been blind, blind because he could not face the thought of it. The thing of which Lianne had warned, seeing it far in advance—from the beginning, perhaps?—yet lacking the courage to open his eyes. This was the thing she'd known only Stefred could tell him.

"I can't make it easy for you," Stefred said, "and harsh though it may sound, I wouldn't at this moment even if I could."

"Because you want me to fail," Noren said, not bitterly but in simple acknowledgment that Stefred's compassion and his duty were at odds. "You've always opposed genetic change, apart from believing it couldn't be brought about safely. You don't think it's the lesser of evils."

"I do think it is. I must be ruthless with you because I want you to succeed."

Noren turned in his chair, looking up at Stefred in utter astonishment. He could not speak.

"I look far ahead, as you do, Noren," Stefred went on. "I can't say it's wrong to put survival of our species ahead of all other goals, important though they are. I oppose you only because it would be self-defeating to put short-term survival at risk for the sake of long-term survival. Now for the first time you've come to me with a plan that entails no such risk. Of course I want you to succeed in it. But it's more demanding than you realize, and you must face that from the start—only by doing so can you become strong enough to deal with the problems you'll meet."

No doubt, Noren thought numbly. If he could find courage to accept exile from the City, he'd have courage to do anything; as usual, Stefred understood him perfectly. "I'm…not sure I can," he confessed. "I've borne everything else so far without cursing fate, without asking why it has to be me who gets hurt. Yet this is so ironic—I'm just about the only person in here who doesn't look at City confinement as a sacrifice—"

"It is not ironic," Stefred said, drawing his own chair close to Noren's and sitting down again. "The fact that for you the sacrifice works the other way is providential. Noren, priesthood itself is founded on voluntary sacrifice. The Scholars who are homesick for the villages would have buried guilt feelings if they returned, and you will be in a position where you can't afford not to feel wholly sure of your worthiness to fill the role in which you'll be cast."

"I don't feel sure," Noren protested. "Oh, I know that I haven't got selfish motives for letting people worship me. But I'm not really qualified to inspire them. I haven't any gift for it; I'm a good scientist, but in dealing with people I'm—inept."

"I would not let you go if it were otherwise," Stefred told him. "That handicap, too, will work for rather than against you."

"How, when I need to win their confidence?"

"You will win it through your symbolic role and your integrity alone; you'll be in no danger of receiving personal adulation. For a natural leader, even one who didn't want homage, there would be that danger: by his very charisma he would, against his will, become a god. That's a concept you may not be familiar with—"

"I've read," said Noren shortly. "The idea's blasphemous."

"To you, yes, as it should be. To villagers it would seem a natural extension of the supposed superhuman stature of Scholars. And that fact creates peril, Noren. Our system keeps power-seekers from the priesthood; it even eliminates those who might be corrupted by the collective power we do have. But it cannot completely protect against the possibility that a natural leader in close contact with villagers might be tempted to use his power to serve unselfish ends. He might impose his own concept of what's good for people upon them; that's one reason such contact has been prohibited. What's more, the people would welcome a godlike leader. They would demand that he take responsibilities they can better exercise for themselves. Someone gifted enough in leadership to assume them would not be the right person to enter the villages as a prophet—but you, I trust."

Lianne had known these things, too, Noren perceived. They must have entered into her initial judgment of him as the only Scholar qualified to bring about genetic change. "What would happen," he ventured, "if I couldn't keep my promises to the people—if the genetic alteration I've designed fails in the next generation, or if the Council refuses to implement it after it's proven?"

Stefred hesitated, frowning. "There would be no harm done," he said, "at least not by your actions. That's why I can safely let you go."

"But the people would lose faith. They'd feel betrayed—they might not trust Scholars at all any more."

"You won't be speaking for the Scholars, though they'll assume you are." He leaned forward and met Noren's eyes unflinchingly. "If the experimental change fails, I will denounce you as no true priest but a renegade, and they'll believe not what you've said, but what's said of you in the formal ceremonies—because the latter will be what they'll then want to believe. Does that risk frighten you?"

"No," said Noren resolutely. With quiet despair he became aware that Stefred had been speaking for some time in simple future tense, assuming that his choice was already firm, and inwardly he knew he was indeed committed. He was not sure he could endure exile or fulfill the role he must assume; beside those things, public humiliation seemed a minor ordeal. Apart from failure itself, it did not scare him.

"It should," Stefred informed him. "I'm not sure you see all the consequences of failure."

"I'm satisfied enough with the vaccine to stake my chances on it."

"You realize that if you are publicly banished from the priesthood, the villagers may kill you?"

He hadn't, but as Stefred said it he knew it for truth, and nodded. How he'd changed, he thought—long ago, when he and Brek had resolved to become real renegades and repudiate the Prophecy, they'd expected death at the hands of the villagers; but now he felt none of the resignation he had then. He no longer had any hidden desire to become a martyr.

"There is something more," Stefred continued. "As you say, if the vaccine proves safe, majority opinion among Scholars may still hold fast against implementation of genetic change.

I will have the power to override the Council decision, secretly if necessary, and I won't hesitate to use it if I am sure the villagers will give up City aid willingly. My highest loyalty is, and always has been, to them and their descendants. But if at the time you've set for the change they're against it, or so divided that interruption of the pure water supply would lead to widespread violence, it will be no better than if the vaccine itself had failed. I'll still have to denounce you and even your own followers may turn on you; if they do, I'll lift no hand to save you. Do you understand why?"

In a low voice Noren said, "It would be the same kind of situation as it was with the First Scholar. People were justifiably angry, and he led them to take it out on him instead of killing others. I have to—to plan it that way from the beginning, don't I...make sure that if I fail, I'll be the only one to bear the blame."

"Yes," Stefred said gently. "I'm trusting you for that, too. I couldn't very well refuse to after all these years of saying you're more like the First Scholar than any other man I've known."

Noren looked around the familiar study, realizing with a shock that after this day he might never enter it again. More than any other place in the City it had been home to him; more than anyone else in his life, excepting only Talyra, Stefred had been family. Now if they ever did meet again, Stefred would be *old*...

He stood up. "We can't communicate, can we," he stated, knowing the answer.

"No. I'll have reports on your actions from Technicians, but you must not send direct word, and you won't know what's happening here."

"It's better if I don't; it won't be good news."

"You'll be despised by all but your secret supporters," Stefred agreed, "and I can't openly defend you. If the Council wants you stopped, I will have only one weapon to ensure your freedom—the argument that you've made promises for which you must take personal responsibility."

Promises. A new age; a new kind of City built by common people, of stone; new seed that would flourish in untreated land. Machines, yes—to villagers any unknown object was a Machine. Knowledge, too, for who was to decide the bounds of knowledge? He could make it all fit the Prophecy, and the people would never know what they must lose.

Stefred's face was drawn with pain. "This is true priesthood," he said, "to take the universe as it is and affirm what we cannot alter. What's humanly possible to change, we will. We must change even our own biological design when survival demands it. But we have no power to reorder the world to match our hopes. If there is no way to preserve our ancestors' knowledge—if despite all our striving, its loss is inherent in the nature of things—then we must affirm that fact without despair. The Prophecy is a metaphor, not a blueprint. It proclaims a future better than the present. That's the only absolute we can have faith in."

His throat aching, Noren stood mute while Stefred embraced him. Then he turned quickly, knowing he must go before tears surfaced.

Stefred called him back. "Noren," he said. "Noren...make a good future for my son."

What a strange way to put it, Noren thought—the children of Stefred's wife must now be full-grown, and he had never mentioned any particular one, nor had he acknowledged other offspring. "The future belongs to the new race," he said firmly. "Perhaps to some of your son's children, Stefred, if he accepts genetic alteration himself in his later life."

"He won't need to. He was born with genes adapted to this world."

"Born—" Noren's breath caught; in shock, he whispered, "Veldry's son...*yours?* But she wouldn't have—"

"Wouldn't have revealed your secret to me, no. But watching you preside at the service for her dead baby, Noren, I guessed; I knew you too well not to realize there was just one reason you could have been suffering as you were. I also knew Veldry well enough to anticipate what she'd do next, and when I saw her begin to smile at men she had previously discouraged, I confronted her with it. She'd had no hope of finding anyone who approved of the experiments; she was ready to sacrifice her pride by offering herself to one of those unlikely to care one way or the other. I spared her that, at least."

"You were willing to take the risk, knowing how my son died, knowing yours might die too or else live with some horrible handicap, and that if he didn't, if things turned out well, you could never tell anyone?"

"Not even you—I couldn't have told you if you were remaining here; the others would read it in your eyes. My stand against genetic change is all that's prevented the idea from tearing the Inner City apart. But did you suppose I could favor your goal and let the burden rest on you alone?" Himself close to tears, Stefred went on, "You must bear the heaviest load; I can't spare you any part of it—but I can't spare myself, either."

"Oh, Stefred." He could neither spare himself nor be spared, Noren thought; the worst, for Stefred, was yet to come. Lianne would disappear, and in that grief he'd be unable to see any purpose.

Abruptly, inspired by unconscious telepathy, Stefred said, "Noren, you mustn't tell Lianne; it would ruin her recruiting system. Unless…it just occurs to me…she may go with you. If she offers, you must accept for the sake of her happiness as well as yours."

"The rumors aren't true," Noren said. "We aren't lovers; I thought you knew that."

"I know that so far your love is unconsummated—but I also know, perhaps better than you do, that it exists. It would be harmless for the two of you to share the village work. I would…miss Lianne, miss her a great deal, but I could train another assistant who'd win novices to your cause."

"No," said Noren steadily. "Lianne has her mission, as I have mine. After tonight we won't see each other again."

In the computer room, after he'd generated the discs of essential data, checked and rechecked, realizing that this was his last opportunity ever to question the computers personally, Noren recalled the secret file once more, for courage. He reread the First Scholar's last words to him: MAY THE INFINITE SPIRIT GUIDE AND PROTECT YOU; AS I DIE, YOU WILL BE IN MY THOUGHTS.

When he'd experienced those dying thoughts in dream form—that most intense transfer of knowledge which, like all other kinds, would now be unavailable to him—they had concerned not genetic change, but the Prophecy. Were the promises indeed one and the same? As Stefred had said, the Prophecy was metaphor. The First Scholar had not composed its words. *It's there in my mind, but I've never been able to frame it as it should be,* he'd thought through his pain. *I'm a scientist, not a poet…* He, Noren, was also a scientist. Would he be able to find adequate words for new promises, or would his sacrifice be futile?

He should wait, perhaps, and compose the words before going. But if he waited, he would wait forever; he would lose courage, not gain it. He might already have lost what had carried him through the day... Motionless, clinging to the console he might never touch again, he found he could not choose a question to be his last.

His head dropped, and he wept.

Lianne found him there long after midnight. Noren turned slowly, reaching out to her. "Lianne," he said in agony, "I *can't.*"

She touched his face with cool, gentle fingers. "You have no choice."

"I do have a choice! No one's path is predestined; no one's required to take on the job of saving the world."

"I didn't mean that. I meant you've already chosen. You may feel you can't go—but can you stay?"

No. It was as simple as that. He could not stay in the City, aware of what he might achieve outside it; if he tried, he would only come to despise himself.

Lianne held him close as they left the computer complex, giving him no chance to look back. They sat on a stone bench in the courtyard, under fading stars. "All this time," she murmured, "all this time, nearly four years, I've known you would go before I did. That you'd give up not just the things you longed for, but those you already had."

She too was an exile, Noren thought, though her renunciation of her heritage was temporary, and he'd done little to ease her loneliness. His arms tightened around her. Now that it was too late, all the pent-up passion he'd denied was rising in him: passion not only of his body but of his yearning to reach Lianne's world. Just when had he stopped measuring Lianne against Talyra? He would always love Talyra, but she had been dead four years; she wouldn't have wanted him to mourn indefinitely. He hadn't waited solely for her sake. He had held back, unwittingly guarding himself against this moment, the moment of the inevitable parting. And now that it had come, it was no easier for his long self-restraint.

"I don't know why I wasted the years," he said with remorse. "I wanted to love you, but I felt—frozen. Sometimes I think I'm the one who's alien."

"I understood how it was with you, Noren. As a child you lost your mother; as a man you lost your bride—you couldn't love only to lose again. You were afraid to give your heart, and I wouldn't have wanted less."

"Yet you too knew we'd lose each other, and you weren't afraid."

"I'd have taken the time we could have rather than none," she acknowledged. "But people are different, born different, and not only because of their genes. You were born to stand apart, as you were born with a questioning mind."

"Maybe it's a good thing, since I'll always have to," he declared. His position would be solitary past the endurance of a warmer person. Furthermore, a Scholar in the villages could love no woman—in the eyes of the people, any such relationship between castes would be shockingly unnatural. It was no longer important that his genes were damaged; no situation where it mattered could arise. And anyway, he would not want anyone but Lianne. He'd given his heart despite himself, long ago. He would not give it a third time even after she was gone from the world.

Would he know when she was gone? Someday the starship would return; would he look up some night and see a light move and know that was the moment when she was lost to him? When the doors of the universe were for him irrevocably closed?

Her face was wet against his, and sobs shook her body. *Oh, Lianne,* he thought, *how could I have deceived myself so? If I'd been as honest about my feelings as about my beliefs, we'd have had what people think we've had…*

"We have the rest of tonight," Lianne said. "We still can have memories."

He took her into the lodging tower, and for a few brief hours of his last night in the City, Noren's spirits were lifted.

Chapter Ten

In the morning, Noren took the blue robe from beneath his bed, opening the storage compartment quietly so as not to wake Lianne—though he knew she was only pretending to be asleep. She was right; there must be no farewell. Neither of them could get through it without breaking. He would need his strength for this day, and for the days ahead.

He had no real plan. "Take things as they come," Stefred had advised him. "You've always been quick-witted and resourceful; rely on those assets instead of trying to deal with what you can't foresee. You have the right instincts. You'll find them more effective than you expect."

Lianne had put it somewhat differently. "You will receive—inspiration, Noren," she'd said seriously. "I don't know how to explain this to you, but I am sure, from many worlds' experience, that it is true. Unconscious functions of the mind play a part in it, but one draws, too, on something outside oneself."

"If that were true universally, Stefred would know," Noren had objected; but he'd recalled as he did so that Stefred wasn't aware even of telepathy.

"He knows," Lianne had replied. "He said, 'May the spirit of the Star go with you,' didn't he?"

Naturally he had, and he'd said it with more feeling than people did on less momentous occasions. Now, suddenly, it occurred to Noren that the common, conventional phrase might—like the equally improbable-sounding prediction of the Star's physical appearance—reflect an actual concrete fact. Was the difference only in the extent of the Founders' understanding?

He took his blue robe and the clothes he wore, nothing else. As a condemned heretic he had arrived in the City with nothing, and he'd acquired nothing during the interval, for as stewards, Scholars were not permitted personal belongings. The data discs he'd generated he took to the Outer City lab, placing them in the custody of the Technician in charge with specific orders about their storage. From there, he proceeded to the City's exit dome. His hand trembling, he pushed the button to slide back the heavy Gates. They began to open, revealing blinding white pavement beyond; Noren touched the button again to reverse them as he stepped through.

From the outside they were, of course, unopenable.

He was prepared for the panic that hit him; having been conditioned to it both by dreaming the First Scholar's death and by his own initiation ordeal, he knew what he would feel. There was no ugly mob now, still he found himself flinching as he approached the platform's edge. Here the First Scholar had been struck down. Here he himself had been pelted with dirt during the reenactment to which he'd been subjected, without warning, at his recantation. He had not been outside the Gates since that day. His trips to and from the outpost had been made by air; Scholars never stood on this platform except during public ceremonies. The first such ceremony of one's priesthood, he'd heard, was a grueling test of nerve: one was sent out alone so that remembered terror would counter one's aversion to mass obeisance. One was not expected to endure either for more than a few minutes; prolonged exposure to kneeling multitudes was unheard of.

Noren started down the long flight of steps, wide steps up which crowds swarmed at recantations and on feast days. The steps, too, held memories. Talyra had stood on them, watching in anguish as he'd faced abuse, humiliation and finally the sentencing. He had believed then that he would never see her again. Would she be living now if there'd been no reunion? She might have died anyway with her first child, no matter who she'd married. That was something he would never know.

Before recantation, he had been on the steps himself; it was there he'd been recaptured after his escape from the village had proved useless. He had been injured and penniless; he'd known it was only a matter of hours until Technicians would apprehend him—but he had reached the walls of the City. And the sight of the City had so stirred him that nothing else seemed to matter. The sound, also...there had been music, his first experience with the awesome electronic music he'd since come to take for granted. It had heartened him. Was it not better, he'd thought, to die defiant than to he dragged to his fate like a work-beast marked for slaughter? A blue-robed priest had emerged from the Gates to preside at Benison, the daily ritual for opening the markets; when that priest had read from the Book of the Prophecy, Noren had cried out against the apparent falsity of the words. He'd kept shouting his protests until Technicians stunned him. The crowd assumed the Star itself had struck him down for his blasphemy. He had known better, and had believed himself doomed to torture and execution, yet inside he had hardly minded—for they had carried him through the Gates into the City. The City...the one place on the earth he had ever wanted to be.

Now, years later, he looked back up those steps toward the again-impenetrable walls and the glimmering towers beyond. They shone in the hot sun of midmorning. He could not gaze at them any more; it hurt too much, hurt more deeply than the sting of his watering eyes.

And besides, at the foot of the steps, a small, eager cluster of people was gathering.

This was, in their view, a blessed day. It was something to tell their grandchildren: the day a Scholar descended the steps, the day they knelt within reach of his hands! There were a few Technicians in the group; these might have seen Scholars at close range before. But the villagers certainly hadn't. They had not been sure whether a Scholar's hands were made of ordinary flesh or were, perhaps, translucent. Noren steeled himself and extended his arms in blessing. He had no right to deprive them of that. This first congregation was composed of reverent people, those who cared about the Prophecy, the future—the ones who did not care had remained in the market stalls. His appearance being unprecedented, no custom compelled anyone to come forward; he had not beckoned; these had approached him as seekers of hope. *A priest gives...* If they wanted a tale to pass down to their descendants, well, he was here to make sure they could have descendants to pass it to.

"May the spirit of the Mother Star abide with you, and with your children, and your children's children," Noren said with solemnity. "I have brought you good news of the coming age."

It was both easier and harder than he'd expected it to be: easier because words did come to him, sincere words that left him feeling no taint of dishonesty; yet harder because he had not foreseen the practical problems that would arise.

He had known he would attract attention, but that was an understatement. People flocked to him. They knelt silently, not cheering—for that would not be seemly—but simply waiting, eyes devoutly raised toward the sky; and after he'd passed, they got to their feet for a better view. Whether they heard what he said was questionable; they were too absorbed by the thrill of his mere presence. But at this stage, that did not matter. He was a long way from asking them to break the High Law. What he must accomplish at first was simply to win their trust—and that he could do only by being worthy of trust. More and more clearly, as the first day passed, Noren understood why Stefred and Lianne had believed he might succeed where equally worthy Scholars would fail. Only his mood of self-sacrifice was making this possible. If he had come to the people in any state other than total despair about his own future, he could never have borne their veneration. As it was, he didn't have to remind himself that he had no ulterior aims.

It was not, of course, necessary for the people to venerate Scholars as they did; that was no part of the Founders' design. No Scholar had ever encouraged the belief that priests were superhuman. It had arisen spontaneously over the generations, and there was no way to stamp it out, for the sole alternative to being seen as transcendent would have been to become all-too-human tyrants. But now, Noren saw, there was some chance he could counter that belief. He could demonstrate his own humanity. He must move very carefully, however. He must retain authority to speak, and given a choice, he preferred mystical authority to individual authority. Better that he should be classed among impersonal beings than that he be considered an idol in his own right.

The fact that he'd be assumed to be superhuman was his chief protection against being recognized as a former heretic. No one in the first weeks would be likely to look at his face, and he'd soon have grown a beard. People saw what they expected to see. As long as he kept away from his home village, where he might run into his father or brothers, there was small danger. His family would be unlikely to speak out in any case, lest they be accused of blasphemy; the provision that only older Scholars could appear publicly was meant to prevent multiple recognitions rather than particular ones. He had been away for six years, and was not the same person he once had been. The years had aged him more than they'd have aged a carefree farmer.

He had no plan as to where to go, but it soon became apparent that without declaration of a destination, he would never get away from the market area outside the walls. People would block the roads; as word spread, they would travel from far and wide, leaving farms and village shops untended. Furthermore, it would soon take on the atmosphere of a carnival. His first listeners might be devout, but they would soon be joined by the merely curious. Before long everyone would want to see the show. Huge crowds always came to the markets for festivals, such as Founding Day and the Blessing of the Seed, for a trip to the City outskirts was a welcome break in humdrum lives. But that was not the kind of foundation he should build on,

Escape, to be sure, would be simple. He had only to command, and Technicians would put an aircar at his disposal; they would take him unquestioningly wherever he ordered. And indeed, if he was to visit outlying villages, that would be the most practical way of getting there, as well as the way everyone would expect a Scholar to arrive. But it didn't seem the best way. *You have the right instincts,* Stefred had said; and instinct told him that though he had full power to command Technicians—a power that couldn't be taken from him unless he was ceremonially banished from the priesthood—he must use it only for the indirect access to lab facilities needed to continue the genetic research. He did not want to ask Technicians, even those eager for the honor, to fill his personal needs. Nor did he want to do what everyone would expect. The whole point was to get people used to changes…

Inspiration, when it came, was a flash of light. He found himself speaking almost as one did in the controlled dreams, not knowing what was to come, afraid, yet at the same time confident. "I will build a new City," he said, "beyond the end of the longest road: a City without walls, without towers; and the unquickened land there will bear fruit. And in this, no Technicians will aid me…"

It was tantamount to a declaration that the sun would stop in its tracks and rain would fall up instead of down. Everyone knew that unquickened land—land not treated by the Technicians' machines—did not, and could not, become fruitful. Such words from anyone but a Scholar would have merited not mere derision, but the charge of presumptuous blasphemy. And, Noren thought grimly, even he had sown seeds of potential retribution. If he did not make good his words, if the genetically altered plants would not grow in untreated soil...well, this was the sort of commitment Stefred had warned he must make. Carefully, he did not specify exactly when the miracle would come to pass; but there would be a limit to people's patience. Omniscient as they thought him to be, he had placed himself at their mercy.

That idea, strangely, was heartening. It made their present adulation much easier to face.

"Beyond the end of the longest road" was a long way, a journey of many days on foot even without stops in intermediate villages. He had made such a journey before; the village of his birth was far out on one of the spokes that radiated from the City, and after escaping, he'd traveled inbound by night, sleeping in farmers' fields during daylight hours. Only at the end, after his injury, had he dared accept a ride in a trader's sledge. Now he would not ride at all. People would be glad to build a sledge for him, to harness a team of their best work-beasts, to spread sand before it as it traveled so that its runners would glide more smoothly than on a routinely sanded road. To them, that would seem fitting. Yet even had he possessed miraculous power to produce wheels he would not have ridden, though he knew his stamina would be taxed.

City dwellers were not hardened as villagers were; in years of confinement, one lost one's physical prowess. Even his labor at the outpost was now far behind him. The oppressive heat, hour after hour, began to drain him, and he appreciated, for the first time, how Lianne felt about it. As a boy he'd been inured to heat, had never known the cool relief of a tower's interior. He could become inured again. In his renunciation of the City, he had not counted physical comforts among his sacrifices. All the same, he found to his surprise that his body's demands were the cause of his first role crisis.

If villagers thought Scholars ageless and sexless, they gave even less thought to such mundane matters as these awesome beings' bodily needs. Noren didn't recall this until he realized that he was thirsty. He had been on his feet half a day in the hot sun, speaking to groups most of that time, repeating the same blessing over and over. No one had offered him a drink of water; it would never occur to anyone that he might want one. He could, of course, ask for it—but that was awkward. No one had pure water in hand, and in any case, how could he pronounce the blessing in one breath and ask for a drink in the next? It would be undignified. He himself wouldn't mind that, but his audience would; he must uphold the ideal image they expected. His mouth got drier and drier. He began to wonder, half-seriously, whether the sacrament of drinking impure water should be established far sooner than he'd planned; but no, he could not yet break the High Law in their presence. There was not even any impure water, since streams close to the City were all diverted to the purification plant. Longingly, as he left the market area, he eyed roadside taverns.

By the time sunset approached he was, by supreme irony, suffering more seriously from thirst than from any emotional burdens.

The blue robe was a hot garment, never designed for long wear. Under it, sweat drenched Noren's clothes. How, he thought in dismay, was he going to wash? How would he manage other bodily functions that might be assumed unnecessary for Scholars? He could not remove the robe except in privacy, and at a farmyard cistern there'd be none; as for excusing himself to use a privy, the very thought was ludicrous.

These concerns overrode that of food, but he'd eaten nothing all day and eventually must do so. This was the one such problem he'd considered before leaving the City. Technicians, when in the villages, bought food; they never took from the villagers without paying. But he could have carried no large amount of money, and in any case, people might be insulted if he tried to pay. No one had ever dreamed of such an honor as seating a Scholar at table, yet an honor it would be, and in that one respect he must let people serve him. He must also, he now saw, request a private sleeping room—though it would mean turning its occupants out—as well as the unheard-of luxury of an individual wash-water jug and slop jar. His hosts would hardly begrudge this, but he disliked the thought of demanding privileges. Furthermore, it wasn't quite the fashion in which he'd choose to prove himself human…or was it? On second thought, Noren decided, the vulgar gossip that would spread would be a healthy thing.

He had not traveled far the first day, for he had spent most of it with the market crowds. By nightfall they had thinned out; after once being blessed, people didn't presume to follow him without invitation. He must eventually, he supposed, choose followers. It wouldn't be fitting to go alone, and he'd rejected the idea of a Technician escort such as would appear with a Scholar before the

Gates. Besides, to build a new "city" he would need help, and it must come from people willing to abandon their past lives, willing to take the frightening steps he would ultimately ask them to. But that was in the future. For now, he could think no further than water and rest.

At the crest of a long hill overlooking the City was a farmhouse. Leaving the last cluster of suppliants, Noren, dizzy with fatigue, climbed the path to its door. To his immense relief the family saw him coming and met him outside. "May the spirit of the Star be with you," whispered Noren hoarsely. The formal greeting was now, and must remain, automatic, for it would be a terrible breach of courtesy to inadvertently omit it. "I should like to share your table if I may."

The farmer, a graying man, was so stunned he couldn't reply; but his wife was a woman of presence. "Reverend Sir, you will be welcome," she said simply. She met his eyes squarely, even from her knees; Noren liked that.

"If I enter your house, you must not kneel to me," he said. "That is fitting only in public places, and I wish to be your guest." He wondered if he would be able to stand on his own feet long enough for the others to rise to theirs.

They gave him a room, obviously their own, and after he'd bathed, a hearty meal. Like all farm and village families, they had ample food and no need to apologize for its quality, since only one type of food existed—he was served bread and stewed fowl, just as he would have been in the Inner City's refectory. They waited silently before eating; he realized they expected him to recite the customary words. It had been many years since he'd done that, though he'd used those words in other rituals. *"Let us rejoice in the bounty of the land, for the land is good, and from the Mother Star came the heritage that has blessed it… And it shall remain fruitful, and the people shall multiply across the face of the earth…"* That took him back to his childhood, even to the time when his mother was alive, and to the later time when he'd burned with resentment at the idea that she'd been led to believe in the Scholars' blessings. What would his mother think if she could see him now?

"I must rise at dawn and be on my way," he told the family, "for I go to build a new City…" They listened solemnly to the new prophecy that had in a single day become more real to Noren than that of the Founders. No one, not even the old man, seemed surprised. It fit; it was right; it was *natural.* It was the business of Scholars to build Cities, to make the land fruitful, to enable the people to multiply. The change was not going to be hard to effect after all. It required only his wit—and his willingness to pay the price.

At daybreak he stood on the hilltop and watched the sun rise. As he'd seen the City first, coming by another road down this same hill, he looked his last upon it. The lighted beacons atop the towers faded as the sky brightened. Sunlight struck the silvered surface of the domes, which from this distance appeared as a single scalloped wall encircling the tall spires within. Inside one of those towers, Lianne would be waking… Resolutely, Noren turned his back on the scene and started down the other side of the hill.

Gradually his life assumed a new pattern, a pattern composed not only of what he must cope with on the journey, but of his blossoming plans for its end. So the First Scholar had felt, embarking upon another "impossible" scheme, hating his own role, expecting no happy ending for himself, yet believing more and more that it would work. That future generations would be saved by it. It was so simple…one committed oneself *first,* and *then* faith came! Noren had never understood that; even after experiencing the dreams repeatedly, he had not. But both Stefred and Lianne had seen.

Stefred, though unable to see the specific way to success until it was pointed out to him, had committed himself by fathering Veldry's child. He would not have done that without believing underneath that a way would be found. There was the child to consider; he would not have risked that child's welfare merely out of kindness to Veldry or desire to support Noren's cause.

Noren, too, had believed strongly enough to take risks. In the end, he had committed himself not to mere risk but to outright sacrifice. Yet in his conscious mind, he'd been uncertain that it would achieve anything; he had left the City less out of faith than out of the knowledge that to stay would be to concede defeat. He had imagined a long period of vagueness—of grayness, like the moss-covered land into which he'd come—during which he must live in utter despair. He'd thought it would be like the time at the outpost, only more permanent. It wasn't. Once his commitment was complete, he felt hope, even excitement. The pieces began to mesh. The plan was really going to enable humanity to survive!

The experimental children, all of them, must live in the new "city." Stefred would be able to arrange that—it had already been agreed that they'd be named by their parents according to a code both he and Noren could recognize. Having them sent where he ordered wouldn't be hard, for village-bound Technicians were accustomed to obeying Stefred's instructions without informing other Scholars. If his interference with normal procedures ever came out, he'd have only to say his aim was to make Noren answerable for those children's welfare. Already, word of the new prophecy would have reached him; he would contrive to delay the adoption of his son until he heard that the settlement was established. He would understand that the children must eat food from unquickened land.

Their adoptive parents also would have to eat it, which meant they must have their own genes altered. This, the human experimentation among villagers, was the part Noren liked least. Yet it wasn't as if it were an untried change, and he'd already resigned himself to the fact that a comparable situation would arise as soon as the children came of age. Better to have them together than scattered throughout the population, and better, too, to place them with families composed of volunteers. The couples would give informed consent; he could tell them the essential truth in terms they'd understand. People would come to his settlement as Technicians sought admission to the Inner City, knowing the hardships involved, but nothing of the real reason these must exist.

Noren's own task, apart from bringing to pass the miracle on which he'd now staked his life, was to choose the residents of—of what? He spoke of it as a new city, but he could not think of it that way in his own mind. The research outpost had been conceived as "a new City beyond the Tomorrow Mountains," but everybody called it simply the outpost. Villages had names: Abundance, Prosperity, and so forth. He named the planned settlement Futurity. He began to talk about it by name. Rumor spread ahead of him; it was not long before people in the villages he entered were already believers in the place, starting to wonder who would be fortunate enough to live there.

They turned out to meet him now in holiday garb, green instead of everyday brown, adorned with the blue glass beads that symbolized religious devotion. They filled the village squares as they normally would on feast days. Their bearing toward him was not so much worshipful as jubilant; his coming was cause for celebration. The farther he got from the City, the truer this was, for not everyone had opportunities to travel—some had lived to old age without a pilgrimage to the Gates, and had not seen Scholars even from a distance.

It was impossible, of course, for him to individually bless every man, woman and child in each and every village along the road. He spoke to those on outlying farms, but in the centers he held services. Once, he thought ruefully, he had shrunk from the role of presiding as priest at small City gatherings; now he was assuming it before hundreds—and on those occasions, he could not stop them from kneeling.

He was also asked to bless wedding parties. Weddings were solemnized by village councils and blessed, when possible, by Technicians as the Scholars' representatives; but naturally people were eager for the unprecedented distinction of a benediction from a real priest. At first Noren wondered how there could be so many weddings. Were these boys and girls marrying hastily simply because of his appearance? No doubt a few dates were advanced, but he soon learned that some couples were traveling long distances on connecting roads from villages on other radials, bringing their families and friends along. His days were long, hot and thirsty, but at night there was invariably a wedding feast—and he saw that when the time came to introduce innovations, there'd be no lack of enthusiasm.

He did not mind weddings or the rites of Thanksgiving for Birth, but services for the dead were another matter. The first time he was called upon he was, unreasonably, stunned. It was the job of Technicians to conduct such services! But no one sent for the Technicians when a priest was present; instead, they thanked providence for their good fortune. And in fact it was whispered that the aged woman who'd died, after outliving her grandchildren, had declared that now—having seen a Scholar with her own eyes—she could depart in peace. Horrified, shivering despite the heat, Noren went through with the service, though of course the Technicians had to be summoned first to bring the aircar, which he was incapable of calling down from the sky as he'd been expected to. Watching it lift away afterward, he nearly lost his self-control. His face was wet with tears. What would happen when there were no more aircars?

Ultimately, when genetic change was complete, recycling of bodies would not be necessary; his new crops would have genes to recover trace elements efficiently from organically fertilized soil. But the people, who knew nothing of the disposal of bodies in any case, would wish to continue sending them to the City as long as the City stood. It was a symbol not to be lightly cast aside. And indeed, thought Noren, did he not want his own body to go there; did he not wish to think that in death if not in life, he would someday return?

He got through that service by rote, as he had the one for his son, without letting himself think of the words. But it wasn't the only such rite he performed, and the words did bother him. *Not in memory alone does he survive, for the universe is vast.* Was it right to tell the people something he wasn't sure of? They trusted him! He owed them comfort, and yet... *Were the doors now closed to us reopened, as in time they shall be, still there would remain that wall through which there is no door save that through which he has passed.* Lianne didn't think such words were foolish, although she had no more real knowledge of the matter than he did. And he had none, after all. He certainly did not know they expressed a false idea—he could not say it was false any more than he could say the Prophecy was. Like the Prophecy, those words were more metaphor than blueprint.

As he perceived this, much fell into place for Noren. Most villagers had a naive view of the Prophecy: they thought Cities would rise overnight on the date of the Star's appearance. The Scholars considered themselves enlightened, yet he'd wondered, lately, whether their view might not be equally naive. Not false, as he'd feared in his despair over the impossibility of metal synthesization, but—well, oversimplified. Too literally tied to the Founders' specific plans. The First Scholar himself had known better than that! He'd made provision for genetic change, knowing that would mean loss of technology; yet the ideas of the Prophecy had all been in his deathbed recording. It was on those ideas he, Noren, was now drawing in his own words to the people, rather than on the interpretation priests were taught, the narrow interpretation that kept them from facing the real world. Stefred knew. It had been he who'd declared it wasn't a blueprint. But he knew, too, that most Scholars would hold to their interpretation as fiercely as the villagers to theirs. They would not pursue truth to a third level.

Was that why he now felt no hypocrisy? Noren asked himself. Because, paradoxically, he still cared more about searching for truth than did others?

One evening as he entered a village, people took him to the house of a critically sick man. He stood appalled by the bedside, his mouth dry with more than the thirst of the weary day behind him. They expected him to cure the man's disease! They believed Scholars could do anything. If he failed, as he inevitably would, they might think him no true Scholar—yet if by chance the man survived, he could not accept the credit that would be accorded him. There were limits beyond which he would not go.

"I can do nothing," he said, inwardly groping for inspiration. "You must call the Technicians; illness can be cured only with Machines."

"The Technicians came yesterday, and said they could not help. But surely, Reverend Sir, if you merely speak the words—"

It was possible. Noren knew from things Lianne had said that faith could often heal; if the man was a believer, and heard, he might recover—even from an illness beyond the skill of City physicians, he might. But he also might not. Some things mind could not do. If only he knew the diagnosis...but no, it was better this way. It was better if he himself did not know the probable outcome.

"May the spirit of the Star abide with you," he said gravely, placing his hand on the sick man's hot forehead, "and if it be fitting, may you be healed; but rest assured that the light of the Star falls on realms beyond this earth." He turned, and to the family went on, "Do you think we Scholars would permit any deaths if we could prevent them? We are but stewards, guardians of the Star's mysteries. The power to give life or take it is not ours. I do not know how long this man will live."

And because this was true, they nodded in acceptance and let him go his way. If he'd been certain the man was dying, Noren perceived, what he had said would not have satisfied them. They'd have sensed a presumption of power at least to foresee. Only by keeping an open mind could he function as a prophet; he must make no predictions, good or ill, unless sure beyond logic that they were genuine.

He had as yet no permanent followers, though people walked with him from village to village. Usually, now, he lodged with the heads of village councils, these being the most prominent citizens, deferred to by others desirous of the honor. It was ironic, considering the scorn he'd once received from the council of his own village that had tried him for heresy. When he asked himself whether his hosts would do the same, he knew that most would. He didn't like to think of what might happen to youths of these villages who dared to express doubts about his status, yet wasn't he serving his original aim? The more heresy he inspired, the better. It was good if boys and girls looked upon him and were set to thinking, good for the world, and good for them, too, in terms of their real fate if they were condemned on that account. But it was not good on the part of those who did the condemning. They were not the sort he wanted in Futurity; he could take neither such men nor those they judged, who, if not sent to the City, would be deprived of their birthright. So he must find some way to make contact with the folk who stayed in the background. Those like Talyra…

Thoughts of Talyra came often to him, for with her he had shared the open land. He had sat with her on the gray moss; walked with her down roads like this, lined with dull-hued fodder and purple shrubs, past the green of quickened fields; taken her in his arms under the wide sky alight with silver crescents and the red bead of Little Moon. The memories, all too poignant, came back—still, he could not wish for those days. That part of his life was gone. His heart would always be in the City…or, when Lianne went, would it go with Lianne? Noren honestly did not know. It hardly mattered; that life was gone, too. Only his goal remained.

Dwellings grew fewer as he traveled outward from the City, and villages were farther apart. There came a night when he stopped at a lone farmhouse once more. The husband and wife were respectful but less diffident than most; were it not for the now-tattered blue robe, he thought sadly, he might have talked with them as friends. Yet he sensed that they were troubled. No family was present, and the woman, beneath her courteous welcome, eyed him with the desperate plea for aid he'd now seen, and helplessly sorrowed over, in too many people to count.

After supper she approached him privately. "Reverend Sir, I wish no favor," she said, "yet for my husband's sake I will speak, since you have paid us honor such as we could not have hoped for. As you see, we have no children. We are undeserving of anyone's esteem. Yet he has not divorced me, shame though my barrenness is on us. If I merit punishment so heavy, can it not take form that falls on me alone?"

"Barrenness is not a punishment," Noren began. But then, having learned much from Stefred's ways, he added, "Do you feel you are justly punished, and if so, why? I warn you that you mustn't lie to me."

The woman drew breath, then met his eyes steadily. "I am aware of no weighty sin. I thought you, Reverend Sir, might enlighten me; for it's hard not knowing what I've done wrong."

If she had been guilt-ridden or had shown false humility, he would not have pursued the matter, but he saw that this woman and her husband were fit parents. Since they could have no children of their own, why not some of his wards? The tradition whereby Wards of the City were placed only with large families, barren wives being considered unworthy, was senseless. Besides, he must take only childless couples, for he disliked the thought of inoculating young children who'd been born with unaltered genes and he did not want to limit the settlement to newlyweds. He alone would have authority to place the experimental babies—that was necessary, since only he would know which were in fact siblings who must grow up as foster-kin lest they later, unknowingly, intermarry—and no one would challenge his decisions.

"You have heard me speak of Futurity," he said slowly, "where barren land will become fruitful. Unfruitful marriages will also be blessed there. I cannot promise that you will conceive a child if you come, but whether or not you do, you will be mother to Wards of the City."

She dropped to her knees despite his earlier prohibition, joy and gratitude illuminating her plain features. Noren took her hands. "It will not be an easy life," he warned. "Get up and call your husband, and I will tell you what the people of Futurity must venture."

Before he left the next morning, they had pledged to sell their farm and come after him. They were mature, reliable people, a good balance to the adolescent couples who would of necessity make up the majority of the Chosen Families. To them, he decided, he would give Veldry's children.

The alteration of people's genes must be done dramatically, for it must be made clear from the start who was free to drink impure water and who was not. Furthermore, people would want the assurance of a rite. They would even want the rite to be frightening; though ordinarily the injection involved was painless, they'd feel better afterward if it were made an ordeal. Again following what Stefred had taught him of initiations, Noren realized that it would be necessary to give the volunteers proof of their own worthiness. Also, almost too late, he remembered that in the case of those yet to be married the injections must take effect before the weddings, and in fact brides must be required to swear by the Mother Star that they were not already with child. He dared not inoculate a woman who might be pregnant; the effect on the unborn baby's genes would be too uncertain.

In the last village, therefore, he waited. He spoke of how Chosen Families must qualify, and word spread, by the traders and by radiophone; before long barren and betrothed couples began arriving from other regions. Most were years younger than himself, youngsters fresh from school eager to embark on a glorious adventure. They made him feel ancient—as, now full-bearded, he indeed must look to them, if they looked beyond his priest's robe at all.

He'd expected to call on the village for help in building, but he soon saw that that would be a mistake. There were far too many volunteer couples; he had to make the conditions hard. They must be willing to raise the new "city" unaided, stone by stone. It was well, and necessary, for them to come anticipating miracles; but all that could be done without miracles they must do for themselves. This wasn't only a screening strategy, he realized. Later, they would take pride in what they'd accomplished.

Gradually, through many interviews, he chose those with the soundest motives. He explained the goal with half-truths, nonetheless valid for being partial. "Families grow, the villages grow, there are more and more people every year—and this is as it should be under the Law. Yet the City does not grow at all. A time will come when the world needs more farmland than can be quickened, more water than can be made pure; the Technicians will have too few Machines to serve everyone. The Law does not say this, for the Law does not speak of the future. The Prophecy does not say it, for the Prophecy tells of the time when the Star will become visible. But the Scholars know it. They know someday the Law must change, and my work is to teach you to live with tomorrow's Law. To this, if you are willing, you will be sealed; but if you choose it, you cannot go back, nor can your children. You will belong to Futurity as Technicians belong to the City..."

They were, Noren feared, spellbound. One by one he listed the hardships: no preexisting village comforts, no buildings except those they raised themselves, no City goods such as traders sold elsewhere. Limited social contacts outside the new settlement. Poverty unprecedented in their world, since they'd have no harvests or craftwork to sell and no time free to work for wages. Mysterious changes in the High Law that would not be spelled out in advance; still more mysterious risks that might extend to their descendants. Most sobering of all, a rule that their children must marry within the community or face charges of heresy. Noren had read enough to know that while many of these provisions would, under other circumstances, be wholly unjustifiable, in most societies it would nevertheless be easy for a self-proclaimed prophet to find people who'd voluntarily comply with them. The magnitude of Stefred's trust in him impressed him anew. What he was doing was dangerous, though it was a lesser evil than extinction, lesser even than the caste system his work would ultimately abolish.

Yet Futurity would indeed produce heretics, or so he hoped. His people, like all other citizens, would be free to choose dissent; and it wasn't as if the dissenters would suffer harm.

He gave orders by radiophone; Technicians from the lab came out by aircar, bringing the genetic vaccine. They did not know what it was, of course, and since they were used to inoculating villagers against disease, they wondered only that he took personal charge of the equipment. They knew nothing of the rite held that evening for the chosen couples alone. The volunteers themselves did not know the true significance of the needle to which they submitted, though since it was a metal object they looked upon it as holy. "It will mark you as pledged to Futurity," he told them, "and ever after, until the fruit of Futurity is spread throughout this world, you and your children will be set apart. I believe the spirit of the Star will favor you, but I have no sure foreknowledge. You are the vanguard, for good or for ill—if your children should sicken, it would be a sign that peril threatens the coming age. Against such peril the world must have warning. What is new must flourish in one place before it can flourish everywhere. Do you accept the role of forerunners, knowing these things to be true?"

Individually they gave assent, elated not only by the honor of being chosen, but by their own excitement. Noren wasn't gentle with the needle; he knew how Stefred, or even Lianne, would handle it, and overcame his reluctance to offer a symbol more memorable than words. The triumph in the initiates' faces told him he'd judged accurately.

But this rite was not the real test, either of them or of him. So far he had not asked them to do anything against their inclinations, nor had he presented them with any conflict between their image of a Scholar and his demands on them. To induce them to break the High Law's taboos would be far harder. With growing apprehension, he faced the thought that the time for that step was at hand.

The weddings were to take place in the new community, and the feast, Noren declared, was to be attended by its members alone. Farewells to friends and relatives must be made before departure. "You will set forth to no household," he warned, "and the moss of the wilderness will be your marriage bed. But from your children and foster-children will come new strength for the world, and the light of the Star will shine upon the City you establish."

So at last, beyond the end of the road, Noren came to Futurity; high on a knoll, looking out toward the Tomorrow Mountains, he chose its site. At sunset the people climbed to it in wedding garb: red skirts for brides, red-trimmed white for those already married, with white tunics for everyone but him. He himself wore, as always, the blue robe—and it occurred to him that he would be the only person there that night who would sleep alone.

They stood in a circle around a blazing moss fire as one by one, the couples exchanged vows and received his blessing. When the solemnities were over someone started a song, and the others joined in while two went to the campsite to fetch ale for the toast. Returning, they said to him in puzzlement, "Sir, most of the jugs are empty; there's not even any water—"

Though he'd been waiting for this discovery, Noren felt a sick chill of fear. If their trust in him was not strong enough, the whole scheme would fall in ruins—and he found himself worrying less over his own fate, or even the world's, than about the feelings of these young people whose wedding night would be spoiled. How had he had the audacity to think he could make the occasion joyous for them?

He kept his voice calm. "This is the mystery for which I've prepared you, for which the rite set you apart from your generation. We drink water fresh from the land, here; fill the jugs from the stream and you will not be condemned. A day will come when the High Law is changed, but you and your children need not wait for that day. Here grain will grow in unquickened fields—did you think you were not to harvest it, though that too is now contrary to the Law?"

Their eyes widened in shock. They had been reared to believe that eating or drinking anything impure was not only sinful, but likely to have dire results. Even those who suspected that prevalent nursery tales were exaggerations knew that to consume impurities, or merely to use pots made of unpurified clay, was an offense equivalent to heresy for which one would be sent to the City in bonds.

After a long pause one woman spoke out, saying, "Reverend Sir, you are testing us, lest having been honored, we might think ourselves above the Law. Perhaps also you test again our willingness to endure hardship. There is no need. We will go thirsty, and hungry, too, if you ask it of us. Rest assured that we won't defile what is sacred."

Aghast, Noren realized they'd naturally take it that way. Having picked the hardiest and most dedicated, he could well imagine their abstaining even through heavy labor within sight of the stream. They might persist until they collapsed, trusting him, ironically, to eventually provide them with sustenance. And though he could pronounce water pure by decree, that would do nothing toward freeing them from dependence.

"This is indeed a test of courage," he said soberly, "but not the sort you suppose. I know what it is to deny thirst, for I have done so; once I came near death thus, seeing that to use impure water would be a wrong. Yet I have also done something else. I have drunk such water deliberately, in dread of the outcome, for the sake of those who may face an age when the City cannot supply the world. The Star did not strike me down for it."

They all stared at him, amazed less by his impunity—for could not a Scholar do as he pleased?—than by the implicit admission that he was neither immortal nor exempt from fear. Noren stood up, opening the fastenings of the blue robe to show the commonplace clothes underneath. "Look at me," he said. "I am human, a man like other men, although it has been given to me to know mysteries. I will not tell you impure water did not harm me. It did, for someone among the Scholars had to pay the price of new knowledge. But it harms me no longer and has not harmed anyone to whom I have done what I did to you in the rite of pledging; the spirit of the Star revealed to me what I must do. From that same source I have knowledge of how to make grain sprout in this wasteland. Someday all will have such knowledge, for does not the Prophecy tell us that a time will come when the Scholars no longer are guardians?"

The young couples remained very still, clinging tightly to each others' hands; but he knew they were responding to him. "I forbade your families and friends to attend your marriage feast," Noren went on, "because it must not yet become known what we do here. Village people would bring you to trial; they would send you to the City for the Scholars' discipline, and from that I cannot, and will not, shield you if you are charged. But once Futurity's land bears fruit, people's feelings will change. They will acknowledge you subject to a new Law and will look forward to the age of that Law: the time when all land will be fruitful and all wedding feasts will be as this one."

Slowly, the faces circling him took on confidence. "We will fill the jugs as you command," said someone at last. And as several went to do so, Noren, striving to keep the mood to which he'd roused them, started a familiar wedding hymn:

May the Star of our hope be with us,
As the joy of this night we celebrate.
May the heirs of our love be many,
As the world of its light we await.

He took the water they brought him and mixed in a scant portion of ale. "This is a night of celebration," he said, smiling, "and who would not wish ale on such a night? Yet it is also something more. That is what the water means: henceforth, when in love we give life to children, we are pledged not to the world that must pass but to the one that must come." Raising his cup, he added, "I will drink first, and on my head be it. I have performed rites and made prophecies, and have not been struck down. Yet should they prove false, in the end I will be stricken.

The Star's spirit will be withdrawn from me; my priesthood will be nullified; I will be accursed in the sight of the Scholars, and indeed of all people, if I lead you unwittingly to harm."

The cups were passed around, in readiness for the toast; people handled them not fearfully, but with awe. Plainly they believed in him. The only thing they did not believe, thought Noren in anguish, was his last statement. They did not guess there was real danger of its becoming the truest prophecy of all.

"To these unions: may they be fruitful and bring lasting joy." Hiding the shaking of his hands, Noren drank; and all the others followed.

The ensuing seasons were hard beyond measure. Looking back on them afterward, Noren wondered how anyone had endured. Backbreaking labor was, of course, taken for granted by farm and village people; the clearing of fields with stone tools and the erection of stone buildings did not dismay them. Hunger was a newer concept. Since the time of the Founders, the full burden of any food shortage had been taken by the Inner City, and a Scholar, by instinct and by training, shrank from the thought of villagers having to subsist on short rations. Yet though native plants could now be safely eaten, their taste was unpleasant; and alone, they were not nutritious enough to sustain anyone whose time was spent doing heavy work—they were no substitute for grain crops. Trusting Noren wholly, the people of Futurity would have expected their land to bring forth a harvest in the first cycle after clearing had he not warned that they must stretch the meager supply of grain their dowries and savings would buy. "I cannot know when the land will bear fruit," he was obliged to tell them. Privately, he was afraid it might not happen before he himself, who took no more than one scant serving of bread a day, was close to starvation. He could have requisitioned supplies from the Technicians, but the power of his scheme lay in forgoing City aid. He must prove it was possible to survive without that; his people must put their faith in the new way.

Delaying work on their own homesteads, they built a dwelling for him, built it tall, at the summit of the knoll, although the stones couldn't be brought by sledge when there was no road. It was not his idea; they did it out of love. Noren could not demur, for he saw that such a building was vital. Futurity was to be a new city, and the mark of a city in their eyes, evidently, was less the presence of actual towers than the presence of a resident Scholar. The Scholar must, to satisfy them, be fittingly housed. As he mounted his steps for the first time—steps unlike any ever built in a village—he found himself aware, with a stab of pain, that this might be where he would live out his years. Many years...even worldwide implementation of genetic change would not free him to leave these people. He owed them more than bountiful harvests.

The steps became the center of the community; he held Vespers there. Each evening after the service, the others gathered around informal bonfires, but he soon found that accompanying them put a damper on the fun. They revered him; they loved him—but they would not tell jokes or sing bawdy songs until he had retired into his house and shut the door. They'd have been shocked to know Scholars enjoyed such activities, and for him to say so would not be seemly. It would deprive people of something they valued. It was his good fortune to have been born a loner, Noren realized, because he could never again be anything but alone.

Once a small plot of land was cleared, his genetic work progressed. He ordered a radiophone sent out, and Technicians in the Outer City labs read to him from his data discs as instructed. When necessary they carried scientific materials to and fro by aircar. If computer analysis of genotypes was needed, they were told to leave the samples in a place where he knew they'd be found by Denrul—who was to have been informed of the situation by Lianne—but Noren communicated no more with Denrul than with Stefred or Lianne herself. His supporters in the City would keep track of his progress, for those who'd assumed the robe were as free to command Technicians secretly as he was. Direct contact, however, was out of the question. The safety of what he was doing depended on his complete repudiation by the City in case of failure; no Technician must be given grounds to testify that Scholars had done more than watch. He was honestly glad they resisted the temptation to send messages.

All the same, indirect contact with the City was harder to bear than the dreamlike detachment that had dominated the first weeks of his exile. Now again functioning as a scientist, he could not forget that his work would lead to the end of science—that his success would mean exile for others as well as for him. To his people, he spoke with hope of "the day when all the world will live as Futurity lives," the day when no land would be quickened, no water piped from within the City's walls. But on that day the City would begin to die. Was it true that in time a means of regaining technology would appear, or was Lianne's faith in this only illusion?

Cities shall rise beyond the Tomorrow Mountains, and shall have Power, and Machines... He used those words in ritual and now considered himself honest. He had, in Futurity, dropped the capital letter from his conception of "cities" and no one had been dissatisfied, so no doubt the same would be true when it came to power and machines. He could accept that. He was willing to search for a truth beyond truth. And yet...Lianne had said that without technology, evolution would stop. That particular truth was more than metaphorical, at least it was unless the Service, too, was naive.

He did not often think of the Service. He did not even think of Lianne as alien. He'd be satisfied, Noren thought grimly, with the City and with the Lianne he knew; but they were as inaccessible now as the rest of the universe.

His plants, after a few terrifying setbacks, grew vigorously. On hands and knees with a stone cultivating tool, his robe cast aside in the hot sun, Noren laughed at the irony: this was the way he'd started, in his father's fields, and he'd despised every moment of it. His brothers had derided him for lack of persistence. If they could see the effort he now expended on nurturing each slender stalk, they would think it a greater marvel than the vivification of unquickened land.

The people of Futurity were surprised less by the plants' growth than by the fact that there were so few. "Did you think I could raise my hand and bring all the fields to life at once?" Noren chided, realizing as he spoke that they had indeed thought so. "It takes work! It is with plants as with people, as you well know: the seed of a few in time engenders many. I will give you seed for planting, but I cannot produce it any faster than these grain stalks can."

So in the first cycle, "harvest" meant only seed for the test garden, though he held the traditional ceremonies. But on that day a greater event occurred. Stefred knew, of course, the date of the harvest festival, for this was fixed according to season zone, staggered region by region for efficient use of land treatment machines in the villages; the invariant climate had nothing to do with it. Thus it was that when Futurity's citizens gathered for the Blessing of the Seed, Noren looked up to see an aircar appear unsummoned, bringing Technician women who gave three Wards of the City into his care. And the oldest of these children had Veldry's features, but his eyes were like Stefred's own.

The arrival of the children, which Noren placed with the couples to whom they had been promised, marked a change in the settlement. While there was still hard work and hunger, living became less camplike and more family-oriented. Many of the brides were pregnant, and though Noren could not banish all worry over that large group of genetically altered babies, sustained by unpurified water from the time of conception, he managed to conceal his mixed feelings. He kept up his dual work as priest and scientist, but was no longer required to lead in practical matters; Futurity elected its own council and began to make civil laws.

The new crop sprouted, a patch large enough to be seen from aircars. Word of green shoots in unquickened earth soon spread, for the Technicians, by whom it was also viewed as a miracle, had occasion to talk in village taverns. Despite lack of a road, people began arriving to see the wonder. Having expected this, the community had built ordinary rain-catchment cisterns so that visitors could quench their thirst, and the absence of pipes to the City was not noticed. The council also built a wall around the test garden; sightseers were charged a fee, not only to obtain much-needed funds for grain, but to keep the precious young plants from being trampled. This Noren approved with considerable relief. His religious services, however, were open to all comers, and he now spoke of a time when the miracle would extend elsewhere. He mentioned, without emphasis, that this would bring changes in the High Law. The idea did not bother anyone. His status as a prophet was firm as long as both the plants and the adopted children were thriving.

The veneration he received still bothered him, and yet, he reminded himself, the quickening of land with Machines had been considered supernatural in the first place. Who was to say what "supernatural" was? He'd made no claims that were not true, and none he was not backing with his life. Was it worse, really, for people to assume what they did, than for Stefred to believe that psychic powers were against nature? If Lianne were to display her gifts openly—not only the gifts he, Noren, had been shown, but others at which she'd merely hinted—the villagers and Technicians wouldn't be the only ones to believe they were seeing miracles.

He was once again besieged with pleas for blessings; people approached him whenever he emerged from his door. During his journey, he'd been so dazed by his new role that, except during rites, he'd pronounced the words of the benediction mechanically. Now he searched the faces of the suppliants and tried to convey personal warmth each time he said them. Once he wouldn't have been able to do this; he perceived that he had grown. He knew more about giving than he had in the City. And he knew the pattern of his years was formed: to give, and receive nothing; to live, as had the First Scholar, without hope of attaining more than the world's future good.

And then one morning as he raised his hands for the hundredth time in the formal gesture of benison, Noren froze, seeing an upturned face so like Lianne's that he must be dreaming.

It was not Lianne, of course; it was not even a woman. The man who knelt before him had…what? Not piercing blue eyes—though the eyes were what drew him, they were green, not blue. Not white hair or near-white skin. The impression of resemblance had been an instant, instinctive thing that didn't bear up under analysis. Or…could it have been a purely mental resemblance? Yes—not likeness, but the touch of a mind similarly trained. A powerful telepathic touch. He knew, in less time than it took to say the blessing, that the skill behind it was greater than Lianne's and would be used at a far deeper level. *Don't panic,* he told himself. *Reach as you would in controlled dreaming, open your mind to whatever experience may come; nothing will happen to which you have not consented.* And in the next moment he realized he'd not told himself this at all, but had been wordlessly informed.

They paused only a brief time; no one nearby noticed anything strange. But to Noren it seemed that hours were passing. There were no words, it was not silent conversation. He sensed none of the man's thoughts as he had sensed Lianne's, and though he reached out for knowledge, he was given none. Instead, all he felt—all the pain and uncertainty and longing, the anguish of exile, the hunger to search out truth, all the fears and regrets of his past, the grief for those he had lost…and, too, all his hopes for the future, all his faith born of commitment to them—rose to the surface at once. He was engulfed, overwhelmed. His head roared and light blazed behind his eyelids; he was reeling…

He opened his eyes and met calm green ones that held not reverence, but something quite like it: a mixture of sympathy and awed, startled admiration. "Reverend Sir, I am honored by your blessing," the stranger said with sincerity.

Struggling to maintain his balance, Noren repeated it. "May the spirit of the Star go with you—wherever you may travel."

"May it abide with you also," replied the man softly, rising from his knees, "and with all people of this earth, until the Star's light falls upon them and the Prophecy comes to fulfillment."

It was a farewell. This could be no one but an alien from the starship, which meant the starship had returned for Lianne. They would be leaving: in mere days, or even hours, they would leave this world forever. Noren knew he had been examined and found equal to his task; he knew, as he had long known, that he would receive no help with it. He had not expected them to relent, had not even wanted them to, in view of the cost—the decision had been his, and he did not wish to alter it. He should now rejoice, for he had just been told specifically that his sacrifices were not vain, that not only survival, but fulfillment of the Prophecy, was judged assured.

But he did not feel like rejoicing. When the stranger had gone, Noren retired into his house and threw himself down on his moss pallet; and for the first time since leaving the City, he wept.

Several days passed. Noren got through them with set face and level voice, but his hard-won, precarious peace had been shattered. No fire of hope warmed his words of blessing. He felt no joy at the sight of the flourishing green seedlings that meant salvation of the world. For him the light had gone out, as in due course, the lights of the City would flicker and then fail. He had saved his people—but he was no longer able to care.

He was not sure why this was so. He had learned nothing from the alien's visit that he'd not been expecting, and the only words said to him had been a confirmation of faith in his world's future. Furthermore, he'd received clear assurance that he need not doubt his fitness to fill the role in which fate had cast him. Why then did he doubt more than ever? Why did he not just fear, but *know,* that his strength would not last a lifetime?

Lianne's departure? But he had known for years that she must leave his world. His last night in the City, he had faced how much that mattered to him; still he had risen from their bed and walked out through the Gates alone. He should be buoyed by that memory, not crushed, for if he had done that, he'd have courage for all lesser things—only he did not think he'd be able to do it twice. It was a foolish point to be unnerved by, Noren thought miserably. That was one test to which he would not be brought again. Lianne was gone.

No. He was not certain she had gone yet; the starship had arrived, but had not necessarily departed...and before it left, Lianne might come to say goodbye.

That was the source of his despair, Noren perceived suddenly. She might come, thinking him strong, and he would not be strong enough. He had the power to make her people stay. He had only to say he was quitting; that he was not a prophet, not a savior, but human; that it was their job to save worlds, not his. They were not gods, but neither was he—and he was alone while they were many. He'd done all that could be asked of him. He could return to the City with Lianne and let them finish what he had started.

As he thought this, lying sleepless on his pallet while dawn brightened the stone casing of his window, he looked up and Lianne was there.

It was telepathy, he realized, not coincidence; he'd never have guessed she might come had he not sensed that she was close. She had left the City by darkness, and under cover of darkness the alien shuttlecraft had brought her here. It must be waiting nearby to return to the starship. They'd hardly deny her a brief visit; Lianne too was human, and in love.

As she stood in the doorway, her hand white against the matting she'd drawn back, he felt her love sweep over him: a far more powerful mental radiance than she'd loosed within the City's walls. He understood that this was the telepathic mode natural to her, and that love heightened it, that physical love would heighten it still more. She had suppressed it to spare him, even during their one night together; she hadn't wanted him to glimpse what he was giving up. She had not wanted to show him what true intimacy was among her kind, what powers his own mind could attain, through love, that no less intense experience could awaken.

But now it seemed she herself was weakening; her thought was more for him than for his world's welfare, or even for the bright realm to which she'd soon return. Their loss of each other was a grief that would be with her always. And Noren found that what hurt most was not anything he had sacrificed, but the heartbreak he had caused her.

He lay motionless, not daring to go to her. "Lianne," he said, his voice flat and remote. "Don't come in. Don't even speak to me. Leave quickly, while there's still a chance."

She moved close, ignoring the words. A blue blur brushed his cheek as she bent down, the sleeve of her robe...how odd that was; he'd never seen Lianne robed before. All these years, despite Stefred's puzzled disappointment, she'd been adamant about refusing priesthood. She had remained unwilling to make a sham commitment lacking permanence. Now, he supposed, she'd had to wear a robe in case people saw her enter his house, and after all, no Scholars would ever know. Yet if she did encounter people, they'd kneel to her! That would be still worse than it was for him. She would feel she had no right to pronounce the blessing.

"Please go," he repeated, not looking at her face.

"Don't you want me here?" It wasn't really a question, and her voice was light; in the emotion he sensed, love overpowered all pain.

Noren sat up, resisting the urge to take her in his arms, knowing that even to kiss her would mean defeat of the cause to which he'd given himself. "You know how much I want you, how much I'll always love you," he said tonelessly. "But you don't know, I guess, that I have limits. Maybe you think I'm as superhuman as the villagers do. By the Star, Lianne—" He broke off, aware that the phrase, in this case, was not profanity; he meant it seriously. "In the name of the Star, I ask you to leave this world before all that's behind us loses its point. I'm on the verge of cracking up right now. Maybe, just maybe, I'll get my nerve back after you're gone; but if you tempt me to keep you here, I'll do it—at the cost of everything we both believe."

She dropped to the pallet beside him and took his face between her hands. "You won't have to," she said. "I'm staying."

Stunned, afraid of the thoughts that idea roused in him, Noren drew away from her touch. "Staying? You'd let the ship go and come back for you another time?"

Very quietly Lianne said, "It won't be coming back, Noren."

He stared at her, appalled. "That's not possible. Your people wouldn't abandon you." He wanted her to stay, yes, but not at that price. Not if she'd be exiled from her heritage, as he was from his.

"They haven't abandoned me," she told him. "I chose."

"Chose *this* world, when you could have the whole universe?"

"Not quite the whole universe. There's a lot more to it than this galaxy, after all. Everybody's got boundaries, and life is life, on one world or a thousand."

"I—I can't look at it that way," confessed Noren dazedly.

"I know you can't. That's one reason I'm here."

"To enlarge my prison by sharing it? Lianne, what good would it do me to know you were suffering, too?"

"Oh, Noren. I'm not going to suffer, not as long as we have love."

Abruptly, he grasped the whole of what she was offering. She would not stay in the City; she was no more free to return there now than he was, for she'd have told Stefred she was joining him so as to spare Stefred's feelings by not disappearing unaccountably. She meant to live here, in Futurity. She would share not only the exile, but the commitment—that was why she had assumed the robe.

But how could she? "Your oath to the Service—" Noren protested.

"I won't violate it. The Oath demands that I put the best interests of your people above all else, but my being with you isn't contrary to them. I won't be intervening. I'll be living just as you do."

As he did. Years without respite from the oppressive heat she found so taxing outside the towers; hard physical labor in the fields, using Stone Age tools she'd never before handled; isolation not merely from her heritage but from such sources of knowledge as she'd had in the City, poor as they were by her own civilization's standards… And, too, the burden of priesthood among people not even her biological kin: people who, once they discovered the healing powers she wouldn't deny them, would venerate her in a way not merely symbolic. Whatever she said now, she would suffer. And she might not always have his love, for there was still danger that the genetic change would prove unsafe, still a possibility that he might fail and die for it. If the people turned against him, Lianne might die too. Or she might be left to grieve—she might outlive him in any case, for the lifespan of their species wasn't the same; she'd already lived more years than he had, perhaps many more, and yet she didn't age as fast. For her to stay with him awhile was one thing, a thing she evidently wanted to do. But she must not send her people away forever.

"Surely someday they'll come back for you," he said.

"No. Besides, I don't want them to. I couldn't bear to have you come to hate me."

"I could never hate you."

"You could, and would, in time, Noren—if the starship were going to return for me, yet not for you."

He was silent. She was right, of course; he wouldn't be able to suppress envy—but he wouldn't have let her know...

"I'd know. I'm telepathic, remember? But even if I weren't, I'd have known, whatever worlds I went to, all the rest of my life."

Noren drew Lianne to him, embracing her, no longer doubting his own self-control. He had feared he'd not be strong; now he knew better. He loved her too much to be anything else. His destiny demanded sacrifice, but hers did not, and he would not let her suffer for his sake. If she must go with the ship or remain permanently, then he must make her go.

"Lianne," he said slowly, "you once said I was born to be apart. That's true. I am what I am, and you can't soften it. Maybe it all has meaning, I don't know—I guess neither of us knows the why of things. Maybe my losing everything, *everything,* is in some way necessary to the future of this world; anyway so far it's seemed to be, and I don't mind paying that price. I'm not paying it for nothing. The man who came from the starship affirmed the Prophecy—"

"From the ship? When?" Lianne broke in, obviously startled.

He told her, perplexed by her surprise. "That was before I told them I want to stay," she said, frowning. "There was no need for such a mind probe, certainly not then. And that man, he's senior to most of us, he deals with basic policy; he rarely leaves the ship personally. I didn't know probes of that kind were ever tried with people of immature species. Was it...painful, Noren?"

"In a way. He warned me not to panic; I assumed it was something telepaths do routinely."

"Not like that. Deep wordless communication is used privately between people close to each other, but a full one-way scrutiny of motives done by a stranger, fast, and in public—very few untrained people could stand up under that. It's a technique we reserve for special occasions. It has been done to me in Service rituals, was done yesterday by the same man, in fact, during my formal leave-taking aboard the starship." She shook her head, puzzled. "I wondered why he didn't argue more against my choice; now I see. But why didn't he tell me he'd met you, or even that he'd been down to the surface?"

"What did he tell you about the Prophecy, about how our civilization will regain technology?" Noren asked. "He knows our evolution won't stop, I could sense that. And anyway, they couldn't have made a decision to withdraw unless they knew the answer."

"He knew," she agreed. "But he didn't inform me; he said that by staying here, I'd forfeit my right to hear what they expect."

"Not even whether the key will appear in your lifetime?" Noren protested indignantly. "Why would they be so merciless?"

"Because they realized that I love you," Lianne told him, "and that I'd pass all my knowledge on to you."

"They didn't trust me not to tell anyone about them, then."

"Oh, yes. If they hadn't trusted you, they wouldn't have allowed me to stay as living evidence. They withheld what they did for my sake—to make sure I really wanted to spend my life with you and wasn't doing it merely to buy knowledge for you that your task doesn't require."

"I couldn't endure having you give up the stars for my benefit," he declared, trying to steady his voice.

"They realized that, too," she said. "They aren't merciless; they simply take a long view of mercy."

Then they were waiting for her. They had trusted him not only with future generations' welfare, but with hers, and had known he would say what must be said to send her back to them. Unless…

"Lianne," he asked, trying to contain the sudden hope, "you told me subtle intervention's permitted, sometimes. If there were a way we could keep our technology without synthesizing metal, some way we can't ever discover, and they could give me a clue to it—would they?"

"Yes. Yes, and knowing you were probed before I left the City makes me wonder...only it doesn't fit. They don't lie, and they did tell me specifically that my decision was final, that no ship will return here for any reason in our era."

A cold thrill, excitement mixed with dread, came over Noren, and he smiled. "It does fit! There's still a chance, in the time before they leave orbit—they knew you'd want to be with me when the clue is offered. They'll surprise you too, or perhaps you'll even be needed to interpret, I know they won't make it simple for either of us—"

She pulled away from him, staring. "Noren, I thought you understood. They've already left orbit. They're light-years away by now."

Shock drained him. "Are you sure?" he whispered, disbelieving.

"Of course I'm sure. If an agent decides to stay on a planet, there are—formalities. They aren't painless because there's got to be a guarantee that it's an informed choice, and not a hasty one; I knew in advance what I'd have to do. I watched the ship go last night. The point of light was there and then it was gone, and the special links with me were just—cut off. Instantly, when the ship went into hyperdrive."

He couldn't speak, but his horror reached her silently. "Noren," she pleaded, stroking his hand, "Noren, don't lose heart now. They didn't tell me the answer, but when they said farewell they weren't grieving, not even for me. Telepathically, I could tell they weren't; and if they'd believed us doomed to live out our lives in tragic futility, they would have been. What we do will lead somewhere, even if we never know where."

"It's not that," he said, "not the thing I'd already come to terms with. It's you, Lianne. Don't you see, I wouldn't have let you stay behind."

"Why do you think I didn't come here till they were gone?" She settled back against his shoulder, her white hair soft against his skin. "I wouldn't have let you decide, and I wasn't sure how to make you believe it'll be all right for me—only now that's easy. You've been probed by one of the most skilled elders of my people, and you *know* he grasped all your feelings. Remember that he probed me, too."

Slowly, Noren absorbed it. *Life is life, on one world or a thousand.* She did not need to see more worlds; her life was here. The rest of the universe existed; it was full of wonders—and just knowing that was enough. Enough even for him, now that he did know. This world was not a prison, but a base: one might choose one's base freely, but one could not escape the necessity of choosing. Might some even, perhaps, on the level veiled in mystery, choose worlds in which to be born?

He held Lianne close. They sat quietly, not even fondling each other. There was time ahead for that, and Noren knew it would be good, that there would be a union of spirit as well as of body that would illumine all the dark years confronting them. Though the doors of the universe were shut, Lianne could open a window; and he no longer feared to look through.

Suddenly, rays of sunlight flooded the room. "It's morning," said Noren, as if waking from sleep. "It's a bright morning."

He stood up, putting on his tunic and then his blue robe over it, and turned to Lianne. "We've got obligations, you know. You aren't going to enjoy being a prophet."

"A culture," she told him, "can have only one great prophet at a time. I serve as a priest, but you are more. That, I think, must be what the mind probe was meant to confirm."

Side by side, they stood in the doorway as people came up the hill toward his dwelling; it was time for Benison. Lianne looked and whispered in astonishment, "Noren, practically all those girls are soon to give birth."

"Well, their weddings were all held on the same day." He smiled. "This is what we've worked toward, isn't it—new life, a new generation that's born adapted to this world? It's a good thing you've had some medical training, seeing as I forgot to include a midwife among the settlers. You got here just in time to deliver a lot of babies."

He took her hand and led her out before the assembled people. "Tonight is to be a feast night," he announced with rising happiness, "for I will ask you to witness my marriage to the Scholar Lianne."

Epilogue

As is well known, the Scholar Noren became a legend among his people. The usual image of him is as a white-bearded patriarch, revered Archpriest to the world of the Interregnum Era; that he was still a young man when he came out of the City is rarely remembered. That his exile outside the walls involved self-sacrifice is never so much as imagined, although those who knew him best did note that in his eyes, even at the moments of his greatest triumphs, was an inexplicable sadness. This seemed something of a paradox, for beneath the wisdom all acknowledged were intuitions of deeper things—things concerning the vast universe of which the Prophecy spoke—and there, he evidently found more light than dark. There is thus little doubt that his consort Lianne showed him visions of realms she had explored, and that she opened his questing mind to more than she herself had seen in them.

In the closing years of the Dark Era, the settlement at Futurity flourished. The first harvests were small; most of the grain was kept for seed and the rest ceremonially consumed by the few Chosen Families then in residence. But word of the miracle spread. As each new crop sprouted, crowds came to see it, and to be blessed by the Scholar who was already accorded a status different from that of other priests, different even from that of the Scholar Lianne who stood at his side. He could have taken power over all the land in those years. People would have believed anything from him—except that his prophecies might yet fail. That knowledge, like the knowledge that such failure would turn men to vengeance, he kept to himself; yet he claimed none of the authority that could have been his. By his word, the City remained the world's center. His task was not to abolish the High Law, but to herald the age of its transformation.

Within the City, where this goal soon became openly known, the Scholar Noren was held in contempt. He was viewed as a defector, and a dangerous one; only the belief that he must stand answerable for his prophecies saved him from seizure. Few of his opponents felt—or wanted to feel—that the Law could be changed with safety, or that the promises of the Prophecy as traditionally interpreted might not be essential to survival. Alteration of human genes, in the second generation if not in the first, would surely prove as ruinous as it was indecent. For this, in the villages, Noren alone must be blamed; only so could the City's life-support role be preserved. And meanwhile, grain was growing in untreated soil, grain that might be consumed by the unfit were it not for Noren's presence. He was therefore left alone; but among the Scholars he was already a scapegoat, not merely for anticipated disaster, but for the lack of progress toward metal synthesization.

This injustice even his secret supporters encouraged, telling themselves that the First Scholar's pose as a mad tyrant had been comparable. Aware that a means of retreat must indeed be left open until genetic change was fully proven, they were obliged to become more secretive than ever, lest their cause be won too soon. Slowly, their number grew. There were more heretics than there used to be, youngsters stirred by Noren's subtle discouragement of the caste concept. With such as these, he was merciless; he stimulated their rebellion and then contrived for them to be condemned, knowing they'd hate him for the betrayal, yet knowing, too, that they must be led to claim their birthright. Once enlightened in the City, their bitterness turned to loyalty, for Lianne had seen to it that recruitment of novices would be continued by her successor. By this means, over the years, Noren won a large following among the Scholars: a following inspired by him personally. The Scholar Stefred, foreseeing this, bided his time. He continued to champion tradition, forestalling the showdown until the outcome was assured.

Genetic work continued, led by Noren outside the City and Denrul within, through the unquestioning Technician intermediaries. The genes of the newborn were tested. More Wards of the City were adopted, and more Chosen Families admitted to Futurity. Changes were made to the vaccine so as to impart heritable immunity to the planet's lethal diseases; offspring of the first families were inoculated against disease like all villagers, but for their own children, and those of couples chosen later, that was no longer required—it would become impossible, after all, once the City's technology failed. This was the last of the genetic alterations indispensable to human survival. When it was complete, Noren went on working: he designed vegetables to supplement the monotonous diet of grain. It was now also safe for the flesh of work-beasts to be eaten, but this he kept from the citizens of Futurity in fear that it would be called an abomination.

Futurity's children came of age. They married within the community as arranged; the few who refused were tried by the council for their defiance and delivered to the City for discipline—to Noren's private satisfaction. He did not send word to Stefred that one of these was his son, for it would not help the boy to be the only known child of Scholars to attain Scholar rank in turn. That much of tradition must stand. But he confessed in his own heart that he'd fostered that child's nonconformity.

The children had children of their own, and all were born genetically healthy. *There will be a time when all the world shall live as Futurity lives,* the Scholar Noren had prophesied, *and this will be in our era, before the Mother Star appears to posterity. Scholars will come forth to bless unquickened fields, and to mark all people, that they may turn from the old Law to the new.* To the day of this event, all villages looked forward with gladness. No date had been given, but within the City, supporters and opponents alike knew the time for the change was ripe.

They awaited Noren's word. For he would choose his day, and they must respond: either in full agreement, or—as many feared—through a split no longer dangerous. The supporters were numerous enough now to take control; they would destroy the water purification plant if need be; but they would not see the castes maintained in the name of the original Prophecy's lost cause.

On Founding Day, the Scholar Noren spoke out, spoke to vast crowds at Futurity rivaling those before the City's Gates. As always, Technicians recorded his words, and those words were soon heard in the Inner City.

But they were not the words anyone expected to hear.

I will build another new City, Noren had said, *on the shores of a great lake two weeks' journey hence; and it will be called Providence. And those in Providence will live as do those in Futurity; but there will be Technicians among them, and all villagers who work there will become Technicians.*

Among the Scholars there was both bewilderment and outrage. Had Noren, at the last moment, succumbed to the temptation to save the City at the price of keeping the castes? Or had he found evidence that genetic change was unsafe after all and so retreated to save his own life? Comparatively few would follow him two weeks' journey into the wilderness, for not enough pure water could be carried to supply anyone whose genes had not been altered; those few would not rise against him for the failure of his promises to the rest of the world. And if they were offered Technician status, they would become his sure defenders.

Thus the Scholars were of a mind to forbid this new scheme. Some believed genetic change should be implemented without delay, while others felt he should be publicly repudiated—and nearly all agreed that he should be brought back, by force if necessary, to give an accounting. But the Scholar Stefred trusted Noren; and because he had not aided him in the past, his word prevailed. The City waited, uncertain and afraid, while Providence was established.

After the new settlement's first harvest, on the day of the Blessing of the Seed, there was yet another prophecy. *When all harvests are as this and no fields of the world need be quickened,* Noren declared, *the Scholars will go back into the sky from whence they once came. By the time of the Star's appearance, they will return; and there will be a new Founding. And from that day forward, our world will be as the Prophecy promises.*

This was clearly impossible. There was not enough metal in the world to restore space travel; all Scholars knew that. The shuttle used in the establishment of the outpost beyond the mountains was still operable, but the starships in orbit were stripped hulls. Though in theory, the process of decommissioning them carried out by the Founders could be reversed, there were not sufficient resources to restore even one; there never would be, even if the life-support equipment unneeded after full implementation of genetic change were diverted to the task. Moreover, were a space journey to become possible, there could be no chance of fulfilling the Prophecy by it. The Founders had searched thoroughly but futilely for a solar system from which metal might be obtained, and the chances of finding one within range were therefore negligible. So it was said that Noren had been too long away from the computers, that his judgment was warped—or worse, that his longings and his power had driven him to madness.

Yet the Scholar Stefred, now the oldest and most respected member of the Council, still refused to countenance any interference. In his thought was that the First Scholar had feigned madness for worthy ends. "Let Noren come to us in his own time," he insisted. "For better or for worse, this world's future is in his hands.

If he is mad, which I do not believe, he nevertheless has the people behind him; they will not break the High Law without his sanction. And if he fails in the end to give it, full blame must rest on him for the promises unfulfilled."

Thus the building of Providence went forward without purpose the Scholars could discern. Perplexed, they reconnoitered from aircars during their trips to and from the outpost. The lake seemed more than a symbol of water now safely used for bathing. Much activity went on there, structures were built at the edge, and people approached these almost as they would holy things like Machines. It was recalled that the Founders' plan for the transition period preceding fulfillment of the Prophecy included a phase during which villagers would earn Technician status by machine-aided work—but without metal, what semblance of machines could Noren have placed on the lakeshore?

Several seasons passed. And then one morning, fair like all mornings, the plaza before the Gates began to fill with people, though no ceremony was scheduled; and word came through Technicians that the Scholar Noren would soon arrive. Without precedent in his years away from the City, he had commanded that an aircar be sent out to him. He had broadcast a message by radiophone, heard in all villages as well as by his contacts in the Outer City: he would appear at the Gates, and many Scholars would come forth to greet him.

The aircar did not drop into its accustomed dome, but instead came to earth in the plaza outside the walls. Before a crowd surpassing any ever assembled there, the Scholars Noren and Lianne alighted; and with them were two citizens of Providence. Technicians cleared a path for them as they ascended the steps, while Scholars indeed came out to meet them, as many as could stand upon the wide platform—and for the first time in history, the Gates stood open after all had emerged. They invited Noren to pass through; but he shook his head and remained on the topmost step, facing the Scholar Stefred.

"I will not enter the City," he said, "until all people of the land are free to do so. I have come today for a different purpose." As he spoke, the man and woman of Providence came forward. They did not kneel, but stood beside him, holding between them a large clay bowl, which they handled as a sacred thing, raising it in the manner of a seed jar presented for blessing.

"These are the firstborn of Futurity," Noren said, "who now show you the gift of Providence. Grant them in my presence their rightful status as Technicians, according to the Law."

Leaning forward, Stefred looked into the bowl, and saw with amazement the unmistakable glint of metal.

"I have at last learned how it can be obtained," said Noren, smiling.

To the people, this was a lesser miracle than the blossoming of unquickened land; having been taught that all metal had been brought into the world by Scholars at the time of the Founding, they viewed a repetition of the event as not especially surprising. But to the Scholars on the platform, it seemed a truly supernatural feat. They wondered, in that moment, if Noren might not possess in truth the powers village tales had long attributed to him.

"This is not my own doing," he told them solemnly. "I must not be credited with it, now or ever, for it is a blessing of the Star."

"And…the Prophecy?" Stefred, his voice hushed with awe, spoke for everyone: all the Scholars who had kept that faith and all those who had in sorrow relinquished it for the sake of their people's assured survival.

"Our faith is vindicated," Noren declared, "if we are now willing to give up our guardianship and turn to other tasks. I did not wish to raise your hopes before I was sure; but to my people last Seed Blessing Day, I told the literal truth. Though there is not enough metal on this earth to fulfill the Prophecy, what is accessible will suffice to restore one starship. In time, we can mine other worlds as the Visitors once mined here. What we lost to them has been amply repaid."

Then to the Scholars, in a voice too low to be heard by the multitude over the music that swelled forth, Noren explained his discovery. The metal could be extracted from lake water and wet soil, not by any method the Founders had known, but by genetically altered bacteria—which was, no doubt, a routine process on worlds less rich in ore than the Six. For it had been suggested to him not by sheer genius, but by a new alien artifact found the previous year near Futurity.

"The *Visitors* used this—this genetic process?" Stefred asked.

"So it appears." Noren's face was impassive. "The artifact contains coded symbols; Lianne and I were able to decipher them. Once I had the fundamental idea, genetic engineering of native bacteria wasn't difficult."

The incredibility of this explanation was apparent. In the first place, it was an almost fantastic coincidence for Noren to have found one alien artifact, the radiating sphere, just at the place where he had crashed in the mountains. That another such coincidence could have occurred was past rational belief; the odds against it were incalculable. And even supposing that it had happened, how could any artifact of those long-vanished miners reveal that they'd used bacteria in such a way? Furthermore, if they'd indeed done so, why had they not completed the job, taken the last traces of metal? Why had the bacteria not gone on extracting it during the interim if there'd been any left—or if they had, why had the Founders not seen?

These questions and more went through Stefred's mind as he listened—but he knew they were, and would remain, unanswerable. He did not suppose that even Noren had answers to them. Yet one could not deny evidence before one's eyes merely because logic said it couldn't exist. Noren was extracting metal from low-grade unminable deposits, and he would not lie about how he'd learned to do so. There was in fact no other way he could have learned. Moreover, his next words confirmed what he had claimed.

"There is also a star chart," Noren went on calmly. "Its symbols, too, are decipherable and can be fed into the computers. Whether or not we find aliens by following where it leads, we need not worry about failing to find planets."

A chart of solar systems unknown to the Founders could not have been derived from any source other than the Visitors.

So the Scholars Stefred and Noren embraced, and many prophecies were affirmed to the people; then all priests withdrew into the City save Noren and Lianne. In the days that followed, the Scholars embarked on new work: some to effect genetic change in the Outer City and villages; some to mine distant lakes; some to prepare for the immense task of refitting a starship. And Noren, from his base at Providence, watched with mixed feelings—for he knew that to equip the ship, the City must die.

Yet in his heart was a great thankfulness. For that death must precede a rebirth, and the rebirth would be to a greater destiny than the other Scholars imagined. Only he and Lianne knew the truth about the scope of such a destiny.

He had indeed found an alien artifact. He had shown it, by now, to the City's scientists; the star chart was in their hands. They would believe the only thing they could believe: that it had been left by the aliens they knew about, the ancient Visitors. His people's history would never record that other aliens had come and gone, much less that discovery of the artifact near Futurity had not been coincidence at all. But Noren knew, knew surely enough to stake everything on faith that its chart would lead the ship to planets that could be mined. For among the symbols decipherable by science, there had been one that seemed meaningless; and this Lianne had known for the Service emblem.

It must be done very subtly, she'd told him long before. So subtly that had he not left the City, it could not have been done at all, not, in any case, in his era. Yet the data contained in that small capsule would make the difference between descent into a permanent Stone Age and ultimate rise to Federation level. It was for this the alien elder had come on that long-ago morning, not merely to probe his mind. The decision had been made then; and the Service had gone away in the certainty that he, Noren, would search out all the knowledge accessible to him.

The Dark Era drew to its close. The people of all villages were inoculated; their unquickened land was sown; they knelt with joy beside the streams of their land while Scholars blessed the water in Noren's name. The people dipped in their hands and drank gladly, knowing themselves one with the earth, with the fruits it could bring forth. And though they still revered the City, they looked to it no more for sustenance.

The Technicians moved from the Outer City to new villages beyond its walls, for the Outer City was not livable any longer. Its power and air conditioning were gone, no water was piped in, all metal that had been used there was sent back into the sky. Every day the shuttle rose and returned. Gradually, the towers too were abandoned, except for the Hall of Scholars where the computer complex was preserved; the Scholars still in the City slept in the open courtyard. The water purification plant was shut down, and no one noted the day on which no more water came through the conduits to village cisterns.

No City goods were now sold in the markets, for there was no longer any way of manufacturing anything beyond what could be made of stone, clay, fiber, wicker and hide. To these crafts the former Technicians turned, taught by village masters, and village craftsworkers thus earned Technician rank. Furthermore, all people in the world could earn it by a few weeks' labor at lakeside mines. It extended to their children, so that in the next generation no one of lesser status would be left. Only the Scholars remained apart, as priests; but it was made known that their offspring did not succeed them. Henceforth priesthood would be an honor to be sought freely, though still attained through mysterious ordeals to which one must submit of one's own will.

Through the years of the starship's refitting, Noren continued to live in Providence, supervising the work there and the training of those who went to other lakes. He had sworn not to enter the Gates until they could remain open, which until the ship was equipped, could not happen. And perhaps he no longer minded exile; he can hardly have wanted to see the City's lifeblood drained. Bit by bit, all he valued within was taken—finally even the computer complex, which had provided the instructions for restoring interstellar travel, was split into components. All that would be left, once the ship had gone, was a climate-controlled data storage vault maintained with minimum power. The City would stand as an empty shell.

Most Scholars did not grieve over this. They were afire with enthusiasm for the space expedition. A large majority were going; among those with scientific training, few but the aged would stay behind. It was a perilous venture, to be sure, and there could be no hope of quick return, for unless they found an alien civilization—which Noren privately knew they would not—supplies were not sufficient for a two-way trip. They would have to build an outpost on a new planet, and stay there many years while they utilized its metal to establish mining and manufacturing facilities. *Not on this world only, but on myriad worlds of innumerable suns shall the spirit of the Star abide...* Metal would, of course, be returned to their people once large-scale mining capability had been developed and more starships recommissioned. But perhaps, too, new worlds would prove more habitable than the old. Many might choose to emigrate to planets with richer resources. The Star might already be visible there, if those planets were within a smaller radius from the nova—priests who were now alive might set eyes upon it! And so might the children of the new race already born. Meanwhile, the world was safe; the stars beckoned; and the Scholars were content. Only the Scholar Noren stood apart.

The Scholars will go back into the sky from whence they once came, he had prophesied, *and by the time of the Star's appearance, they will return; and there will be a new Founding. And from that day forward, our world will be as the Prophecy promises.*

But Noren would not live to see that day. In his time, the world would be far poorer than before, since all but remnants of its technology must go with the ship—and only he could lead the people through that hard age. Only from him would they continue to believe the promise.

He could not go with the ship himself.

It is not certain when this knowledge came to him. Perhaps he knew from the start, from the hour he first held the star chart in his hands and perceived the unlooked-for outcome of his endeavors: the doors of the universe would be opened for his people within his own lifetime. Yet it was his dream, his most cherished wish, and through him it had come to pass...must he not have felt, at least for a little while, that the universe might be opened for him also?

He never confessed this, except perhaps to Lianne. He kept working. There was time for one last genetic project before the computer complex was dismantled, and as his final act as a scientist, he gave the world trees. For them to have sturdy trunks was not possible with the shrub species available to start from; had this not been so, he would have aimed for a wood-based technology in years past. But dense thickets could someday provide shade. Knowing from Lianne what a lakeshore settlement should look like, he planted masses of them beside the water, hiding the ugly traces of the completed mining. They were, naturally, mere seedlings, and in a land where tall plants were unknown, his prophecies about what they'd become were soon mixed with legend.

The time of embarkation came. Having endured the departure of her own people's starship, Lianne was well prepared to uphold him through the farewell rites, which were formal and were held before the Gates. It was a day of rejoicing. Noren filled the role expected of him, and no one noticed that she kept closer than usual to his side. When in the end the Scholar Stefred came to them, with sorrow in his eyes unlike any before seen there, Noren perceived that he was not glad to go; for him, too, the hour of parting was bitter. "Why?" Noren asked. "Why leave this place against your wish when you cannot live to return to it?

We will need priests here; who will judge their worthiness and teach them to dream?"

"Lianne can do that," Stefred replied. "This is my world, and for its people I've lived; I would not choose to die in exile. But my presence here would tear it asunder. The Scholars staying are loyal to me, while the people are loyal to you—and it is you who are most fit to be Archpriest."

So at last, when the shuttle had ascended on its final trip, the Gates of the City were thrown open, never again to be sealed; and the Scholar Noren went in to his tabernacle. It was a symbol still, a holy place, a place not to be defiled by the people now free to enter. He would see that they entered with reverence. He stood with Lianne between the silent towers that could not, in their time, be relighted; crescent moons illumined the courtyard. And Noren knew he had now come into his own.

Afterword

Warning: this Afterword contains major spoilers! If you haven't yet read all three of the novels contained in this book, please don't read it first.

I'm happy to have this trilogy back in print and available in one volume so that it will at last be read as a whole. And yet, originally I didn't envision a three-part story. When I wrote the first draft of *This Star Shall Abide* I didn't foresee how long it was going to get.

It grew to include a second volume before its initial publication in the early 70s; my editor at Atheneum felt that the first wasn't complete and did not want to issue it without a planned sequel. So, although I was then writing only for young people and *Beyond the Tomorrow Mountains* wasn't of interest to readers as young as some who liked my earlier novels, the two volumes appeared in sequence. Hardcover books for young people, however, are sold almost exclusively to libraries—and librarians tended to put all mine together in the children's room, which is rarely visited by the more mature teenagers and adults. So *Beyond the Tomorrow Mountains* wasn't often found by the people most apt to enjoy it. It never had a paperback edition, and my British publisher, who evidently did think the first book could stand alone, never issued the sequel at all.

I believed, at that time, that the story was finished. It was about faith in the face of impossible odds; I didn't want to weaken it by letting Noren single-handedly and unrealistically save his people. Furthermore, I had no idea what could save them—I'd done such a good job of making survival without metal-based technology impossible in their world (because under no other circumstances would I have justified their desperate social measures) that there wasn't any solution, or so I thought.

However, much later when I was writing a nonfiction book about genetic engineering, it dawned on me, to my dismay, that I had been mistaken. I had known nothing whatsoever about genetics until I began to research it; once knowledgeable, I realized that there was no good reason why genetic engineering could not have enabled Noren's people to survive. This appalled me, because genetic engineering had become a topic of public discussion, and what if new readers assumed I'd simply ignored it for plot purposes and justified the social evils in the story on false grounds? So I wrote *The Doors of the Universe,* which was published eight years after the other two novels.

The uncanny thing was that after I finished it, the story was obviously better as a trilogy and seemed as if it had been planned that way all along. Many things in the first two volumes looked—even to me—as if they had been "planted" for their relevance to the third. And it has bothered me that many of the original readers never learned that a third volume existed; even recently, on the Internet, I've seen the story referred to as a duology. *The Doors of the Universe,* dealing as it does with Noren as an adult, was never really a Young Adult novel; yet it had to be issued in the same series as the others. As a result, many librarians again put it with books for younger readers than its intended audience. Since the teenagers who'd read the preceding volumes had by then grown up, the majority of them never discovered it.

But some did—and more who'd liked *This Star Shall Abide* (published in England as *Heritage of the Star*) heard about the other two volumes, yet were unable to find copies. In the past two years, since opening my Web site, I've discovered to my surprise that a great many adults have been searching for them. I've received a lot of e-mail from readers who remember this story, have reread it over the years, and want to find the parts they may have missed. To them I owe the opportunity for this new edition, which will reach a whole new group of readers as well.

In preparing the books for reprinting, I have made some minor revisions. (Nothing big—some of my recent e-mail has come from people worried that I might change too much!) The main ones were in references to computer technology. I wrote these before desktop computers existed, based on my own experience programming real-time systems in the late 50s and early 60s. I'm amazed that I got as much right as I did—for instance, I guessed networked computers could replace a large central one—but a few crucial points are now outdated (for details, see the explanation at my Web site). Changing them didn't affect the story; I've merely altered some terms and statements … and removed the quotation marks from computer "game" now that the idea of playing a game with a computer isn't so strange as it was to young readers in 1970.

Another thing I changed was phrasing that now sounds sexist, such as many references to the survival of "man" and "mankind." Personally I think these are perfectly good words that don't imply male more than female any more than they imply our own species as distinguished from the hypothetical human species of the story. But I have given in to today's majority opinion because I don't want anybody to read in implications that I didn't intend. I've also tried to make clearer that although the culture of the villagers in the story is indeed sexist, that of the City is not. What did the feminist reviewers who objected to sexism in the books expect of a society that had reverted to backward, pre-technological customs?

There were some reviewers who stated that the colonists in the story came from Earth, despite the fact that Earth's solar system does not have Six Worlds that are similar, as that of the Founders did. Originally this mattered to me only because it's not credible that the religion of the story could have replaced the all the religions of our own planet, which are based on somewhat different concepts of deity. But the fact that I'd assumed a hypothetical system of origin proved very fortunate when I came to write the concluding volume and brought in the Service from my other novels, which may—or may not—include starfarers of Earth descent. Here again, it worked out the same as if I'd planned the whole story from the beginning.

The final revision I've made for this omnibus edition is the elimination of some explanations that were needed to make the separate volumes clear if read independently. It's better as a single narrative!

There are more comments at my Web site on questions people have asked about the books.

www.teleport.com/~sengdahl/

I enjoy hearing from readers, and I hope to meet you there.

Sylvia Engdahl
Eugene, Oregon
October, 1999

Sylvia Engdahl Biography

Sylvia Engdahl was born in Los Angeles and received her degree in 1955 from the University of California at Santa Barbara. After teaching for a short time, she switched to the then-new field of computer programming, starting as a trainee with the RAND Corporation (later the System Development Corporation), which was developing the SAGE Air Defense System. For ten years she did assembly-language systems and utility programming for SAGE, working at sites in Massachusetts, Wisconsin, and Washington State before returning to California, where she became a Computer Systems Specialist.

In 1967 she left programming and moved to Portland, Oregon as companion to her elderly mother, a situation she chose both to get away from Southern California and to gain time for writing. She began her writing career as an award-winning author of science fiction for young people. Her first novel *Enchantress from the Stars* was a 1971 Newbery Honor Book and winner of the Children's Literature Association's 1990 Phoenix Award, given "from the perspective of time" to the best book for children published in the year 20 years prior to the award date—however, the book is enjoyed by many adult readers, as are her five later novels for more mature Young Adults. She has also written nonfiction for young people, and is currently concentrating on a major adult nonfiction project.

Ms. Engdahl is a long-term advocate of space exploration, an interest she first developed at the age of 12 in 1946, when the subject wasn't widely discussed by the public. She has always believed that extraterrestrial expansion is essential to human survival (her views on this are presented at www.teleport.com/~sengdahl/space.htm) and during the late 70s she did graduate work in anthropology focused on the evolutionary significance of space colonization. Her major goal as a writer has been to share her enthusiasm for space.

She has been a strong devotee of online communication since first logging on to BBSs in 1984. She was a volunteer moderator for Participate® on the Source, an early conferencing system, and from 1985 to 1997 was an online faculty and staff member of Connected Education, Inc., under the directorship of Paul Levinson. Via Connect Ed she taught "Science Fiction and Space Age Mythology," a Media Studies course dealing with pop-culture SF, for graduate credit from the New School for Social Research in New York.

At present Ms. Engdahl lives in Eugene, Oregon, where she is settled, along with two cats, in a permamently-sited mobile home. When not writing or doing web design and desktop publishing work, she can usually be found online.

Sylvia Engdahl's personal website is at:

http://www.teleport.com/~sengdahl

She can be reached by e-mail at:

sengdahl@teleport.com

Artist Tom Kidd Biography

Tom Kidd is a widely known fantasy illustrator. He has received four Hugo nominations and has won four Chesley Awards and the Anlab award. His work has appeared on the covers of well over two hundred books and magazines, ranging from Good Housekeeping and Readers Digest to Savage Sword of Conan. His work has been displayed in the Delaware Art Museum, the Society of Illustrators, and the Cleveland Museum of Science. He has designed robots and created architectural designs for a theme park, and is working on a large-scale book about airships.

William Morrow recently published an illustrated edition of The Three Musketeers with sixteen full color illustrations by Tom. He has also just finished work as a conceptual designer on an animated feature for Walt Disney Studios, and is now at work illustrating The War of the Worlds for Morrow. Tom lives in New Milford, Connecticut with his wife Andrea.